THE HOUSE
OF ALWAYS

ALSO BY JENN LYONS

The Ruin of Kings
The Name of All Things
The Memory of Souls

THE
HOUSE
OF
ALWAYS

JENN LYONS

TOR

A TOM DOHERTY
ASSOCIATES BOOK
New York

THE HOUSE OF ALWAYS

A Tor Book
Published by Tom Doherty Associates
120 Broadway
New York, NY 10271

www.tor-forge.com

Tor® is a registered trademark of Macmillan Publishing Group, LLC.

The Library of Congress Cataloging-in-Publication Data is available upon request.

ISBN 978-1-250-17567-0 (hardcover)
ISBN 978-1-250-17566-3 (ebook)

Our books may be purchased in bulk for promotional, educational,
or business use. Please contact your local bookseller or the Macmillan Corporate
and Premium Sales Department at 1-800-221-7945, extension 5442,
or by email at MacmillanSpecialMarkets@macmillan.com.

First Edition: May 2021

Printed in the United States of America

0 9 8 7 6 5 4 3 2 1

To my husband, Michael,
the foundation my world rests upon.

PRÉCIS

After Kihrin D'Mon was tricked into giving up the sword Godslayer and waking the demon king Vol Karoth, the Eight Immortals tasked him and his companions with informing the king of the Manol vané that it was his turn to conduct the Ritual of Night. The ritual had been created by the voras to imprison Vol Karoth, and two times since to re-imprison him. It could only be performed by an immortal race, who would be mortal after—the vané were the only race left who could do it.

Not all the vané wanted to cooperate. Kihrin, Janel, Teraeth, and Thurvishar found themselves drugged and dumped into the Korthaen Blight to die. With Vol Karoth awake, the Blight had become a land of unpredictable and wild magic. As a result Thurvishar was unable to cast spells which would allow them to escape. Scrounging what supplies they could find, the four stumbled upon the dragon Rol'amar in a fight with a band of morgage. Realizing these people might be willing to help, Janel ran into the fight and the group was (eventually) able to successfully retreat and hide from the dragon.

But not, unfortunately, from Vol Karoth, whom Kihrin had been sensing ever since waking in the Blight. A projection of the fallen god appeared in the middle of their new camp and began killing everyone, all the while calling for Kihrin to join him. The four fled while the morgage covered their escape, and what resulted was a painful and exhausting trip back to the court of the vané king.

Meanwhile, Kihrin's mother, Khaeriel, who had kidnapped his father, had taken Therin to the Manol, where she enchanted him to fall in love with her in preparation for retaking her throne. Relos Var visited her while she was at her safe house, but was distinctly disapproving of her actions even as he handed over an object she apparently needed—the harp Valathea. He informed her that her son was still alive. After Var left, Talon appeared and pledged loyalty to the vané queen-in-exile. Together, all three traveled to a vané holy site called the Well of Spirals, where vané can, among other things, make new bodies for themselves. Khaeriel revealed that the harp Valathea was in fact the tsali stone of the real, actual Queen Valathea, the cursed wife of the overthrown Kirpis vané king, Terindel. However, while readying Valathea's resurrection, Talon helped Therin break Khaeriel's control. He escaped into the woods, discovering to his surprise that they were in the Kirpis forest—back in Quur.

Meanwhile, Kihrin's group made their way to the same location (the Well of Spirals) just a short while later, just missing Khaeriel, but instead succeeding at meeting with her brother, King Kelanis. Unfortunately, they discovered too late that the vané who didn't want them completing the ritual was the king himself. Kelanis had them thrown into a prison known as the Quarry, which kept their prisoners well behaved by keeping them heavily drugged.

A number of forces conspired to break the group out again, from their own efforts to Talon and the now resurrected Valathea. Eventually they escaped, and were reunited with not only Valathea, but her husband (and Teraeth's father) Terindel, Kihrin's father Therin—and his mother Khaeriel. But the family reunion only grew more awkward when Kihrin revealed that he didn't think Kelanis was wrong to refuse the ritual—it was the wrong solution to the problem. Kihrin's relationship with Janel evolved and he also, finally, admitted his feelings toward Teraeth, but that admission was interrupted by Rol'amar the dragon, who had tracked Kihrin down. In the fight, Kihrin's father Therin was slain, and Kihrin—channeling Vol Karoth's powers—destroyed Rol'amar.

Afterward, Khaeriel made a deal with her grandmother, the goddess Thaena: if Thaena would agree to Return Therin, Khaeriel would agree to perform the Ritual of Night. The group split up at this point. Kihrin and Thurvishar left for Kishna-Farriga to try to track down the wizard Grizzst, who theoretically knew the most about imprisoning Vol Karoth. Janel and Teraeth returned with the vané to the Manol capital, intent on taking back the vané throne.

Thurvishar and Kihrin began their search, but ran into Senera, Xivan, and Talea, who were tracking down the witch-queen Suless. Kihrin learned that it hadn't been Relos Var who'd sent a Daughter of Laaka to destroy his ship so many years earlier, but Thaena herself, framing Relos Var in order to gain Kihrin's trust. After they continued to run into each other, Thurvishar and Kihrin joined forces with Senera, Xivan, and Talea, who agreed to help with Kihrin's quest if the two men would help with theirs. They were able to track Suless to the lair of the dragon Baelosh, but not in time to save Xivan's husband or son, whom Suless murdered. Suless herself was killed during a fight between the dragons Sharanakal and Baelosh, but it was a ruse: Suless had possessed the one person out there readied for such a transfer—Janel.

Meanwhile, back in the Capital, Teraeth, Janel, Khaeriel, Terindel, and Valathea went into hiding while waiting for Parliament to hear their case. They were taken by surprise when Senera, Xivan, and Talea ambushed them to rescue Janel, but Suless escaped in the confusion before they could explain their good intentions, taking Janel's body with her. Suless promptly took shelter with King Kelanis.

Kihrin and Thurvishar tracked down Grizzst to a brothel, discovering that Grizzst was the leader of the Gryphon Men that Thurvishar's father, Emperor Sandus, and Kihrin's adoptive father, Surdyeh, had both belonged to, and was ultimately responsible for Kihrin growing up at the Shattered Veil Club. They also learned that Grizzst had been helping Relos Var this entire time, but after Grizzst realized how closely linked Vol Karoth and Kihrin seemed to be, he switched sides. Kihrin and Thurvishar determined that Relos Var had trapped the last warding crystal—if anyone finished the Ritual of Night, it would free Vol Karoth rather than imprisoning him. Kihrin secretly messaged Terindel, warning him to do whatever it took to delay or sabotage the Ritual of Night.

When the time came for the trial, Janel escaped Suless's control, but at a high price: Janel was forced to take the final steps toward becoming a demon, and Suless learned the trick from her. Valathea and Terindel double-crossed Khaeriel, taking the crown for themselves. But Teraeth suspected this was something more than ambition when Terindel gave his cornerstone, Chainbreaker, to his wife before she fled. Terindel then called on Thaena and agreed to honor the bargain made with Khaeriel—with Terindel performing the ritual himself. Therin was Returned and Terindel performed the ritual, but it failed. Confronted by Thaena, Terindel finally admitted the truth—the ritual couldn't succeed because the vané weren't an immortal race. They were just an offshoot branch of the voras, who became mortal the first time Vol Karoth was imprisoned. They'd been using their magic to artificially prolong their lives using the Well of Spirals, but they weren't truly "immortal"—so there was nothing to sacrifice. Every race had already given up their immortality. Thaena killed Terindel, forced the vané to crown their son Teraeth, and kidnapped him in order to prepare a new ritual that would sacrifice not the vané's immortality, but the vané themselves.

Kihrin destroyed the last crystal, forcing Relos Var to help him or let the vané die senselessly. The Immortals fractured, with Taja, Khored, and Tya offering to help Kihrin and Ompher, Galava, and Argas siding with Thaena. A giant battle occurred at the Well of Spirals, and in the aftermath, Taja, Argas, Galava, and Thaena were all dead—with Thaena slain by her own son, Teraeth.

Afterward, Kihrin embarked on a dangerous plan to bring Vol Karoth under control. He broke Talon out of prison and took her to Kharas Gulgoth, where he instructed Talon to kill him so she could eat his brain and perfectly impersonate him afterward. Kihrin's soul entered Vol Karoth's prison, secure in the knowledge that he'd be able to overcome a weakened, damaged deity.

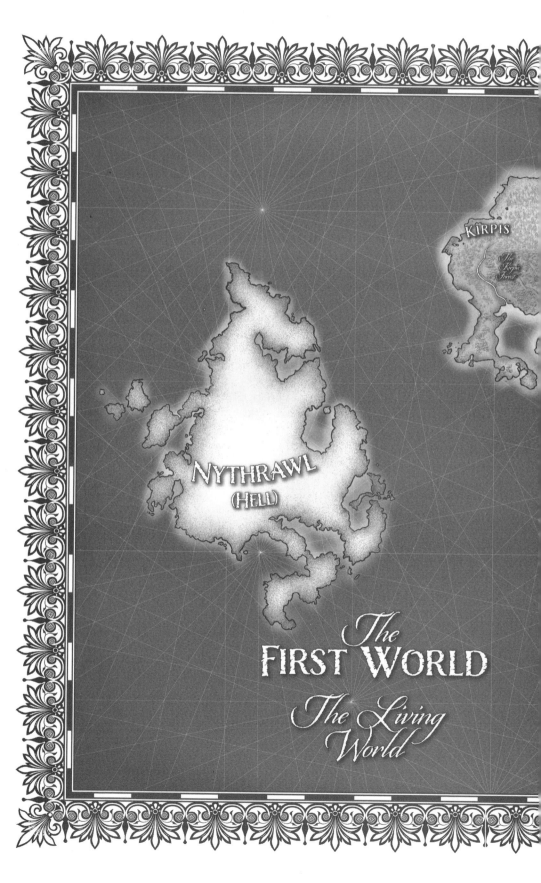

KIRPIS

The
Kirpis
Forest

NYTHRAWL
(HELL)

The
FIRST WORLD

The Living
World

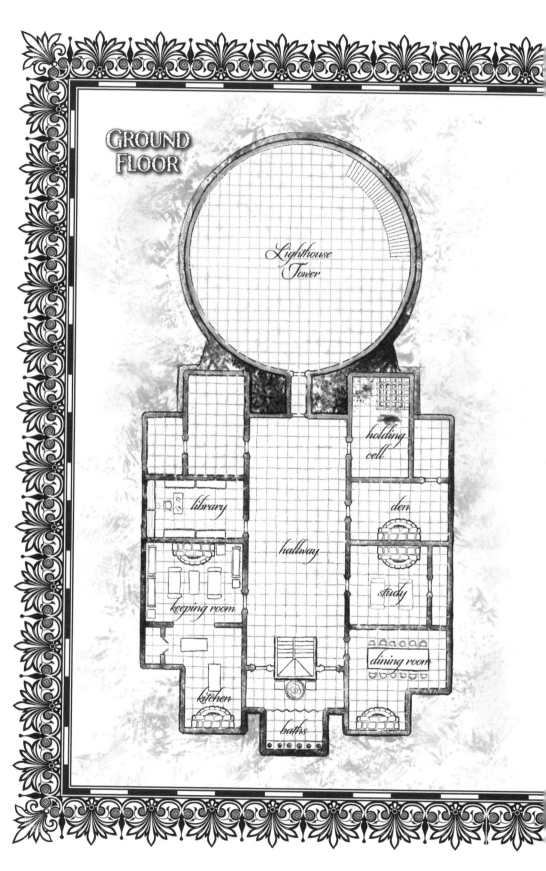

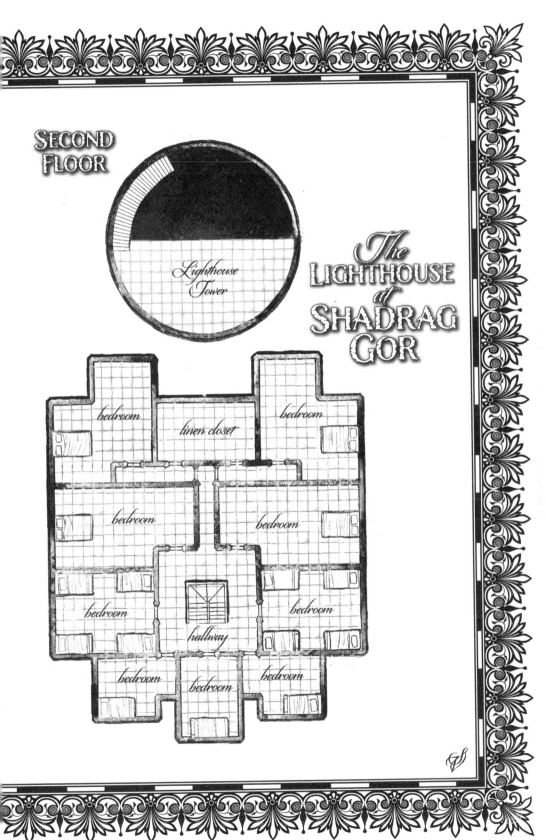

SECOND FLOOR

Lighthouse Tower

The LIGHTHOUSE at SHADRAG GOR

bedroom

linen closet

bedroom

bedroom

bedroom

bedroom

bedroom

hallway

bedroom

bedroom

bedroom

THE HOUSE
OF ALWAYS

Dear Lord Var,

Let me tell you of the moment when I first knew I would betray you.

Your grandson, I think, has known for ages this would be the inevitable result. He saw it long before I did. I didn't want to see it.

Such is love.

For I did love you. How could I not? You saved me. You gave me meaning and purpose. You were my polestar. No crime proved too unspeakable to commit in your name, no atrocity out of bounds in pursuit of your goals. And it's only now that I understand how much you manipulated me, how much you used me, how much I was never meant to rise to your level. I won't say you were the father I never had, because I remember my father. I don't miss him. He was a violent, broken man—but he never used me the way you have.

But anyway: that moment.

I stood in the center of Kharas Gulgoth and gazed upon all you had wrought. Your sin, your vanity, your astonishing hubris.

It would have been different if your plans, or Thaena's plans, had succeeded. Funny how you committed such similar crimes in pursuit of contradictory goals. If Thaena's chosen pawn had conducted the ritual that you and Grizzst had twisted, you would have freed Vol Karoth. And if Thaena had succeeded in her plans, she would have sent him back to sleep, at least for a few more centuries, but only at the cost of the entire Manol vané nation.

But Thaena failed. And so did you, although I'm sure you don't consider it such, given the Immortals who lost their lives that day. Argas, Galava, Taja. Thaena herself.

I knew your goals were not yet won as I stood just a few feet from Vol Karoth's silhouette, not dying.

Not dying, not because Vol Karoth was neither asleep nor freed but because Vol Karoth was distracted as he grappled with his younger, better self.

That was the precise moment I knew you were wrong.

No matter how smart you are, no matter how old, no matter how wise, you are incapable of comprehending a solution that hinges on your own sacrifice. He had done a thing you would never do. All your explanations of necessity and pragmatism, lesser evils and greater goods, taste of ash and smoke.

I suppose I should note that if you ever read these words, it means you will have won. Entirely plausible; I am too cynical to think righteousness is any guarantee of victory. If I have one consolation, however, it is this: the knowledge that you will never be able to pry the Name of All Things from my cold, dead fingers and use it to discover the truth. It will never be able to answer your questions again. You can guess. You will never know.

You will have the story I narrate, the explanation I give, or you will have none at all.

So allow me to explain.

Allow me to explain where you made your mistakes. Allow me to explain why I can no longer blindly trust your judgment nor follow your commands. Allow me to show you why—even if you win—you will always be wrong.

Allow me to explain why I switched sides.

Your formerly obedient servant,
Senera

Thurvishar—

S wrote this just before the end. Then she threw it out before you could see it. I saved it from the fire before it was too damaged to read. Now, I'm slipping it into your copy, because I know she wouldn't want me to.

That's just the kind of petty bitch I am. You're welcome.

—Talon

My dearest Thurvishar,

If you're reading this, then you're the last one.

I wasn't sure which of us it would be.

One might, if one were so inclined, speculate on what you're feeling in this moment. That you might imagine yourself teetering on the razor-sharp divide between victory and destruction. The stomach-clenching anxiety of knowing you have rolled the dice and made your bets and there is nothing left to do but watch the bones dance and land and decide the fate of the whole world.

My apologies for the comparison, but Relos Var might have some insight on what this feels like.

This is a battle ended in an eyeblink, in the beginning of an inhalation, in that space between surprise and the wineglass shattering against the cold stone floor. A battle that had and has and will take place entirely within the mind and entirely within this inviolate and sacred space, the Lighthouse at Shadrag Gor. And whether we do our jobs well or poorly, it is a battle no one else will ever know happened. Not unless we tell them. If we even can.

Did Gadrith ever tell you the Lighthouse's history? Often the things right in front of us are the sights we overlook, the objects we fail to see. There seem to be a thousand stories about its origins, all of them outlandish and nonsensical. The Name of All Things is no help here—the Cornerstone cannot divine the history of entities older than itself. My favorite, though, is that a D'Lorus wizard whose lover had been sentenced to death the next morning was responsible. He won permission from his high lord for a single night, and so brought his lover with him to the Lighthouse. They spent a lifetime together before dying of old age in each other's arms—all before the sun rose the next morning.

It's a ridiculous story, but I cannot help but feel you would like it.

I am quite sure the Lighthouse tower itself is voras and unspeakably ancient. What its purpose might have been I don't know. I suppose it's even possible that it was a lighthouse. It is an elegant structure, thick and stonelike but without a single crack, mortar, or seam. I have never heard of the tower needing repair. The attached manor is more modern, more fugitive, and more livable. I like to imagine you walking through the manor room by room, starting in the cellar and working your way up, making sure everything is put away, everything is clean. It may be centuries, after all, before the Lighthouse is used again. Any perishable item not locked away under preservation spells will crumble to dust.

You'll probably wish you had cleaned the kitchen and repaired the damaged spot on the wall, put away the soup supplies, the rice, the spices. But there is, quite ironically, no time for such domesticity. Instead, you will check on the bodies.

Knowing you, you'll pretend it matters whether or not we are comfortable. Perhaps you'll even tuck us in.

Yes, I suspect you will.

You will also, I think, give some thought to this second blade's edge: there is no way to know which of those bodies will wake and which will not. Even to you, even in this place, we must all seem dead: without pulse and without breath. I do not envy you the feeling of knowing it is all out of your hands.

When you come to my side, I like to imagine you'll make the effort to smooth a blanket over me, fold back the top so it won't bunch under my chin. You'll slide a pillow under my neck before you take the brush out of my hair so it won't prick needlelike against my scalp. Perhaps you'll craft a flower to replace it. (I'm fond of Osmanthus blossoms.) You'll try very hard not to think of how it looks like I'm lying in repose.

You will wait.

Until there is no more waiting possible. And then you will choose whether we live or die.

But know this—even though I have lived a life as full of thin, small regrets as a cherry tree is full of petals in spring, this will be my largest: that I could not be there with you, right then, to share the space between never and always while waiting for the sun to rise.

PART I

WHERE ALL
PATHS LEAD

1: A KIND OF RESCUE

Talea's story
Twenty-four days after the Battle of the Well of Spirals
The Main Island of Devors, Quur

The emergency bells rang out all over the island, fast and loud, magically amplified. Talea regarded the Devorans running from the dining hall, noting how unprepared the priests all seemed to be. These people had been so certain of their fortress library's inviolate, impenetrable defenses. They'd grown sloppy.[1]

Now the priests would pay for it. Everyone would pay for it.

Talea found little satisfaction in I told you so. She'd have gladly traded gloating opportunities for a little more serious preparation. For example, the panicking priests, monks, and assorted scholars running around like shocked rabbits weren't paying attention to Talea's group. Personally convenient, yes, but it demonstrated a fundamental flaw in training. When being attacked, the first thing one should always do was secure any unknown variables.

Talea being the definition of *unknown variable.*

She rushed to the ramparts along with everyone else. Tempest rains left the stonework slick, visibility shuttered to vague shapes crawling in the distance. The rains hadn't muffled the sound of fighting, the retort of the scorpion war machines, the screams.

The Lash's attack on Devors had begun.

"She got here faster than we thought," Galen said, exhaling.

"Didn't they say this was impossible? What of the wards?" Sheloran D'Mon whipped around as she scanned the defenses. Her expression suggested she wanted to conjure the abbess through pure indignation to begin scolding her.

"Someone must have disabled them," Talea said, "but I don't know where they keep the controls."

"I do," Janel Theranon said. She stood behind the assembled group, arms crossed over her chest, an unamused scowl twisting her mouth. "I know where they are."

"Really? How?" Sheloran squinted at her, eyes narrowed with suspicion. Which made sense. If you'd never seen a Joratese person in your life before,

---

[1] In their defense, they hadn't been attacked in over a century. But one would think the people screaming that the end of the world is nigh would be the ones most prepared for their world ending, yes?

let alone a Joratese person dressed like a vané knight, then Janel would be strange indeed.[2]

"Because I used to be married to the man who created them," Janel answered. "Assuming they haven't changed the location in a few centuries, it's this way. Come with me." She headed into the complex without checking to see if anyone followed.

Talea raised an eyebrow at Teraeth. He stared at her with a face wiped clean of emotion. "Wasn't me."[3]

She wanted to stop and talk to the man. Talea wasn't stupid enough to ask why Teraeth's manner suggested a thread pulled taut enough to snap; she knew what had happened to him at the Well of Spirals. Years wouldn't be enough time to recover from being forced to kill your own mother. He'd had weeks at best.

But there was no time to talk, not even if Teraeth had been willing.[4] Not with the bells ringing and Janel running. They followed her, joined by Thurvishar. The rest trailed behind like dangerous little ducks who'd imprinted on the wrong mother.

Janel ran to a large room off the main courtyard, where the warding array had been hidden under mosaic tile flooring. Kalindra Milligreest stood in the center, staring down at the broken tiles. Clearly, she too had known where the controls were kept. The woman was still dressed in Quuros mourning clothing appropriate for the High General's daughter-in-law, now laughably unsuited for a siege. What Kalindra wore wouldn't have stopped a gentle winter shower, let alone typhoon rains and sword blows.

Kalindra startled as everyone filed in. "I came here as soon as I heard the bells," she said. "Someone sabotaged it—" She pointed to the discarded pickax left behind.

The whole group stared. The shattered stonework revealed elaborate glyphs, ruined. Entire sigil sections were missing, making it impossible to know the original pattern's form.

"Is there any way to repair this?" Janel asked Thurvishar.

"Possibly," the D'Lorus wizard said, "but the damage is already done if the goal is to keep out attackers—I have my doubts it was ever going to be capable of keeping out a kraken."

"I'm going down to the docks." Galen unsheathed his sword. "You're welcome to join me."

"Just try and stop me." Galen's wife, Sheloran, smiled as she spread her metal fan—her personal equivalent of drawing a blade.

Janel nodded but made no move to follow. "Teraeth and I will stay here.

---

[2] I have to assume she'd been taking advantage of the fact that Teraeth is technically still king of the Manol and presumably has access to all the best armorers. And his predecessor's wardrobe, which was considerable.

[3] The "husband" referenced must have been Terindel, to whom Janel was married in a previous life. He rarely used magic. That is not the same as not knowing any magic. Honestly, though, I never would have guessed the Devoran Library wards had been placed by none other than Terindel the Black. I have . . . questions.

[4] He wouldn't have been.

We're going to guard Thurvishar until he's repaired these wards. Then we find out whether or not Thurvishar is wrong about the kraken."

Teraeth's scowl turned murderous. "Do I get a say in that?"

"If you'd rather stay near the fighting—" Janel glanced at him, expression uncertain.

Teraeth snorted. "If I want to stay near the fighting, I'm sticking near you. Don't pretend you're not chasing after that kraken the moment he's finished."

Talea couldn't tell if the man was angry or proud.

"Never killed a kraken before," Janel admitted, trying to smile. "Today's a good day for it."

That seemed to satisfy Teraeth's expectations.

"I'm with the kids." Talea pointed toward the door the others had taken. Qown had already sneaked through; Talea was willing to bet metal Janel hadn't even noticed he'd been there. She'd barely looked away from Teraeth the whole morning.

Talea left without waiting for Janel's acknowledgment. As she stepped outside, a cask hit one of the towers with explosive force. The Lash's pirate ship, the *Cruel Mistress*, had turned its own war machines on the monastery.[5] Talea didn't understand why the harbor defenses weren't responding in kind. Clearly, something had gone wrong there too.

It had to have been an inside job, but they'd need to survive it before they could ferret out their saboteur.

The real problem became obvious as soon as they reached the docks: the initial dead pirates, sailors, and assorted sea life had all climbed ashore with murderous intent. Everyone they killed promptly animated and joined their side.

Galen and Sheloran began fighting from the start. All three—Galen, Sheloran, and Talea—had an unspoken agreement to keep any stray blades, claws, or teeth from reaching Qown. Talea reminded herself, again, that she needed to teach the healer to fight, but this wasn't the place to learn. Battling the roaming dead required beheading and amputation; her sword suited that need perfectly.[6] Galen's did not. Talea found herself rescuing the D'Mon prince as often as she guarded his healer.

The rain made footing on the docks slippery, although that worked to the disadvantage of the dead husks too. Everyone was soaking wet, miserable, and fighting for their lives. To make matters worse, a huge shadow had fallen over the docks, visible through the downpour, which could only be the kraken herself. Any moment, Talea expected a tentacle to smash through the wooden planks and stone pier foundations.

Then it would really be a party.

---

[5] It really is one of the most infamous pirate ships ever documented. Accounts of ships being attacked by the *Cruel Mistress*, helmed by the Lash, go back centuries, but I had assumed—like everyone else—that it was simply a title and ship's name being handed down from one pirate to the next.
[6] Talea and Xivan both use a Khorveshan curved sword known as an *imchii*. They are slicing weapons made from folded metal, and exceedingly sharp.

A space formed around them, a gap between waves of undead. Talea knew right away that this wasn't a lucky break. Just the opposite.

Xivan walked into view.

Talea's ex-lover looked angry. Xivan had changed clothes for the occasion too. She wore silk, gold-embroidered lace, jewels; some irreverent prankster must have convinced the Lash all good pirates dressed to make a Quuros high lord blush. Talea's traitorous heart warmed to see her.

Xivan spotted them, sighed, and strolled in their direction. She wasn't in any hurry.

"Take Sheloran out of here," Talea said to Galen.

"Oh, I think not," Sheloran responded.

"Please–" Talea started to say.

"No, Talea, dear. I mean the way is blocked." Sheloran gestured backward with her fan. Several lines of husks–Devoran priests and Quuros soldiers this time–lay between their position and the stairs.

"Hand over Sheloran D'Talus," Xivan said. "The rest of you may leave."

"Sheloran D'Mon," the princess muttered. Galen flashed his wife a smile.

Talea stepped forward and unbuckled the spare sword. It was now or never. "Is this you or the Lash talking? Or Suless?"

Xivan's eyes widened. "How do you know about–" Her gaze slipped past Talea. She let one short, mocking laugh escape. "Oh, I see. Hello, Qown. I didn't recognize you back there. Having hair's a new look for you."

"We know it's not your fault," Qown said, "but what happened isn't Sheloran's fault either."

"Oh, I know that now," Xivan replied. "If only I had a choice." She frowned as Talea tossed a sheathed sword down to the wooden dock. It skidded to a halt at Xivan's feet.

"You dropped this," Talea chirped.

"What's this?" Xivan scowled.

"I'm returning your sword," Talea clarified. "I asked Sheloran to fix it. I know I'm sentimental, but I thought, hey, if the woman I love is going to kill me, she should at least do it with her own sword. It's . . . you know . . . tradition."

"I don't want to kill you," Xivan said. "Please get out of my way. *Please.*"

Talea smiled. "We both know that's not going to happen. Pick up your sword."

Xivan looked heartbroken. "I told you–I don't have a choice. This isn't like a gaesh, Talea. She can make me do anything she wants. I can't even kill myself resisting the order."

Talea set herself into a proper dueling stance. "Pick up your sword," she repeated.

Xivan kept her eyes on Talea. She stepped on the scabbard's edge and levered it into the air so quickly, it looked like she'd kicked the sword into her hands. She glanced down at it. "Nice scabbard."

"Do you like it? I had it made just for you." Which was even true.

It was, in fact, the whole point.

Xivan looked like she might cry. She tossed her old sword aside and pulled out the new one, which came free from its sheath with a satisfying ring.[7]

Talea hadn't told the others that the odds of Xivan keeping the scabbard had only been 26 percent. Most people would keep the sword and toss the sheath, especially if they already wore one. Xivan's preferred fighting style needed both hands free.

"Please," Xivan pleaded, "just hand her over."

"You have to fight the Lash's control. I know you can. You're stronger than this."

Xivan tucked the scabbard—scrimshaw carved with red roses, impossibly beautiful, because damn if Sheloran didn't have *standards*—under her belt; Talea exhaled.

Talea wasn't sure if this was a situation like being gaeshed, where the broken control would be obvious, or if Xivan would only gradually realize the Lash no longer held her strings.

But Talea was out of time: Xivan attacked.

Talea easily avoided the first slash, deflecting the blade as she stepped to the side, but she wasn't naïve enough to think it would be an easy fight. She was fighting the woman who'd taught her everything she'd ever known about swordplay. Talea didn't hold back. Easier to do when Talea knew Xivan would shrug off most attacks short of decapitation.[8] But it wasn't a worry—Talea wasn't anywhere close to getting through Xivan's defenses.

Maybe Xivan wondered why the others weren't interfering with their duel. Maybe she put it out of her mind as a distraction.

Then something terrible happened: it stopped raining.

Since it was the rainy season, Talea hadn't considered that this rain might not be natural. In hindsight, it made sense; cutting off long-distance sight worked far more to the Lash's advantage than to the Quuros soldiers defending Devors. Rain made aiming the Quuros scorpion war machines impossible.

The rain had also blocked Talea's view of the Lash.

Talea had underestimated the kraken's size. She was simply enormous, so huge that the sea monster's body pushed her pirate ship to the side. It slammed against a dock, shattering both.

Talea could only stop and stare.

A sharp, cold pain blossomed as Xivan's sword slammed into Talea's stomach. Xivan pulled the sword back in shock, but it was too late. The pain was incandescent, terrible. Talea fought not to drop her sword and curl in on herself.

Talea took a wobbly step backward.

"What have you done?" a voice thundered above them, deep and vast.

---

[7] You know, if Talea had simply glued that sword into its damn scabbard, this all might have ended right there, but no one had asked my opinion. And I had no idea this was happening.

[8] I'm not sure about decapitation. I suspect that would mostly be inconvenient.

Talea smiled through the pain. The Lash wouldn't complain about Talea being stabbed. So all odds pointed to the same result: the Lash must have tried to control Xivan using the Cornerstone Grimward. And she had failed.

"It worked!" Talea said, triumphant. She held a hand over her wound, feeling the warm blood wash over her fingers. She hoped she didn't spill her intestines all over the dock. It would be so inconvenient. She was so happy the injury almost didn't hurt. Almost.

Actually no, it really hurt. A lot.

"Help her!" someone yelled.

Xivan shook her head. "You little fool. Why did you–?"

"Xivan, why can't I see through your eyes anymore?"

Xivan turned around. "What?"

One of the kraken's arms smashed a ship. Just smashed it to tiny pieces as though it were a toy.

"Oh, that is–" Teraeth's voice came from somewhere in the back. "That is quite a bit bigger than the last kraken I encountered."

"Talea!" Janel's voice.

"You can't see through my eyes–what a tragedy. I guess I'll fix that right away." Xivan gave the sea monster a rude gesture, sheathed her sword, and pivoted back to Talea's group. "We need to leave."

"Are you still trying to kidnap me?" Sheloran asked.

"No," Xivan said. "No, absolutely not. But Suless is here somewhere. *She* wants to kidnap you, if not worse, and I can't stop her."

"Talea told me Suless is a demon now," Sheloran pointed out. "Aren't de- mons just souls? Couldn't you simply eat her?"

Xivan stared at her, mouth agape.[9]

Qown ran over to Talea's side. "I've got you. Let me see your wound."

"Not here," Xivan said. "We need to–"

Magical energy formed a wall over their heads just as one of the Lash's tentacles slammed against their location.

"I can't maintain this for long!" Thurvishar shouted as he trembled from the strain. "Might I suggest a retreat?"[10]

"I'll delay her." Janel started walking toward the end of the dock.

Which was the moment the whole world went dark. The Lash roared with a combination of confusion, anger, and, strangely, joy. Massive wings flapped over everyone's heads.

Drehemia the dragon, lady of secrets and shadows, had arrived.

"I take it back," Talea muttered. "It can get worse."

"You never said that," Xivan told her.

"I thought it, though," Talea admitted. "My bad. Can you see?"

"Not a bit."

"I can," Galen said. "Talea, here. This is Xivan's hand. I'll grab hers–"

"This is a terrible idea," Xivan muttered.

---

[9] Perhaps she could, yes, but I am reminded of the Zheriasian proverb about the hungry beggar and the beached whale.

[10] Considering how immune most kraken are to magic, that you could maintain it at all is nothing short of extraordinary.

"If you have a better one," Galen said as he started to pull them in a direction Talea assumed led to the stairs, "you're welcome to try it."

Apparently, Xivan didn't have a better idea.

As they formed a chain, a bright light appeared overhead, cutting through the darkness. Thurvishar's voice rang out: "Turn that off! Don't draw the dragon's attention!"

But it was too late.

Talea looked up. The dragon had landed on the top of the cliff, claws clutching at the crumbling monastery walls. She was beautiful in the light—dark purples, indigos, and deep sea greens rippling over her scales. Her eyes were the night sky, black and full of stars. Somehow, even as a dragon, Drehemia managed to convey a sense of complete insanity.

She opened her mouth and screamed. Talea didn't know what the shadow dragon would breathe at them, but she knew she wouldn't like it.

"Drehemia!" the Lash's voice cried out.

The dragon's head whipped around; she growled at the kraken.

"Stop this," the Lash ordered. **"Please, darling. Talk to me. Remember me?"**

Drehemia spread her wings and flew down to meet her lover, claws extended. It didn't at all look like Drehemia intended on giving the kraken a loving embrace.

"Oh," Talea said absently. "This seems familiar."

Xivan's hand tightened in hers.

"Run," Janel said. "Everyone run, right now."

Talea felt light-headed. She didn't want to run. She wanted to lie down on the floor, maybe take a nap. She could feel—oh, but it hurt. Qown hadn't had a chance to do anything to help. He'd probably been the one to make the light. Despite Thurvishar's warning, Talea was glad he hadn't dropped the spell. She shuddered to think how difficult escaping would have been otherwise.

As they fought their way through the dock area, a new enemy arrived. These were Quuros, just as the animated dead had been, but living. They were also bestial, lost in rage. They attacked anything around them, including each other. And those they killed were promptly animated by the Lash.

Drehemia. The dragon had to be responsible for this.

"Where to?" Kalindra yelled out.

"Somewhere underground," Galen said. "Away from the darkness and the Lash!"

They smashed their way through the lines of dead and mindless. Talea noticed quite a few of their enemies spontaneously lit on fire, which she assumed was Janel's work. Halfway up the stairs, Talea stumbled. Xivan picked her up and carried her after that.

They ran up several flights and then through a service tunnel. They exited into a larger room, a storage space for supplies.

"Where's Nikali?" Galen asked Kalindra.

"With his grandfather," Kalindra said. "I don't know where they went! I need to go find him right now!"

"Who's Nikali?" Teraeth asked.[11]

"My son," Kalindra answered. At which point, she kept running, serious about the find him right now part.

Janel said, "Let's go," and ran after her.

Everyone else followed Janel, until the entire group exited into a large open courtyard filled with statues and perfectly groomed hedges.

And looming over all of it, Drehemia herself.

"Shit."

It might have been Qown who said that, but Talea wasn't positive.

The dragon perched on the wall surrounding the courtyard, her attention focused on the Lash below. She faced the other way. Or at least, she'd faced the other way when they'd all run panting into the area and found themselves a dozen yards from her twitching tail. She must have heard them. Drehemia's head whipped around to stare.

At that exact moment, a gate opened in the courtyard.

"Damn it," Talea murmured. "I already admitted it could get worse."

Senera and a Yoran woman Talea didn't recognize stepped through the portal. The other woman saw the dragon first and yelped. Senera glanced up above, did a double take. The wizard uttered a single emphatic curse and then shook her head as if the dragon were someone else's problem.

Talea was more than reasonably sure Drehemia was everyone's problem.[12]

Then, Senera gestured, forming an ornate yellow series of glyphs and sigils in the air. The arcane symbols expanded in an eyeblink to fill the whole courtyard, then sank down to ground level, still glowing.

Talea had seen that before. So had Janel.

"No, stop!" Janel shouted.

Relos Var had used that trick before. It created a gate entrance. Under everyone's feet.

The entire group fell through, and the portal shut over their heads.

---

[11] Given that Teraeth's father Terindel had used the name Nikali as an alias for decades, it was a reasonable question.

[12] As you will see, I wasn't planning on staying that long. Still, my heart did skip more than a few beats.

2: The Lies We Tell

Kihrin's story
Inside Vol Karoth's prison, just after Kihrin's death

The ruins of the city where I died stretched out around me . . .

Perhaps calling it a ruin was unfair. It was not, in fact, ruined at all.

Nor was it where I'd died, in this lifetime or the last.

It was a memory of such places, however. The city's buildings stood proud and tall, but no trees lined the streets, no grass decorated the verge. The buildings–inanimate, mineral, lifeless–lay pristine as they wrapped around dusty streets. I felt a strange disconnection–as if the city only existed when I directly gazed at it, dissolving and re-forming as I moved my field of view. I couldn't help feeling, staring at the buildings stretched out before me, that I inspected a corpse. Nothing living moved around me. No scent–good or bad–perfumed the air. Even the colors were washed out, faded.

The daytime sky loomed a dull leaden gray less like cloud cover than a physical cap over the heaven's zenith. I couldn't see the sun. I'm not sure a sun existed.

Only then did I examine myself. I wore funeral white, just a misha and kef with sandals, but the sword at my belt surprised me. It wasn't Urthaenriel. It was, in fact, the thriss-crafted blade I'd worn for years while training on Ynisthana. Nameless and serviceable, with not a drop of magic owed to its existence. No realer than the clothes, the city, the . . . everything.

Including me.

My illusionary reality manifested in a hundred subtle ways, from the lack of scent to the way I didn't feel hunger, weariness, or discomfort. Possibly a failure of imagination on my part. Or perhaps neither hunger nor exhaustion were necessary to communicate this particular metaphor.

A wasteland. Bereft of life, hope, or joy.[1]

But I wasn't alone here. Somewhere out there a lurked a god. A haunted, tortured god. The whole reason I'd come.

If only I had a clue where to find Vol Karoth.

So I searched. I walked through deserted streets for endless spans. I had no way to track time. No way to tell the passing of hours or minutes when no sun moved across the sky, the seasons never changed, my body had no needs, and counting to myself had long since grown tiresome. Oh, I had time. Time to contemplate how arrogant it had been to assume I could just step inside Vol

---

[1] But not, it would appear, of melodrama.

Karoth's prison and right all wrongs with a finger snap. That I could fix all the mistakes when I barely understood what was wrong.

Then, after some interminable time, I felt him.

Vol Karoth was a hollow place just under my sternum, like the gut twist of loss that scrapes one's insides clean and leaves only stupefaction in its wake. He lurked in the back of my throat, in the unbidden sting of tears with no cause, in the creeping sour taste of malice under my tongue. Vol Karoth was empty and dark and endless. A bottomless cup that could never be filled.

Before I found him, he found me.

There was no warning before the ambush. One moment, I was walking along, and the next . . . a surge of anger, of hatred, of darkness barreled toward me. I parried the blow; even then, the force of his swing pushed me back along the street. Stones splintered underfoot. A sound wave blasted outward. Had this been the real world I would have been dead.

Vol Karoth slammed into me, darkness and shadow given form. I couldn't see his face—he existed as nothing more than an outline—but I knew his expression would have been the most hateful and malicious scowl.

How dare you.

His voice was a raspy whisper, a hollow echo bouncing down long, empty streets.

Now you return? Now you think to conquer me? You fool.

"Wait," I stammered out. "You wanted me back—"

It was hard to explain oneself while fighting for one's life. His sword strike bounced past my defenses and sliced a line of brilliant pain along my arm.

Explain how you think I'm a mistake. Explain how you think you can control me. Dominate me. How you can destroy me, take my place. Do you think I cannot recognize betrayal? Was I not born in the fires of betrayal?

So I had a problem.

This wasn't a child. This wasn't someone injured and hurting, whose will wasn't strong enough to fight off a more spiritually mature opponent (myself, I had naïvely assumed). Vol Karoth was a full-grown adult. A full-grown god. A full-grown god who saw through all my plans, knew what I'd intended to do, and laughed at my intentions.

Is it fun, I wonder? To think yourself so much better than me? Than our brother? But the two of you are not so different.

He never stopped attacking.

I wanted to ignore his words, but it was difficult when he began comparing me to Rev'arric. "Don't—it's not like that."

Is it not? Don't try to hide how you feel. You can't. Not from me.

The next strike fell along my hip. I screamed as I stumbled backward.

I expected you to be better. His voice was grim, amused, hateful.

I didn't know what to do. I was keeping him back, but only barely. I didn't think I'd be able to do so forever. He seemed in no danger of becoming fatigued; I had the terrible suspicion it wasn't possible for him to become fatigued. He'd stay here in this prison, with all this power, never tiring, never waning, all his hatred focused on me. Forever.

So I did the only thing I could: I ran.

His howls rang behind me as I tripped, stumbled, fell–

And then I found myself somewhere else in the city.

What had just happened? I wasn't sure. I stood up. I was still in Karolaen. In the distance, Vol Karoth bellowed. Somehow I had managed to escape him.

My heart seized up at the idea of him locating me. He wouldn't stop searching. He would track me down; he would kill me; he would recover everything he'd lost and more. He'd use me as clay to rejoin the battered shards of his soul. Then he'd be free to unleash himself upon the universe.

I had . . . I had done the stupidest thing imaginable, hadn't I? I'd thought I was saving the world, but I'd done just the opposite.

I'd doomed everyone.

I stifled hysterical laughter.

I ran out into the wasteland, away from the city. Maybe I could lose myself out there so Vol Karoth couldn't find me, but I didn't hold out much hope.

I didn't hold out much hope at all.

Senera's story
The Lighthouse at Shadrag Gor
Twenty-four days after the Battle of the Well of Spirals

Senera timed it perfectly. She'd spent a week chaining spells together. The moment the gate dumped out everyone at the Lighthouse at Shadrag Gor, she completed the final swirl on the last sigil. She doubted anyone noticed. It would have just been another flash as the circuit completed and the swirling energies overhead closed the gate.

That had been the easy part. Magic was always the easy part.

The hard part was always people.

"Before you try to kill me," Senera said as everyone stumbled or pulled themselves to their feet again, "you need to know I've brought you all here to help Kihrin."

The witch spoke the words in a rush, hoping to let them hang on the air before Teraeth or Janel left her too busy fighting for her life to engage in banter. They weren't the only ones she worried might react poorly to what she'd done, but they were the most volatile.

She took quick stock of her kidnap victims. There hadn't been time to sort through the people she wanted versus those she didn't, no time to do anything but bring the whole and entire group, damn the consequences. Teraeth, Janel, Thurvishar–she'd had to bring them, obviously. Galen was also essential. But the others? Kalindra, maybe, since she and Kihrin had been lovers. Talea, though? Xivan? Senera didn't even know why Talea was there. Perhaps Xivan had brought her, although she had no idea what Xivan had been doing on Devors either.

Or why she was dressed like the main character in *Pirate Queen of the Desolation*.[2]

---

[2] It's a House D'Jorax theatrical production. Quite elaborate. They use an aquarium.

Galen's wife, Sheloran, was also present, whom Kihrin had met exactly once.[3] Lastly, two people with highly suspect loyalties: Qown, who still worked for Relos Var; and Talon, who only worked for chaos and mischief.[4]

Senera knew it was an odd tableau; a situation where analogies of kindling and matches might yet prove apt (even if her "guests" were soaking wet). The Lighthouse's arrival room was circular, large, and devoid of windows. Ascending and descending staircases led to other floors, while a small passage joined the Lighthouse to the manor beyond. Painted black glyphs lined the stone interior. Most of the people she'd kidnapped wouldn't consider them strange only because most of the people she'd kidnapped had never been to Shadrag Gor before.[5] If they had, they'd have recognized those glyphs as new.

But none of them, not even Thurvishar, understood their purpose.

There was considerable irony to her scrambling, desperate fight for time, here, in this place, where time seemed in infinite supply. Yet she rushed for each precious second, for a chance to explain.

"You can't expect us to believe—" Janel had already gone for her sword.

"Just hear me out!" Senera cried. If she could just explain . . .

But she had even less time than she'd believed. The Lighthouse at Shadrag Gor wasn't a safe place anymore. Senera had no one to blame but herself; she'd made it that way.

In that moment, Vol Karoth struck.

The world changed.

Inside Vol Karoth's prison. The arrival.

I'm not sure how many times Vol Karoth and I fought or for how long. It seemed like forever.

We fell into a routine. He always found me. No matter how far I ran or how well I hid, he eventually arrived with a sword in his hand and hate in his heart. Time had no meaning, so I couldn't be certain how long it took him each time. It was forever, and it was instant.

Then we would fight until I became so exhausted I stumbled or he slipped a blow past my defenses. Then I would find myself somewhere else. At which point, the whole game would start up again, a cycle I hadn't figured out how to break, let alone defeat.

Vol Karoth had just finished a swing powered with so much energy it had shattered one of the buildings behind me, when we felt the others arrive.

I couldn't tell you how I knew.

It's not like people appeared out of thin air. But I felt them. Twelve souls, several of which meant so much—everything—to me.[6]

---

[3] Twice. I forget he'd technically run into Sheloran a second time when Kihrin returned to the Capital and was captured by Gadrith.

[4] Talon was the Yoran woman. Yes, I brought her, but in my defense, would you have let her out of your sight?

[5] Here I am forced to acknowledge that a shocking number of them had, in fact, been to Shadrag Gor before.

[6] You have no doubt noticed by this point that the math doesn't work. That's because we didn't know about our stowaway.

"No," I whispered. What? How? We were inside Vol Karoth's prison, weren't we? Nothing should have been able to get to us here. The one thing I had been able to count on was that no matter what happened to me, at least the others would be safe.

You brought friends.

"No." I ducked away from the slash before charging him. I flipped, dodged the blow I knew he'd aimed at my legs, tagged him along the arm instead. It was a meaningless act of defiance, but I wanted him focused on me. "Leave them alone. It's just you and me. And we don't have to be enemies."

Oh? You're ready to surrender, then?

"Have it your way. I guess we do have to be enemies." I jumped up as he slammed his sword down on the ground, fracturing the stone paving underneath.

You don't want me hurting your friends. But they aren't your friends. You don't have friends. Friends are a lie.

"They're not. You used to have them too, you know."

Vol Karoth laughed at me.

No, I never did. That was a lie too. But what you call friendship ... ah, what a joke. After how you hurt them. Shall I show you?

I felt a sweep of panic. "No, you don't have to—"

Let's look at the lies we tell ourselves.

The world changed.

3: Secret Plans

Teraeth's memory
Grizzst's Tower at Rainbow Lake
Twenty-two days after the Battle of the Well of Spirals
Before breakfast

Janel set a plate of jam-smeared sag bread on the table next to Teraeth's bed. "I would've made porridge," she said, "but you're the only one who has any clue how to cook."

Teraeth stared down at the plate, frowning. When had he last eaten? He wasn't hungry. He mostly slept. It seemed preferable to the alternative: thinking.

Thinking led to remembering. And if he remembered, he relived what had happened over and over. His father's death. His mother, forcing him to be crowned king against his will. Kidnapping him. Trying to sacrifice him as an act of genocide.[1]

His mother's death at his own hand. In the end, it hadn't been Relos Var who'd killed Thaena. He had.

Teraeth had known two things when he'd seen his mother, Khaemezra, toss Urthaenriel down to the floor: she'd unwittingly broken her magical control of him, and if he hesitated even for a moment, she'd take Kihrin's life.

Teraeth made his choice. It wasn't even a hard choice.

At least, it hadn't been a hard choice at the time.

It turned out choices could linger like a wound, reminding a person every waking second of their consequences. Choices were ghosts; they haunted.

"Teraeth."

Teraeth tried to collect himself. What had he been doing? What was−? He stared at the food, then at Janel. She'd started braiding her laevos flat against her skull. Or wait, no. She always did that before she slept, didn't she?

She wasn't preparing for sleep now. Janel wore red-and-gold mail, with a motif of flame and scales. She dressed for war, not lounging around a wizard's tower. She clearly intended on going somewhere. Leaving.

Teraeth knew he should get up. He knew he should eat, bathe, dress−but he couldn't make himself move. It all seemed so unimportant. No, insignificant. What did it even matter?

---

[1] Had Thaena successfully forced Teraeth to finish the ritual, it would have resulted in not only his death, but the death of every citizen of the Manol nation. I am only somewhat comforted in the knowledge that the tenyé cost of such an act is usually far too high for any individual or group to provide. War is easier.

What did anything matter?

"I want you out of bed, Teraeth," Janel said again. "It's been almost three weeks. That's enough."

He closed his eyes.

Janel yanked the sheets off the bed. "Time's up. You've had your chance to wallow in guilt, and now you have to work. You have people who need you, a crown to abdicate, and a very short list of enemies to kill."

Teraeth rolled over. "Leave me alone."

"No. Personally, I'd let you be Kihrin's problem, but I can't: Kihrin's missing." Her voice crackled with anger.

He felt plunged in cold water.

When had he last seen Kihrin? He wasn't sure. He remembered Kihrin being around a lot in the days after . . . what had happened. Dim memories of falling into deep, possibly drugged slumbers wedged between Kihrin and Janel, as if both were afraid to leave him unsupervised for fear of what he might do to himself. Kihrin had seldom been around during the day, and then he had simply . . . not been around.

Teraeth hadn't noticed. No, that wasn't true. He'd noticed. He'd just thought it was . . . appropriate. Exactly what Teraeth deserved. Between Kihrin and Janel, at least one of them had been smart enough to back away before they ended up hurt.

Teraeth turned to her. "What?"

"He left to do . . . something." Janel stared off to the side as if she could see through the walls to wherever Kihrin had hidden himself. "Thurvishar keeps saying nothing's wrong, but Thurvishar's a damn liar. Kihrin's been gone for five days without a note, without saying a word to anyone. He wouldn't do that."

An even colder splash of water that time. The shock of fear and worry. He sat up and swung his feet over the side of the bed. "What the fuck?"

"Yes!" Janel said, gesturing toward him. "What the fuck, indeed. That's exactly how I feel. Where are you? Where's your mind? I need you focused. I need the Teraeth who doesn't accept failure. I need the Teraeth who hates injustice. I need the Teraeth who's afraid of nothing!"

Teraeth stood. "I hated the injustice of Quur because I was a hypocrite too blinded by my mother's bullshit to see that she was the one keeping Quur in shackles the whole time. I was afraid of nothing because I was a fool whose mother was the literal Goddess of Death! Failure had no consequences. I couldn't die! And you're the fool if you think failure is something you can reject. Some failures are final. There are some failures from which you can never return!"

"Not yet!" Janel screamed. "I need your help! I need you to be here with me now, do you understand me?"

"You want a Teraeth that doesn't exist anymore. He's gone. I lost him!"

She loomed so much larger than her true size. Janel shouted at him with tears running down her cheeks. "Then go find him! Listen to me. Listen!" She paused, panting, then lowered her voice. "I. Need. Your. Help. Do you understand? I am asking for you to help me. Do I need to beg?"

Pure ice. Facedown against a glacier. He blinked away the sting. Teraeth hadn't thought . . . Janel was admitting she needed help, that she needed *his* help. Janel, for whom going to someone for help meant submission, meant admitting vulnerability. She would rather chew off her own arm.[2]

"Five days," he said.

"Yes. So it's well past time for you to wake up." Janel's face twisted. "Thurvishar knows something." She threw a pile of glittering cloth at him. "Get dressed. We have work to do."

Teraeth was embarrassed by how long it took to track down Thurvishar. He blamed it on assuming the wizard would be trying to avoid them. Instead, the D'Lorus high lord sat in the main room of Grizzst's tower, reading a book. Teraeth hadn't been paying much attention, so he almost didn't recognize the place; Thurvishar had made significant progress organizing and cleaning the wizard's library in the several weeks since they'd arrived.

He'd never questioned why they ended up at the tower. It had just happened. Neither Kihrin nor Thurvishar had wanted to go back to the Capital, Teraeth hadn't wanted to go back to the Manol, and Janel wasn't sure she even had a place to go back to in Jorat.[3] They had defaulted on staying at the now unoccupied tower, mostly because Thurvishar had wanted to look through Grizzst's notes.

He was still doing that when Teraeth and Janel found him.

"Where's Kihrin?" Janel asked, wasting no time on such frivolous questions as "How are you?" or "Figured out how to defeat Relos Var yet?"

Thurvishar raised his head. The man had always been good at keeping an expression off his face, but it didn't stop Teraeth from recognizing the dread lurking in his eyes.

Thurvishar closed the book and set it aside. "I don't know. He's overdue. We set aside a location and time for a meeting. He missed it, but that doesn't mean there's cause for panic."

"And how long ago," Teraeth asked softly, "was this meeting supposed to take place?"

Thurvishar gave him a wary look. "Three days ago."

"Three days ago," Teraeth repeated. "And were you planning to say anything? Go looking for him? How was this supposed to work?" He stepped forward suddenly and took note of the moment when Thurvishar flinched.

"It's . . . complicated."

"Simplify it," Janel pressed. "It's not that we don't trust you, Thurvishar—"

"Speak for yourself," Teraeth said. He wasn't feeling in a friendly or forgiving mood.

Janel crossed over to Thurvishar's table. She clearly wasn't feeling in a friendly or forgiving mood either. "Where did he go, Thurvishar? What was he doing?"

"Ah, well," Thurvishar said.

---

[2] Joratese people—especially Joratese men such as Janel—often have a difficult time asking for help because of the cultural belief that protection bestows fealty and thus accepting assistance is an act of capitulation to a greater authority. An act of weakness, in other words. I cannot roll my eyes hard enough.

[3] Ironically, she probably had the most stable "ask no awkward questions" safe haven of all of them, but she hadn't kept up with current events in her absence.

Teraeth waited.

"Don't make me feel the need to be rude," Teraeth said, "because you know I'll hurt more than your feelings."

The wizard pressed his lips together. "Kihrin thought you'd try to talk him out of it."

The air vanished from the room—or at least from Teraeth's lungs. He knew Kihrin, after all. He knew how much of a well-intentioned fool the man could be, all in the name of some greater good. How reckless he could be. How self-sacrificing. "What did he think we'd talk him out of doing?"

"He returned to the Blight."

Everything stilled, a moment of silent shock that so often heralds a blur of outrage, shouting, violence. Maybe under different circumstances. Now Teraeth just felt dizzy. Hollow. Unbalanced. No, no, no.

"He what?" Janel's voice was deceptively calm.

Thurvishar exhaled. "I couldn't have stopped him. The single location he can teleport to without any assistance is Kharas Gulgoth."

Teraeth grabbed the desk's edge, his lungs burning.

"You let him—" The timbre of Janel's voice betrayed her loss of temper, and Janel was even more capable of murderous rages than he was. Teraeth nursed his grudges along with careful sips until the final poisoning came due. She'd let it out all at once, explosively.

"Janel, please try to stay calm," Thurvishar said, a basic error in judgment as far as Teraeth was concerned. Telling Janel to stay calm rarely had that result. It was ridiculously satisfying to watch her direct her temper at someone other than himself.

"Calm?" Janel's eyes could set the whole room on fire. Which happened to be literally as well as figuratively true. "You're telling me that with Kihrin out there in the Blight, when we know Vol Karoth would love nothing more than to *devour him whole*, I should stay calm?"

"That might have been the wrong choice of words," Thurvishar allowed. He pushed his chair back from the table. "But I'm not going to apologize for Kihrin's decision."

"You should have—" Janel started to say.

"What? Tattled on him? Treated him as though he were a child who shouldn't be allowed to make up his own mind?" Thurvishar stared at them both, no longer nervous. Now he just looked annoyed. "Why don't you stop for a good, long minute and think about why Kihrin might not have wanted to tell you the truth concerning his plans. Why he didn't think he could trust you to work with him."

Teraeth flushed. "How dare you—"

"Oh no," Thurvishar interrupted. "How dare you. With the whole world at stake and thousands dying, how dare you say he's not allowed to risk his own life. I understand that you both care for him. The idea that he's in danger is painful. But you don't have the right to lock him away in a cage." He shook his head. "I don't know what I was thinking. I should have left a letter."

"Thurvishar." Janel managed to pack an amazing amount of venom into one proper noun.

"He was right," Thurvishar said. "Kihrin was right to not tell you. You're both proving it this very moment."

Janel narrowed her eyes. "No, you don't get to put this on us! I refuse to accept—"

"I don't care," Teraeth said.

Both Thurvishar and Janel stopped to look at him.

"I don't care who's to blame," he said. "I care about where Kihrin is. I care about what happens next." Teraeth was lying. He cared a great deal about who was responsible, but acting on that emotion wouldn't get him what he wanted. So he pushed it all down—his anger, his rage, his despair. He'd done it before. He was good at it. "You wouldn't have done this without a plan for what's next. What was that supposed to be?"

Thurvishar sighed.

"Just answer the question—" Janel looked ready to set the entire room ablaze.

"I can't," Thurvishar snarled. He corrected himself. "No, I won't. You both know this"—he gestured around the room—"isn't safe from eavesdropping by our enemies. So no, I don't believe I will tell you just yet. We've already said far too much."

"So where to, then?" Janel said. "Shadrag Gor? Where do we go so you'll be comfortable telling us the truth?"

"Yes, fine. Shadrag Gor." Thurvishar's face twisted in frustration; he swept all the papers off the table, sending them flying. "I can't find what I need here, anyway. I've spent days reading through these damn papers, and for what?"

Teraeth leaned against a wall and said nothing. He couldn't believe it. Except no, of course he could. It was a perfect cap to the perfect ruin of everything he held dear. Kihrin had gone back to the Blight. He must have found something. Thought he could do something to deal with Vol Karoth. Something dangerous and stupid, of course, which was the reason he'd gone alone.

And hadn't come back.

"These are C'indrol's notes."[4] There was a funny catch in Janel's voice. She'd picked up one of the scattered pieces of paper and stood there reading it.

Thurvishar lifted his head from his chest. "Yes, well. Kihrin assumed you'd be able to remember what you did to separate his souls from Vol Karoth's, but I realized after you sat down for our talks that you don't." A rueful, unhappy smile touched his lips. "I had hoped something in Grizzst's copies of C'indrol's research notes on ousology[5] might have held a clue. No such luck."

Janel's hand started to shake. She let the page fall from her fingers as she stared at Thurvishar with wide eyes.

---

[4] While I understand you're perfectly aware of who C'indrol was, I am operating under the assumption that, at some point, these accounts will reach a wider audience. So: C'indrol was a voras researcher and later politician who secretly continued both their research and an affair with S'arric prior to his corruption into Vol Karoth. C'indrol died during the destruction of Karolaen, and was reincarnated as Elana Milligreest and, later, Janel.

[5] The study of souls and magic dealing with souls. Grizzst based much of his work attempting to resurrect the Eight on C'indrol's research.

Teraeth felt his own pulse quicken with dread. "What did you just realize—?" He held up a hand before she could answer. "No, don't tell me. Don't say it aloud. Thurvishar's right about that much."

Thurvishar scoffed.[6]

Janel balled her hands into fists. "You're never going to find the answers you need in this room. Grizzst didn't have all of C'indrol's notes, and he had no idea more existed. I doubt Grizzst knew Elana Milligreest created a library to store information. Every scrap of information. If she ever wrote down what you need, it's there."

Thurvishar blinked several times. "She—what? How have I never heard of this?"

Teraeth was glad Thurvishar had asked the question so he wouldn't have to.

Janel's smile was vindictive. "You have. You've heard about it all your life. It's become so famous for gathering up every shred of anything even tangentially related to Xaltorath's stupid prophecies that most of the damn things are named after the place."

"The Devoran Prophecies?" Thurvishar asked. "The Devors Islands?"

"The monastery there, yes," Janel answered.

"Fine." Teraeth walked over to the other two. "So let's go. You can find the information you need and then explain to us—somewhere secure—what is going on. And, Thurvishar?"

The wizard gazed at Teraeth like he knew exactly what he was about to say. It didn't matter. Teraeth would spell it out, anyway, just to make sure there were no misunderstandings. "Kihrin had better not be dead, or you'll be joining him."[7]

Teraeth's reaction
The Lighthouse at Shadrag Gor
Twenty-four days after the Battle of the Well of Spirals
Just after arrival

"What was that?" Janel asked. "What just happened?"

Teraeth opened his eyes after the vision faded. Or rather, Teraeth's vision returned, as he'd never closed his eyes in the first place. No sooner had they arrived in the Lighthouse then he'd been overwhelmed by that memory, as sharp and painful as if he'd just experienced it again. Now he was in a room he recognized even though he'd only been there a few times before.

The last time, however, when his mother had brought him, had been recent and memorable. Teraeth had stayed there for three weeks before Thaena had been ready to sacrifice him.

This was the Lighthouse at Shadrag Gor. He nearly laughed. They were in the right place, but he didn't like how they'd gotten there.[8]

The main tower was a huge, tapering, multi-floored structure of perfectly

---

[6] Please. You were right about all of it.
[7] I can see how that ended up being quite awkward.
[8] You're welcome.

fitted stone, thick wooden planks underfoot, creaking circular stairs leading farther up or down. Dim mage-light provided the only illumination. The
whole place smelled of fresh paint and the musty scent of confined spaces.[9]
Someone desperately needed to open a window, which was a shame, because
there weren't any.

Someone had painted the place since the last time he'd visited. Not in the
sense of redecorating but in the manner of some sort of occult ritual.

All the people surrounding him had been there at the end on Devors,
and thus snatched up when Senera arrived. A few were unfamiliar, but the
majority he already knew, including one he wouldn't have expected—his old
sect-sister and former lover, Kalindra. Two he didn't recognize: an elegant,
slender young man with long hair and a Yoran woman who was probably one
of Xivan's Spurned mercenaries.[10]

And all of them except for Senera and the Spurned woman were sopping,
wet cloth plastered to wet skin. It was unreasonably cold inside the Lighthouse too—or at least it felt that way to someone soaking wet—which just gave
Teraeth one more thing to be angry about.

"Janel," Senera said, hands raised, grimacing, "I don't know what just happened. I'm not responsible for that."

"Then who is, Senera?" Janel's grip tightened on her sword. She still wore
the same red-and-gold armor she'd worn when she woke Teraeth up that
morning. Teraeth belatedly realized it must have come from the Manol, the
same as his own clothing, which meant she must have traveled back there at
some point during the last several weeks. He'd missed it.[11]

"Did we all see that? Did we all see the same thing?" Galen D'Mon asked.
He was dressed oddly too, wearing his agolé as a sash instead of the more
traditional Quuros manner. That was an affectation Teraeth had only seen
on Zherias, which implied some odd things about the Quuros prince's recent
travel history. "I wasn't sure if it was just me hallucinating, except I can't
imagine why my mind would have picked that." He glanced at Teraeth, and
then quickly looked away.

"I should be surprised if we didn't all see it. But as to what caused it—" The
woman standing next to Galen made a distasteful face, as if someone had forgotten to wash the silverware. She looked like someone had dunked her into
a bathtub fully clothed, but also like that bathtub had been made from solid
gold and filled with milk and rose petals. He remembered Galen's wife from
Gadrith's attack on the Blue Palace, but he'd forgotten her name.[12] Her gaze
fell on Teraeth. "That was you."

"Yes," Teraeth said. "That was me."

---

[9] I'd have thought the smell of paint would have faded, but even with the Lighthouse's time dilation, I hadn't been gone for more than a few days.

[10] The man would be Qown, whom Teraeth had never previously met, and the woman would be
our favorite bad coin, Talon.

[11] It's a minor detail, but I'm curious about this. Did you transport her? If not, how did she manage
this? I must make a note to ask.

[12] Sheloran D'Mon, formerly of House D'Talus.

She stared at him as she moved her wet hair away from her face. "Thaena's truly dead?"

"Yes. That was also me."

"Talea," Galen muttered. "Wait. Talea was hurt—"

Talea groaned as if to punctuate his point. Xivan laid Talea down on the floor, her expression frantic. Thurvishar summoned up brighter mage-light to reveal blood had washed Talea's stomach and hips red.

Galen pulled Xivan away from the other woman. "I think you've done enough."

Xivan didn't fight him.

"Qown!" Sheloran gestured frantically. "What are you doing hiding over there? Talea's injured!" The royal princess looked close to tears, despite her otherwise excellent posture. She whipped back around to glare at Talea. "And you! You said you'd be a fool to fight Xivan by yourself."

"I'm fine, Sheloran," Talea—who was clearly not fine—protested. "But hadn't you noticed I'm a bit of a fool?"

Teraeth hadn't missed the magic word Sheloran had yelled, however, and neither had Janel. Her eyes widened as the long-haired man hurried over to Talea's side. Teraeth couldn't help but notice the way the man avoided Janel's eyes.

"That's Qown?" Teraeth mouthed to Janel. She nodded.

Teraeth was surprised. Janel had always described Qown as if he were an impoverished monk, the kind who had taken every vow of self-denial—pleasure, material possessions—in favor of living a life with all his concerns wrapped around others and nothing left for himself. This man didn't look like that. He was doing a fair impression of a Zheriasian rake, his agolé worn as a sash in the same manner as Galen.

"Whatever you did," Kalindra growled, pushing herself toward Senera, "reverse it! Reverse it right now! That monster is still attacking, and my son is back there!" Her hair spattered water in an uneven circle around her as she held a dagger with shaking hands. Her eyes were wild.

"This is Shadrag Gor," Thurvishar explained.

Teraeth sighed. Like Kalindra knew what the hell Shadrag Gor was. She'd never needed to know. And she was a newly widowed mother with a child in jeopardy. She had no patience whatsoever. Who could blame her? The woman crossed the room, fast the way only a Black Brotherhood assassin could be. Teraeth didn't think she meant to kill Senera. More likely threaten, put that dagger to her throat, make her point a little . . . clearer.

But Kalindra's blade slammed against a warp of iridescent magics and rebounded.

Teraeth sighed as Kalindra started to swing again. "Kalindra, stop."

Complicated emotions played over the woman's face as he addressed her. Anger. Worry. And, interestingly, shame.

"Teraeth?" Kalindra looked around as if hoping their location had shifted back to Devors between eyeblinks. "What are you doing here, anyway?" she asked. "What happened?"

"Later," Teraeth said, his voice thick.

Kalindra shuddered. "Teraeth, I need to go back."

"We will," Teraeth growled. "After I have my answers. Time moves differently here. Only seconds will have passed when we return. There's no need to hurry. There's no point." He stared at Thurvishar. "Someone said he was going to explain matters."

"What was that about Kihrin?" Janel asked Senera. "And why did you show us Teraeth's memories?" Steam rose from her clothing as she spoke. Teraeth wasn't sure if she was purposefully drying the water from her clothing or if her body temperature was just running that hot.

"I didn't do that." Senera lifted her chin, but she still seemed nervous. Her gaze lingered on the tall, black-clad, and only living member of House D'Lorus.[13] "I'm fixing your mistake," she told Thurvishar.

He rolled his eyes to the heavens as if praying to every kind of divine being out there. "You checked."

"Of course I checked!" Senera growled. "Don't tell me you didn't think I would!"

"Thurvishar, are you talking about Kihrin?" Janel's voice was a warning wrapped in velvet.

Thurvishar ignored Janel, his focus entirely on Senera. "What have you done?" he asked. His gaze flickered to the strangely painted walls. "Senera, what is this?"

"Kihrin and Vol Karoth are fighting for dominance," Senera explained. "What did you think was going to happen?"

"But why are we in Shadrag Gor?" Thurvishar asked, still frowning.

"Never mind that," Teraeth cut in, raising his voice. He was out of patience himself. "Where is Kihrin?"

Before Senera could reply, the world changed.

[13] I realize that's a gray area, depending on Tyentso's legal status as emperor.

4: BALANCED ON THE EDGE

Kihrin's story
Inside Vol Karoth's prison
Just after Teraeth's vision

I came back from Teraeth's memories to find myself still the same distance from Vol Karoth, both of us still armed and circling around each other. The city looked much the same—bleak and dry and washed with gray. Vol Karoth was the same black shape cut out of reality.

Disbelief and rage cycled through me, but I stamped down on those emotions as unproductive.

"What was that?" I asked him. "You think showing me Teraeth's memories is some sort of gotcha?"

Oh, but it wasn't just his memories, Vol Karoth said. ***It was his reaction to what you did. Because you betrayed him. You betrayed both of them with your lack of trust. With your lack of faith. With your secrets. Did you enjoy hurting them?***

I shuddered and tried to retreat, but I knew too well that I'd hear his voice for some time when we were in this kind of proximity to each other, even if I couldn't see him.

"Fuck you," I told him. "I was protecting them."

And now they're here. Well done.

"Leave them alone," I said.

I didn't bring them here. Thank Senera for that. And let's look at your "friends," shall we? Murderers and terrorists. Traitors. More than one assassin. What a fine group of upstanding people.

"Better than you," I spat. Not exactly my finest retort. He was hitting pretty close to the mark when "Yeah, but what are you?" was my big comeback.

You're a hypocrite. Vol Karoth seemed bizarrely angry about the whole thing. He sounded insulted.

"I never claimed not to be." I stepped away from him, trying to put some distance between us.

The thing was, I could feel the people in the Lighthouse. I mean, I knew everyone who was there: Janel and Teraeth; Galen of all people; his wife, Sheloran; Jarith's widowed wife, Kalindra (*my* Kalindra,[1] which I guess just proved Vol Karoth had a point about me and assassins); Thurvishar; Senera;

---

[1] Although Kihrin's affair with Kalindra lasted for less than six months while he was on Ynisthana, I suppose it held an exaggerated importance because of his age, and because of how they parted—forcibly, at Thaena's command.

Qown; Talea; and Xivan. Oh, and one more, just to make it extra hilarious: Talon. Enough for quite a party.[2]

I felt their presence in a manner far beyond simple recognition. It's like each of them was a book, something I could pull down from a shelf, flip through at my leisure. I wondered if this was how Thurvishar felt about being a telepath, because it was terribly intrusive. I didn't want to go stealing through people's memories, but I couldn't help it. I just knew things.

Teraeth and Kalindra were both a mess. Janel was furious. Thurvishar was both furious and worried. Emotions were running pretty hot, as it happened. Hell, Xivan had been the person who'd stabbed Talea, which would have had me a little more bothered if I couldn't tell just how guilty Xivan was feeling about that.

And Galen . . . wow. *Galen.*

But Senera was the one who had my attention the most at that moment, both because I was annoyed at her for bringing everyone here and putting them at risk but also . . . also, I was proud of her. Really proud.

I considered Vol Karoth. It felt like a lull just before he was going to charge again, and the dark god didn't disappoint. I managed to block him for long enough to dodge to the side and roll, bringing me a few feet farther away when I stood.

"You want to see the people I call friends?" I smirked. "Okay, let's do this."

I opened the book of Senera's mind, found the particular memories I wanted, and shoved them at Vol Karoth the same way he'd done to me.

The world changed.

Senera's memory
Twenty days after the Battle of the Well of Spirals
The Lighthouse at Shadrag Gor

Senera closed the cover of Thurvishar's book and leaned back. There were a few details that she hadn't known and a few more that were uncomfortable and best forgotten. Thurvishar had delivered the account into her hands almost shyly, his expression sheepish, as if it were a damn bouquet of flowers. Most of his allies would kill him if they found out Thurvishar was handing his notes over to the enemy like this.

And Senera absolutely was the enemy. She knew this. They both knew this. This was fact. She had the body count to prove it.

So she'd retired to the Lighthouse at Shadrag Gor to read the book. She had to see . . .

She had to see what would need editing before showing the manuscript to Relos Var. It's not that she had anything to hide, *because she didn't,* but she'd been certain Thurvishar had included little sabotages, subtle suggestions that Senera might not be completely loyal. Thurvishar knew the value of turning Relos Var against her, to force Senera to turn against Relos Var. She'd been right to be that paranoid, because more than a few such traps existed in the chronicle.

---

[2] He missed one, and I don't think that was coincidence. Vol Karoth was blocking his perceptions.

Senera didn't know what was worse: that Thurvishar dared to guess at so many of her inner thoughts and feelings, or that he'd so often guessed correctly.[3] She'd needed to excise large portions before the final account would be safe to pass along.

She wanted to be furious at Thurvishar for daring to tell parts of the story from her perspective, as if he had any way of knowing . . . but he did. Ah, he did.

She knew the nature of his witchgift.

Spitefully, she pulled out the Name of All Things. Senera asked the Cornerstone what Thurvishar had purposefully edited out of the manuscript.[4]

When Senera finished, she stared at the pages in shock, in dull, stupefied horror. If Thurvishar had been there, she'd have slapped him. How could he be that . . . that . . . stupid? That purely and unarguably stupid? In all the history of the Twin Worlds, had anyone else ever been that completely stupid? How could either of those fools possibly think that such an absurd, ludicrous, obstinate, demented plan would work?

Except it might work. She knew it might work. Maybe. There was the tiniest chance . . .

Then she asked one last question: *Where is Talon now?*

Senera left Shadrag Gor once she had the answer.

It didn't occur to her until much later, until much too late in fact, that what she should have done—what Thurvishar's *enemy* would've done—was first tell Relos Var.

A few hours later, she stood on the outskirts of Stonegate Pass in eastern Khorvesh, scanning the skies. She took care to stay away from any imperial sky watchers who might prove an inconvenience. The air was hot and dry. It might almost have been considered a lovely day, under different circumstances. Senera took no notice of the weather, except to be thankful it was clear enough to see.

She waited the entire day and still saw no sign of the mimic. Senera despaired that she'd miscalculated projecting Talon's likely path. The sun set to the east, and the blanket of night reached out to cover the land, and still there was no sign of her.

Until there was.

Senera might have missed it in daytime, but she'd learned some tricks from Qown he'd never meant to teach. She'd been searching by heat as well as by sight, and Talon ran hotter than a bird should. So either Talon, or a magical adept trying the same trick, flying out of the Blight.

So: Talon.

Senera waited until Talon had flown past the line of sight of anyone at Stonegate and then made her move. As attacks went, hers was simple: she wove an invisible net in the air, a spiderweb hanging without supports, while

---

[3] I had always believed my own mental defenses were better than that.
[4] I caught myself just in time to tack *that isn't sexual* to the end of that question or I'd have little doubt I'd have been transcribing pornographic scenes for days.

she waited with ready glyph-inscribed sheets of paper. Talon hit the net and tumbled; Senera used the distraction to transform the glyphs into skeins of light and shoved the bundles of tenyé created toward the mimic's flailing shape. The glyphs hit and triggered. That quickly, the fight was over.

A bird fell from the sky and landed in a glowing tangle of chain and spell-work. Talon fell just next to a clearing, surrounded by chaparral and scrub brush, the sort of place where Senera had been told they grew the most amazing olibanum. The air smelled of balsam resin and old, dried wood.

By the time Senera reached the crash site, Talon had attempted multiple escapes and had each time failed. She no longer looked like a bird. The shape she'd taken made Senera's stomach knot.

Talon looked like Kihrin. Exactly like. The monster had copied every detail perfectly.

"What the fuck, Senera?" Talon scolded her in Kihrin's voice. "If you wanted to talk to me so badly, you could have just asked."

Senera bent down next to the mimic and grabbed her by the hair. "Did you do it?"

Talon—and it was absolutely Talon because Kihrin had never learned a spell to change into a bird—stared at her blankly. "Could you be more specific?"

"Did you kill Kihrin?" Senera sneered.

"Senera..." Talon looked at her like she'd gone insane. The act was so good that for a second Senera wondered herself. "I'm right here."

"Talon, I asked the Name of All Things where to find you," Senera told the mimic. She saw the precise moment when Talon stopped pretending, when she realized the game was done.

Talon's eyes widened. "That... Why were you even looking for me?"

Senera let go of Talon's hair. "Thurvishar gave your plot away."

Talon started cursing.

Senera felt a profound degree of annoyance with herself, at how troubled she was by the idea of Kihrin's death. They weren't friends. They'd never been friends. She didn't even like him.[5] "Did you kill Kihrin?" she asked one more time.

"You didn't ask your stone?"

"I did. But I want to hear you admit it." She grabbed Talon's arm and dragged the mimic to her feet. "Let's take a trip."

Talon eyed the woman. "Where?"

"Kharas Gulgoth," Senera said as she started to cast the spell to open a gate. "Don't worry. I know the way."

Talon began struggling again, for what good it did. "Are you out of your mind? You know what's awake in the center of Kharas Gulgoth? You can't go there. That's insane!"

"Well, you are the expert on insanity." Senera pinned one of the binding glyphs in midair so she could use both hands to cast the spell. When she finished, she picked up the glyph again. "Let's go visit Vol Karoth, shall we?"

---

[5] Yes, fine. In the interest of veracity, I will admit to some degree of exaggeration here.

Senera ignored the mimic's struggling and dragged her. She had to cast another spell to manage it; she wasn't strong enough normally. That one, she'd learned from Janel.

The thing was, Senera knew perfectly well how foolish this was. Relos Var had told her all about the expected outcomes of what would happen after Vol Karoth woke. But for that same reason, she knew she had a small but definite window before she faced her own annihilation.

Enough time to slip in and see for herself. Enough time to know for sure what Thurvishar and Kihrin had done. And as a consequence, decide what she would do in return.

If people were going to bandy words like *insane* around, it wouldn't be because she was suicidal.

The gate opened. Senera pulled Talon through.

It wasn't perfectly dark in the center of the Blight, but only because of magic. The buildings glowed. Only they had long ceased to be buildings. What Senera saw instead was the web of magical supports that had once outlined structures now crumbled beneath them, atrophied by Vol Karoth or age or both. The rainbow hues of Tya's Veil washed the night sky. The air smelled of nothing.

But neither Senera nor Talon were disintegrating. Nothing was disintegrating. Not buildings, not paving stones, not flesh.

Senera looked up to the top of the main building. Seven rays of light streaked to the center from distant horizons. They would continue to do so even though four of the Immortals who powered those wards were clinically dead. The prison still held, even if it no longer trapped its occupant in a state of slumber.

But something was wrong. Vol Karoth wasn't fighting to break free anymore. He wasn't pulling on tenyé so hard it literally broke apart all physical matter in proximity.

Something—someone—was distracting him.

She stared at the prison, not quite able to force herself to take the next step. Then Talon started laughing. When the wizard glared at her, Talon said, "Oh, but you've come all this way. Don't you want to go see for yourself?"

She pushed down her temptation to hit the mimic. Also, Talon was right. Senera did want to see for herself, because apparently, the Arric family weren't the only ones capable of acts of extraordinary hubris.[6] She walked inside the great hall and studied the fallen god of the sun.

The room must have been grand, elegant, once. Someone even tried to repair parts of it, which must have been damaged when nine proto-dragons had fled into the firestorms accompanying their births. Now it was a corpse, which didn't smell of . . . anything. Not sulfur or fungus, not dirt or desert or decay. The wards provided light, but they just emphasized how utterly dark the figure they trapped truly was. Senera studied the god of annihilation and felt something lodge in her throat.

---

[6] Yes, I realize from a legal standpoint I might be considered to qualify, but we both know my marriage to Relos Var was never more than a necessary tactical fiction.

This was without a doubt the bravest act that she had ever seen, the most literally selfless. Kihrin had to have known he couldn't come back from this. Even if it worked–even if everything went right, *which it couldn't*–he'd stop being Kihrin. He'd return to being S'arric or Vol Karoth. He'd sacrificed his souls answering the question the Eight Immortals and Relos Var never dared.

It killed her to know it was a sacrifice utterly made in vain.

"I assume Kihrin's in there somewhere," Talon said. "I wonder what they're talking about."

Senera narrowed her eyes and didn't dignify the mimic with a glare. "Was that the plan? Kihrin and Vol Karoth would just . . . talk?"

"Of course not!" Talon protested. "Kihrin's a complete whole soul, and Vol Karoth's a tattered remnant of one. Kihrin's going to–" Talon stopped and stared at Senera, apparently realizing she had been about to spell out the entire scheme.

"I'll find out no matter what," Senera reminded her.

"Will you?" Talon no longer acted like a struggling, defiant teenager. "That sounds like something Thurvishar would say." There was something in Talon's gaze–Kihrin's gaze, because she still looked like him–that reminded Senera so much of Kihrin when he had one of those annoying little moments of inspiration, of insight. Senera felt a chill. She had to keep reminding herself this wasn't Kihrin.

But Talon had all of Kihrin's memories, and if she really had slain Kihrin, she even had his mental map. Talon was as close to being "Kihrin" as it was possible to be without actually possessing the man's souls.

"I'm nothing like Thurvishar." Senera clenched her teeth. The problem was that, even without using the Name of All Things, she had a reasonably good idea exactly what Thurvishar and Kihrin had tried to do. "You thought Vol Karoth was a child," Senera said. "You thought Kihrin would be able to just take over."

Talon didn't answer. She watched Senera like a fox waiting for the startled mouse to move. It felt that way even though Talon was still bound.

Senera's gimlet eyes glared. "You idiots," she sneered. "Vol Karoth's not a child. He's all the darkness and hate and malice that ever existed inside the leader of the Eight Immortals, inside the man so talented it drove Relos Var sick with jealousy. And anyway, Kihrin and Thurvishar forgot about time, didn't they?"

Only then did Talon seem uncertain. "Time? What do you mean?"

"I mean there's literally no time!" She waved her hand toward the trapped silhouette in the center of the room, which seemed to be floating. But only if one didn't understand he had literally destroyed everything within twenty-five feet of himself, carving a perfect sphere out of the nearby physical matter, and hadn't yet had *time* to start falling. "Time's slowed to a crawl for Vol Karoth. That means it has for Kihrin too. He'll have no chance to do anything before Relos Var is ready with his plans, before Relos Var frees Vol Karoth. And that means Vol Karoth will very much still be in charge when he's unleashed on the world. Those idiots didn't think this through!"[7]

Senera realized she was shouting.

Talon stared at her again. And then, slowly, the mimic smiled.

"What do you have to be happy about?" Senera said. "Do you think I'm going to let you live?"

Talon's smile didn't falter. "I think if you meant to turn me in to Relos Var, he'd be here right now, and we wouldn't be having this 'conversation.'"

Senera felt her heart stop. She felt the whole world, or maybe just her whole world, come to a stuttering, horrified, paralyzed stop.

She . . . she hadn't told Relos Var.

Senera hadn't even thought to tell Relos Var. She'd only ever thought about ensuring he didn't find out.

Talon's smile grew wider. "Because here's the thing, ducky. You just looked at the big shadow man hanging up here, knowing that Kihrin sacrificed his life for the chance he could screw up all of Relos Var's and Xaltorath's plans, and you didn't think he was an idiot. Naïve, maybe. A bit too quick to rush to action, sure. But not an idiot."

"I did—"

"Don't pretend. You're not hard to read when you're shouting. What you thought was: Relos Var would never be selfless enough to do this."

Senera exhaled.

"You did, didn't you? You don't have to admit it. It can just be our little secret." Talon lifted her chin. "Var's perfectly content to sacrifice others for his cause, to have someone else pay the price, but to step up to the altar himself?"

"Shut up."

"Oh no. Not himself. He's too important. Too essential. A universe without Relos Var is a universe that might as well be lost, isn't it?"

"Shut up," Senera repeated.

"He'd have never done this, not even if he knew for an absolute fact that It. Would. Work."

"Shut up!"

"And so the question I have for you, Senera—"

"Please stop talking," Senera said, her voice hitching on the last word. Her legs felt like they might crumple beneath her any second.

"—is, what are you going to do about it?"

Senera wiped both eyes with a thumb. "That fucking bastard."

Talon raised an eyebrow. "Relos Var?"

"No, Thurvishar!" Senera spat out. "That . . . that fucking brat! Do you really think he didn't know I'd check? Of course he did. He knows I'm not that gullible. He did this deliberately, knowing that either I have to betray Relos Var—the man who saved me and to whom I owe *everything*—or I will have let this all have been for nothing. Thurvishar's just given me his life, and made

---

[7] It is possible I didn't give you enough credit here, but a full analysis of the temporal anomalies of Vol Karoth's prison will have to wait.

it my choice whether or not to save it. Because Relos Var will kill Thurvishar for this, kinship be damned. Relos Var will free Vol Karoth too early, and he'll find a way to deal with what Kihrin's done. Relos Var will win! He'll . . . he'll . . . win . . ." Senera trailed off as she realized what she was saying. What it meant.

Senera fell to her knees. She grabbed the edges of the tiles with her fingers and dug into the marble, as if the sharp edges on the cut stone might remind her of who she was. Tears dropped down to splash against the floor, which should have been covered with dust but, of course, wasn't.

"Aww. Did somebody just realize they don't want him to?"

"Yes!" Senera admitted, her heart breaking. "No! I want the world Relos Var promised me! I want a world where nobody is better or worse just because of who their parents were. All I ever wanted was a world where children don't grow up in chains. I'm willing to do anything to make that world real!"

A dark emotion flickered across Talon's face.

"But instead of freeing the oppressed, it turns out his solution is just to chain everyone." Senera laughed darkly. "I suppose it's a kind of equality."

Talon walked over and crouched down beside Senera. The idea of restraints had always been absurd, anyway. "So now it comes to this. Which side are you on? Because this time, you get to choose. Actually, this time, you have to choose. Sorry about that."

"Don't lie. You're not even a tiny bit sorry."

"No," Talon admitted. "But hey, it's not like I'm going to judge you. I'm the last person in the whole world who would. It's kind of my thing. You want to switch sides? I say go for it."

Senera turned her head and stared hatefully at Vol Karoth. "Kihrin and Thurvishar want to do this? Fine. We'll let them try. And I will show you, Talon, exactly what I'm going to do about this."

Senera opened her satchel and pulled out her paints. She freed the brush from her hair and began to work.

The world changed.

5: Lessons in Betrayal

Senera's reaction
The Lighthouse at Shadrag Gor

Senera knocked her head back against the Lighthouse tower wall. "I. Am. Not. Doing. This."

"So is someone reading our minds?" Thurvishar asked. "How is someone defeating–"

When Thurvishar stopped talking, Senera looked up to see what was wrong.

Teraeth held a knife to the wizard's throat.

"What did I tell you would happen if Kihrin died?" the assassin said in a low voice.

Behind them, the room erupted into noise, shouts.

"Shut up!" Xivan screamed. She had a voice that carried when she felt like it, perfectly pitched to cut through any amount of clamor.

The room fell silent.

"Thank you," Thurvishar said, careful not to move.

"You're welcome," Xivan replied. "Teraeth, what the fuck are you doing? You look like hell, by the way."

"Right back at you." Teraeth didn't turn his head.

Senera scoffed. Xivan looked healthier than she had in ages. If Senera hadn't known better, she'd never have guessed the woman wasn't alive.[1]

"Teraeth," Senera said carefully, "I can't let you kill him."

"Teraeth, stop," Janel said. "Please."

Thurvishar hadn't said a word other than the thank-you. He held his chin up, baring his neck. But Senera didn't think they were getting through to Teraeth. He was about to do something horrible.

Faintly, strains of music floated through the air. Everyone paused.

The music might have been playing earlier, but if it had, everyone had been talking too loudly to hear it. In the awkward, tense silence, it was perfectly audible.

It sounded like someone in another room was playing a harp. Which would have been fine–although no, it would *not* have been fine–except Senera knew she'd only been gone from the Lighthouse for a few seconds of exterior time.

The Lighthouse had been empty when she'd left. The odds of anyone else being here now . . .

---

[1] I just assumed she'd been dining really well. On sailors and pirates, presumably.

Teraeth jerked the knife away from Thurvishar's throat. He turned and threw it, so it embedded in the opposite wall, quivering. As he stepped toward the doorway hall leading to the manor, the music faded as if someone had walked outside or shut the door.

"That's Kihrin," he said. "How is Kihrin playing the harp when Kihrin's dead?"

"I don't . . ." Janel's voice trailed off. She sounded lost.

"I'll be right back," Teraeth said. He darted down the hallway without waiting for a reaction or permission. Under the circumstances, Senera didn't feel like trying to stop him. Janel looked like she was debating whether or not to follow, but questioning Senera won out on the priorities list.

"Senera—" Janel started to say.

"What is going on?" Xivan interrupted.

"I don't know!" Senera said. I *don't know* was a phrase she hated. "This has gone off in a direction I hadn't expected."

"And just what did you expect?" Janel asked.

Senera bit the edge of a thumbnail. "Not this." Senera narrowed her eyes at Thurvishar, who had a faint scarlet line across his throat. Teraeth shouldn't have been able to get anywhere near the wizard. So what was that? A test? A demonstration of trust? Guilt?[2]

"Who else is here?" Sheloran asked.

"No one," Senera said. She was lying, but there shouldn't have been anyone else there capable of playing music. That didn't mean there wasn't technically anyone else there.

Not all the current guests of the Lighthouse were visible.

No one moved. There was no place to sit. By long-standing tradition, the landing—long ago designated for the opening of gates into the Lighthouse—was kept clear of furniture. No one encouraged lingering in this room, even though the odds of two different entries into the location crossing paths were so low as to define impossible.

They were all waiting for an explanation.

Thurvishar turned to Senera. "What did you do?"

"I think we all saw what she did," Sheloran said.

"No," Thurvishar said. "I mean after the vision ended. You had a plan, Senera. You were going to do something. So what was it?" Instead of waiting for her answer, he rotated in place and tried to trace the twisting maze of painted sigils and glyphs.

"This is a trap," Janel responded.

Senera supposed she'd earned that.

"Maybe," Xivan answered, "but I'm curious as to its exact nature."

Senera rubbed a temple. "Oh, fuck all of this," she chuntered. "Do you seriously imagine I would conjure up an illusion like that just to make you trust me?"

"Yes," answered half a dozen people, including, to Senera's infinite chagrin, Talon.

---

[2] I would still like to know what you were thinking here.

Senera exhaled. "Do you all think I'm stupid enough to expect it to work?"

That time, her question was met with silence.

Talea struggled to sit up. "Qown, stop. It's fine. I'm fine."

"You're not!" Qown protested. "That sword blow sliced you open and . . ." He frowned at her, blinking.

"I'm fine," Talea repeated. "You're good at this, remember?" She patted his hand.

"Right," Qown said. "I . . . am." He looked confused.

Talea pulled herself to her feet and tutted over the blood staining her wet clothing. She'd left a red stain on the floor behind her. She then grinned at Senera. "Senera! How have you been? How's Rebel doing?"

"Maybe this isn't the right time, Talea," Senera answered. With everything that was going on, all the chaos surrounding them, it naturally followed that Talea would be mostly concerned about Senera's dog. "And she's fine."[3]

"Oh, I'm so glad to hear that," she said. "But funny you should mention time. Because that's what you did with the glyphs, right? Something with time. If the problem is that time is too slow where Kihrin is trapped in Kharas Gulgoth, maybe doing something with the place where time moves too fast is the solution?"

Senera stared. When . . . It was damnably annoying how the woman occasionally proved herself to be far more insightful than anyone gave her credit for. She was just so sweet and cheerful and simple. Normally.

Thurvishar transferred his attention from the walls to Senera. "Wait, how would that even be . . . Talea's right, isn't she?"

Talea didn't wait on the official answer. She pulled a gold coin from her pocket and started lacing it over and under fingers as she leaned against a wall.[4] Senera turned back to Thurvishar.

"Yes," Senera said, "she's right. As I said, the reason your plan wasn't going to work was because you didn't have enough time."

Thurvishar studied the glyphs on the walls again, finger on his chin. "You sympathetically linked Shadrag Gor and Kharas Gulgoth."

"No," Senera replied. "I sympathetically linked Shadrag Gor and *Vol Karoth's prison.*"

"But that—" Thurvishar stopped, then swallowed down a laugh. His gaze was openly worshipful. "That's brilliant."

Senera turned away, hating herself for the way his praise brought the blood to her cheeks. His utter sincerity was the worst part about it. "It's not brilliant. I missed something. These visions—" She waved a hand in irritation. "Nothing in the glyphs should be causing this. I don't know what is. I missed something."

"Maybe it's not a what," Thurvishar said, "but rather a who?"

Before she could respond, Teraeth returned, his face a scowl. "The Lighthouse is empty. There's no one else here."

"I could have told you that," Senera said. "Oh wait. I did."

"Then where was that music coming from?" Janel asked.

---

[3] I left her with a sitter.

[4] The coin Talea received from the Goddess of Luck, Taja, was silver, for the record.

"Maybe it was one of us playing a prank?" Qown suggested. "Did someone craft an illusion, you know, as a joke? We won't be angry if you did."

No one spoke.

Teraeth broke the silence. "Speak for yourself. I'll be plenty angry; it was in poor fucking taste."

Galen's wife, Sheloran, turned to Senera. "When you say you linked this tower and Vol Karoth's prison, what do you mean?"

"She did what?" Teraeth hadn't been there for that part of the conversation.

Senera sighed, but before she could respond, Qown interrupted, his attention focused on Sheloran. "You know who Vol Karoth is?"

Sheloran raised her chin as she fanned herself. "Some of us received a classical education, Qown."

Galen blinked. "Mind sharing with the rest of the class, Red? Because I have no idea who Vol Karoth is."

"Is that a hand?" Xivan asked.

"Vol Karoth," Senera said, "is the demon god of destruction who's been imprisoned for longer than Quur has existed and if freed will wipe out all life on the planet and then eat the sun as dessert."

"Finish eating the sun," Janel corrected. "He's already taken a few bites."

"Talea—" Xivan's voice held a desperate, terrified note. "Talea, this is important. Don't move."

Senera didn't see the problem. Not at first. Then she realized her angle was off. Five irregularly spaced black dots marked the stone wall next to Talea, just a few inches to the right of her head. If Senera shifted a few feet to the side, they resolved into five slender cylinders of absolute black. And Xivan was right; it looked like the fingers of a hand, just beginning to emerge from the solid stone wall.

Senera felt her gut twist. The ground threatened to drop away. *What a fool she'd been.*

"Go that way," Xivan said, pointing to her right, Talea's left. "Just take a step, Talea. Then another."

Talea tucked away the coin and did as Xivan asked. When she had traveled a half dozen steps away, she turned. "I see. Oh. That's not good, is it?"

"Oh, sweet fields," Janel said. Her eyes were wide, her mouth dropped open. She whirled to face Senera. "Don't claim you don't know what that is!"

A shudder raced through Senera's body from scalp to heel. "No. I wouldn't do that." She felt her hands start to shake. "I am so sorry. I've made a mistake."

Janel stared at her as if they'd never met before. For a moment, she looked terrified.

Kalindra Milligreest scowled. "Would someone mind explaining to me, then? Because I don't have any idea—" It was almost comical to watch all the color flee the woman's face, leaving her skin the color of ash. She must have figured it out even as she complained. "Thaena help me," she muttered and then flinched at her accidental naming of her dead patron goddess.

"That's Vol Karoth, isn't it?" Sheloran's voice was very quiet. "Right here. In front of us. That's *his hand*."

THE HOUSE OF ALWAYS

"Yes." Teraeth might as well have been answering if he wanted a drink. She almost envied his lack of emotion.

Senera bit down on a finger, a nervous habit she couldn't stop. Nobody needed to spell out what that meant. Vol Karoth . . . Vol Karoth, the Dark Sun, Vol Karoth, the Ender of Everything . . . was stepping through the Lighthouse wall. She'd only meant to combine mental spaces, to allow the people Kihrin loved most to lend him their strength and support. Vol Karoth himself had been meant to remain trapped inside his prison.

Someone should have explained that to Vol Karoth.

Senera came close to laughter—bitter, horrible laughter—as she watched all her plans crumble. No. As she watched her plans transform into acid, eating away everything they touched.

Vol Karoth's freedom was now *inevitable.*

The corrupted Immortal would simply walk into the Lighthouse, which the wards of the Eight were never designed to protect.

Oh, they'd hold for a while. They might even hold for years. But what did that even mean when weeks in the Lighthouse passed by in minutes, centuries in months?

It would not be long before Vol Karoth simply . . . walked out.

And Relos Var would get exactly what he wanted, the way he always did.

The room had remained silent as they all stared in horror at those five dark, unholy fingers.

"What happens when he finishes walking through the wall?" Galen asked.

"Oh, that's easy," Senera said. "He kills everyone, and he starts with—"

The world changed.

Kihrin's story
Vol Karoth's prison
Just after Senera's memory

Vol Karoth stood with his head tilted to the side when the vision ended, his body posture suggesting contemplation.

Then he started to laugh.

Did you just try to defend your friendships by showing me someone betraying her mentor and turning against her life's work? I didn't expect you to argue my side for me, traitor.

I swallowed as the floor seemed to shift underneath me. I might have miscalculated.

"No," I said, "I showed you that people can change! Senera is capable of becoming a good person."

Senera is a terrorist who has murdered thousands. But suddenly that's acceptable because she's switched sides? How convenient for Senera. How convenient for you.

I backed up. "So redemption is impossible? Once a sin is committed, it can never be forgiven?

Are you somehow empowered to give that forgiveness? Last I checked, she didn't murder you. Do you think the men, women, and children she killed in

Jorat care if she's asked a Quuros royal prince for forgiveness? That she wants to be redeemed? This isn't redemption. All she's done is add betrayal to her list of sins.

"It's not like that," I protested.

True. You're right. It's not like that. Because she hasn't even asked for forgiveness, has she? She won't. Did you not listen to her? She doesn't care about any of you. She cares about creating her perfect impossible world where everyone is equal. She's never cared who she has to kill to get there. That's not absolution. That's another Rev'arric in the making.

I felt a shudder. That . . . that actually made sense.

I was certain I shouldn't be agreeing with Vol Karoth.

I see it's time for another lesson, Vol Karoth said. *Fortunately, your so-called friends have an almost infinite supply of examples.*

The world changed.

6: The Hand in the Wall

Xivan's memory
Six days after the Battle of the Well of Spirals
The mountains of the Dominion of Yor, Quur

The trip back to Yor from the Kirpis forest was instantaneous.

Xivan had assumed it would take days, if not weeks—time to reach a city, time to convince some idiot to open a gate so they could return home. Senera had left without them, after all. But Tya—yes, *that* Tya, Goddess of Magic—had asked them where they wanted to go. When Xivan had answered, "Back to the Spurned," Tya had just waved a hand and . . .

And they were back in Yor. As if they'd never left. As if Tya had brought her back to a time before Xivan had been quite so acquainted with failure. The Spurned camp hadn't even moved, still trapped in the same stone-and-ice canyon where they had been wintering the worst of the Yoran storms. The bitterly cold air frosted the tips of Xivan's eyelashes with tiny crystals. It made Talea's breath freeze as soon as it left her body. Even for Yorans, this weather was a bit much.

They had only stayed to make sure Xivan and Talea could find their way back. The women greeted her with cheers and warmth that provided no succor at all. She couldn't so much as look at them without thinking of other white-skinned witches, of Suless's hyena eyes, of the bodies of her child and husband, left hanging to bleed out.

These women had once worshipped Suless, and if she had been willing to overlook it once, that had all changed. Still, she tried to do the right thing. She tried to pretend it didn't matter.

But it did. It mattered a great deal.

Her husband was dead. Her son was dead. She'd given Urthaenriel away, and Suless was—Suless was out of her reach. Janel had said the Queen of Witches had become a demon, who could travel anywhere she wanted, at will.

Suless was no longer confined to base matter, no longer trapped in the Living World. Xivan had no ability to chase after her. No recourse if she caught up to her. Suless could toy with Xivan forever. And would. Just for the sheer, ugly, petty joy of doing so. Xivan didn't know if Suless had hidden her husband's and son's souls or if she'd eaten them in the manner of all demons.

She suspected the latter.

Xivan didn't sleep really, not in her current state caught between the Living

World and the Afterlife, but she did dream.[1] And for every night since their return, she roused herself from a sleeplike stupor to the sound of her own screaming, dreaming of blood and death and betrayal. When Talea tried to shake her out of it on the sixth night, Xivan pulled her sword from next to their sleeping blankets and swung at her lover. It was only by blind luck that Talea managed to duck out of the way.

"What's wrong? What can I do?" Talea asked her, kneeling. Pretending Xivan hadn't just tried to kill her.

It was still night, the darkness of the Yoran mountains so absolute the world seemed to end outside the limits of the dying Spurned campfires. It was, as always, freezing, but Xivan realized the cold was from more than the climate.

She'd gone too long without eating.

"Find Senera," Xivan croaked, rubbing her eyes.

"I'm not sure–" Talea wrung her hands, fumbling with some excuse.

"Find Senera!" Xivan screamed. "And get away from me!"

Talea fled while Xivan put her head in her hands. Just for a moment. Then she threw off her blankets and put on her boots.

This couldn't end like this. She refused to let it end like this.

Suless wasn't going to win.

Xivan stalked out of the camp and waited near a frozen stream, crouched down, watching the darkness. Leaving Janel alive, she decided, had been a moment of weakness. If Xivan had killed Janel while Suless had still possessed her body, Xivan would have ended Suless's threat for good. Instead, she'd given Suless time to fucking *ascend*.

Talea didn't come back for several hours. When she did, Senera was with her, looking put out. "Xivan, are you stupid? Maybe you don't want to be contacting me right now. Let's not remind Relos Var of what you did."

Xivan lifted the corner of her lip. "What I did was help kill Thaena. Was that not what your master wanted?"

Senera gave Talea a look, as if somehow implying she should have talked more sense into Xivan. Then Senera turned back to the duchess. "Pretty sure he wanted that and also for you to keep the gods-damned sword. And in any event, don't assume I'm at your beck and call. I only have one master, and you look nothing like him."

Xivan didn't grace that last bit with the courtesy of a response. "I want to know where the Stone of Shackles is."

Senera blinked. "You what?"

"The Stone of Shackles. I want to know where it is. I'll pay any price you name."

Senera looked more than a little confused. "Xivan . . . why do you want to know? It can't possibly–" Her eyes widened. "You want to go after Suless."

Xivan slammed her hand down against a slab of rock, creating a loud report. "Yes! The Stone of Shackles won't care that she's a demon. The Stone of Shackles works perfectly well on demons. Just tell me who has it."

---

[1] If you've ever wondered if beings such as Xivan and Gadrith dream, consider that curiosity now satisfied.

Senera stared at her, considering. Finally, she said, "Let's return to camp, have some tea, and I'll see what I can do."

Without saying another word, Xivan turned around and headed back.

Xivan paced while Senera did everything *but* consult the Name of All Things. Talea stood by the side, watching Xivan nervously. The women who hadn't been woken by Xivan's screaming were almost certainly awake now, as Talea added more logs to the fire and went about the business of faking good hospitality.

One of the Spurned served Senera buttered tea, which she drank with the appreciation of someone who had spent years among the Yoran mountain peoples. But finally, Xivan lost her patience.

"Well? Are you going to use the Name of All Things or not?" she snapped.

Senera raised an eyebrow at her. "I had hoped you were going to–"

"What?" Xivan said. "Let this go? Just forget about the lives that bitch has taken? About losing the only people I care about?"

Talea shot her a strange look.

Senera sighed. "Relos Var won't let you keep it," she explained. "Not after you gave up Urthaenriel. He has plans for the Cornerstones. Even if he allowed you to chase after it, he would want it turned over."

"What's he going to do, steal it from me?" Xivan asked.

Senera looked at her sideways. "Do you have any idea how easy it is to take the Stone of Shackles from someone like you if one knows how it works? Yes, he'd take it from you. And you wouldn't like how."

Xivan scowled. "Fine. I only want it for a little bit. He can have it back when I'm done." She waved a hand toward Senera. "Now do your thing."

Senera drank her tea.

Xivan stopped pacing. "Well?"

Senera shrugged. "I don't need to ask a question when I already know the answer. If it were easy to recover, Relos Var would have already done so."

"I don't care. Just tell me who has it, and I'll take care of the rest." Xivan clenched her hands into fists. "Just tell me." She knew better than to pull out her sword and threaten the woman with it, but it was a difficult urge to resist.

Senera narrowed her eyes, and Xivan sneered at the judgment she could see there. When Senera didn't answer, Xivan said, "Don't play hypocrite with me. I know you've already had your revenge against all the people who ever wronged you as a child."

"Yes," Senera said dryly. "Now ask me what good it did. Ask me what it changed. Ask me how it made a damn thing better."[2]

"Fuck you. Tell me where it is."

Senera raised both eyebrows. She set the teacup aside, stood, and started to walk away.

"Senera!" Xivan shouted. "Name your price. Want me to go after Kihrin and reclaim the sword? Fine. Want me to vow my services to Relos Var? I'll do that. Just tell me where it is."

Senera whirled back. "What I want is for you to let this go, but you aren't

---

[2] It's not a period of my life I like to talk about.

going to, are you?" She gestured toward the camp. "You have people who need you now. Talea needs you."

"Fuck these people!" Xivan shouted, too angry to care that every single one of them could hear her. "Do you think I give a damn about my husband's cast-off whores? They were nothing more than an amusing way to pass the time. Tell me who has the necklace, Senera!"

Senera's mouth settled into a thin, unhappy line. Still judging. Xivan so badly wanted to smack her face into some other expression. "High Lady Lessoral of House D'Talus now owns the Stone of Shackles," she finally said. "And you will never get it away from her."

"You said it was easy—"

"I said it would be easy for Relos Var to take it from *you*," Senera corrected. "High Lady D'Talus is in a different class."[3] She unfolded a piece of paper from her belt, held it up where it almost seemed to float for a moment, and then twisted a hand just so before punching forward. The markings glowed yellow and lifted off the paper, which crumbled to ash. A moment later, the glyphs expanded, circled in midair, and turned into the distinctive spiral quicksilver of a gate opening. Beyond was the silhouette of the Capital City.

Xivan narrowed her eyes. Relos Var had always been able to open gates instantly, but Relos Var was in the same league as literal gods. Senera had found a way to shortcut the process. When had that happened?[4]

Senera left—but the gate didn't shut behind her.

The camp was cold and still and silent. No one said a word.

Until Bikeinoh[5] said, "Hon, we can't stay camped out here. The last storm was costly, and we'd do a lot better if we found a—"

Xivan rolled her eyes as she turned. "Weren't you listening? Do whatever you like. I don't care."

More silence. Then a lot of women started talking at once.

"Be quiet!" Xivan screamed. "Get it through your thick skulls. I'm not one of you. I don't like snow, I don't like your land, and the only reason I was ever here was because of the man who ordered you all killed. Why would you ever think I was one of you?"

Talea shook her head. "Xivan, you don't really mean—"

"I do," Xivan said. "I really do mean that. I don't give a fuck about a bunch of women who were more than happy to be passed around like chained dogs. You want to stay with these bitches? Help them take over Yor? Help them destroy Yor? I don't really care. That's your choice. But I'm going to the Capital."

Talea's expression was one of shock, surprise, and hurt—Xivan felt a flash of guilt, which she quickly shoved back down again. The Spurned had always been nothing more than a diversion, a way of reminding her husband how much she'd disapproved of his ridiculous, foolish harem. They'd meant nothing in and of themselves. Had they really thought she was going to gallivant

---

[3] For one thing, she's not alive purely because of a ritual Relos Var himself performed, and that does make a difference.

[4] I had a week to kill and spent a healthy chunk of it in Shadrag Gor.

[5] The oldest of Azhen Kaen's wives, after Xivan, and leader of the Spurned, when Xivan and Talea are away. Or just leader of the Spurned, now.

around the countryside, quelling the local Yorans or starting a revolution against the empire?

Then they were naïve fools.

She'd almost reached the gate when Xivan turned back to Talea. "Are you coming or not?"

The look in Talea's eyes was unreadable. She tucked the silver coin she'd been fiddling with away. "You know I'll go wherever you do."

"Then do so." Xivan entered the gate.

The world changed.

Xivan's reaction
The Lighthouse at Shadrag Gor

Xivan shuddered and made a point of not looking at anyone else. Especially not looking at Talea. Or Janel. Or Senera.

Damn it all to Hell. She didn't need to ask to know everyone had seen the same vision, the same memory. From her point of view.

"Fuck!" Teraeth screamed at the almost-blank wall. "Stop doing that!"

Xivan shuddered again. She didn't know if the escaping god of annihilation was actually responsible for these visions, but it didn't seem a huge jump to imagine it must all be connected.

"Well, I think that speaks for all of us." Kalindra looked exhausted and terrified, although covering both with black humor.

"Everyone!" Janel said. "We can discuss the visions later. Teraeth, were does that hall lead?" She pointed at the passageway he'd taken earlier when searching for the music.

"Living spaces," Teraeth answered, never taking his eyes from the fingers emerging from the stone. "It's safe."

"Then everyone go," Janel said. "Out of this room, right now!"

To be fair, no one needed to be told. As soon as Teraeth answered the question, people started to move, all of them eager to be as far away from the hand emerging from the wall as possible, on principle if for no other reason.

Besides, other rooms might have things like fireplaces, blankets, and warm drinks. Xivan might have been incapable of catching a cold, but that didn't mean she enjoyed being sopping wet.

The main Lighthouse tower had been thick, even stone with no visible seams. How it had been constructed could be lumped under the heading "magic" and then ignored. The rest of the Lighthouse was both structurally and materially different. Someone had built this addition to the Lighthouse more recently, using rough-hewn stone blocks fitted with mortar. The main Lighthouse tower seemed immune to age, but this area was looking its years.

Thurvishar took the lead; they raced through the rooms. First, a main hallway, likely the nexus of the entire manor house, numerous doors branching off to unknown locations. Then Thurvishar led them to a set of adjoining rooms: a kitchen and keeping room, probably meant as a servant gathering area while meals were sent out to wherever the dining room was located. Couches and chairs filled the area before the fireplace, enough to seat all of them.

Everyone stopped.

Thurvishar began using magic to dry everyone off. Of course he knew a spell for that.[6] Xivan wasn't going to complain. Who knew velvet could hold so much damn water? Once she was dry enough to not make sloshing noises with every step, she picked a spot against the wall and put her back to it. She looked down at her sword and grimaced. She'd sheathed it still covered in blood. Still covered in Talea's blood.

And if the woman hadn't so much as glanced at Xivan, she could hardly blame her.

But that wasn't Xivan's biggest problem, which was stunning in its simplicity: What next? Not just for her but for everyone. It's not like they had any way to fight Vol Karoth. They'd run to another room in Shadrag Gor, but that only removed Vol Karoth from their sight. It did nothing to alleviate the danger.

Galen turned to everyone else. "Not a trick question or anything, but how do we stop this from being the room we die in?"

Kalindra snorted as though Galen must be an idiot for not knowing the obvious answer. "We leave. This is the part where we *leave*." She gestured angrily at Senera, who seemed the obvious method for making that happen. She'd brought them all there, after all.

"We can't," Senera said woodenly. She sank down into one of the chairs.

"Of course we can," Kalindra said. "Open another gate. It should be easy for you."

Senera didn't respond.

"Why can't we leave?" Thurvishar asked Senera. "What happens if I try to open a gate right now?"

"It won't work," Senera said.

"I don't believe you," Kalindra snapped.

"I don't care," Senera responded. She still hadn't looked at her. She hadn't looked at anyone since they entered the room.

Qown made a low, panicked sound in the back of his throat. He was staring at Senera with wide eyes. Xivan didn't know if this was general "Oh god, oh god, that was Vol Karoth in the other room" panic or some more specific sort of panic she didn't yet understand.

"Qown, go make Senera some tea," Xivan suggested. If nothing else, he needed the distraction.

Qown didn't respond either.

"Qown!" Xivan repeated, louder.

The healer visibly jumped. "What? I . . ."

Talea tugged on the man's sleeve. "Oh, would you? It would be so kind of you. I'd do it myself, but you always make it so much better than I do."

Qown blinked. His gaze flickered from Xivan to Talea. "Uh . . . right. Yes. Of course. I'd . . . I'd be happy to." He retreated to the kitchen, still visible from the keeping room, but now opening cabinets and looking through the supplies.

Janel crouched down next to Senera. "Come on, Senera. Tell us what you've

---

[6] Learned from Kihrin, if I'm remembering correctly, who learned it from Tyentso.

done." Her voice sounded suspiciously kind. From the way Senera's eyes narrowed, she wasn't falling for it any more than Xivan had.

"I told you what I've done," Senera's voice dripped acid, "or Talea did, anyway. So even if we could leave, and I will stress one more time that *we can't*, anyone who somehow found a way isn't going to be able to return in time to make any difference. The time dilation won't allow it."

Xivan felt her gut twist. Because she'd understood what Senera meant. She'd rarely if ever been to Shadrag Gor herself, but she knew why the Lighthouse was so famous. She knew that time ran faster inside its walls than it did outside. Much faster. Weeks might pass by here and only be minutes to the rest of the world. Gadrith D'Lorus has used that trick to prepare rituals before anyone had a chance to respond. Thaena had done the same when she'd attempted to sacrifice her son and, by proxy, the entire Manol nation. But this once, it wouldn't work to the advantage of the tower's guests.

"There's no one to help us," Senera continued. "We can't leave and bring back help to deal with Vol Karoth. No one will reach us in time. It's just us. If we don't fix this, Vol Karoth escapes. We leave and we don't prevent our deaths, we guarantee them. Because unless it takes Vol Karoth centuries to finish passing through that wall, this will all be over and done with before anyone else—including gods—can arrive." The Doltari wizard looked as close to tears as Xivan had ever seen.

Janel swallowed visibly and closed her eyes.

Kalindra began cursing. Galen had a hand to his mouth as if he might be sick. And across the room, Teraeth didn't move at all.

"And one more thing," Senera snapped, "last I checked, I grabbed the lot of you in Devors while you were in the middle of being attacked by Drehemia the gods-damned shadow dragon. The last thing you should want to do is start the clock back up on that unholy mess before you're ready to deal with it."

"Oh, it's quite worse than that," Sheloran said, "but I suppose you weren't there for long enough to notice the giant undead kraken and her army of mind-controlled soulless puppets."

Senera stared. "No," she finally said. "I missed that part."

Footsteps echoed loudly from somewhere upstairs.

Everyone's eyes drifted up toward the ceiling. The noise was unmistakably the sound of someone walking.

"You checked upstairs . . . ?" Janel said to Teraeth.

"I'm telling you, no one's here," Teraeth said as he drew his knives.

"I'll go look," Xivan volunteered. "The rest of you stay here." Talea started to say something, and Xivan knew that it was going to be some nonsense about not going alone. "What are they going to do," she said to Talea, "kill me? I'll shout if I get into trouble." She drew her sword, which came free from its scabbard with a loud, satisfying, and wholly unrealistic ring. Xivan looked down at Talea's gift scabbard in surprise. They'd lined the damn thing with ceramic, so her sword made a sound like it was being sharpened against a stone every time she drew it. Ridiculous.

She loved it.

Xivan appreciated the excuse to leave the suffocating room. At least everyone had been too scared of the damn shadow god to round on Xivan herself and demand explanations. That would come soon enough. Just as soon as everyone calmed down and stopped losing their damn minds.

The footsteps bothered her, though. For one, because Teraeth was thorough by habit. While no one was immune to being fooled by the occasional illusion, she didn't expect that it happened to Teraeth often. But the other reason was because of that whole "time dilation" issue. The sheer odds of hitting Shadrag Gor at the same time it was already occupied verged into ludicrous.[7] It sounded like Senera had come straight from the Lighthouse to grab them. That gave a would-be trespasser a window of seconds.

So Xivan took it seriously. She paused to wipe the blood off her sword using one of her outlandish lace sleeves and then started making her way upstairs. The halls were well lit thanks to centuries of wizards adding their own enchantments to the ever-present mage-lights, but she'd have preferred something with a real flame. The air was bitterly cold.

Xivan paused. She'd just "eaten" before arriving here. The ice of Hell itself shouldn't have felt cold to her.

And yet . . . she was freezing.

She exhaled and watched as a puff of air made soft clouds in front of her. So the cold wasn't just her imagination either.

Xivan kept going.

She searched every room. Many were plain, although she passed a number of bedrooms containing the most luxuriously ornate stonework she'd ever seen.[8]

All of them were empty.

Still, she felt . . . something. Xivan didn't hear or see anything, but she had the same itch at the back of her neck she always felt when she was being watched. She didn't feel alone.

She felt . . . in danger.

Xivan stopped in the upstairs hallway, her back to a wall, both hands on the hilt of her sword. Nothing moved. Nothing appeared. The hall was quiet.

Nothing.

Feeling foolish and jumpier than she'd felt in years, she returned to the others.

Her steps slowed as she approached the open doorway. Voices were raised, and it wasn't difficult to hear what was being said.

Oh. Of course. They'd waited until Xivan was gone to talk about her.

"–how are you okay with what happened?" Galen's voice, sounding so much like Kihrin for a moment that it made Xivan flinch. "Red, she stabbed Talea!"

"She was being magically controlled," Talea explained. "A control that has now been broken. It worked!"

"And that bit about the Spurned?" Janel's voice was so soft, Xivan almost

---

[7] Note that it has happened. In particular, Qown and Thurvishar ran into Gadrith D'Lorus. But in that case, it tilts the odds quite a bit when one of the party involved is immortal and willing to spend centuries locked in a tower performing magical research.

[8] I assume that is your doing, Thurvishar.

didn't hear it. "How letting me live was a mistake? Was that also because she was being magically controlled?"

Xivan squared her shoulders and walked into the room. "No. It wasn't. I was just being a bitch."

"You were in a bad place," Talea said.

Xivan glared. "Don't apologize for me, Talea. I'm a grown woman, and I'll own my own mistakes, thank you. There's no excuse for what I've done." She sheathed her sword. "But you should know, I didn't find anyone upstairs." She gave Teraeth an acknowledging nod.

Teraeth paused from scowling at nothing. "How is that even possible?"

"I'll say it again, sound illusions aren't difficult," Qown called out from where he was setting the tea to steep. "Maybe someone left them here to be triggered? As a bad joke?" He looked hopeful for such a mundane, if tasteless, explanation.

"Then why didn't it trigger when I was here earlier?" Senera said.

"Maybe because you're the one who's doing this?" Kalindra snapped.

Janel said, "No. Not Senera's style."[9]

Kalindra looked willing to argue the point.

Xivan turned to Talea. "How did you break the Lash's hold, anyway? I was being controlled by a Cornerstone. That's not something you just casually block with a spell."

"Oh, we, uh . . ." Talea gave her a sheepish, embarrassed smile.

"We used the Grail of Thaena," Sheloran offered as though that was nothing of particular note. Didn't everyone have one of those in the pantry?

Teraeth made a strangled noise. "That's not a thing."

"Yes, it is," Kalindra said.

Teraeth raised an eyebrow at her. "Kalindra. No, it isn't. The cup I used to use for the Maevanos ritual was just a cup. It had no special powers."

"Sure, that cup didn't, but *the Grail* exists." Kalindra pointed at Xivan. "Either that or we just blocked the Lash's control using the power of wishful thinking. But since I was the one who led these people to it, let's just assume the Grail is real." She smiled wryly. "What do you know? Turns out your mother didn't tell you everything, Teraeth."

"Wait, what? What exactly are you talking about?" Senera looked like she'd just eaten something sour.

"The Grail of Thaena?" Thurvishar had been quiet during the entire conversation, but at this, he raised his head and started to look interested. "How have I never heard of this before?"

"What does it do?" Senera asked. "How was it created?"

"Oh, now you've done it," Janel whispered. "The wizards didn't know something."

Sheloran and Galen both looked helplessly at Kalindra. And Kalindra looked at . . . Talea.

What. Since when was *Talea* the expert on magical artifacts?

---

[9] It's a sad commentary when you've been enemies with someone for so long that they know your little quirks like this.

That embarrassed smile was back. "Ah . . . it was a secret?" Talea said. "And Tya made it. But really, that's kind of not important right now."

"Not important?" Senera stood up, vibrating with righteous anger. "We're trapped here with an evil god, and you're casually telling me we have a magical artifact with us that I didn't even know existed! Why didn't you say something? Does one of you have Urthaenriel while we're confessing hidden weapons?"

"Calm down, Senera. Not where you need to be focusing your energy right now." That comment came from the woman who looked like a Yoran Spurned, but who could not possibly be one. Xivan would have recognized her. She'd done a commendable job until that point of staying in the background, staying quiet. But Xivan hadn't forgotten she'd arrived with Senera.

And if that vision of Senera's was accurate, then the last person Senera had traveled with hadn't been a person at all. Xivan would have been positive it was Talon except her advice to Senera had actually been helpful. In fact, it had sounded like—

It had sounded like something Kihrin might have said.

"Fine," Senera grumbled.

Talea shrugged a shoulder. "I decided not to bring Urthaenriel. You know I don't like carrying that thing."

Thurvishar gave her a hard look.

"It's fine," Janel said, probably to reassure herself as much as anyone else. "We'll assess what we're working with and figure out a plan—"

The world changed.

7: Waking Up

Kihrin's story
Inside Vol Karoth's prison
Just after Xivan's memory

I shut my eyes as the vision ended, then opened them again as I remembered where I was. I managed to bring my sword up just in time.

Your "love" is nothing but slavery. Your "friendship" is nothing but an exchange of obligations. You can't show me a single example from these people where their love isn't anything more than an excuse to pardon hurting each other.

He swung again, the blow so strong it pushed me to a knee. I felt the strength in my arm start to give way . . .

The world blinked as I found myself in another part of the city.

I dragged myself to a staircase and sat down, panting for breath. I evidently needed to be a lot more careful with the memories I picked. That one with Senera hadn't worked out so well. I could feel Teraeth's reaction—his despair—like wading through the waters of a murky, numbing cold lake. But there were memories further back . . .

A heavy rain of ash fell over the harbor, piling up along the crates and coating the pier like a blanket of dirty snow. The sky to the east was red from the ongoing eruption of Ynisthana's volcano. The air cracked with lightning through towering black clouds that strangled the night sky.

The other side of the gate on Ynisthana led to a harbor town in Zherias, an odd shanty sort of place that existed as a stop for fishermen, traders, and pirates looking to unload their merchandise. Only a few people permanently lived there, with everyone else a migrant population who sailed in for a few weeks at a time before continuing on to other ports of call.

This made it wonderfully easy for the Black Brotherhood to slip in without anyone noticing. Most of the Brotherhood members had holed up in safe houses in town before dispersing for wherever Khaemezra set up the new training camp. I sat on a crate, watching—

I felt myself violently yanked from the memory, returned back to haunted, empty streets.

No. I already know this story. Try again.[1]

---

[1] I should point out that no one in the Lighthouse saw this snippet of memory.

"What, I can't use my own memories? What about . . ." I kicked at dust and let the sentence die an early death. I knew without having to ask that I wasn't going to be able to exploit a loophole, show him an example of my history from Teraeth's point of view, from Thurvishar's, from Janel's. Fine.

I wondered how much of what we were doing was to prove a point and how much was just because the dark god of annihilation wanted someone to tell him a story. This didn't really seem like a child asking for a god-king tale before bedtime, though, or like someone who was lonely.

I didn't think I'd be doing myself any favors to point that out, though. Just the opposite.

I'd have to try something else.

It took me longer to recover that time. I paced the city streets, hiding from Vol Karoth while I tried to find something solid, something good, I could send his way. I had to hope that the memories I picked wouldn't be twisted by Vol Karoth into something more negative than I had imagined. But I had to do *something.*

This time, I picked Galen, and again, pushed the memories at Vol Karoth. The world changed.

Galen's memory
Two days after the House D'Mon massacre
The Black Gate of Thaena, the Capital City, Quur

Galen D'Mon took his first breath in two days and opened his eyes.

He wasn't aware of exactly how much time had passed, just that there had been a dark and fathomless sleep, something more permanent and final than the hours between bedtime and breakfast.

He woke in the private chapel of the Black Gate, a small, womb-like space in contrast to the great cavernous cathedral that had previously been his only other experience with the church of Thaena. A priest hovered over him, dressed in white trimmed with red, his hand set flat against Galen's chest. Galen sat up, gasping, his head whirling. He felt dizzy and sick, ravenously hungry but also nauseated.

"Galen?"

Sheloran stood next to him, also dressed in white and red, for once wearing no jewelry, her hair pulled back in a tight knot. She was tense, tightly wound. Her red eyes were even more red, bloodshot from crying. Why had–?

Galen looked down at himself. He wore white. No red. Someone had tied the robes tightly across his chest in a mourning knot. Funerary clothing.

The last few moments of his life came back to him, and he fought not to gag. Miya. Lady Miya had–

He noticed he was alone, save for the priest and Sheloran. No sign of his grandfather. No sign of anyone else either.

"All praise be to Thaena," the priest intoned, "whose merciful blessing and forgiveness has granted unto this man the chance to make right the sins of his life, to forge anew the bonds of goodness, to free him from the shackles of an unrighteous life–"

"Get out," Galen told him.

The priest first looked startled and then offended. "It is not proper to—"

"You've been paid," Sheloran said. "I need a moment alone with my husband. This has been very traumatic for us both. I'm sure my father will also want to give you his 'thanks.'"

The priest had tired, baggy eyes. There were stains down the front of his robes. He inhaled and nodded. "Yes, of course." The priest managed to put an arrogant spin in his abrupt turn as he left the room.

Sheloran helped Galen off the altar and over to a bench. He was shocked at how shaky he felt, how weak. Sheloran pulled him close to her and held him. He took a shuddering breath and fought back the nearly overwhelming urge to start crying. He concentrated on stroking her hair. The little gestures and touches they'd been forced to cultivate to protect each other from gossip had at some point turned into genuine acts of comfort.

Galen started to ask her how long he'd been dead but realized that was the wrong question.

"Who survived?" he asked her instead.

She shook her head. "No one."

Galen didn't quite process that, couldn't understand. He frowned. "I don't ... But ..."

"Miya's gone," Sheloran said. "Presumably, she fled. The suspicion is that she took High Lord Therin with her, but whether or not he was still alive when that happened ..." She sighed and looked away. "She killed everyone else. Momma came and petitioned the Black Gate to have me Returned, and then I petitioned for you." Sheloran patted his knee.

"My strong Red," he told her. "Thank you."

"You're welcome, Blue," she said primly.

Then Sheloran burst into tears.

This time, Galen was the one who pulled her into his arms and let her shake there. He felt the tears falling down his cheeks, his throat so tight he thought he might choke. "Thank you, thank you, thank you," he whispered. "My sister, my dearest friend. What would I do without you, hmm?"

Sheloran backed away, wiped her eyes. "I should have done more. I should have been able to—I couldn't even hurt her! I tried!"[2]

"Yeah, well." He brushed a thumb over his own eyes. "The centuries-old vané sorceress turned out to be good at magic. Go figure, right? You can't blame yourself."

"You sound like Momma."

"It's why your mother likes me," Galen agreed. "Mind if we stay for a little while longer? I need to make a few more petitions." He felt hollow inside, emptied out. His little sisters' bodies would be stored there somewhere. Oh gods. So many dead, and he wasn't fool enough to think Thaena would Return them all.

---

[2] I suspected this. Just as I suspect the depiction of this scene in the first chronicle may have elided Sheloran's involvement.

"Of course," Sheloran said. "Momma had them gather all the bodies and put them under preservation spells."

"And that's why I like her," Galen said. "Just one of the many reasons." He didn't want to do any of that, of course. He didn't want to deal with petitioning for the Return of family members, for the organization of the house—

Hell. It was all him now.

The thought slammed through him, so hard and lethal he felt himself slump backward as if the blow had been real.

He was High Lord. He—Galen D'Mon—was High Lord of House D'Mon. Even if his father was still alive, Galen was quite sure Therin had made good on exiling Darzin from the house and striking him from the books before everything had gone wrong. Galen had been Lord Heir, no matter for how short a time. So that meant Galen had now inherited.

The thing he'd never wanted. The title he had always dreaded. The reason he had never been good enough for his father or his grandfather. That he would be too weak, too kind, too soft.

Sheloran took his hand. "We'll get through this."

"We aren't ready, Red," he told her. "This is . . . This is too soon."

"I know," she said. "We thought we'd have at least two more years. None of the right pieces are in position yet, we haven't—" She made a fluttery hand motion. "Nothing's ready."[3] She cleared her throat. "Darzin's dead. I have confirmation. They found his body outside of Arena Park. So . . . no question on that one."

"How did he die?" Galen asked. He felt his hands curl up to fists against the wood of the bench.

"Decapitation," she answered. "Some sort of sword, I imagine."

Galen felt the tears threaten to well up again, the temptation lurking behind his eyes, in the back of his throat. But how little of that was actually sorrow took him by surprise. He'd expected grief. It was his father, after all. He knew he should feel grief. But he didn't. Not the tiniest portion. Instead, he only felt relief and a spike of intoxicating satisfaction.

What was it Miya had said? She could finally breathe?

It felt a little like that. Galen could finally breathe.

"That's one Return I won't be petitioning," Galen said at last.

Sheloran squeezed his hand. "No, I should say not."

When they'd finished cleaning away each other's tears, Galen and Sheloran left the small chapel to find that Sheloran's parents were waiting. Neither of the D'Talus royals looked like they'd had much rest recently. The fact that High Lord Varik D'Talus had been persuaded to leave his workshop spoke more eloquently of the state of emergency in progress than any amount of rushing, shouting imperial soldiers could have. Next to him, Sheloran's

---

[3] Someday soon, I really do need to sit down and find out the details behind this plan. I'm very curious as to how they intended taking over House D'Mon.

mother, the divinely exquisite Lessoral, stood posed and regal in a gown so pared down from her normal elaborate jewels and silks that she was nearly in disguise. Only her bright, unnaturally red hair and bonfire hot eyes gave away her allegiance.

"My children," Lessoral said as soon as they entered the room. She rushed forward to hug her daughter, and then a second later hugged Galen as well, completely ignoring his squawk of surprise. A squawk that only became more awkward as Galen realized Varik had also joined the group hug.

House D'Talus was the most physically affectionate group of people Galen had ever encountered. Even after two years, he still found himself taken by surprise.

"I'd ask if you're all right," Varik said when he pulled away, "but I believe I already know the answer. Sheloran filled us in on what happened."

"I'm so sorry," Lessoral added, which Galen knew was less a statement of guilt than her own boundless sympathy. "I assume you'll want to register your petitions for the rest of your family before we leave?"

"Yes," Galen said. "Thank you."

They did this, with High Lord D'Talus promising to cover any donation costs before Galen had a chance to assess the status of the House D'Mon treasury. The fee proved to be a stunning amount of metal. If High Lord D'Talus hadn't been the man who literally ran the empire's mint, the priests might have balked at his request to take the promise of payment as good. As it was, Galen wasn't sure that many royals had ever died at once, not even during the Affair of the Voices. It was . . .

Well, it had been very nearly the whole and entire family, hadn't it? All in a single day. And Galen didn't know who could even *be* Returned.[4]

He could only hope.

After all the paperwork was filed, the high lord and his contingent of guards escorted Galen and Sheloran over to the House D'Aramarin Gatestone. Galen's feet slowed, and he found himself coming to a halt as he realized where they were heading.

"We're not . . ." He paused, confused. "We're not going back to the Rose Palace?"

"Or at least the Blue Palace," Sheloran said. "I'm sure there's so much cleaning that needs to be done." She seemed lost. "The blood alone . . ."

The D'Talus couple shared a look.

"Oh, darlings," Lessoral D'Talus said to them, "the Capital is just . . . not a safe place to be right now. We both agreed you should go to one of the summering estates until the situation is more stable. There's a Hellmarch in progress, and we haven't even begun to catch you up on everything that's gone wrong. You've always liked our manor up in the mountains. You'll be safe there."

---

[4] Mostly the children. It's tradition to Return the youngest first, but that meant a great many of the members of House D'Mon were still dead when Thaena and Galava ceased honoring Return requests, several weeks before they themselves were slain at the Battle of the Well of Spirals.

Galen felt a peculiar floating sensation. A sense of familiarity. He remembered his grandfather Therin telling him that Galen's job was to stay safe. That Therin was sending him away to estates. For his own protection.

Galen felt an odd, sharp snap inside of him, like he'd just jerked awake unexpectedly from a long sleep.

"No," he said.

The high lord turned back and frowned at him. "What was that?"

Galen exhaled and rubbed the back of a hand against his lips. "No." He straightened. "No. I'm not going to an estate in the country until this is all over. I'm not leaving the Capital. I won't run."

Lessoral got that look in her eyes that meant she was about to go into good-mother mode. "Galen, sweetheart–"

"My grandfather Therin was clearing out the Blue Houses. He was ordering everyone back to the Blue Palace. That means we're in the middle of a demon invasion and there are no physickers out there in the city." Galen scowled. "Maybe Therin—probably Therin—would have sent them back or was pulling them so he could organize mobile teams or something, but now he's gone, and that means no one's been giving anyone orders for days. I can't imagine that the situation has done anything but deteriorate. I can't leave."

Lessoral's gaze was sympathetic, and for the first time that Galen could remember, it made Galen angry rather than comforted. "Galen, I commend that sentiment, but you're in no position to help. Putting yourself in danger isn't helpful."

"But, Momma," Sheloran said, "he's right. We have resources and connections, and it would be nothing but cowardice to turn our backs on that now of all times just so we can . . . I don't even know. Be safe." She reached forward and picked up the hands of her parents. "You know I love you both, but did you raise a daughter who would hide while this was happening?"

Lessoral glared at her husband. "She's your child. Heroism never came from my side of the family."[5]

"I'll have you both know I've learned all my terrible habits from Galen," Sheloran said. "You know how D'Mons are."

"Ha!" Galen cleverly retorted.

"It's going to be dangerous," the high lord said, but he didn't sound like he actually disapproved. Just the opposite, really. Then he reached behind him and picked up a large, flat box, which he handed to Sheloran. "I suppose you'd better be prepared."

Sheloran's mouth dropped open, then she hurried over to the side to open up the box. Inside were two items—a chain shirt of links made from metal so fine and light it wouldn't be much more difficult to wear than a well-made chemise. On top of that rested a folding metal fan, lacy and delicate in appearance.

Galen didn't doubt for a second the fan was a weapon that had been built

---

[5] Rarely have truer words ever been spoken.

to exacting military-grade standards. And High Lord D'Talus understood he was sending his little girl into battle.

"I don't get anything?" Galen teased, because he knew he could get away with it.

Varik D'Talus snorted. "I gave you my daughter. Wasn't that enough?"

8: Wizard, Healer, Dragon, Spy

Galen's reaction
The Lighthouse at Shadrag Gor
Just after Galen's memory

Galen blinked as the vision ended. Sheloran murmured in dismay.

"So that happened," Galen said. "Not sure why we needed to share it with the whole room, though." While he spoke, his wife wandered back over to his side, moved a lock of his hair out of the way, and kissed his cheek before nestling into his arms. She had the air of someone who wanted comforting.

Really, she knew he was the one who wanted comforting.

"That was sweet," Talea said.

Xivan growled.

Galen blinked at her. He'd have asked her what the hell her problem was, but it was painfully obvious they didn't have that kind of time. He concentrated on Senera. "Oh, I'm quite a fan of that whole 'being raised from the dead' idea myself, but why am I reliving it? And why are you all reliving it with me?"

"I don't know," Senera admitted. "I didn't expect . . . this. I knew Vol Karoth and Kihrin would be fighting for dominance. I'd hoped that we might be able to provide moral support. That's why I grabbed people who are emotionally significant to Kihrin." She gestured toward Galen, then Teraeth and Janel. "Apologies to the rest of you. It was an all-or-nothing proposition."

"I'm important to Kihrin?" Galen felt shock arc through him. "I'm not, though–"

"Oh no," Talea said. "Kihrin was lying when he told Gadrith he didn't care what happens to you. Don't think for one second you're not important to him. You're really important to him."

Galen's mouth dropped open. How could Talea possibly know about that? He was absolutely certain he'd never mentioned any of that to her. Sheloran was the only one who'd known . . . but as he looked over at his wife, he saw her surprise and knew she was just as nonplussed as he was.[1]

"Yes, well," Sheloran said, "certainly Kihrin's important to Galen too. But a question: If Vol Karoth is physically present here in the tower, one assumes that means Kihrin's here too, doesn't it?"

"Don't you remember the vision?" Teraeth spat. "Kihrin's . . . Kihrin's dead."

"They have a word for souls that linger after the bodies are gone," Sheloran

---

[1] While Talea and Xivan stayed with Teraeth, Janel, Khaeriel, Valathea, and Terindel, Talea read both Thurvishar's first chronicle and mine. More bothersome, she's evidently remembered them.

answered him primly. "And also a word for the house they occupy when it fills with strange inexplicable sounds."

An awkward and uncomfortable silence filled the room.

Galen felt a moment of elation, almost giddiness. *Yes, of course.* That would explain the harp, the footsteps. Kihrin was there. Maybe quite literally there with them. Vol Karoth was trying to break through, but Kihrin was haunting the place. And that meant Kihrin could be Returned . . . That euphoria came crashing back down.

Thaena was dead.

No one was Returning anyone.

Sheloran cleared her throat. "Even with Thaena gone, there has to be a way. My understanding is that the greatest difficulty in Returning someone is pulling their souls across the Veils. So while I'm not suggesting we get our hopes up—"

"Grizzst resurrected Galava," Thurvishar said. "So it's possible. I had hoped I could use Wildheart to grow a body for Kihrin, then rejoin his souls using Grimward."

Teraeth flatly regarded the wizard. "You should have mentioned that earlier."

"I didn't want to get your hopes up," Thurvishar admitted.

Janel walked over to the Manol vané man and laced an arm around his waist, tucked her head into his side. "We'll get him back, Teraeth."

"We will," Teraeth said, "so I can *kill him.*"

Galen studied the black-skinned vané man. He'd never met many vané. Just the one other, really, and he was trying not to think about Miya. "We met once before, didn't we? When Kihrin came back to the Capital?"

Teraeth stared at him evenly. He nodded.

"Good," Galen said. "Well, Janel's right. We're going to get him back. I promise you that. We're going to get my brother back."

"You know he's not actually your brother, don't you?" Senera said.

Galen made a moue. "He's my brother in all the ways that matter." Which Galen knew made no sense at all, but he'd spent the last four years of his life believing Kihrin was his older brother. Even if that wasn't true—Kihrin was his uncle, evidently—it still felt true.

Senera raised a hand in his direction. "As long as you know."

Thurvishar turned to Senera. "This has to be a side effect of what you did."

"How?" Senera seemed indignant. "Nothing in the sigils I drew causes this. And even if Sheloran's right about Kihrin haunting the Lighthouse, have you ever heard of a haunting that does this?"

"And yet," Janel said, "here we are."

"Senera, perhaps it would help if you went over exactly what you did," Thurvishar said. He seemed to be losing his patience. "You combined the Lighthouse here with Vol Karoth's prison. Fine. How was that supposed to work? Use small words."

Senera glared. "I would really like that cup of tea first. And it's cold in here. Someone should light a fire."

"You're stalling," Janel said, although she did head over to the cord of wood tucked next to the fireplace and begin building a stack.

Senera held up her hand. It was shaking. "It's just that I'm scared to death, you see. I'd take something more alcoholic if I didn't think I was going to need all my faculties."

Nobody asked what she was scared of. That seemed unnecessary. And scared to death definitely seemed to be the defining mood of the moment.

"I need a few minutes," Qown said. "The tea's almost ready."

Janel paused from lighting the fire to turn back to Qown. "So do I want to know how you ended up involved in all this, Qown, or should I just assume the answer rhymes with *egos scar*?"

Galen looked up. "Wait. You two know each other?"

Janel laughed bitterly. "I thought we did, but it turns out I never knew Qown at–"

The world changed.

Kihrin's story
Inside Vol Karoth's prison
Just after Galen's memory

I felt a bubble of laughing delight rise out of me as Galen's memory ended. Not that there weren't sad moments to it, of course, but the idea that Galen had lived–that he had people who cared about him–that he'd refused to leave the city because he could help people . . .

Well, it didn't surprise me that he would do that. I'd always known Galen was a good person. It just meant Darzin hadn't corrupted it out of him.

Then I felt a shadow slip over my souls, a feeling like the world had dimmed, just the tiniest amount. I threw myself to the side as Vol Karoth appeared and began to attack. He seemed angry for some reason.

"Oh, I'm sorry, are you annoyed that people might actually be decent?"

It's a lie. A self-deception at best. He didn't want to leave, because he had a power base that needed to be nurtured, a power vacuum that he needed to step into, and because he didn't want to hand over the high lord position. This wasn't about altruism, this was about survival.

"You can claim that," I told him as we circled each other, "but you and I both know perfectly well that's not what his memories show. His memories show that he cares–his wife cares–hell, his in-laws care. They're not bad people."

Everyone is a bad person if you judge them honestly.

I scoffed. "Everyone's a bad person if you want to twist their motives, but that's not going to convince me. I'm not going to believe you just because you said it with conviction."

Amusing. Wrong, but amusing. That memory you showed was no realer than the lies we tell ourselves. Those in power always step over bodies to get there, and we lie and tell ourselves we're still good people regardless of the blood. Belief has little relationship to truth. We warp our memories to serve our goals, to make our sins seem pure. We change the facts to justify our desires. It's not truth. Truth doesn't exist. Let's find some examples . . .

"I told you to leave them alone!" I pressed my attack this time, which must have taken him aback if only because it was unexpected.

I thought I might have even been making progress, but then I realized he'd just been toying with me. Hot liquid agony opened up along my stomach as his sword slipped past my defenses, shearing open skin in a scarlet line. I retreated, concentrating on healing myself.

It was never your decision. They involved themselves. Now they're pieces on the board. And how exactly would you keep me from them? His laughter was thick and dark, a horrible and pleased mockery.

"I thought you were interested in me."

You care about them. It's close enough.

I exhaled slowly. The sad thing was that he was right, and I honestly didn't know how I could stop him. Distract him, maybe, but not stop him.

"All right," I said finally. "But if they're not really my friends, because friendship doesn't exist, then why would I care what happens to them? Why would that matter at all? Seems to me that you can't have it both ways."

Yes, but you still believe. You still believe they love you. That they love each other. You want to be lied to. You relish the self-deception. Stop caring about them and I'll have no reason to keep using them.

"Oh, just like that. Just . . . stop caring about them."

Just like that, Vol Karoth agreed. *Here, let me help—you already knew this one was a traitor, after all. Let me show you how it wasn't just the one time . . .*

Qown's memory
One week after the destruction of Atrine

~~Father Zajhera~~ Relos Var and Qown exited the magical gate into a back street of the Upper Circle of the Capital City. Qown had only been to the city twice before. Both times had been as a child, and in neither case had he gone to the Upper Circle, where the richest and most powerful lived.

And yet neither money nor power had saved them from the Hellmarch. The air stank of a whole city's firing, with elements of that stench suggesting roasting flesh and scorched earth. A large proportion of the city had lost . . . well. At best, their homes, and at worst, their very souls. It had truly been a cataclysm almost beyond imagining, and yet people lived on, because there was no other choice.

No one noticed their arrival, but Qown checked the area using his Cornerstone, Worldhearth, just to make certain. Then he turned back to his teacher.

Technically, the man's real name wasn't Father Zajhera, but technically, his real name wasn't Relos Var either. The wizard appeared as Father Zajhera now because it suited his plans to continue using that identity for as long as possible. So there he was, looking like the wise old patriarch of the Vishai faith. Unlike Relos Var, who always appeared quite average and easy to overlook, Father Zajhera was a tall, distinguished man who drew the eye, with dark brown skin and Kirpis cloudcurl hair he wore knotted into locks. He smiled easily and had kind eyes.

It was easy to trust Father Zajhera. Less easy to trust Relos Var.

And yet Qown had vowed his loyalty and his life to both.

"Why are we here again, Father?"

Relos Var smiled at him but, instead of answering, began to walk. The streets seemed curiously empty, either because the guards discouraged foot traffic, or, even more likely, because everyone was hiding. The demons could reappear at any time.

"We are going to a funeral, dear boy." The priest tilted his head. "Sadly a far-too-common occurrence of late. Indeed, there have been so many dead that the D'Talus forges have been doing double duty as crematoria. Western Quur is learning the hard way what eastern Quur has always known: it's best to burn the bodies."

They passed the fire-gutted shells of what must have been palaces, mansions, manors as they walked. Even if nothing else had burned, few hedges had survived the fires. The Upper Circle appeared naked, broad lawns and expensive homes shamelessly revealed for anyone to ogle.

Relos Var walked with the brisk air of a man certain of his destination. They exited an area of violet mage-lights and entered a different, red-lit section of the Upper Circle. As the Royal Houses were conveniently color-coded, this was necessarily the district controlled by House D'Talus, which might have explained why the smell of smoke and burning flesh was so thick in the air.

"Whose funeral?" Qown rather doubted Relos Var would be attending anyone's funeral out of sorrow. Relos Var had been preparing for thousands of years for these upcoming months and weeks, which would see the culmination of so many plans. Sentimentality had no place there.

"Jarith Milligreest," Relos Var answered. "I never met the young man myself, but I understand he was a real fan of my work." He smiled even as his voice slipped into a register far more appropriate for wizard than priest.

Qown couldn't help but wonder if "fan" was being used ironically[2] . . . and then the second part to that name sank in. Jarith Milligreest would be related to Qoran Milligreest, the high general of Quur.

Qoran Milligreest, who was also Janel Theranon's illegitimate father.

Qown concealed his flinch. After all, Janel Theranon—the person he'd so recently served and so recently betrayed—wouldn't be there. As far as he knew, she wasn't on speaking terms with her father.

He hoped. But then, if she were, Relos Var wouldn't have been quite so carefree about attending. Janel would recognize Relos Var as easily as she would recognize Qown.

The two men walked until they reached a sad, bent gate that did nothing to defend the periphery of the estate grounds—the walls themselves had been smashed, burned, or both to varying degrees. Qown expected the first guards they met to turn them away, but unexpectedly, Relos Var showed them a chit—some kind of permission slip or pass—and they allowed the Vishai priests through.

The ceremony itself had been set up in the courtyard of the manor, underneath a gigantic mural of a battle scene. A sea of mourning white filled the space, the brightly colored edging on agolé, misha, and raisigi betraying Royal House origins. Incense hung thick in the air, but it only turned the ever-present stench into something even more malodorous.

---

[2] Oh, it was. Relos Var found Jarith's talent for recognizing the real threat endlessly amusing.

Qown could only say "sorry" so many times as Relos Var pushed through the crowd. There was no place to stand, let alone sit. Qown had grown cynical enough to suspect the crowd size was less due to Jarith Milligreest's popularity than to a political desire to shelter under the umbrella of his father's military protection. People were sucking up while they could.

"So we're here. Now what?" Qown asked.

"Patience," Relos Var said.

"But—" Qown bit his lip and made a studied examination of his fingers; he needed to clean his nails. He'd always thought of himself as a patient person, but everything about this situation had his frayed nerves unraveling even more.

"You will gain a man's trust," Relos Var said, still looking forward even as he spoke. "By whatever means necessary. That shouldn't be a difficult task. You're very easy to trust."

Qown swallowed, but he also nodded. He knew how Relos Var had trained him—he was an easy man to talk to, an easy man in which to confide. He'd spent his whole life convincing people to tell him all the things of which they were most ashamed.

"That man is attending this funeral," Relos Var continued. "We just have to find—" He broke off as someone walked up to the front of the crowd, near where the covered body rested under the supervision of four Thaenan priests.

The man himself was young but had a tired, haggard look about him all too common in these demon days. His hair needed grooming. He hadn't slept. He was tall and thin, dressed in the same white as everyone else, but the clothing appeared ill-fitting and possibly borrowed. Or just kept at the bottom of a linen chest, a remnant of a time not so long ago when funerals were rare.

Despite all of this, he was by far the most beautiful person Qown had ever seen.

"And there he is," Relos Var whispered. "Galen D'Mon."

Qown couldn't stop himself from frowning at Relos Var. The man standing up in the front of the courtyard wasn't wearing blue—his white agolé wasn't even edged in blue—but Qown knew who Galen D'Mon was. Kihrin D'Mon's nephew. Darzin D'Mon's son. Far too close to men Qown had no desire to ever meet again.

Although Darzin was apparently dead, so that was lucky.

Relos Var either didn't notice or pretended not to notice Qown's discomfort. "Jarith's cousin, once removed. Honestly, it's extraordinary he's here, considering what he's been through."

Before Qown could ask Relos Var what he meant by that, Galen D'Mon pulled a sheet of paper from under his agolé. He gave the audience a tight, unhappy smile and said in a voice magically carried to the farthest corners of the courtyard, "I was asked to say a few words before the priests begin. I'm supposed to tell you how Jarith Milligreest is the 'best of men.'" He paused.

Qown cocked his head to the side. The prince's wording suggested the possibility Galen was about to do something else. The crowd perked up. The funeral had just turned exciting. Scandalous.

Relos Var leaned forward.

From the front row, someone said something, a sharp note of protest, but it wasn't magically amplified. Galen didn't even glance in that direction.

"The funny thing is," Galen continued, still smiling but now ignoring the piece of paper in his hand, "most of the time when someone's asked to say that, they're being asked to lie. If I'd been asked to say that about my father? I'd have been lying. The only good thing my father ever did in his entire life was die quickly. But I don't have to lie about Jarith; he really was the best of men. He reached out to me, after–" Galen broke off whatever he'd been about to say. "We were friends," he amended. "And he really was a good man. Heroic, selfless, kind, generous. The world is so much poorer for his loss."

A combination of relieved sighs and disappointment settled through the spectators. This wasn't to turn into some kind of horrible castigation of the high general's son, after all.

"What haunts me," Galen said, the corner of his mouth quirking upward with bitter irony, "is that Jarith and I died on the same day.

"One week ago, he was slain while defending this city. Whereas I was murdered." Galen swallowed, looked down. Even from this distance, his eyes seemed too bright. "I was killed by . . . by my grandfather's favorite slave as I was about to flee the city to hide and stay safe. And that's just so unfair–"

Someone said something again. Whatever it was, Galen heard it that time, and his head snapped in that direction.

He ripped up the piece of paper in his hands, and his smile turned so dark, bitter, and hateful–

Qown inhaled. Darzin. Galen reminded him so much of Darzin D'Mon just then. That was the smile–the look in his eyes–Darzin always wore on his face just before he was about to take pleasure in another's pain. Something foul where he could delight in the chaos that followed.

Galen pointed backward then, toward the priests. "Guess which one of us that bitch Thaena Returned?"

The priests froze, wide-eyed, clearly not prepared or willing to do anything about an angry teenager venting embarrassingly and publicly.

"Isn't that hilarious?" Galen continued. "She brought me back, but not him. Which makes no sense, because he's the one who deserves to be standing here right now, not me."

"Galen, that's enough." General Milligreest's voice was loud enough to be recognizable.

Galen D'Mon laughed and didn't even look at him. Even from the distance, Qown could see how wild his eyes looked, how hateful. "Thaena must really want me to be high lord. Joke's on her, though; I'm never going to hold that title."

Galen pointed to the front benches, where a tall woman with short-cut hair sat next to the high general. "That's my aunt Tishenya, who's come back to the city. I have to assume she's here to usurp my title. My aunt Gerisea's back too, which absolutely means my aunts are going for a power grab. And why not? Everyone in Quur knows the easiest time to kick someone is when they're already on the ground, and only a truly great person–someone like Jarith–could have resisted that temptation. But take some honest advice, Aunt

Tish—my father always liked Gerisea best. So if I were you, I wouldn't drink anything she gives you, and I'd never let her catch you in a room alone. He hated Jarith, and that should tell you something. My father didn't like good people."

The woman said something, but Qown couldn't hear what.

Galen just smiled more brightly. "Oh, and speaking of my father . . . did all of the rest of you know he's the one responsible for this catastrophe? It's true. My father summoned the demon prince that started this Hellmarch—"

"By all the gods!" someone swore from the front, quite possibly the same aunt Tishenya Galen had just indicated.

Galen laughed in delight. The crowd seemed frozen, fascinated, clearly wondering just how deep the man was going to bury himself and his family.

"But as long as I'm standing here being so ridiculously honest for once in my life, I'd like to point out that not one of you has any right to feel righteous about your innocence. Because there isn't a one of you who wouldn't have murdered a family member to grab the same prize he was aiming at. It could have been any one of us. We're all terrible. We've built an empire off summoned demons, gaeshe, slaves, and pain. Or we used to. We've delighted in the misery of the less fortunate, built our thrones out of the skulls of our conquered. And guess what? Apparently, slaves don't enjoy being slaves! Shocking, isn't it? So now the bill comes due."

Someone must have said something to him. Galen snorted and replied, "I couldn't be more sober. But maybe the cost I paid for Returning from the dead is that I no longer give a damn about playing your games or kissing your asses."

Milligreest stood and moved toward Galen, who raised his hands. "I'm going, I'm going. But don't pretend everything's fine. Don't lie to these good, worthy people and tell them everything is going to be fine. It isn't. The empire is falling, and some of us might even be unlucky enough to live to see it crash. I don't think I'll be one of those, though." Whatever magic was amplifying his voice, it hadn't shut off yet. "Maybe it's just as well Thaena didn't care enough to bring Jarith back. He'd have tried to save us. And we don't deserve it."[3]

Qown stood there, mouth open, too stunned to react. It was rather like being blinded. Dazzled. Galen's fury had been absolutely incandescent. Something inside Qown twisted—confusion and admiration and something heated.

Galen D'Mon pushed his way through the crowd and headed to the courtyard door. No one tried to stop him; indeed, no one seemed to want to touch him. The crowd melted back to clear a path for this beautiful, angry young man. Qown could hardly breathe for the shock of it all.

Qown was struck by an overwhelming sense of apprehension. There would be consequences for what Galen D'Mon had just done. The high lords would never tolerate . . . that. That sort of honesty. That sort of disrespect. He'd be shunned, if not much, much worse. He might as well have

[3] I am honestly so disappointed I missed being here for this speech.

brought a noose to the services, handed out invitations for his execution later.

Then Qown felt an equally overwhelming sense of disappointment. Whatever Relos Var's plans for this royal had been, surely Galen had just neatly dashed them, turned himself into something less than useful. Which of course meant they had come there for nothing; there was no reason for Qown to ever meet Galen at all.

"He prefers men," Relos Var said, leaning toward him. "Don't let the wife fool you. She's as interested in men as he is in women, which is to say, not in the slightest. They've done an impressive job of covering for each other, though."

"Oh, I see," Qown said absently and then startled, looking up at his teacher with wide eyes. He knew he was blushing. He had to be. This was not a discussion they'd ever had. "I'm sorry? Why would you tell me that?"

Relos Var shrugged. "I thought you might like an extra tool at your disposal. Galen has father issues of the sort one seldom has the pleasure of exploiting. Darzin abused him horribly. His mother treated him slightly better, but she had her own issues with alcohol, so she did her son no favors. I suppose you might say he has mother issues too. Don't underestimate Galen D'Mon's desperate need to be loved."

A strange sort of dizziness nearly overcame the priest. He forced himself to exhale slowly. "Are you . . . Sir. Are you suggesting that I . . . seduce . . . the man?" He cleared his throat and lowered his voice. "*Him?*"

He very nearly laughed at the idea. It was ludicrous. For so many reasons! First of all, most obvious of all, because Galen was a royal prince who looked like that. Whereas Qown was . . . Qown. A man who had always been best described by adjectives like *ordinary* and *unassuming* or, his personal favorite, *kind.* He'd never had any illusions about his appearance. If Relos Var chose to be unremarkable, Qown never had to fake his homeliness. He had gone from being fat and plain to thin and plain, but in neither case had anyone ever given him more than a glance of interest. Suggesting otherwise verged on mockery.

Relos Var sighed and gave him a knowing look that managed to completely misinterpret the reason for Qown's hesitation. "You do realize that your vows are no longer binding, don't you? You have moved beyond the order." The wizard shrugged. "I leave your strategy up to you. Despite what some might tell you, seductions don't require sex. I only want his trust. How you acquire it is up to you. Become his confidant, become his lover, become his mentor. Whatever you prefer. Just make it work."

Qown inhaled. He was good at confidant. He could do confidant in his sleep. He was not going to . . . embarrass himself . . . by trying for anything else.

Besides, Qown had no interest in romance or sex. Qown didn't run with horses.[4]

He did *not.*

---

[4] I find it amusing that Qown still uses the Joratese idioms for sexual preferences, but then I have to admit they are far more straightforward than anything that exists in Guarem.

Qown chewed on his lip before bowing. "I'll do as you command, Father."

"Excellent. Now we should hurry. We'll need to catch up to Galen before Gerisea gets her claws into him, assuming he returns to the Blue Palace. Why don't we arrange for an appropriate introduction?"

The world changed.

9: True Loyalties

Qown's reaction
The Lighthouse at Shadrag Gor
Just after Qown's memory

The vision cleared.

Qown dropped the brick of tea he'd been holding and backed up, wide-eyed. He locked eyes with Galen across the room. The shock and horror of it all numbed his mind. Everyone must have seen that. Everyone. Galen saw that. And so many people in the room already knew Qown was capable of betrayal . . .

But Galen . . . Galen hadn't known.

"I can explain," Qown said. "It's not what you think–"

Galen's face had gone ash gray. He pulled away from his wife, staring at Qown as if the man were an open wound, an infection.

"And how exactly would that be 'not what we think,' Qown?" Sheloran asked. "Because it certainly looks like you're working for Relos Var."

"That's because he is," Janel said. "It was a shock to us too."

Galen swallowed once, looking at Qown. He still hadn't said a word.

Qown shook his head. "Please don't believe–"

Galen spun on his heel and walked out of the room.

Qown started to chase after him, only to have Sheloran snake out a hand, still holding her fan, and block his way. "Let him go."

"Lady Sheloran," Qown pleaded, "I would never–" He swallowed down bile. Truly, he felt like he was about to be sick. "I would never try to seduce your husband. I just–" He stammered even as he turned bright red from shame.

Oh light. What Galen must think of him . . . Galen was so happily married too! His wife was one of the most beautiful people Qown had ever seen. And yes, Relos Var had said Galen liked men, but it was just impossible to think that he was . . . that he . . . clearly, Galen liked women just fine!

Sheloran narrowed her eyes at Qown. "You're an idiot."

"Qown, you're still working for Relos Var, aren't you?" Janel asked. "Whether or not you planned on seducing Galen, Var wanted you to earn his trust," Janel said. The last bit wasn't phrased as a question. "Because Galen is related to Kihrin. Because he's important to Kihrin."

"I don't think that's true at all," Qown said miserably.

"Really." Janel raised both eyebrows.

Qown cleared his throat and bent over to pick up the brick of tea. But he also realized he couldn't ignore Janel, and everyone was staring at him.

Teraeth pointed to Qown while looking at Senera. "So why did we bring along one of Var's unrepentant minions, anyway? Just curious."

Senera shrugged. "I couldn't leave him behind. He was in the area of effect."

"You could've killed him," Teraeth said.

"There was no time," Senera admitted.

"What," Qown said, resolutely trying to ignore the way Senera and Teraeth had just discussed how killing him hadn't happened simply because it hadn't been convenient. "It wasn't because of Kihrin at all! I mean I don't—" His stomach twisted again. "Yes, fine. Probably. But Janel, you know how Relos Var is! There were multiple reasons. There are *always* multiple reasons. I think Var wanted me to get close to Galen because he's married to Sheloran."

Everyone paused.

"That doesn't even make sense," Kalindra said.

Xivan sighed. "Sheloran's mother. That's who you're talking about. Relos Var wants to get close because . . ." She paused and frowned as if she'd wanted to say more but couldn't.

Talea gave her a sympathetic smile.

"Because High Lady Lessoral D'Talus has the Stone of Shackles," Qown said. "I think so, yes."

The Spurned Qown didn't recognize spoke up again. "We have no idea what's in the rest of this Lighthouse or even if someone else might already be here. Someone should follow Lord D'Mon to make sure he's all right." Since that had apparently been explanation, not permission, she launched herself after the prince.

"Not you," Senera growled. "*You* don't leave my sight."

The woman halted. She rolled her eyes and sighed but didn't try to leave the room after that. Qown blinked at her, realizing she was the only person he didn't recognize. Even Teraeth was known to him—at least by reputation and description. This woman was dressed as one of the Spurned, but neither Xivan nor Talea acted like they knew her.

Qown shook his head and sighed. He couldn't believe—he spared Senera a glare.

She noticed. "Yes?" When he blushed and didn't answer, she said, "If you're giving me that look because you're wondering how I could be betraying Relos Var, you might want to give serious consideration to doing the same. He's not your friend. He never was."

Qown swallowed uneasily. He'd never thought Relos Var was his friend. Relos Var hadn't been his friend even when Relos Var had been Father Zajhera, his mentor, his superior. Relos Var was just . . . the smartest man around. The one who knew how to get them all out of this mess. Which Qown had thought Senera knew.

So he was having a hard time understanding why Senera was suddenly changing her mind about that. Qown poured himself a cup of tea and sipped it, not looking at anyone.

Then sputtered and stared at his teacup in shock.

It was ice cold. Which made no sense. He'd boiled the water himself. He'd boiled the water himself just a few minutes beforehand.

"Don't like the taste?" Teraeth said. "You made it."

Something in the man's tone suggested he wasn't talking about tea. At which point Teraeth slowly pulled one of his knives clear of its sheath.

Qown dropped his cup, ignoring the way cold tea splattered everywhere, and backed away.

"Teraeth–" Janel said carefully. "What are you doing?"

Teraeth's lip curled. "Cleaning house."

Qown felt his pulse begin to race. "I didn't . . . I haven't–"

"Teraeth, let's not be hasty," Thurvishar chided. "Believe it or not, you can't solve every problem with a blade."

The Manol vané man cocked his head as he examined the edge of the knife. "Are you sure about that?"

Then Teraeth moved, fast.

Shockingly fast, but he didn't close with Qown. Instead, he slid behind the woman Qown didn't recognize. In a single, smooth, economical motion, Teraeth ran the dagger across the woman's throat.

"Let's find out," Teraeth said.

The world changed.

Kihrin's story
Inside Vol Karoth's prison
Just after Qown's memory

Vol Karoth attacked the moment the vision ended, which made sense, since he'd started the damn thing and certainly had known when it would end. I can't say I dodged out of the way. I felt the blade slice down across my side, skipping painfully over ribs. If this had been the real world . . .

Well, if this had been the real world, I'm pretty sure I'd have been dead many times over by that point. The attack was bad enough that I ended up transported elsewhere. Again.

"Fine!" I screamed into the shadowed sky. "Like you said, I already knew Qown was a traitor. But this time, you're the one who screwed up, because Galen's speech was great!"

I didn't understand why Vol Karoth seemed to feel he had to convince me that he was right. What did it gain him? Maybe nothing. So much of his actions just seemed to be whim or sadism or some other dark emotion I couldn't quite comprehend.

And I didn't know if he was anywhere close enough to hear me. I hoped he wasn't, honestly.

I patched myself up and limped over to a step, sat down, and put my head down between my knees. After a moment, I scoffed and pulled myself back up again.

"You want to tell a story," I said. "I've danced to this tune before. Let's keep going."

The world changed.

Qown's memory
The Upper Circle, the Capital City, Quur
Just after Jarith Milligreest's funeral

Qown had no idea what he was doing.

On a fundamental, deeply personal level, he just had no idea. None.

He felt restless, anxious. He wanted to help people. He wanted to make things better. Qown didn't understand how helping some Quuros royal—no matter how pretty—would do any of that. He found himself fighting the terrible suspicion that Relos Var didn't trust him and now had no use for him. Relos Var was thus keeping him distracted with some essentially trivial mission whose primary importance was to keep Qown out from underfoot.

This wasn't a great feeling. What was the point of standing up for his principles and doing the right thing if it was followed by not being able to do anything at all?

At least, Qown reflected as they walked, it was a beautiful day.[1] The smell of smoke and all it represented put a bit of a damper on that enjoyment, as did the burned-out shells of mansions they passed in the Upper Circle, but overall . . .

Relos Var stopped mid-stride. An angry, frustrated expression replaced his beatific smile.

"Father—?" Qown didn't see any reason for Relos Var's change in mood.

The wizard narrowed his eyes. "I didn't expect anyone to move this quickly."

Qown tilted his head.

But Var didn't answer the unspoken question. He grabbed Qown by the back of his agolé and teleported.

They appeared at a location much like the one they'd just left—a Quuros city street—but there were important differences. The clash of metal, the smell of blood. An ornate carriage of dark wood, blue enamel, and gold trim stood unmoving in the middle of the road, doors ajar. Someone had cut the harness straps tying the horses, who had taken the opportunity to bolt. The horses hadn't gone far. They lingered up the street, suavely pretending they'd always been hanging out by that apple cart.

Perhaps the most obvious difference was the people attempting to kill each other. Those dressed in plain clothes far outnumbered those wearing the uniform of House D'Mon. That margin grew with each passing second. A guard standing on the roof of the carriage seemed to be in a particularly bad position as he fought off two men armed with spears. An ambusher on the ground was on his knees, hands wrapped around his own throat as his face turned purple. He was choking to death, but it was unclear why.

Magic was a safe assumption, but poison couldn't be discounted.

Qown started to move forward.

"Wait." Relos Var put a hand out to stop him.

"But we have to help them—"

That was when Galen D'Mon leaped from the carriage doorway. His ap-

---

[1] Please note that this contradicts other accounts that describe the weather that day as awful. Is this significant? Hard to say. It definitely speaks to the issue of unreliable narration at work here.

parent goal lay across the battlefield, where one of his guards had just fallen. The surviving soldier now faced two attackers by himself. Galen drew his sword across the throat of the choking man as he passed and kept going. He didn't see the ambusher with a spear running up behind him.

"Look out!" Qown called at the same time as the guard on top of the carriage. Relos Var's hand tightened on Qown's shoulder. Galen heard the warnings and slid to the side, the movement so graceful it could have been dance instead of combat. He dodged the spear stab but couldn't draw close enough to reach this new opponent. Meanwhile, the two men behind him dispatched the soldier Galen had meant to rescue.

Which meant Galen now fought three killers by himself.

The guard on top of the carriage did something unexpected and jumped off, swinging down his sword like an ax. The assassin with the spear—the one who'd been trying to ambush Galen from behind—tried to bring his spear in line to counter this new threat. He failed; both men went down in a jumble of sharp edges and writhing cloth. It removed one of Galen's attackers but also freed up two more assassins.

Qown pulled himself from Relos Var's grip. "No," he said. "We have to help them."

Qown didn't know any combat spells, although he'd have been horrified to admit he knew a number of spells that would have been just the thing for wiping out entire towns.[2] Still, he'd learned some non-healing magics in the past few years because of their utility in his work: illusions.

He cast a spell and hoped no one noticed how it precipitated the ringing of the Watchmen's bell, too close to be coincidence. Qown wasn't so naïve as to think this would make the attackers scatter, but they must have been counting on the fact no one would be able to respond to this attack in time to do anything. If the assassins thought they were about to be discovered . . .

The men didn't run, but they did pause to determine if Watchmen were on their way.

Galen took advantage of the distraction. The D'Mon prince ran a sword through the thigh of one man, neatly severing a major artery before bringing his weapon up in a perfect silver arc to plunge through the second's chest. Both men dropped.

With only two attackers left, those men fell to the ground too, grabbing at their throats, choking.

Sheloran D'Mon walked around from behind the carriage, fanning herself with an ornate shanathá metal fan so beautifully fashioned its cost would have fed several families in Eamithon for the rest of their lives. If not for the blood splattered across her white dress, raisigi ripped to reveal silvery mesh, she might have been bored at a party. Her face was carved from stone; her eyes burned.

Qown ran to the two choking men. One of them pulled a knife from his belt and started prying at his own neck, slicing the skin. The assassin tried to speak, but nothing coherent escaped him.

---

[2] I still can't believe you let him research Quuros war magic.

"No, stop!" Qown cried out. "What are you doing? Stop it–" Now he had a man choking *and* bleeding to death.

The guard who'd leaped from the carriage staggered to his feet, although not easily. Blood drenched the man's uniform. If not all of it was his, too much of it was.

"Damn it," Galen growled as soon as he saw the D'Mon guard. "No, you're injured. Stay where you are. Don't move." He threw an arm under the man. He seemed at a loss for what to do. Galen looked around, wide-eyed. He spotted Qown and Relos Var. "Wait," Galen said, "Vishai priests. You're Vishai priests." His eyes opened wide. "You're healers. Help me! He's bleeding out."

Relos Var walked over as if he hadn't been content to just watch from the sidelines and see how it would all play out without him. "Of course. We're always pleased to serve."

Qown was still trying to figure out why the two assassins were dying. One man, he supposed, since the first one had managed to slit his own throat. He reexamined that one, ignoring the blood. Something hard and sharp was lodged in the man's trachea, presumably what he'd been choking on.

A shadow crossed over him. Qown looked up.

Sheloran D'Mon stood there, staring down at him–at the attacker–with an unreadable expression on her face.

"Nightrunners," she murmured. "A Khorveshan mercenary company. One assumes they decided to expand their repertoire into assassination."

"Lady?" Qown had no idea what she was talking about. "Please, did you see what happened to these men . . . ? If I can cure him–"

"You can't," Sheloran D'Mon said. Their eyes met; hers were red and full of fury that showed through nowhere else in her posture. She did something then, a curious little curl of fingers and a tight, flicking motion.

The other man on the ground spasmed; sharp metallic spikes punctured his throat, from the inside out, as if a dozen blades had spontaneously erupted from his vocal cords. The man died immediately, drowning in blood, nearly decapitated.

"Light!" Qown cursed as he scrambled back.

As Sheloran strolled past him, she gestured, a come-hither motion. The small blades inside the dead man's throat quivered, shrank, and melted into tiny bloodless metal blobs, which sailed through the air to land on her fan, blending into the lacy metal filigree until they were all but invisible.

She never looked back at the priest.

Qown closed his eyes for a moment, forced himself to take a deep breath. Somehow she had . . . How had she . . . ? Had she thought Qown wouldn't notice what she'd done? She must have known. She just didn't seem to have cared.

He put the concern out of his mind. He had more important things to worry about. There were still injured.

Not many injured, though. Almost no one, attackers or defenders, had survived this clash. These ambushers had known what they were doing. Khorveshan mercenaries, apparently, if the princess was right. The guards had died from well-placed wounds, all to vital organs or important arteries, guaranteed to kill quickly. The guards had made a good show of themselves, but they'd been outnumbered.

Qown suspected the assassination attempt had truly failed, however, because no one had looked past Sheloran D'Mon's façade to realize she might be more than she seemed. Whatever she'd done wouldn't have worked at all against wizards.[3] Anyone with talismans or simply a strong enough natural aura would have been able to effortlessly keep her from affecting a foreign object worn close to their bodies. But against normal people? Lethal. So very lethal.

Red eyes, Qown remembered. So House D'Talus, the Royal House in charge of smelting, smithing, and metal crafts. And she certainly could control metal. Illegal for her to do so as a woman, but she'd made no effort to hide her skill.[4]

Sheloran closed her fan and bounced it off the palm of her other hand as she crossed over to Galen. "We can't stay here, Blue. We need to head back to the palace right away."

"Once he can be moved—"

The nearly unconscious guard Relos Var was treating mumbled something.

"What was that?" Galen asked Relos Var, who was closer.

"I do believe he said, 'The driver stopped for them,'" Relos Var volunteered. "Is that important?"

Both D'Mons looked back toward the carriage. The driver still slumped over in his seat, throat slit and blood spilling down his House D'Mon uniform.

"I see," Galen D'Mon said. "Then no, we can't go back to the palace."

"Oh?" Relos Var asked amiably, fingers still channeling tenyé through the guard's body. It was a bit like talking while cooking, the hands continuing their work even while the person held a conversation. "And why is that, my lord?"

"Because that means it was an inside job," Sheloran answered, spreading that fan of hers to cover the lower half of her face.

The world changed.

---

[3] I'm not certain that's true.
[4] Not illegal, but Qown hadn't heard about Tya's proclamation at Atrine by this point.

10: The Malice of the World

Qown's reaction
The Lighthouse at Shadrag Gor
Just after Qown's memory

Qown hesitated as autonomy returned. Then the shouting started as people reoriented themselves to the aftereffects of Qown's memories of the ambush and reacting in various ways to Teraeth's unprovoked attack on the Spurned woman. Qown ran forward to see if he could heal the woman in time. Possibly others had the same idea. He wasn't the only one in the room who could heal, after all.

Senera didn't move.

Meanwhile, the woman Teraeth had attacked clutched her throat, blood spilling through her fingers. Her head slumped forward, her form teetered . . .

"Must you be so dramatic," Senera said.

Teraeth had stopped paying attention after the vision hit, as if he didn't give a damn that he'd just murdered someone. He'd pulled back from the bleeding woman and now stood, shoulders slumped, eyebrows drawn together, staring down at the floor. When Senera spoke, he raised his head and growled, "I'm not being dramatic–"

Senera said, "I wasn't talking to you."

The woman with the slit throat started laughing.

Everyone paused, confused.

As the Spurned woman raised her head, her body . . . shifted. White hair turned golden, her height grew, the "lethal" neck wound stopped bleeding, her entire body changed. "She" stopped being a woman at all.

She now looked exactly like Kihrin.

"Light!" Qown backed away from her. He knew the stories. That was a mimic. That had to be a mimic . . . [1]

Teraeth's expression didn't flicker. "I thought that was you, Talon."

Talon wrapped herself around Teraeth's arm and purred. "I missed you too, Your Majesty."

Senera sighed.

He shrugged her away. "I should have killed you when I had the chance," Teraeth said.

Talon made a moue. "Kihrin was pretty glad you didn't, but I agree with you, if it makes you feel any better."

---

[1] While the legends paint them as demons, and Qown was assuredly taught not to believe that, I'm not surprised he took this as seriously as he did. Mimics deserve their reputation.

Teraeth said, "It doesn't." He wiped off his dagger, sheathed it, and walked over to the other side of the keeping room, setting his back against the wall and sliding down until he was sitting. His expression was haunted, lost. A sob escaped his throat as he dropped his head.

"That does it," Janel said. "I'm setting her on fire."

"Wait," Thurvishar said.

"Not this time–" Janel started to say, voice dripping hatred.

"Janel, stop!" Thurvishar shouted. Before Janel could create an inferno hot enough to melt flesh, he wrapped the mimic in energy, trapping her.

Janel rounded on him. "Don't test me, D'Lorus. Not after what you've done."

"Wait. She's the one attacking, and I'm the one who's imprisoned–" Talon protested.

"Shut up, Talon," five or six people said simultaneously.

"Oh, come on," Talon said, "you had to know I was here. Did you think Senera was going to leave me behind while she betrayed Relos Var?"

"Janel, please." Qown interposed himself. He thought it might have been the first time he'd addressed her since they arrived. It was definitely the first time he'd looked her in the eyes.

She had an expression on her face suggesting her willingness to set the world on fire. Then her gaze refocused on him.

Qown swallowed. "I'm not defending her. But let's not kill anyone before we've figured out what's going on and who's doing this. Don't you agree?"

Before Janel could answer, Thurvishar said, "Qown, please check Teraeth. Something's wrong."

Qown wasn't positive if Thurvishar had asked the question because he was genuinely concerned about Teraeth or because he wanted to distract Janel. If it was the latter, it worked. Janel turned around and studied the vané man. He hadn't moved from his position on the floor, head lowered, arms resting on his knees.

Janel touched the side of Teraeth's face, put a hand on his shoulder.

"Teraeth?" Janel's voice was soft.

"Is he well?" Sheloran D'Mon asked. "He seems very . . . still."

Janel pushed at Teraeth's shoulder. The man fell over like a large bag of rice, sliding down and out over the floor. Qown gasped and ran over, while Janel grabbed Teraeth's wrist and felt his pulse. Then she backed away, eyes wide, shaking.

"His heart isn't beating," Janel whispered.

Qown picked up Teraeth's wrist from where Janel had dropped it.

Janel was shaking her head. "No, he can't be dead. Qown–"

"I'm checking, I'm checking!" He had no intention of ignoring the man. Teraeth didn't seem prone to fainting.

But Teraeth hadn't fainted.

He was dead.

He had no pulse. He was dead, he was–

Qown forced himself to stop. He'd spent too many years around Janel, a person who looked indistinguishable from the dead every time she went to sleep, to take something like this at face value. There were explanations that didn't require Teraeth to be permanently removed from the picture.

Janel had to have known that too, but she wasn't thinking rationally. "Is he dead?" Janel asked in the most broken voice Qown had ever heard from her.

"Help me bring him over to the fire. It's so cold in here. There's a chance–" But Qown never finished the sentence.

The world changed.

Kihrin's story
Inside Vol Karoth's prison

I felt the moment Teraeth's mind vanished from the Lighthouse. It was like trying to read by candlelight. If just a single candle snuffs, the effect is obvious. Maybe you wouldn't notice it under other circumstances, but when it's one of the only lights in the room, it's impossible to ignore.

"What have you done?" I shouted. I didn't know where Vol Karoth was or if he could even hear me.

Laughter echoed through the city. He'd heard me just fine.

I felt him, knew that he'd appeared behind me. He felt satisfied. Smug.

"What have you done with Teraeth?" I asked again.

If you really want to know . . .

That's when the vision hit.

Teraeth's prison
Just after Qown's memory of the D'Mon carriage ambush

Teraeth couldn't move. He was trapped in place, chained into the middle of a vast array of magical energy. The octagon-shaped rings were carved with runes and sigils, all engraved into a tiled marble floor that had previously never known a flaw or scratch. More marble in the rising columns and archways that crisscrossed the room, large enough that it had been the obvious choice for the ritual. Now it just seemed mocking. He'd never be able to look at this place the same way. He wished it had been somewhere else. Anywhere else. He could see the dark sky through the windows lining the upper levels of the building, clouds churning as a thunderstorm loomed over them all.

The hall itself amplified every sound, which made it all the more horrible that the entire area was so still and quiet. No one was making any noise.

There was no one left to do so.

The bodies lay at the edge of his peripheral vision, close enough to allow him to make out details and identities. There, Kalindra. Over there, Janel. In front of him, Kihrin.

All of them, dead.

And still he couldn't move, even with the knowledge that he was the one who'd killed them, that as the ritual finished, he was the only one left. Was this supposed to feel like victory? It didn't. It felt like far too high a price to pay. Nothing could be worth this.

"Now, now," a weather-tossed thunderstorm of a voice whispered, and

Teraeth's heart wrenched to hear it. His mother crossed in front of him. "It's all going to be over soon. Just one more life to sacrifice, to keep all the others safe."

"Mother, please. I don't want this," he whispered.

"What you want doesn't matter," she whispered back. Her expression was benevolent, her smile kind. She was holding Godslayer in her hands. "Now you'll earn your due."

"Mother, please!" He knew even as he begged that she wasn't listening. Something about this whole scenario felt wrong somehow, but it was all lost under the ponderous weight of pain, guilt, and betrayal.

She raised the sword up high. "This will only hurt for a second."

That was a lie.

The sword came down and pierced through him, not just physically but spiritually. He felt it sever something important inside himself. Something vital. He didn't know how to recover what he'd just lost. Maybe it was impossible. The world faded until it was only pain and hate and the knowledge that he was born to be betrayed, created as a sacrifice.

Never meant for anything more than this.

He woke to find himself unable to move, trapped in place in the center of a magical array.

It all began again, in an endless loop.

Janel's reaction
The Lighthouse at Shadrag Gor

Janel's eyes widened with horror and fear when the vision ended. Hers were hardly the only ones.

"What–" Qown looked down at Teraeth's body. "I didn't . . . Who's doing this?"

"Vol Karoth," Senera whispered. "It has to be Vol Karoth."

Sheloran's mouth was a thin, hard line. "A better question might be: Why?"

"He took Teraeth's souls," Janel murmured. "That vision implies imprisonment. Not destruction." Maybe that was just wishful thinking on her part, a stubborn refusal to accept the worst, but why show them that vision unless there was a point to it?

It seemed like gloating.

She smelled the copper tang of blood in the air. And the room seemed . . . darker.

"Vol Karoth hasn't destroyed Teraeth," Janel said firmly.

"Not yet," Kalindra said.

Xivan stared at Kalindra with narrowed eyes. "Was pointing that out really necessary?"

Kalindra crossed her arms over her chest. "She shouldn't get her hopes up."

Janel didn't tighten her fist around her scabbard, but only because she'd long since learned that was a fantastic way to wreck scabbards. She suspected the problem here was something more than just Kalindra's fantastic lack of empathy.

Xivan must have come to a similar conclusion, because the duchess walked up to Kalindra. Too close. Perhaps not the smartest move when facing an opponent almost certainly better with knives than swords, but then again, Xivan wasn't concerned about being stabbed. It made the differences between the two women obvious—for all that both were Khorveshan and wore their hair in a similar style, Xivan was taller and more athletic, more clearly a soldier.

"We've all lost people," Xivan told her. "The wounds are raw and bleeding for all of us. We'll know soon if another injury's been added to the pile. So no. She *should* get her hopes up. Hope might be all we have."

Kalindra scoffed. "Oh, that's hilarious coming from you."

Janel had no idea what that was supposed to mean, but the venom the woman was throwing at Xivan was even worse than what she'd been staring at Janel a moment earlier.

Possibly Kalindra was just angry at everything.

Janel could tell it was about to escalate. Xivan didn't look like she was in a mood to put up with anyone's shit. So best to take control while it could still be done.

"This is about Kihrin." Janel interposed herself. "Vol Karoth isn't showing this to us. He's showing it to Kihrin."

"But why?" Qown asked. He sounded so young.

Janel worried on the inside of her lip. The answer seemed obvious enough, but she'd been wrong about this sort of thing before. "If I had to guess, to show Kihrin that Vol Korath's keeping Teraeth as a hostage. We have to figure out a way to stop—"

The world changed.

Inside Vol Karoth's prison
Just after Teraeth's vision

I had to stop myself from lunging forward when the vision ended. Had to stop myself, because this was Vol Karoth and something that foolish was going to get me killed. Destroyed. Unmade. Pick the most appropriate word.

"What did you do with Teraeth? Bring him back!" I screamed.

Oh, but he's here. I've brought him here. Or rather, we have. Thank you so much, by the way. I couldn't have done it without you. Although Senera helped.

"No. No, I—" I backed away from Vol Karoth. "That's not true."

The witch has spread the borders of my prison, and now I share it with you and twelve other souls. And when they know despair, when they surrender to the pain, when they give up, that's when they're mine. But I couldn't have taken Teraeth without you. You're the one who helped put my sword into his hands to slay his mother. You're the one who abandoned him to come here. You're the one who died. Did you not understand how that would hurt him? Or did you just not care? What does it matter if you betray the trust of the ones you love, so long as you win?

My gut twisted, razor sharp, brittle shards of guilt cutting into me. I hadn't realized—I hadn't thought—

I steadied my sword. Even if all that was true, I refused to believe he'd just absorbed Teraeth, eaten him the way a demon ate souls. If Vol Karoth could so simply do that, he'd have already done it to me.[2] He'd have done it to the other Immortals four thousand years before. He might be titled "King of Demons," but that didn't make him one. Not truly. "Where is he?"

I forget. Why don't you give me what I want, and I'll remember.

"What do you want?" I started backing away. I needed Teraeth. I needed to get him out of here, away from Vol Karoth, who would keep twisting Teraeth's nightmares until he found a way to break him. And with everything Teraeth had been through, I didn't know if or when he could recover.

You and I are born from the same roots. We want the same things. You want my surrender, and I want yours. The difference between us, Kihrin, is that you have nothing to bargain with. Tell me: Just how many people in this Lighthouse do you care about? They have always been your weakness. And you care so easily.

I'd have fought to keep my expression blank, but I knew there was no point. He knew exactly what I was feeling, and so he knew the depths of my horror at his words. He would chip away at the rest of them—at Janel, at Galen, at Thurvishar and Talea—until they were his. Until I was his. And then there would be nothing to stop him.

Vol Karoth was wrong. I did have one bargaining chip. "You won't be able to stop Relos Var. You need me for that."

Yes, I do. And I'll have you when you come back to me.

Maybe . . . I didn't have any bargaining chips.

I ran, but his laughter followed, mocking.

Ah, little sprout. You cannot run from yourself. Or this.

The world changed.

Kalindra's memory
Several hours before Jarith Milligreest's funeral

Kalindra watched from the upper story as the servants set up benches for the funeral. The smell of burning wood and fired stone filled in the air, while birds, irate at being scattered from their normal orange tree lookout posts, scolded the staff. In theory, it was daytime, but the dark clouds made that knowledge more a question of faith than fact. Kalindra appreciated the honesty of the weather.

There would be no more beautiful days ever again.

The servants were taking longer than normal because there were so few of them. So many had died, and even more had run off, under the entirely mistaken impression that anywhere else would be safer than the Capital. She was tempted to go down there and help, but it would upset her father-in-law.

Nikali woke from his nap, screaming. She crossed swiftly to his bed and sat down next to him.

"Shhh," she said, putting a hand on his head. No fever. Probably just a nightmare. He had enough inspiration for those to last a lifetime. "It's all right, darling. I'm here."

He was all tears and phlegm, little hands screwed up and jammed into

---

[2] I have nothing to say on this, except to point out Kihrin was quite wrong.

his eye sockets. "I want . . . want . . ." He began crying again before he could articulate what he actually wanted, which might have been anything from a glass of water to his favorite blanket (never mind that it was wrapped around him) to a breastfeeding he sometimes forgot he'd been weaned from.

Kalindra pulled her son into her arms and stroked his hair. "I'm here. I won't let anything hurt you."

Lies. The lies parents tell their children.

"Momma, doll man scares me," Nikali sobbed into her chest.

She felt a chill she couldn't explain. Kalindra clasped her son to her. "Doll man, sweetheart? One of your dolls scared you?" She looked around the crèche, but any toys that were not to be kept in Nikali's constant company had been put away.

The toddler shook his head. "No! The doll man. He was—" His face scrunched up, and another bout of tears stopped any attempt at communication. "I want my dada!"

Kalindra's heart broke. She knew she had tears running down her own face, but what could she do? She held her son to her. "Me too, little one. Me too."

She wiped his tears and let him cry until his breath calmed and he floated off to sleep. Kalindra tucked him into the cradle and pulled his favorite blanket over him, setting his favorite stuffed animal, a white elephant, next to him.

"You should be dressed by now," her father-in-law said from the doorway.

Kalindra looked up. Qoran Milligreest wore funeral white. He had heavy, dark circles under his eyes that spoke to how little sleep he'd had in the last week. Very little, and what capacity he had supported by magic. Every time the situation seemed as though it couldn't possibly get grimmer, it did. She wasn't sure where the bottom was, but the universe seemed determined they would reach it.

She scoffed as she realized he waited on an explanation. "Your grandson had a bad dream," she muttered as she motioned for a maid to take her place at her son's side. She left the nursery and entered her bedchamber.

Her father-in-law followed her, irritation clear on his face. He picked up the white dress some servant had left for her and threw it across a bed she had loathed to use for the last week. "Let the nurses handle Nikali's bad dreams. It's your husband's funeral. You will attend it."

"I will not have a servant substitute for having a mother," Kalindra said. "He only has one parent left."

Kalindra immediately regretted her words.

Qoran inhaled, but the fact that he didn't raise his voice didn't stop the feeling of awful, ugly violence his anger so often invoked. It was an unreasonable feeling; Kalindra had never seen him raise a hand to anyone outside a battlefield. "I know that," he said. "And I care."

Kalindra stared at him. "If you cared, Jarith would already be Returned."

Qoran flinched. "I told you—"

"Thaena was supposed to Return him. She can't have refused. She wouldn't."

Under the weight of Qoran Milligreest's flat, tired stare, all the blood flowed to her cheeks. She turned away from him, resting her hands on the balcony railing. How could she begin to explain? It's not like she could admit to being anything other than the lowborn, unorthodox commoner his son had insisted on marrying, could she?

Here's a funny joke, General. Ever hear the one about how your son married an assassin?

And not just any assassin. She was one of Thaena's angels. The idea of Thaena denying her request to see a loved one Returned was . . . unthinkable. And yet Thaena *had*. The Goddess of Death had refused to answer her prayers, refused to communicate with her at all.

No rebuke. No explanations. Just silence.

Kalindra had started to wonder if "loved one" was in fact the heart of the problem. She'd come to Khorvesh on orders, more than a little bitter about her assigned mission. She hadn't wanted to leave Kihrin, even if her duty demanded it. Yes, he was younger than she was by several years, but she'd still cared.

Except the prophecies had spoken of a different outcome to Kihrin's love life.

> In the shadows of death's throne
> The hawk and the lion will reunite
> Demon's seed and demon's own
> Wander in the darkening blight[3]

But apparently, Kalindra hadn't been meant to fall in love with Jarith either.

"It is not our right to question the gods," Qoran said softly. Kalindra silently complimented herself on what a fine job she did of not punching him in the throat.

"Are you sure?" she said instead.

"Daughter—" He put a hand on her arm. She didn't shrug it off, although the temptation was strong.

She wondered just when she'd fallen in love with her husband. But Jarith had been so easy to love. Before she'd quite known what had happened, she found herself swept up into the arms of a man who'd been everything she'd ever wanted and more. She'd thought herself the luckiest woman in the world to have had what started out as "duty" turn into something far more personal, far more pleasurable.

Now it didn't seem like luck at all.

She missed him. She missed Jarith so much it made her insides ache, made her sick with horror. She kept feeling him, like he was about to sneak up behind her, wrap his arms around her waist. He would kiss the side of her neck, laugh into her ear, and tell her how beautiful she was. She kept waking in the middle of the night expecting to turn over and find him there, and . . .

Her Jarith was dead. Dead and not Returned, and for the first time in her entire life, she hated, hated, *hated* Thaena.

All she wanted was Jarith.

[3] The Devoran Prophecies, Book 32, Quatrain 353.

"Kalindra, I'm sorry." Qoran shook his head. "This . . . I know this is hard. But we—"

"Where's Eledore?" she asked.

Qoran wrinkled his nose and looked away.

"You don't know, do you?" Kalindra said.

"We'll find my daughter," Qoran said. "She's done this before."

Kalindra didn't feel like arguing the point or pointing out just how good Eledore was at not being found when she didn't feel like it. Kalindra also knew just how close Eledore had been with her older brother—she would be looking forward to his funeral every bit as much as Kalindra. Meaning either woman would have rather done themselves personal injury than attend it.

"And when you do, are you sending her away as well?" Kalindra asked.

Qoran frowned. "I'm not sure what—"

"No, don't try to pretend you don't know what I mean."

He sighed. She wondered if he would tell her to mind her business and do what she was told. But it seemed he hadn't spent so long in the Capital as to have picked up that bad habit.

"It's for your safety. I have a job to do, and it's harder and harder to do it when I have to be worried about my own family. Devors is the securest location outside the imperial Arena in the entire Quuros Empire. The magical wards there have held in place for over four hundred years."

"It's an island filled with nothing but a bunch of very boring monks who spend all their days accumulating very boring prophecies." Her laughter was weak and watery, but oh so bitter.

"Not so boring these days," Qoran mused.

She scoffed under her breath. No, not so boring at all. And there was a part of her . . . Oh, she hated to admit the old man had a point, but he did.

Veils, she missed Jarith so much.

"Very well," Kalindra said. "I'll have my maid start to pack."

Qoran raised an eyebrow. "You're not going to fight me?"

"I only fight you when you're wrong," Kalindra snapped.

Qoran gave her a sad smile. "You know, I've questioned my son's judgment in many things, but never why he chose you."

Kalindra inhaled. He probably thought he was being comforting. "I'll go change."

She wasn't conceding to his wishes because he was right. It was because Devors lay close to where she needed to be. Because she was an angel of Thaena. She knew a great many secrets.

Including how to get Jarith back. With or without Thaena's permission.

As she watched them prepare for the funeral, the world changed.

11: A Window into Night

The sensation of returning to the present, returning to the Lighthouse, disoriented Kalindra. No one said a word.

Kalindra felt nothing but dread. She'd hardly needed to see her own memories paraded around for everyone else to know that none of their secrets were safe. That didn't stop the reality from feeling like a violation. She was a woman who'd always cherished the power of mystery, who kept her past and her sins hidden from everyone around her. If Jarith hadn't known about her background with the Black Brotherhood, neither Teraeth nor Kihrin had known about her history before joining it.

Jarith was dead. Kihrin was dead. And Teraeth was . . .

People weren't even looking at her, turning their heads away as if to pretend they weren't seeing her so . . . revealed. She couldn't stand it.

Kalindra ran from the room. She ignored Xivan yelling behind her.

As soon as she made it out into the main hallway, she knew she'd made an error in judgment. She wasn't dressed warmly—an absurd idea in the Capital, or indeed in Devors, rain or not. The hallway was so cold she felt like she'd been dunked in ice water and left outside in the Yoran winter. She'd have been far better off putting up with the pitying looks of those hypocrites while staying by the fire.

She stared down the hallway at the small tunnel connecting the manor with the Lighthouse. It wasn't difficult to imagine movement. A dark shadow shifting at the edge of her vision . . .

The hallway visibly dimmed.

Kalindra darted through a doorway leading off from the hall. The room was warmer but still cold enough to make her breath frost. It was a sitting room, with couches arranged facing each other before a large window looking out over a landscape smeared into streaks of green and brown by thick, seeded glass. The room was austere and minimalist. Mostly stone, with a few pieces of cloth or wood to provide what might be laughably considered "comfort"—a cushion here, a table there.

Kalindra sat down on a couch and laced her fingers together in her lap.

Then Galen said, "How was that supposed to work, anyway? Were you feeding information back to the rest of your little cult, or did they just want you in position for when the order finally came down to assassinate the high general?"

Kalindra turned around.

Galen leaned against the stone wall in the back, his arms crossed over his chest. He must have been there when she'd entered, brooding in the darkness. The room wasn't well lit; she hadn't seen him.

"Galen, I . . ." Running from a room again would look ridiculous, but she was sorely tempted.

He didn't respond. He just glared at her and waited.

"Both," she finally said. "Please believe me, Galen, my target was never Jarith."

That did nothing to console the man. "Would Thaena have told you if it was?"

Kalindra felt something in her stomach twist. She couldn't meet Galen's eyes.

No. Thaena wouldn't have.

"I can't believe–" Galen started to scold.

Oh good. The flare of pure anger she felt was a blessed relief. "No. Just stop. You think I didn't love Jarith? Was anything in your memories that were dragged out and shown to that crowd a lie? Because mine were all true."

"Sure," Galen said. "You loved him. But not enough to tell him the truth. You didn't tell him the truth, did you?"

Kalindra stared off at the window. It was raining outside. "Tell him the truth? No. They frown on that in assassin school." She choked down her bitter anger. It was hardly the worst of her secrets, and she had no reason to think the forces determined to make her share like this were going to stop.

"Did he even have a choice, or did you use some kind of–"

Kalindra was done with apologizing for this. "I'd drown myself in filth before I'd use a spell to make someone fall in love with me. I understand why you were Jarith's friend. But did he ever tell you why he was yours?"

Galen narrowed his eyes. "What are you talking about?"

"Did he ever tell you why he approached you, after he came back from Stonegate Pass? Why we started inviting you and Sheloran over for dinner every week and always made such an effort to include you in our lives? It's not like he had to. And frankly, his father would have been much happier if he hadn't. Or perhaps you hadn't noticed just how *done* Qoran was your family?"

Doubt crept into the man's blue eyes. Suspicion. "He's my cousin," Galen offered, but the tremor in his voice suggested he knew what a poor excuse that was.

Kalindra didn't bother making her laughter light and friendly. "No, Darzin's his cousin. The cousin he hated. And you are that hated cousin's son. So why would he try to befriend you? Certainly not some scheme to get in Darzin's good graces. Try again."

Galen swallowed. "Fine. Why did he?"

"At first? Because I asked him to. I suggested that maybe you needed more friends in your life. People who weren't just around because you were a good political connection. Don't act like I never cared just because I had a master you didn't know about."

Galen said, "And I suppose the fact that this let you do double duty and get close to House D'Mon is just–"

"Get over yourself," Kalindra snapped. "I did it because for the six months I was *fucking your brother Kihrin*, he never stopped talking about how he was going to storm the Blue Palace to get you back. Which I knew would never happen, so the least I could do was try to see to it that your life wasn't completely miserable. You're welcome."

An emotion she couldn't identify crossed Galen's face, tucked out of sight as soon as it appeared. He scowled, started to respond, and then swallowed that too.

"Kalindra? Galen?" Thurvishar called from the hallway. They had exactly that much warning before the wizard, with uncanny luck, ducked into the sitting room. He smiled at them, but as his gaze slid past them toward the window, his expression froze.

Kalindra looked back at the window again and startled, standing upright and backing away.

The rain had turned to blood.

"There is no way that is good," Galen said. He too was retreating to the door.

"Oh, it's much worse than you know," Thurvishar said.

"What do you mean?" Kalindra asked.

"The Lighthouse at Shadrag Gor doesn't have windows."

Kalindra felt her skin prickle.

All three of them stared at the rebelliously existing window. What would happen if she opened it, if she stepped through? Where would it go? Then she remembered the green land beyond she'd seen before it started raining and felt a chill that had nothing to do with the temperature.

Because Shadrag Gor was on an island in the far northeastern section of Yor. They should have been surrounded by storm-tossed seas, not land.

"Are you sure—?" She didn't finish the sentence as she saw the look on Thurvishar's face. He was sure.

"You're trembling," Galen told her.

"It's cold," she responded. Which was true and not at all why she was shaking. Kalindra knew better than to think he accepted that explanation.

"Why don't we go back?" Thurvishar suggested. "It'll be safer."

"Safer?" Kalindra stared at him. "Teraeth's corpse suggests otherwise."

Thurvishar didn't seem concerned. In fact, he gave her a small smile. "That's why I came to find you," he said. "Teraeth's alive."

Later, after they'd returned and Kalindra sat down by the fireplace, she turned to Thurvishar and said, "Your definition of 'alive' needs some work."

Teraeth still looked dead.

"His souls are untethered," Janel said. She handed Kalindra a teacup peace offering, holding it in both hands for a few seconds until steam rose from it. "It's just that unlike me, his souls aren't slipping into the Afterlife." She glanced over at Senera. "Tell them the rest of it."

The white-skinned witch, Senera, had dragged over a table from the kitchen and was using it as a workstation. She had a small inkstone sitting next to an open journal, as well as a fine camel-hair brush.

"There's a great deal I can't determine," she said, tapping on the inkstone with the sharpened end of the brush, "because Vol Karoth is like Urthaenriel–a null space. But even that can be informative, depending on which questions the Name of All Things refuses to answer."

Kalindra's focus snapped back to the rock, apparently not an inkstone at all. Right.[1] She remembered the look on Khaemezra's face when Teraeth had told her that Relos Var had the Cornerstone that would let him answer any question. Or almost any question, apparently.

She forced herself to drink her tea while it was still hot.

Thurvishar sat down on the arm of a couch. "We know Vol Karoth has a physical form as well as a psychic form. I suspect, although can't prove"–he inclined his head toward Senera–"that this psychic form is more like a psychic space, something that can exist and be visited even while Vol Karoth is imprisoned."

Kalindra forced herself back to the conversation. "I'm not following?"

"Five hundred years ago," Janel said, "Elana didn't break Vol Karoth's prison, but she was still able to reach Vol Karoth's souls and affect them. Therefore, his souls must not be imprisoned the way we think they are."

More than a few faces around the room looked confused, but they seemed content not to interrupt, at least for the moment.

Kalindra was not one of those people. "You're saying if Vol Karoth was truly imprisoned and unreachable, Elana shouldn't have been able to free S'arric so he could be reincarnated as Kihrin at all."

Janel looked uncomfortable. "He was imprisoned. But prisons are seldom impenetrable. Vol Karoth couldn't escape, but it's possible to 'visit,' if you will."

Thurvishar waved a hand as if this was old news, which it probably was–for him. "When Senera merged Shadrag Gor and Vol Karoth's prison, she also merged this psychic space. That's where both Kihrin and Vol Karoth are right now."

"I hate to disagree, but I do believe Vol Karoth is just down the hall," Sheloran said. Her voice was carefree, but her knuckles clenching her fan were white.

"His physical body is just down the hall," Thurvishar agreed. "His souls are on a mental layer that's parallel to our own. We can't see this psychic space. It's possible that they can't see us, but communication can occur between the two layers."

"Communication? What kind of communication?" Kalindra asked.

"Forcibly sharing memories, for one," Talea said.

"Teraeth's souls have been taken into this psychic space, but he's not dead," Thurvishar said.

"At least not yet," Kalindra added.

"Oh, for fuck's sake." Xivan slammed her arm down on the couch. "Would you stop that?"

Kalindra ignored her. She looked over to the couch where they'd laid his

---

[1] Oh, but it was. I did use it for making ink, after all.

body. Janel sat down sat next to Teraeth's body. She held Teraeth's hand and gazed at him with an expression Kalindra could only describe as wretched.

Kalindra scowled. So the woman cared about Teraeth too. Fine.

Janel looked over then. "Much as it pains me to say it, Kalindra's not wrong. We're operating under a time limit. Remove souls from the body for long enough, and eventually, the body receives the message 'You should be dead' and makes it true. If we can't get his souls back from Vol Karoth's psychic space . . .'"

"He'll dehydrate or starve to death." Qown was holding his own teacup so tightly he was in serious danger of shattering it. "But . . . wait. Thurvishar, could you use Wildheart to keep his body alive?"

"*Wildheart?*" Kalindra scowled. "How many Cornerstones do you people have?"

Thurvishar, Senera, and Qown all raised three fingers.

"Oh, fuck me," Kalindra muttered.

"Even if he does, Qown, it doesn't matter," Senera said, "because death is inevitable if you stay away from your own body for too long. If we can't figure out a way to pull Teraeth's souls back from this other mental plane, he'll truly die. And being an angel of Thaena is no help when Thaena herself is . . ." She made a vague motion.

"Dead," Kalindra snapped. "Just say dead." She tried not to feel like the word was a dagger into her heart. It still didn't feel real, but the silence on the other end of her connection to Thaena whispered the truth.

"Gods," Galen murmured.

Thurvishar said, "Also I think . . . I think I can transport myself into that space. I can sense the edges of it. I'm reasonably sure it would work."

"Well, great! Do that, grab Kihrin–" Galen said.

"But I'm not certain I'll be able to come back," Thurvishar mused.

"*Don't* do that, then," Senera said.

"But I do think we could do what Kihrin and Vol Karoth are doing," Thurvishar continued.

"What? What do you mean?" said several voices at once.

Janel waited until the wall of questions died down and then turned to Thurvishar again. "Explain, please?"

Thurvishar pondered his answer before stating, "If we assume that Kihrin and Vol Karoth are somehow responsible for these visions, why are we seeing them? My theory is that it's unintentional. This is more like opening a door and pouring a lake through. It doesn't matter who's on the other side. Everyone is getting drenched. But the advantage to that is that we don't need to aim. We don't need to know exactly who is on the other side or overcome their defenses. We too could open a door and pour memories through."

"Yes, but whose memories?" Sheloran said. "It's quite rude to point out the flaw in your theory, but wouldn't that require the very targeting you say isn't happening?"

"It's not a perfect metaphor. I don't as yet even understand why they're choosing these particular memories . . ."

Talon guffawed. "Oh, come on. That's obvious. Vol Karoth and Kihrin are arguing with each other."

Everyone stared at the mimic. Even Senera rolled her eyes. "Talon, you can't know that. We haven't established why someone's targeting us—"

"This isn't about *us*," Talon said. "And trust me, if there's one thing I know how to recognize, it's when two different personalities in the same mind are having a fight." The mimic pointed at "his" temples for emphasis.

"Would you please stop looking like him?" Janel's voice was raw.

Talon studied Janel for a long beat. Kalindra could hardly blame Janel for finding it unnerving. She found Talon's resemblance to Kihrin unsettling, and she hadn't seen him in years.

"Anything for you, Janel," Talon told her, sounding like she meant it. Her shape morphed into a Quuros woman with wheat-gold skin who looked nothing like the person who, ultimately, was the reason everyone was in this mess.[2]

Thurvishar cleared his throat and continued, "What I mean is that we could do the same, but projected back into the psychic space. Our own shout. It would at least let Kihrin know we're here."

"Assuming he doesn't already," Senera said.

"Do we want to catch Vol Karoth's attention?" Qown asked.

"He already knows we're here," Talea pointed out.

Thurvishar said, "This is an experiment. We need to find out what we can do, how possible communication even is."

"If you're looking for volunteers to be the next person to reveal their memories," Kalindra said, "count me out."

"I think Qown should go next," Galen said.

Qown twitched in his seat, but he neither responded nor turned around to look at Galen.

There was a pause as everyone waited for someone else to speak.

"I'm serious," Galen repeated. "I think Qown should be next."

Qown looked over that time. "Why? What good would it possibly—?" The priest exhaled sharply. "You know what, fine. Yes. I'll be next." He moved from his seat at the table and over to one of the couches next to Thurvishar. He looked at the wizard expectantly. "I'm next."

Thurvishar raised an eyebrow. "You're sure?"

"Why not? At least this way, people won't have to ask whether or not I was lying." He glared at Galen.

Kalindra laughed under her breath. Someone needed to sit the boy down and explain that the cost of being a spy was indeed that those one betrayed would never trust them again. And would be completely justified to feel that way. There was no sense being offended when this was the prize his metal had purchased. How had he thought that was going to work out?

She thought of her own words with Galen a short time earlier and stopped smiling. So maybe it still hurt when you made the mistake of caring.

Always, always a mistake to care.

---

[2] The woman she turned into was Lyrilyn, Talon's original body. This becomes important later.

Thurvishar crouched down on his haunches before Qown. "I want you to concentrate on a memory. Keep it clear in your mind."

"Any memory?" Qown's voice was tremulous.

"It's up to you," Thurvishar said.

Qown stared at him with clear dread and guilt in his expression. He swallowed and nodded at Thurvishar. "Yes, I'm ready."

"This shouldn't hurt," Thurvishar said, "but I can't be entirely certain what's going to happen, so please be prepared." He locked eyes with the healer.

The world changed.

12: A Fair Trade

Qown's memory
The Upper Circle of the Capital City, Quur
Just after the assassination attempt on Galen D'Mon

In the end, Relos Var drove the carriage, as he was the only one who knew how. The others rode inside.[1]

The D'Mon carriage suggested impossible levels of wealth, lined with blue silk, decorated with gilt trim. Either those were blue crystals nestled amongst the carvings, or–Veils–those couldn't be real sapphires, could they?

But it wasn't all gold and luxury. The bloodstains served as a bracing reminder of just what had brought them there.

Qown forced himself to concentrate on more important matters, such as the injured. Of the seven guards and two royals who had left the funeral together, three remained alive. Galen D'Mon held his arm against his body, surreptitiously cradling it. Worse, a darker stain had begun to spread along his sleeve.

"You're bleeding," Qown told the prince.

Galen D'Mon looked up from examining his guard, in turn uncomfortable with the fussing being made over him. "It's nothing. Finished seeing to my man."

Qown summoned up a ball of mage-light and held it toward the prince's arm. That was a lot more blood than "nothing." "Is every D'Mon as stubborn as you?" Qown bit down on saying anything else as his sense finally caught up with his indignation and reminded him that there were proper ways to address royalty–and not a single word he'd said qualified.

He'd been expecting a certain amount of selfishness from any Quuros royal–especially from Darzin D'Mon's son–but this man was ... well, he wasn't acting the right way. Of course, if he had been, he wouldn't have given that disastrously honest speech at the funeral.

"Oh yes," Sheloran answered, more amused than scandalized. "Every single one. Let him look at your arm, Blue. You're no good to me dead."

"You're injured too, Red," Galen reproached.

She snapped open her metal fan. "You're bleeding," she said. "I'm not."

Qown coughed. "Apologies, Your Highness, but we can't be sure of that. We'll need to look over you both. And your guard." Qown glanced at the injured man. "I'm sorry, but what's your name?"

The guard's voice was weak. Despite Relos Var's efforts, he barely seemed

---

[1] It's possible either Anlyr or Galen knew how, but since they were both injured, it must have seemed reasonable to allow another to take over.

conscious. "Anlyr." He shifted his eyes toward the high lord. "I wasn't here last week, my lord," he said. "My sister was getting married."

Qown had no idea why the guard had felt the need to explain that. Possibly he was feverish.

Galen D'Mon's mouth quirked. "Are you apologizing to me for still being alive, Anlyr?"

The guard let out a short, surprised laugh before wincing and falling silent. Qown snuck a better look at Anlyr. He was young, in his early twenties. The sort royals would keep around as much for accessorizing as protection. Handsome, with deep brown eyes and a face meant for poems and heartbreak.

Not the sort Qown would think wise to keep around a wife like Sheloran, but maybe Galen was just that confident of his wife's fidelity.[2] Relos Var had said Galen just wasn't interested in women, but Qown was finding that difficult to believe. Galen clearly cared about his wife a great deal.

"Don't apologize," Galen said, his expression turning grimmer, "you'd have only put yourself in the path of forces you couldn't possibly have defeated." His gaze grew distant. "One man can't stop the ocean."

Qown shifted seats so he sat next to Galen, pretending it didn't bother him. He examined the prince's sleeve. The wound wasn't so serious that he'd die from blood loss, but that didn't make Galen immune to complications later.

Galen scowled at him. "Must you?"

"Yes, Your Highness," Qown answered. "I must."

The royal tried his best to cow the priest into submission, but that was always going to be a losing battle. Qown had been bullied by Galen's father, Darzin, had met Gadrith, knew Relos Var; Galen was a lightweight in the intimidation department.

Qown eyed the fabric. Blood had clotted and begun sticking to the cloth. There was no help for it. "This is going to hurt," Qown warned. "Let me numb the pain first."

"Will it keep me from being able to fight?"

Qown frowned. There was no physical resemblance, but Galen reminded Qown of Janel just then. That same twisted sense of priorities. "It's not . . . I mean, only for a short while."

"Then skip it. Just get on with it."

The two men locked stares. Galen had a stubborn, determined look on his face. Had Qown been giving the matter thought, he'd have agreed he mirrored the expression. But he wasn't, distracted as he was by both Galen being incredibly muleheaded and the realization that none of the sapphires in the carriage were bluer than the man's eyes.

Qown looked away, shook his head, and ripped the fabric from the wound, breaking open the still-forming scab.

Galen didn't flinch. Qown might have thought someone else had beaten him to numbing the wound if he hadn't been so certain such wasn't the case. Galen should have reacted differently. It would have been normal to react differently.

---

[2] Why yes, I imagine he probably was. At least around men.

"At least that wasn't my favorite shirt," Galen said. "This is why I hate wearing white."

"Didn't you feel that?" Qown found himself staring at the man's eyes again.

"I did," Galen admitted, "but it's just pain."

Sheloran sighed.

Qown felt more than a little appalled. People responded to repeated trauma in any number of ways, each as different and myriad as herbs in the Temple of Light garden. It wasn't uncommon for people to become hypersensitive to pain, hypervigilant to anything that might cause them discomfort, their bodies a beacon, every nerve screaming. But the reverse was also possible—people so out of tune to the song of flesh and nerves they could no longer feel its signals, blunting the edges of qualities like pain. Or pleasure. Or happiness.

Whatever Galen D'Mon saw in Qown's wide-eyed stare, it amused him. Despite the open wound, despite the discomfort, Galen gave Qown a soft smile.

Qown flushed. He looked down at the wound instead, which seemed a far safer target for his attention. He clasped his hand over it as if his fingers were a cloth bandage to stop the bleeding. Qown concentrated on spells to clean out the wound, reattach muscles and nerves, fuse the skin back into place.

"How old are you?" Galen D'Mon asked suddenly.

The question almost broke Qown's concentration, but he kept it for long enough to finish the spell. Qown moved his hand away. "You were right," he said. "It was nothing." He didn't answer the question.

There was no shame in the answer. Qown was old enough. Older than Galen, certainly. Just . . . younger than most people ever realized. He'd always looked old for his age. His mother used to say he was born ancient. If someone were to ask Janel how old he was, Qown confidently expected she would answer incorrectly.

"What are priests of Vishai, anyway?" Sheloran asked. She leaned against one side of the carriage, fanning herself. One might think this was a pleasant outing to the baths if one ignored the splashes of blood against the white cloth. "I thought I was familiar with all the local gods."

Before Qown could answer, Galen did. "It's not the name of a god. They're an Eamithonian mystery cult. Celibates." Galen gave Qown a sideways look of amusement before returning his attention to his wife. "You'd like them." His voice was teasing.

She laughed. "Excuse me? I can't imagine how."

"Healers, or so they like to claim—"

"I'm right here," Qown said, "healing your arm."

Galen leaned back in his seat. His eyes had a glassy look about them as if this were all incredibly funny or he was drunk. Which meant the shock was setting in.

He ignored Qown. "Obviously, the Vishai can't operate without a Blue House license. Except they don't like to charge for their services, so guess who's always defaulting on paying their dues? Father used to go on and on." Then Galen winked—winked!—at Qown.

Sheloran laughed. "You're right, Blue. I do like them."

The carriage came to a halt. The wooden ceiling creaked as Relos Var helped himself down.

The guard, Anlyr, seemed prepared to rise from his deathbed to be the first to leave the carriage. Instead, he was too weak to fight off Qown as the healer grabbed him by the elbow and helped him. Galen and Sheloran followed last.

"Forgive me, my lord, but this place isn't . . . ," the guard began to say, then shut his mouth. No doubt he was reminding himself of the same proper etiquette Qown had been so prone to forgetting.

"It's safer than the Blue Palace right now," Galen said, "which I realize isn't saying much."

"Where are we?" Qown asked.

Sheloran snickered behind him. "You've never been to the Culling Fields?"

They stood on a broad street, with the large, grand buildings of the Upper Circle in the distance. More immediately, a parklike area with trees and shrubs sat on his left, while on the other side of the road lurked a few meager buildings. A large, dark stone tower that had suffered greatly in the recent Hellmarch and a two-story whitewashed brick building, atypical of the normal Quuros style only in that it had several large glass windows, now shattered. There was no signage, no identifying markings. A few people moved around inside.

Relos Var left the horses by the side of the road. He didn't bother to remove their tack, suggesting he didn't expect to be there long. Which was probably prudent, given Galen's funeral speech, its consequences, and the assassins.

Although the assassins had moved so quickly, Qown thought it unlikely they'd been a response to the speech itself.

Despite his injuries, Anlyr insisted on opening the front door for everyone else, which wasn't locked, only closed. The inside of the tavern stood almost empty, likely because of the hour. People had more important things to do than go carousing in taverns.

Also, it wasn't open for business.

Workmen piled broken furniture in a corner for repair or kindling. Scorch marks and signs of violence marred the walls and floors.

A woman sat at the bar, head down on a countertop littered with liquor bottles, while another woman stood behind it. Qown couldn't see any other details from the first woman besides her long, dark hair, but the second one wore a man's misha and an exasperated look. When they walked inside, she noticed them, and that expression turned into recognition.

"Oh gods. Galen. Are you lot all right? Was it a demon attack?" The woman walked out from behind the bar. "Sit down, sit down." She pointed at Anlyr. "You too, damn it."

"I'm fine," the guard protested.

"'Fine' is a state rarely accompanied by bloodstains," Relos Var said dryly. "Now sit down and allow me to finish healing you."

"No, Taunna, it wasn't demons," Galen said, "but I did just survive my first assassination attempt. I feel so grown-up now."

As he spoke, the woman seated at the counter raised her tear-streaked face. Her eyes were a beautiful amber color, if otherwise glossy and red from sobbing.

She saw Galen and rubbed a hand over her face. "Hey, it's my cousin. Hello, cousin!" She raised a glass in mock salute.

"Eledore?" Galen said. "Is this where you've been hiding?"

Judging from the unfocused look and the dead bottles, Eledore was quite drunk.

Galen walked over to the bar and took a seat next to the woman. He pushed aside several empty glasses and threw the bartender, Taunna, a reprimanding glare. She shrugged in response.

Qown frowned as Sheloran walked over to Eledore's other side. The princess claimed the remaining bottle of sassibim brandy and poured the contents into a glass for herself. She took a single sip and then set the bottle to the side.

Out of Eledore's reach.

"Who is that?" Qown asked Relos Var, who had watched all of this with a slight smile on his face.

"Eledore Milligreest," Var whispered.

Oh.

"I didn't see you at the funeral," Galen told Eledore.

She snorted. "I won't tell Jarith if you don't." Then she plucked at Galen's bloodstained shirt. "I thought we made a deal you weren't going to die again."

"I won't tell Thaena if you don't," he responded. "When did you get back into town?"

"Yesterday," she answered. "I just . . . can't. You understand, don't you? Daddy wanted me to make a *speech*."

"Oh, I think Galen's said enough for everyone." Sheloran threw her husband a look simultaneously fond and scolding. "Now how is it that in the two years that we've been married, I have never met this woman?" Her voice was light and breezy, but there was a noticeable tremble lurking under the surface. The second sip of brandy was far more generous than the first, before she recovered her fan and opened it again.

"Oh, Daddy sent me away," Eledore explained. "For my 'safety.' I've heard stories about you, though." She examined Sheloran critically before turning back to her cousin, a feat that required her to turn her entire body on the stool. "Jarith was right, you know. Your wife has amazing tits."

The bartender dropped her face into the palm of her hand.

Qown coughed, while Galen visibly bit back on a laugh. "Ah yes. I've been told."

Galen glanced back at the table where Qown and Relos Var sat, and Qown realized his embarrassed cough must have betrayed his eavesdropping. Galen leaned past Eledore and said to his wife, "Would you mind, Red? I should talk to the priests."

Sheloran waved her fan demurely, covering her lower face. "Of course, Blue. I'm sure I can find something to discuss with Taunna and Eledore. The magnificence of my breasts, if all else fails."

Galen laughed, regarded his wife with obvious fondness. Qown, on the other hand, had turned several shades of red and was trying to pretend he wasn't listening.

Dorna would have found Sheloran adorable.[3]

Galen gave an insouciant bow to the bartender before heading back to their table. Halfway there, his eyes met Qown's.

To be fair, Qown had been staring.

Galen reminded Qown a bit of Kihrin, more than a bit of Darzin, and yet he also wasn't like either man. He caught Qown with those bluer-than-blue eyes, studied the priest, and then did something exceptionally unnecessary.

He grinned.

Galen D'Mon was handsome in the same way Qown assumed all the men of the D'Mon family were probably handsome, but it was ridiculous and unreasonable—absolutely unacceptable—how that smile transformed him into something transcendentally beautiful. He was pure sunlight. Qown felt the floor drop out from under him, dizzy even though he still sat, with no chance to lose his balance. His pulse roared through the veins in his ears.

Qown kept his face perfectly expressionless as he forced his attention elsewhere—what an interesting lamp sat against that wall—all too aware that it was ludicrous that just being smiled at by some Quuros prince would be enough to force all the blood to his cheeks.

To use the Joratese expression, if Qown ran with horses—which he most certainly did *not*—he would run with mares, not stallions. This . . . this . . . overwhelming abundance of feeling was simply the result of being unused to anyone giving him that sort of look, man or woman. That was the only explanation. Qown huffed under his breath.

If Galen noticed, he didn't say anything.

Relos Var wrapped a cleaning spell around his hands as he finished healing Anlyr. "That should do the trick. For best results, please try not to let anyone stab you for at least three days."

Anlyr chuckled. "I'll be sure to keep that in mind." He stood and bowed as Galen approached the table.

"With your permission, my lord, may I make a suggestion? If you'd be willing to stay here for a short while, I can venture next door to the Citadel and bring back more men. That way, you'll still have a proper escort when you leave and, um, a driver for the carriage." He didn't make any further comments on the security of the tavern, but he did frown at the room as if he might conjure up bars on the windows and barricade the door.

Galen shrugged. "If you like. But there are two Milligreest women here. I've never been safer."

Qown looked again at the bartender. It hadn't occurred to him that she might also be a Milligreest, but it was certainly possible. She did look Khorveshan.[4]

"Hey, you all want something from the bar?" the same woman, Taunna,

---

[3] Dorna was Janel's nurse, but I believe the more salient point here is that she *runs with mares,* to use the Joratese expression.

[4] What? Are all Khorveshan women automatically Milligreests?
Fine. He might have a point.

called over to them. "Might as well. For a tavern that's not open for business, we seem to be doing plenty of it today."

"I would love a glass of wine," Relos Var said happily. "Something Kirpis, please."

"Do you have tea?" Qown examined the alcohol lining the shelves doubtfully.

Taunna narrowed her eyes. "Why not? It's not like Galen's old enough to drink anything else.[5] Might as well put a pot on to boil."

Galen didn't rise to the bait; he simply claimed the chair Anlyr vacated. "So I'm going to assume all this goodwill and healing—not to mention that you haven't left—has some expectation of reward."

Relos Var waved a hand. "Less a reward than a business opportunity, my lord."

Galen cocked an eyebrow. He spared Qown the briefest glance, but Qown was giving a close inspection to the opposite wall, sitting as straight as possible, and doing his very best impression of a statue.

Statues never blushed and were rarely, if ever, flustered.

Relos Var regarded Galen with stern severity. "Do you know the Way of Vishai, my lord?"

"If this is about to turn into evangelizing, we're done here."

"Oh no, my lord," Relos Var said. "Nothing like that. But our order has always had two main interests: healing and demons. I cannot help but think the empire currently rests in a state where both those expertises might be valued. If rumors are true, the Physickers Guild has lost a great many people; you'll need all the healers you can gather to your banner."

Galen's expression flattened. "Maybe you haven't heard, but I'm not the High Lord of House D'Mon."

Var shrugged. "I'm sure you'll sort that out."

"Even if I did, I'm not sure you understand just how thoroughly I've salted my own fields. Those assassins we met on the road won't be the last."

"No," Qown corrected, "but those men couldn't have attacked you for what you said at the funeral. Not unless they'd been able to see into the future or someone knew what you were planning to do in advance. Did you . . . did you tell anyone what you were going to do?"

Galen scowled. "*I* didn't even know what I was going to do."

Relos Var beamed at Qown. "Just so! I'm sure what you said—shocking as it no doubt was to royal sensibilities—wasn't their motivation. Far more likely one of your aunts arranged that attack after you were Returned in spite of their best efforts to ensure otherwise. How inconvenient for their own ambitions."

Galen didn't seem surprised by this revelation. "So shouldn't you be making this offer to them?"

"Well, no. They won't suit my needs—oh, bless you, child. Truly, you are an angel." Relos Var took the wine from Taunna's hands and sipped appreciatively before setting it down again on the table. "I have no faith in their ability to see the larger picture. Whereas, if I can help you both keep

---

[5] This was not true. She was teasing.

your position and your heads, I believe you'll be far more trustworthy and grateful." Relos Var offered the wine to Qown. "You should try this. It's delightful."

Qown did his best not to sigh at his teacher—who knew Qown didn't drink alcohol—and instead shook his head. "No, thank you, Father."

"Hmm. Your loss."

Galen rubbed his temples. "You're not going to keep me in power. Everyone knows what a miserable high lord I'd make. Even the people who like House D'Mon—a truly small number, I assure you—want me gone for the house's own good. The only reason anyone tolerated me as heir was because my father had younger brothers and—" A sick, bitter look flashed across Galen's face. "I can't believe he ran. *Again.*"

"I'm sorry?" Qown didn't have to fake his confusion. "Who ran?"

"My brother—" Galen inhaled. "Never mind. It's not important."

Who his brother was clicked in a half second later. Galen was wrong; it *was* important. This was why Relos Var was there. This was why Relos Var was interested in Galen. Because where Relos Var was concerned, it was always about Kihrin.

Brothers, indeed.

It made Qown feel more than a little ill. Galen had no idea what he was being dropped into. Qown couldn't help but think of Janel and her rants about Relos Var's game pieces. It was unfortunate, if necessary.

He reminded himself how necessary this all must be, even if he didn't yet understand why.

Galen scowled. "A business opportunity. You have healers. Even if I were in a position to approve this, which I must emphasize, I'm not, what would you want in payment for this?"

"Well, there is the matter of license dues . . ."

Galen stared at Relos Var for several long, disbelieving seconds. Then he began to laugh.

Relos Var took it all in with quiet amusement—to a point. Then he frowned.

"You want forgiveness for license fees." Galen guffawed, his body language mocking. "You know, if you'd come a few days ago, we might have had a deal."

Confusion washed the benevolent expression from Relos Var's features. "I'm not sure I understand."

Galen cast his gaze on the two men in disbelief. "You didn't hear? The gods themselves came down from heaven in Atrine and declared an end to license fees. Anyone who wants to practice magic can." He waved his fingers at the two priests. "Congratulations. You've paid up your guild fees, because you don't owe any."

A wave of lightheartedness nearly overtook Qown. "But that would mean . . . the Royal Houses—"

"The Royal Houses are like roaches," Galen complained. "Don't worry about us. We'll figure out some justification to survive. If nothing else, the gods only said we can't make magic illegal. Nothing was mentioned about free access to education. Right now, we are the only port in the seas if you want to learn how to cast spells."[6] He scoffed as he sipped his tea. "Even if some of us never had the opportunity, as my aunts are so eager to remind me."

Qown's mouth worked silently. He wasn't sure if he should think Galen naïve, trustworthy, or just cynical for giving away that information. He might have been able to force the Vishai into an agreement under false pretenses.

Relos Var straightened. "Then from the sound of things, you need us even more."

Galen set down his cup. "What are you proposing? And since license fees can't be what I use to pay you, what do you want from the deal? Again, please note that what you're asking is impossible, if for no other reason than, again, I'm not high lord. You'll want to talk to my grandfather. Good luck finding him."

The pretend priest returned Galen's sneer with a flat look. "I heard what happened to your grandfather. Even if he's not dead, he's not coming back. Which means you're allowing a lifetime of your own expectations to limit your vision. Before you call the idea ludicrous, consider my offer. Your aunts want you out of the way, but their situation is even more precarious than yours. Do you know who the other high lords want in charge of a Royal House even less than a young, irate prince willing to tell them all to go to Hell? A *woman*."

Galen started to protest, then stopped.

Qown watched his teacher plunge in the metaphorical knife and twist. He was really quite good at this. "The damage that's been done to House D'Mon's reputation is incalculable. The fact that your aunts weren't in the Capital when the Hellmarch started won't save them if the High Council decides to enact retribution or, worse, demand a payment against damages."

Galen flinched before he recovered, pulling himself upright. "I don't hear a proposal in that."

Var smiled. "House D'Mon doesn't have enough healers left alive to deal with even the normal workload the Blue Houses demand, let alone the casualties we've seen from the Hellmarch. That's not even acknowledging the pestilence we know will soon spread . . ."

Galen's blue eyes focused on Relos Var's every gesture, but he didn't interrupt.

"I'm offering priests of my order—wearing your colors—dispatched to every part of the city to tend to the wounded, the sick, the dying. My people won't take orders from Tishenya or Gerisea. They will be under your authority alone. If you should die an untimely death, they'll return to Eamithon, leaving your house without desperately needed personnel."

Qown kept his expression neutral. Because for Vishai priests to leave their posts, to stop nursing those who needed their services, was unthinkable. What Father Zajhera suggested—

He blinked. Right. Relos Var, not Father Zajhera. How did he keep forgetting?

---

[6] Not true. Just wait until people realize how many priests are really just sorcerers with a different education track.

No matter what Relos Var promised Galen, Vishai priests would run true to their own tenets. So either Relos Var was underestimating the moral character of the religion he had himself created, or he was lying.

"Such a powerful show of goodwill might stay your aunts from making any continued attempts—" Relos Var cocked his head as Galen snorted. "Or it might not. But the option is yours. It will give you something quite valuable: leverage."

Galen drummed his fingers against the tabletop. Less irritation, Qown suspected, than contemplation.

"And in addition," Relos Var said, leaning forward and lowering his voice as if they were in a crowded room instead of an empty one, "it is my understanding—as you yourself just implied—that you, de facto head of house, have never been able to absent yourself from house duties for long enough to attend the Academy."

"What a diplomatic way of phrasing it," Galen murmured.

"My point is that you are—through no fault of your own—not trained in the healing arts." Relos Var gestured toward the door Anlyr had exited through on his way to the Citadel. "You'd have hardly needed our services otherwise."

Galen narrowed his eyes. "Your point?"

"My point is that I assume you're still unable to absent yourself from house duties for long enough to rectify that oversight, but we Vishai are also excellent teachers." Relos Var paused as Taunna returned with a teapot and two cups. She set all three down without fanfare and retreated to the bar, this time sitting next to Eledore.

Galen reached for the teapot at the same time as Qown, but the Vishai priest beat him to it because Galen pulled back his fingers.

Galen's hands were shaking.

"Allow me," Qown murmured, pouring for them both. The tea was a Kazivari jasmine-scented green. Expensive.

"Thank you." Galen took a quick sip of the still-too-hot liquid before setting the cup down and returning his hands to under the table.

Qown pretended not to notice.

Relos Var continued, "Why should you leave the Capital and spend a half dozen or so years in Kirpis attending the Academy? You don't have time for that. However, if you're amenable to the idea, we will provide you with your own personal tutor in the magical arts. You have obvious talent. It would not take long to bring you up to a skill level comparable to your house physickers." His smile was kind, his posture, sympathetic. He was so very, very good at this. "At the risk of seeming arrogant, I feel our training methods are superior to the Academy's in every way."

Galen's expression turned from calculating to simply . . . shocked. Disbelieving.

Qown studied the prince. He had a hunch . . . He sat up straight, set his tea on the table, and slipped his vision past the First Veil. Qown was curious to see what Galen's aura looked like.

Strong. Now, Qown had seen stronger. Relos Var's was outlandish, and

Janel's nearly as bad, but Galen's was respectable. Qown would have assumed him a proficient sorcerer.

But if Galen had never learned magic at all . . .

Oh, what potential had been wasted. And by a Royal House! Whatever could have possessed them to leave a talent like this untrained?[7] To leave an heir like that untrained. The tragedy of it made Qown angry, which Galen noticed and frowned at in turn.

Galen returned his attention to Relos Var. "Since I wasn't handling the accounts, how many healers are we discussing? That you'd be putting at House D'Mon's disposal until the end of the crisis?"

"If we emptied our churches and monasteries, a little over two thousand people. All those healers who can use magic, of course. Twice that number if–" And here Relos Var stumbled verbally, before laughing. "What I mean to say is that if licenses and gender are no longer a concern, around four thousand people."

Galen stared at the man.

Qown doubted the Blue Houses had ever possessed more than two thousand people in the Capital City, let alone twice that. If Galen returned to his family with that sort of reinforcement, what were the odds they wouldn't suddenly decide to perceive him as useful? And meanwhile, Relos Var could take over Galen's teaching. He was, after all, exceptionally good at it.

Galen D'Mon seemed to be thinking at least along the same lines. "And the teacher? You, I suppose?"

"Alas, no. Much as I would love to take you under my wing, so to speak, I am too busy at the moment. My apprentice here, Qown, will remain behind to see to your education."

What.

Qown fought down pure, fluttery panic. No, no, no. Not with this man. "You're leaving me? But I thought my job was going to be–"

He'd wanted to exorcise demons, push back the Hellmarch. Something important. Something helpful. Something that mattered. Not babysitting Darzin D'Mon's spoiled, temperamental, suicidal, impossibly pretty teenage son who'd probably never known a single day of–

Qown forced himself to calm down. Galen was, after all, Darzin D'Mon's son. Of course he'd known adversity. The man was so inured to pain he barely acknowledged it. Qown couldn't accuse him of being pampered. Indeed, exactly the opposite. His childhood must have been torture.

"No, no, Qown. All things in their time and place. You're one of the best students I've ever trained and a fine teacher yourself. This young man needs you. I understand staying in the Capital wasn't what you had in mind, but we all serve the greater good." Relos Var gave him a significant look.

Trust the plan. Qown knew he had to trust the plan.

"I'd rather not have a teacher who doesn't want to be here," Galen said, raising an eyebrow at Qown. "No offense."

---

[7] Oh, I do imagine Darzin didn't want to make it easy for his son to kill him, having already provided the boy with so much motive.

"Apologies," Qown said, bowing as much as he could while still sitting. "It is not the idea of teaching you that bothers me. I had simply hoped I might be allowed to handle a demon."

A dangerous glint sparked in Galen's bright blue eyes. "Let's not be premature," he said. "You hardly even know me yet."

It took Qown a second.

Qown knew he'd lived a sheltered life. He wouldn't have understood the innuendo at all if not for time spent with Dorna, but he had and so he did. Demon. D'Mon. Handling. He froze, aware he had no idea how to react but was turning bright red.

Galen D'Mon sat back in his chair, gave the slender priest a little quirked smile, and drank the rest of his tea.

Qown looked away, swallowing the temptation to practice every Joratese curse word he'd ever learned from Dorna. Or, and this was a lovely thought, throw his own tea in the smug royal's face. Punch him. This was . . .

Galen was just like his father, wasn't he? Except subtler about his bullying, cleverer when it came to getting under one's skin. Smarter.

It bothered Qown. It bothered Qown a great deal. He knew Galen wasn't flirting with him.[8] For one thing, Galen was married to . . . well, basically the most beautiful woman in the entire world and clearly doted on her. And Galen knew the Vishai order was celibate–he'd been the one to explain that very fact to Sheloran. So this had to be purposeful, said purely to shame.

Relos Var must have noticed Galen's wordplay, but if so, he gave no outward sign. "Does that intrigue?"

Galen squinted at the old man. "You haven't named your price. Like I said, license fees are no longer an issue."

"Sponsor a temple in the Ivory District for us."

Qown stopped sulking. Even if the Vishai faith was now legal, that didn't mean the religion was, well . . . as Galen had said, it was considered something of a cult, too poor to have their own temple in the Capital's Ivory District. That required royal family support–even sponsorship.

It was far more valuable than a reduction in license fees.

Galen seemed to understand the ramifications at once too. "If I give you a permanent position in this Capital, how long will it be before you've simply replaced House D'Mon? After all, you don't charge for your services. You can't tell me that would change." His laughter was black. "My own fault for telling you the truth, I suppose."

"With all apologies, my lord," Relos Var said, "if you hadn't, it just would have made things more awkward when we discovered the truth for ourselves later." He slid his fingers against the table as if moving coins, even though none were present. "But I think we could make an arrangement to not provide competing services with the Blue Houses for at least, oh, the next five years?"

"Five years? How lovely to know exactly when my house will cease to be relevant–"

"Wouldn't that be lovely," Qown murmured.

---

[8] Yes, he was.

Galen glanced over at the priest. "What was that?"

Qown set down his teacup. "I apologize. I didn't mean to say that out loud."

"Did you just say," Galen said, "it would be lovely to know House D'Mon will be irrelevant in five years?"

Qown's eyes widened. "Oh no, my lord. I was just wondering if any of us will still be alive then."

Everyone at the table fell silent.

Qown bowed his head. "I do apologize. The last few weeks have all been a bit . . . much." He sank down in the chair, aware that Relos Var was glaring at him, and not in a cute, scolding way.

Galen D'Mon started laughing. "Yes," he said. "It's certainly been 'a bit much.'"

Relos Var said nothing.

Galen turned back to the old man. "I'll take him. And you'll get your temple—assuming your people are as skilled as you claim and assuming I live. So; a lot of conditions. None of it may work out. And if you've lied to me, the deal's off."

Relos Var didn't seem offended. "I understand." He drained his glass before setting his hand on Qown's shoulder. "I'll leave Qown with you. Where would you like me to start bringing in our people?"

"He can contact you?"

Qown narrowed his eyes, resisting the temptation to protest that he was still. Right. There.

"He can," Relos Var answered.

"I'll let you know," Galen said.

Relos Var smiled, pleased. "Then we have a deal."

13: The Shelter of Devors

Kihrin's story
Inside Vol Karoth's prison
Just after Qown's vision of Relos Var and Galen's deal

The vision took us off guard, I think. We hadn't been expecting it. I initially assumed Vol Karoth was somehow responsible, but it didn't feel like something he'd show me. It wasn't dark enough—and he wasn't gloating.

That was when I realized that when we'd been sending the memories we'd pulled from my friends to each other, we must have been sending them to everyone trapped in the Lighthouse as well.

So they'd sent something back.

I was so stunned I almost didn't notice when Vol Karoth resumed his attack. I blocked his strike, but his sword still danced across my shoulder, a sharp, jagged splash of agony. I hissed as I fell backward, feeling that curious jarring slide as reality shifted around me and put me . . . somewhere else. My blood splattered against the dusty gray rocks.

Damn it, I thought, *there has to be something . . .*

Why do you keep hiding? If we're truly not enemies . . .

"Why do you keep stabbing me, then?" I shouted. "I'll stop hiding when you stop stabbing!"

I hadn't traveled far that time. I still felt him. Presumably, he still felt me. An aching dread crawled along my spine, settled down in the pit of my stomach.

I feel you.

I dove to the side in time to avoid the sword blow slamming down into the ground where I'd sat a moment before.

"I'll repeat myself," I said, staring at the silhouette that was . . . nothing. "You're not my enemy. Rev'arric is."

I had to admit it was growing increasingly difficult to say those words and mean it. Veils, I'd fucked up.

You live in a universe of illusion and lies, and you refuse to see the truth. I am your enemy. Everyone is your enemy. Just as everyone is mine.

"So no luck visiting on birthdays, huh?" Even if Vol Karoth had a visible expression, that wouldn't have made him smile. No sense of humor. "Look, how can you say that when you've seen how these people care about each other? If Teraeth was despondent, it's because he cares about me." I pressed back against him with my sword and then kicked him back. It wasn't anything that would damage him, but better than nothing.

You want me to show you how evil—

"No," I said. "I know how evil people can be. I'm not claiming evil doesn't exist. But you're trying to tell me *only* evil exists. Only selfishness exists. That's a lie."

Vol Karoth backed up, lowered his weapon, cocked his head in a way that made me quite certain I knew the expression on his face—eyebrow raised, eyes narrowed, mouth quirked in one corner. It was unnerving as hell whenever he did something that reminded me of how we'd once been the same person.

You think they love you.

"I know they love me," I said.

He scoffed. *I'll prove you wrong.*

Fear gripped me. "No, no, you don't need to—"

Deljari. Deljari vanis.

The words echoed through the air, spiraling out across the wasteland. I knew that they hadn't been said to me.

"What have you done?" I said.

You've brought them here. Let's bring them closer. And while we're at it—

"No, don't do anything else!"

Why don't we say hello to our twelfth guest? The one you don't want to admit is in the room.

I could both feel and hear his laughter, a cold shock traveling across my skin. The world changed.

Qown's reaction
The Lighthouse at Shadrag Gor
Just after Qown's memory of Relos Var and Galen's deal

The world returned, if somehow colder than previously.

Galen raised an eyebrow at Thurvishar. "Was that what you planned?"

"Yes," Thurvishar said, "and it worked."

"Did you have to show *everything*?" Qown drew himself up, glaring at Thurvishar.

He knew it could have been worse. Later events had been more embarrassing on a personal level. But even so . . .

Thurvishar seemed amused, probably because it wasn't difficult to guess why Qown might be upset. "Yes, I did."

Galen's eyes were still narrowed, his expression angry. He hadn't forgiven Qown yet, which was incredibly unfair considering . . . well. Fine.

Qown could admit it was fair.

Qown exhaled. "I really didn't—"

Deljari. Deljari vanis.

"What was that?" Sheloran asked. They'd all heard the sound, or rather felt it, a whisper in their minds.

Qown didn't recognize the voice. It was male and smooth and ever so faintly desperate. But the language . . .

"That was voral," Senera said.

"That was Kihrin," Kalindra said.

Talon shrugged. "I guess he knows we're here too."

"That wasn't Kihrin," Janel corrected, her voice quiet and grief-stricken. "That was *S'arric*."

Galen frowned. "Every time you say that name, I keep wondering if you're talking about my great-uncle."

Janel stared at him, blinking, before she turned back to Thurvishar. "Someone needs to bring him up to speed."

"Oh, I can—" Qown swallowed the rest of his sentence. It seemed unlikely he would be allowed to explain anything, since Galen still wasn't looking at him.

"Fine," Galen said. "I'll assume that wasn't my great-something uncle Saric. But what did he say?"

"Send reinforcements," Janel translated.

"You wanted communication," Qown told Thurvishar. "I think we have it."

Sheloran said, "'Send reinforcements' seems a lot to ask when we can't reach where the help is needed."

"We can," Thurvishar corrected.

"You said you didn't know if you could come back," Senera snapped. "Don't do something stupid. Especially don't do something stupid when we know it's a trap."

"Send me," Janel said.

"Janel—" Thurvishar started to protest.

"No, send me," she repeated. "I make the most sense. My souls are already untethered. You just need to push me in the right direction. I've done similar things before."

"Every night when you go to sleep," Qown said.

Janel twisted to look over her shoulder at him. "Yes, but this time, I'm going someplace a whole lot scarier than the Afterlife."

Galen made a face.

Sheloran's smile was wan and thin. "Yes, that really was one of those sentences you just never think you're going to hear until . . . there it is."

"Would you like more tea before you go?" Talea offered Janel a cup. "It's cold, but you can fix that."

Qown frowned. It couldn't be cold; he'd just made it.

"It's a nice gesture, but I don't know how long I'm going to be unconscious," Janel said as she refused it. "I don't want a full bladder."

"You did hear me say this is a trap, didn't you?" Senera said. "Because this is a trap."

Janel snorted.

"It could be—" Thurvishar started to say.

Senera gestured. "No vision has interrupted us. Vol Karoth's waiting for us to respond to that call before he sends something else. The only reason to do that is to set a trap."

"Or Kihrin's genuinely in trouble," Janel answered back. Then she sighed. "Yes, fine. It's a trap. But that's why I'm not rescuing Kihrin."

Thurvishar blinked. "You're not?"

"No," she said. "Because if what I find is anything like what I think is going to be there, then I know where Vol Karoth is keeping Teraeth. That's who I'm going after." She pointed to his body. "If he is being used as a hostage, let's stop that."

Thurvishar pursed his lips. "All right. I agree."

Janel lay back on one of the couches. Qown wasn't sure what Thurvishar did. The exact details of the spell weren't visible to the naked eye. After a few minutes, Janel's chest stopped moving. She was, much like Teraeth, dead to the world.

Qown could only hope not literally so.

It must have done something in any event, because shortly thereafter, another vision struck. The world changed.

Kalindra's memory
The Monastery on Devors
Later in the evening after Jarith Milligreest's funeral

It was nighttime when the Gatestone flared to life, spiraled into a circle, and disgorged two people before shutting down.

Three people, but no one noticed the third.

An austere, prim man wearing tan robes waited for Kalindra Milligreest's arrival. His expression suggested her presence was a personal insult. No one else was present, however, so she stepped toward him. "This isn't the reception I expected."

He studied her, eyes narrowed, chin up. "You're Kalindra Milligreest?"

"Who else would I be?"

He turned red, somehow even angrier. "Confirm your identity, now."

Kalindra stared, her expression disbelieving. "You thought the guards on the other side weren't checking before they let people through? Yes, I'm Kalindra Milligreest."

"You were supposed to be here earlier."

Kalindra shifted her child on her hip, who was sleepy-eyed from having been kept up past his bedtime. "So someone made a mistake. Fine. In the meantime, why don't you show me to my rooms?"

The monk narrowed his eyes and considered her. "No weapons allowed."

"Oh, for fuck's sake," Kalindra said, then grimaced at her son. "You didn't hear that, sweetheart." She glared at the man. "Do you really think I'm going to slaughter all the librarians with a dagger?[1] Why don't you just show us to a room where we can sleep, and we will sort this all out in the morning."

The monk ground his teeth a few more times before answering, "Follow me. You're too late for meals. The wake-up bell rings an hour before dawn, and it is already past curfew. You will not socialize with or distract the priests—"

"Are women not allowed in monastery?" Kalindra interrupted.

The priest paused, frowning, as if Kalindra had broken a rule by asking questions. "Of course they are. They are kept separate from the men."

"Great," Kalindra said. "This is going to be fantastic. I already love it here. I feel so safe." She shifted Nikali in her arms and started walking. "Where's my room?"

The priest hurried after her. "Wait. There are rules."

---

[1] Which is not to say she wouldn't have been capable of doing exactly that.

"I'm sure there are," Kalindra muttered as she looked around. "I can't wait to hear them."

The island of Devors was two islands, treated as one. A lush swath of jungle green painted the windward side, while the leeward side sheltered temperate fields of grain and scrub brush. The islands were home to farmers and craftsmen, most of whom had never left their home.

But that wasn't what everyone thought of when someone mentioned Devors. What people thought of was this: the monastery at the edge of the great Pajanya Cliffs, old and hoary, built up over centuries until it resembled a collection of clamshells stacked up in messy columns. The currents that had once brought rains to Khorvesh now broke storms on the island chain, smashed against picturesque rocks, and sent ocean spray hurtling up into the air. Only a single safe harbor for hundreds of miles in any direction, the monastery itself could only be reached by that port, a narrow strip of land, or by Gatestone. The magical protections around those buildings had been carved into the foundations. They had never fallen—not to demons, god-kings, or dragons. Legends said Ompher himself had created them. The monastery served as home to the largest library in the world[2] and to several thousand men and women who had dedicated their lives to one singular mission: recording and interpreting the prophecies that had become synonymous with their island's name.

"Milligreest!" the man called out behind Kalindra, his voice sharp and angry.

She turned around.

He narrowed his eyes. "Don't cause trouble."

Kalindra regarded the man coolly. "What's your name?"

That brought him short. He was unused to this idea of women asking questions, wanting to know information, *existing*.

"Oliyuan," he offered grudgingly.

"Fine. Oliyuan," Kalindra said, bouncing her son on her hip. Nikali was, for the moment, in a good mood, if a bit squirmy because he wanted to look at the waves. "I don't want to cause any trouble," she said, "but you need to understand that I have the high general's grandson here. And the high general is going to have his way, even if you don't want me here, and even if I don't want to be here. But what will make this worse for both of us is if any harm should befall this child"—she hiked up Nikali at this, who giggled—"because you insisted on making me follow rules that were never meant to meet the needs of mothers and their children. Do you understand what I'm saying?"

A tic developed under Oliyuan's left eye. "Is that a threat?"

Kalindra smiled. "Yes."

Oliyuan raised his lip in a sneer, quickly suppressed. "I'll take you to your room."

Her room was a cell.

That might well have been true for most monks who lived there. The main purpose of the Devors monastery was to protect and shelter pieces of paper, not people. This was a thick-slabbed, six-foot-by-eight-foot room just large

---

[2] I am quite certain the dreth would disagree with that.

enough for a pallet on the floor and a washbasin. A lonely window high up on the wall would allow for some insignificant quantity of light during daytime, and overall, the entire room felt designed for punishment more than rest.

Nikali started crying immediately.

Before Kalindra could turn back to the door, it slammed shut. And locked. "Hey! Hey!"

"Wait here," the man said.

Then he walked away.

Kalindra banged against the metal door, which echoed, hollow and loud, like a drum. No one responded, and after a few minutes, she stopped to wipe the tears from her son's eyes and hold him close.

She never noticed a sliver of shadow disconnecting from her body, sliding away and passing through the door as though it were made of smoke.

Jarith's memory

The shadow left the cell. It was simplicity itself to do so.

They hadn't been able to sense him earlier, when he'd hidden, crouched and lurking in the dark spaces of his widow's souls. It had been one of the hardest things he'd ever done—to stay quiet and still and soft, applying no pressure, causing no injury. Her fire was right there, her heat so close all he had to do was reach out . . . But no. He could not.

His name was Jarith Milligreest. He was a man. His wife's name was Kalindra. His son's name was Nikali. He loved them both. It was wrong to hurt people he loved.

He had a list. It was a small list, but he held on to it tightly. It was all he had left of himself, this vow that there were people he would not hurt, would not kill.

Oliyuan wasn't on that list.

The man was returning to the barracks where he'd left Kalindra, but he wasn't alone. There were two other men with him. Not monks.

More importantly: not on his list.

Soldiers. Quuros soldiers, who wore good armor under their dark sallí cloaks. Both had the aura of sorcerers and the studious demeanor of men who had spent a great many years stationed on the island. Long enough to become believers to a religion formed not of gods but of lines on paper and the promise of saving the world from a foretold apocalypse.

Their expressions suggested they were about to perform an unpleasant task—for example, murdering a mother and her child. Unpleasant, but necessary. There were prophecies about Kalindra. By their conviction, killing her would save so many lives that there could be no question that it was worth doing.

Jarith felt differently. Kalindra could not be allowed to die. She was on his list.

None of the men noticed the literal shadow pulling itself into cohesion just behind them.

Jarith formed a rough body for himself. Then he crafted blades, stabbed them through the necks of the two men, and ripped outward, away. A bright red line of hot blood splattered against the carved-stone floor. Oliyuan barely had a chance to notice before he met the same fate, this time with Jarith crossing both swords over the man's neck and slicing down hard.

The rage already boiled in his veins by then, though, so he didn't stop. Jarith stabbed and sliced long after the men were dead, then graduated to ripping and tearing. By the time he'd finished stealing their fire, what was left was a pile of cold meat that could never be mistaken for human beings.

The demon left the bodies at the base of the Founders statue.

The world changed.

14: WHAT DEMONS ARE

Inside Vol Karoth's prison
Just after Jarith's vision

I narrowed my eyes at Vol Karoth. "It doesn't do much to prove your point if you're going to lie about it."

That was the truth.

For a moment, my mind just . . . blanked. Stuttered.

What? No.

I didn't want to draw a conclusion, interpret what it meant. Then my mind did it, anyway, because if Vol Karoth was right and he'd told the truth, then Jarith wasn't dead. And if Jarith wasn't dead, how would that even be possible? Was it possible? I'd seen Jarith's corpse at the temple of Thaena, face locked in frozen horror after he'd been killed by Xaltorath–

After he'd been killed by Xaltorath.

Of course.

Damn it all to Hell, a phrase that was more ironically appropriate than I needed at just that moment.

I don't need to lie. Vol Karoth sounded amused. **Your so-called friends are everything I said, and so much more. Literal demons in several cases. When are you going to learn?**

Jarith had been murdered by Xaltorath, but Jarith's souls hadn't been devoured by Xaltorath. Instead, the demon had infected him, turned him from a bright, compassionate, and noble man into a creature of darkness, the shadows curling around him, his face a blank mask. Jarith's treatment at Xaltorath's hands must have been much less gentle than his sister Janel's.

Xaltorath had even gloated about it to Janel when they had told her, *I made you a brother . . .*

The odds were good Xaltorath had done it as a lark. They'd probably wanted nothing more than just to see the look on Janel's face when she realized she'd been tricked into devouring her own kin. No reason other than that–petty maliciousness–but then again, that followed, since Xaltorath's core would always belong to their first lifetime: Suless.

There was no coming back from that. Jarith had been turned into something worse than dead: he was broken, a creature that existed to feed on souls and pain and fear. He was forevermore a monster.

Kalindra was never getting him back. There would be no resurrection. Not by Thaena, not with any Cornerstone. The best–very best–she could possibly hope for was that he might keep himself enough under control not to turn that rage and hunger on her, on Nikali, on everyone he'd ever loved. It was a testament to the man's will that he'd held out as long as he had. I knew what Xaltorath would have done to him, to try to force him to become something so vile that destroying him would seem a mercy, the revelation of his true identity a tragedy.

Hate flared through me. The grim determination that I would find a way to destroy Xaltorath once and for all.

But it wouldn't recover my friend.

Hot tears fell down my cheeks as I went to my knees, head bowed.

I'm going to win this, Vol Karoth told me. The cruelest laughter lurked in his voice. *But it's your turn.*

It was. I knew it was.

But I had no idea what to show Vol Karoth that wouldn't prove his case for him. All I could feel was pain.

Kalindra's reaction
The Lighthouse at Shadrag Gor
Also just after Jarith's memory

Kalindra thought she could hear the world hold its breath when the vision ended. The shocked silence, that profound. Her mind, a blank, numb sea.

When thought returned, it was this: that it never would have worked. Never. All her plans were dust. Thaena hadn't refused to Return Jarith because she hadn't approved of Kalindra's love or even because a demon had consumed his souls. She'd refused because Jarith could never be resurrected. Nothing could bring him back. Not Thaena, not the Cornerstone Grimward. All the sacrifices that she had made, the crimes she'd committed—unnecessary and absurd. She'd been searching for a knife only to find she already held it, the weapon so sharp she'd never noticed it had sliced open every vein.

"The doll man," Kalindra murmured softly, remembering the words her son had used. How the doll man had scared him.

Her breath froze in her lungs. Her husband was a demon, and her husband had shown himself to their son. There was no point in screaming, although part of her wanted to. There was no point in tears, although she very much wanted them too.

There was no point in any of it, since none of it could bring Jarith back.

Not as a human.

She looked to the side and accidentally met Galen's eyes. The moment she did, she knew that he was thinking something very similar. He'd been chasing the same thing, after all: Jarith's resurrection. Then his look shifted into something like pity, and she had to fight not to throw a knife at him.

Kalindra grabbed one of the blankets Thurvishar had crafted off a couch. If she was going to go off into one of the other rooms, at least she wouldn't be cold.

Except Talea blocked her way. She had a hand on the hilt of her sword.

"Move," Kalindra said.

"It's not safe out there," Talea told her. Her expression was so kind. So sympathetic. Kalindra wanted to stab it.

"Get the fuck out of my way!" Kalindra screamed.

Talea did.

Kalindra's victory was short-lived, however. Footsteps pounded behind her. She started to turn back, to shout at Talea that she didn't need a damn escort. But it wasn't Talea.

It was Xivan.

The woman grabbed Kalindra's wrist, her other arm around her shoulder, and half carried her, half threw her past one of the other doorways. This wasn't a sitting room. Kalindra had the briefest flash of stone walls and a cage nestled into a corner. Her attention, though, was on the undead bitch fighting her. Xivan hadn't pulled her sword. That was a mistake. She twisted her foot around Xivan's and yanked, sending the other woman crashing to the ground. But Xivan rolled up quickly and tried to move past Kalindra.

Too fucking easy. Kalindra redirected the strike and used Xivan's momentum to toss her down to the ground. She followed that up immediately with a twist of the arm that should have finished the fight—dislocated Xivan's arm, put her in indescribable pain. It didn't. It didn't even though Kalindra felt the pop of the other woman's joint breaking free of its socket. Xivan didn't seem to notice.

Seriously, Kalindra *hated* fighting dead people.

Xivan yanked down, so Kalindra had to release her and roll or face the possibility of ending up sprawled on top of the other woman. As she stood to her feet, Xivan kicked, using Kalindra's step back as an opportunity to stand up again herself.

Kalindra had her knives out then. And still Xivan hadn't drawn her sword.

It made Kalindra pause. It made her think.

Undead were anathema to Thaena, but they were usually created by demonic possession, or more rarely by a sorcerer skilled enough to have devised some form of remote control. Something like Xivan was rarer and far more dangerous.

Kalindra was giving serious consideration to exactly how she could make Xivan's situation more permanent when she realized Xivan wasn't closing the gap between them. The woman was just standing on the other side of the room, watching her with an unreadable expression.

Xivan wasn't her enemy. Not in this place, not facing what was coming for them. They had so much worse to worry about.

This was wasted energy.

Kalindra put her knives away. She cast her gaze around the room, but there was no place to sit except for a three-legged stool tossed into a corner. This was either a storeroom or a jail cell or probably both—it wasn't meant to be comfortable. "Damn it."

"We can keep fighting, if you like." The corner of Xivan's lips curled into something that couldn't exactly be called a smile. "It always makes me feel better. I make a shockingly good sparring puppet."

The anger bubbled up in Kalindra, exited out as a hard, hateful laugh. The horrible thing was that Xivan wasn't wrong. It did feel good. It felt like soaking in the hot springs on Ynisthana, washing herself with a pumice stone until the grime and the dead skin were scoured.

"I don't need your pity," Kalindra snapped.

"That's good," Xivan said as she pulled her dislocated arm back into place. She didn't even wince. "Because I have none, least of all for you."

Kalindra turned back to face the other woman. "Excuse me?"

"You lost your husband during the Hellmarch? Fine. I lost mine three weeks ago. Shall we compare scars? See who's bled the most?" Xivan's sarcasm was thick, black, and bitterly amused.

"I think I'll win such a contest since you don't bleed. Three weeks? For a widow, you didn't waste any time finding a replacement, did you?"

A huff of air escaped Xivan as the words hit. "Talea was never a replacement. Was Jarith a replacement for Teraeth? For Kihrin? Or did you realize that for reasons you couldn't begin to fathom you'd found yourself lucky enough to find one of the few good, perfect people in this world? That against all expectation they loved you, even though you don't deserve that love in the slightest."

"Are we talking about me here?" Kalindra raised an eyebrow.

"Don't be coy," Xivan answered. "I know you."

Kalindra almost demanded her to explain that, to describe what Xivan thought she was seeing. But as she looked into the flat white stare of that dead woman's eyes, she had the sudden irrational fear that Xivan might not be lying. That Xivan might, indeed, *see* her. And know exactly what she was.

Know exactly how filthy, exactly how wrong Kalindra was. That one murderer might recognize another. The poor fools back in the other room might think themselves hard, but they, all of them, killed for *causes.* Because they believed in the righteousness of their actions.[1] Even dear Teraeth had always been a shadow champion of justice, killing not out of selfishness or real malice but because he thought he was making the world better at the edge of a knife.

But Kalindra knew what it was like to kill for reasons that couldn't be defended. And she was suddenly struck with the certainty that Xivan did too.

Kalindra said, "Do you think you have the right to judge me?"

Something around Xivan's eyes shifted. An infinitesimal softening. "No. I don't."

Kalindra broke the stare. The acceptance was somehow worse. She couldn't stand it anymore. Instead, she put her back against the iron bars, leaned backward until her head hit the cold metal.

Silence stretched out as neither woman spoke.

"You remind me of Jheshikah," Xivan said.

"I'm sure that would mean something if only I knew who the fuck Jheshikah was."

"One of my husband's wives. Thirty-second, I think? Something like that. Anyway, her anger was like the tides. She'd scream, retreat to another room,

---

[1] She was forgetting Talon, but even without that, it's human nature to justify our actions. The vast majority of us refuse to accept the idea that we might be the villains of the story—even if that's demonstrably true.

think of something else that had to be said, come storming back, run away again . . ." Xivan smiled. "Maybe next time you're upset, you might want to consider standing your ground."

"Oh, fuck you." Kalindra crossed her arms over her chest, aware of just how much the sullen little girl this made her look.

"Isn't it funny? To think that you and I are probably the oldest ones here," Xivan said. She didn't say the next part—*and yet you're acting the most like a child*—out loud, but Kalindra heard her fine.

It did nothing at all for her mood to know that Xivan was right. Kalindra was absolutely acting like a child. Jarith's little sister Eledore would be shouting at her to grow up, and that was saying something.

"Anyway," Xivan said, "I think you're missing an important point."

Kalindra ground her teeth. "And what would that be?"

"None of the visions have been from the point of view of anyone not physically present in the Lighthouse," Xivan stated.

Kalindra stared at her for a second, not comprehending. Then she remembered. She remembered how part of that last vision had been from Jarith's point of view. She straightened, even as all the blood in her body tried to pool down by her feet, leaving her dizzy and sick.

"He's here," Kalindra said, her pulse roaring staccato around her. Her thoughts were broken panes of glass, slicing her open as she tried to grab at them.

Jarith was *here.*

The thought wasn't as comforting as it should have been. Jarith was now a demon, after all, and while apparently Kalindra was "on the list"—that didn't seem to be true for anyone else. In fact—

Kalindra reexamined her encounter with Xivan. Other than the first initial grab, she'd never tried to attack Kalindra, had she? Had she realized that there was a chance Jarith might come to Kalindra's rescue? Or had Xivan been counting on the fact that Jarith wouldn't want to show himself while Kalindra was still around to see him?

"Yeah," Xivan said. "He is. Somewhere. That's the other reason no one should go off alone. Whether or not Vol Karoth can reach us may be in doubt, but Jarith certainly can." She gestured to the door. "If you're ready, we should go back. They're waiting on us, and if you have any questions you want to ask about Jarith, well, Senera and her pretty rock are in the other room."

"Right," Kalindra murmured. She felt dazed.

They returned.

Thurvishar was talking about demons when they came back. It sounded like she was walking into the middle of a class lecture.

"—came from another world," Thurvishar said.

"More precisely," Senera interrupted, "from another universe." Her gray eyes flicked over to the doorway as Kalindra and Xivan returned.

Thurvishar smiled fondly at the woman, not even seeming to mind the correction. "Yes, just so. But Xaltorath is not from another universe. One could argue he shouldn't be called a demon, but he behaves enough like one that it's usually not necessary to make the distinction. Except in times like this."

Most of Kalindra's career had been spent dealing with assassinations and talk of prophecies, occasionally attempts to counter Relos Var, even her share of hunting demons in the Afterlife, but very little on Xaltorath. She was starting to feel like her education might have been neglected.

Sheloran handed Kalindra a handkerchief. Kalindra stared at it for a moment and then realized it was for her tears. Which meant she'd been crying. She angrily wiped her eyes and sat down across from Thurvishar.

"Times like my husband being turned into a demon?" Kalindra asked.

"Turned into a demon by Xaltorath," Thurvishar said. "When a demon infects someone—"

"I know how this works," Kalindra snapped.

"How nice for you. Not all of us do," Galen said.

Thurvishar cleared his throat. "Demons are like wasps."

No one said a word.

Senera sighed. "I know what you mean," she said. "*They* don't."

Thurvishar blushed. "Just as a wasp lays eggs in a host, only to have those eggs hatch and eat their way out, a demon will 'infect' a host soul. There's still a great deal of debate as to whether the host is transformed, becoming a demon, or is eaten to provide nourishment to a larval form, which develops into a demon."

Kalindra felt her stomach churn. If Thurvishar had meant for this to be comforting, he was truly an idiot. "It's both," she said. When people looked at her, Kalindra shook her head. "The lower souls are eaten, but the upper souls are not. Thaena—" She stopped and inhaled deeply. "Thaena always said that when she captured a demon, she made a point of untangling all the combined souls in order to put them back into the river of reincarnation."

"Interesting," Senera said.

"In either case," Thurvishar said, "the new demon does seem to be a kind of 'offspring'—they inherit qualities from their 'parent.'"

Senera sighed. "Which is Thurvishar's way of saying we have no idea what Jarith can do or even how he'll behave. Certainly that vision implies he's barely holding on to the tattered shreds of his humanity."

Kalindra made a low keening sound.

"I'm sorry, Kalindra," Thurvishar said. "Jarith was a good man."

"If you'll remember, you once called him a fool," Senera pointed out.

"Challenging me to a duel was foolish," Thurvishar said mildly. "He was still a good man."

The banter would have been adorable in other situations. Here, now, it made Kalindra want to throw things at them both. Sharp, poisonous things. Kalindra felt her heart clench, painful and breath-stealing. She felt flayed.

She breathed deeply and tried to wrestle her despair under control.

"Do you people mind?" Kalindra managed, somehow, not to shout. "I don't give a damn what your assessment is of my husband's intelligence or character. I just want him back."

"Why would Vol Karoth show us that?" Sheloran asked. "It's upsetting, yes, but it also proved that all hope isn't lost. Jarith is recoverable. Janel, after all, stands as proof that someone with untethered souls can still survive."

Talon laughed. "You think Vol Karoth believed for a second we'd give a demon a pass? No, no. He was trying to foment unrest. Have us chasing every shadow thinking it had to be Jarith. Ideally, fan this into a situation where we stop trusting each other. Easy to do with me, of course; I'm inherently untrustworthy. But the rest of you? You all could be friends. Or are friends. Maybe you lot can band together and prove that friendship really is all we need to defeat all the evils in the world. Wouldn't that be a hilarious joke?"

"Shut up, Talon," Senera said. "I like you better when you're pretending to be Kihrin."

"She has a point, though," Thurvishar said.

Everyone stopped.

Talon turned to Thurvishar and blinked several times, slowly. "I do? What point? Please tell me. I promise I won't do it again."

"Vol Karoth is trying to break Kihrin, and to do that, he needs to prove Kihrin's opinions wrong. He has to prove friendship is a lie. Compassion is weakness. Love is delusion. Being a good person won't save you from becoming a demon, metaphoric or otherwise. So yes, whatever visions we are sending him need to pick apart those arguments." Thurvishar gave Galen a studied look. "Do you think your story might qualify?"

Galen winced. "You have met my family, yes?"

Thurvishar glanced at Sheloran. "As a matter of fact, I have. There are some notable bright points in all that darkness."

Sheloran smiled. "Was that a compliment?"

"It might have been," Thurvishar admitted. "It's too early to say for sure."

"Some of us," Xivan said, "shouldn't be part of that sort of 'storytelling.' We wouldn't help Kihrin's case."

Talea threw the woman a worried look. "Oh, I don't think it's that bad—" But she let the rest of her protest slide away in response to the expression on Xivan's face. Talea gave one quick, guilty glance at Sheloran and didn't say another word.

"Talon, take over for me. You know what to do," Thurvishar said.

"Says who?" Talon stood up from her chair. "Wait. What are you going to do?"

Thurvishar turned to her. "You watched what I did with Janel. You're a mimic. Mimics are telepaths. You're telling me you can't reproduce that?"

Talon's expression took on a sullen, pouting look. "The way my powers work is passive. I read. I don't send. It's completely—" She glanced at Thurvishar's expression and paused, swallowing. "Yes, fine. I can do it too. But the better question is, why can't you?"

"Because I'm going to help Janel track down Teraeth and Kihrin." He moved over to the couches where both of them lay. Then he frowned and glanced over at the fireplace. "It really is cold in here. We should get some blankets out of storage and move to the bedrooms upstairs."

Senera stood up as well. "Thurvishar! You said if you sent yourself into Vol Karoth's mind, you didn't know if you could come back. How has that changed?"

"It hasn't," Thurvishar replied calmly. "I'm taking a calculated risk."

Senera's complexion reddened. She pointed a furious finger at Thurvishar. "No. Stop learning terrible habits from Kihrin. We can't afford to lose you!"

"Don't you mean you can't afford to lose him?" Talon said, grinning wickedly.

Kalindra couldn't help it: she laughed. And then immediately shut up as the blazing look of fury in Senera's eyes suggested it was probably a bad idea to bait wizards.

Thurvishar, however, just smiled and moved over to Senera. For a second, it looked like he was going to take her hand, but he never touched the woman. He just stared at her with uncomfortable, embarrassing intensity.

"I'll be fine," he promised her. "I'm not planning on dying today."

Before Senera could respond, Qown interrupted, "I d-don't think we should move people upstairs, though. It's difficult enough to keep everyone warm. We'd have to keep watch on them. I'm not sure how safe that would be." He fidgeted, all but biting his nails.

"Whatever you think is best. I trust you." Thurvishar was still looking at Senera, so it wasn't completely clear who he was addressing.

"Trust me?" Qown blinked.

Only then did Thurvishar look over. He took in the healer, then glanced down at Janel's unconscious body. "With this? Yes." Thurvishar turned away from the others and began to gesture. It wasn't clear what he was doing at first, then sections of the stone wall began to visibly distort and twist. Within a matter of minutes he'd formed a set of stone platforms—bunk beds—several layers deep. It would give them somewhere to transfer the bodies without being forced to let Teraeth, Thurvishar, or Janel out of the group's sight.

"Thurvishar, I won't let you do this."

He gazed at the pale woman fondly. "And how exactly were you planning to stop me?"

Senera just stared.

Sheloran made a motion to the door. "Do we need to give you two some space? We could just wait next door while you . . . figure this out."

Senera turned red and didn't respond.

With that, Thurvishar sat down on the lowest bed, winked at Senera, and closed his eyes.

No one said anything.

Mocking laughter drifted down the hallway. No one had to ask where it was likely coming from. Kalindra's heart seized.

"Oh . . . I think this might have been a mistake," Talea said.

"Really? You think?" Senera was all but snarling. "Fine. Who wants to be first?"

Silence.

"Someone had better volunteer or I'll let Talon choose," Senera snapped.

"What about you?" Kalindra suggested, right back to Senera. Kalindra had no particular desire to continue with her own experiences. As Xivan had said, some stories wouldn't be helpful.

Sadly, Kalindra had the terrible suspicion that her story would be used whether she wanted it or not–just by Vol Karoth, rather than Kihrin.

"We can't use Senera," Talon said. "We need hopeful memories."

Senera glared at the mimic. "What Talon means is that after we left the Korthaen Blight we came straight here to the Lighthouse and then to Devors so I could bring you lot here. Which means there's nothing to tell."

"I'll go," Galen said. "It's fine."

"Are you sure, sweeting?" Talon's voice was the definition of solicitous concern.

Galen stared at her for a long minute, eyes flat. "Yes."

Talon smiled. The world changed.

15: WORDS THAT KILL

Janel's story
Inside Vol Karoth's prison

The building in the center had been part of the university system, itself in the center of Karolaen. If Janel hadn't remembered it on her own, it had certainly featured prominently enough in Kihrin's memories—or perhaps more accurately, in S'arric's memories—when they'd accidentally stumbled across them.[1] It made sense the building would be prominent here too.

The last time she remembered seeing this place, it was a ruin save for the scraped-clean globe of negative energy at the center, the man-shaped silhouette that had created it floating inside.

If she was wrong . . . Janel pushed the thought aside. There was no reason why Vol Karoth would have shown Teraeth inside the space where Vol Karoth himself—S'arric—had been ritually sacrificed by his brother. And it was in general an odd choice. The dream hadn't even been a faithful re-creation of the Ritual of Night. It had been a strange mélange of rituals: the Ritual of Night, the ritual Thaena had devised to destroy the Manol vané and thus retrap Vol Karoth, the ritual that Relos Var had used to turn S'arric into Vol Karoth.

Why? Was Vol Karoth trying to imply that Teraeth was in the same position he was? Demonstrably untrue. Or was it perhaps that Vol Karoth just couldn't view any event save through the lens of his own life? The implications sent tremors racing along her skin, tingling down the backs of her hands. A taste of bile lingered in her throat.

She explored the periphery of the building before realizing she'd had to take the blunt approach. The double doors to the university's great hall were closed; Janel yanked on them so hard they almost came off their hinges. She ran inside just in time to see Thaena stabbing her son through the heart with Urthaenriel.

How real would that weapon be here? How much authority, how much verisimilitude, did a memory have in a wasteland built of memories? In a place like this, the idea of Urthaenriel might work nearly as well as the real thing. But there was nothing to be done. She darted into the ritual circle while Teraeth screamed, grabbed the sword away from Thaena, and swung at the woman. The fact that it worked at all was probably all the proof that Janel would ever need that this wasn't the real Goddess of Death.

Even as Thaena's body fell, Janel used the sword to slice at Teraeth's chains.

---

[1] I assume this refers to the attempt Kihrin and Janel made to access the memories of previous lives while they were in the Manol Jungle.

"Teraeth!" she screamed. "Wake up!" When he didn't respond, she reached up–Janel had to stand nearly on her tiptoes to manage it–and kissed him.

For a few seconds, nothing. Then his arms tightened around her and he kissed back, so violently it felt less like romance than struggling to hold on to the edge of a cliff, fingers digging in hard enough to bruise in his desperation not to fall. He broke away only to take a deep, shaky breath and stare at her with haunted eyes. "What–?"

"We need to leave," Janel said. "Questions can wait."

"Janel." Teraeth's voice was shaking with need. Before he said another word, he grabbed her and pulled her close again, one hand cradling her head, the other around her waist. He was shaking. "You're alive. I didn't lose you."

"Never," she agreed. "But we need to leave. It's not safe–"

"What the fuck are you doing here?" Kihrin demanded.

Janel's pulse spiked and skipped. Kihrin stood in the doorway, face twisted in anger. Purple shadows darkened his eyes. His features were too gaunt, as if he'd been starved. As if this were a physical place where he *could* starve. Everything about him felt sharper, harder, barbed.

"Kihrin–" Teraeth said as he started to reach for him. There was no time for Janel to explain why that might not be wise. How that might not be Kihrin.

He flinched from Teraeth's touch, backing away from both of them. He looked furious, fearful, not entirely sane. "No, what the fuck are you doing here? You're going to mess everything up. Didn't that idiot Thurvishar explain what I was doing?"

"I didn't–" Teraeth shook his head. "I don't even know what I'm doing here, let alone what you are."

"You said you needed reinforcements." Janel kept her voice low and gentle as if reminding a child that they were throwing a tantrum over being denied the toy they already held. She eyed the doorway Kihrin blocked and then the wall. How much would it hurt to slam through the stone?

"I never said that," Kihrin snapped.

Teraeth gulped air, clenched and unclenched his fists. "Okay. You never said that. Janel, where are we?"

Janel eyed Kihrin warily. The likeness wasn't perfect, but that didn't prove anything. Wouldn't Vol Karoth try to fool them with an exact likeness? Kihrin at his best? This version looked like he'd suffered, like he'd been fighting for weeks. It seemed more authentic than a pristine, perfect version of their lover.

"We're inside Vol Karoth's upper soul," she answered. "Inside his mind."

Teraeth visibly swallowed and took Janel's hand, ran his thumb absently over the back of it. "Okay. I guess that's a thing that's possible. Anyway, we're here now, so we might as well help."

"No," Kihrin said. "No, you can't help. In fact, what you're doing right now is the opposite of helping. However you got here? Do that again and get the fuck out."

"Kihrin–" Janel began to say.

"No," Kihrin interrupted. "You'll just make it worse. You're giving *him* a weapon. Fuck, why do you think I ran off without telling you? There was no way I was ever going to be able to deal with Vol Karoth as long as I had the rest of you dragging me back. You'd have just messed everything up. Like right now."

Janel said nothing. She still couldn't tell if it was really Kihrin or not. Kihrin when angry was perfectly capable of cutting words. Of cruelty. Vol Karoth . . . Vol Karoth would surely just appear as himself, wouldn't he? Was he capable of this sort of disguise?

Maybe she was trying to think of excuses for why this couldn't be Kihrin, because then she could ignore how much his words stung.

"Kihrin, seriously?" Anger replaced despair and guilt as the expressions of the hour on Teraeth's face. "It wasn't my choice to be here."

"Well, it sure as hell wasn't mine." Kihrin scowled at both of them. "Now fuck off."

"You don't mean that," Teraeth said.

Kihrin raised an eyebrow. "I do mean that. Do I have to spell this out? Fine. Janel's a demon now, and I kill demons. And you?" His laughter scratched against Janel's skin, stinging like nettles. "You were never more than a physical attraction I wasn't willing to admit I felt. Well, I've admitted it now. But I'm not going to let Relos Var win just so you can sit on my dick, so maybe you should leave and let me do what I need to."

Teraeth didn't flinch. He didn't move. His face just turned perfectly blank, holding no expression at all.

Kihrin rolled his eyes. "What? No protest that you love me? Just as well. We both know how well you treat the people you love. You loved your mother, didn't you? Look where it got her."

Janel felt Teraeth tighten his hold on her hand, the way someone might if they were in pain. And she knew in the aftermath of that injury that she'd been wrong; Vol Karoth was perfectly capable of hiding his knives before he struck. Kihrin, for all his flaws, his temper, his impulsive, reckless dives off verbal cliffs, would never say those words. He'd never wield them with such scalpel-sharp precision to maim and bleed. Not to Teraeth. Not to Janel. Even if Kihrin thought pushing them both away was the only way to save them, there were lines he wouldn't cross.

"Leave him alone," Janel said, appalled at the shake in her voice. "He's not the one you're mad at."

Kihrin met her eyes then. And oh, this was so much worse than she had ever thought. He had eyes here. He wasn't just a black outline. She could see the hate, the accusation, the absolute malice and know that he'd saved it all for her.

"You're right," he said, voice soft and fatal. "He's nobody. You're the one who made all this happen. Do you ever stop late at night and think about all the people who've died because of you? *Millions.* Do you think my brother would have turned against me if he hadn't discovered that I was having an affair with the person responsible for making sure he wasn't approved for the Guardian project, right under his nose?"[2]

Janel shuddered and took a step back. Gods.

"What was he ever going to think except that I'd stolen what he deserved?"

---

[2] So, with the caveat that a great many assumptions are being made here, I have so far pieced together the following: that a romance between S'arric and C'indrol was forbidden (but they were having one anyway) and that C'indrol was the 'friend' whom Valathea had once said tried to persuade her that Relos Var was dangerous and not to be trusted.

Kihrin—no, it wasn't Kihrin at all—stepped farther toward Janel, face twisted with hate. "And then you came back as Elana and made it a thousand times worse. You're right; Teraeth isn't the person I'm mad at."

"Teraeth, run," Janel whispered.

But he didn't. He blinked dully at Kihrin, the frown slow to form but finally settling over his expression. "Oh," he said. "I see. I understand now."

Kihrin looked away from Janel to scowl at him. "Understand what?"

"You're not Kihrin," Teraeth said. "You're Vol Karoth."

Teraeth said the words before Janel could stop him. She had no idea if what he'd done was smart or stupid. Maybe Vol Karoth would've been content with verbal knives if his identity had remained concealed. Maybe not.

Before she could find out, the world changed.

Galen's memory
The Culling Fields, The Capital City, Quur
Just after the meeting with Relos Var

Once the old priest was done making his deals, he left, leaving his younger companion behind. He never looked back. Galen wasn't quite sure what that indicated.

The Vishai priest left behind a room that just missed being silent. Taunna, Eledore, and Sheloran were still speaking to each other in soft murmurs. The workmen had renewed their repairs. And the younger priest, Qown, still sat across the table from Galen, drinking tea. He seemed eager to rest his gaze on any surface that wasn't a D'Mon.

Galen had the distinct impression Qown didn't like him. There was a time where that might have bothered him too.

They didn't even have enough time for the tea to cool before the front door opened and his guard returned, this time with soldiers in tow. Damn man must have run from the Citadel to have made it there and back so quickly. Anlyr, Anlyr, Anlyr. Galen repeated the name to himself several times, embedding it into his memory. He was grateful that Qown had asked the man for it earlier—it saved Galen from having to awkwardly admit that he hadn't had the faintest idea in the world what his own guard's name was. And Anlyr had just won himself a promotion—if nothing else for the commendable skill of having survived.

Said guard bowed to Galen, perfectly, with practiced elegance. "My lord, I have brought you an escort to take you and Lady D'Mon to the Army Gatestone."

Galen made a face. "Oh. Well, that's going to be a bit awkward, I'm afraid." He smiled apologetically and waved a hand. "We won't be going to the Kirpis estate."

Across the table, Qown watched, his face blank.

Anlyr tried—and failed—to hide his consternation. His expression could best be described as a combination of resigned and pleading. "Of course, my lord."

Red went over to the table at that moment, leading a still-quite-drunk Eledore. Galen suspected his cousin teetered on the edge of passing out. "Where are we heading then? To my parents'?"

Galen stood, setting his tea down. The priest scrambled to his feet a moment later—someone had evidently told him one didn't remain seated when a high lord was standing, which was both humorous and wrong.

"Yes," Galen confirmed, "I don't see any other choice. But if you'd rather go to the Kirpis estate . . ."

Sheloran made a moue. "Don't even think about it."

Galen smiled at her, eyes crinkling at the corners. "Now whatever did I do to earn a wife so loyal?" She narrowed her eyes. Galen suspected she'd only just managed to resist the temptation to stick her tongue out at him.

Sheloran humphed. "As if you don't remember. But you know Momma will use this as yet another opportunity to try to make us leave the city."

Galen shrugged. "I know, but I won't. It would feel like running."

"The count I used to serve liked to call it a 'strategic retreat,'" the priest volunteered.

Both Galen and Sheloran turned to look at the man. It probably came off as astonishment that Qown would dare interrupt the conversation, because he immediately flushed. "I mean, uh . . ." The priest cleared his throat. "Tactically necessary in order to regroup and reassess future enemy engagements?"

The corner of Galen's mouth quirked. So the little priest wasn't quite fresh off the monastery. Had it been an Eamithonian count? How interesting. But alas, this wasn't the time to indulge idle curiosities.

"Or in other words," Galen said, "a dead man fights no battles. If only that were always true." He then examined Eledore, who rested her head on Sheloran's shoulder. "I'm afraid we'll have to leave her here. Do you think Taunna–?"

"I'm sure she'll make sure any wayward Milligreest lambs are returned to their flock," Sheloran agreed.

"I could sober her, if you wished," Qown offered. He had a look of vague disgust on his face.

Galen felt himself bristle, which was ludicrous, because he loathed drinking. He wasn't pleased by Eledore's binging either. But he felt, irrational as it was, that Eledore was his cousin, his family, and damned if some random cloistered priest from Eamithon was going to chastise her inebriation. Besides, she had just lost her brother. Galen could sympathize, even if he didn't have anyone in his family whose loss would pain him enough to make him want to numb the wound that way. Her family seemed to actually care about each other. It was just one of the ways they were so fundamentally different.

Sheloran sighed and shifted Eledore until she was snoozing away happily in one of the chairs. "Perhaps we should go."

Galen said, "I'm tempted to use the safe house instead. I don't want to cause your parents any trouble."

Sheloran rolled her eyes. "Trouble from whom, exactly? A pair of absentee sisters attempting to take over a house too broken and dishonored to survive on its own? I think House D'Talus will somehow manage to weather this storm."

"If there's one thing I've always loved about you, Red, it's your humility," Galen said, grinning.

"You mean my faith in my family," Sheloran corrected.

"No, that's just the part I'm jealous of." He reached out and booped his wife on the nose before turning to the soldiers. "Escort us back to the Red District, if you'd be so kind."

Anlyr nodded, visibly relieved to be heading someplace with thick walls and a significant working guard contingent.

A few minutes later, everyone was bundled back into the carriage, trying their hardest to ignore the blood splatters and stab marks and all the evidence of the earlier fight. Sheloran sat across from him, fussing over the bloodstains on her agolé.

Qown sat next to him, so straight and proper someone might have tied a piece of string to his spine and pulled tightly. His face was completely free from any expression, but Galen thought he sensed a deep-seated discomfort. Something a little more profound than just having been left with a bunch of royals.

Galen watched the man until Qown glanced in his direction and then immediately stared forward again.

Galen grinned and took the opening. "So how does one join a cult of celibate religious fanatics, anyway? Were you repenting a misspent youth? In mourning because your true love died?"

Qown's nostrils flared. "That's . . ." He seemed about to make the same sort of denouncement one of Galen's old tutors might have said: absurd or ludicrous or idiotic. He seemed to remember himself at the last possible second, inhaled deeply, and said, "I very nearly joined House D'Lorus."

Galen blinked. "Really."

Qown nodded, just the tiniest tilt of his head, and pursed his lips. "I grew up in a village near the Temple of Light, so when the House D'Lorus recruiters came, Father Zajhera showed up as well. He convinced my parents that he would be a better teacher than anyone at House D'Lorus."

Galen found himself bemused at the answer. He was just having a hard time imagining anyone turning down an offer from a Royal House. Maybe Qown wasn't in fact very talented.[3] If they didn't offer a lot of metal, that would certainly explain why the priest's parents had refused. Then again, had no one told them House D'Lorus ran the Academy? There was no better education than that. Then the other implication of what Qown had said caught up with Galen. Because there was only one reason any royal recruiters ever came searching among peasants.

"So you must have had a witchgift," Galen finally said. "What was it?"

"I'd . . . rather not say."

Galen raised an eyebrow.

"It's personal," Qown replied defensively.

"We're going to be spending a lot of time together," Galen pointed out. "And I won't judge."

Qown stared at Galen, frowning, brows drawn together. Then he raised a finger and wrote in the air, which would have been a cute affectation if the words hadn't glowed bright yellow and lingered.

---

[3] As if Relos Var would waste his time with someone untalented.

You forgot to mention being a sword carries a price.
That the final cost of strength is always more
than metal or flesh can pay.

Galen sucked in his breath, surprised by more than the witchgift itself. He fought down a sense of almost giddy surprise, not quite sure if he should be delighted or wary at the priest's choice of poem. He decided, to hell with it.

"Maybe you didn't know this truth," Galen continued, quoting the next verse:

having spent your whole life plucking flowers
to fill that hollow space inside you
where a soul might once have found good soil.

Qown's eyes widened in shock. "You read Kavis Tel?"

Sheloran made a choking sound and hid most of her face behind her fan. Galen flashed her an admonishing look that meant "Do not spoil this for me." Galen put his hand to his mouth and bit down on the side of his thumb, desperate to stamp down on the impulse to ask what other poems of "Kavis Tel" the priest might know well enough to quote by heart. If he had a favorite. If he'd had the slightest clue what Galen had been trying to say when he wrote them. Probably not that particular poem, anyway, since it was extremely unlikely Qown had ever experienced the unique pleasure of meeting Darzin D'Mon.[4]

When Galen didn't answer, Qown flushed bright red. "Oh, I'm sorry. I didn't mean to imply–" To compensate for his embarrassment, Qown somehow managed to sit even straighter, a feat Galen wouldn't have thought possible. His grandfather Therin would have loved this man's posture. "My apologies, my lord. Please believe I meant no disrespect. Kavis Tel is one of my favorite poets."

Galen laughed, unable to stop himself, then looked away before he could betray anything more. He studied the wall for a moment, as it occurred to him that the whole reason for the pseudonym was gone now. His father was dead. His grandfather was . . . who knew where. Why worry about embarrassing the house when there was almost no house left to embarrass? There was no one at all to stop him from openly publishing poetry if he felt like it. And still a hundred reasons why he never would.

Galen decided it was safest to change the subject. Or rather, return to an earlier one. "So your parents just gave you to this priest. Were they paid?"

Qown frowned. "I-I don't know."

"House D'Lorus would have offered metal. They usually do if they find someone promising enough."

This made the priest frown even more. "My parents wanted what was best for me, and they didn't feel that road lay with House D'Lorus."

Sheloran muttered, "Must have heard rumors about the human sacrifices."

---

[4] And yet Qown very much had. Ah, but it's such a small world sometimes.

Qown looked down at his hands. "I don't—they're not all terrible in House D'Lorus."

Galen cocked his head and threw Qown an odd look. "Really. And just how many members of House D'Lorus have you met?"

Qown shifted uncomfortably, visibly swallowed. "Two," he admitted. "I've met Thurvishar D'Lorus."

Sheloran looked as surprised as Galen felt. Thurvishar D'Lorus was not exactly one of his favorite people, even if he'd been declared innocent of his part in the Hellmarch.[5] Anyway, he wasn't a socially active person. Meeting Thurvishar—even casually—wouldn't have been easy. "And the second being his grandfather Cedric, I assume?"

"No." Qown paused a split second before continuing. "Thurvishar's father, Gadrith."

The carriage fell silent, with only the sound of the wheels rolling over the paving stones and the creaking wood of the joists filling the air.

Gadrith D'Lorus had been dead—or undead—for longer than Galen had been alive. It hadn't even been two weeks since Gadrith D'Lorus had finally died for good. Many years too late, in Galen's opinion. And here was this priest, who claimed to have somehow . . .

Galen simply stared.

Qown shifted, uncomfortable. "It was several years ago. I was at the court of the Duke of Yor and Gadrith was . . ." Qown winced and left the sentence hanging. "I met him by accident. I'm told I'm lucky to still be alive."

"You were a guest of the Duke of Yor." Galen's tone was perfectly flat.

"That might be the wrong word."

"Then what would be the right word?"

"Hostage."

Galen stared harder and then knocked the back of his head against the carriage wall, releasing a single, startled laugh. "You're a lot more interesting than you appear, priest."

Qown flushed again. "Thank you?" Then his eyes flickered down to Galen's waist.

Galen almost leaped to some incorrect conclusions about where the man rested his gaze, when he realized the priest was staring at Galen's sword hand, holding a white-knuckled death grip on the hilt of his dueling blade. Which had been true for the entire trip.

The whole reason Galen had started talking to the man was because he was desperate for a distraction. Any kind of distraction. Anything that might make it a little easier to pass the time while they waited out a second ambush that might come any second. There was no way to know if the assassins were already on their way. Galen thought they'd done as well as could be expected the first time—certainly much better than anyone had given them credit for.

---

[5] As Quuros law designates crimes committed by a gaeshed person are the responsibility of whoever holds the gaesh, Gadrith D'Lorus and Darzin D'Mon took full credit for the Hellmarch from a legal perspective. I'm sure you're relieved.

Sheloran, in particular, had picked up some new tricks with admirable speed, but then, she had a lot more magical training than Galen.

A thing Galen might also now admit publicly, even if he'd continue to hide the poetry.

"Have you read all of Kavis Tel's work?" Qown asked Galen, who blinked because it was as if Qown had been reading his mind. Although if that were actually true, Qown certainly wouldn't have asked that particular question. "I admit I only chanced across his writing a few years ago, and then had to hunt down the rest of it, as it's rather obscure. Some of it is really quite . . . provocative . . ."

Galen raised an eyebrow.

Qown immediately flushed. "Not like that. Free-spirited."

"What a polite way of saying 'treasonous,'" Galen replied, "but yes, I've read all his work. Sometimes more than once."

Sheloran snorted, and Galen fought not to smile. The priest looked a little lost, no doubt because he couldn't possibly imagine how a royal might like poems about hope, beauty, the equality of all people, and other such myths.

"Father Zajhera speculated that his work was related to the prophecies, but I never found any evidence of that. I researched it quite extensively."

Something jolted the carriage. Galen and Sheloran both sat upright. Galen unsheathed his sword a few inches, and Sheloran snapped open her metal fan.

But it was just a pothole. The D'Mons settled back down, exhaling. Sheloran reached over, took Galen's hand, and squeezed it. A moment later, the quality of the lighting outside changed, and although it was still daytime, it was possible to see a red tint to all the shadows.

A loud voice from up above proclaimed a request for entrance, and Galen relaxed a little more. The timing was correct. They should in fact have reached the Rose Palace by this point. Which was as close to a definition of "safe" as Galen had yet found in this awful, evil city. The sound of metal grinding against metal rang out, followed by the grating hiss of the front gates opening. The carriage moved forward again, followed by a hard, final clang as the same gate shut. It might have sounded ominous to someone else.

Galen should have kept talking. He would have liked the distraction from thinking about what he'd done. Because ultimately, there was no hiding from this. Any chance he might have had of convincing Aunt Tishenya that he could be controlled—that he'd play nice and roll meekly to the side—had just been eradicated. And the most concerning thing about it was how much Galen just. Didn't. Care. He should care, right?

It was probably shock, he told himself. Shock from . . . Gods. So many things, it was easy to lose track of which trauma should hurt the most. He'd just been left numb and cynical and lost.

The carriage pulled to a halt, swaying as the guards whom Anlyr had borrowed from the Citadel climbed down from the top. Someone opened the door. Galen motioned for the others to leave first. Qown did, followed by Sheloran and lastly himself.

The House D'Talus guards came out to meet them, bowing.

"I know Mother's not back yet," Sheloran said. "Is my father available?"

The guard took on an apologetic air. "Ah, I'm sorry—"

"He's in his workshop," Sheloran said, because Sheloran's father was always in the workshop except for those moments when Lady D'Talus reminded him to eat, sleep, or join her in bed. "It's fine. We'll wait in the Lotus Court." Sheloran began walking toward one of the doorways that led deeper into the palace.

"My lady—" the guard began, but it was clear she wasn't listening.

Galen started to follow her, when he realized they were missing a person and turned back to find his prospective teacher still standing there, his mouth dropped open.

Galen couldn't help but chuckle. There wasn't a single Royal House in the city that didn't have an impressive palace—it was always a constant battle to outdo each other. House D'Talus, for its part, insisted on being as House D'Talus as science, magic, or circumstance could allow.

Thus everything was made from metal.

Of course, that didn't do the conceit justice. The entire first court was sculpted from metal—gold and silver, copper and tin, drussian, shanathá, and alloys Galen had no idea what to call, although he assumed House D'Talus did.[6] The metal formed beautiful rosebushes, flowering with perfect metallic delicacy. It mimicked wooden beams and the sharp silken-smooth texture of marble. Graceful trees made sounds like silver bells as the wind blew through foliage that had grown from a forge rather than the ground. The air smelled sharp and hot, heated metals of all sorts blending to create a fragrance layered over the magically crafted scent of roses. While not all the metal was red, the mage-lights expertly reflected off shiny surfaces to create all the different shades of carmine, ruby, scarlet, and crimson one might ever imagine.

The Rose Palace indeed. It always made Galen smile, but Sheloran loathed the first court with all the enthusiasm of someone who'd grown up surrounded by steel and iron and just wanted to see a lily.

Galen held out a hand to Qown. "Well?"

The priest snapped out of his shock and blinked at the royal with flushed embarrassment. "I'm sorry, you don't want me to wait here?"

Galen sighed. "There's no reason to keep you waiting at the stables. You're not a horse." Galen's gaze swept past the priest to the soldiers who had escorted them. "Gentlemen, thank you for your company, but we'll be fine from here."

The men bowed to him. "Yes, Your Highness."

Galen waved a finger at his single surviving guard. "Anlyr, you're with me as well."

Anlyr looked relieved. Galen reminded himself to ask the man about his background. He clearly took his bodyguarding duties seriously.

Galen turned around and followed his wife into the rest of the palace.

The prince took a strange sort of glee in observing the reactions of his two

[6] Did you know there's apparently a shanathá alloy called sheloran? House D'Talus takes its metallurgy very seriously; the naming of children less so.

servants. Anlyr did a fine job of acting unimpressed—no doubt concerned about the pride of House D'Mon—but Qown was not so successful, and for once, his response was easily interpreted.

The Rose Palace wasn't done with its surprises. They crossed another full court, with catastrophically high walls and all the defenses of a military fortress, and then came to another, much smaller gate. This one had been built to be inhospitable to carriages, horses, or any creature larger than a normal human. Sheloran set her hand against the metal surface, let the warding spells do their job, and motioned for the rest of them to follow.

Galen found himself thankful, again, that House D'Talus had never severed ties with their daughter, the way so many Royal Houses would do when a child married into another house, and presumably adopted other loyalties. And he owed quite a bit to House D'Talus's willingness to break with that tradition. For example: being alive.

Galen felt the radiant heat of the metal as he passed through the doorway and then turned and grabbed Qown by the hand when the priest reacted exactly how Galen had suspected he might: freezing in place, mouth agape at the incredible view. This had the immediate effect of both snapping Qown out of it and also making him blush bright red. He quickly jerked his hand away from Galen's, wearing an expression of shock.

"Don't stop in the doorway," Galen said. It was probably a bad sign that he found Qown's indignation as adorable as he did, but it was so much fun to see that expression on the man's face.

Qown inhaled sharply and turned to look at the view.

It was, of course, an exceptional view, if one completely out of place with the rest of the palace.

This court contained a lake.

Galen wasn't sure just who had created it, but it had been meticulously maintained since—a perfect and lovely lake, upon which a number of pavilions had been built, so they just skimmed the surface of the waters. If there was any metal to be found anywhere, its nature had been carefully concealed. The fragrance of flowers mixed with the scent of water and green, living things. Befitting the name, lotus flowers grew in profusion over the surface.

Qown took one look and then started scowling.

"You don't like water?" Galen asked.

"No, I–" Qown swallowed and then started again. "I'm just wondering why none of this was damaged in the Hellmarch."

"Ah," Galen said. "Probably because demons have never attacked it."

Qown's expression switched to disbelief.

Galen just gave the man a lopsided smile. He had no answers for the man, since he didn't know himself. He'd always presumed that Lessoral and Varik were responsible.[7]

Galen was quite fond of the Lotus Court. It was . . .

Soft. Everything was soft and lovely, from the breezy pink silk curtains on the pavilion windows to the velvet carpets lining the bridges that led to them.

---

[7] Likely so, yes.

Everything smelled soft and looked soft and felt soft. He had never in his life found a better place for napping. Just after his marriage to Sheloran, he used to use any possible excuse to sneak over here and do just that, claiming that he was enjoying some time alone with his wife.

Which he was. Just not in the manner his father would have expected.

"Excuse us," Sheloran said, "but some of us would like to have tea today."

Galen laughed. "Apologies, my dearest wife. Let's fix that without delay."

Sheloran sighed. "Blue, don't you start."

Galen raised his hands. He'd play the game for as long as she let him. "Aw, come on. Have a heart."

She growled at him. Galen laughed again and moved ahead of his wife, almost skipping his step as he ran most improperly to be the first one inside the pavilion.

16: In Darkness

Teraeth's story
Inside Vol Karoth's prison
Just after Galen's memory

Teraeth was surprised to discover he could still see the visions, even here. This one with Galen, the little brother / little nephew Kihrin had always cared so much about.

But Teraeth looked at it all through a thick, numb fog where nothing really mattered. Even Janel, even Kihrin—they both mattered, of course they mattered—but he couldn't muster up any emotional connection beyond that. His heart had been soaked in ice, abandoned to the elements—he had no feeling anymore.

But Kihrin's image flickered in front of him, staggered backward as though touching a hot flame. Any chance Vol Karoth might have had to deny Teraeth's accusation or deflect attention died stillborn as Teraeth saw the telltale clues of a shattered illusion. He knew he'd been right.

"Teraeth!" Janel yelled.

He felt a sharp pain, almost mistaken for pleasure because it was such a pure sensation. A tiny slice of oblivion erupted from his stomach in a spray of blood, where Vol Karoth had plunged a sword through his core. The illusion of Kihrin vanished, replaced by the dark god's silhouette. Teraeth shouldn't have been surprised by how much it hurt, but it was . . . Gods. It always shocked him how much injuries in the Afterlife felt just like their real-life counterparts. This was no different. It hurt like dying. Worse than that, because he had never been afraid of dying.

He was afraid of this.

Even as Vol Karoth pulled his sword from the wound, Teraeth had the sense that the Immortal's attention wasn't on him. He'd been attacked as foreplay, as prelude. It had nothing to do with hurting Teraeth.

Teraeth stumbled back. Blood spilled over his hand as he clutched the wound.

"No!" Janel's voice was unsteady, rough, her eyes a pyre. She pulled her sword and swung at Vol Karoth.

Teraeth started to draw his weapons as well, but there was the small problem of the stomach wound and the way his "metaphorical" intestines wanted to spill from his "hypothetical" body.

Vol Karoth laughed, dark and ugly.

I will kill the two of you and take back what is mine. Your love is paper and ash. Your love means nothing.

Janel swung at Vol Karoth. He blocked the sword blow easily, then reached out with his other hand and grabbed her sword arm.

Which Vol Karoth disintegrated.

Janel's eyes widened with shock and horror as she fell back, one arm just . . . gone. Like flame eating the edges of thin paper, obliterating it in an instant so not even the evidence remained.

"No!" Teraeth screamed and rushed forward.

Vol Karoth laughed.

A hand landed on Teraeth's shoulder.

"Actually, you asshole, their love means everything," Kihrin told Vol Karoth.

Kihrin—the real Kihrin—had one hand on Teraeth, the other on Janel. He looked even worse than Vol Karoth had imitated, covered in bruises, cuts, dirt, and blood. Something ephemerally darker slouched in his shadowed blue eyes: despair. But under that hopelessness still lurked a spark of the Kihrin that Teraeth knew and loved.

The world lurched in shuddering dislocation, and then they were gone.

Galen's reaction
The Lighthouse at Shadrag Gor
Also just after Galen's memory

The vision cut off. Everyone found themselves once more in the Lighthouse.

Galen sighed. He didn't particularly mind leaving off at that point, if he was being honest. He knew what came next. But he had the itchy feeling that someone was staring at him. Galen looked over to see it was Qown. The man was glaring. Why in the world—

Galen quirked his mouth. Oh. Right.

"Kavis Tel," Qown muttered, managing to glare even more. It was almost comically adorable. "How is that even possible. Kavis Tel!"

"In my defense," Galen said, "even if it wouldn't have embarrassed House D'Mon, using a pen name was just a smart precaution. Besides, I first started writing poems when I was twelve; most of them are objectively terrible."

"None of them are terrible!" Qown nearly screamed.

"Ah, you think so? It's nice to have a fan," Galen said.

Xivan's eyebrows were making a break for the ceiling. "I saw the same vision as everyone else, so what am I missing?"

"You're not used to that feeling by now?" Talon said. "That's weird."

Xivan's eyes narrowed. "Seriously? You're picking a fight with *me*?"[1]

Kalindra chuckled with a sour sort of mirth. "On the plus side, I'm pretty sure that fight would never end."

"That's a plus?" Talea asked her.

"It would give them something to do?" Kalindra said. "And we could watch."

"Oh, now girls," the mimic said, grinning. "I'm sure Xivan has plenty to do." She winked at Talea, just in case anyone missed the innuendo.

Galen scrubbed his eyes with the butt of his palms and sighed.

---

[1] As if Talon isn't capable of picking a fight with anyone, including deities.

Sheloran waved her fan idly in front of her face. "Perhaps we might, I don't know, keep a bit of focus? For example, that was all very nice, but do we have any way to know if it actually helped?"

"It wouldn't have helped if I'd kept going," Talon protested. "The next part isn't really so . . . you know . . . pleasant. So I thought, why not just focus on Galen flirting with Qown?"

"He wasn't flirting!" Qown protested. "That was not flirting. That was just being polite."

Sheloran gave her husband a look that clearly said: Can you believe this?

Galen chuckled. "Adorable. But no, Qown. I *was* flirting."

Qown stared at him, wide-eyed, and turned bright red. Which was also adorable. Before the priest responded, however, the fire in the hearth died and the light in the room turned dim.

A voice cut through all the stunned silence.

If you're going to tell the story, don't leave out the best parts.

"Oh fuck," Talon said, "that is *not* Kihrin."

The world changed.

Qown's memory
The Upper Circle, Quur
Just after their arrival at the Rose Palace

Qown watched as Galen skipped ahead toward the pavilion doors. "We'll have the servants send for some food—"

Galen threw open the doors and froze.

Qown wasn't sure why at first, then he saw that the room was already occupied by a group of people.

And to the last, they all wore blue.

The oldest woman, dressed immaculately in sapphires and blue silks, eyes like azure razors, stared at Galen and clearly didn't like what she saw. Then she smiled, a slow, slimy smirk that reminded Qown so strongly of Darzin D'Mon he flinched.

"Oh, well now, this is so much more convenient. Whoever would have thought you'd come to us." The fingers of her hands started to crackle with electricity.

Galen said, "Hello, Aunt Gerisea."

Gerisea D'Mon regarded her nephew with wicked delight. "Why don't you sit down?" Sparks fell from her fingertips, cascading down to the floor as if it were a small waterfall made from lightning. The tranquility lasted for barely a second, and then the lightning lashed out and leaped from Galen to Anlyr, who had just enough time to draw his sword before being reminded that it was an excellent conductor of electricity.

Lightning wasn't a bad choice for an offensive spell. Spellcasting required thought, after all, and anything that paralyzed thought made that difficult. Even if Galen had—like Gerisea—been hiding his magical training, he'd probably still have been rendered helpless by the attack.

Under other circumstances, Qown might have thought the attack idiotic, but it was a matter of timing. Gerisea probably assumed all the high lords were at

Jarith Milligreest's funeral. Lady D'Talus was, and Lord D'Talus apparently never left his workshop. Under normal circumstances, at a "normal" funeral, they wouldn't return for several more hours. Gerisea D'Mon probably thought she had at least another hour before she'd have to worry about interruptions. More than enough time to clean house.

But no one was paying attention to Qown, and Sheloran had stayed behind to talk to one of the servants. Had Gerisea seen Sheloran, she probably wouldn't have even made the attempt. Killing Galen was a house-related squabble, after all. Killing High Lord D'Talus's precious little girl . . .

"Galen's being attacked!" Qown cried out.

Sheloran's reaction was immediate. She sliced her fan through the air as she ran, the blurs proceeding her belonging to more of those tiny balls of metal she'd used so lethally during the assassination attempt. Qown followed close behind.

"What do you think you're doing?" Sheloran said when she reached the pavilion entrance.

The lightning stopped.

The older woman raised her hands and scowled. "This doesn't involve you."

Qown wasn't sure if Gerisea had noticed the little floating metal balls of death. In any event, whatever metal they were made from wasn't a terribly good conductor of electricity.

"Oh, I think it does," Sheloran said primly. "I was extremely fortunate to find such a suitable husband. You shall not ruin that for me."

Then Sheloran started screaming. High-pitched, hysterical screams, loud enough to make Qown wince and contemplate plugging his ears, interspersed with "Guards!" and "Help me!"

Gerisea glared at Sheloran with absolute loathing. Then her eyes flicked to the side and widened as she noticed one of those tiny little silver-gray orbs floating right next to the throat of one of her companions. A reminder, perhaps, that she wasn't the only royal in the room who'd lied about her ability to use magic.

Gerisea glowered and waved a hand. "Everyone throw down your weapons," she told the people with her.

"But, Mother—" one of the other people, young and handsome and about Galen's age, began to protest.

"*Now*," Gerisea D'Mon growled.

Qown heard the pounding of feet along the wooden walkways leading around the lakeshore. Shouting, the jangling of mail. A giant wall of fire sprang into life in the distance, wide enough to completely span the outside circumference of the Lotus Court. A bell began ringing.

Once it was clear that the guards would be there in seconds, Sheloran stopped screaming and just stood there staring hatefully at Gerisea, faintly smug.

"I didn't realize you knew her," Qown whispered.

"I don't have to," Sheloran whispered back. "I know her type." She held out her fan and watched as the metal sailed back to it, flattening out into the shape of a lion's head—the House D'Talus family symbol and a reminder of where they were.

Then the guards were all upon them, firmly but politely ordering everyone to put down their weapons and separating them. A group of people who were probably sorcerers trained in healing of some sort (not, perhaps, to the extent of someone of House D'Mon, but enough for immediate first aid) bent over Galen and the guard, Anlyr, and began treating them.

Qown raised a hand. "I'm a healer. I could—"

"Don't move," a guard snapped. "Not until we've sorted everything out."

Qown swallowed, but did what he was told.

At which point, Gerisea D'Mon burst into tears.

Everyone froze, even the guards. Gerisea wasn't just crying, she was sobbing, tears streaking down her cheeks, breath gasping from her lungs. "I'm so sorry—I didn't—he came at me—I was so scared—" The woman's children were clustered around her as much as the guards allowed, trying to comfort their extremely "distraught" mother.

Qown had to hand it to her: her performance was exceptional, custom designed to wring empathy from the most jaded, cynical heart. She was still a sobbing mess when all the guards parted for the royal who walked into the pavilion. He must have been Sheloran's older brother, dressed in a surprising amount of black (although the undershirt peeking out from under his misha was a bright, vivid scarlet). He also wore a black leather apron around his waist, his sleeves rolled up to the elbows, his hair tied back in a messy ponytail. He was beautiful and perfect and exceedingly angry.

"High Lord!" Gerisea cried out, bowing to the man while on her knees. "Please—I was so frightened. He came at me with a sword, and I had to protect myself! I didn't mean to hurt your daughter!"

Ah, Qown thought. So not Sheloran's brother. He supposed that if you had enough metal, you could buy all the youth you wanted, and House D'Talus, by definition, had all of it.

"Father," Sheloran began, "this woman was attacking—"

The people with Gerisea began to talk all at once.

"Silence!" the high lord said.

The high lord scanned the room, his gaze swinging past Qown to Sheloran, where it lingered for a moment. That look didn't seem completely friendly, and Qown found himself wondering if Sheloran marrying outside the house meant that the high lord might not view her with total paternal affection. Then the high lord's gaze whipped back to Qown.

"Who are you?"

Qown bowed. "I work for High Lord Galen D'Mon."

"I didn't ask you who you worked for. I asked you who you are."

Qown straightened and swallowed. "My name is Qown, my lord." He gave a careful and (he hoped) correct bow and forcibly stopped himself from looking over at Gerisea. He hadn't wanted to say his name in front of that woman. She was still sobbing, but Qown wasn't fooled—she was listening to every word.

The high lord walked over to him. He wasn't any taller than most Quuros men, but he seemed tall. Maybe it was the anger or the fact he could order Qown's death with a flick of his fingers.

"What happened here?" High Lord D'Talus asked Qown.

Gerisea's sobbing increased in volume. Sheloran gave her an exasperated stare but then straightened, swallowing uneasily. Her eyes, as she stared at her father, seemed too bright, on the verge of tears kept back with great effort.

It was, Qown thought, a much superior acting job. It made Sheloran seem as if she were putting on a brave front for the dignity of the houses she represented.

But that didn't rescue Qown from his own predicament. He felt himself start to shake. He had no idea how to play this, if there was a smart thing to say or do, so he defaulted to the truth. "We . . . we just walked in, and that woman attacked Galen. My lord would never threaten his own aunt."

"He's lying!" one of Gerisea's children said.

The high lord exhaled. His hand came down on Qown's shoulder like an iron bar. "I have no doubt of that." Qown couldn't tell which statement he was commenting on—his or the accusation of lying—but he pulled Qown forward, then pushed him toward two of his guards. "Take him."

Qown felt himself sliding into a panic. No, no, he had to believe . . . the high lord couldn't just dismiss what he'd said. "But I—"

"But, Father—!"

"Silence! You've done enough," the high lord snapped. He turned back to Gerisea, reaching over to take her hands. "Oh, sweet lady Gerisea, I'm so sorry you had to go through this unfortunate incident. Believe me when I say that I never meant for any of this to happen. I will make very certain the appropriate parties are punished." He let her go then and gestured to the rest of his people. "Escort Gerisea D'Mon and her children to the gates, and make sure they reach the Blue Palace safely."

Gerisea's eyes widened. "Wait, but our meeting—"

"Oh no," the high lord said, "I know you're much too distraught to talk about 'politics' in your current condition. I wouldn't dream of taking advantage. We'll have to do this another time. But don't worry. I'm sure it wasn't anything so important that it can't wait."

Gerisea started to protest, but then pressed her lips together and gave the man a long, even stare. The high lord returned it with the friendliest of smiles. Finally, Gerisea nodded. She bowed to the high lord, then swept out of the room. She did spare a look for Qown, though. It reminded him enough of her brother Darzin that he had no trouble interpreting it.

It meant: *You're a dead man.*

17: The Arrogance of Heroes

Kihrin's story
Inside Vol Karoth's prison

Oh, it hurt to see Janel and Teraeth. It had hurt even more to find myself screaming at them while they couldn't hear me, couldn't see me, while that bastard Vol Karoth told them lies in the most hurtful possible way.

It almost, almost overcame the fierce bloom of pride I'd felt when Teraeth spotted Vol Karoth's deception and called him on it.

If seeing them hurt, having them here with me also made me ridiculously, unreasonably happy. It felt like breathing clean air after a thousand years of acid bile clouds in the Blight. But I didn't want to lose them, and dear gods, Vol Karoth had ended up being so much stronger than I could have ever dreamed possible. I was barely surviving, and I'd seen just how much damage Vol Karoth had been able to do in seconds . . .

That first vision, whatever had caused it, had bought me the time I needed. I couldn't even find it in myself to be mad at Qown, except in the most general sort of sense that if he managed to hurt Galen, I would make it a point to find a way to kill him. Admittedly, a ludicrous notion when the easy metal was still on me killing everyone.

We reappeared on a street on the far side of the city, next to a tall building that might have been anything in better times.

"Come on," I told them. "Let's get you both out of sight. It always slows him down a little."

I sat Teraeth down as soon as we were inside an inner room. There wasn't any furniture. There was never any furniture in any room. No decorations, no functional décor, nothing with purpose or grace or need. Just vast buildings full of empty rooms, silence, and dust.

Teraeth was the worse off of the two, at least in the short term. He was still bleeding, and his dark face was gray from pain. Vol Karoth hadn't been trying to kill Teraeth; he'd been trying to make it hurt. He'd very much succeeded.

"Janel–" I looked over at her. "Are you–"

She waved me away as if it were perfectly normal to have an arm dissolved. "I'll be fine. Take care of him first."

"Right. Let me help," I said as I knelt next to Teraeth. But even as I did, I couldn't stop myself from grimacing. This was all my fault, after all. All. My. Fault. "Damn. You shouldn't have come."

"Idiot," Teraeth growled, although it looked like it cost him. "I wasn't given a choice."

I closed my eyes, tried to blink away the sting of tears. "I know. He used how upset you were—"

That was when the next vision hit.

"Fuck!" I muttered. I blinked away the images.

"So I guess that means at least one of your sisters is *also* a massive asshole," Teraeth said.

"She's a D'Mon. The odds were always in favor of that." I placed my hand against his stomach wound, let the tenyé slip through my fingers toward him. The energy curled around the edges of his injury, binding, closing, healing. When we parted, he grabbed my other wrist, and we just stared at each other. His eyes were shining, ebullient—which was ridiculous because our situation was so dire it made me shudder to think of it. He still looked at me like I was every sunrise the world had ever seen. Then his emerald gaze focused, sharpened, and he looked past me, to Janel.

When I turned back to her, she'd either ripped off most of her armor or had dismissed it and was concentrating on the horrifying stump of her arm. As we watched, the flesh of her shoulder stretched out, warped, began to take on the cast and scale of a normal limb.

I straightened. I hadn't known someone could do that. Or rather, I hadn't known a human could do that.

And then remembered that humans couldn't.

"Damn," Teraeth murmured, expression unreadable. "When . . . Janel." He sat up. "When did you finish becoming a demon?"

I sat down on my knees and scrubbed my fingers against my legs. I suppose she hadn't had a chance yet to tell Teraeth what had happened. I couldn't blame her for wanting to put off that particular conversation for as long as possible. Some might have considered it cowardly, but it was a cowardice I could hardly rebuke. You know, considering my own.

"Since Suless," Janel said softly. "I had to. It was the only way to escape her after she'd taken possession of my body and tsali'd me. Unfortunately, Suless learned the trick of it herself. A problem for another time, I'm afraid."

Teraeth shut his eyes and sighed. "That's why you told Xivan that Suless was beyond her reach."

The shape of her mouth could only laughably be compared to a smile. "It's worse than you know. I'll tell you later."

"Why didn't you tell me before—?" Teraeth bit off his words and inhaled deeply. "Right. Sorry. I was about to ask you an unhelpful question. See? I can be taught."

Janel smiled at him fondly.

"Um." I raised a hand and waved fingers at them. "Much as I hate to . . . Look, Vol Karoth said some horrible, hateful, untrue things back there, but he was right that you both need to leave. Please. It's not that I'm unhappy you're here—because I'm so happy—but I can't stop him from killing you. He's just so strong." I shuddered and ran a hand over my face. I really had no idea what I was going to do. I just knew who I couldn't bear to lose while doing it.

[I'm afraid Teraeth can't leave, Kihrin, at least not on his own,] Thurvishar's voice said in my mind.

Janel raised her head. "Thurvishar. What are you doing here? You said you couldn't follow me."

I blinked. "Wait. What? Where are you?" I turned in a circle around the room, but if he was standing there, he'd learned a better invisibility spell than I'd ever known.

[That's not an easy question to answer. It might be most accurate to say I have traded a physical manifestation for cognitive clarity.]

"Most accurate, huh?" I made a moue. "What if you were trying for less accurate but more in a language we understand . . . ?"

A few seconds punctuated the silence. Then: *[The more I can see, the less I can do. And I'm trying to see a great deal in order to help you.]*

"Can you return?" Janel was talking to the ceiling, which verged on comedic considering that it wasn't obvious where Thurvishar's voice was coming from.

[I believe so. I'm attempting to keep a strong link to my physical body—the other reason you can't see me.]

"Right. Fair enough." I rubbed my eyes and thought about next steps. Not . . . being caught . . . something . . . something. I still had no idea. "Keep a watch out for my shadow, would you? It would be nice to have a head start on running for our lives this time."

Janel squinted at me. "I take it fighting him hasn't been going so well."

"I . . . may have underestimated the situation," I admitted.

Teraeth rubbed a thumb into his temple. "Oh, I should kick your ass. You may have 'underestimated the situation.'" His laughter was dark and thick and mocking. Not so long ago, I think I might have lost my temper about it or at least would have been embarrassed. Those days were gone.

I didn't answer. What was there to say? I sat down next to him and put my head on his shoulder. He wore the same green silk with gold seashell that I first remembered from Ynisthana, and I wondered if he even realized. I wouldn't have thought that outfit would be associated with pleasant memories, inasmuch as I would very much associate it with the Black Brotherhood and his mother. I was struck again by how real this all felt. His skin, the scent of him, the flat planes of his chest, which that damn shirt had always shown far too much of. I mourned for the totally inappropriate circumstances, because this was hardly the time or place to do any of the things I had wanted to do about that.

Janel slid between our legs, sitting on her knees, just the tiniest sliver of her thighs brushing against mine. She wore an outfit I'd only ever heard about: her family heirloom, the shanathá mail she'd inherited from her adoptive grandfather. So a gown of midnight blue links that shone with an iridescent luster, ending just above long, tight riding boots of soft leather. And since none of this was real, she'd just skipped the details that might otherwise have been necessary and practical—the arming jacket, the bodice.[1] Honestly, even if I logically knew the shanathá armor was very practical and sturdy, it still seemed like she was wearing jewelry more than armor. I kept seeing flashes of . . .

---

[1] Not the same sort of garment as a raisigi. A joratese bodice is meant to be worn under clothing. The garment is sewn with dozens of narrow channels which are then strengthened with reed. The

I was distracted, is what I'm saying.

I squinted and studied a wall. Some sort of brickwork?

"Since we're here, we might as well help," Janel said.

"I don't see how you can," I said.

"There has to be something. We just need to figure out our enemy's weaknesses, study his patterns," Janel said. I didn't think she was nearly as confident as she sounded, but damned if she wasn't going to keep a positive attitude about the whole thing.

"Why me?" Teraeth asked softly. "If he can grab souls from the Lighthouse, why hasn't he taken everyone?"

At least I knew the answer to that. "He said . . ." I exhaled. "He said when people give up, that's when they're his."

Janel and I both looked at Teraeth.

"It was just after we'd learned Talon had killed you," Teraeth said. His whole body was tense with remembered pain.

"Excuse me," said Janel, "but I believe the correct term is committed suicide by mimic."

Teraeth scoffed and gave her a black smile.

Janel leaned forward and gave Teraeth a gentle kiss. Then she slapped the top of my head.

"Hey! What was that for?"

"*Suicide by mimic*," Janel repeated.

I laughed, although it was not at all funny. For the record, I thought it was funny. "You should still stay away from me. He'll target me. If you avoid me, then at least there's a chance—"

Teraeth growled. "Don't you fucking dare suggest he'll leave us alone." I felt his arm tighten around my waist. He was literally not letting me go.

Janel sighed. "I'll repeat what Thurvishar just said: Teraeth can't leave. I'm reasonably certain I can, but Teraeth is trapped here in this hellscape with you. Don't you think that if Thurvishar could just yank Teraeth back to his physical body, he'd have done it by now?"

I inhaled sharply. "But if we can't get Teraeth back into his body . . ."

"I die," Teraeth said. "Believe me, I'm aware of how this works."

I felt a wave of regret wash over me, and I turned my face away. Right up until Teraeth pinched me. "Hey!"

"If I'm not allowed to wallow in guilt, neither are you." Teraeth shifted so I had to put my arm around him to keep my position. The net result of it was that we were basically in each other's arms with Janel placing a hand on each of our legs for balance. The fact that we were sitting on the ground in a room with no furniture, with a mad god looking to kill us . . .

I inhaled and attempted to concentrate, although these two weren't making it easy.

"All right," I said. "Teraeth can't leave. And neither can I. But—Janel—you

---

whole thing is then laced tightly over the breasts using cord. I don't find the garment particularly comfortable, but as it does an excellent job of minimizing movement, I can understand why it's considered so essential to such a physically active culture.

can. And you should. And then we'll work on getting Teraeth out of here, and then–"

Janel was not impressed with my logic. She stared flatly at me. "You hypocrite."

I flushed. "I'm not claiming–"

Janel wasn't done talking, though. "Are you listening to yourself? Did you stop for even five seconds while you were planning all this to consider that we're not eager to see the man we love die right in front of us either? Did you think of our feelings *at all*?"

I seemed to have had something caught in my throat. "I'm not saying–wait. Love? *We* love?"

Hey, the last I'd checked, Janel hadn't been willing to admit to "love." We hadn't known each other for long enough, she'd said, as if we hadn't known each other across lifetimes and millennia.

"Oh, for fuck's sake," Teraeth muttered.

Janel flushed. "Yes, we. Because certainly I throw myself into the minds of dark gods of annihilation for just anyone, all the time." Her eyes narrowed with frustration and annoyance. "Don't change the subject."

"Oh, but could we, anyway? Because I'm perfectly aware of just how badly I've fucked this up."

"You were playing hero," Teraeth growled. "Sacrificing yourself for the cause. It's the one thing you and Relos Var have never disagreed on."

I winced. "Oh, when you play dirty, you don't mess around, do you?"

"You," Teraeth said carefully, "started it."

I exhaled.

Janel wasn't finished, though. "I'm glad you're aware that you've made mistakes, but I'm not sure you realize why. You probably think it's because you underestimated Vol Karoth, but that's not the issue for Teraeth and me. Your miscalculation with us was the same one Relos Var loves so much: arrogance."

I blinked. A feeling of surprise and anger bubbled up inside me. "I'm sorry? Arrogance? You know, I think I take exception to that. Quite a lot of exception." Suddenly, I wasn't feeling quite so in the mood to cuddle.

"Go right ahead." Janel crossed her arms over her chest and straightened. Given that Teraeth and I were all but lying down, it made her for once seem taller. "Let's put aside for the moment how arrogant it is to think that the fate of *the whole world* must rest on your shoulders alone. Let's instead talk about the arrogance of assuming that Teraeth and I wouldn't understand."

That trapped the air inside my lungs. Fuck.

"You just assumed that you had the right to make decisions about our happiness for us without consultation. And don't bother denying that's what you did, because one of the conditions of our happiness is *you*."

"I was trying to protect you!"

"Oh yes, because clearly that worked out so well." She waved fingers at me, and it took me a second to realize that was the arm Vol Karoth had disintegrated. "You weren't protecting us, Monkey.[2] You were hiding."

---

[2] Considering that "Monkey" was a nickname originally given to Kihrin by Kalindra, I'm dis-

I shuddered. Oh, she was angry. I guessed they both were. I wasn't in a good position to see Teraeth's face, and I didn't even want to try for fear of what I'd see in his eyes, but . . .

I'd assumed I'd either have solved the issue by the time I met up with them (and thus it wouldn't be a problem) or I would be dead and it . . . wouldn't be a problem. It hadn't occurred to me that I might end up in a between state where I was dead but also available to be yelled at.

Fuck. Thurvishar had been right. I should have told them. And yes, maybe they'd have talked me out of it, but . . .

But they'd have been right to.

I pondered if Teraeth would let me hide my face in his shirt and never make eye contact with anyone ever again. I already knew the answer was no. I could feel how tense he was. He was letting Janel do the yelling, but he didn't disagree with a thing she was saying. So I untangled myself to sit up, turned to face both of them, and picked up Teraeth's and Janel's hands.

"I understand why you're both upset," I said, "but this really seemed like it would work, and I . . . okay. Yes. You're right. I knew you wouldn't agree and that you'd try to stop me."

"Really. You knew that." Teraeth used his voice like a razor. "Without asking us, without giving us any chance to hear your reasons or make a case for any other approach. You knew we'd never tolerate the idea of you sacrificing yourself for the greater good. Even if it was the right thing to do. Even though both of us have done the same thing in past lives. Even though we would have made the exact same sacrifice in a heartbeat. You really thought we were that selfish?"

"I wouldn't call it selfish after everything you've already lost," I told him. "Haven't you sacrificed enough? What kind of person would I be if I asked you to give this up too? Why the hell would I expect you to just calmly be okay with this?"

Teraeth's scorn was acid. "Refresh my memory: Who exactly helped you blow up an entire fucking volcano again? I'm *exactly* the brand of idiot who would be okay with this."

"Also, it would have been his choice," Janel said quietly. "And it would have been my choice. Whether we agreed or not—at least we would have known."

"Admit it, Kihrin," Teraeth said, "you were hoping it would be over one way or the other before we ever found out."

I exhaled loudly and didn't answer.

No one said anything for a while. I kept trying to think about next steps, and my mind kept skittering away from anything that resembled a reasonable solution. Mostly because there was no such thing as a reasonable solution. Presumably, Teraeth would only be able to leave once Thurvishar figured out a way to help him escape Vol Karoth's control or we'd dealt with Vol Karoth himself. And I still had to deal with a nasty, grumpy god of evil who hated the world and most especially me.

---

appointed that Janel never used it within the other woman's hearing. I bet Kalindra's reaction would've been priceless.

"I was so convinced he was a child," I whispered. "Scared. Alone. Full of misery and pain. That I could help him. Except he doesn't want my help. He just wants to destroy everything."

After a moment, Janel said, "Nothing you just stated is necessarily wrong."

"Clearly, it is; he's not a child."

"Of course he isn't. You're here."

I blinked and shifted to look at her. "I'm sorry?"

She gestured around us. "This isn't Vol Karoth's prison, Kihrin. This is Vol Karoth's upper soul. This is his mind. Teraeth and I—we're here, but we have bodies—"

"But you're a demon now—"

"Shh. I still have a body. I haven't given it up yet. But you, Kihrin, are here for good. You're not linked to a normal body. Your normal body is dead." Her eyes burned as she said that last part.

"And I am deeply regretting that . . ."

She continued speaking. "Vol Karoth is probably less childlike than you thought he'd be exactly because the link between you is bolstering his intelligence. To defeat Vol Karoth, you're going to have defeat—" Janel chewed on the inside of her lip.

"Myself," I said.

"Yes," she said. "I suspect so, anyway."

"Good luck with that," Teraeth said.

"Asshole, you're supposed to be supportive." Ah, how I lamented a lack of anything to throw at him.

He pondered that before shaking his head. "No, you'll have to find someone else for that. I'm not good at supportive. I'm more of a stabber."

"Really? I never noticed."

I stood up to break physical contact with both of them—it was impossibly distracting—and walked over to an interior doorway leading to a courtyard, well away from any windows. I was pretty sure it wouldn't matter—if Vol Karoth were close enough for a window to make the difference, he'd be close enough to sense me. Still, I just needed to walk, move, do something.

Then I froze as I realized what I was seeing.

"Kihrin?" Janel asked behind me.

"There's a tree," I said.

In that narrow square of open land, a spindly, dead tree reached its branches up toward the sky, dug roots into rock-hard, dry ground.

"Is that a problem?" Janel sounded confused.

"I've never seen a tree here before," I explained. "Nothing living, ever. Not a blade of grass or a stalk of weed or patch of mold."

I had no idea what it meant.

"Are you sure that wasn't here all along?" Teraeth asked.

I gave him a look.

"Okay, fine. It's probably new," Teraeth agreed. "But what does it mean?"

I bit my lip. Still had not a single clue in the universe. It seemed like a good sign, though. A single dead tree is hardly a miracle, but since this was Vol Karoth's mind, it was a sign that something had changed. The question was: What had caused the change? Was it the arrival of Janel and Teraeth? Something else? That vision of Galen's? The ones neither Vol Karoth nor I had caused?

"Thurvishar? Are you still here?"

[Yes. Trying very hard not to pay attention, however.] It was his voice, even if we couldn't see him.

"Why wouldn't you be trying–" I paused. It occurred to me that he was probably trying to give us at least a modicum of privacy or the illusion thereof. "Never mind. Look, whatever you're doing back at the Lighthouse, keep doing it, all right? At the very least, it's distracting him."

[I'll let Talon know. Stay out of trouble while I'm gone.]

"You think that's possible?" Teraeth sounded skeptical, but I wasn't sure if it was to the idea of distracting Vol Karoth or staying out of trouble.

Probably the latter. He knew me.

"I think we wouldn't be sitting here if that vision hadn't happened," I said. "Might as well see if we can push it further. I just don't know if it's really because–" I stopped talking as I felt a chill.

"What is it?" Janel's voice dropped to a whisper.

It was a bit like being outside when a cloud crossed over the sun. I felt the cold in the air, an invisible breeze ruffling the hairs on my skin. I'd been through it enough to know exactly what it meant, and the dread as much as anything else sent my pulse hammering against my heart.

"He's found us," I said.

18: The Court of Iron Roses

Qown's reaction
The Lighthouse at Shadrag Gor
Just after Qown's memory

"That wasn't how that ended!" Qown screamed at nothing as the vision stopped. "You're not telling the whole story either!" He turned to Sheloran. "You were there. You know that's not how it ended. Your father was just getting that awful woman to leave without a fuss. He didn't believe her." Qown took a deep breath. "He was nice. He apologized."

"Qown," Sheloran said. "It's fine. Really."

"It just made him seem like some kind of terrible person," Qown said quietly. His hands were shaking. It had been just like being there, so that he remembered the fear and the anxiety and all the ways that it had gone wrong . . .

"He's a high lord," Xivan said. "By definition, he's a terrible person."

Sheloran glared. "That is not true."

Xivan shrugged. Her smile was just a little too flat to be genuine. "Isn't it? Why don't we ask the former slaves in the room?"

The temperature in the room had plummeted with the fire out, so Qown knelt by the fireplace and worked on lighting it again. These days, he was almost as good at fire spells as Janel, so it didn't take him long to have the fire crackling again.[1]

But the fire somehow didn't seem as bright or warm as it had been previously. Even the mage-lights seemed to have lost some of their power.

Qown thought it was a very bad sign.[2]

Kalindra snorted in response to Xivan's comment, a rare moment of solidarity between the two women.

"Oh, please." Senera looked up from her papers. "Please tell me the one where your parents aren't like the other royals. That they treat their slaves kindly and that makes it all okay. Go ahead and tell me that House D'Talus doesn't use slaves in the mines. I haven't had a good laugh in ages."

So perhaps it was cold in the room for reasons other than temperature.

"Let it go, Red," Galen said.

The lower half of Sheloran's face was hidden behind her fan, but the way her eyes were narrowed suggested she was very much not letting it go.

---

[1] I imagine having the Cornerstone Worldhearth was some help here too.
[2] And Qown was right, wasn't he?

Qown stood up from the fireplace. "I'm sorry. I didn't mean to start a fight. Let's just be nice . . ."

"Sure," Talon said, "because heaven forbid we make the royalty uncomfortable."

Qown sighed. He might have agreed with her—he did agree with her in principle—if he didn't know Sheloran and Galen were the last two royals in the whole damn empire who deserved to be yelled out for supporting slavery. Which Talon probably knew perfectly well. But Talon was a little damn demon, and there likely hadn't been enough yelling in the last five minutes to make her happy.

"We'll have all the time we want to make them uncomfortable once we're out of here," Kalindra said to Talon. She crossed to the other side of the room. Qown wasn't sure if she intended to check on Teraeth or if she just had a difficult time staying in one place when she was upset—but either way, Talea blocked her path.

Talea looked like nothing so much as a guard standing watch. A coin danced across her knuckles for a moment, then she pocketed it and met Kalindra's gaze coolly. She didn't move out of the way.

"And just what do you think you're doing?" Kalindra snapped. "Babysitting?"

Talea shrugged. "Just keeping an eye on them. Wouldn't want any of them accidentally falling on a knife several times while they slept."

Kalindra frowned. "Why would I—"

"Oh, was that a slam at me?" Talon said. "I feel like that was a slam at me." She faked a gasp. "I'm insulted."

"I wasn't going for that," Talea admitted, "but I feel a lot better knowing you took it that way, so thank you."

"What happened between us?" Talon mourned.

"You murdered my twin sister," Talea said flatly.

"But besides that . . ."

"And then you *ate her.*"

Talon made a face and then nodded as if to concede the other woman had a point.

Kalindra backed away from the one-woman barricade. "Okay, fine, I forgot we had a man-eating monster with us."

"More than one," Talon volunteered happily. "We should start making a list."

Qown looked around, wide-eyed. It was easy to forget, sometimes, that Xivan was exactly the same as Gadrith. And somewhere in the Lighthouse, a demon lurked, and their diet was sadly all too predictable as well. Indeed, Talon stood out in that at least she ate flesh.[3]

"Right," Kalindra said. "And while we're sitting here hoping that the god at the end of the hall never finishes taking a step, what happens when the monsters locked up in here with us grow hungry?"

"Hmm. That reminds me. I should make us something to eat," Qown

---

[3] I've found no evidence mimics are required to be cannibals. That, I believe, is the result of how they most efficiently gain memories from their victims as well as hide the bodies.

volunteered, mostly because he really, really didn't want to think about the consequences of what Kalindra had just said.

"You might want to be a little more careful with your wording while people like Xivan and I are in the room," Talon said cheerfully. "We might think you were volunteering."

Qown blinked at her, and then his eyes widened. "Obviously, I didn't mean you can eat any of us."

"Was that obvious, though?" Talon's smile was just a little too wide.

"I'd rather not be lumped in the same category as you," Xivan said. "And I have no intention of harming anyone here."

"Oh, come now," Talon said, "don't tell me you're not a little hungry?"

"No," Xivan said. "I'm not." She frowned then as if she'd just said something strange.

"That's fine," Talon said. "I have no intention of hurting anyone here either."

Everyone stared at the mimic in disbelief.

"Kihrin doesn't like it when I kill his friends," Talon explained.

Qown noted the use of present tense. Unfortunately, there was no way to know if that meant Talon didn't consider Kihrin dead, or if Talon considered Kihrin . . . part of Talon, talking to her right at that very moment. Sometimes it was easy to forget that Talon was insane.

And then there were times like this.

"So . . . yeah. I'll just . . . cook something," Qown said.

Sheloran walked over. "Lentil soup, you think? Do we have the ingredients for that? Something spicy would be just the thing to take some of this chill off."

Qown dragged his gaze away from the vampire and the mimic. "What? Oh yes, I think we do. There's some onions and garlic in the box, if you'd like to help with the chopping. Do you mind?"

"No, not at all," Sheloran said, smiling at him. "Do we have the right spices?"

"We do. Thurvishar's always done a good job of keeping the pantry stocked." Qown found himself smiling back. He was just so glad she was still talking to him. Plus, it was nice to have a helper; she'd picked up the cooking basics quickly for someone who'd grown up with servants doing all the work her whole life.

Mostly, it was nice to think about . . . something else.

Qown eyed the ingredients. "We should toast the spices."

"You're right, we—" Sheloran frowned and lit the fire again, because the tiny fire had died immediately instead of catching. This time, she concentrated until more than just the tinder caught. "If only we had clarified butter."

"We have that as well," Qown said. "There's a preservation box that keeps perishables from spoiling."

Sheloran stared. "All the ice in the world won't keep food from going bad for as long as it would have been sitting here, Qown."

"That's true," he replied, "but this isn't a cold box. I don't know how it works—"

"Thurvishar created it," Senera said distractedly. "It's ingenious." She seemed to have no idea that she'd just said a complimentary thing about her rival.

Although Qown was starting to feel like rival might be the wrong word for that relationship.

Talon's chuckle was chilling. "Oh, so does that mean it's story time?" She happily drummed her fingers against each other. "I love story time. And being back here in the Lighthouse, well, it's making me all nostalgic. I really should go find a rock."[4]

Senera straightened. "Talon, what are you plotting?"

"Senera, they think I'm untrustworthy," Talon explained, all wide-eyed innocence. "But don't worry. I'm not going to jump ahead. I mean, Qown is right; Vol Karoth cut off the story far too soon."

"Nobody wants to sit here and listen to you talk," Kalindra said.

"That's fine. I wasn't going to talk." Talon smiled, then tilted her head to the side and gave Qown a wink. "We'll just keep going with your story, won't we, ducky?"

"What?" Qown nearly dropped the bag of lentils he was holding. "No, I don't want to do that—"

"Oh, I'm sorry. You misunderstand. I wasn't asking permission."

The world changed.

Qown's memory
Still in the Lotus Court section of the Rose Palace

Qown didn't dare move. The guards had him locked in an iron grip, fingers digging into him so hard it was impossible that he wouldn't have bruises to show for it.

Lord D'Talus watched the woman go. As soon as the D'Mons were out of sight, he turned back to his guards. "Release him. Now will someone explain what happened here again without the hysterical woman trying to drown it out with theatrics?"

Sheloran nodded. "Assassins attacked our carriage on the way back from the funeral, Father. They killed almost all our guards, apparently with inside help from the carriage driver. So we knew it wasn't safe to return to the Blue Palace. Where else could we go?" She gave Galen's unconscious body a concerned look. "I certainly didn't expect his aunt Gerisea would be here, which was rotten luck. Since she thought you and Mother were gone, she took advantage of the opportunity to be rid of Galen. Did you know Gerisea was a sorceress?"

Lord D'Talus's face twisted like he'd just bitten down on an unripe persimmon. "No, but it doesn't surprise me. Therin never really cared what his children got up to as long as they weren't caught."

"The nerve of some people," Sheloran said dryly.

"Indeed. Now come over here and give your father a hug." He held out his arms to Sheloran.

"Daddy . . ." She rushed into her father's arms. "It really wasn't my fault this time."

He kissed the top of Sheloran's head before letting her go. "It wasn't your fault last time either. I'm just glad nothing came of it." Lord D'Talus then

---

[4] That took me a second. She was referencing how she recorded the conversations she had with Kihrin in your first chronicle.

gestured toward one of the men tending to his son-in-law. "Nothing did come of it, right? He'll recover?"

"Just stunned, my lord. They should be up and around in a few minutes."

"Good." Lord D'Talus scanned the group with a clear expression of distaste on his features. "They're a mess. Bring everyone new clothing and show them to the baths. My wife will want to speak with them when she returns. If anyone needs me, I'll be in the workshop." He gave his daughter a glare that would have been terrifying if he hadn't been hugging her just a moment before. "Make sure no one needs me."

With that, High Lord D'Talus swept back out of the room.

The next few hours turned into a blur. Qown was firmly escorted away from the others and taken to the very large, private D'Talus bathhouse. A number of attendants promptly took his clothes (he could only hope they intended on cleaning them) and set about yanking him through a series of hot and cold baths before subjecting him to a vigorous scrubbing and massage. After that, he was rinsed off once more and finally allowed to just sit and soak in a large heated indoor pool, which was empty of anyone else.

Or . . . not. He hadn't been there for more than a minute when the doors opened and Anlyr was escorted inside.

Qown turned away and studied the engraved metal walls. He immediately chided himself. He had no idea why he was letting himself be so flustered by just–everything. It's not like he'd never been in a public bath before. But it had been a few years–bathing was strictly a very private activity in Duke Kaen's court–and what he might have once not even thought about suddenly seemed embarrassing and awkward.

"You know, this isn't how I imagined my day would go," Anlyr said, splashing water as he made his way over to Qown. "Would you have ever predicted it? Not one but two assassination attempts?"

Of course. Anlyr was the sort who loved to talk while soaking after a bath. A perfect match with the smile and the cheerful eyes. Qown had a sudden brief bout of sympathy for Senera whenever Talea would bounce after her, chattering away.

Qown swallowed. "No, absolutely not."

"I was a bit out of it back there, but how did you end up with us? You didn't work with House D'Mon before this, did you?" Anlyr's eyes were bright, his smile friendly.

"Uh, no. I'm a priest of Vishai." He paused and reflected that he was probably going to have to explain–again–what that meant. Qown felt a peculiar sense of floundering, almost resentment, at the idea. He didn't want to have to keep explaining his beliefs.

But Anlyr surprised him. "Oh, I should have known that. I have a cousin who joined the Vishai. But if you don't mind me saying, I never would have expected a priest of Vishai to end up with the D'Mons."

Qown blinked and raised his head, looking at Anlyr. "Wait. You're from Eamithon?"

"Oh yes," Anlyr said. "Sterenale. That's just a–"

"I know where Sterenale is. I'm from Vanoizi."

"Really!" Anlyr straightened, clearly delighted. "That's just an hour down the road! That's fantastic. My brother has a bakery in Vanoizi. Colarin's."

Qown's mouth dropped open. "Colarin's? I know Colarin's! They have the most amazing black lentil sag . . ."

"Oh, you should try their caraba. Astonishing. And those tiny little dibis . . . And stop, stop. You're making me hungry and homesick." Anlyr laughed and splashed water in Qown's direction.

"Hey, you were back there a few days ago. I haven't been back in years . . ." Qown stopped smiling and looked to the side. This was the second time someone had brought up his birthplace in one day, and he wasn't enjoying it any more with repetition.

Anlyr put a hand on Qown's shoulder, broad fingers clasping him. "I'm sure you can go back." He was suddenly standing very close.

Qown stared at him, wide-eyed, and flinched backward away from Anlyr's touch and Anlyr's . . . everything.

Anlyr started to say something, then he seemed to realize how nervous Qown looked and instead backed away. "Ah, right. Sorry about that. I know Vishai take vows. I apologize if I made you uncomfortable. I wasn't trying to make a play at you."

Qown started to laugh it away, offer his assurance that he hadn't taken it that way at all. Then he realized that most people wouldn't have assumed Qown *would* take it that way. Most people would have thought he was flinching because of the violence of the day, because he'd been caught off guard, because he was a cloistered, introverted priest who wasn't used to being around other people so much. They wouldn't have assumed Qown's hesitation had anything to do with attraction.

Qown blinked. "Yes, you were."

He felt absolutely astonished. He'd never in his life . . . well, almost never. A few times in Jorat, but they'd always seemed so impersonal. He'd always felt he was being approached because it would be a bit rude not to approach. Good manners and all that. Absolved of all responsibility once Qown said no, which he always did. Never because someone was actually interested. And this beautiful man—practically from his hometown—no, it was impossible.

It made no sense at all.

Anlyr's expression brightened into a wide smile. "Sure, but if you're not interested, I'm allowed to say I never meant it that way. Those are the rules." He shrugged. "If you're working for the D'Mons, you're not a Vishai priest anymore, are you?"

All the moisture evaporated from Qown's throat. He stood very straight and stared at the wall with renewed dedication, while his mind floundered and slipped under. That wasn't . . . That couldn't be . . .

But did the Vishai faith even exist? Did it even exist when he knew perfectly well that it was all a fraud perpetrated by Relos Var to further his own agenda? Could it be worth continuing to follow if he knew that his church had been built on a foundation of lies? He only worked for Father Zajhera as a front for truly working for Relos Var, and Relos Var didn't demand a vow of chastity.

He only demanded obedience.[5]

Qown wondered if it might be possible to think about something else, anything else. He took a deep breath and attempted to force himself into a state of calm. Anlyr seemed nice. He was certainly brave. And he'd been through a great deal that day. He didn't deserve Qown being upset at him for reasons that ultimately were none of Anlyr's doing. If anything, Qown was just surprised that someone on this side of the Dragonspires would be bold enough to make this sort of advance. In Jorat? Sure. But here . . . ? Maybe this was something that had always existed, though, and Qown had just never been paying attention enough to see it.

Meanwhile, Anlyr had no idea what Qown was thinking, only that he'd stopped smiling and seemed upset. "Hey, forget I said anything. I'll just, uh . . . We'd best not linger, anyway. Not if the high lady really is waiting to interrogate us. That should be fun."

"For certain definitions of fun, I suppose." Qown forced down his heartbeat, slowed his breathing. He could do this. There was, ultimately, nothing at all to be ashamed of, was there? "Let's see what we have to do to find our clothing."

Clothing turned out to be easily acquired. It wasn't Qown's clothing, however, which the attendants had mysteriously lost, even going so far as to claim they never received any robes in the first place. They proved resolutely impervious to any of Qown's attempts to convince them to materialize his original priestly garments. What he was given instead were very plain linen robes that were at least without anything like decoration or pretension—although, in Qown's opinion, they were far too thin. They seemed more like the sort of garments one might wear at a bath, if one intended to stay at the bath and not go out in public. Temporary, placeholder garments. It actually got Qown's hopes up that they might intend on returning his Vishai robes.

Anlyr was given a guard uniform for House D'Mon.

After they'd both changed, they were escorted into a sitting room, where they were served a meal. Qown suspected this was some sort of area for guests—not nearly as nice as what the royals themselves would enjoy, but far better than one might ever expect outside one of the palaces. And then there was the food: saffron-laced butter rice, cooked in a rose-shaped copper pan until seared with a perfect crust, decanted right at the table, and drizzled with a tart cherry sauce; sorshi balls—coconut, cherimoya, and sugar apple—dusted with different-colored powdered sugars; hot-spiced dakerra, served a perfect medium rare, along with herbed sag bread for rolls; and, to crown it all, a delicate kevra sorbet.

---

[5] Or, to quote Relos Var from just a short time earlier: *"Become his confidant, become his lover, become his mentor. Whatever you prefer. Just make it work."* I think we can safely say Var was not expecting celibacy.

If Qown found out this was what the servants ate, he was going to seriously reconsider his life choices.

As soon as they were finished, several servants in House D'Talus colors arrived.

"If you would," one of the servants said to Anlyr, "I will escort you back to Lord D'Mon."

Anlyr stood. "Yes, that would be fantastic. Thank you."

Qown waited a moment, but the guard left with the servant behind him, and nobody had indicated he should follow. He stood up, intending on possibly following, anyway, when one of the other servants turned to him. "If you would come with us, please."

"Where are we going?" Qown asked.

"The temple," the man answered as if that did in fact explain anything.

It very much did not. It especially did not as Qown exited into one of the open areas and realized two important facts about this temple. The first was that it was still inside the Rose Palace—very unusual. Most temples would be in the Ivory District in the Capital. Royals seldom kept their own holy sites beyond the occasional chapel.

The second important piece of information was that this was a temple dedicated to Caless, goddess of sex.

"Oh no," Qown said, turning around.

But House D'Talus servants seemed to expect that and found it amusing. One of them grinned. "It's fine! Lady D'Talus wants to talk to you, that's all."

Qown stepped back. "Lady D'Talus is in there? In a temple to Caless?" He felt a spike of dread tear through him. Because it wasn't the fact that Caless was the goddess of sex that made him feel chilled.

It was that he had an odd sort of connection to Caless, who was Suless's daughter. Once, that wouldn't have meant anything to him, but once, he thought Suless was just a long-dead remnant of half-forgotten god-king tales. The idea of god-queens being real and horrible and perfectly capable of ruining lives was much more believable now than it had once been. And unlike Suless, whom everyone had long believed dead, Caless was very much alive and reputed to be every bit as wicked as her mother. Wicked, in this instance, having all kinds of nefarious sexual connotations as well as moral ones.

"Sometimes, yes," the man said. "Now please come along."

He forced himself back under control, reminding himself that this was what Relos Var had asked him to do, and it would look odd for him to refuse. The temple itself was strangely lovely, a small building of lacework, carved stone, and orchid flowers, with architectural elements that suggested sexuality without openly depicting anything lewd or obscene.

A priest came to meet them at the door. He wore his head shaved bald and had a line of gold earrings piercing each ear. His eyes were lined with black kohl, and he wore an agolé with no garment underneath save for extremely baggy kef, leaving his well-muscled chest bare. At his belt, he wore a long, curved knife.

"Ah, so here's my victim," the man said.

Qown stopped.

The priest started laughing. "Oh, I'm so sorry, I couldn't help myself. I bet you thought I was going to ask if you're a virgin next. The look on your face is priceless. I'm Aryahal. I'm going to help you with your disguise."

Qown blinked. "I'm sorry. My what?"

"Come forward. Let me look at you." The priest made a shooing motion to the servants who had escorted Qown. "A disguise. Something about having made enemies recently and you shouldn't look so much like exactly what you are. You very much do look like a priest. Such soulful eyes. I bet you could convince a scorpion to confess its sins." He frowned, pausing thoughtfully. "Are you . . . are you Vishai?" He seemed faintly incredulous.

"I'm, uh . . . yes?" Qown wondered if he could possibly make a run for it.

"I thought you might be." The priest gestured toward one of the low couches. "Have a seat. We should talk."

Qown moved over and sat down, feeling uncomfortable and strange. He wondered where Galen was and was honestly tempted to go run somewhere to use Worldhearth to find him. The only problem was that searching through the Rose Palace was a bit like staring into the sun—there were so many heat sources, it tended to make everything blur together.

"You pay a license fee to House D'Mon, yes?" Aryahal asked.

"Well, I used to—"

The priest held up his hands. "The priests of Caless don't tend to have the same relationship with House D'Mon that Vishai priests do, but that's only because House D'Jorax and House D'Mon have been feuding for the better part of the last three hundred years over which of them should claim us. House D'Jorax because Caless is inaccurately grouped under 'entertainment' or House D'Mon because body modifications might be considered 'healing.' So while our orders have rarely crossed paths, it might be accurate to say that your church and mine annoy all the same people."

Qown started to protest, but then stopped. He frowned. "Inaccurately grouped . . . ? Caless is the goddess of sex, the goddess of . . . uh . . ." He knew he was blushing, but couldn't stop himself. "Prostitutes."

Aryahal's lips turned downward. "Caless is the goddess of love," he corrected. "And love is not an emotion that the Royal Houses have ever found useful. Sex, on the other hand, is a tradable commodity." He drew himself up. "But that's not important. What is important is that I have been asked to provide you any physical alterations to your appearance that you might desire. You saved the daughter of the high lady, and as a result, she is feeling generous. Anything you like. Eye color, skin, anything. Always hated your nose? We can fix that."

Qown stared at the man. He knew enough about healing spells to know how such things might be performed, but he knew of no method for doing so that wouldn't be incredibly, intensely, unbelievably painful.

"Thank you, but I don't need any of that."

Which is when a woman's voice snapped, "You stupid boy, it's not about what you want. It's about saving my daughter's life."

Qown turned in his seat and then fought not to let his mouth drop open. Standing behind him, at the entrance to the temple, was a stunning woman dressed in red ombré silks, with red hair—scarlet red, crimson red, not any natural color—piled up high on her head before falling back behind her like a red cloak. Despite her appearance, she struck him as being like the Rose Palace itself—smooth, made of steel, and full of thorns. The only thing about her that wasn't some shade or tone of red was a blue crystal she wore nestled in her cleavage—a rough-cut piece of indigo gemstone set in a lavish gold cradle crafted to look like flames.[6]

The priest was on his feet immediately, bowing. "My lady."

High Lady D'Talus sailed into the room, the transparent layered silks of her dress unfurling behind her as she walked. "I'm sending my daughter and her husband into hiding for a few weeks while we attempt to see if we can find a diplomatic solution to this mess. But that does me no good at all if the very identifiable Vishai priest whom my son-in-law insists is coming along with him still looks the same as the man that Gerisea D'Mon managed to get a good, hard look at. Her assassins will find you, and then her assassins will find Galen and Sheloran. Unacceptable. So. You will change your appearance. You will be in disguise. You will keep your head down. You will stay out of trouble." She gave Qown a searching gaze. "Am I understood?"

Qown met her eyes and then had to fight not to flinch. Her eyes weren't D'Talus red. They were red like Janel's—red and orange and gold, like a flame. Then he remembered she was waiting on an answer. "Yes, my lady."

She frowned. "Honestly, I don't even understand why he's bothering." Then her hand lashed out, far faster than Qown would have expected, and grabbed him by the chin. She turned his head to the side, then back again. "There's nothing wrong with your bone structure. Reasonably good symmetry. Your skin's a bit loose. It makes you look older than you are. Were you starved?"

Qown's eyes widened. "I . . . I was, uh . . . I spent a few years with people who didn't really eat much other than meat, and I don't eat meat, so . . . I lost a lot of weight."

"And you haven't gained it back since?"

"No, I . . . My studies keep me busy. I forget to eat." Which was mostly true, although it was really that when he used Worldhearth, it was far too easy to ignore the needs of his physical body—including hunger.

"You're malnourished," she announced. "And it's just as unhealthy to starve yourself as it is to overeat. Assuming overeating was the issue and not a metabolic imbalance, which I'm more inclined to believe. Fix that, Aryahal. I want his skin looking like he's bathed in ass's milk and roses every day of his life."

"Yes, my lady."

She continued to study Qown even as she removed her hand from his jaw. "Give him hair; that's the easiest change. Striking hair, so people notice that first. Oh, and change his eye color."

"That's very kind, but I don't—" But they weren't listening to Qown.

"D'Mon blue?" Aryahal asked.

"Tempting, given most people don't know how careful Darzin D'Mon was

---

[6] Yes, for those keeping track: that would indeed be the Stone of Shackles. While Kihrin did destroy it, it reformed, as no one had simultaneously slain its matching dragon, Rol'amar.

to not flood the world with Ogenra, but people would question why he's not running off to present himself. Any D'Mon Ogenra out there who's not an idiot is going to be showing up and asking for formal admission to the house, no matter how embarrassing their background. No, make it gold. The way Palnyr D'Kaje goes through concubines, it's a wonder half the Lower Circle isn't yellow-eyed."

"Is that—is that really necessary?" Qown asked, starting to feel thoroughly horrified.

"Yes," Lady D'Talus answered harshly. "It really is."

"I thought you wanted me to be unnoticed, though? Isn't it going to look weird when a blue-eyed royal and a yellow-eyed royal are spending time with each other?"

The corner of her mouth quirked. "My son-in-law tells me that you can do a trick with writing in light, yes?"

Qown swallowed and nodded, feeling irritably betrayed that Galen D'Mon had told someone else about the witchgift he'd revealed in confidence. But that wasn't the real problem. The real problem was that impersonating a royal was a capital offense, which this woman undoubtedly knew. "Yes."

"Perfect for the witchgift of a lamplighter's guild reject slumming in the Lower Circle then. Yes, that will do nicely." She pointed to the priest. "Hair, eyes, skin, raise the cheekbones a bit, fix his teeth. Don't forget his nails. Bring him to the others when you're finished."

The priest nodded. Qown fought down his panic and stared at his hands, feeling ugly and embarrassed. He'd never paid attention to what he looked like. It had never mattered.

Lady D'Talus turned to leave. Indeed, Qown thought that she had and didn't realize that wasn't the case until she spoke again, much softer. "Who's done this to you, Qown? Who twisted you like this?"

He startled and stared back at her, wide-eyed.

Lady D'Talus stood at the doorway, and the expression on her face was not the haughty arrogance that it had been just a few minutes before. She did, however, look angry.

"I'm sorry? No one's . . . no one's hurt me." He refused to think of Relos Var, of how the wizard had gaeshed him. That had been for his protection, because the alternative would have meant his death.

She scowled. "Do you know what you should be doing right now?"

"No, I–"

"You should be telling me to go fuck myself."

He swallowed. "Oh no, Your Highness. You're a royal–"

She waved that away. "I'm a royal who's ordering Aryahal to change your bone structure, your muscles, your eyes. And you know that's going to hurt. You know just how much that will hurt. You're not my slave. You're not Galen's slave. You're a free man who's known Galen D'Mon for less than a day. You shouldn't be meekly submitting to treatment like this from anyone. You should be walking out that door and saying, 'I quit,' because no one has the right to do this to you against your will. But you're not. Why?"

"I was asked to—I mean, you said it would endanger—oh stars." He found himself floundering. He was supposed to have some sort of smooth lie for this, right? Some sort of justification for why this was important enough to him to make it worth his while to put up with this treatment. Something that wasn't "Because my master, Relos Var, ordered me to stay by Galen's side and earn his trust, and so that's what I have to do even if it means letting you change what I look like when I see myself in a mirror."

Lady D'Talus cocked her head and studied him as she stepped back toward him. "You Vishai talk a lot about love and selflessness. How important it is to love others, sacrifice for others, put the happiness of others before your own. But do you know what I have learned in all my years? And don't let my appearance fool you. I'm older than I look. I've learned that all that sounds sweet but means very little if you've never learned to love yourself. You are allowed—no, you are entitled—to think of your own health and safety first. Someone has taught you that you aren't worth the same love you would give a stranger. That someone deserves to be slapped quite hard."

Qown didn't have any idea what to say. He found himself blinking back tears and wondering just who the hell this woman was and how she had managed to just . . . dismantle him . . . so easily.

Lady D'Talus's expression softened, just a little. "I've known far too many like you, and you never last long. The world grinds you to pieces." She gestured, not at Qown but behind him, to the priest. "All right. We're done here."

"You weren't serious about doing all that, then?" Qown asked.

"Oh no, you silly child. I'm still saving your life, whether you want me to or not." Lady D'Talus told him. "But there's no law that says you have to be awake for it."

Aryahal stepped up behind Qown and set his hands against his temples. Everything turned to the softest velvet, wrapped inside a veil of sleep.

19: Make It Darker

Kihrin's story
Inside Vol Karoth's prison

"Can we run?" Janel whispered. I didn't know whether to be relieved or deeply worried that she wasn't even considering fighting, but then again, Vol Karoth had pretty handily demonstrated how futile fighting was.

"You two should," I said. "But the closer he gets to me, the harder it is—" I paused and bit my lip. "We can feel each other." He was a dark stain nestled up right against my heart, heavy and numb.

You might as well come out. I know you're here.

"We're not leaving you," Teraeth whispered.

"And how much good are you going to do if you stay?" I knew, knew, just from looking at both of them that Teraeth was right; neither was going to leave me. Which meant that I either needed to run—which we'd already established wasn't going to work—or . . .

I jumped out of one of the windows.

Teraeth and Janel both cursed behind me. I'd certainly not won myself any points for repeating exactly the same thing they'd just revealed they were furious at me for doing previously. I just didn't see any alternative. None of us were powerful enough to take on Vol Karoth.

The jump down would have killed me if this had been the real world, but lucky me, this wasn't. So I landed softly in the middle of the street and hoped it hadn't been too obvious where I'd come from.

Vol Karoth whirled in my direction.

I stood up and brushed myself off. "I'll make you a deal," I said.

Vol Karoth paused. The whole world seemed to pause, and given the nature of what the world was, perhaps that was even true.

A deal? What kind of deal?

I was stalling.

There was no plan. Or rather, the plan had fallen apart when I'd realized to my horror that Vol Karoth wasn't going to be some small child I could kiss on the forehead and make all the hurts go away. Vol Karoth was as bad as Relos Var, as bad as Xaltorath—but the difference was that Vol Karoth was here and I couldn't avoid him.

I had to figure out a solution.

Scratch that. Thurvishar, Teraeth, and Janel. They had to find a solution. Clearly, I wasn't contributing anything useful.

"I'll surrender," I offered, ignoring the gasp that signaled that those two idiots hadn't used this time to their advantage to escape, "but only if you can prove that you're right. That love is a lie. That friendship is meaningless. That people will always desert you. But"—I raised a finger—"you can't lie. No making shit up. It has to have really happened. And"—this was the most important part—"you have to agree not to attack anyone else. No trying to kill my friends."

And you expect me to believe you'll just . . . give up? I'm not a fool.

"We both know what you want, and we both know it will be much easier to obtain if I don't fight you. You win, you prove to me that you're right? Why would I fight after that?" I swallowed down thick, sticky despair. "Why would I even care enough to do that? You won't have to worry about whether or not my word is good. I won't want to do anything but give up."

Vol Karoth cocked his head. At some point, the sword in his hand had vanished. I hadn't noticed.

And if you win?

"Let me take over," I said. "You let me do what I need to."

This time, his voice was quieter, but much sharper. *And you trust me to honor such a bargain? That would make you the fool.*

"If you won't do it, then we're right back to where we started." I gestured around the cold, vacant remains of a dead city. "Chasing each other around, fighting. But I think we're both going to get pretty bored with that, so I'm offering an alternative."

Like I said, stalling.

Stalling for what, though, I didn't know.

Fine. We have a deal, and it's my turn.

The world changed.

Qown's reaction
The Lighthouse at Shadrag Gor
Right after his memory at the Rose Palace

Qown lunged at Talon as soon as his vision cleared. "You! You—! How could you!" He had no idea what he would have done if he'd actually succeeded at reaching the monster. He didn't have any weapons except a bag of lentils, which sprayed—oh, just everywhere. But he didn't think he'd ever been this angry or embarrassed in his entire life. It was just awful. All of it. Awful.

And it wasn't even a lie. Talon hadn't changed a thing.

The mimic laughed as she bounded out of the way, dodging around one of the couches. "Oh, Qown, sweetheart! I was helping you. Didn't you want someone to prove you weren't trying to seduce Galen? But now Galen knows you're far too much of a fumbling panicky mess to ever do something like that on purpose. You did it entirely by accident!"

Qown stood there, panting, nearly growling. He refused to look at Galen.

But that didn't change the fact that Galen was in the room, that he had heard, felt, seen, experienced the whole thing. "Talon," Galen said. "Your name is Talon, right?"

Talon stopped smirking like a child that had just been caught sneaking papers in class. "Uh . . . yes. Weren't you paying attention? I think we've established that by now."

"Okay, Talon. Mind leaving my healer the fuck alone?" Galen kept his voice level. It somehow managed to be simultaneously polite and intimidating.

"Uh . . ." Talon scrunched up her nose. "Sure?"

Qown dared to sneak a peek then. Galen wore a pleasant smile and a kind expression that showed nothing of what was roiling underneath. Except that smile was just a little too bright, just a bit too forced. He held himself with too much tension. Qown had grown comfortable enough reading the man to know that underneath that mask, Galen was furious.

Meanwhile, Talon had the strangest expression on her face. She gazed at Galen with fond pride, like her baby had taken his first steps. Qown frowned at her. Why . . . ? He wagged a finger between them, his own problems forgotten for the moment. "How do you two know each other?"

"She ate Kihrin," Galen reminded him.

"Oh, that's not the only person–" Talon shrugged, looking almost embarrassed. Almost. "I worked for your father, Galen. Truthfully, I've known you for years."

"As who?" Galen demanded.

"You so do not want to know," someone muttered.[1]

"Let's not," Senera interrupted before Talon–or anyone else–could answer. "I have zero interest in watching that fun little drama play out. That's not why we're here."

Which told Qown that the answer would very much have been something Galen would've hated. He decided not to push it. Not right then.

"Fine. Let's go over why we're here one more time, then," Kalindra said. "Because I don't understand how any of this"–she gestured around the small room–"is helping Kihrin. That's why we're here, right? Not to force us to share our memories and private thoughts. This isn't some sort of sacred confessional."

Sheloran began sweeping up lentils. "For that matter, all of us can't be so pivotal to his failure or victory. I only met Kihrin once." She pulled out a pot and started measuring more beans again, set a fire going with a snap of her fingers.

Kalindra was still pacing back and forth, but finally she stopped. "I'm out. Just . . . I'm out. I don't want any part of this. I'm not going to be any help to Kihrin. Go ahead and open up a gate, Senera. Send me home."

Senera sighed. "We can't leave."

Kalindra leaned over the table. "Why? You explained that I won't be able to come back. Fine. I don't *want* to come back. Just let me go."

Senera stood up. "Perhaps a demonstration might make this clearer."

She did the same trick she'd done before, the one that had Qown squinting because–yes, that was *his* writing spell she'd somehow modified to

[1] Talon killed and took the place of Galen's mother, Alshena.

speed up the gate creation process. She pulled up the glyphs, let them linger in the air for a second as lines of yellow energy, and then pushed out until the shapes hit the wall and folded in on themselves in the swirl of a magical portal opening.

Except . . . this looked wrong. A rainbow sheen of colors lay over the open entrance, thick enough to make it difficult to see what was on the other side. Qown dropped the herbs he'd started chopping and walked over. "That—are you causing that?"

Senera scoffed. "No, of course not. I told you I linked Shadrag Gor with Vol Karoth's prison. Come on, Qown, you're not this stupid."

Qown flushed and started to protest, but then what she'd just said sank in. If she'd linked those two sites, yes, it meant time had probably been affected. Faster for Vol Karoth, slower for Shadrag Gor. How much slower was an interesting question, but it also meant that Vol Karoth—and Kihrin—had access to Shadrag Gor. What did that mean for the wards?

"We're inside Vol Karoth's prison too," Qown said. "So we're trapped by the same ward crystals keeping him locked up."

"By the wards powered by the Eight Immortals, yes," Senera said. "Until we figure out how to help Kihrin defeat Vol Karoth, Vol Karoth is freed, or both. I didn't say we shouldn't leave, I said we *can't*." She gave Kalindra a cool look. "You're not going anywhere. None of us—"

The world changed.

Xivan's memory
The Upper Circle of the Capital City, Quur
Six days after the Battle of the Well of Spirals

"Well, I have to say it's looked better," Talea commented as they both stood in front of the smoking ruin.

Upon arriving by Senera's gate to the Upper Circle, Xivan had made her way over to a particular section near the center set aside for visiting dignitaries from around the empire. Yor, in particular, had a house at the duke's disposal under the assumption he'd use it when visiting the Capital. He never had.

Unfortunately, at some point in the last two weeks, the entire edifice had burned to the ground. Xivan wasn't even sure anyone had bothered to put out the fire—she suspected it had eventually died down from lack of fuel. Some of the embers in the ashes still glowed red.

Xivan raised an eyebrow at Talea. "You say that like you've been here before."

Talea shrugged and took the older woman's hand. "I say that like it's a smoking hole in the ground, but as a matter of fact, I have been here before." She shrugged. "My first owner's town house is about a mile"—she pointed—"that way."

Xivan studied her carefully. "Would you like to see if it's still there? We could set it on fire. I bet no one will notice. Half this city seems to have burned down in the last month."

Talea smiled, clearly delighted. "Aw, that's so sweet. But it's fine. My old owner had his throat ripped out. I'm good."[2]

Xivan had a moment of . . . concern. Two armed women walking alone would be fine in many parts of the world, but not here in the Capital City. Then she remembered that they were honestly wearing so many furs their gender might not be evident to a casual observer. Talea would overheat soon and need to remove hers. Xivan didn't have to. As long as she didn't draw any attention to herself, most people would assume they were a couple—true enough—and let them be.

And anyone who didn't would have a sword ripped through their liver as Xivan drained their souls.

"But where are we going to stay—" Talea blinked and opened her eyes wide, astonished.

Xivan followed her gaze. The next building over—which had not burned to the ground—was the Joratese embassy. Xivan had always thought it looked a great deal fancier than the Yoran house, but that was probably because it had been built by Atrin Kandor, and the Yoran house had been built by Gendal, as an afterthought, and probably to the barest acceptable specifications. In any event, an old woman was walking up to the building, baskets in hand, annoyed and muttering to herself. She must have been Joratese, because she had parti-color skin, in her case, black and white splattered over each other like wet paint.

Talea began waving her hand and crossing the street before Xivan could stop her. "Excuse me? Excuse me! Is your name Dorna?"

The old woman stopped. "I didn't do it. You can't prove a thing."

Talea started grinning happily. Xivan sighed and followed.

"You're Dorna, right?" Talea put a hand to her chest. "I'm Talea. I'm a friend of Janel's. I mean, we both are. She's told me so much about you, I feel like I know you." She gestured back toward Xivan. "This is Xivan Kaen."

"Oh?" The old woman narrowed an eye and scrutinized them both. Then she nearly dropped the basket. "Oh! Oh, I know who you are. And you—" She paused, finger still pointed at Xivan. She tucked the finger back into her fist. "You're taller than I thought ya'd be. Just as scary, though." Dorna tilted her head toward the burned Yoran house. "I'm guessing y'all need a place to put up for the night? Any friends of Janel's is welcome here, of course. Especially if you have news about what the little beast's been up to. She don't write, and I'm about ready to give her a piece of my mind over the matter. Come in, come in, might as well take your tack off and make yourselves comfortable. I was fixing to start a tamarane shield roast going.[3] If you've never tried it, you're in for a treat."

---

[2] By a Joratese slave, as I recall, who then took her own life. For a culture so obsessed with dominance and submission, the Joratese are remarkably intolerant of slavery.

[3] One of the eight styles of cooking meat in Joratese cuisine. The Joratese don't often eat meat, but they have a highly codified culinary tradition in contrast to the typical Quuros manner of cooking meat, which comes in precisely two categories: roasted or boiled.

Dorna opened the door and walked inside, clearly expecting them to follow.

Talea grinned as she turned back to Xivan. She flipped the silver coin in her hand and caught it with a laugh. "This was so unbelievably lucky!" She turned to follow Dorna inside.

Xivan bit her lip and frowned.

"Yes," she said. "It really was."

They spent the rest of the evening talking to Dorna and, perhaps more interestingly, to Ninavis Theranon, who was in the Capital to petition the High Council to acknowledge her claim as Duchess of Jorat. Xivan thought Hell would catch on fire before that happened, but she admired the attempt. And both Ninavis and Dorna proved anxious to hear any news about Janel. They were so persistent in the matter that finally, Xivan relented and told them as much as she knew.

But she didn't know what to say when it came time to describe the Battle of the Well of Spirals.

"I–" She grimaced.

"Who won?" Ninavis asked.

"No one," Xivan said. "We all lost. Argas is dead. Thaena's dead. Taja and Galava too–"

"What?" Dorna stared at her, open-mouthed. "*Galava?*"

Ninavis frowned at the old woman's obvious distress. "I thought you were an angel of Tya."

"Oh, I am, foal, I am." Dorna looked absolutely heartbroken. "But Galava–oh sweet fields. There's no Festival of the Turning Leaves without Galava. There's no–" Her voice broke, and she wiped her eyes. "Anyone in Jorat who's ever prayed to have their body match their souls was praying to Galava. And she always listened. Without her, that's all gone. Gone! Oh, I just weep for those poor dears who won't ever have the same chances–the same choices–that I did. That Aroth did.[4] Oh, it's not fair . . ." She made a hand into a fist and slammed it against her thigh. "Xaltorath. I would pull apart every seam that bastard has if I could!"[5]

Xivan wasn't quite sure she understood, but the tears made it obvious enough that whatever it was Galava had been to the Joratese people, it was irreplaceable.

Talea, being Talea, crossed over to where Dorna was sitting and threw her arms around the woman, who broke down crying.

Ninavis gave them both a sad look and walked over to Xivan, clearly meaning to give Dorna some space. "So I'm to understand we're neighbors." She was a lean, leathery woman with a vicious wine-stain birthmark across half her face–or, well, she was Joratese, so it probably wasn't a birthmark in

---

[4] Aroth Malkoessian, a Joratese nobleman to whom Dorna was evidently married at one point. Neither are the sex they were at birth, which evidently caused a rift, as Dorna "runs with mares" exclusively.

[5] Dorna's witchgift is the ability to split or join seams. I've never seen her use any other spell.

the traditional sense.[6] One had only to examine Dorna to realize that normal ideas about skin tones were absolute nonsense in Jorat. Xivan had learned that herself the first time she'd seen Janel take a bath and realized the black "socks" on her arms and legs weren't makeup or affectation but an actual change in skin tone.

"Not neighbors for much longer," Xivan said.

Ninavis tilted her head. "You're not planning to take over as Duchess of Yor?"

Xivan snorted and drank some more of the ara they'd given her. She couldn't get drunk, but the memory of ara was nice. Azhen had been quite fond of the stuff and went to great effort to import it for his use.

So maybe the memory of ara wasn't that nice.

"I've lost any reason I might have ever cared to be Duchess of Yor," Xivan admitted. "Why in all of Hell's frozen fields would I put myself, put Talea, in a position where people who will hate us both for no other reason than our sex and our nationality can plot to kill us at their leisure? Yor doesn't want to be ruled by the Quuros, and at least for my part, the feeling is quite mutual."

"Ah. A pity. I could have used a friendly face when I go before the High Council meetings." Ninavis paused. "Tyentso counts, but I wouldn't mind knowing one of the other dukes is on my side. But I understand your position. Truthfully, if you'd told me six months ago that I'd be standing here today, I'd have told you to go fuck yourself. I'm a thief and an outlaw, and I never thought that would see me end up as one of the nobility."

"Funny, sounds to me like you have the perfect qualifications."

Ninavis squinted at her. "You're not noble-born either, are you?"

"Me? *No.* My mother taught sword fighting, and my father was a blade-smith." She smiled ruefully. "It's how they met. She kept coming into the shop asking him to repair her sword until he finally realized she was breaking it on purpose just for the excuse. It's how I met Azhen too. Although he was just commissioning a sword. But he paid extra to be able to watch it being made and so he was in the shop for weeks and . . ." She shrugged. "You?"

"Farmers," Ninavis said. "Farmers going as far back as I know. And now look at us." It wasn't entirely clear if she meant that in the sense of "look how far we've come" or "look how far we've fallen."

Xivan laughed bitterly. "Fate makes fools of us all."

Ninavis raised her glass. "I'll drink to that."

They stayed the night. Ninavis had given them a room to share after Talea made it clear they were a couple, a thing that didn't cause even the slightest bit of eyebrow raising or snide looks. Logically, Xivan hadn't expected it to, given Janel had always claimed her attitudes on sex were common in Jorat, but emotionally was a different matter. Even in Khorvesh, where same-sex pairings between women were considered "just a normal part of growing up," it was generally expected that women would eventually settle down and

---

[6] Actually, she's Marakori, so it is a birthmark in the traditional sense. It just looks unremarkable if one is pretending to be Joratese.

marry a man, as was one's duty. If they were particularly attached to one of their battle sisters, then they'd arrange to marry the same man.

Talea was young enough to still be allowed to play with other women without raising eyebrows. Xivan was not.

And then there was the other issue, the one that they had been studiously avoiding discussing, which was quite simply Xivan's status as a vampire, forced to feed off souls to survive. No matter how alive she looked or felt just after feeding, a great many of life's pleasures simply didn't exist for her anymore. Sex was one of those pleasures. She was perfectly willing to make Talea feel good—delighted in it, even—but she knew it bothered Talea deeply that she couldn't reciprocate. And she could already see, even after only a few weeks, that Talea was starting to withdraw. Starting to not push the matter. Knowing Talea, she was probably starting to worry that she was being too selfish. That it wasn't fair to Xivan. Talea wouldn't want to be a bother.

It made Xivan angry. Sometimes, Talea was just too much. Too good, too kind, too selfless. And while Xivan loved her for it, it was always a reminder of everything Xivan knew she was not.

Because Xivan was not kind, not good, and she was very, very selfish.

That evening after they had said their goodbyes and gone to their room, Xivan pushed Talea up against the wall and kissed her as though she were twenty years younger. As if she were still that naïve Khorveshan girl so full of want for the person she'd so loved she'd been stupid enough to follow the man all the way back to the frozen hell that is Yor and then too stubborn to leave.

When she paused, Talea's eyes were dark with lust and her lips flushed and swollen. "What—you don't have to do—"

"If I did something you didn't like, you'd tell me to stop, wouldn't you?"

Talea blinked, surprised, blushing. "Of course."

Xivan stared at the girl. That was part of the problem, wasn't it? She was a *girl*, at least compared to Xivan, who was literally old enough to be Talea's mother. Talea had her whole future ahead of her, a brilliant, shining future because Talea was such a brilliant, shining gem of a girl. She should have lovers and adventures and all the opportunities that came with being young and beautiful. What did Xivan have?

The grave.

Everyone Xivan loved had been rewarded for it with a personal escort across the Second Veil.

"I think you're lying," Xivan whispered. "I think you'd let me do anything I wanted. Anything at all."

A flicker of fear crossed Talea's face and then confusion. "Xivan, why—"

Xivan grabbed Talea by the hair and dragged her over to the bed. When they got there, she pulled down until Talea's neck and back formed the most beautiful arc, until she was in danger of falling backward. Then Xivan began undressing her, working off the fastenings and buttons with one hand while she latched her teeth to Talea's neck, bruising that lovely skin with bite marks, biting down until her brown flesh turned white and then red. Marks that would bruise. Marks that would hurt.

But Talea gasped and moaned and most certainly didn't tell Xivan to stop.

Once she had Talea disrobed—or at least disrobed enough—Xivan threw her back on the bed and was on her like a rabid wolf. She pinched Talea's nipples hard and kneaded her hips, dug her fingers into Talea's soft flesh with viselike force. And while Talea was still recovering from this absolute onslaught, Xivan pushed two fingers into her sex, thrusting deep and fast. She added a third, and then a fourth and finally Talea started to look uncomfortable. Finally, the moans sounded less like pleasure than pain. Finally, the look in Talea's eyes was the look Xivan deserved.

"Xivan, please—"

But Xivan didn't stop. She put her other hand around Talea's throat, not hard enough to truly suffocate, but impossible to ignore.

"Stop it!" Talea said and then rolled, kicking Xivan away and landing in a crouch on the floor. "Xivan! What the fuck is wrong with you!"

Xivan stared at her for a second, then sat down on the edge of the bed. She was still fully dressed. She hadn't taken her clothes off at all.

"Everything," Xivan said. "You surprised me here, Talea. I really didn't think you'd stop me." She absently wiped her hand off on the linens and wondered at how numb she felt.

Far worse than normal.

"I've been pawed at by enough people who only wanted to make me bleed, thank you very much." Talea started picking up her clothes. "What is wrong? Talk to me."

"You're too good," Xivan whispered.

"What?" Talea stopped and stared at her. "That doesn't even make sense."

"Why do I get to keep you?" Xivan wasn't looking at Talea. She was staring at a wall. "Why do I get to keep this perfect, beautiful girl when I couldn't even save Azhen or Exidhar? When I couldn't even kill Suless? Why do I get to be happy with you when I don't deserve happiness?" She realized she was shaking, and she couldn't stop.

"Oh," Talea said. "Never mind. It does make sense." She dropped to her knees in front of Xivan, pretending not to notice when Xivan flinched as Talea touched her legs. "Love, you were never going to save Azhen or Exidhar. Never."

Xivan Kaen's jaw clenched. "Don't—"

"No, hear me out. Azhen was going mad. It wasn't a matter of if he was going to get himself killed but *when*. He'd just ordered Janel's and Qown's executions. You don't think Relos Var was going to kill him for that? Oh, Var would've been sad about it, but that wouldn't have stopped him."

Xivan paused, feeling suddenly light-headed. She'd never thought about that.

"There's only so many ways that was ever going to play out," Talea argued. "A dozen other paths that all lead to Azhen dead. The probabilities are just . . . so obvious. Suless could just as easily have killed everyone in the palace that day, and then your granddaughter would be dead too. And if everything else had gone your way—everything—Azhen Kaen still would have died fighting

Morios. That was the whole point of having that spear, right? That was the best outcome you could hope for, because Azhen couldn't win. Once Suless took him, he was a dead man. She wasn't going to let you rescue Azhen. It's not your fault that your husband and son are dead."

"I couldn't kill Suless," Xivan said.

"Aren't we still here to kill Suless?" Talea reminded her. "Isn't that why we're here in the Capital? Did we fail at that before we even tried?"

Xivan swallowed and forced herself to look at Talea, really look at her. She reached out and touched the woman's cheek. "I hurt you," she said.

"Yes, you did," Talea agreed. "I would appreciate it if you never did it again."

"Or else?" Xivan said.

Talea closed her eyes, so quickly it might have been mistaken for a blink. "Or else no matter how much I love you, I'll leave." Anger flashed through her lovely brown eyes. "I didn't fall in love with the kind of woman who would . . . do that. What were you doing, Xivan? Were you trying to convince me that I'm too good for you? Were you trying to drive me off?"

"Something like that." Xivan stared at her hands. "Everyone I love dies, Talea."

"And someday I will too. That doesn't mean you should cut yourself early, just because you know there's a blade with your name on it out there somewhere."

Xivan screwed her eyes shut and wished she could cry. She so badly wanted to cry. Or maybe scream. Maybe both. "I'm sorry."

Sorry for so many reasons. Because she wasn't done hurting Talea, and she knew it.

Gods, it would have been so much easier if Talea had stormed out of there, vowing to never come back. Although, truthfully it would just have been easier for Xivan. Talea would never have to know how she'd been betrayed, and now she would learn. Now Xivan would have to watch her eyes as she realized. Although it would all depend on how the meeting went. It would all depend on Lady D'Talus's price.

"Sorry isn't enough. Those are just words."

Xivan opened her eyes again. "I know. But right now, they're all I have. I know they're not enough."

Talea stared at her, not smiling at all. "They certainly won't be if you ever treat me like that again." Then she stood up and took Xivan's hands, pulling her up too. "Now come to bed and hold me until I fall asleep. Then you can slip out and go find your next meal. In this town? It should be the easiest one you've ever hunted."

Xivan kissed her on the forehead, then on the cheeks, and finally on the lips. Talea helped her undress and then climbed into bed with her. Xivan was struck once again by the knowledge that it must feel exactly like sleeping with a corpse. Talea never acted like it did. Not even once.

"And I'm not perfect," Talea muttered, head nestled up against Xivan's chest. "How dare you say that."

Xivan didn't smile. "Yes, you are. Now go to sleep."

The next morning, they said their goodbyes and left for the estate of House D'Talus. Knowing that it would look strange if they walked, Xivan hired a carriage to deliver them and left a message at the front that the Duchess of Yor wished to speak to Lady D'Talus. It would have been an odd, almost unprecedented request—the Royal Houses and the dominions rarely interacted publicly—but at least Xivan was in a position where she could make it. This would have been a much more difficult task had she been trying to gain such an audience with no title at all.

True to her suspicions, after a minor wait, both she and Talea were ushered inside and taken to a sitting area.

Xivan was reminded once again that Talea was probably more used to the Royal Houses than she was, when Xivan found herself the one fighting not to gawk. In contrast, Talea seemed bored by the opulence around them.

They waited nearly an hour, which Xivan didn't take as an insult. She was the one who had dropped in with no warning. Who knew what the high lady was doing, what she was interrupting? She was lucky the woman was deigning to see them at all. And House D'Talus had not been inhospitable—servants had brought out tea and a light breakfast.

"Are they just taking our word for it?" Talea asked as she grabbed yet another biscuit.

"What?" Xivan stopped staring at the door for long enough to face her.

"Are they just taking our word for it?" she repeated. "That you are in fact the Duchess of Yor? Seems a bit trusting, don't you think?"

Xivan frowned. Yes, it did. And Royal Houses did not have a reputation for being trusting.

As she was about to reply, the door at the end of the room opened, and a woman entered, flanked by several servants. It seemed impossible that this wasn't the high lady—her gown was a luscious affair of embroidered ruby silks not quite as red as her hair. The jewels on her arms and waist might have been sold to feed and house an army.

And she wore the Stone of Shackles around her neck. At least, Xivan assumed it was the Stone of Shackles. It matched the description.

Behind the high lady stood a pair of servants—beautiful, strangely androgynous, dressed almost as gorgeously as their mistress but in clothing that clearly afforded them far greater freedom of movement. Even though they were beautiful enough to be velvet boys (or girls? Xivan kept changing her mind about which term was more appropriate), they struck her as more likely bodyguards. And behind those two were a half-dozen men who clearly were House D'Talus guards, complete with weapons and shimmering red gold mail shirts.

"Your Grace," High Lady D'Talus said, "to what do I owe this most unexpected visit?" Her red eyes flickered from Xivan to Talea and back again. Xivan felt recognized, and she wondered where the high lady might have ever run into her. House D'Talus had not been one of the houses her husband had ever courted—far too much of D'Talus's wealth and success had come from supporting the empire for it to ever be interested in its overthrow. It had always seemed like a nonstarter.

"Your Majesty," Xivan responded, bowing. "I was hoping you might indulge me while discussing a sale. I am most interested in arranging for a particular purchase."

"I see." Lady D'Talus waved to her people. The guards promptly retreated, although Xivan didn't doubt they would manifest again in seconds if the royal needed it. The two personal bodyguards took up positions on opposite sides of the room, still as statues. "Yes, I have a curiosity I'd like your help in satisfying as well."

Xivan paused. "You do?"

"Please sit." Lady D'Talus gestured to the couches. "There's no reason for us to be uncomfortable."

Xivan realized she was in danger of making a faux pas, not to the high lady but to her lover. "My apologies, this is—"

"Talea Ferandis. I know."

Xivan felt a chill. This was not starting out the way she'd expected.

"I'm sorry?" Talea said. "What did you just call me?"

"Ferandis. It's your family name." Her gaze lost a little of its chill, which it had managed to convey even though her eyes were red as fire. "Did no one ever tell you?"

Talea stared at the woman, open-mouthed. "I—"

"Ah, my apologies. I thought you were aware." One of her two personal servants materialized and poured the high lady a cup of tea. She took it, nodded to her servant, then addressed Xivan. "I was wondering if you might be able to tell me about a very odd suit of armor your husband ordered. Pure shanathá, lined with lead. Incredibly expensive. All the paperwork suggests my husband signed off on the fabrication, but he didn't. Our records do suggest it was delivered—to Yor."

Xivan's chill turned into something else. The woman had neatly wrested control of the conversation from the very start, throwing Xivan and Talea both off-balance. They hadn't even brought up the reason why they were here yet, and already they were approaching the matter from a position of debt and quite possibly an accusation of criminal fraud.

Xivan scowled and tried to remember if she knew anything about her husband ordering any armor. Her memory came up blank.[7]

"If the duke ever commissioned such a set of armor from House D'Talus," Xivan said carefully, "I'm afraid any knowledge of it—and probably the armor itself—was destroyed along with my husband."

"Ah. So that rumor is true."

Xivan nodded. "It is. He was murdered by Suless."

The high lady's response was unexpected. She seemed to tense, her nostrils flaring ever so slightly, and abruptly set down her cup, so the ceramic made a loud snap against the tabletop. "So that rumor is true as well. I never quite believed it."

---

[7] This was in fact the armor Qown ordered for Janel to use to protect herself from the razarras ore in the catacombs of the Ice Demesne.

Xivan frowned. "That Suless murdered my husband and my son?"

"No, that she was still alive."

"Apparently, she was—" Xivan's mouth twisted. "My husband was keeping her as a slave."

"And Cherthog?"

Xivan blinked. "I'm sorry?"

"Where was Cherthog in all this? The God-King of Winter. He was the one who held Suless's gaesh originally. Was his death also a fabrication?"

"I . . . I honestly don't know. I assume he's dead."[8]

"We can only hope," Lady D'Talus said.

The high lady was perfectly still, studying Xivan with those red eyes. *Strange,* Xivan thought. Those eyes really did look the same as Janel's, not quite the right color for House D'Talus, which would have been more of a pure crimson. Yet nothing else about her was reminiscent of Janel. This woman was all sensuality and delicacy, her face and clothing more appropriate for a velvet house than a battlefield.

Lady D'Talus raised her hand. "I need the room. I'll let you know when to come back."

To Xivan's surprise, the two bodyguards left. She would have expected someone to protest, someone who was under the high lord's authority rather than the high lady's. But if that was the case, Xivan saw no sign of it. The two people cleared out of the room with precise and commendable speed.

When they were gone, Lady D'Talus turned back to Xivan. "Your Grace," the high lady said, "just why are you here?"

"I want to buy the Stone of Shackles from you."

The high lady stared at her and blinked, just once. Then she began to laugh. That noise was best described as unkind and, at worst, mocking.

"Oh," she said. "I don't think so. No."

"I do, though. I have no other motive for being here."

"No," High Lady D'Talus said, waving a hand as she stood. "I mean, my answer is no. My people will show you the way out."

Xivan also stood, feeling angry and panicked. If she had a pulse, it would be racing. "You haven't even heard what I'm offering."

The high lady paused, her expression incredulous. "What could you be offering. Coin? House D'Talus runs the mint. Gems?" She waved a hand. "The dominion of Yor has been the poorest in the empire since it joined. Even Raenena has more wealth.[9] You have nothing I want."

Xivan clenched her fingers. "I'm offering fifty trained war wizards who have no allegiance to the empire, Academy, or any other Royal House." She ignored Talea's shocked gasp.

Lady D'Talus raised an eyebrow. "Fifty?"

"All superlatively trained, all talented at magic. Each one is worth a hundred men."

---

[8] He is. I checked. I assume Suless killed him not long after her escape.

[9] Somewhat disingenuous, since Raenena also has most of the mines. What Raenena lacks is the population to fully exploit it.

"Xivan!" Talea stared in shock.

"Be silent," Xivan told the woman. "If they are mine, then they are also mine to give away." She turned back to High Lady D'Talus. "Fifty wizards–fifty women–no one would ever suspect. And they're yours. Surely that is more useful than a necklace whose only value is encouraging you to make sure the assassin who slays you is pretty?"

"You have fifty trained women, and you're going to sell them to me for a magic rock." Xivan couldn't tell if that was approval or condemnation. "Why do you want the Stone of Shackles so badly? For the same reason Gadrith wanted it? Because you think it can restore your life?"

Xivan blinked. That . . . that hadn't even occurred to her. It also hadn't occurred to her that Lady D'Talus would be able to tell she wasn't alive. "I want it because Suless is not only alive and free, she's become a demon."

For the first time, an expression of fear entered Lady D'Talus's eyes, but that emotion was quickly tucked away.

Xivan continued, "The only way I can deal with a demon is by using something they can't defend against, and the only thing I know of that fits that definition is the Stone of Shackles." Xivan shook her head. "I don't even need it permanently. I'll give it back. You can keep the women. Just let me have it for long enough to kill Suless!"

"What possible reason could you have to think me stupid enough to accept your word?" Lady D'Talus's expression had stopped being something adjacent to friendly. "You'll just give it back? When there is no power in the universe that can compel you to do so?"

Xivan growled, "I am a woman of my word!"

"Are you? Because I think there are fifty women under your authority who might disagree." Lady D'Talus was shorter than Xivan, but she still radiated an awful aura of menace and threat.

Xivan lost her temper. All her plans depended on the whims of some fickle, spoiled brat who would dare to be self-righteous about her Spurned when gods knew how many slaves she owned herself. Hypocrite. At least Xivan had turned her husband's wives into people capable of protecting themselves. At least no one would ever force themselves on those women again. It was probably far better than High Lady D'Talus could say. "They would understand it's a necessary sacrifice if it means I kill Suless!"

The high lady's laughter mocked. "Would they *really*?"

"You have no idea what she's done!"

"I know a great deal better than you."

"How could you possibly know a thing about it? She's been locked up in Yor for longer than you've been alive!"

"Because she's my mother, you stupid little girl!" Lady D'Talus's eyes blazed. "If anyone is going to kill that bitch, it's going to be me!"

Xivan took a moment to process what Lady D'Talus had just said, what it meant. Because it seemed unlikely that she was a witch-mother, and equally unlikely that Lady D'Talus had been, like Janel, singled out for special attention. And as far as Xivan knew, Suless only had one true, biological child . . .

"*Oh fuck,*" Talea said. "You're Caless. You're the god-queen Caless."

"You'd be amazed how many god-kings live in the Royal Houses," Caless said. "If we're going to have to pretend to be mortal, why not do it in style?" The ironic smile fell from her lips then. "But I shouldn't have admitted that."

Xivan felt a spike of panic. "Talea, run."

Talea tried, but the doors slammed shut before she could reach them. Caless reached out her arm. Her eyes flashed blue, and Talea simply fell to the floor as though her legs had stopped working entirely. A second later, Xivan understood that it was something very much like that, as the muscles in her thighs stopped responding. Her legs folded under her.

Footsteps walked toward her, accompanied by the swish of silken fabric sliding against itself.

"I'm not a good person," Caless explained. "Most of the time, I don't pretend to be, but I just want what anyone wants. To protect my family, to live well. And I have tried so hard to make those things happen. I do understand your desire to have revenge against my mother. I don't even think you're wrong to want it. I just don't believe you're strong enough to succeed. The last thing I want is the Stone of Shackles in my mother's hands. Giving it to you would really be almost as good as giving it to her." She grabbed Xivan's head by her knotted locks and pulled her head up to look into her eyes. "But I'm not going to kill you, just because you're not playing at the same level as an immortal god-queen."

Caless's words tasted bitter in Xivan's mouth. Only now did she remember Senera's warning: *Lady D'Talus is in a different class.* Xivan had thought Senera was talking about political connections, consequences, what would happen if the Empire of Quur discovered Xivan had assaulted a high lord's wife.

But no. Senera had meant something far more literal. Relos Var hadn't taken the Stone of Shackles from High Lady D'Talus, because he couldn't—at least not easily, not without a major, massive fight that would draw attention. Of all the gods worshipped in the entire empire, Caless certainly ranked in the top ten. She might not have been as strong as one of the Eight Immortals, but she had a lot of worshippers, and that meant she had a lot of power. And she was one of the very oldest, with only two god-kings who were older: her mother, Suless, and her father, Cherthog.[10]

Xivan had made a horrible mistake.

"Do you know how the Stone of Shackles works?"

"Yes, but you—" Xivan's throat clenched. Caless wasn't talking about the switching of souls. She was talking about gaeshe. Gaeshe that were, thanks to the stone's returned existence, once again possible.

Talea must have realized what she meant as well. Her breath quickened, shuddering against the edge of tears and terror. "Please don't," Talea whispered.

---

[10] Indeed, every other god-king owes their existence to Caless, since she's the one who "let the secret out of the bag" so to speak, and taught her lovers the secret of becoming god-kings.

THE HOUSE OF ALWAYS

"My father owned this Cornerstone for over a thousand years," Caless told Talea. "I know how to use it as few others do. Don't worry. I'll be gentle."

The last thing Xivan remembered was Caless holding the stone around her neck with one hand, and reaching for Xivan's chest with the other, and then nothing but darkness.

20: WHAT THEY CAN'T SAY

Kihrin's story
Inside Vol Karoth's prison

When I came back to myself after Xivan's memory ended, I had two sets of arms linked under my own, and I was being dragged away from the street corner. I wasn't sure where Vol Karoth was. Maybe he'd let us go.

It was my turn, after all.

"Run," Teraeth said.

"I'm trying. Let me go!" I scrambled to recover my feet and my dignity.

"Too slow," Janel muttered, ducked, and lifted me up over her shoulder like I weighed no more than a bag of rice.

"No, wait–" I started to protest, and to my infinite embarrassment was soundly ignored.

Without missing a beat, Janel ran into one of the buildings. This one didn't seem to have been housing originally. The main hallway was wide enough to make it more appropriate as a public space than private residence. Smaller rooms branched off from the main one, with wide cutouts in the walls that might once have held market carts or tables or perhaps even panes of glass.

"Janel, set me down!" I thrashed and tried to slip out of her grip.

She finally tossed me down in a very undignified heap on the ground. I wrestled myself into a sitting position, rested my elbows on my knees, and rubbed a knuckle into my eye. "Janel, what the fuck? What was that?"

"That was me rescuing the idiot who thought any of this was a good idea," Janel growled.

Okay, she was still mad at me.

But I wasn't having it this time.

"No," I said. "You don't get to be angry at me for back there. Who ran to confront Rol'amar by yourself without asking anyone? Did you have a good reason? Yes. Did you have time to explain it to us? No. Sometimes it's about trust." I squinted at her. "Although nice job on completely ditching the idorrá/thudajé dynamic."

She flushed red and looked away. "I was trying out the whole 'we're all equal partners' idea you're so fond of."

"I'd like to point out that also requires trust."

"So what happened back there?" Teraeth sat down next to me. Right next to me, so our legs touched and our sides. "Because I thought we just had this talk. Right before you threw yourself at Vol Karoth. I was there. Weren't you there? I could have sworn you were there."

"I wanted to keep you both safe," I mumbled.

Teraeth threw an arm around me, and I let him, leaning against his shoulder. It felt nice. "Monkey, you can't do that. Because we aren't safe. I'm certainly not safe. Maybe Janel can go back—"

"I can't."

Both of us straightened again. "What was that?" I asked her.

She paused from pacing back and forth. "I tried earlier. I can't go back. He's blocking me. Thurvishar isn't fully 'present' here, so he seems to be fine, but Vol Karoth is . . ." She sighed. "Who am I kidding? It's not because Thurvishar didn't fully enter this space, it's because it's me. Maybe he'd let someone else leave. But not me."

"Vol Karoth's not very happy with C'indrol," I agreed.

She gave me a piercing stare. "He hates me, Kihrin. Maybe more than he hates Relos Var."

"Naturally. It hurts more when the people you love the most betray you," Teraeth said.

Janel and I both froze.

We both knew he wasn't talking about C'indrol or Relos Var.

Janel sat down on the other side of Teraeth. "I didn't mean—Teraeth, I'm sorry."

"Why? I'm the one who cut off her head."

I bit my lip. We hadn't talked about this after we'd brought Teraeth back from the Well of Spirals. Teraeth hadn't wanted to talk about this. I couldn't blame him. How does one even begin to have that conversation?

"Thaena hurts too," Janel said. "The betrayal hurts. I trusted her."

"*You* trusted her?" Teraeth turned his head to stare at her.

Janel bit her lip, reached out to tuck a strand of Teraeth's hair behind his ear. "Just because the betrayal was greater for you doesn't mean it didn't hurt me too. I thought she was on my side. I never imagined she saw me as nothing more than a convenient tool. I'm sure Kihrin feels the same."

"You know I—" He pulled his arms away from both of us and leaned forward. "I don't think she even liked me."

"No, Teraeth—" The denial was automatic, but what hurt so much was that I honestly didn't know if he was wrong.

"I think she *appreciated* me. You know, the way I wasn't a dragon and usually did what I was told. But I don't think she loved me. Maybe when I was younger, but after I started remembering being Atrin . . . ? No, not so much."

Janel straightened. "Teraeth . . . should we be talking about this?" She looked around as though Vol Karoth might appear at any second, and to be fair, maybe that was the appropriate response.

But I frowned. I felt sad. I even felt a little angry, but what I mostly felt was a very strong desire to bring Thaena—Khaemezra—back from the dead so I could shake some sense into her and maybe scream at her a lot for treating her son this way. Because Teraeth deserved far, far better, and if I was being really and truly honest with myself, so did Khaemezra. She'd . . . forgotten. Forgotten what was important. She'd convinced herself that all the cruelty was acceptable as long as it accomplished the right goals. Maybe was even deserved.

"No, we should," I said. "We should talk about it. Because if we don't, you'd better believe Vol Karoth will use it against us later. If you two are going to insist on staying here—"

"Oh, we insist," Janel said. "Not that we have any choice, mind you, but even if we did, we'd insist."

"I have a little choice. For example, I chose to stay right here glued to Kihrin's side," Teraeth said and laced his arm around my waist for emphasis.

"That's going to make walking difficult," I pointed out.

Teraeth shrugged. "You should have thought of that before you threw yourself into the god of evil's mind."

"It seemed like a good idea at the time," I said.

Teraeth shifted next to me so he could give me a truly impressive sideways glare. "Did it? Did it really? Just how drunk were you when 'killing yourself so you could try possessing a dark god' seemed like a good idea?"

Janel snorted.

I sighed and pulled away from Teraeth's grip. "Okay, you two. You know what? I was perfectly sober. Thurvishar was perfectly sober. You two weren't there when Vol Karoth showed up later, when it started to become obvious that what C'indrol had done"—I motioned at Janel—"had injured Vol Karoth in a way he hadn't recovered from. He was operating at the level of a child. A young child. He should have been so damaged on a spiritual level that I should have been able to walk in here and make him do whatever I wanted. I know what Janel—what Elana—did to both of our souls, and you know it too, Teraeth. Maybe we're not demons, but we're really close to being something like that. It should have worked!" I exhaled. "But it didn't work, and I don't know why."

"You still should have said something," Teraeth said quietly. At least he didn't sound angry this time, but the disappointment was worse.

"Yes," I growled. "Evidently, I should have!" I sat back down again, aware of the awkward silence that fell over the three of us. "We were talking about your mother."

Teraeth scoffed. He clearly had no intention of returning to that subject.

"Honestly, he seems to be doing much better since we escaped from Vol Karoth," Janel told me.

"Of course I am," Teraeth said. "I always do better when I have an enemy. When something can distract me from"—he grimaced—"everything. I don't want to talk about this."

I grabbed his hand and laced my fingers through his, tucked him under my chin. On the other side, Janel nestled up against his body.

Teraeth hesitated. "Right at the end, I realized that my father . . . wasn't who I thought he was. I always thought he was so selfish. That he didn't care about saving anyone else. And then I realized that I'd horribly misjudged him, but it was too late to make it right. Just the same way I'm *always* too late to make things right. For just once in my existence, I would like to show up in time to make a difference. If I'd realized what was going on earlier . . . if I'd been able to do something . . ."

I shifted, put my arms around him as I kissed the top of his head. I felt Janel's weight shift too. "This isn't your fault, you know." My eyes met hers. She knew I wasn't just speaking to Teraeth.

"It feels like my fault," he mumbled into my collarbone.

Janel didn't believe me either.

"Last I checked, you weren't the Goddess of Death or the king of–okay, ignore that last statement." I rubbed my cheek against his head. "Fuck, what a trio we make."

"We need a plan," Janel said gently.

"Yes, that would be nice," I agreed. I didn't offer one up, mind you. I had no idea what to suggest.

Silence wrapped around the three of us.

Finally, Teraeth groaned and extricated himself for the tangle of limbs that was Janel and myself. "You are so fucking lucky I love you," he muttered as he stood. "Clearly, we need information. If this city is a reflection of Vol Karoth's mind, then it follows that the answers to why your plan didn't work are here too. We just need to find them."

"You make that sound so easy," I said.

"But he's right." Janel stood too, brushing herself off. "Because as much as it annoys me to admit it, your plan should have succeeded. We need to find out why it didn't."

"It'll be fun," Teraeth said. "Like hunting for pirate treasure without a map or clues or any idea what 'treasure' looks like."

I stared at him. "We need to work on your definition of 'fun.'"

He smirked. "We ever find a bed around here, and I'll be happy to show you."

Xivan's reaction
The Lighthouse at Shadrag Gor

Everyone opened their eyes after Xivan's vision faded. Qown immediately turned to Xivan. "Seriously? You were going to sell the Spurned?"

Xivan sighed. "I wasn't in a good place."

"Clearly," Kalindra said. "Explicitly so. Oh, and next time you want to remember having sex, mind making it good sex? As a personal favor."

There was an uncomfortable pause, and several people in the room actually blushed. Ah, there it was. Just in case Xivan had any doubt that everyone had indeed seen that.

She refused to look at Talea.

"I don't know," the mimic said into the gap in conversation. "I think betrayal's pretty hot." She paused as everyone stared at her. "Just me? Fine. Be that way. I don't judge what gets you dancing." She sighed and rolled her eyes. "Okay, okay. 'Yes, I do,'" she said as if repeating something another person said.

Qown looked around. "Um, no one said you didn't."

Talon sighed. "Kihrin did. I swear, he won't shut up. He's really going to be such a killjoy. Eat Kihrin, I said. We'll reconnect, I said. It'll be good, I said. Why did I ever agree to this?"

Everyone stared at the monster and then by silent, mutual agreement turned to each other instead. Xivan had expected people to stare at her, give her hateful, accusing looks, but mostly no one wanted to meet her eyes.

Instead, everyone was staring at Sheloran.

The royal princess stood perfectly still. She might not have even reacted to the vision except she held her fan so tightly her knuckles shone white through her brown skin. Her jaw tensed, a sharp line against her throat.

Then she started to tremble.

"Oh," Talea said. "So I guess you didn't know about your mother."

Xivan clenched her teeth. It made sense. Of course Sheloran hadn't known. Hell, there was a better than even chance the High Lord of House D'Talus didn't know what his wife truly was.[1] Why would Caless tell a teenage girl?

Sheloran blinked, wide-eyed and staring. She turned to Galen. "I thought . . . I thought she was a priestess . . ."

"I know, Red. So did I." He pulled her to him and put his arms around her. The moment he did, she let out a sob, immediately followed by a sharp inhale. She wiped her eyes and straightened, turning toward Talea and Xivan.

"I'm so sorry," Sheloran said. "I had no idea my mother had done that. Would do that. Could . . . Please . . . accept my sincerest—" Her voice stuttered, stopped. Her lower lip wobbled. It had probably occurred to her how ridiculous and trite it was to try to make apologies for gaeshing someone.

Some sins were unforgivable.

The girl was probably about five seconds from completely breaking down. Unlike the time she'd cried in the earlier vision to counteract that D'Mon woman, this time it would be real.

"It's not your fault," Talea said. "You didn't do anything wrong."

Xivan shouldn't have felt those words like razors, but she couldn't help it. Because it was Xivan's fault. She had done something wrong. She had no excuses.

And Xivan had no idea how to even begin to say she was sorry.

"It's why I was concerned Suless would go after you," Xivan told Sheloran. "Because you're her granddaughter. That makes you a target." Xivan shrugged. "Most people would want to protect their family, but that's Suless for you."

"My mother's a goddess," Sheloran murmured. She sat down, and it seemed of no particular consequence that there was no chair, couch, or cushion for her to sit down on. She just collapsed to the floor with her legs folded under her.

Galen knelt next to her.

"We don't have anything to drink around here, do we?" Kalindra asked. "This seems like a good time for it. You know it's a real shame Teraeth's not conscious. You two could compare notes on having goddesses for mothers." Her voice was surprisingly free of the mockery Xivan would have expected. Mostly, she just sounded tired.

"Janel too," Qown murmured.

"Really? Who?" Kalindra raised an eyebrow.

---

[1] I wouldn't take that bet. I think he knows perfectly well.

"Tya," he said.

"Oh, well, that does explain a few things—"

"Would you all shut up!" Sheloran shouted. Xivan thought it might have been the first time—barring that whole shouting-for-the-guards incident in that earlier memory—that she'd heard Sheloran raise her voice in anger. "Don't you understand? She lied to me. My whole life—" She took a deep, shuddering breath. "We were going to change things. We were going to make Quur better, change all the terrible things that are wrong with the empire. I was going to . . . I was supposed to make it better—"

Xivan felt her throat tighten.

Sheloran found her voice again. "But she's Caless! Caless is *everything that's wrong with Quur*. She's the reason everything is wrong with Quur! She is held up as the archetype of every reason why women are weak and fickle and not to be trusted. Why we shouldn't be allowed to use magic. She's had millennia to fix Quur, and she's done *nothing*."

No one said anything. What was there to say? The silence stretched out. At least they didn't hear footsteps overhead this time. Or scraping sounds out in the hall.

Qown stared at Xivan. "Did Caless really gaesh you, I mean—?"

Xivan glared. As if she needed to answer a question like that.

"I believe we can assume that's a yes," Senera said. "And far be it from me to say, 'I told you so—'"

"Fuck you, Senera," Xivan said.

Senera's stare went cold. "How's revenge working out for you so far, Xivan? All warm and happy?"

"I'm not going to sit here and be lectured on morality by a mass murderer," Xivan growled back.

"Fine," Senera said. "Why am I even bothering? I've wanted to spare you some pain, but you just won't stop until you've rammed that knife through your own heart, will you? So be it. But you still have something to lose, Xivan."

"You have no idea what I've gone through—"

"Do not," Senera whispered, "make this a contest. You will lose."

Something about Senera's silver-eyed stare stopped Xivan cold. She thought about what she knew of the wizard's background. Growing up in slavery among House D'Jorax—the entertainers' house who controlled Velvet Town, for fuck's sake—with that body and that face and absolutely no one in the whole world to protect her. With the knowledge that anything could be done to her, anything at all, and the law said it was fine, because slaves were property and not people. Not so different from Talea's background on the surface, but somehow Talea had come through it all with wide eyes, a deep empathy, and a heart so large she'd save the world if she could. While Senera had wrapped all that pain into a hard, brittle shell around herself so nothing could ever hurt her again. It occurred to Xivan, just then, that such a shell had probably been forged in the blood of every person in the Capital who'd ever wronged her. She'd likely waded through gore on her way to Relos Var's side.

So maybe Senera knew something about the cost of vengeance.

Xivan grabbed her cup off the table and stalked over into the kitchen, mostly because everyone was gathered someplace else.

She paused at one of the tables and tried to collect herself. She even poured herself a cup of tea, not because she needed the tea but just because the little rituals were sometimes comforting.

She paused at the smell.

Xivan frowned. Something smelled wonderful. Cumin and ginger, cardamom and pepper, butter and the hot tang of peppers—Xivan stopped, stunned. She was smelling the lentil soup Qown and Sheloran had made, which smelled unspeakably, illogically delicious.

Her stomach rumbled. *Impossible.*

Before Xivan knew what she was even doing, she'd emptied out the cold tea and ladled a helping of soup into her cup. She hesitated with the edge of the cup at her lip, let the spice-laced steam dance under her nose. Surely she was going insane, hallucinating. She hadn't felt hungry—hungry for food—in over twenty years. She hadn't tasted spices or savored the richness of a Quuros stew for a literal lifetime. Such pleasures were for the living; she no longer qualified.

Xivan drank in gulps, forcing herself to stop to chew, to remember how to chew. The soup was so delicious she felt near to tears from the experience.

A feeling of unease, close to being chased down by panic, nearly overwhelmed her.

Talea walked into the kitchen.

The two women stared at each other.

"It's going to be okay," Talea said.

Xivan nodded numbly. Then she said, "Are we? Are we going to be okay?"

Talea's expression tightened. "I don't know."

Xivan nodded. "I deserve that."

"You've proven that you're in no position to judge what you do or don't deserve," Talea told her. "That's always been the prob—did you just eat a bowl of soup?"

Xivan set the bowl down on the table and swallowed. "I was hungry."

"You were . . . hungry." Talea didn't move, but her eyes did, tracing Xivan's outline as if she were checking to see if she'd been replaced by a mimic. She peered through the doorway to the other room where Talon was clearly still visible, then back at Xivan.

"What's happening to me?" Xivan asked quietly.

Talea put a hand on Xivan's arm. "It's . . . I'm sure it's nothing bad."

Xivan reached for the scabbard at her side, shaking it so hard the sword inside rattled. "Is it because of this? This scabbard you gave me to break the Lash's control?"

Talea eyed the carved scrimshaw with a rueful expression. "Probably."

"What's it doing to me?"

Talea shrugged and shook her head. "It didn't do anything like that to me. But, uh . . ."

"But you're not dead."

"No."

Xivan forced herself to focus. "You know the worst is yet to come. On so many levels."

"I know." Talea took her hand. "But let's go back."

Xivan didn't fight her.

The others were still talking, probably had been the entire time that Xivan had been in the kitchen. Galen looked particularly pale. Possibly someone had taken the time to explain exactly what was going on with Kihrin.

Talon cracked her knuckles. "Shall we do this?"

Without waiting for anyone to respond, she did something.

The world changed.

21: THE SHATTERED VEIL CLUB

Qown's memory
The Lower Circle of the Capital City, Quur
The day after Qown entered D'Mon service

Qown woke to find himself staring at a mask. He managed not to scream, although it was a close thing, slowly focusing on the fact that the ceiling of the room he was in was simply covered—covered—in masks. Masks everywhere. They were all sorts of styles, many unfamiliar, surely from far away countries. None of them seemed friendly or nice.

It was extremely creepy.

The bed he was on was comfortable, covered with a thick red velvet cloth and a great many pillows. The floor was carpeted in a large, thin red rug, tough-textured, woven with stripes of color and glittering with sequins. The mage-light wasn't red, but it seemed likely that Qown was still somewhere on the D'Talus grounds. The air smelled like cinnamon and frankincense, mixed with a more complicated incense.

Qown sat up and immediately knew that Lady D'Talus had made good on her threat; his hair fell in front of his eyes. He brushed a hand through the mass and realized not only had she done as she'd claimed she would, she'd gone a bit overboard. His hair reached nearly to his waist. He staggered to his feet, noticing more changes. He'd been dressed in kef pants of the highest quality, dark brown, and was wearing a wrinkled but perfectly elegant pale off-white silk misha embroidered with lilies. The agolé draped across the chair next to the bed was even more ornate, and the boots were . . . astonishing, really. Exquisite. Qown had the immediate thought that Relos Var would love them, but it was a thought largely drowned out by shock and panic.[1]

A mirror lay against the wall on the far end of the room, next to a large wooden wardrobe and glass-topped circular table. He stumbled over to it and stared.

Lady D'Talus had indeed made good on almost all her promises. Qown was a little relieved to note that he was still . . . well . . . him. Still recognizably the same features, the same cheekbones, the same nose. But his hair looked like there had never been a day in his entire life where servants had not washed it, combed it, and layered it with the finest oils. And his skin, while unchanged in color, was so perfect it was nearly poreless and without a single blemish or

---

[1] The man does love his shoes.

mark anywhere. The dark circles under his eyes were gone; he couldn't deny that he finally looked as young as his actual years.

But there was one change that she had not made, or rather, one change that she had not made as promised. Qown looked at his eyes and hissed, unable to stop himself. Heat rose to his cheeks. Not shame but anger.

Lady D'Talus had turned the color of his eyes *orange*.

Not House D'Kaje. House D'Erinwa. The slavers house. The house that had, once upon a time not very long ago at all, been the house in charge of gaeshe. Never mind that it was a death sentence to impersonate a royal, but to impersonate someone from House D'Erinwa? Of all the sick, twisted . . . Of all the Royal Houses, this was the house he hated the most. This was the house Qown would gladly have destroyed if it was in his power, even though he hated violence, even though he had always told himself he valued human life above all things.

He stopped himself. It was, he supposed, a way of ensuring his cooperation with whatever strange scheme Lady D'Talus had come up with to protect her daughter. All they would have to do to keep Qown in line was drop a friendly note to House D'Erinwa letting them know that an impostor was mimicking one of their own. And that would be that. He'd have witch-hunters after him. People with ridiculous, ironic, and horrifying names like Humility, Grace, or Mercy.

"Ah, you're up. Very good, my lord," someone said behind Qown.

He turned around. A man close to his own age had opened the door. He had the red hair of a Marakori native but the accent of someone who had grown up in the Capital. His clothing was not nearly as nice as Qown's, but good enough to suggest he wasn't in danger of starving. The clothing looked nothing like House D'Talus livery. He had a tray in his hands, which held several bowls and a tea set.

Qown had never seen the man before.

"I'm sorry, I–" Qown put his hand to his head as though nursing a headache, which was true enough. "What happened?"

He chuckled. "You were so drunk when your man brought you in last night, I'm surprised you remember your own name, my lord. Anyway, I thought it best to put you in here to sleep it off. Keeps the riffraff from taking advantage."

"Ah, um . . . and you are?" Qown decided not to mention that he did not, in fact, remember his own name, or at least he was reasonably certain that whatever fake identity they'd created for him was unlikely to be "Qown."

"Oh right. I'm Merit. I run this delightful establishment." He grinned at Qown as he set the tray down on the table in front of him. The grin struck Qown as rather predatory and just a bit vicious. "If you need anything or anyone, just let me know."

"Thank you, Merit," Qown said. "Wait. You mentioned my man. Where is my man right now?"

"Eating breakfast, I assume. Would you like me to fetch him for you, my lord?"

Qown stared. "Yes. Please."

When the man left, Qown looked at the food. Vanoizi-style poached quail eggs in a spiced tomato sauce, not poisoned, with accompanying sag bread and seeded loquats, also not poisoned. The tea was not tea but coffee, again, not poisoned.

Three years in Yor had made the habit of checking for poison automatic. One never knew when ~~Wyrga~~Suless had slipped something into the pot.

Qown sighed, slid on the boots (they fit perfectly), washed his hands, and relocated the tray over to the glass table, where he could at least sit down on a chair while he ate. No sooner had food crossed his lips than the door opened and another man walked through, one far more familiar.

He was dressed in clothing that suggested he'd done a lot of drinking the night before and hadn't yet changed his shirt. His black cotton misha was rolled up at the sleeves and unfastened partway down the front, and he wasn't even wearing a sash or agolé over his dark burgundy kef. His hair was short, tousled, and uncombed. His eyes were . . . brown. Just brown, although they still managed to suggest dark, fresh-turned earth in private, secluded bowers. His fingers were smudged with ink.

But it was still Galen D'Mon.

"My lord," Galen greeted loudly enough for anyone nearby to hear as he closed the door behind him. "I trust you slept well."

"What. Have. You. Done?" Qown demanded. "This is—what—" He gestured to himself, frantic.

"Shh," Galen said. "Now it's all right to be a little temperamental. Royals often are. But let's not get too carried away."

Qown stared at him.

He couldn't remember the last time he'd found himself so desperately wanting to punch someone.

Oh right. That had *also* been Galen D'Mon.

"Lady D'Talus said she was going to make my eyes yellow, not orange. Why did your mother-in-law do this to me?" Qown asked, and then he gestured at Galen. "And how did you change your eye color? That's supposed to be impossible! It's supposed to be a curse!"

Galen traitorously directed one of *those* smiles at Qown as he sat down in the other chair and started eating Qown's breakfast. "Oh, it is. Honestly. My eyes are still blue. But did you know that if you know what you're doing, you can make a very fine film that fits over the eye and has a colored lens? And Lessoral—or Lady D'Talus to you—really knows what she's doing. You would think it would hurt, but it doesn't at all." Galen stared at his hands, seeming to realize only then that they were stained. "Oh sorry." He quickly found a washbasin and washed his hands too, although it did nothing for the ink stains.

"Oil," Qown murmured.

"Sorry?"

"You'll want oil to get rid of the stains. Rub it in until the oil turns dark, then wash that off."

"Huh. Never knew that." Galen returned to the breakfast table and poured himself a cup of coffee.

Merit must have suspected Galen would join him, Qown realized. There were two cups.

Qown took deep breaths. "Why? Can we please go back to why?"

"That was my doing. I asked her to go with orange instead. Because people are looking for Galen D'Mon," he said. "But nobody's looking for a down-on-their-luck royal from House D'Erinwa." He pointed a finger at me. "D'Erinwa is in even direr straits than House D'Mon, if you can imagine. With all the gaeshed slaves they used to keep? Oh, it was a bloodbath. Royals murdered left and right. I don't even know who's high lord over there right now, so no one will question why the odd stray royal is lurking down here in the Lower Circle keeping their head low until the dust settles."

Qown felt his stomach flip. "We're in the Lower Circle?"

"Mmm-hmm." His eyes danced with mirth. "You're *slumming.*"

Qown inhaled. "Why am I pretending to be House D'Erinwa? Why wouldn't it be you if you've found a way around the god-touched curse?"

"Oh no. I'm much too tall. Besides, I'd look terrible with jacinth eyes. It's quite breathtaking on you, though."

Qown ground his teeth. "I didn't agree to any of this! This is outrageous!"

Galen paused while eating a tomato and gave Qown a shrewd eye. "Oh, that's perfect. Just like that. I knew you'd make a terrific royal."

Qown attempted, somehow, to calm himself down a third time. "You're laughing at me."

Galen paused. "Maybe a little," he admitted, the smile faltering on his lips. "But not in a mean way. I'm not . . . I'm not mocking you. I promise that. I actually do need your help."

Qown knew he was failing to calm down. "If you needed my help, maybe you should have asked. Instead of—" He gestured around, latching onto a question that mattered not at all but at least wouldn't have him screaming. "Why do you have all these masks here?"

Qown was the calm one. He was always the calm one. Why was he being so completely and totally not the calm one this time?

Galen shrugged. "Not a clue. They were here when I bought the place. You should try to eat something." He saw the look on Qown's face and sighed. "I'm not going to make you do anything. If you don't want to help me, that's fine. It's up to you. You can stay here, anything you want will be brought to you, and you can hide out for a couple of weeks until the meeting with my aunts is arranged."

Qown looked around the room. "This is a hospitality house?"

"Oh no, it's a velvet house," Galen said, "called the Shattered Veil Club."

"A brothel?" Qown said. "We're in a brothel!"

He waved a hand. "Sort of. Technically. The area up front is where the brothel is. These are the private quarters of the velvet house's owner, a terribly mysterious figure called the Veiled Lady, who may or may not be Zheriasian and only rarely makes appearances." He shrugged. "I'm told the previous owner really was Zheriasian and really was mysterious. So we just sort of went with it. Why toss out a perfectly good reputation for being terribly mysterious?"

"But this 'Veiled Lady' isn't the owner. You are. You own a brothel." Qown glared. He wondered, fleetingly, if Relos Var had any idea in the whole world. "I thought that Merit person owned the place."

"He runs it for me. Close enough." Galen shrugged and stood. "I do understand. I do. Lady D'Talus can run roughshod over people if you let her. She has the same personality as an entire herd of elephant matriarchs. It's almost impossible to refuse her. So please accept my apologies and enjoy yourself here. If all goes according to plan, we'll be back inside the Blue Palace within a month at the latest, and you can shave off all that gorgeous hair and dress as poorly as your vows demand."

Qown stared at him. "It's a brothel," he repeated.

He seemed a bit stuck on that point.

Galen cocked his head. "So don't have sex with anyone. That's your objection, right?"

Qown scowled. "Won't that look odd? Why would a royal stay at a velvet house and not sleep with any of the velvet girls?"

"Okay, so do have sex with someone. Velvet girls, velvet boys. Sleep with all of them. I don't care. It's on the house."

"I have taken a vow!" Qown screamed. "That means something. I'm especially not going to take advantage of velvets–"

"Oh, live a little. Maybe you'll even pull the stick out of your ass," Galen growled. He'd absolutely stopped smiling.

Qown clenched his fists at his sides. He didn't know a great deal about Velvet Town–it wasn't a place he visited if at all possible–but he knew enough. Most of the prostitutes who worked there were slaves, or desperate, or some combination therein. Very few had any real choice in the matter. And for all that House D'Talus had a temple of Caless set up inside their walls, Qown rather doubted the velvets in the Lower Circle were treated like they had value, intrinsic worth.

Although it did seem odd, that Caless connection. Qown felt as if he were staring at something, but just not quite at the right angle to really see it.

Anyway, Qown had taken a vow. It meant something, damn it. It did. Even if the Vishai faith was . . . fiction.

"I'm quite comfortable with my stick–" Qown paused. "I'm fine. I'm just not a good liar. I'll only give your plan away."

Galen walked up to Qown. Rather too close, and it was an unsubtle reminder that yes, the man was uncomfortably tall. "You don't know what my plan is. You never asked." Then he walked past Qown, clearly headed for the door.

Qown almost let him go, but he couldn't rein in his curiosity. "Fine. What's your plan?"

Galen gave him a wry smile just before he walked out the door. "I'm going to steal wagonloads of slaves from the Octagon and set them free. Enjoy your breakfast."

Qown stared after the man for a span of breathless heartbeats. He wasn't completely certain what the answer he'd been expecting would have looked like, but he knew it would have borne absolutely no resemblance to the one Galen had just given him. House D'Erinwa was in absolute chaos, Galen had said. And this was probably just a bit of interhouse warfare, kicking a house when, as Galen himself had said, they were already on the floor, but–

Oh, it was insane. It was insane and magical, and if it worked, it would make Qown so happy he'd just about burst. Because it would feel so good–so amazingly good—to actually be able to do something he knew for a fact was in the right. There wasn't much moral gray area to slavery. It was bad. End of debate.

"Damn it all to Hell." Qown scrambled to find his agolé and then ran out the door to catch up to Galen.

Sheloran's memory

It was a reasonably quiet morning at the velvet house. Some idiot was apparently making an ass of himself and being thrown out, but it looked like Raorin had that well in hand. Clarea—the velvet girl who presumably had lodged the complaint—looked like she was about five seconds from knifing the man if he caused any trouble. Which he wouldn't, if he had even the slightest idea what was good for him. It was one of the principal rules of the Shattered Veil Club that all the men and women who worked there had absolute and inviolate authority over who they would or would not take as customers, what acts they would or would not perform with those customers, and for how much.

No one who tried to force any of those issues was ever welcomed back.

Sheloran was contemplating her odds of sneaking off and grabbing something to eat before Galen returned. Much as it was hilarious to roam around in veils and make mysterious statements, it did make it rather difficult to eat in public. It was fine; honestly, she had so much work to do, there was little time left over for food, anyway.

Mostly, she faced a problem: Darzin D'Mon had died too soon.

Sheloran controlled more businesses in the Lower Circle than anyone but her parents or husband realized. Blue Houses. Orphanages. Kilin. Gambling dens. Too many velvet houses. But what she didn't fully control—not yet—was the Shadowdancers. That plan had required at least another year and the grooming of a replacement for Scabbard willing to accept orders from a woman. They'd made great progress in shifting the Shadowdancers into a more useful organization for Sheloran's purposes, but Scabbard still thought he took orders from a man.

And there was no way he would calmly accept transferring that fealty to a nineteen-year-old princess.

So that was a problem. One she still didn't know how to solve.

She played with the edges of her veil and wished she had her fan, but it was too distinctive. Still, she always thought better when she had something to do with her hands. She opened one of the folders in front of her and studied the papers inside. Perhaps looking at them in public wasn't the wisest course of action, but she had two guards standing a respectful distance away to make sure no one interrupted her. And even if they did, a velvet house madam looking at slave ownership papers was hardly a unique occurrence. It's just that these papers were fake.

Galen entered then, looking like he'd just spilled coffee on his favorite misha. When he crossed to her table, she said, "So I assume the talk with our new friend went well."

"He's infuriating," Galen said in a way that suggested he meant the opposite.

"This was your idea." Sheloran returned to looking at the papers. Scabbard had done an excellent job. If she didn't know better, she'd think them genuine.

"We don't need him," Galen muttered, never moving his eyes from the courtyard door.

"Need has nothing to do with it," Sheloran said.

Galen looked at her.

"Do you think just because I prefer flowers, I can't judge the quality of a sword?" Sheloran teased. "Mother did an excellent job cleaning him up. Oh yes, and he loves your poetry."

Galen sat down next to her and pretended to busy himself looking over the papers. "I have no idea what you're talking about."

"Uh-huh." Sheloran raised her eyes to meet her husband's. "Don't let him distract you too much. We're in a precarious position right now, and there's very little he can do to improve it. He can't really help us, and you've always been too trusting." She sighed to herself. She might as well be telling the clouds to stay away from the sky. She honestly had no idea where he got it from, considering his parents.

Galen shrugged. "Doesn't really matter. He wants nothing to do with this."

"Hmm." But then she saw how Galen's eyes brightened, and she turned in the direction he was facing.

Qown had entered the room.

Galen's memory

Galen hadn't really expected Qown to follow him into the main room of the Shattered Veil Club after he'd dropped that teasing exit line about freeing slaves. He'd hoped Qown would, but that wasn't the same thing. Galen's goals could be accomplished without the Vishai priest's help—what kind of fool would he be if he'd hung all his plans on a man he barely knew?—but he didn't deny Qown's cooperation would make it easier.

That's why he waited a few seconds after leaving. So Qown would have a chance to see him entering the main hall of the Shattered Veil if the Vishai priest chose to follow.

When Qown entered, his eyes were so wide when they finally grew accustomed to the lighting levels in the room that Galen took pity on the poor man. He'd probably never even stepped foot inside a brothel in his entire life. And Galen had some sympathy. The first time Sheloran had taken him to one, Galen had been reasonably certain he was going to literally die from embarrassment. Then Galen and Sheloran had had one of their very few fights, because Galen had been incensed by the idea that—even after he'd told her about his father's slaves—she'd thought he'd want to imitate Darzin in any way. But the house she'd taken him to didn't use slaves; the men and women who worked there considered their work a holy rite. And it turned out that the shame was something he was welcome to kick to the side along with the clothing.

The Shattered Veil Club had been a present from his mother-in-law, because he had once complained he had nothing of Kihrin's to remember him by. As to how she'd known that this was the particular velvet house where Kihrin had been raised . . . Ah well, Lessoral had her ways, evidently.[2] He'd spoken to enough of the staff he'd coaxed back to work there to confirm her sources had been correct.

Anlyr left the shadows as Qown entered, sticking to the man's side as though he were assigned to guard Qown and not Galen.

Galen left Sheloran's table to go stand at Qown's elbow. "Ah, I'm sorry, my lord. I'm sure your head must still be hurting you terribly. Come sit over here and shield your eyes from the light. I'll fetch you tea." He guided Qown over to their table, along with a very bemused Anlyr. He was just a touch too professional to ask questions, but clearly a thousand of them lurked under his bitten tongue.

Qown leaned over toward Galen and whispered, "I hate you."

Galen laughed in spite of himself. "Do you, though? I wonder."

They returned to the table with Sheloran. The pot of tea was already there, set up next to a tray of fruit and nuts. The papers Sheloran had been working through were stacked to the side, as well as several crow quills and a bottle of ink. Galen would transcribe them later; Sheloran had atrocious handwriting.

Qown nodded to the guard. "Anlyr, how are you feeling?" The question sounded diagnostic. Any lingering pain? Did the wound heal completely?

The guard smiled. "A little . . . uh . . . This is not how I thought my week would go."

"Why a velvet house?" Qown whispered to Galen and Sheloran. "There are plenty of other places to hide."

Galen raised an eyebrow. "Are there?"

Because there really weren't. Any royal would stand out like a bonfire against the night sky at any tavern in the Lower Circle. Maybe the Temple of Caless, since Sheloran's mother had maintained her ties with the church, but there were multiple reasons Galen would really rather just not. And also, how exactly would that differ from a velvet house?

Galen poured tea for his "lord" and set the cup in front of Qown. "Velvet houses are wonderful," he explained softly. "People are always coming and going. It's impolite to ask anyone's name. You can rent a room all to yourself, no questions asked. The food is remarkably good. What's not to love?"

Qown reached over and plucked up one of Sheloran's pieces of paper before she could stop him. He gazed at the document critically. "It's indecent," he grumbled under his breath.

Sheloran audibly sighed.

"Truly obscene, yes, the idea someone might enjoy themselves without judgment," Galen replied. He kept the smile on his face but knew it probably didn't reach his eyes. "How dare we be so lewd."

---

[2] One does have a much easier time understanding how Lessoral D'Talus has one of the most astonishing spy networks in Quur once one realizes that it's a rare velvet house that doesn't have an altar of Caless set up in every bedroom.

"That's not—" Qown turned red and stared down at the page again. "Why are you doing this?"

Galen wasn't about to answer that question.

Qown moved on. "And is this how you're going to do it? Just walk over to the Octagon and present this?" He set the forged slave certificate back on the stack.

"Yes," Galen said. "It's risky, though, so it would be better if the person handing over the documents was unquestionably House D'Erinwa. They're less likely to ask the wrong questions that way."

"It would be better still if these were good forgeries," Qown muttered under his breath.

Galen saw Sheloran freeze and knew he had as well. It was certainly . . . interesting that Qown had immediately spotted that the documents weren't genuine. Galen had been under the impression that they were excellent counterfeits.

Galen blinked and leaned back, not sure if he was insulted or amused. "And what would you know about D'Erinwa ownership papers?"

Qown bit his lip and looked way. Instead of answering, he took a minute to drink his tea. "Would one of you answer my question? Why are you doing this?"

Galen leaned back into the alcove. His back was to the wall, and there were no rooms behind him. It didn't prevent eavesdropping—magic still existed. Hell, lipreading still existed. But it was a sensible first step. "Ever seen the hostile succession of a Royal House? Those times when it doesn't go smoothly, when different sides are fighting for the title?"

Qown swallowed and shook his head. Sheloran didn't say anything; she was going to let Galen handle this. Anlyr just watched.

"Me neither, but I've read about it," Galen said. "And most of the time, when there are factions, the winner will do away with any members of the loser's faction. That means family members may end up killed, slaves sold off, servants turned into slaves and then sold off. The sorcerers themselves are usually too valuable and difficult to replace to be treated so, but everyone else is fair game. It gives the new lord a little stockpile of cash they'll need and makes sure that they don't have to worry about disgruntled servants of their dead enemies sneaking in a quick bit of revenge along with the after-dinner tea. But in a case like Tishenya and Gerisea, where neither has lived in the Capital City in decades, well . . . everyone in the Blue Palace is, effectively, 'the other faction.'"

Qown's eyes widened. "Oh no."

"Oh yes. They're selling off the whole house. Not the healers, of course. But everyone else. Whether they used to be a slave or not."

Anlyr leaned forward, suddenly interested. "Wait, everyone—?"

Galen gave his guard a wistful look. "You're luckier than you know to be here, Anlyr, and not reporting back for duty."

Anlyr gulped visibly.

"No, but—" Qown was starting to sputter in outrage, his eyes wide.

Galen put his hand on the priest's leg, under the table. "Remember where you are."

Qown flushed red and inhaled. "How could they do that? Those people didn't commit a crime. You can't just snatch someone up and declare them a slave."

Sheloran's laughter was mocking. "Why not? The empire does it all the time. Do you think anyone pays attention to the people screaming that they've been unjustly enslaved?"

"If a Royal House says you deserved it," Galen added, "then you must have done something, yes?"

The Vishai priest—who had probably never looked less like a Vishai priest in his entire life—scrubbed a hand over his face and closed his eyes. Then he started fishing under his misha, until he pulled out a tumbled stone held in an elegant gold clasp and necklace. He frowned at the chain. "Did your mother-in-law do this? I used to keep this thing tied up with twine."

"I'm sure she felt that twine wasn't befitting a royal prince . . ." Galen frowned. "I'm surprised you can even stand up straight if you're running around with that thing pulling at your neck all the time. It looks heavy."

Anlyr also frowned at the rock, and at Qown, but he didn't say anything.

It was a pretty rock, Galen thought, even if it wasn't precisely what he might call a gem. It was a bit like an agate, he supposed, but the raw exposed center of the stone transitioned through different shades of red, orange, and yellow, twinkling to the point where it seemed like a flame burned in the center.

Honestly, it was the most House D'Talus piece of jewelry Galen thought he'd ever seen.

Without looking at him, Qown said, "If you try to do this after they've already been sold, you'll have both House D'Erinwa and whoever won the bid to contend with, yes? The best way to handle this is before they go up on the auction block. Make it so they never do because House D'Erinwa thinks the slaves have already been sold. Then you can just have someone . . . collect them."

Galen studied Qown for a moment. "I'm afraid you misunderstand. I don't have enough metal—not nearly enough metal—to buy even a fraction of them. And that's not even counting the fact that cost would be at least double if I tried to do so at a privileged sale."

"I realize that," Qown said. "I-I can fix that."

Sheloran laughed.

Galen raised both eyebrows. "And how, exactly, would you manage that? Please don't try to tell me that a man in your . . . situation . . . has that sort of metal lying around?"

Qown started to look nervous. "No, of course not. But they'll think those slaves have been sold, and they'll set them aside. If you move quickly, you can leave with them before they have any idea otherwise. I-I can do this. I'll just alter the order books."

Both Galen and Sheloran turned to face Qown fully then.

Galen wasn't sure what bothered him more, the idea that this man was this naïve about the way the Quuros slave trade worked or that a fucking Vishai priest was actually being serious about what he could do. "If altering the order books were easy to do, I'd have asked my in-laws to do it yesterday when I figured out what was going to happen. But it's not. The order books are kept in a sealed, magically protected vault that is trapped to the stars and buried under a hundred feet of alternating-material strata, as well as being protected by several dozen guards and half a dozen witch-hunters. The paper is enchanted so only a very specific kind of magical ink can even be used to write on its pages. And you think you can alter the order books? I'd like to know how."

Qown swallowed. "This was a bad idea. Never mind. I'll just—"

Sheloran grabbed the priest's hand before he could make a serious effort at standing. "Explain yourself. Now."

Qown started to say something, stopped, then opened his mouth again. Galen sympathized. Sheloran was using that tone of voice she'd clearly learned from her mother, the one that never raised to the level of a shout but implied all kinds of horrifying ends to anyone who crossed her. It made for an appalling contrast when compared to her normally sweet tones.

"It's the stone," Qown finally said, scratching at the edges of it with a thumbnail. "I can use it to see things at a distance. Affect things at a distance. They'll never see me, and their wards can't stop me. I can . . ." Qown stopped and sipped his tea, collected himself. Then he whispered, "I can spy on anyone."

Galen didn't say anything for a span. He watched the room. Nobody seemed to be paying attention.

"Is that a Cornerstone?" Sheloran softly asked.

"Worldhearth," Qown answered.

Galen felt stunned. He didn't know much about Cornerstones, but he knew a little. He couldn't help but learn a little after what had happened. The Vishai healer was carrying around an artifact. Sure. Naturally.

"And you think you can do this?" Galen asked softly.

Qown nodded. He took a deep breath. "I have before."

"You've forged purchase orders? With slaves?" Galen leaned forward, lowered his voice again.

"Not exactly. It was a different Royal House."

Galen stared at the man a little harder. He didn't seem like the type to be a particularly good liar, and what would be his motivation besides? Galen would want to test it, after all. And if he was serious about what that magic rock could do, Qown was taking an enormous risk by telling Galen.

As big a risk as Galen was taking by telling Qown about his plans in the first place.

"Which house?" Sheloran asked carefully, like it didn't matter.

"Yours," Qown answered, his voice very small. "I mean . . . D'Talus. It was House D'Talus."

Galen blinked. Forging orders for House D'Talus would in fact be harder than House D'Erinwa. House D'Erinwa didn't have Varik and Lessoral running things. And whatever else could be said about Varik and Lessoral, they were stunningly competent. And if they hadn't caught Qown . . .

. . . this might work.

"I take it back," Sheloran told Galen. "I suppose he can help us, after all."

22: An Early Spring

Kihrin's story
Inside Vol Karoth's prison

"Merit's not dead? Ha! Merit's not dead!" I bounced around a back-alley street on the outskirts of the city, in one case literally kick-jumping off a wall before I landed again. What can I say? I was in a good mood.

Teraeth blinked. "The man running the velvet house . . . ? Why would you even care?"

"I agree," Janel said. "Is he an old friend of yours?" Janel paused in our walk and leaned back against a wall, stretching out a leg. I stopped to watch her, because Janel's legs deserved an audience.

We hadn't as yet found anything significant, but we had started to notice the way the city both was and wasn't Karolaen. Parts of it seemed newer, even so far as to be reminiscent of sections of the Capital, while other parts were even older than the ancient city, architecture that dated back to the voras's original settlements on Nythrawl.

What it meant or how we could use it was less clear.

I walked over and took up a section of wall next to her, mostly for the excuse to be within touching distance. "Merit and I used to belong to the same group of thieves in the Lower Circle."

"The Shadowdancers?" Janel squinted. "I didn't think you were friends. Didn't you threaten him with blackmail?"

"Sure, but if Merit hadn't liked me, he'd have found a way to screw things up. Blackmailing him was just giving his conscience a salve so he didn't have to feel bad for ringing out the Shadowdancers." I paused. "But it does kind of make me wonder what Merit was doing running the Shattered Veil Club. Or working for Galen, for that matter."

"Priorities?" Teraeth said. "Does this matter?"

I sat back down again and exhaled. "No. But it's still nice to find out that someone you thought was dead is still alive. And Galen—" I smiled. "Wow, Galen's come a long way, hasn't he? I always thought he was going to . . . I mean, when I ended up on that slave ship, with no idea when or even if I would see him again, all I could think about was that Galen was going to be all alone. But I think he came out okay. Although Darzin used to be the one who controlled the Shadowdancers, and Therin before him, and Pedron before that. So really, this is just following the family tradition."

"The freeing-slaves bit is new, though," Teraeth mused. "I really hope I have the opportunity to rub that in your mother's face, Kihrin. You know, that she might have managed to murder the only good pair of royals in the whole empire."

"You're a bad man, Teraeth."

"This is not a secret," he admitted, then immediately paused and looked thoughtful.

"No," I said. "You're right; it's not a secret."

Teraeth spared me the briefest grin before he returned to his thoughts.

"What is it?" Janel asked.

"I was just contemplating that Vol Karoth doesn't seem particularly creative."

I laughed. "I just felt the weirdest desire to defend him."

"He's not, though," Teraeth said. "He seems to only be capable of working with what secrets are already in someone's memories or his own memories, which is why I was jammed into that very strange ritual sacrifice that was far more in keeping with S'arric's experiences than my own. So I was just thinking that secrets benefit him. The things that he knows that no one else does."

"He clearly can read our minds," Janel said. She didn't have to explain how uncomfortable the idea made her.

I scrunched my nose. "Technically . . ." I rubbed a finger under my chin. "Technically, we both can. Go looking through everyone's memories. Everyone who is at the Lighthouse seems to be accessible to me, although some are growing less so with every passing second. I've avoided that because, well, it's rude. I wouldn't want someone else tripping through every dirty thought I've ever had." I held up a finger to Teraeth. "I know you wouldn't judge. Even so."

"I might judge a little," Teraeth admitted. "Or at least critique."

I rolled my eyes.

"But once any of you join me here"—I pointed down at the ground—"you seem to no longer qualify as easy to read. Just for your information."

"Ah, a bit of bright side," Janel said. Then she turned to Teraeth. "So what are you suggesting? We ask Thurvishar to pass along that everyone needs to share their darkest secrets? We brought that up. I somehow doubt everyone has confessed to all their issues."

"Then those issues will be used against us," Teraeth said. "I understand how laughable it is to have me be the one suggesting honesty is our best weapon here, but . . ."

"Hey, don't look at me," I said. "I've had two different wizards and a mimic spelling out every secret I ever had for anyone who takes the time to read about them. Pretty sure I have no more secrets to divulge."

"That's not true," Janel said. "I don't really know your preferences in bed at all." She gave me a serious, piercing stare. Someone who didn't know her would probably have missed the faint way the corners of her lips turned up, the tiny signs that she was doing everything in her power to keep from grinning.

A laugh bubbled out of me, quite out of my ability to stop it, flaunting itself in the face of every challenge before us. "Are you and Teraeth ganging up on me?"

The two shared a look.

"Yes," they both said together.

"Uh-huh. I see." I stared at them both, the feelings in me sparkling and warm. I'd have labeled the feeling as "happiness" if it wasn't anchored down by the knowledge that I didn't get to keep my loves.

Or more, I suppose, that they didn't get to keep me.

I took Janel's hands in mine, traced the dark skin with my fingertips, then closed my hand around her wrists. Janel wasn't a small woman, but she was still thin enough in comparison that I could manage that with one hand. I raised her arms over her head and set my hand against the wall, trapping her like a pair of shackles. Purely performative, of course. This was Janel, after all. She could free herself whenever she felt like it.[1]

"My preference," I said, not whispering because I wanted Teraeth to hear this too, "is usually for reins. And a hard ride."

She swallowed visibly, but she didn't look . . . displeased. I bent down and grazed the side of her neck with my teeth. Janel gasped.

I felt movement next to me. Teraeth said, "What happened to you liking being tied up?"

I nipped at her ear while I eyed him. We were basically out in the open, but it didn't really matter when the whole city was deserted, did it? "I knew I shouldn't have told you about that."

Teraeth eyed us both with more than a little interest. "Nothing to be ashamed of. Not a thing anymore?"

I sighed, gave Janel a gentle kiss on the temple, and let her go. This wasn't really the time or place for this, even if I knew both my dear partners would be enthusiastically willing, anyway. So I figured I might as well be honest.

"No," I said. "Three months in the rowing galley of a slave ship cured that nicely."

Janel straightened and pushed herself away from the wall. "What?"

"Remind me to tell you about the scars sometime," I told her. I stepped away from both of them. "Any other secrets you feel like sharing? Because our sexual proclivities hardly seem like the sort of thing Vol Karoth is really going to use to mess with our heads, and he already knows that I'm in love with both of you."

"I hate it when you spoil all the fun with rationality and logic," Teraeth muttered. "We could've had confessions. Demonstrations."

"You just wanted the excuse to get into my pants," I told him.

He grinned. "You have met me, yes?" Teraeth pushed his hair out of his eyes and started to walk down the street.

But then we both realized Janel wasn't following.

She hadn't moved from the wall where I'd left her. She'd crossed her arms over her chest and was staring at the far side of the street. Finally, she scoffed and shook her head, looking at the ground.

"Janel . . . ?" I hated the way my heart was starting to hammer inside the cage of my chest.

---

[1] Could she? I see no reason to think Janel would be any stronger than Kihrin in this particular location.

"I do have one secret," Janel said, sighing, her posture very much that of someone psyching themselves up to reveal something unpleasant.

When neither of us said anything, she shrugged and looked away.

"Janel." It was Teraeth's turn that time. "You know there's nothing you can say that will change how we—"

"I'm pregnant," she said.

"—feel." Teraeth's eyes went very wide and more than a little panicked. He ran back over to her side. "I'm sorry. Did you just say . . . ?"

"I did. And I am." She sighed. "You wanted secrets . . ." Her eyes met mine. "It's why Suless stabbed me back in the Manol. She knew I wouldn't abandon my body, even after I finished my transformation. The baby would have died."

Teraeth asked the big question: "Who's the father?"

Wow. There were . . . there were options, weren't there? We still didn't know what Suless had done while she was possessing Janel's body, and while Suless had never shown much sign of being particularly interested in fooling around with, well, anyone, it seemed unwise to discount the god-queen of malice's capacity to make a special exception just to be a petty bitch. Which made King Kelanis a possibility, as well as Teraeth.

But I didn't ask. I knew who the father was.

"I am," I said. "Aren't I?"

The whole world seemed to hold its breath, but the look in her eyes was all the answer I needed.

"Yes," Janel said.

I walked back over to the alley, set my back against the wall, and slid all the way down into a sitting position. Fortunately, the one good thing about exploring the deserted city lurking in the mind of a quasi-dead god was that the alleys were shockingly clean.

I was not at all sure how to interpret how I was feeling. Overwhelmed. Scared. Absurdly, inappropriately pleased.

"I wanted to be further along before I said anything," Janel continued, "but Teraeth's right; Vol Karoth will try to use it against us. There's very little chance he doesn't know."

"Good luck using that against me," I said. "If he thinks it'll make me unhappy, he's out of his tiny little divine mind." I stopped and floundered. "I mean . . . assuming you . . . I mean I shouldn't assume."

"I'm keeping it," Janel clarified. "Makes me laugh, though."

"Laugh?" My voice might have broken on that.

Her smile was warm and bittersweet. "This isn't the first time I've tried to free you from Kharas Gulgoth while pregnant. It's just that this time, I'm carrying your child instead of his." She tilted her head toward Teraeth.

"Eh. It's his turn," Teraeth said.

Janel flicked her fingers against his shoulder. Then she scowled at me. "And I am still beyond angry at you. How dare you kill yourself to get out of helping me with this. Take some responsibility."

"Well, technically, I—" I shut up as she glared at me so fiercely it was a wonder the street didn't catch on fire. I cleared my throat. "Thurvishar thinks it might be possible to make me a new body with Wildheart once this is all over, but, uh–" I sighed. "Fuck, I'm so sorry. You know I'm not coming back from this. Even if we win, I can't–" I exhaled. "There's this rather large hole in the universe that's going to destroy everything, and someone has to fix it."

"It doesn't have to be you," Teraeth snapped.

"Yeah, it kind of does," I said. "It's literally what Vol Karoth was created to do, and he's the only one who can, so if I can somehow find a way to make this"–I gestured around me–"work, then yeah, it'll have to be me."

"That's not true," Teraeth said.

"It is–"

"It's not!" Teraeth shouted. "Saying it is just means you've given up on find-ing a better solution. Fuck you, Kihrin! I'm not going to lose you!"

I glared at him. "You think I don't want to be around for this? How dare you! I'm not–"

Janel turned her hand into a fist and slammed it down onto the street, which cracked.

Both Teraeth and I got the hint. We shut up.

Her voice was soft and sad and more than a little bitter. "The surest way to suffer defeat in a battle is to walk into one planning not to win. You've already taken your loss as granted, which does nothing more than guarantee that result. That is unacceptable."

When I turned to Teraeth, he shook his head. "Oh no. I'm not on your side. You're really going to just sit there and tell us that *Relos Var's* plan is the only one that can work?"

I started to answer and then stopped. Because that was . . . that was actu-ally a good point.

Janel added, "Winning, in case you're curious, means you're still around to enjoy it afterward. It does not mean you have sacrificed yourself to save the whole world. We're going to find another way. You're smarter than this. *We* are smarter than this."

"I don't–" I stopped and swallowed. Gods. I was going to have a child. Janel was going to have a child. Taja–

Taja. The Luck Goddess must have known. Maybe she'd even helped the odds. Looking back, the answer the Goddess of Luck had given me hadn't at all been "Don't worry about it, she's not pregnant," had it? The one and only time we'd slept together, and of course Janel ended up pregnant. What luck, indeed. I felt a fluttery sense of excitement neatly drowned out by pure blind panic. I wasn't ready for this. The whole universe wasn't ready for this. It didn't matter that we were already on a sort of time line. This made it so much worse. When I thought of all the people, gods, entities, and demons–oh, most espe-cially demons–who would try to use a baby against us, against me, I felt more than a little queasy. Neither Xaltorath nor Suless would let this go.

Fuck, *Relos Var* wouldn't let this go.

And then the dread twisted again. If Janel couldn't figure out a way to make it back to her own body . . .

She must have had some idea what my expression meant, because she leaned over and kissed the side of my mouth. "If we can't find a solution to this, it won't matter if I'm here or if I'm back at the Lighthouse. Everyone's dead, anyway."

"That doesn't mean I like it," I protested. Next to me, Teraeth snorted in agreement as he brushed his fingers across the side of Janel's neck.

"It would be rather odd if you did, wouldn't it?" Janel said. "Let's figure how to fix this mess first. And after that, we have seven more months to solve the rest of it."

I laughed. "Sure. Nobody's been able to figure this out in over three thousand years, but I'm sure we can sort it all out in the next seven months. Really, Janel, I thought you were going to ask for something tough. This'll be easy now that we have the proper motivation. Thank you for that."

"Don't sell yourself short, Monkey. You helped."

"Fantastic job." Teraeth picked up Janel's hand and squeezed. "I'm feeling very motivated."

I stood up and gestured toward the doorway. "Let's keep moving."

Galen's reaction
The Lighthouse at Shadrag Gor
Just after Qown, Galen, and Sheloran's memories

Galen turned to Talon as the memories ended. "Could you pick one of us and stick with that, please?"

Talon grinned. "No, ducky. Be less interesting next time."

Kalindra blinked at Sheloran. "What on earth were you doing in the Lower Circle?"

Sheloran sighed, fanned herself, and didn't answer.

"I admit, I find myself wondering the same thing," Senera said, scowling as though someone had just dug spikes under her nails to force that statement.

"Isn't it obvious?" Sheloran raised her chin and made a special effort to look extra haughty.

Galen laughed in spite of himself. They'd seen her plans from her own point of view, but they still hadn't made the connection. And Sheloran didn't feel like explaining. It was downright adorable. No one trusted anyone, even after literally seeing through each other's eyes.

Perhaps *adorable* was the wrong word.

"Red's doing what she always does," Galen offered. "She's saving everyone. Whether they want to be saved or not."

"Taking control of an underworld gang hardly seems like saving anything but your own purse," Kalindra said.

Sheloran collapsed her fan with a sharp metallic click. "That's because you're not paying attention, which is frankly a huge disappointment given your background and training. An underworld organization has resources, connections, all the right Watchmen on the payroll, secret routes into and out of the city, even trained sorcerers and teachers. If such an organization is seen as less of a threat than the Royal Houses and guilds, they even have loyalty. Think of what you could do with that."

"To what end?" Xivan asked.

"To provide the civic services the government is failing to offer, obviously," Sheloran said, "as well as maintain a system for smuggling escaped slaves out of the city, destabilizing the power structures of oppositional organizations, and eventually forcing the High Council to open Voice nominations to the general population. The fact that it will also have the effect of making us ridiculously rich is just a bonus." She added, "It was a ten-year plan."

Everyone stared.

Talon began laughing hysterically.

Xivan pinched her nose. "The babies have a ten-year plan. Of course they do. Makes perfect sense. The smartest person in any room is a teenager. *Just ask them.*"

Sheloran turned red.

"Isn't she great?" Galen said, beaming. Seriously, he had the best wife.

Senera sighed. "Okay, I applaud your goals, but if we get out of this, we need to talk."[2]

"It's nice to have a plan, but uh . . . if there really are more god-kings in the Royal Houses, you might want to uh . . . go over that plan again." Qown's brows were drawn together. He looked concerned as he distributed bowls of soup to the group.

"Oh, and that's not even taking into account what happens when those same god-kings figure out that a healthy chunk of the Eight aren't around anymore to force them to behave," Talea said. "It's going to be a mess."

Galen frowned. It was going to be a mess, anyway. Part of it was his fault. He'd said too much, been far too honest. Even if Galen could go back . . .

Well, he wasn't sure he could. House D'Mon was all but finished, and his hand had tossed in the last grain of rice to send the whole thing crashing down.

He wanted to laugh at Senera's concern. It wasn't exactly difficult to see the older people in the room dismissing Sheloran's plans as the cute, enthusiastic overreach of a teenager with no awareness of the realities of the world. Some of the people in this room were also trying to change things in Quur, in several cases violently, and often for decades. They'd probably told themselves that their inability to fulfill those goals meant they simply couldn't be changed quickly. Not in ten years. Maybe not in a hundred years.

But they didn't know Sheloran the way he did. And they clearly didn't understand how the march of history could move with sickening lethargy, resisting every pull and push, only to spin about on the edge of a coin, moving so quickly it left one breathless and tossed upside down.

This was the year *everything* changed.

Still thinking over politics and revolutions, Galen absently put the spoonful of lentil soup to his mouth. He immediately spat it back out again and stared down at his bowl in shock.

It had rotted.

From the sounds of disgust and retching from the others, he wasn't alone in his experience. Qown was staring down at his bowl, aghast. "It was fine two minutes ago!"

---

[2] I owned the rock that lets me answer any question, am a competent wizard, and worked for Relos Var, and we didn't think changing Quur could be accomplished in a single lifetime. I admire her bullheaded enthusiasm, but by the Veils . . .

"This looks like someone left it out on the table for two weeks," Kalindra complained. "Tastes like it too."

There was a tense moment. In particular, Qown and Senera shared a look. Then both ran outside into the hallway. Galen followed, hand on his sword for all the good it would do him. At least Sheloran had her magic.

The hallway was freezing cold, and the end of it, where the tunnel led out into the Lighthouse tower, was pitch-black. Galen could still see through it, but he was all too aware that he likely was the only one for whom that was true. Everyone else was staring into the black, unable to hide their growing dread.

"I see his head," Galen said. "And part of his chest, most of his hands and forearms." He felt the dread grab tight around his throat, that gut twist that reminded him that while they'd been talking and joking and sometimes shouting, Vol Karoth had been slowly escaping.

"I'd like to go back inside now," Sheloran said.

No one said a word in response. Everyone just slowly left the hallway and returned to the keeping room. It was warmer, and brighter, but not louder; no one knew what to say.

Finally, Qown asked Senera, "Do you think time is fluctuating unevenly?"

Galen didn't understand the ramifications at first. Then he realized that if the food really had rotted because too much time had passed, then their attempts to gauge how long they might have before Vol Karoth would escape were meaningless.

He could be free any moment.

Before he had a chance to say anything, the world changed.

23: ALONE WITH THE HATE

Xivan's memory
The Upper Circle
Two days after arriving in the Capital

Xivan woke with a blinding headache, an indescribable feeling of loss, and the sure, certain knowledge that she had irrevocably and completely messed up. She was lying on grass, and as she raised her head up, she realized she had been dumped in something that looked like a park. Xivan looked again and realized it was Arena Park. The grass was wet with early morning dew. Since it had been midmorning when they'd left to go visit House D'Talus, Xivan assumed they'd been unconscious for at least a day. Nothing about their clothing had changed. Nothing at all had changed except for the one small detail that changed everything.

Talea lay on the ground next to her as well, crying.

Xivan reached out to touch the woman. "Are you hurt?"

"Don't touch me," Talea said and rolled away. "You–she–" Talea closed her mouth and took several deep breaths. She patted herself down and barked out a short, painful laugh. "My lucky coin's gone. It must have fallen out of my pocket." She stood up and started carefully going back over her clothing. She let out the most despairing sound when she found nothing.

Then she began walking away.

It took Xivan a moment to realize that Talea was *leaving*. "Talea!" she called out.

The young woman turned around. Her eyes were hard. "Yes, master?"

Xivan flinched. "I'm not . . . I'm not your master."

"You're not? Funny, because I seem to recall a conversation just recently where you tried to sell me."

"Not you." Xivan stood up and ignored the wet, damp feeling of her kef. "I didn't mean you."

Talea put a hand to her heart. "I'm one of the Spurned. How could you not have meant me? And even if that were true, really? You were going to sell Bikeinoh? Nezessa? You've known them and trained them for years. And you were going to sell them to a Royal House? Do you have any idea what a Royal House will do with fifty battle witches?"

Xivan sighed. She'd known it would come to this. She'd known and she'd just been forced to watch that boulder roll downhill, gaining speed with every bump. "What was I supposed to do? She was right. I don't have enough metal."

"No one has enough metal!" Talea screamed. "And she wasn't wrong,

Xivan! You don't have Urthaenriel anymore. You don't know how to use . . ." She hissed as if in pain. "You don't know how to use that damn necklace. And if you had it, Suless would laugh, and Suless would find a way to take it from you, and you still wouldn't win! Janel has a chance! Kihrin has a chance! *You don't.* And as long as you insist on doing this alone without them, you never will."

"I won't apologize, Talea," Xivan said.

"I know you won't. And you kept your word; you didn't touch me like that again. Yet you still found a way to rip out my heart. And it's too much. I thought I fell in love with a woman of honor and conviction, a great woman who was going to do great things because it was her nature, as natural as the sun coming up in the morning. But I was wrong. You're just like Azhen. You're so focused on this one meaningless thing, you're going to let everything else burn to get it." She shook her head. "I can't bear to watch."

Xivan didn't say a word. She just let Talea go.

Really, it was better this way.

After Talea was gone, Xivan brushed herself off and went to a nearby tavern to think things over. She had been needlessly rushing ahead, and look where it had gotten her. She needed information, and she needed it fast. Unfortunately, she suspected Senera was done with helping, and it's not like she could force the wizard to do so.

She needed to know the extent of the command chain she'd been given. She quickly discovered that the gaesh responded, if nonlethally, to even thinking about forbidden actions. She had a hard time even contemplating telling anyone that she had been gaeshed by Caless, for instance, or that Caless had been pretending to be a royal for gods knew how long.

Xivan wondered if the high lord knew, or if he just considered himself lucky that his wife was so young-looking and beautiful, even after all these years. Probably thought it was because of cosmetic magics, probably bought from–ha!–the church of Caless. At some point, Lady D'Talus would have to have an "accident" or retire to the countryside where she could die peacefully in her sleep, yes?

She was forbidden to talk about the gaesh, forbidden to reveal what she knew about Lady D'Talus or the Stone of Shackles. She was also forbidden from trying to steal the Stone of Shackles.

But Xivan had something she wanted more than the Stone of Shackles now. She wanted her gaesh. Her gaesh, and Talea's gaesh, and she wanted Caless to pay. She wanted Caless to bleed. If she couldn't attack Caless directly, she could still find a way to accomplish her goals. If she'd learned anything from Suless, it was that.

So she walked around the Ivory District until she found the Temple of Galava, where they kept the birth records.

The Temple of Galava was empty. It's not that people didn't care. Candles and flowers had been left on the altars and prayer mats. Even while Xivan stood there, a young man who looked like he probably worked as some sort of groom came in, lit a candle, and burst into tears. The sound of muffled crying echoed through the large building.

Xivan fought off a sense of bittersweet irony just being there. She was, after all, not a creature of Galava's. Just the opposite, or at least, she would have been just the opposite if Thaena had been willing to claim her, if Thaena hadn't decreed her kind and any like her anathema. So she was trapped, belonging to neither goddess.

Fortunately for her sense of self, both goddesses were now dead.

She searched the church grounds until she noticed a man in Galava's green robes duck into a back room, and followed him. He had evidently gone to a rectory for the priests of the order, although many of the doors had been thrown open, clothes and vestments strewn, beds now empty. They must have felt it when she died. They must have known at the precise moment it had happened, that Galava would be answering no more prayers ever again.

"This is a private area."

She turned around to see a priest, although the agolé he wore was stained as if a great deal of wine had been spilled down the front. He looked very tired and quite possibly very hungover as well.

"That's all right," she said. "You can help me. Do you know if the royal families keep their birth records here?"

The priest seemed taken aback. "Well, yes, but I don't see—"

She pulled a pouch of gems from her belt—a child's set of shiny rocks compared to what House D'Talus could levy, but still more than a priest ever saw in his lifetime. She tossed the bag to him. "I want to see your records."

That seemed to sober him. He visibly straightened. "Oh no. I'm sorry. Those are private."

Xivan sighed. Why did everyone want to do things the hard way? She walked up to him, quickly, before he could run, grabbed him by the back of his robes, and threw him into one of the cloister rooms, shutting the door behind her. It was thankfully empty, containing only a cot, a small box for personal effects, and very little else. The priest scrabbled as he hit the edge of the cot and fell to the floor.

"It wasn't a request," Xivan said. "Now I'm offering you money, and considering your goddess is dead and soon everyone will know it, I don't see how any of you lot are going to be on the receiving end of donations for a long time. You can take the money and give me what I want, or we can get to know each other better." She pulled the knife from her belt, thinking as she did that it had actually been rather polite of the high lady to leave them with their weapons. She pretended to examine the edge. At times like this, it was best to stick to the classics. "Let's start with your fingers. You don't really need your fingers to pray, do you?"

He began to scream, so Xivan stuffed his agolé into his mouth. She settled back on her heels next to him. "I hope you realize the position you're putting me in here. If I have to gag you, how will I know that you're ready to cooperate? I might well go through all your fingers before you can make me understand. That doesn't seem like a good strategy to me. What do you think?"

Wide-eyed, the priest shook his head.

"Okay, better," Xivan said. "Now if I pull this agolé out of your mouth, will you scream?"

He shook his head again. When she removed the gag, he added, "Please don't do this."

"You know what I want," Xivan said. "I'm not unaware of the situation you're in. And Galava isn't around anymore, so who will heal your injuries, regrow your fingers? House D'Mon? Maybe, but you'd need a lot of metal—" She jingled the bag. "Doesn't it make more sense to just help me from the start, keep the metal and your fingers?"

The priest nodded.

"Good," Xivan said. "Now I'm going to help you up, and you're going to remember that I have this knife and I'm not at all afraid to use it, and we're going to walk over to where they keep the records. Deal?"

He swallowed and nodded. "Deal."

"Good man." She grabbed his arm and pulled him to his feet. Xivan was pleased with how quickly he'd folded, because truthfully, she hadn't really wanted to start severing fingers. She would have done it, but it always made a mess.

Together, they walked over to another hallway, another, slightly more administerial grouping of rooms, and eventually to a relatively small room filled with glyphs and magical sigils, but no paper, no boxes.

"Wh-what are y-you looking for?" the priest managed.

"This is the record room?" She was skeptical.

He nodded vigorously. "It is. The actual records are kept in a vault, but this is an access point. There's another access point in the Soaring Halls." He pulled a scroll from under a desk. "Who are you looking for?"

"I want all births in House D'Talus for the last fifty years," she said.

All the color fled the man's face, and it occurred to Xivan that he must think he'd signed his own execution order, since if Xivan didn't kill him, House D'Talus would. Which . . . honestly was a possibility. Assuming they ever found out.

"Don't start having second thoughts now," Xivan warned him. "I'm giving you enough money to leave the Capital and settle down in a nice quiet town in a beautiful house and never worry another day in your life. The only way you'll mess that up is by being scared or being greedy."

The priest looked at her sideways and finally nodded. "Yes. I see." He stepped forward and removed a large scroll from underneath the main table. It didn't seem like it could possibly be large enough to hold the records of every birth, and she didn't see any other scrolls. However, Xivan just took it as granted that magic was involved.

He unfolded the scroll, wrote something down, unfolded the scroll again, wrote something down again, and finally unrolled it one last time. Then he said, "Here they are. Thirty-seven births during that time period. Would you like to see?" He pointed down to the scroll, so she could see the list of names, dates, and parents.

Xivan studied it. She couldn't directly ask for what she wanted, but she didn't have to. "That one," she said, pointing to a specific name. It was the only one listed as the offspring of Lessoral D'Talus and Varik D'Talus.[1] Interestingly enough, she'd seen a birth listing for Varik D'Talus. She hadn't seen one for Lessoral. Xivan wondered if the woman was even claiming to be a member of House D'Talus or had just married into it.

It didn't matter. What did matter was she had a single daughter, in her late teens, named Sheloran. And Sheloran would not be a god-queen. Sheloran would be vulnerable.

Let's just see how Caless liked how it felt to lose someone *she* cared about.

Xivan's reaction
The Lighthouse at Shadrag Gor

Galen surged forward, hand on his sword. "You bitch!"

Xivan had her sword drawn an instant later. The sound of metal rang out as Talea followed suit. Qown dropped his bowl again and seemed about to bodily interpose himself. Xivan scowled and tried to push the damn priest out of the way. She wasn't really worried about Galen—he was a decent swordsman as far as she could tell, but not at all a match for her. Even if he scored a hit, Xivan would likely be able to just ignore it. Sheloran and her magic were a different story.

Qown and his magic were very much a different story.

And Xivan had to just hope that Senera stayed the hell out of it.

Everyone began shouting at once, Xivan included.

"Just put down your damn weapon!"

"I don't want to fight you!"

"You lay a single finger on Sheloran—!"

"Even if Lady D'Talus is Caless, that doesn't mean we need—"

"Please! Let's not fight about this!"

"You hypocrite! How are you any different from Suless?"

Okay, that last one hurt. Before she could say or do anything, however, a rather large tentacle holding a fish—a wet fish!—slapped Xivan across the cheek. And everyone else across the face as well, all simultaneously. Everyone's breath frosted in the air.

Everyone paused, stunned.

Talon retracted her arms. "Would the children stop playing for a moment? Mommy's trying to have a conversation." She turned to Talea. "Could you repeat that last bit? I don't think everyone heard."

Talea, looking extremely flushed and flustered, crossed her arms over her chest. "I said, I don't really care if Lady D'Talus is secretly the god-queen Caless. I'm fine—" The corners of her lips turned down in a small, adorable frown. "Huh. Should I be able to talk about this?"

Senera cocked her head. "I admit I had assumed Caless would have gaeshed you to keep that a secret."

"She *did*," Xivan growled, incredulous at what she was hearing. "She very much did. Talea, how . . . how are you doing this?"

---

[1] You may remember Galen commenting in your first chronicle that Sheloran was the youngest of the D'Talus high lord's daughters, not an only child. More on this in a bit.

"Talea hasn't secretly been replaced by a mimic," Talon volunteered. "I know 'cause I'm the only mimic in this Lighthouse, and I'm still right here." She paused, though. "You're not Jarith, are you?"

"No!" Talea said.

"Had to check."

"Okay, what the fuck?" Kalindra said. "You can't just 'break' a gaesh."

"And yet . . ." Galen said. "Talea seems to have done something pretty interesting."

"You mean impossible," Kalindra corrected.

"Doesn't impossible qualify as interesting?" Sheloran asked.

"How does one cure a gaesh?" Qown asked Senera.

"You mean besides destroying the Stone of Shackles?" Senera shook her head. "Remove the soul fragment from the container housing it—usually by destroying said container—kill the person who's gaeshed, let the damage heal in the Afterlife, hope no demon grabs them while that's happening, and then Return them. It's not a particularly clean solution, but it can work. Not easily, and until recently, the Goddess of Death would probably try to stop you, but the theory exists." She pulled her Cornerstone out of her shirt and sat down at the table. "Keep talking. I'm going to ask a few questions."

Talea pulled a chair out from the table and sat down, bemused. She started ticking off points on her fingers. "Lady D'Talus is secretly Suless's daughter, the god-queen Caless, she has the Stone of Shackles, and she gaeshed both of us to keep us from revealing that fact." She chewed on her lip. "Huh. Yup, not feeling any impulse to die or anything. Doesn't even hurt." She looked over at Xivan. "Do you want to try?"

"No. I really don't, thank you." But Xivan had the horrifying suspicion she probably could have done so safely. She just didn't want to do it out here, in front of everyone.

The room fell silent.

"Well, well, well," Senera muttered, stopping to turn the paper she used.

"Did you find out anything?" Talea asked.

"Possibly. I asked if you were gaeshed, and it said no. I asked if you had been gaeshed, and the answer was yes. I asked why Talea Ferandis was no longer gaeshed, and it answered because your soul has been healed. I asked who healed your soul, and the answer was Taja."

"Oh." Talea's voice was very small. She looked vaguely guilty.

What she didn't look was surprised.

"Talea . . . ?" Xivan stared at her. "Is there something you'd like to tell us?"

Senera leaned back in her chair, tapped the Cornerstone on the table. "Is the Goddess of Luck not dead?"

"No," Talea said, swallowing, pain flashing across bright eyes. "Taja's dead. I saw her die." Talea gestured back to Xivan. "We both did."

"Hmm." Senera stared at the woman for a moment longer. "As it happens, the Name of All Things agrees with you."

"Then why did you ask?" Talea didn't seem upset, just a bit exasperated.

Xivan's focus snapped back to Senera as the woman said, "I asked because people don't always give the same answers to the same questions, and it doesn't mean anyone involved is lying. Nuance is a tricky thing. If there's something we've overlooked . . ."

The answer was so immediately obvious, the words were out of Xivan's mouth before she'd had a chance to consider what she was saying. "What about your lucky coin? I know you said it wasn't important—"

"Oh yes," Senera said, "because my dying last act is certainly going to be to empty my purse of loose change I can hand to strangers."

Xivan ignored the interruption. "—and you lost it when we woke up after being kicked out of House D'Talus. You thought it must have fallen out of your pocket. What if you didn't lose it so much as you used it up? Is it possible that the coin healed you?"

"Is it possible that, I don't know, maybe Taja had a motive *other* than giving alms?" Senera said.

Talea's mouth twisted to the side. "I suppose that's possible. I mean . . . I don't really know. But the coin is gone."

"And you're not in danger from the coin," Senera said. "I asked that too." She scowled. "I hate not knowing the right questions to ask."

"Oh, you poor thing." Kalindra's voice was so dry and dull and heavy that almost everyone in the room turned to look at her. She was sitting on the floor with her back against the wall. She looked like she'd seen her own death.

"Kalindra, are you feeling all right?" Galen knelt next to her.

"I'm fine," Kalindra said in a voice anything but.

"Kalindra—"

"I'm fine!" she snapped.

She did not look fine to Xivan. She looked like she just needed one, maybe two more pushes and then she'd walk into Vol Karoth's loving embrace of her own free will, all the while thanking him for oblivion. Xivan's mouth felt dry, her tongue thick.

She knew what it felt like. It was hard to look at Kalindra and not think of herself with a husband and son, of the hollow feeling of knowing that you could in fact lose everything and yet somehow still exist. Except . . .

No. This probably wasn't how she'd felt. This was closer to how Azhen must have felt, wasn't it? The slow, creeping horror of realizing that the person you loved wasn't dead—technically—but hating yourself for wondering if death might not have been the kinder option. And what did one say to that, that made the least bit of difference?

I understand. My husband went through this. Of course, it drove him insane. Yours too?

Xivan turned to Talon. "You've got to do something."

Talon blinked at her, wide-eyed and starting to laugh. "Me? And just what do you think I can do . . . ?"

Xivan's hands closed around Talon's shoulders, although she knew Talon could easily escape her anytime she felt like it. "You're a telepath," Xivan said. "There has to be something. Something in Kalindra's mind. Something in Jarith's mind, if you can find him."

That caught Kalindra's attention. To Talon, she said, "Can you find Jarith?"

Talon looked uncomfortable, caught out. "It's not that easy. His mind is . . .

It's like a tapestry that's been unraveled. It's just threads everywhere in a giant messy tangle, and none of it makes any sense, let alone forms a pattern."

Senera blinked. "You can sense him?"

"Only in the thinnest definition of that term, which means nothing about him makes any sense!" Talon protested. "And this is coming from *me*."

"Look for the parts that are locked away," Senera suggested. "Damaged and tied off. That's where you'll find the important memories."

Talon glared. "You're not helping!"

Senera raised an eyebrow. "I *am* helping. Because Xivan's right. If Vol Karoth is feeding off our emotional states, then Kalindra must be a buffet. This isn't charity. This is survival. If we can help her, then we should." With that, she went back to whatever question she was asking that Cornerstone of hers, writing with perfectly neat, exact script.

"You mean I should," Talon corrected with narrowed eyes.

"As you say." Senera didn't look up from her writing.

"Do I get a choice—?" Kalindra started to voice an angry question. She stopped and closed her eyes. "Fine. If you can do it, you should. I'd be grateful."

What was that look in Talon's eyes? Sympathy? From *Talon*?

The mimic closed her eyes and seemed to be concentrating. Everyone just . . . watched. Unlike other attempts, this wasn't fast. Whatever she was looking for wasn't so easy to locate. Talon seemed to be struggling, searching.

"Why do people have to be so complicated?" Talon whined. "But fine, I guess this snarl will have to do."

The world changed.

24: Sacrificial Rites

Kihrin's story
Inside Vol Karoth's prison

"We need a plan," Teraeth said after we "returned" from another always-pleasant stroll through Xivan's quest for revenge. Of course, this was also something like the sixth time he'd made that statement, and it wasn't bringing us any closer to accomplishing it.

"Stay alive?" I said. "Or as close as some of us can come to it."

Janel cocked her head at me. "That's a shitty plan."

"Thank you," Teraeth said. "I happen to agree."

"Look," I said, half spoken word and half deep sigh, "I get that things went a little . . . off the path."

Janel stopped walking so she could cross her arms over her chest and glare up at me. "A little off the path is what happens when you hire a Marakori to be your tour guide, and you end up at her cousin's cellar house while he charges you three times the going rate for a room. A little off the path is when all you want is a relaxing drink at your favorite bar and a fight breaks out between supporters of your tournament favorites and some thorra from a visiting stable. That's a 'little off the path.' This is the King of Demons killing everyone we care about, the world ending, and your soul getting devoured."

"And let's not forget the King of Demons is Janel's ex, in this scenario," Teraeth offered.

Janel lowered her head and took a deep breath.

"I really don't think Janel's forgotten that, Teraeth," I offered.

"My point," Janel said, "is that the literal End of Everything is perhaps not the time when you want to go on the defensive."

I blinked, bemused. I looked at Teraeth, but he just raised an eyebrow at me and waited. I raised a finger, reconsidered, lowered it again.

"It's just . . . ," I said.

"Yes?" Teraeth said.

"Well . . . ," I said.

We all stood there in silence for a moment. And there is no silence like the silence in the fake Kharas Golgoth inside Vol Karoth's mind.

"Right now, he has all the advantages," Janel said. "We need to change that. Stop reacting like a scared foal, put on your adult boots, and *think*."

She was right. Of course she was right. I was thinking like Rook, the Shadowdancer Key who hid while Gadrith and Darzin D'Mon performed unspeakable rituals on hapless vané. I was thinking like the minstrel's son.

But Vol Karoth . . .

Vol Karoth was thinking like Solan'arric, only without anything that might pass for moral qualms.

"Let's break it down," I said after letting out the breath I hadn't realized I'd been holding. "We're in his mind."

"So how is that possible?" Teraeth asked. The look on his face told me it wasn't a rhetorical question.

"I don't know," I admitted. "He's a horrible dark god created by a horrible ritual that went horribly wrong."

Janel nodded slowly. "Exactly. There's something there."

"Something horrible?"

She waved away the (admittedly poor) attempt at humor. "I was talking about him." She pointed at Teraeth. "He's onto something."

"Ohhh, do I get a prize?" he asked.

She ignored him even harder than she'd ignored me. "Let's question assumptions; either we're in Vol Karoth's mind like we think we are, in which case, the geography here must be representational. Or we're not in his mind, in which case we're . . . where?"

"Representational?" I raised an eyebrow at her. "I realize it's all a metaphor, so how is that different from the Afterlife?"

"Because the Afterlife's rules are set, just as the Living World's rules are set. But if this is Vol Karoth's mind—or at least some sort of mental projection, then that means that the Vol Karoth we've been fighting isn't really Vol Karoth. It's a projection, like the one we encountered in the Korthaen Blight, but mental instead of physical. It also means . . ."

"Yes?" Teraeth prompted after a few moments of silence.

"What's the word for it when one soul inhabits another, living mind?" Janel asked, looking directly at me.

"Oh. Shit," I said.

"Hello?" Teraeth waved a hand.

"Possession." I turned to him. "We're not 'just hanging out' in his mind. We're possessing Vol Karoth's mind. Like . . . well, like demons. Or ghosts."

"And that means that all of this"—Janel gestured around the city—"is along the order of a talisman he has created to keep us distracted, because ghosts can have a real effect on the minds of those they inhabit."

"So what we need to do—" I started, but Teraeth already had the bit in his mouth and was running with it.

"—is fight the city, not the scary demon-man."

"Right," Janel said. "So . . . absent the presence of a Morios, how does one fight a city?"

"Dunno," Teraeth said. "But we're still gathering intelligence. So let's explore the city. That building there, for example." He pointed at a door. I blinked at it.

It was an excellent choice. It didn't really match. I didn't recognize it, but it seemed rougher hewn than the doors around it.

I looked at Janel. She looked at me. We both shrugged. "Sure," I said at the same time she said, "Works for me."

We walked through the doorway.

It wasn't the largest of buildings nearby, nor the smallest. A wide, sliding door divided the entry room roughly in half, with stairs leading up toward the back. If there had been furniture, we might have had an inkling as to the structure's intended purpose.

"So now what?" I asked Teraeth.

"Look for anything interesting," he said. "We don't know what will be important yet. I'll look upstairs."

"You and I can look through the first floor," Janel told me.

Teraeth nodded and put actions to words, swiftly striding across the room and skipping up the steps.

"Wouldn't it be faster if we split up?" I said.

She tilted her head in my direction. "It's adorable that you think we're letting you out of our sight after what you've pulled multiple times now."

I glared at her, to which she seemed utterly immune.

I went for a closer look at the sliding door. A rail ran along the wall above the door, which hung on rollers. The workmanship was precise. A memory fidgeted in the back of my mind, but before it could fully rise up and reveal itself, Teraeth's voice came from above.

"Up here," he called.

We went up there.

The ceiling on the second floor wasn't as high, but the floor was large and open, lacking the dividing wall of downstairs. But that wasn't the interesting thing about the room.

The interesting thing about the room was what it contained: Teraeth . . . and a couch.

The style of it struck me with a visceral sense of familiarity that reached across my mind and pulled that other memory to the fore. I recognized the style of both the couch and the sliding door despite the fact that I'd technically never seen either in my life. The fabric was pale gold, velvety, and wrapped around thick padding. I've seen plenty of beds that looked less comfortable.

"Huh," Janel said as we all drew closer to the tempting resting place.

"Something must be going right," I said. "This is the first time I've seen furniture in the whole city."

"Yeah," Janel said. "So why's it here? Trap?"

"Seems kind of obvious," Teraeth said. "Unlikely to be trapped." Which he underlined by sitting down and patting the fabric next to him.

"Teraeth," I sighed. And they were yelling at me for being reckless.

"So evidently, it's not trapped," Janel commented.

"I mean it's not quite a bed, but still . . ." He gave me a teasing glance.

"We're information gathering," I reminded him, smiling. I'm pretty sure he wasn't serious, but he wasn't going to pass up the chance to mess with me a little either.

Janel, however, was studying the couch with a frown on her face.

I sat down next to Teraeth, then promptly shifted so I was lying down with my legs slung over the back. "What is it?"

"Does the couch seem familiar?" Janel asked.

I looked down at the fabric. "I don't think so. It's not a House D'Mon–" I paused. "This was my mother's couch. I mean—" I shook my head. I was still not used to these flashes of multiple lives. "S'arric's mother's couch." I shook my head. "Fuck, I hated this couch."

I couldn't remember why, though. All I could remember was that the couch was a sore point. It was like remembering you had a fight with someone, but not why you'd been fighting or what words had been exchanged.

"Change it," Janel suggested as she took position on one of the arms, riding it in a manner not too dissimilar to what one might do to a horse. Which was hard to look away from, if I'm being honest. "Change it into something that is a happy memory."

"Well, I don't know—"

Teraeth didn't say anything, but he watched me carefully.

My teacher back in the Shadowdancers, a woman we all called Mouse, had a couch that she'd somehow managed to stash in the small back-alley store she used as a base of operations. I assume she'd had some of the larger, burlier folk in the Shadowdancers do the actual moving; the thing must have weighed four times as much as she did. Anyway, it was a ridiculously fluffy, overstuffed thing that no self-respecting merchant or freeman would be caught dead having anywhere in their house.

Naturally, I'd loved it without restraint; when you jumped on it, you *bounced.*

Teraeth chuckled and ran his fingers over the stuffed woven fabric. "This is a happy memory? It looks like it's home to a dozen mice and at least three rabbits. Although it's comfortable, I suppose." He stretched out against it to emphasize that fact, setting his feet in Janel's lap. "So I guess that answers that question."

I jerked my gaze from studying his legs. "I'm sorry, what?"

Teraeth laughed. He hadn't missed what had distracted me. "What Janel asked. How do you fight a city? I say, you don't. *You occupy it.*"

Janel grabbed one of Teraeth's feet, quickly stripped off the sandal, and began to massage it. Teraeth made a noise, and yes, I was distracted again.

But no. I concentrated on what he'd just said. They were both right. If I could change a couch, why not something larger? A room, a house . . . the city itself? If these things were reflections of Vol Karoth's mind, what happened when I turned them into reflections of myself?

Before we could explore that idea any further, however, the world changed.

Jarith's memory
Stonegate Pass, Khorvesh, Quur
Three years before his death

When Jarith came back from patrol, the emperor was sitting in his office.

The hilarious thing about that—the seriously laugh-until-one-cried thing—was that his secretary, Hivar, had no idea. Jarith just walked back inside, still sweaty and dusty, wanting nothing so much as a bath and several gallons of mint tea, when Hivar had said, "Would you like me to block off your afternoon?" Which was Hivar's exceptionally polite way of saying, "I know you've just returned from a three-day tour of the most miserable outposts on the borders of the empire. Maybe you should rest before you spend three more days filling out forms?"

As Jarith's mother wasn't stationed at Stonegate, his secretary had decided to fill in on her behalf.

Jarith gave the man a wry smile. "One report won't kill me."

"Oh, you say that now . . ." But Hivar didn't try to stop him, and Hivar didn't mention that anyone was waiting for him.

Because likely, he just hadn't known.

Jarith realized the moment he stepped through the doorway and saw the unassuming man sitting there.

He'd only met the emperor on one previous occasion, but it wasn't one he'd likely soon forget. Sandus still dressed in a way that might easily be mistaken for an itinerant musician, although his patchwork sallí was a little too nondescript. With the man's hair and his clear Marakori features, Jarith imagined that most people probably assumed he was some sort of vagrant, and probably one a bit light with other's property at that. Only the thin copper circlet on his head betrayed his true authority. He no doubt carried the Scepter of Quur on him as well, but Jarith couldn't see it.

Jarith closed the door behind him before bowing.

"That's not really necessary," Sandus said, smiling as he stood.

"Your Majesty, I . . ." Jarith swallowed. He could think of no good reasons, no good reasons at all, for the emperor to be sitting in his office. "Has something happened to my father?"

Sandus's face stuttered in surprise, and then he shook his head. "Oh? No, nothing like that. Nothing like that at all."

"Is it Kihrin? Because if—"

"Instead of you asking me questions until you hit upon the right one, perhaps instead listen to what I have to say?" Emperor Sandus chided, not unkindly.

Jarith crossed over to his desk and sat down and managed not to fidget like a schoolboy for at least three minutes.

"I'm here because of prophecies," Sandus explained, looking like that admittance hurt him somewhere deep inside. "Hmm, that's a rather indirect way of addressing what's important here, I suppose. I'm here because of that girl you've started seeing."

Jarith blinked. They'd have sat here for a long time if Sandus had been waiting for Jarith to hit upon that right guess. "Kalindra? But why—" He paused and swallowed. He liked to think he wasn't an idiot, even if the world occasionally challenged that assumption. He examined the wall for a moment before turning back to Emperor Sandus. "Who does she work for, then?"

Jarith tried to wrestle his pulse back under control. Because if there was one thing he knew, it was the ridiculous lengths that the Royal Houses seemed to be willing to go to gain leverage on council members—and on his father. And then they'd try to blackmail his father over his affairs—or blackmail his mother about hers—only to have the high general laugh in their faces. His parents kept no secrets from each other. Certainly not their lovers.

Sandus looked sad. "Your father taught you to be paranoid." He hesitated. "Not that it's a wrong impulse in this case. Thaena."

Jarith felt all the hairs raise up along the back of his neck. "I'm sorry? What do you mean, Thaena?"

"Kalindra is a member of an organization called the Black Brotherhood. Assassins, mostly, but they do other jobs. I would imagine most people think they're a cult, but they answer directly to the Goddess of Death."

"And you know this because of . . . prophecies?" Jarith felt dazed and feverish, his gut lined with hot lead. "So you could be wrong, then. The Devoran Prophecies are vague. Father says they're wrong too often to be believed."

"Oh, that is true," Sandus acknowledged. He was idly thumbing a ring on one of his fingers, the only other piece of jewelry he wore besides the circlet. It was a red stone—ruby or possibly spinel, engraved with something. "But it led me to taking a look at her and I am reasonably sure of my facts in this particular case. She's a Brotherhood assassin." Sandus paused. "Given current events, if her mission has anything to do with you, it's more likely to be protection than harm."

Jarith let out a deep, shuddery breath. "Your Majesty—"

"Please, just call me Sandus."

"*Your Majesty*," Jarith continued, "have you told my father about this?" But even as he asked the question, he knew it was absurd. If Qoran Milligreest knew that someone, anyone, was trying to get close to his family, no matter what their reasons, they would be arrested already.

No. They would be dead.

And it wouldn't be the Emperor of Quur breaking the news to him.

"No," Sandus said. "I haven't. It isn't any of his business."

Jarith stared.

"Well, it isn't," Sandus protested, looking a little flustered for a split moment before the kind paternal mask slammed back into place. "And please understand, there's been a Black Brotherhood member in proximity to your father for years.[1] A situation which only recently changed, largely because of me.[2] So I imagine this is just Thaena replacing the last person. Nothing malicious. She's just not of a sort to bother explaining herself. Goddesses are often like that." Sandus reached forward and tapped the top of a stack of papers. "But it is your business, and I thought you deserved to know so you could decide what to do. This young woman is just doing her sacred duty to her goddess, but you're the one sleeping with her. You're going to have to decide if that's a thing you can continue doing when you know she's lying to you, no matter how well-intentioned those lies might be."

"You're telling me so I can . . . not do anything?" Jarith was starting to regret he hadn't found them a bottle of brandy and poured them both a drink before this started.

"If you like," Sandus said. "That's up to you."

"You just told me that she's seducing me to—"

"No," Sandus said. "I didn't. I'm sure her assignment was to get close to your family. There are plenty of other ways she might have done so. I doubt

---

[1] Terindel, I imagine.
[2] Yes, he's definitely referring to Terindel.

her orders were specifically to seduce you." He added, "I have been told that the Black Brotherhood gives its members a great deal of latitude to decide how a mission is to be accomplished."

"If she knows her cover's blown, would she leave?" Jarith finally asked.

Sandus gave him a very considering gaze. "I have no way to know that."

"Right." Jarith exhaled. "Right. Of course you don't."

Sandus was still staring at Jarith with uncomfortable intensity. "You're not going to turn her in, are you?"

"My father would kill her!" Jarith's snap was instantaneous. He quieted. "I mean. He would certainly have her arrested."

"And you'll keep seeing her?"

Jarith paused. Sandus waited on the answer so expectantly. So intently. As though it wasn't trivial at all.

"Yes," Jarith said slowly.

A flicker of emotion crossed Sandus's face, so quickly Jarith would probably have missed it except, well, he'd been looking for some clue. Sorrow. Resignation. As if Jarith had just announced he was running out into the Korthaen Blight the next morning, naked and weaponless. Done something foolish.

Sealed his own fate.

Jarith stood up. "Thank you," he said, bowing with all the politeness his father had ever ingrained in him. "I appreciate the warning, Your Majesty."

The corner of Sandus's mouth quirked. He seemed to understand he was being dismissed and found the experience amusing. "Certainly. It was the least I could do."[3]

And with that, he vanished.

Jarith sighed, letting the echoes of the man's presence slowly drain from the room, although there was nothing to be done about the slick taint of distrust and suspicion his news had left behind. That would stain, difficult if not impossible to clean.

He fled the office and headed out to find her.

Stonegate Pass was built on fear. The fear that the morgage might once more swarm through the gates of that fortress to rampage over the empire. The fear that another race's desperation might prove stronger than Quuros loyalty.

The fear that sooner or later, everyone gets what they deserve, even empires.

Because of that fear, the architects of Stonegate had never stopped building, each generation adding to the fortress and its surrounding walls. They built higher and stronger until there was no chance—none at all—that the morgage would ever invade through that narrow cleft into the heart of Quur ever again. They ignored all the paths still open: north through the Dragonspires, east through the Kulma swamp, or simply anyplace along the western cliffs that wasn't Stonegate Pass.

---

[3] I don't know why people say things like that. The least he could have done was not show up at all.

Often, Jarith truly wondered if anyone back in the Capital had ever looked at a map.

But it wasn't his place to call his superiors idiots except in the privacy of his own mind. He made his way down the labyrinthine passages until he reached the town that had grown up in the military fortress's shadow. The town (also called Stonegate) was larger than visitors typically expected, but that's because Stonegate had existed for a long time. Long enough for generations to have lived there and have sent their sons to serve on the fortress's walls. Long enough for all the amenities a soldier might ever want to become firm and traditional fixtures: velvet houses and taverns, smithies and stables. There were at least seven licensed mercenary companies, some of whom also operated as fighting schools.

Jarith had met Kalindra of Nevale in a local tavern when one of his men decided to be a little too pushy about demanding her company. As Jarith had picked his man off the floor, after, she'd pointed out how considerate she'd been about not breaking any limbs. Jarith had thought it was considerate; he'd also never seen anyone who could fight like that without a single weapon drawn. When he'd asked her about it, she'd just laughed and told him that if he wanted to know more, he could pay to take her classes at the Ten Metals fighting school like everyone else.

So he had.

Jarith nodded to the man at the front gate as he entered the compound, Kalindra in the normal courtyard she used for training drills, leading a group of students. Later, she'd make them repeat the drills while she roamed their ranks, correcting them with a sharp eye and sharper tongue. He had gathered that of all the teachers at the Ten Metals, she was considered the harshest. Her classes filled up months in advance.

He could believe that she was an assassin. Or at the very least, he could believe that she was someone to whom violence came easily. As good as he was with a sword, he knew perfectly well which of them would win in any fight without one. She would be lethal indeed in any situation where her opponent was unprepared.

But . . . surely, she hadn't been ordered to seduce him. Kalindra wasn't the sort of person Jarith imagined seducing anyone, let alone seducing someone on orders. She didn't flatter or charm, never appeased, made no attempts to mollify. Nothing about her was yielding or soft. Kalindra was a lithe whip of a woman made of scars, calluses, and temper. If her honesty offended other people, she considered that their problem.

All of which objectively made her a massive bitch, but he'd also seen how she was with the younger students. How patient and kind, never mocking them while somehow managing to never lie either. How her eyes shadowed every time she saw a powerless person, be it child or slave, mistreated. And while she never did anything—at least not that he'd ever been aware of—Jarith had noticed something almost like a pattern to what happened to the worst offenders in town. The bullies and abusers, the ones who were happy to exploit their power—namely, they tended to have "accidents."

Maybe he was being naïve. Maybe she was the perfect woman to seduce him.

When the lesson was over and a dozen children had retreated, scrambling outside to play because they hadn't burned off enough energy practicing sword forms, he stepped forward. "Kalindra? Are you free for a few minutes?"

Her smile was wry. "For you, I'll make the time." She motioned over toward a room to the side where they stored supplies.

The moment she closed the door behind them, he pushed her against it. Her back only just touched the wood before she flipped them over so she was pushing him. They wrestled with each other to see who could grab the other by the wrists. The lone high window of the storeroom painted the sides of their faces with ghostly light.

The whole time, they never stopped kissing. She pushed him as he worked his way down the side of her neck, biting.

"Stop, stop!" she said, laughing. "You know I love this, but Dervala gave me dirty looks and cold tea for two weeks after the last time he caught us in a classroom."

He almost said, "Since when has that ever stopped you?" but instead, he put his hands on the sides of her cheeks and gave her a softer, gentler kiss. "You're right. I just couldn't–"

The delight in her eyes turned into something else. "Jarith, is something wrong?"

Jarith rested his head against hers, smelled her hair. She still smelled like sweat from the class layered under the scent of roses because Kalindra always insisted on using the most ridiculously flowery soaps. But he also wasn't answering, and he knew that with each passing second, Kalindra would grow only more worried and frustrated.

"You know you're a good person, right?"

She pulled back and stared at him for an endless second, then flushed. "If you're just here to mock me–" She reached and tried opening the door. Tried, but she'd flipped them around, which meant he now blocked it.

"No," Jarith said. "I'm not making fun of you. It just . . . it just occurred to me that you might not know. How good you are. That maybe someone should let you in on the secret." He caressed the side of her face. "You can hide it from everyone else, but not from me."

She stopped pushing and met his eyes. Neither of them moved.

"Something happened. What happened?"

Jarith paused. This had been a mistake. He'd just been swept up in the need to see her, to tell her how he really felt about her. He opened his mouth to say something, anything. The words hung in the air, unspoken.

"Jarith." Her expression was swiftly shifting from confused and worried to angry.

He leaned his forehead against hers, rubbed his hands over her shoulders. "I just realized today that what we have is precious and I was taking it for granted. And you . . ." He inhaled. "You mean so much to me. Because you are good and because I know you care."

Kalindra stared.

Jarith could feel the compliments slide off Kalindra like water off palm leaves. She never paid any attention to anyone's attempts to tell her that she'd done well or was good; she only ever heard the criticisms. It made him want to scream, want to take her by the arms and shake her until she understood. Which would only result in him having at least one broken arm and sabotage the entire fucking point.

"Are you drunk?" Kalindra finally asked him.

"No, I–" He swallowed, fought down the temptation to mumble a prayer to Khored. Jarith wondered for a fleeting crystal moment if he should tell her. Tell her that he knew the truth. Tell her that he knew where her true loyalties lay.

But he was too scared she'd leave.

"Marry me," he said instead.

Kalindra laughed and then stopped laughing as she realized he was serious. "What?"

"Marry me," Jarith repeated.

"No," Kalindra said.

It was Jarith's turn to look confused and incredulous. "No?"

"No!" Kalindra repeated. "Gods, no! How can you even ask me a thing like that? You don't know a thing about me, Jarith. I'm a horrible person."

"You're not."

She looked appalled and then angry. "You don't . . . you don't know that! You can't make a snap judgment like . . ." She was so angry she was rendered near speechless and sputtering.

"Kalindra." He kept his voice soft, his movements gentle as he reached for her. "Marry me."

"No," she said again, but her expression softened. "Ask me another time."

He did. The fifth time, she said yes.

25: HELL'S DOORS UNLOCKED

Kalindra's response
The Lighthouse at Shadrag Gor

Kalindra rubbed her hands over her eyes. She was crying, unable to stop herself, and also laughing.

She wondered if she might be going just a little mad.

He'd known. Jarith had known all about Kalindra's secrets—or at least about the secret that had really mattered. She wondered how the emperor had found out, but then answered her own question immediately: the fucking prophecies. Apparently, Kalindra was a predictable, anticipated commodity. Not terribly difficult to identify as an angel of Thaena if one knew what to look for.[1]

She found it difficult to grapple with the idea that Jarith had known and not only hadn't flinched but had kept running forward . . . Kalindra wanted him to show up so she could scream at him. So she would ask—no, demand—that he explain how he could possibly have been that stupid.

He'd known and he'd married her, anyway. He'd given her a son. Why would he do such a thing? Why would he make her family? She'd always known he was a little naïve, a little too trusting, but this . . .

He'd known exactly what she was and he'd loved her, anyway. She didn't understand how it could be possible. Now her loving Jarith? That was different. That had been easy. Anyone would love Jarith if given even the tiniest opportunity. Jarith was kind and diligent and so fucking good. In contrast, she'd always known he would have despised her if he'd known the truth.

Except apparently, she'd underestimated just how good he was.

Someone wrapped their arms around her. She didn't fight it, too shocked and upset to react normally. After a moment, she realized she was crying on Galen's shoulder.

"Why would he do that?" she whispered. "Why?"

"Because he was Jarith," Galen answered, which shouldn't have been an answer but somehow was.

A harsh, loud scratching sound filled the air, coming from somewhere upstairs. It sounded very much like something dragging a weapon across a stone floor.

Senera asked, "Still no one upstairs, I assume?"

---

[1] And one shouldn't forget that while the ultimate leader of the Gryphon Men cabal was apparently Grizzst, Emperor Sandus was the active leader. And that was quite the spy network. It's difficult to say just how much they know.

Xivan replied, "Do you feel like checking this time?"

"Not especially, no."

Kalindra raised her head and wondered, just for a moment, if the person rattling around upstairs might be Jarith. Did she dare take that risk? Did she dare go hunting for him?

But she never found out. The world changed.

Jarith's memories
Stonegate Pass, Khorvesh, Quur
One week after the Capital Hellmarch

It didn't know its own name.

It didn't exist, really, not in the way most creatures define existence. It had no face or name or body. No memories of who it was or what it had been.

Just the dark and pain.

It was hungry, and it was cold. There really wasn't any difference between these two states of being. It was an empty void that existed only to devour. Any goals or dreams it might have ever had in its life were reduced to that.

It was in a city, with no knowledge of how it arrived there. Just the sudden awareness of its existence in a cluster of buildings, a forest made of stone and mortar, quicklime and clay. The scent of burning wood hung thick in the air, the world tasting of fire and fear. The terrified fear of the herd—of the prey—was sweet and rich, the hunting so easy that even someone as weak as it was had no trouble feasting.

They were all so solid, so corporeal. Limited. But it was a massive collection of such prey congregating in one place, a giant herd that screamed and ran, their tenyé flickering with the warmth of their bodies, the sweet taste of their fear. It was not the only one of its kind present, but they all seemed to be in much the same situation it was: hungry.

At first, it filled itself on the fires that rose up all around the city, turning flames to ash and then to ice. But it wasn't enough, and there was so much prey. So many people filled with so much life, so many emotions.

Many of its kind took on physical forms to attack, to better rend and tear and frighten, but it did not. It was too weak. It didn't have enough control.

That didn't mean it wasn't still dangerous.

It found an injured life-form. Probably he had managed to slay the demon who had caused his injuries, but not before receiving the mortal wound that would kill him. He must have known he was dying, though, and he was scared.

That fear tasted so good. So it fed.

The moment it did, it realized it had made a mistake. Or, no. It wasn't a mistake, exactly. But as the man's soul and memories spiraled through its consciousness like a ribbon unspooling from a spindle, it encountered the trap that all demons must deal with sooner or later.

Namely, who defines a demon's sense of self? As every lower soul was eaten and every upper soul absorbed, a demon's identity was subsumed into a whirling maelstrom comprised of all the other souls proceeding it. That first infected soul was less a consciousness than a seed, the personality it would

later develop growing and evolving as more and more souls merged together
into a seething ball of hunger and need.

And possibly–probably–it would have been like that in this instance as
well, except for one little quirk of luck: Hivar remembered Jarith.

So when it–when he–killed Hivar and devoured his souls, some of those
memories that had flooded over him, cool and bright, had included very specific memories. Memories of himself. Memories of Jarith.

And Jarith woke.

Perhaps not fully. Not completely. But enough to know his name, enough
to remember that he had once been a man. Enough to know how much he'd
lost and exactly who he had just betrayed. Hivar had congratulated him on
his wedding, had been there with a wry smile and a last round of drinks when
he'd been transferred back to the Capital. Hivar had–

Jarith screamed and screamed and screamed. The people couldn't hear
him, and the demons didn't care.

Jarith still didn't have a body: he wasn't strong enough to craft his own.
The best he could do was a swirl of darkness, like ink spilling into water.

He fled into the Blight.

Kihrin's story
Inside Vol Karoth's prison

We were all quiet when those visions ended. They'd come hot on each other's
heels, close enough that we hadn't yet moved from sitting on my re-creation
of Mouse's couch. There'd been no warning, but that had been true for several
visions now, from both sides.

I was no longer participating in the conversation.

"Fuck." Teraeth pulled his feet away from Janel and righted himself, putting a hand to his forehead. Janel slid down from the arm of the couch and
just sat there.

I closed my eyes and tried not to think about . . . oh, how exactly was I supposed to not think about Jarith? I spent a few minutes cursing Vol Karoth and
his delightful little gift of knowing exactly how much Xaltorath had broken
my friend.

Janel scowled. "I still cannot believe . . ." She sighed. "What am I saying?
Of course Xaltorath would be so base and petty as to try to arrange Jarith's
destruction at my hand."

Teraeth raised his head. "What?"

I threw an arm around him, kissed the top of his head, even though I had
to stretch a little, because he is taller than I am. I assumed that in the time
I'd been gone, lost in his own grief, Teraeth certainly hadn't made an effort
to read through the other chronicles. It's unlikely Thurvishar would have
offered either, under the circumstances. "Xaltorath tried to trick Janel into
eating Jarith. Very maternal. 'Won't you be a good child and eat the demon I
brought you? It's fresh.'"

Janel shuddered, so I threw the other arm around her and drew her in to rest her head on my chest. "I hate her so much," Janel said. "You know she didn't have to . . . do that. She didn't have to do any of that."

I kissed the top of her head too, which was much easier. "I thought we'd established that she—they?—is a petty bitch. Does she need any more reason than that to hurt you?"

Janel drew short, pausing as some idea occurred to her. Her eyes blazed as she stood. "In this case? . . . Yes. I think she does."

Teraeth and I looked at each other.

"What did you just realize?" Teraeth asked her.

Janel put her hands behind her back and began to pace, lost in her own thoughts, not so much as glancing at either of us for several moments. "She didn't turn Jarith into a demon because of me. Or rather, if she had turned Jarith into a demon purely to hurt me, then none of what follows would make any sense. Xaltorath clearly tried to strip Jarith's mind and reduce him to nothing but malleable hate, and then she dumped him into a major population center. That should have resulted in him cannibalizing his way through a veritable swath of souls to the point where Jarith's personality would have been destroyed in the tumult of a thousand souls battling each other for dominance. Which means that when I ate him, I *wouldn't* have recognized him."

"Huh," Teraeth murmured. "You have a point."

There was something wrong with that logic, but it took me a moment to put my finger on the fault. Then I saw it. "But you can identify individual souls. That's what happened when you tried to eat Xaltorath, wasn't it? You could identify the unique constituent parts."

Janel didn't seem the slightest bit unsettled. I saw immediately that she'd already considered and dismissed that point. "She didn't know I could do that," Janel said flatly.

Teraeth scowled. "How can you be sure?"

"She'd have never let me anywhere near her if she'd thought I could do that," Janel said. "Now that she knows, the only reason I'm still alive is because she thinks she needs me as leverage more than she needs me destroyed."

"Leverage? Against who?" I said.

Janel just gave me a look.

"Oh," I said. "Right."

Janel pointed at Teraeth with an amused flick of her fingers. "*Your* emotional connection with our darling Anointed Hero wasn't so predictable."

"Nice to know I can still surprise someone," Teraeth said.

Janel smiled as she gave him a bow. "But I believe the point of the original argument still stands; Xaltorath wouldn't have tried to destroy Jarith's personality if her entire motivation for doing so rested on me identifying that same personality so as to understand the enormity of my sin. Thus, she had a different reason for targeting him." Janel held out her hands to both of us—an invitation to stand. "My suspicion is that if Xaltorath really is repeating the same loop of time, manipulating it with each repetition until she gains the result she wants, then in one of those previous time lines, Jarith was much more of a problem."

As we both stood, Teraeth chuckled. "Oh, not just in a previous time line. I think Xaltorath's fucked up here. If Jarith can pull himself together, he's going to be a problem for Xaltorath *now*."

A slow, quiet smile spread across Janel's face. "Gods, I do hope so." She kissed both our hands, eyes glimmering with mischief, before dropping them as she headed for the door. "We should keep going. We have a lot to redecorate."

Kalindra's reaction
The Lighthouse at Shadrag Gor
Just after Jarith's memory

If Kalindra didn't cry this time, it was only because she'd already shed all her tears, leaving only a pervasive, thorough numbness.

Her gaze flickered around the room. Galen was still next to her, arm thrown around Kalindra's shoulder. Kalindra honestly wasn't sure which of them was comforting the other. Maybe both. Talea lingered over near the stacked bunks where Thurvishar, Teraeth, and Janel's bodies were laid. Senera and Qown had formed a sort of scholars' area to one side, commandeering one of the tables and using it to spread out several journals, stacks of paper, and inkstones (one of which was *that* inkstone). Xivan paced over by the door, occasionally giving stricken glances toward Talea, and Sheloran sat primly on one of the other couches, eyes closed and practically hiding behind her fan. Talon held up one of the walls.

When Senera set down her brush, Kalindra could all but feel the whole room flinch.

Before Senera could even open her mouth, Qown chirped, "Finally! Some good news!"

Kalindra was up from the couch before Galen had a chance to pull her back down. "What?"

Senera visibly winced while Qown didn't seem to have any idea what he might have said wrong. "Oh yes." He turned to face Kalindra. "This is very promising. Much better than I expected. If that vision was supposed to upset us, well." He drew himself up. "It didn't do a very good job."

As Kalindra's jaw began to ache, she realized she was grinding her teeth. How the ever-loving fuck was a vision showing her husband as a demon so lost and broken he didn't even remember who he was until he murdered one of their oldest friends "good news"?

"Hoookay," Talea said as she slid over in front of Kalindra. "We're all going to pause for a second, and the scary lady with the knives—as opposed to all the other varieties of scary lady present—is going to let the man explain what the fuck he's talking about." Talea gave Kalindra a stern look. "Right?"

Kalindra glared. Xivan was right about Talea. Kalindra could see the resemblance to Jarith. He'd have liked Talea. "I wouldn't stab him just for being an idiot."

Talea cocked an eyebrow.

Kalindra crossed her arms over her chest and huffed. "It would be like hurting a puppy for chewing on a shoe."

Qown's eyes widened as it seemed to finally sink in that he might need to watch what he said. "I, uh . . . um. What I mean is, the level of self-awareness and cognition between this vision, which seems to have occurred during nascent development, and the later vision we saw with the both of you on Devors, are significantly different."

Senera tilted her head. "Yes. We know this. Thurvishar has several eyewitness accounts of Jarith going after other demons. Once in the Manol and then again later at the Well of Spirals. In both cases, the description was consistent. A man-shaped being formed of shadows with a featureless, eyeless porcelain mask. A fondness for using swords–I'll assume Khorveshan imchii."

Kalindra didn't know what she was feeling. "He was hunting demons?"

Qown nodded enthusiastically. "That's what I mean! Independent ideation, consistent bodily autonomy, self-identification. From this vision, I would expect him to be just leaving nascent development for the Imp stage, but this is . . . this is Malice-level development at the very least. That's so fast."

Senera looked like she might be in physical pain. "Qown?"

The priest looked over at her. "Yes?"

"Malice level?" She gave him a flat stare. "What are you talking about?"

"What do you mean?" Qown blinked. "I'm talking about Jarith, obviously. Oh. I, uh . . ." Qown's expression turned to embarrassment. "I'm sorry. I suppose I should have first explained the ranking system I created to describe the stages of demonic development."

"Yes," Senera said dryly. "You should have."[2]

"Right." Galen choked back black laughter. "Your specialty is demons, isn't it?"

Qown threw him a vaguely hurt look. "You don't have to say it like it's some sort of vice. It could be very helpful in this instance."

"Qown!" Kalindra snapped. "Who cares about the ranking system? So my husband is more demonic than you think he should be. How is that a good thing?"

"Because he's still Jarith," Qown explained. When he saw the blank look on Kalindra's face–on more faces than just her own, Kalindra was willing to bet–he stood up from his chair and began gesturing. "So most demons are infected–the nascent stage–and then put through what I call the Imp stage. That's when their minds and personalities are broken down through a combination of torture, forced inhumanization, and deprivation combined with a violent merging of multiple souls. In many ways, demons are the spiritual equivalent of Talon–"

"Excuse me," Talon interrupted with mock outrage. "I most certainly am not–oh. Hmm. You know, actually, that is a fair analogy." She flicked her fingers. "Carry on."

"Talon is a physical accumulation of memories, but demons are a spiritual accumulation of souls. They are not a single entity by the time you or I would ever meet one. It usually isn't an exaggeration to say that a demon isn't the person you once loved anymore because they literally can't be." Qown scanned the

---

[2] Yes, I did sit him down and make him write out the full ranking system. It's in the back.

room and held out his hands, clearly waiting for the "Aha!" of understanding. It didn't come.

"And?" Kalindra said.

"But Jarith is still Jarith," Senera said.

"No, he isn't!" Kalindra protested. "He doesn't remember who he is. He has a list he repeats to himself. That's not the same thing at all!"

Qown shook his head. "It's not, but it's a thousand times better than most other demons. He's skipped the Imp and Spite stages and landed directly on Malice—which is the stage where a demon can travel around on their own and have their own unique personality and appearance. Demons who reach that stage aren't salvageable—normally. Your husband might be the exception."

"Don't give her false hope, Qown," Senera said. "You can't promise that Jarith can be saved."

"But if there's even the slimmest chance," Qown said, "doesn't she deserve to know?"

"Yes," Galen said firmly. "She does. We both do." He seemed to be daring Senera to contradict him.

Kalindra breathed in and out for several long counts. She wasn't sure she agreed with Galen. She wanted her husband back. Obviously, she wanted her husband back. But at the same time, she didn't know if she could stand it if that turned out to be a false, impossible hope. It would be too much.

She wondered if Vol Karoth knew that. If what otherwise might have seemed like a colossal misstep—giving them something that seemed like a glimpse of light—was really just a colossal drop into darkness.

"There really isn't anything else I can pull from Jarith," Talon said. "Not the way he is right now. So . . . if no one minds, I think I'm going to return to picking on the mortals."

"Which one—?" Galen started to ask.

The world changed.

26: The Alternative to Peace

Qown's memory
The Lower Circle of the Capital City, Quur
Two weeks after arriving at the Shattered Veil Club

Sheloran tapped Qown on the shoulder a second before she leaned over and whispered, "Mask room in fifteen minutes." She fluttered away a moment later, laughing as she greeted some other guest.

Sheloran was covered, head to toe, in colorful printed Zheriasian robes, her head covered by a Zheriasian-style veil. And in a rare nod to the overall disguise, she'd gone without her fan (it must have been a hardship). All part of the "Veiled Lady" act, which she used when she was at the Shattered Veil Club. It was difficult for Qown not to think of her—both of them, Sheloran and Galen—as children playing dress-up, but then he remembered just how illegal what they were doing was. The last two weeks had left him with the very real impression that both had gotten themselves involved with criminals and criminal enterprises that carried real risks. He'd learned names and faces, even if some of those were neatly hidden behind code names and aliases. Someone called Scabbard. Others named Crow, Sharp, and Dapper.

All of this had been in place long before they'd fled down to the Lower Circle to escape Tishenya and Gerisea D'Mon. And if it made matters much easier, Qown couldn't escape the feeling that he was touching on the fringes of something much more dangerous and illegal than he'd been aware existed. He'd have complained to Relos Var, but one, how could Relos Var have known, and two, it had made smuggling out people so much easier.

He tucked his supplies back into a small case, cleaned up everything, and retreated back to the mask room, where he'd been spending his nights. By the time he made it back there, Galen and Anlyr had beaten him to it and were waiting along with Sheloran. Qown entered and closed the door behind him.

"Good news," Galen said, waving a piece of parchment. "Our long suffering is finally over. By which I mean, we've set up a meeting with Aunt Tishenya to explain our position."

"That's wonderful," Qown said, feeling truly relieved over the matter. "When and where?"

"Tomorrow, midafternoon at the Culling Fields. We'll have a table right in the open, plenty of security."

"Plenty of crowds," Anlyr corrected. "Plenty of vulnerability and plenty of opportunity for ambush."

Galen frowned at the man. "Tishenya would be an idiot to try anything there."

"My lord, I don't recommend any plan that relies on an enemy's ability to not be an idiot." Anlyr tilted his head. "We should plan for both stupidity and cleverness."

That won Anlyr a warm smile, while Qown forced himself not to bunch his hands into fists. It wasn't like Anlyr was wrong, anyway. He just wished Anlyr would be right while not looking at Galen like he was the next course at a banquet. At the very least, wasn't that sort of thing unprofessional? Guards were supposed to, you know, guard. He found some solace in the fact that Sheloran seemed to agree with him. Or at least he'd caught her giving the handsome D'Mon soldier a speculative look on several occasions when they were in private, when Anlyr wasn't paying attention. Qown was certain it wasn't a look of approval.

"It's fine," Sheloran said, "we'll have High Lord and Lady D'Talus watching—"

Galen made a face. "We won't."

Sheloran turned to her husband. "What was that?"

"It's an internal House D'Mon matter. If we bring House D'Talus into it any more than we already have, then we wouldn't have a crate to stand on when my aunts brought their contacts into matters. Tishenya was married into House D'Kard—I'd really rather not have the *Watchmen* involved in this. No Voice of the Council either. You do not want the High Council interferring. They'd panic just because of the precedent and ruin the whole thing. I've sent messages to your mother to make sure she knows what's going on, and she approved."

Sheloran seemed less than pleased. "Did she?"

"Don't be mad at her. She's already done a damn sight more for us than anyone would have expected." Galen flashed his wife a brilliant smile.

Sheloran drummed her fingernails against the glass tabletop. "Blue, if this goes wrong, it will go very wrong, very fast."

"If I may suggest, my lord," Anlyr said, "I would recommend that I forgo the uniform and stay in the crowd."

Galen studied the guard. "Aunt Gerisea saw you."

"But wasn't focused on me. With all respect, guards are all but invisible."

"I'd also like to take a hair from everyone's head," Qown said.

Everyone paused and stared at him.

"In case something goes wrong," Qown said. "It makes healing much easier. It's a trick I learned from—" He waved a hand. He didn't want to bring up how it was a trick he'd learned from Senera, of all people. "Well, back east."[1]

"Right," Galen said. "In case something goes wrong. Fine. Qown, you're with me. Taunna is saving a table for us and will make sure nothing that reaches said table is drugged. So. Let's do this."

"I'm just saying you're going to need to learn to see past the Veil," Qown found himself telling Galen later. They'd taken a carriage to the Upper Circle without incident and set up shop at a table in the back of the tavern. Anlyr

---

[1] It's not a "trick." It's just being efficient.

was working the crowd along with several of the Culling Fields' own security, while Galen and Sheloran settled back with their servants and a spread of finger foods and teas.[2]

Qown had brought books with him, under the assumption that at some point he should actually do his job—the one where he was supposed to teach Galen magic. Which is where the problem had started.

"Do I really, though?" Galen seemed supremely uninterested.

"Yes. You really do! Learning to see past the First Veil is the first piece of magic any wizard is expected to learn—"

"I thought that was their witchgift."

"You don't learn that," Qown said. "You just ... do it. And anyway, you don't have one, so we should start with this."

Galen cocked his head to the side. "That's an interesting assumption."

"What? That you don't—" Qown blinked at the man. "You don't, do you? I mean, you don't have a witchgift."

Galen picked up a piece of fruit rolled in spices. Qown had been somewhat bemused to discover that Galen was a great fan of Capital street foods, the spicier the better. He'd even gone so far as to claim that non-spicy food gave him indigestion, which was ludicrous and totally not how the human body worked.[3] Qown looked away for a moment as Galen sucked all the chili powder off the mango before finally eating it.

"It's rude to assume I don't."

Qown frowned at him. "Very well. Here I am, not assuming. I'm asking. Do you have a witchgift?"

Galen leaned forward until he was far too close. He stared at Qown for a long, awkward span of seconds. Then the corner of his mouth quirked. "Yes. I do." He leaned back in his chair and picked up another piece of fruit.

"Of course you do," Qown muttered. "Why not? And what is your witchgift?" He held up a finger. "Don't say it's personal. I told you mine."

Galen threw back his head and laughed. "Oh, you are so much fun to tease. Please never change."

Qown felt himself growing red. "So you were just teasing me? You were lying when you said you had one?"

"Oh no." Galen's smile didn't go away, but it settled into something wistful and bittersweet. "I developed it a few years back. I was in a bad place. After my brother, Kihrin, ran off, my grandfather Therin set his foot down about my father beating me, so—" He sighed. "So my father took to locking me up in the palace dungeons."

Qown couldn't stop himself from gasping. "What?"

Galen shrugged. "Technically speaking, he wasn't laying a finger on me."

A horrible slithering feeling crawled over Qown's spine.

"The dungeons are small," Galen explained. "And there's no light. Not a bit of it. And you can hear things ... skittering and crawling ... out in the darkness."

---

[2] At some point during all this, Therin D'Mon must have been in the same room, but no one in Galen's party noticed.

[3] No, but it is how the human mind works. I could see Galen having a stress reaction to food that reminded him of his father, and Darzin D'Mon didn't like spicy food.

"I . . . I can't imagine—" Qown's heart shrank at the very thought of it. And yet he could imagine so easily, because Darzin had always been the worst sort of person, who reveled in nothing as much as another person's fear.

"Now since my maternal grandfather is High Lord of House D'Aramarin," Galen said, "it would have been nice if my witchgift had involved teleporting in some fashion, yes? Even better, making a gate. Ah, that would have been so nice. But no."

"So what is it?"

"I can see in the dark. That's it. I can't even make a light. That would have been *useful.*" He shook his head. "I never told my father. I think he just would have taken it as another reason to be disappointed in me."

"Probably." Qown swallowed something painful and sharp. "I've met your father," he said very quietly.

The casual, mocking nostalgia Galen had wrapped around himself fell away, a blade fully unsheathed. "You what? When?"

"Not recently," Qown admitted. "It was . . . several years ago. When I was in Yor. I didn't like him. He was perfectly awful. It doesn't surprise me to hear that he treated you that way. He must have been very insecure."

Galen exhaled and leaned back in his chair, made himself comfortable again. "Sure. Not the word I'd use, but let's go with *insecure.*"

Sheloran tapped the space in front of Galen with her fan. "Not to break this up, but your aunts are here."

Two women had entered the tavern, accompanied by a small but very competent-looking contingent of guards. Were he the type to bet, he'd be willing to make a wager or two that these men had previously worked for House D'Kard before they came to work for House D'Mon. On the other hand, some of the men looked Khorveshan.

Qown found himself wondering if they had ever belonged to a mercenary company.

Qown gathered up all the books and put them away in his bag before he took a respectful step back. Sheloran and Galen remained sitting.

"Nephew," Tishenya said coolly.

Gerisea said nothing, but her blue eyes flickered around the table as though sliding razors across throats. Her gaze swept past Qown without a trace of recognition.

"Please, have a seat. Would you like anything? I can have the bartender bring over an unopened bottle."

"No, I—"

"Yes, please," Gerisea interrupted. She punctuated that with a small sneeze and immediately pulled a handkerchief from her agolé. "Apologies, but I have a slight cold. I'm sure the wine will be medicinal, not to mention we could all use a drink."

Galen smiled tightly and waved over to the bartender, who wasn't Taunna, but some other man whom Qown didn't know. Galen's instructions to the man for several sealed jars of plum wine were vague enough to ensure that he couldn't possibly be asking for something prepared in advance.

Qown immediately corrected himself. That was naïve. He hadn't prepared anything in advance, but it was always possible.

After the jars had been picked open by Galen and glasses poured for everyone, a moment of tense calm fell over the group.

"We were told you had an offer," Tishenya said.

"I'm just beside myself with excitement," Gerisea added before sneezing again.

Qown frowned. He didn't trust Gerisea one bit. Qown checked the wine. He checked the glasses. Nothing was poisoned.

"Less an offer than a redefining of terms." Galen motioned to one of the waitstaff, who brought over a tray carrying several sets of paper. He handed one of the sets to the older of the two sisters. "I'll wait while you look these over."

Tishenya scanned the documents. Halfway through, her eyes widened and she started over, reading more carefully. She lowered the pages to stare at Galen with an open mouth.

"So I've spent the last week or so checking," Galen said, picking up his wineglass and swirling the contents around, "and inheritance laws for the royal families are remarkably, um, what is the term? Common law. There's no law that's ever been passed that explicitly spells out how inheritance has to work. I found at least four occasions in various house histories where a high lord just . . . changed . . . who was eligible to inherit. So that made me think: What if there was a way to legally solve all our problems?"

Tishenya held up the first page. "This makes you high lord."

"What?" Gerisea squawked. "Let me see that." She tried to grab the page away from her sister.

"A formality," Sheloran said. "Galen can't change the legal inheritance standards for House D'Mon unless he is high lord. If both of you, as his only remaining family, acknowledge Galen is high lord, then it's indisputable."

"But our father–" Tishenya started to say.

"Is either dead or not coming back," Gerisea finished. "But I'm sorry. You honestly think that we're going to entertain a fiction this outlandish? Name you high lord? Why in all the Veils would we do a thing like that?"

Galen gestured toward the papers. "Because that second document stipulates that, in the event I ever become high lord, my first–and *last*–act of office shall be to change the inheritance laws of the house to disregard gender, effective retroactively." Into the stunned silence of the two women, Galen looked at Tishenya and said, "You are my grandfather's oldest child. If gender were not at play, there would be no contest or dispute about inheritance, because you would have always been heir and later high lady. And everything about you suggests you'd be good at the job. So take it. I remove myself from succession. You become lady of the house, Gerisea becomes lady heir, and who is next in line after that becomes an issue for one of Gerisea's children to sort out among themselves before the crown is ever in danger of reaching me."

Tishenya stared at him like he'd just covered himself in bright yellow paint, but Gerisea just sneered. "You honestly expect us to believe that you'd willingly abdicate? Reject the wealth that would be yours as high lord? No one just gives up power."

Galen rolled his eyes. "Oh yes, because House D'Mon is what I think of when I imagine 'wealth' these days."

Sheloran started laughing. When the two women gave her a look, she flicked open her fan with an insouciant twirl of her wrist and smiled at the D'Mon sisters. "Oh, he married me. I don't think he's giving up power at all."

Gerisea did not look impressed. "You're the youngest of a half-dozen daughters. I hardly see how marrying you improves his prospects."

Qown fought to keep his expression blank. It hadn't seemed like Sheloran had siblings when they visited the Rose Palace. Had they all been married off?

Sheloran, meanwhile, found that statement endlessly delightful and laughed as she hid behind her fan. "Ah. Well, then, that's hardly your problem, is it?"[4]

"Indeed," Galen said, who also seemed amused. "That reminds me. I did strike a deal to supply the house with a few thousand healers who normally are with the Vishai, but I'm afraid the deal was with me. The head of that order was very explicit about the deal being off if I can't continue to act as liaison. Because I'm dead or imprisoned, for example."

"A few thousand!" Tishenya grabbed her glass of wine and took a large drink.

"You're lying," Gerisea said, but the accusation was perfunctory. Her expression of distaste and disdain had softened as Galen had continued to explain his terms. Now, she looked thoughtful.

"Oh, I'm not," Galen said. "Four thousand, three hundred, and eighty-six people, all at your service for the next five years. We'll need to build them a temple, but it's still a sweetheart deal. You'd be fools not to jump all over it."

Gerisea picked up her wineglass and stared at it. "Lord heir," she mused just before taking a sip.

"And gained without a fight." Galen pursed his lips. "Well. Without any more fighting. Which we really can't afford to do. There aren't many of us left."

Gerisea started chuckling, which turned into full-blown laughter. "And here I thought there was nothing you could say to save your ass. Well done."

"Thank you," Galen said dryly.

Tishenya pushed the paper to Galen. "Sign the inheritance change first."

"Naturally." Galen pulled the quill pen and ink back over from the other side of the table and signed the document with a flourish. "Now I believe it's your turns." He reversed the page and offered the quill to Tishenya.

She took the quill, gave the page one last look, then signed and passed both pen and paper to Gerisea.

Gerisea signed; Qown remembered to breathe.

The younger sister grinned and picked up her glass. "I think this deserves a toast, don't you?" She rolled her eyes. "Come on. I'm not asking anyone to murder a baby."

Sheloran had drunk a little of her wine, but Galen had not. Qown remem-

---

[4] From what I've been able to divine, Sheloran *is* an only child; however, a half-dozen other girls were raised alongside her as daughters of House D'Talus—apparently as decoys.

bered what Taunna had told him about the man never drinking and wondered if this would be an issue.

But it didn't seem to be. Galen picked up his wine and stood. "To new beginnings and family." He raised his glass, waiting until everyone else did the same, and then tipped back his glass.

Everyone set down their glass, but as Gerisea did, she turned to her sister, accidentally knocking her glass over and spilling wine on her agolé.

"Damn it!" Gerisea said. "I'll never get this clean." She muttered to herself and then looked around, raising her voice. "Would someone bring me another glass? Now." That brought on a coughing jag. Gerisea brought the cloth to her lips and kept it there.

Tishenya watched her sister with a small frown on her lips. Qown found himself frowning too, although he couldn't say exactly what was engendering that reaction. Maybe anything out of place, no matter how innocent, would have, considering everything they'd been through. He felt a fleeting moment of regret that he'd been too busy for the last two weeks to take the time to spy on the D'Mon sisters in more than the most casual way. The problem with that, though, was always one of timing; the odds that he'd just happen to drop in during the few minutes they were making their plans had not worked in Qown's favor.

Then it clicked: she was faking the cough. She'd been faking the sneeze. It was all an excuse to keep that cloth near her face. The wine wasn't poisoned though, so why spill the glass? Qown looked over at the bartender who'd taken the glass away, who was now over at the side, staring intently at the tiny bit of liquid that still remained. He had pulled a small blue bottle out from somewhere, holding it up as if for reference . . .

"Galen, throw away your drink!" Qown warned.

Even as he was shouting that, the wine in everyone's glass turned from pale gold to blue and then aerosolized, billowing up and out of in large, fluffy blue clouds of gas. Qown recognized it, of course. He still had nightmares about the damn stuff. Lysian gas. Someone had turned their wine into Lysian gas.

It was enough to kill everyone at the Culling Fields.

Someone else in the room screamed and shouted, "Demons!" which wasn't true, but at least convinced everyone to scatter.

Time slowed down as the adrenaline rush hit him. People were collapsing all around the bar, choking on the insidious blue smoke. Tishenya, her guards—Gerisea's guards too, because whatever protection was on that handkerchief of hers was only going to work for her. Qown pulled out the bundle of hairs he'd gathered earlier and used it as the focal point for drawing the air glyph.[5] Qown didn't feel triumphant, however. Galen and Sheloran were violently coughing.

Gerisea picked up the paperwork and then stepped away from her shaking sister, who had already breathed in a lethal amount of the gas and was now choking to death on it. "Honestly, I'm a little sorry it turned out this way, but I couldn't stop the avalanche once it started. If I'd had any idea he was going to propose that—" She shrugged and turned to leave. She paused long enough to take note of the glowing glyph on Qown's forehead and laughed. "Perfect."

[5] See? More efficient.

Then she screamed and kept screaming, scrambling backward, sobbing with that handkerchief covering her mouth. Pointed at Galen and the others as if in accusation.

Qown felt his insides twist. Anyone who survived this was going to remember a meeting of royals and five survivors with glowing glyphs on their foreheads. It wouldn't be a great leap of logic from there to conclude that they must have been ready for it—must have planned for it. Were responsible for it.

Galen stumbled forward. "Clear everyone! Get out!"

Anlyr came out of the smoke then, good air swirling around his head. His sword was drawn and bloody—Qown didn't ask how it had gotten that way.

"We have to get out of here," Qown said. "If we go to House D'Talus—"

"We can't," Galen said. "If we go to House D'Talus, we only implicate them."

Qown realized Galen was right. Gerisea had set this up so it would be difficult to tell who was at fault. She'd probably intended to blame it on Galen, and that would prove only easier to do now that they would survive the attack. They couldn't flee to another Royal House.

"Everyone outside first," Galen ordered. "Then we'll figure out next steps."

Qown grabbed someone's abandoned mug of pepperleaf beer. The four of them ran outside, along with any tavern customers or help who'd been quick enough to get out. But many of them had stopped, thinking that would be safe. Qown knew better. He knew how Lysian gas worked; it would keep expanding until it had filled up nearly a half-mile-square volume. In a city as crowded as the Capital, that was a lot of people dead. Thousands. Either Gerisea didn't know that or she didn't care, assuming that any Royal Houses in the area would have enough mages on staff to deal with the danger. Using Lysian gas on a Quuros city without clearance was an automatic death sentence, but she probably thought that was a benefit, rather than a flaw.

Qown stopped when they reached the path through the park outside.

"What are you stopping for?" Anlyr said. "Don't be a fool!"

"Shut up and don't interrupt me." Qown stared at the beer. Then he stared at the blue smoke. Qown had spent *years* figuring out exactly what he would do if ever confronted by Lysian gas again. Like hell he was going to let thousands of people die like this.

Never again.

He cast his spell, felt it reverberate through the spreading smoke, a wildfire chain setting everything ablaze as it lit and spread outward.

Then the entire mass of blue smoke shivered, flashed, and collapsed as a shower of alcohol. Notoriously sticky, sweet alcohol since he'd used pepperleaf beer as his focus.

There was no time to clean anything up. They kept running.

Qown's reaction
The Lighthouse at Shadrag Gor

As soon as Qown's memory of the disastrous meeting with the D'Mon sisters ended, Galen turned to Senera. "Can you find out if Taunna Milligreest survived that? We didn't have time to check on her."

Senera paused, shrugged, and repeated the question. "Yes," she answered. "She did. And since I didn't see any soldiers trying to arrest you back in Devors, should I assume the Quuros Empire isn't under the mistaken belief that you're all mass murderers?" She waved vaguely at Galen, Qown, and Sheloran.

Qown exhaled. "No, they're not. I'm not sure how they figured it out, but they must have."[6]

"Good, because that's a complication . . ." Senera's voice trailed off. She looked past Qown at something on the other side of the room, her jaw slack and her eyes staring.

Sheloran gasped.

He turned around. His pulse spiked and he felt a sharp jab of stark fear.

The bodies were gone.

Not just the bodies of Thurvishar, Janel, and Teraeth. The stacked beds Thurvishar had created were missing too. The wall looked exactly the same as it had when they'd first entered the room, without any modification at all.

No one said a word for a moment as everyone seemed to realize the problem at the same time. Then everyone was shouting or talking at once.

"Quiet!" Xivan shouted, because she still had a voice to cut through the clatter of whole armies.

"They could still be in the Lighthouse." Talea sounded tentatively hopeful.

Senera stared at the Name of All Things, at her journal, scowling. Qown expected her to ask the Cornerstone for the answer, but to his surprise, she didn't. Senera slammed her journal closed. "I can't trust its answers. Not here. Not against Vol Korath. If he took their bodies . . ."

Xivan immediately began shouting orders. "Two teams. Nobody goes off alone. Kalindra, Talon, Senera, you're with me. We'll check downstairs. Everyone else, check upstairs."

No one questioned the orders. It made sense to bring Senera along to keep tabs on Talon, and Talon along to keep her in sight, and Kalindra . . .

Well, honestly, Qown wasn't entirely sure why Xivan had picked Kalindra instead of Talea. This didn't seem like the time to ask.

They were still searching rooms when the next vision hit.

---

[6] Several possibilities immediately spring to mind. One, that the Culling Fields is the last place in the world where one should be performing clandestine meetings due to the overwhelming likelihood that someone present will be magically monitoring/recording events. Two, Thaena wasn't yet dead, so questioning any of the slain witnesses and D'Mon guards, including Tishenya, was thus possible. Three, the air sigil is uncommon in the Capital, but thanks to Janel and her friends, very common in Jorat. A group of people knowing how to defend themselves against Lysian gas isn't the automatic mark of guilt Qown thinks it is.

27: An Understanding Among Equals

Kihrin's story
Inside Vol Karoth's prison

I found myself wishing that I'd been more inclined to learn illusions. Because it turned out that such would have been more than a little advantageous when trying to re-create an entire city. Not that I was trying to change the city all at once. I was changing it bit by bit, building by building—sometimes brick by brick. And the most difficult part of it all was that by definition, I was leaving a trail behind me, the change in buildings, plants, and furnishings an obvious sign of my passing.

That wasn't a fantastic feeling when I was struggling to remember what the streets of my childhood looked like. Or to find any happy memories that I remembered well enough to re-create at all.

"Is that what you think a palm tree looks like?" Teraeth squinted and looked dubiously at the plant I'd created.

"Yes? It's those palm trees they had on the island. You know, the ones with the black seeds." I had fond memories of those palms. The fruit was delicious.

"Unemre palms? They don't look like that."

"Boys." Janel put a hand on both our arms. "May I point out that it doesn't matter? What matters is that Kihrin's adding the plants at all. He could be adding wax vines and poison ivy and it wouldn't matter."

I beamed at her. "Thank you. You know, if someone told me that I'd be running around the mind of a dark god trying to re-create my favorite memories of various locations—"

"Badly re-create your memories," Teraeth corrected.

I narrowed my eyes at him while I left the cluster of palms I'd just created off to the side. I wasn't so much re-creating a place I'd been—say the Capital—as mashing together a lot of places I'd been into a single weird pastiche. "Fine. Next time, it's your turn."

Teraeth held out his hands. "I would help if I could. I have a lot of nice, correct memories of places."

Janel walked backward, scanning the area as we traveled. Teraeth didn't seem like he was paying attention, but I knew that wasn't the case; both of them were keeping watch for me so that we'd have warning if Vol Karoth showed up again.

Janel turned her head. "Teraeth's nice memories or Kandor's nice memories?"

"Irrelevant." Teraeth had something in his hands, and I blinked for a moment as I realized it was a batch of unemre figs, stolen from the tree I'd just created "incorrectly." I laughed and rolled my eyes, then demanded he hand me one. "I've done a bit of traveling in this life, and Manol parties are amazing, but Atrin Kandor was even more widely traveled and lived for over a thousand years."

"Most of which was bloodshed and conquest," Janel reminded him.

"Maybe bloodshed and conquest is a good memory for Teraeth," I said and then ducked as he grinned and threw a seed at me.

"It wasn't as bloody as you'd think," Teraeth said. "But I was, as you may recall, rather enthusiastic about architecture. Not to mention I have some wonderful memories of the imperial palace."

"Especially the bedroom," Janel said dryly. "At least you never had a harem."

"Oh, but I did," Teraeth said.

Janel stopped walking and stared at him. "What?"

I swung around, ready to play peacekeeper if it was needed. Janel didn't seem angry, though, just surprised and perhaps confused. "No, you didn't," she protested. "I'd remember that."

"You'd have taken advantage of that," he corrected.

"Only if they were willing," she said.

"Which they would have been because you've always been cute." Teraeth's grin was a friendly leer. "Anyway, I did have a harem—when I first became emperor. Centuries before I met you. I got over it; turns out that's nothing but drama. Palace intrigues and who poisoned who and which one of my concubines was pregnant—and that last bit was always good for a laugh."

I motioned for both of them to keep walking. It was a bad idea to stop. I let them talk while I concentrated on re-creating my favorite kilin in the Copper District, an establishment that had been in the same family for generations and that cooked up the most amazing tangri stew with fresh-baked sag if you didn't feel like renting a cooking space to make your own.

"Good for a laugh? How so?" She squinted at him.

"People think the imperial throne of Quur is this god-given role set in stone—"

I raised both eyebrows. "That's because it is. Was."

"Sure, but there were a lot of people who would have welcomed a transition into a familial inheritance, with my children taking positions of power. You know, so one could marry into the family and it would mean something. The easy solution to that was to never have children. Which meant anyone who claimed I had sired any was trying to pull a fast one. It was cute right up until it really wasn't." Teraeth offered Janel some of the fruit, and to my surprise, she took it.

"I was just special, then?" Janel seemed amused by the idea. "Because you weren't around for the birth, but we most certainly did have a son."

Teraeth looked away. "I had, uh . . . decided I wanted children." He wisely left off the part where he'd married Janel's previous incarnation precisely because he thought she'd be especially fertile. Her own plans had apparently not been an important part of his decision-making process.

Atrin Kandor had been an asshole. I didn't point it out only because I knew Teraeth was already well aware.

"Why?" Janel said. "What changed your mind?"

"I just . . ." Teraeth chewed on the inside of his lip. "It seemed like it was time. I can't really explain it."[1]

I finished making the kilin and paused for a moment to inspect my handiwork. I thought I was improving, but I desperately wished I'd spent more time learning how to craft illusions from Doc. Anyone who thought this was easy could go eat glass.

Teraeth turned to Janel. "I never meant to leave you alone, you know. If I hadn't died, none of this would have happened, would it? You wouldn't have gone to the Blight. You wouldn't have tried to free S'arric. This wouldn't be—like this."

Janel's expression turned stricken and probably mirrored my own.

"Don't do that to yourself," I told Teraeth, putting a hand on his shoulder. "There are far too many could-have- or might-have-beens. This isn't your fault."

Janel took Teraeth's hand. "I object to your statement entirely. Xaltorath wanted Elana to do what she did, and that meant your days were always numbered."

"I suppose so. It's a shame, though. I would have liked to have met our son . . ."

At which point, Teraeth stopped walking and pulled his arms away from us both.

My gut clenched, because I knew why he'd stopped. I knew exactly what thought process had just been triggered inside his head. I didn't know if Janel was aware of the conversations between Teraeth and his father—my teacher, Doc—but I certainly was. So I knew how bitter Doc had been that Teraeth's mother, Thaena, hadn't told him about their son, hadn't allowed any contact while Teraeth grew up. In hindsight, it made ruthless sense; Thaena must have been concerned that Doc would have corrupted her son, made him question her authority.

I could tell by the withdrawn and gutted look on his face that Teraeth was remembering those conversations.

"Teraeth?" Janel turned to him, took one of his hands.

I glanced around us. It was still a gamble to stop, but one I felt we needed to take. So I stepped up to Teraeth and laced my fingers through his other hand. I tugged the two of them over to an empty space, which might well have been a park had any trees or plants grown there. Now it seemed like a vacant lot filled with empty, skeletal fountains bereft of water.

Teraeth sat down on the edge of one such fountain without any resistance at all. He was lost in his own misery. "I wish . . . Fuck. I wish a lot of things," Teraeth whispered. "I wish I'd had a chance to know him as something other than an enemy or a legacy to overcome."

"I liked him a lot," I said. "Doc was a good man." Which had been the problem, hadn't it? Because while Doc had been a good man, almost no one

---

[1] If Xaltorath was telling the truth (always a dangerous assumption), then Emperor Atrin Kandor made the decision because he was being manipulated by the demon. But since Xaltorath only claimed that their goal was to have Kandor marry Elana Milligreest, it would be rash to assume that Xaltorath is also responsible for Elana's pregnancy.

had actually known it. He'd happily let everyone paint him as the villain, even when he'd been anything but.

"Doc?" Janel frowned. "Doc wasn't our son, he was—"

I cut her off by shaking my head. "We're talking about his dad now." I jerked a chin at Teraeth. "Trust me, it makes sense if you were there for part one of this conversation." Which, I should point out, Kihrin wasn't, but he had read about it later.

Janel nodded and then kissed Teraeth's knuckles. "Don't expect me to say differently." She hesitated before adding, "I liked him too. And your father did a good job of raising our son."[2]

Teraeth and I both paused. I watched Teraeth's eyes go from lost and unfocused to sharply glittering with wry pique.

"You had to make it weird," Teraeth said.

The corners of Janel's lips quirked. Oh yes, she'd known exactly what she was saying. "I made it weird?" she protested with overly dramatic innocence, going so far as to put a hand to her chest.

Unfortunately, her attempt at lightening the mood failed. Teraeth slumped, eyes staring downward. "No, no, you're right. My mother did that. I just . . . I don't know how to feel."

I touched his hair. "You're allowed to hate Khaemezra."

Teraeth's head snapped up again, his expression torn between indignation and guilt. "Kihrin," he chided.

I met Janel's eyes. She gave me an encouraging nod.

"No," I told him. "She was going to force you to kill yourself and drag an entire nation down into the Afterlife with you. You are *allowed* to hate her. My own feelings about Khaemezra may be harder to sort out because there's all this . . . history . . . but at the end of the day, she was . . ." I searched for the right word.

"Craven?" Janel offered.

"She was scared," Teraeth said.

I stood up, if only to go to a knee in front of him. "We were guardians, Teraeth. The Eight Guardians. We weren't guarding our own immortality. We were supposed to be protecting everyone else. She volunteered for this. We all did. And she betrayed that. It's almost funny how mad it makes Vol Karoth."

Janel straightened, her eyes flickered with surprise. "What do you mean?"

I shrugged. "I get the sense that the injustice and the hypocrisy of the world offends him. Just makes him furious. He'd rather destroy it all than let it exist in a state of perpetual sophistry. And while I can say that he's definitely wrong to want to burn it all down, I can't say the anger doesn't have some justification."

Teraeth shook his head. "I don't recommend listening to anything Vol Karoth has to say."

I chuckled. He was trying to sell me a cloak I'd already stolen. "Oh, I am

---

[2] To summarize: In Teraeth's past life as Atrin Kandor, his widowed wife, Elana (who was one of Janel's past lives), married Kandor's bitter nemesis, Terindel, who raised Kandor's son as his own. And Terindel, being an immortal vané, eventually sired Kandor's reincarnation, Teraeth. And yes, it gives me a headache too.

never going to agree with him about the whole 'let's destroy everything because oblivion is so peaceful' idea, but where does one draw the line between good and evil, anyway? How do we say that it's fine that we're just waving our hands and absolving Senera? Or Talon?"

"Or me," Teraeth said.

"Pretty sure your kill count is a lot less than theirs," I said.

Janel patted Teraeth's knee. "Not if we're counting past lives. Then Teraeth wins the contest easily."

He narrowed his eyes at her. "Thank you. I think." But he didn't seem upset. Just the opposite. Teraeth leaned over and delicately, deliberately bit the side of her neck. Janel gasped and closed her eyes. He then straightened and smiled at me like he was sitting in a classroom and honestly had been paying attention the whole time.

"You're a terrible tease," Janel mourned.

"I'm a fantastic tease," Teraeth corrected.

I coughed and fought the desire to laugh. But this is something I really wanted to talk about, so I tried to keep focus. "My point is, if you take an honest look at the people we are allied with, as well as who we are, there's a lot of blood on the floor. I'm supposed to look Galen in the eyes and tell him that my mother, the woman who broke his neck and murdered him in a fit of rage, is probably going to live out her years in the Manol—quite probably as queen if you abdicate the throne—with no consequences for her crimes? But how do we address that she was a slave for years, that House D'Mon has owned slaves for all of its existence? Is it unjustified for her to have taken her revenge for that? Why do my parents get to retire happily to live idyllically when Thurvishar's parents died horrible permanent deaths? Where's the justice in that?"

Janel's expression returned to a serious mien. "It's not a contest."

"If it is," Teraeth said, "Khaeriel and Therin are winning."

Janel shook her head. "There's no great slate board where all the sins of your existence are added up. I've never seen anything to indicate that the sins or virtues of one life bleed over into the next. Reincarnation has nothing to do with justice."

"Easy for you to say," Teraeth retorted. "Add up the body count of all your lives, and you're the saintliest of all of us."

I was surprised at how much that idea seemed to upset Janel. She visibly drew back, brow furrowed, and looked off into the distance. "I don't . . . I don't think that's true."

I frowned. There was something there. Something that we needed to talk about. Before I could ask the question, however, I noticed our shadows sharpen on the ground around us. It was as if the sun had just come out behind the clouds.

Only there was no sun in this place.

I looked up and saw I was wrong. There was a sun. It was incredibly bright, blindingly so, and to my surprise, seemed to be growing brighter.

Then I understood what it meant, and the fear kicked fire through my veins. It turned out that Vol Karoth hadn't needed to track me down. Finding me was inconsequential when he could attack the entire city, all at once, and leave it nothing but ash and shadow.

"Run," I said. "Find a place to—"

But the idea of hiding was ludicrous. Maybe if we'd been underground, in a deep basement, or sheltered in the central university hall. Instead, the three of us were caught entirely in the open when that giant ball of plasma pulled from a still-yellow sun came slamming down on the entire city of Karolaen, annihilating it with fire. Everything exploded in light and heat.

The world turned white.

Xivan's memories
The Upper Circle of the Capital City, Quur
One week after the Battle of the Well of Spirals

By the time Xivan returned to the Joratese embassy, she was embarrassed to discover that she'd missed Ninavis, Dorna, and the rest of their group. They'd either managed to finagle their meeting with the High Council or they'd realized they stood no chance to do so and so had left. Which was a shame; Xivan would have appreciated being able to stay there instead of some hospitality house of far inferior quality.

But the world was what it was. So Xivan retrieved more of her husband's funds from their account at the Temple of Tavris, bought herself clothing respectable enough to remind people that she was actually someone of importance, and rented out a ridiculously expensive suite at one of the few hospitality houses in the Upper Circle. Truthfully, she was only looking for the excuse to linger at the taverns, sip a truly mind-boggling amount of wine, and listen to the gossip roll around her.

It didn't take long at all for that gossip to include the name she was looking for.

"Did you hear what Galen D'Mon did at the funeral for the high general's daughter? I heard he literally summoned a demon!"

"No, it was the funeral for the high general's son, not his daughter. And you're thinking of Galen D'Mon's father. Galen's the quiet kid who married Sheloran D'Talus, remember?"

"She's the high lord's youngest daughter, isn't she?"

"Only daughter. Only child, in fact."

"Huh. I could have sworn they had other children. But you say she's the only one? I wonder what they're going to do about that? What does one even call that: Lady heir? Oh, that sounds terrible."

"I would imagine when Galen and Sheloran have children, their second son will end up as Lord Heir D'Talus, just like the first one will be Lord Heir D'Mon."

"Oh, I don't think so. The new emperor's ruined that."

"New emperor? Oh just call her what she is: empress. And how do you figure?"

"Well, if a woman can be emperor, then a woman can be high lord, can't she? And if a woman can be high lord, then Galen D'Mon isn't even in the running. The oldest child of Therin D'Mon is a woman."

"Was, you mean. Didn't Galen D'Mon kill her? So much for being the quiet kid!"

"I wouldn't be placing any metal on Galen D'Mon being crowned lord anytime soon. And I still think he was the one who summoned that demon."

"Pfft. Go drink your wine."

It didn't take long after that for Xivan to discover that Galen and Sheloran D'Mon had apparently gone into hiding. Therin D'Mon's oldest daughter, Tishenya, had died, and so now the other daughter, Gerisea, had taken over the Blue Palace.

Which was inconvenient in terms of being able to track down Sheloran, but extremely interesting in terms of what kind of protection Sheloran would have once Xivan managed it.

She hired a calligrapher to make her a letter of introduction and sent it by courier to the Blue Palace. There was no sense doing this in a rush. She'd already learned that lesson from Lessoral D'Talus.

She soon received a response, delivered by runner. Xivan took note of the fact that said runner didn't wear the livery of House D'Mon.

When Xivan arrived at the Blue Palace, the entire complex had the same tension as the hours before the arrival of a hurricane. Or perhaps in the middle of one. A great many people were running about and looking exceedingly put upon. Most of the people in charge looked Khorveshan, and an uncommon number had blue eyes.

She waited in the First Court until someone took notice of her. It took longer than it should have, considering.

"Duchess Xivan Kaen of Yor to see Lady Gerisea D'Mon," she told the doorman. In deference to the people she visited, she had worn her sword, and her clothing was lavish, but still of the Khorveshan style. And she'd made sure to feed that morning, so it was difficult to tell that she wasn't a living person.

They brought her to a sitting area, where harried servants served her mint tea and trays of pressed honey-layered pastry, cut into delicate shapes. She had no idea if it was any good—she might as well have been eating dirt for all the flavor it had.

Finally, a woman whom Xivan assumed was Gerisea D'Mon entered the room. She was much taller than the average Quuros woman—indeed, much taller than the average Khorveshan woman—and undeniably lovely, her probable age comparable to Xivan's. She also dressed lavishly, with gold bracelets lining her wrists, a veritable fortune of sapphires around her neck, her agolé dyed a perfect indigo blue and then embroidered and beaded with gold.

Xivan didn't stand. "Gerisea D'Mon, I assume?"

"Yes," the royal admitted as she sat down opposite Xivan. Her eyes traveled down Xivan's body and then back up again. Xivan had the feeling that if this had been under different circumstances, she'd have been asked to show her teeth. Xivan couldn't decide if the appraisal was sexual or not. "How extraordinary. But you don't even look dead. I thought you'd at least be pale. Gadrith was pale."

Xivan's hackles raised. "Have we met?"

"Oh, not directly, no. Darzin mentioned you from time to time, especially after that business with getting him kicked out of the Ice Demesne. He was so mad at you."

"Yes, clearly, I was right to stay up at night sick with worry about his opinion."

Gerisea laughed. It was a nice laugh, polished to profession, no doubt practiced until it conveyed the perfect amount of insouciant charm. "Ah, I'll miss him. Anyway, since we've never met in person, I don't really know for sure that you're the Duchess of Yor. I apologize for being almost unforgivably rude, but I'll need to see some proof of that. These days have been strange enough that any number of people might show up claiming to be anything."

Xivan simply nodded. It hadn't been unexpected. And fortunately, she had been able to recover her husband's signet ring when she recovered his body. She handed the ring over. She assumed there was some sort of magic on it to prevent impersonation or counterfeiting, but she'd never bothered to check.

Gerisea stared at the ring as though accusing it of crimes, but finally handed it back. "Thank you, Your Grace. I admit I'm intrigued by the reason for your visit, but I'll also be honest: you've come at a bad time. I hope you're not wasting my time."

"Of course," Xivan said. "I understand. Which makes my request all the more unfortunate since I've come asking for your assistance."

She raised a perfectly groomed eyebrow. "I understand the duchy went through some unpleasantness recently. You must have had enormous casualties."

Xivan kept her expression calm. In her mind's eye, she pictured the flash of light as the entire palace had melted in a column of fire reaching up into the sky. A great many casualties.

"A few," Xivan said, setting her teacup down. "But it tangentially relates to my request. You see, the witch responsible for that business escaped, and I have been looking for her ever since. I recently discovered that she has a relative living here in the Capital who may know her whereabouts. Unfortunately, that has been somewhat complicated by the fact that Sheloran D'Mon has gone into hiding."

Fortunately for her dignity, Gerisea hadn't been drinking anything. "Sheloran D'Mon? Well, I–" She pulled herself up. "Unfortunately, you're correct; I have no idea where the young lady might be."

"I imagine if you did, she wouldn't be with us anymore."

Gerisea studied Xivan, then drank her tea. She immediately set the cup down again, no doubt also finding it too bitter. "House D'Mon's relationship with House D'Talus is currently strained. My argument is with my nephew, not with his wife, Sheloran."

"Whereas my argument is with Sheloran," Xivan said, "but I share a strong desire to keep the young woman alive, so I'm glad we have an understanding."

Gerisea cocked her head and gazed at Xivan oddly. "Just exactly how are you hoping I might help you?"

"I want to find Sheloran. You quite obviously want to find Galen. I am proposing we join forces. While I am a duchess and that carries some weight, this is the Capital, and your word carries more. I've become a skilled tracker over the years. Perhaps a new set of eyes on the problem is exactly what you need."

The woman leaned back against the couch and studied Xivan. "You're Khorveshan."

"I am." Xivan didn't elaborate. She had no idea if Gerisea would consider it important that Xivan hadn't been raised as some kind of nobility, but it was best not to tempt fate on the matter. "The climate of Yor never suited me, but I would like to finish this one thing before I retire." She paused. "Perhaps if our alliance proves strong enough, you might provide advice on who I nominate to take my place as regent. I have a granddaughter who will one day be duchess, but I'd rather devote myself full-time to helping her mother raise her and leave ruling the Dominion to another." As potential bribes went, it wasn't particularly subtle, but Xivan had learned enough from her husband to know that the weak spot of any royal was the promise of legitimate power.

Gerisea's mouth quirked. "I'd be happy to offer such advice when the time comes. I know how difficult raising a family can be." She paused. "I don't want to hurt Galen, you understand. I have no grudge against the young man. Indeed, before he ran off he set up a potentially lucrative business deal with the Vishai of all things, and without him, the whole deal falls apart. I just think my brother did a poor job of raising the next high lord, and this house won't survive with Galen at its helm. If he's willing to step down, there's no reason he can't live the rest of his life quite happily."

Somewhere else, lay unspoken between them. Exile would be the best he could hope for. But given what she'd already seen of Gerisea, Xivan was reasonably certain that all this was a lie. Galen wouldn't survive to see the next sunrise the day he was returned to his aunt.[3]

"You don't have to explain your reasons to me," Xivan said.

"I wouldn't want you to think that my nephew's health is less important than Sheloran's," Gerisea explained. "He is family, after all, and family matters to me."

"A woman after my own heart," Xivan said as she stood. "I won't take up any more of your time."

"I'll have my captain of the guard meet you in the First Court," Gerisea said. "He can fill you in on what information we have. For example, we do know they're not staying at the House D'Talus estate."

---

[3] Oh no. I'm sure she'd have waited until she found a way to steal that Vishai contract before she murdered Galen.

"Yes, thank you. That would be helpful."

"Of course. Now if you'll excuse me, the empress is throwing a thank-you party for the Royal House high lords, and I wouldn't want to be unfashionably late."

Xivan bowed, one equal to another, and left to go find the captain.

28: Guarantees of Justice

Xivan's reaction
The Lighthouse at Shadrag Gor

"Gerisea," Talon murmured.

Xivan glanced over at the mimic as the vision ended, but if Talon had any further commentary to provide about the members of House D'Mon, she kept it to herself.

Xivan barely paid attention to the vision, even if it had been from her own memories. They had bigger problems, like what had happened to Janel.

As well as Thurvishar and Teraeth, of course.

The hallway outside was bitterly cold, much darker than it should have been. Much darker than earlier when Xivan had chased Kalindra into this same hall.

But what did *time* mean, anyway? She was losing track of it in this place. Time crumbled around her, blended together, stretched out like dough.

Senera looked down the hallway. Xivan didn't need to ask her what she was looking at. It was obvious enough that she was attempting to catch a glimpse of Vol Karoth, not more than a hundred feet away.

"How bad is it?" Kalindra asked.

Senera didn't answer.

"Senera!" Kalindra snapped.

The woman shook her head as she ran a finger over her bottom lip. "What? I–" She seemed to snap herself out of whatever fugue had gripped her. "He has a leg free now. Let's not go that way."

"You think?" Talon said. She began opening doors and peering inside. "You know this place has more than two floors, don't you?"

"We'll explore the basement after we're finished here," Senera said.

"But what about the other–" Talon started to say.

Senera whirled around. "The other levels are accessed through the Lighthouse. Do you think it's safe to enter the Lighthouse tower right now?"

Xivan glanced down the hallway. She couldn't see anything, but she had to imagine anyone in the same room as Vol Karoth right now would quickly find bits of themselves splitting off and floating away.

Talon chewed on her lower lip and looked remarkably sheepish.

"Great talk," Kalindra said, "but these rooms aren't going to search themselves. Let's eliminate the obvious before we start worrying about worst-case scenarios." Making good on her promise, she immediately turned on her heel and headed into one of the rooms.

"Kalindra!" Senera snapped.

"I've got her," Xivan said and—since she was closest, anyway—bolted through the same doorway. The room beyond was utterly uninteresting to her—absolutely riveting to Senera, Thurvishar, or Qown—some library or private study. All the books in question were held inside glass cabinets no doubt dripping with preservation spells. Like the other rooms, the furniture—elegant and graceful—was made from stone. The room notably didn't hold any bodies save their own.

"What part of 'nobody goes off alone' was unclear to you?" Xivan growled. "It was the definition of 'nobody,' wasn't it?"

Kalindra rolled her eyes. "Since you're here, I'd say my definition is holding up to—shit!" She ran past Xivan, toward the door she'd just used.

Or rather, toward where the door should have been. But there was no door—just a smooth, blank wall with peeling plaster chips and the feeling of great age.

"Oh, I'm an idiot," Kalindra said, crossing her arms over her head and resting her forehead against the blank wall.

"Huh," Xivan said.

"Don't you fucking dare say it," Kalindra snapped.

"Which part? The 'I guess we can agree on something' part or the 'I'm astonished you can admit it' part?" Xivan searched the room, but it was reasonably obvious that there'd only ever been one way in or out, which was now simply missing.

"No, *Mother*, the 'If she's an idiot, what does that make me for following her?' part."

Xivan put her hand on her sword hilt, but it wasn't in reaction to Kalindra's need for the last word. Rather, it was a reaction to the spike of dread in the room, the way all the corners seemed darker than they should be, and slanted in wrong directions from the mage-lights.

She had no idea what either of them would do if a threat manifested—neither she nor Kalindra seemed to know any magic. And if this was Vol Karoth's doing, would she even be able to correctly recognize a threat if she saw one?

"Worried," Xivan said absently.

"What?"

Xivan glanced at the younger woman. "What does that make me? It makes me worried. As in worried about how we're going to get out of here in general and worried about how you're holding up in specific."

Kalindra seemed taken aback. "I'm fine."

Xivan gave the woman her iciest stare. "Perhaps now is not the time or place to be lying to anyone, least of all yourself."

Kalindra sat down on top of the desk, kicked her legs out, and laughed. "Coming from you, that's pretty good. What was that last vision? A healthy depiction of acceptable coping mechanisms? Or you doing a whole lot of lying to yourself and compounding bad decision after bad?"

"That follows, does it not?" Xivan examined where the door used to be with her fingertips. If it was an illusion, it was a fantastically good one. She couldn't feel any seams or indication that this had ever been anything other than a wall. "You and I have a great deal in common."

"Oh yeah. We're both women. We're both widows. We're both dead–oh wait, no. That last part's just you." Kalindra shook her head and gestured toward where the door used to be. "And stop being worried. Senera and Talon know where we are. They'll probably bust through the wall any second. Maybe you don't want to stand so close to it?"

Xivan moved back toward the desk. "Why do you hate me so much?"

Kalindra scowled at her. "I appreciate that you don't sugarcoat things, but this isn't the time for our little girl talk."

"You have something better to do?" Xivan bowed and gestured for her to proceed.

"Wow," Kalindra said. "You just bowed *sarcastically*. That takes some skill."

"Have you been to Yor?"

Kalindra laughed and rolled her eyes, but the reaction was missing its normal razor-sharp edge. "Fine," she said. "And it's nothing personal. I hate you because you're an abomination. You shouldn't exist."

"Why would you ever think I'd take that personally?" Xivan said, smiling. "And abomination according to whom? The goddess Thaena? The goddess you hate?"

"Yes, you're right. I am a hypocrite. Completely a hypocrite. I just . . ." Kalindra visibly clenched her jaw and looked away. "You wouldn't understand."

Xivan resisted the urge to sigh. "But I'm here and your Jarith is dead–or at least you thought your Jarith was dead. How is that fair?"

Kalindra met her eyes that time, shocked.

"Perhaps I do understand," Xivan said.

Kalindra held that gaze for just a moment–the briefest look–before she quickly glanced away. "He didn't deserve this," Kalindra said. "He doesn't deserve what's happened to him."

Xivan remembered someone in her youth telling her that every cynic was an idealist who saw the world too clearly. She also remembered thinking the person who said that was an ass. It didn't make them wrong.

"There are no guarantees of justice in this world," Xivan murmured.

"Oh, fuck all the way off."

Xivan knew her expression was the worst sort of scowl, but she didn't seem to be able to force a different one to lay claim to that country. "It would be easier, wouldn't it? If justice were guaranteed. If you knew you'd pay for your sins. If you knew someone out there was paying attention. That the people who deserved to be punished would be."

Kalindra made a soft sound, as if someone had just come up behind her and efficiently applied a knife to her lungs. She closed her eyes as if in pain. "I thought . . . I thought that was my job."

"Would you like to hear a joke?" Xivan said.

Kalindra stared at her with glassy eyes. "Why do I think I won't like the punch line?"

"You might," Xivan said. "Here it is: my husband deserved everything he got."

Kalindra blinked.

Xivan's shoulders shook with a silent gust of laughter. "I can admit that now, can't I? He *earned* what happened to him. Suless murdering him was poetic justice." She swallowed thickly. "But my son was innocent except for letting a pretty girl turn his eye. He deserved better than to die screaming for his father's sins."

Kalindra's hands clenched against the wood of the desk, turning her knuckles white from the strain.

"Look, I–" Kalindra grimaced. "I mean–" But then she looked past Xivan, eyes wide. "The door's back." Kalindra hopped off the table and ran over to the door before Xivan could so much as respond, throwing it open to the hallway beyond.

Xivan frowned. She was going to need to do something about that woman's impulsiveness. Or perhaps it was just that Kalindra had been on the verge of saying something real, something vulnerable and true. These were the moments, in Xivan's experience, where a person might actually look at themselves, where seeds of change might start to sprout.

Xivan didn't think it was coincidence that Vol Karoth allowed them to leave before that could happen.

"We found the bodies," Senera said as soon as they were all in the hallway. "They're upstairs."

Xivan wanted to run, but instead–because she was trying to set a good example–she waited for Kalindra, Senera, and Talon, and stayed together as they rejoined the others.

Talea, Galen, Qown, and Sheloran had pulled down most of the dividing walls upstairs, leaving the rooms beyond much more open, both to each other and to the hallway outside. From that vantage, it was easy to see that Janel, Teraeth, and Thurvishar's bodies were laid out on the elaborate stone beds. The latter reminded Xivan uncomfortably of crypt slabs, especially given the remarkably fine decorations of curling leaves and blooming flowers that embroidered their sides.

"Ah good," Galen said. "Now everyone's together again." He looked relieved, but still deeply worried. Xivan could relate.

Talea was giving her a considered look as she approached. The woman's gaze slid between Xivan and Kalindra and then back again. Her expression turned calculating.

Oh.

Xivan had sent Talea upstairs because she'd thought it would be less dangerous. She hadn't considered that Talea might assume a different motivation.

Xivan walked over to Talea. "It's not like that," Xivan whispered.

"Oh?" Talea whispered back. "You haven't adopted yet another bitter, upset young woman who desperately needs some direction in her life? Because that would not be unusual for you." The corner of her lip curled into the beginnings of a smile.

Xivan bit down on laughter, her concerns evaporating. "Never mind. It is like that." She stared at Talea–beautiful, wild, extraordinary Talea–and offered the woman her hand.

A second later, Talea was in her arms. Xivan didn't care who saw. All she cared about was that Talea was there, real and solid. She didn't know if Talea had forgiven her, but then again, she hadn't yet asked for forgiveness, had she?

She just knew that she still loved Talea more than words could say.

"I'm sorry," Xivan whispered. "I'm so sorry."

"Don't you dare abandon this one," Talea whispered as she drew back. "You can't treat her the way you treated the Spurned, do you understand? People are not assets. We're not *tools*."

Xivan's throat clenched. She rested her head on Talea's shoulder, nodding. "I owe the Spurned an apology, don't I?"

"The biggest apology," Talea agreed. "You might need to bring them presents. Flowers? Hmm, no. Flowers are for funerals. Maybe a pet?"

Xivan laughed. The Spurned would probably view any animals she might give them as livestock, which was almost certainly not what Talea meant. Before Xivan could make that statement, though, the rest of the conversation in progress intruded on her awareness.

"So why did Vol Karoth do that if he was just going to allow us to find their bodies again?" Senera scowled as she glanced into the rooms. Janel and Teraeth were in one room, Thurvishar in the next.

Sheloran made a face as she fanned herself. "Because we were starting to feel like we were safe, I imagine. Perhaps this was his way of reminding us that we're not."

Qown had just finished checking the bodies and was looking down at Janel's unconscious form with a concerned, even shocked expression.

"Is she all right?" Xivan asked. She fought down the temptation to slide into dread and worry.

Qown startled and stood. "She's . . . fine. We may need to start magically supporting them, though. They need nutrients and fluids, but their metabolisms are slow at the moment, so it should be fine." For now. He gave Janel another worried look.[1]

"So let's take them downstairs again?" Talon suggested, but she sounded uncertain.

"Don't bother," Xivan said.

Qown gave her a scandalized look.

"Don't bother," Xivan repeated. "He's made his point. We can't protect them. And if he's powerful enough to steal their bodies and drag them here, he's also powerful enough to kill them. They're as safe here as they were downstairs."

"Except it's ice storage up here," Qown protested. "At least it's warm downstairs." He paused. "Warmer, anyway."

Xivan frowned. That was a valid point.

"Fine," Senera said. "We'll take their bodies back down, and Talon can start on the next vision."

The mimic laughed gleefully. "Who's my next victim?"

Next to her, Talea said, "I am."

---

[1] I assume he noticed the pregnancy.

Kihrin's story
Inside Vol Karoth's prison

I came to lying on my back staring up at the gray-washed sky. Not dead.

Or at least not dead by certain definitions. Not gone, anyway. Just to be sure, I poked myself here and there. Feeling it, I decided I was still myself for certain values thereof.

I sat up and looked around.

Where once there had been a huge city, sporadically littered with my attempts at civic beautification projects, now I sat in a vast crater, the stone smooth and hard as if it had been melted and allowed to re-form.

Which, I reflected, was exactly what had happened.

I stood, looking down at myself. Limbs and extremities all accounted for, as were my clothes. All I was missing were the loves of my lives.

"Janel!" I yelled. "Teraeth!"

No sound but the dim, sharp echo of my voice ringing back from the stone. I tried again.

"Teraeth! Janel! Where are you?"

A chill ran down my spine and caused the hairs on my neck and arms to stand up; I was tied to Vol Karoth, but I had always assumed I could be destroyed, even here, or why would he have kept attacking me? Now I had to face the possibility my existence was more complicated than that.

And possibly the same rules didn't apply to the ones I loved. Were they . . . ?

No. I refused to accept it.

"Thurvishar!" I yelled. "Thurvishar! Are you there?"

A disembodied voice spoke in my mind. *[I'm here. What in the world was that? What just happened?]*

"Vol Karoth remembered the destruction of Karolaen and treated us all to a re-creation. The city is gone, and Janel and Teraeth are . . . gone. Are they . . . can you find them? Please, gods, find them and tell me they're okay!" My voice quavered, broke on the last syllable. Surdyeh would have tsked at me.

[I'm here, so I'm sure they—] Thurvishar's voice started to say, but I'm afraid I cut him off rudely.

"Find them!"

[I will,] he said and left me to the silence of the early days of the Blight.

I stood there for some time, waiting for him to return. Then, having seen all I was going to from that particular spot, I began walking. What direction I went, I had no idea; the sun had once again done its disappearing act into the featureless gray sky.

After a thousand steps, I rubbed my eyes, which had begun to blur. Then, blinking, I realized it wasn't my eyes; a dark smudge of something blotted the horizon.

I turned toward it. Anything, at this point, was better than nothing.

Another timeless time passed as I drew nearer to the smudge, and slowly, it resolved itself into a plateau, perhaps a mile wide and half that in height. As I grew closer still, I could make out buildings on top of the plateau.

I stopped. I knew this, and yet it was different from what I knew.

This was Kharas Golgoth. Only . . .

Only every other time I'd been here, desert or alkaline swamp came right up to the edge of the place.

Was Vol Karoth literally putting himself on a pedestal?

Despite my dread and weariness, I rolled my eyes.

[Oh, there you are–]

I jumped two feet into the air, spinning as I came down. A blade was in my hand before my feet touched stone. Before I could attack the nothing in front of me, the recognition of the voice penetrated my weary mind. "Thurvishar." I chuckled. "Sorry."

[No, my bad,] Thurvishar said. *[Hang on.]* Slowly, a semitranslucent outline of him appeared, reminding me of nothing so much as the ghostly outlines of where building edges used to be in the real Kharas Golgoth. *[Better?]* he asked.

"Well, at least I know where I'm supposed to look now," I said. "What did you find?"

[They're here,] he said. *[Teraeth is walking toward this place also, although he's farther out and roughly one hundred and thirty degrees to the right around the plateau. Janel's up there–]* His outline pointed toward the city above us.

"And she's okay?" I pressed.

[She's trapped in the mind of a mad god, while also trapped in a time-warping lighthouse that said mad god is slowly breaking into so he can kill everyone. I'm not sure fine is the word I would use, but she is alive and, last I saw her, appeared healthy.]

I pinched the bridge of my nose between finger and thumb. "Okay," I said. "Have you seen a way up there?" I, also, pointed toward the top of the plateau.

[No,] said Thurvishar, *[but you can make one.]*

"Last time I made wholesale alterations to Vol Karoth's scenery, he burned a city to ash. I'm not super interested in repeating the experience." I felt like cursing more. Cursing a lot more. All of this meant what we'd been doing had been working or had at least been annoying Vol Karoth enough so he'd been forced to do something drastic.

But now we were starting from scratch.

Thurvishar shrugged. *[Then stay down here. But if I might make a recommendation; meet up with Teraeth and then make a stairway. Just don't make it a nice stairway. Don't give it any emotional connection to your past, and maybe he won't notice.]*

I licked my lips, gazing up at the cliff side looming above me. Then, "One hundred and thirty degrees to the right, you say? Okay, then." I turned to my right and began walking.

Our legs wobbled as we crested the lip of the cliff and stumbled into a main avenue. Teraeth bent over to catch his breath while I turned to look behind us at the mile-long winding staircase we'd just ascended.

I must have made a startled noise, because Teraeth turned swiftly to look.

Behind us, the avenue stretched for a thousand yards before emptying out into what appeared to be a market plaza of some sort. What wasn't there was a cliff descending into a smooth-stoned crater caldera.

"What the hell?" Teraeth summed up my thoughts exactly.

"Thurvishar?" I asked.

He appeared a moment later. *[Sorry,]* he said, *[I was checking in on Janel. Yes?]*

I bit back the urge to ask how she was; if anything significant had changed, he'd have mentioned it. Instead, I pointed up the avenue. "Shouldn't there be a whole lot of really long fall right there?"

Thurvishar looked to the side. *[Interesting,]* he said.

We waited for a moment. Then Teraeth again spoke for both of us when he said, "What is it? Spit it out, man."

[We're back in Karolaen.]

"Really?" Teraeth said. "I hadn't noticed that. Any other shiny bits of brilliant wisdom to share?"

"The better question," I said, nudging Teraeth with an elbow, "is why?"

[I'm not sure,] Thurvishar said. *[Perhaps, Vol Karoth prefers to stay in this city instead of the other one.]*

"They're the same place," I said.

[But not at the same time,] Thurvishar corrected. *[It might be simpler to refer to Kharas Golgoth as the post-destruction city and Karolaen as the city as it stood before.]*

"Fine. So he'd rather pretend he didn't blow all his favorite dance halls to pieces," Teraeth said. "How does that help us?"

[It may not,] Thurvishar admitted. *[Or perhaps it does. It speaks to his ability to improvise, to imagine. Not sure if that'll help us or not, but it's interesting.]*

"Mkay," I said. "Where's Janel?"

[Oh,] Thurvishar said. *[Right. This way.]*

We followed him.

29: ALL THE LUCK IN THE WORLD

Talea's memory
The Capital City, Quur
One week after the Battle of the Well of Spirals

Only later would Talea reflect on the fact that she managed to walk as far as she had without being accosted in some manner. For a woman—even an armed woman—to be alone on the Capital City streets, upper or lower, without harassment was almost unthinkable. Maybe it was because so many were hiding, because the demons were still showing up like unpredictable, deadly little sparks and then vanishing again.

Maybe she was just lucky.

In any event, she managed to leave Arena Park and travel down several nameless, too-familiar streets before the tears blurred her vision to blindness, and she broke down crying. She found herself seated on a step, part of a small side entrance to someone's house, head against her knees, sobbing.

Leaving Xivan had been the hardest thing she'd ever done, and it wasn't lost on Talea that she never could have if she hadn't met Xivan in the first place. Not from the practical, logistical side that one can't leave a person one's never met but because Xivan had spent so many years building Talea up. So many years helping her work through her own pain. Teaching her the sort of behavior one should—and should not—tolerate in a lover. Because Talea had come to her possessing no context—none at all—for what a healthy relationship might even look like. She had longed for love the way a prisoner dreams of freedom, and it was probably predictable and sad that she'd fallen madly in love with the first person she'd met as a free woman who treated her as someone worthy of respect.

But predictable or not, Talea had.

So it was the bitterest sort of irony to see Xivan breaking the relationship rules that she had herself established. Talea wasn't ready to forgive her. Not for this. Not when it was so abundantly clear that Xivan wasn't at all sorry for her actions.

Once she'd cried herself out, Talea kept walking as she thought about the situation and her options. Talea supposed she could take over the Spurned. She would have never even considered the idea before, but she never would have imagined Xivan offering to sell the Spurned either. She had always assumed . . . she had always assumed that the whole point of the Spurned was that they weren't slaves anymore, weren't possessions. That their loyalty was earned rather than bought and sold, not mandated at the end of manacles and chains.

Then again, Talea had never been as good at magic as many of her other sisters in the Spurned. Plenty might well challenge her for leadership, and they'd be right to. So what did she want to do with her life? Darzin D'Mon was dead, and she was a free woman. She didn't have a great deal of money—Xivan had always carried the metal—but she had a sword and knew some spells, and there would always be a demand for that. She wasn't too worried about where her next meal would come from.

She was still very worried about Xivan.

Talea had known Xivan was in pain, but this was beyond Talea's worst nightmares. She could almost see the black cloud of hate wrapping itself around her lover, not really so dissimilar at all to the black cloud that had once wrapped around Xivan's late husband, Azhen. She wondered if Xivan had given any thought to just how much power the duchess was handing over to Suless, how much glee the god-queen would take to find out that her hunt had so obsessed and consumed Xivan's existence.

When Talea reached a gate, she stopped walking, at which point, she looked up and realized she was standing outside the main entrance to the Octagon. The slave auction house.

Her heartbeat stampeded through her veins. She had to close her eyes for a moment.

Of all the buildings in the Upper Circle that had burned to the ground, why was this one still standing?

Because there was no justice in the world. Murad was a sham.[1]

The smart thing to do was turn around and leave. Talea had no business going to the Octagon. She didn't even have the metal to buy a slave, let alone the will. What did she think she was going to do? Free them herself? Fight off every guard and sorcerer tasked with keeping House D'Erinwa property under lock and key? It was a ridiculous notion.

Talea walked through the entry and entered the slave house.

It wasn't easy to walk through the halls of the auction house and be on her best behavior. She didn't really want to be. And she kept expecting someone to try to stop her, to demand an explanation for being there. A few times, she thought the guards were about to, but at the last minute, they'd be distracted by some distraught relative or a screaming patron demanding justice for having missed a bid, and Talea would walk by before they could stop her.

She had no idea where she was going. She was just picking the turns at random, sauntering down the marble hallways as if she had every right to be there. It was probably that, more than anything else, that kept the guards from stopping her. These were strange days. Three months ago, they might have thought to stop a beautiful girl with a curved Khorveshan sword at her side. These days, it seemed too risky.

Talea could taste the storm in the air, the sense that something was about

---

[1] Literally so. The so-called God of Justice was the God-King of Slavery first, and it's best to never forget that. "Justice" in Quur exists for one reason: to keep the slave pits full.

to happen. Which made no sense because there wasn't a cloud in the sky. Still, that feeling . . .

A guard left his post to help with a woman who collapsed from exhaustion, grief, or some other mysterious motive. Talea stepped through the door he'd been guarding. This was less smart than roaming the open halls, but she felt like she was following the scent of a particularly delectable meal back to the kitchens. Not that she smelled anything but sandalwood oil and the cleaner used on the floor, but it was the sense of the thing.

As if potential had a scent.

To her surprise, the passage led to an outside courtyard, with a separate entrance for those well-heeled individuals with enough money and prestige to ensure privacy. A horse-drawn wagon parked there, the sort that moved cargo of the human variety. It was full to the brim, people crying or staring, long past the point of tears. A driver sat on top of the wagon, ready to lead horses and people to a new location. People who had all been sold, who were heading to their new homes and new owners and new horrors. It was guaranteed that the horses would be treated better.

Next to the wagon, a man in the fine clothing of a royal was handing over a sheaf of papers. He said something outside the range of Talea's hearing to the man in House D'Erinwa colors, and then climbed on top of the wagon.

That sense of storm intensified. A different door across the way banged open. A dozen soldiers came running through, including a richly dressed man in House D'Erinwa colors. "Stop that man! Close the gate!"

The man being pointed at took one step toward the gate, must have realized he'd never make it in time, and then turned back toward the overseer. "I'm sorry. Is there a problem?"

The overseer angrily gestured toward the clerk, still clutching the sales receipts in his hands. "Give those over! Let me see those!"

Talea watched as the buyer checked the doors, the armed soldiers, the gate. Looking for a way out.

She could almost taste the lightning building in the air, the tallest objects nearby sending out leads to draw the strike.

The overseer began to laugh. "Ah, you should've quit while you were ahead, Casar. You pushed your luck for the last time."

Talea leaned over and picked up a rock. She felt outside herself, disconnected.

The buyer looked indignant, but underneath that laced a hint of anxiety. "I have no idea what you're talking about. These are legal bills of sale."

"That no one paid for. You think this house doesn't track every throne, chance, and chalice? No money changed hands." The overseer shook the papers for emphasis. "The masters would like to ask you a few questions about how you managed that, though . . ."

Close now . . .

"Still don't have any idea what you're talking about," Casar said. "How dare you! I want to speak with Lord D'Erinwa!"

"Oh, you will. But you'll talk to our torturers first."

There!

Outside the gate, a woman's scream rang out as large cracks appeared in midair, the very fabric of the world splintering and falling away as a dozen demons forced themselves to this side of the Veil. The guards all rushed in that direction.

"Demons!" someone screamed.

Talea threw the rock at the flank of the rear horse drawing the wagon. The poor beast had already been close to bolting because of the demons just a short distance away, so it didn't take much to startle it. That began a chain reaction with the other horses. They all tried to run. The lead horse reared, and her hooves came down hard on the gate.

The gates were closed, not barred. They sprang open under the horse's attack.

The buyer, Casar, recognized his chance. He climbed up on the now moving wagon. In the back, Talea did the same, holding on to the side by the wooden bars on the small windows. Crossbow bolts thunked as they hit the walls of the wagon; people shouted and screamed. In the chaos, the demons were only too happy to switch targets once the guards of House D'Erinwa presented themselves.

A demon spied the wagon and set it on fire, while another took a swipe at Talea. She dodged the strike and lifted herself rolling up and onto the top of the burning wagon. The people inside were screaming. Talea needed to do something or they were all going to be burned, herself included. Up ahead, she saw a glint of silver, and a signpost she recognized. If she was very lucky . . .

She staggered forward, dodging the fire still spreading on the wood. "Turn here!"

The nobleman looked back, did a double take. "Who the fuck are you?"

"I said turn here!" She grabbed a rein from the driver's hand and yanked. Before the driver had a chance to regain control, the horses turned, the wagon sliding several feet in the back from the sharpness of the movement. They found themselves galloping down an alley between bathhouses. As they did, a trio of servants came to a balcony and tipped over a large tub of soapy, scummy water.

It drenched all of them and smothered the fire.

"Taja!" the driver screamed; prayer or curse or both.

Talea began to laugh and then stopped, choking off the sound as she caught another glimpse of silver—a child with silver ringlet curls staring down at her from one of the upper windows, so fast she could have told herself she'd imagined it.

Casar clapped the driver on the shoulder. "Come on. Let's head to the meeting place." He looked back at Talea. "I don't know who the hell you are . . ."

"I'm the reason you got away. Depending on what you intend on doing with these people, that may make me your friend."

He studied her while they turned down another street. The driver finally managed to wrestle the horses under control and assumed a steadier, sedater pace. Nothing to see here. No one running from anything.

"I'm freeing them," the "nobleman" finally said. "It's kind of become a thing. That bastard back there was right, though—I pushed my luck too far."

Talea smiled. She'd known that would be the answer—nobody "stole" slaves from the Octagon for profit, because there was no place to sell them. That left a rumor so nebulous and vague that even Talea had never believed those whispers she'd heard back when she herself had lived a life in chains—that there was a secret network who stole slaves for reasons other than profit. Who stole slaves and freed them and asked for nothing in return.[2]

"Then we can be friends," she said. "I'm Talea. What's your real name?"

The man laughed as he pulled the wig off his head, revealing a shock of bright red hair. "Merit."

Despite the bad start, the rest of it followed with shocking smoothness. In a different back alley, another set of wagons of the non-slave variety waited, and the people they'd transported were unloaded, unshackled, and then divided between them. Merit switched out his agolé for something more pedestrian and set a nicely anonymous sallí cloak over it all. He looked back at Talea. "You coming or staying?"

She studied the wagons. "What's going to happen to them?"

"Safe house. Then . . . well, it depends. They'll be split up, taken different places. Hidden. The first thing we'll do is remove the slave brand."

Talea nodded. That had, in fact, been one of the first things Thurvishar had done after her own purchase—the act that had convinced her perhaps he wasn't just playing a cruel game when he promised he'd free her. She narrowed her eyes at Merit. "And why would you want me along? You don't know me. You don't know if you can trust me. So it's either a trap or . . ." She smiled. "You don't seem stupid, so should I assume the trap?"

Merit laughed. "Yeah, you're right; it's stupid. But you've been my lucky charm so far, and I'm not planning to take you anyplace you'll be able to ring on later."

Talea knew the look and all its unspoken meanings—namely, that he thought she was extremely pretty and was hoping to celebrate his survival with a little something extra. She suspected it wasn't diplomatic to spell out for him that the odds of making that happen were pretty much zero. He seemed nice enough, depending on that whole "trap" angle, but she was certainly not ready to replace Xivan, not even for a quick bit of fun.

He surprised her, though, when the wagons headed down to the Lower Circle. She'd thought they might head to one of the storehouses in the Copper Quarter, or maybe the Harbor District, but he pulled to a building right next to a Blue House and began unloading people. Openly, without a trace of hesitation. And since most of them weren't wearing manacles, it suddenly occurred to her what this looked like. Not a brazen slave escape at all but refugees from another demon attack, being taken to a Blue House for healing.

---

[2] While such a network does exist, none of the people involved with this one had any connection. Irony steps in to join the party when one realizes the abolition movement that Talea is referring to here is run by the Vishai.

If the injuries themselves weren't necessarily obvious, that didn't mean they weren't there.

She felt a thrill. The D'Erinwa slave masters had only noticed a discrepancy because they'd noticed the lack of metal. Whatever methods these people were using to forge bills of sale, it wasn't something the Royal Houses had yet tracked back to their source. House D'Erinwa would have no idea where to look.

But . . . it was a Blue House. How the hell had these people managed to subvert a Blue House?

"Come inside?"

Across the street, a little girl with silver hair stood on the steps to the clinic. She shook her head at Talea: no.

Talea swallowed. No matter how much this man liked the look of her, he wouldn't be working alone. Surely, his friends wouldn't be so willing to overlook her presence when the only explanation for her being there at all was the luck of the draw. And an operation like this was too dangerous and too risky to just take her word that she'd stay silent.

She smiled at him. "Sorry. Can't. I need to meet an old friend."

And then she ran.

There were shouts behind her, and she was sure at least a few people gave half-hearted chase, but she ran until she lost herself in the crowds on Simillion's Crossing. She curled up against a wall, bent over, panting for breath, and to her surprise, grinning like an idiot.

"It's fun, isn't it?" a voice said.

Talea looked up and found herself staring at Taja.

The goddess still looked like a little girl, barefoot and with scabs on one of her shins, a simple ribbon tied around the waist of her short white shift. But the hair was unmistakable, as were the wings and the ancient eyes.

Talea started to say something. The Goddess of Luck shook her head and put a finger to her lips.

"This way," the little girl said and motioned for her to follow.

Which she did. She followed the Goddess of Luck across that street and down an alley, ducked into a tenement and walked up the stairs to the top floor, climbed a ladder to the roof, and from there ended up on a flat rooftop garden overlooking a surprisingly nice view of the city. That view was an untrustworthy liar; it made the Capital look alive and vibrant, a place where one might actually want to live and not just survive.

When they were finally there, she turned to Taja, beaming. "I'm so happy you're still alive!"

"But Taja's not," the little girl who looked like Taja said. "I'm so sorry. I hate to disappoint you, but I'm dead. I mean, Taja's dead."

Talea felt that in her heart, an aching, horrible pain. "But–" She wiped her face. "You're here. I can see you."

"*Only* you can see me. To anyone else, you're talking to the plants." The girl shrugged. "Sorry about that. You might want to make sure we're alone before having any important conversations."

"So I'm going mad?" Talea would have thought going mad might be less obvious than seeing people who admitted they couldn't possibly exist, but there it was.

"No," the little girl said. "You're not."

"Those statements seem at odds with each other," Talea replied. "Do sane people have visions no one else can see?"

"Only when Immortals are involved—and that's the case here. Tya and Taja spent a lot of time thinking about what to do in case the Eight Immortals were ever killed again. It's a galling position to be in, you know, to be this powerful and yet know that all it takes is for Galava to die and the rest of the gods were, uh—"

"Fucked," Talea offered.

"Right. So they figured out a solution. Unfortunately, not a great solution. But I'm sure Taja thought that since she was over fourteen thousand years old, she'd had a good run. Except she left some projects in a delicate state and needs someone to finish them for her."

"So . . . that's where you come in?"

"Oh no," the little girl said. "That's where *you* come in."

Talea just stared at her. "You're not . . . you're not going to rewrite my mind so your soul can take possession of my body, are you? The way Suless did to Janel?"

The little girl's eyes widened in amazement. "Oookay, I think I'm beginning to understand why Taja picked you. Uh, no. There are both logistical and moral reasons that wouldn't work."

"Those reasons being?"

"Well! For one thing, mortal bodies can't contain the amount of tenyé Taja needs to exist, so your body would, literally, *explode*." She widened her eyes in mock surprise. "And second, eww. That's horrible. She would never."

Talea exhaled in relief. She walked over to a chair and sat down.

And immediately found herself with a lapful of small child.

"If you're not Taja," Talea said, "what do I call you?"

"Call me Eshimavari," the little girl said. "I mean . . . Eshi. Call me Eshi."

"Okay, Eshi. And if you're not Taja, why are you here?"

"To help you figure things out. You're not being prepared to be a host for some immortal consciousness or anything. You're more like . . . an angel," Eshi explained. "Sort of. Although in your case, instead of being the angel of an Immortal, you're the angel of the . . . memory . . . of an Immortal. Taja's not actually here, which is the other reason Taja couldn't possess you, even if she wanted, even if I wanted. Her souls are spread out across the universe right now and . . . yeah . . . I'd call that death, wouldn't you?"

"I don't want her to be dead," Talea said, her voice stuttering.

"Shh." Eshi wiped her cheeks with chubby little fingers. "It's okay. I know this is all happening very fast."

"What is it you need me to do?"

"We'll get to that in due time. Right now, I'm more concerned with what you want to do. What my darling little girl needs to be happy."

"I don't know." Talea closed her eyes and thought about it. What did she want? "I want to go back home. I mean, I want to go back to the Spurned."

The child leaned back and regarded her. "Is that what you really want?"

"No, I really–" Talea's lip quivered. "What I really want is Xivan back, but I don't think I'm going to get what I want this time."

The Goddess of Luck–or rather, a memory of the Goddess of Luck–kissed the tip of Talea's nose. "Not right away. Let's make that a long-term project, shall we? In the meantime, let's see who we can run into to help with that other matter."

Talea squinted. "Going home?"

"Eventually. We have a few stops to make first."

Talea's reaction
The Lighthouse at Shadrag Gor

Talea had a thin, uncertain smile plastered on her face when the vision ended, because of course, everyone was staring at her. Which she'd expected, but even so, it hurt a little. Not all the looks were supportive. Kalindra looked openly skeptical, and Senera's expression was . . . considered. Whether that consideration was on the matter of Talea's sanity or some other problem revolving around her revelations wasn't yet clear.

Not-Actually-Taja wasn't visible right at the moment. Evidently, she was going to let Talea work this out on her own.

"You really think–" Senera started to say, and then stopped and reached for the Name of All Things.

"Oh, for fuck's sake. She's telling the truth," Talon said. "If you really must ask your pet rock a thousand questions, go ahead, but she's telling the truth. She really is seeing all that. And if it's not real, someone's doing a hell of a job of faking it."

Sheloran cocked her head. "What do you mean?"

"I mean that unlike the rest of you fine people, I–and I equals Kihrin here–have met the real, actual Taja when she felt like running around as a little girl, and Talea's memories are identical. She didn't just remember any ol' adorable little silver-haired moppet–she remembered *Taja*. As I am under the impression Talea only previously met the adult version, and then only for a few minutes at most, why on earth would she get that detail right if she were going insane? Do you think you could draw what Galen looked like when he was eight just because you've seen him full grown now? Trust me, that was Taja." Talon paced as she rolled her eyes, all but throwing her hands up in the air.

"Thank you," Talea told her, surprised at the defense.

"Anything for my"–Talon paused–"friend."

"You mean sister," Talea corrected. She knew exactly why the mimic was having these little attacks of conscience, and it wasn't out of anything like a sense of friendship. Talon's memories of Talea's twin sister, Morea, were messing with the monster's head.

The mimic froze. "I'm not–" Talon visibly swallowed. "Don't tease."

"So are you still seeing Eshimavari?" Senera asked Talea carefully. She was eyeing her with a wariness Talea found upsetting.

"Yes," Talea said. "I'm not seeing her right now, mind you. She comes and goes."

"And tells you what to do," Kalindra said, making it sound like Talea was "compromised" or had been suborned or some other silly nonsense.

"No!" Talea said. "She just tells me the odds. And lately, she doesn't even really need to do that. I can figure out the odds on my own."

This did nothing to alleviate the worried look on Senera's face. "Have there been any other . . . symptoms?"

"Symptoms?" Talea laughed. "You make it sound like I'm catching a disease."

Senera didn't reply.

As if to break up the awkward silence, Sheloran yawned and then said, "Do we have any idea what time it is? If that's a question that even has any validity under the circumstances."

"It feels late," Kalindra said, "but I can't say for sure."

"Why don't we sleep?" Galen suggested. "It's not like we don't have bedrooms and heating spells."

Qown shook his head. "There are, but it's Vol Karoth's turn . . ."

Galen paused and turned to look at Qown. "Please don't take this as being directed at you, but honestly, why would I give a damn whether or not it's Vol Karoth's turn? What's he going to do, send a vision worse than the nightmares we're already enjoying? And don't try to tell me you don't have nightmares, Qown, because I know better."

Qown turned red and hid his mouth behind a hand. "I just . . . He's still coming through the wall."

"Which he'll probably still be doing eight hours from now," Galen said. "If we're tired and miserable, I fail to see how we're going to be in a better position to figure out a solution. Also, why are we playing that bastard's game? I apologize for the language, but fuck him. He's going to throw horrible visions at us, fine. Nothing says we have to be awake for it. And then, once it's our turn again, we can just . . . sleep."

"I could use the sleep," Talea admitted. "There's really no reason we can't, is there?"

"Why hasn't Vol Karoth already sent us a vision?" Kalindra mused. "He's usually faster than this."

"Presumably, our friends are keeping him occupied. We'll need to find the linens and make the beds first," Senera noted. "We don't keep the bedding out in the open. It would rot away before the next person visited."

Sheloran closed her fan and tucked it into her belt. "If someone doesn't mind showing me what to do, I'm happy to help."

30: GRAY HEART

Kihrin's story
Inside Vol Karoth's prison

"Run!" Janel cried out.

"Ha," I said as I blocked Vol Karoth's swing and felt my whole arm go numb from the strain. "I'd just fucking love to. You first!"

"Not without you," Teraeth replied as he tossed a handful of daggers in quick succession at Vol Karoth's back. I'd love to say it made a difference but . . . nah.

"It's not a race!" Janel screamed. "We can all go!"

Why do you even bother? You know you can't win against me.

"That's never stopped me from trying before." I struck back, although I really wasn't trying to injure him. I didn't think I could injure him. It was like trying to ignore nothing, trying to wound a thing that didn't exist. How do you take from a thing that's already a negative? So I was trying to trip, destabilize, keep him off-balance until the next event distracted him—either the visions sent out by Talon or the ones sent out by Vol Karoth himself.

We had come out of Xivan's vision to find Vol Karoth advancing on us with naked blade in hand.

As we fought, I almost stumbled myself as I noticed an odd spot farther down the street. Trees. Plants. Which should have been one of those good signs except for two problems. One, none of it was in color. It was all washed gray, the undertone to a painting that hadn't been finished. And two, I hadn't created them.

But then Vol Karoth was turning to lash out at Janel, who barely managed to pull her shield up in time. So I had to concentrate on distracting him, rather than investigating what the hell was up with that stretch of road. Something about it was odd beyond just the weird color shift. It felt like the wrong piece of a puzzle hammered into a different position.

Teraeth noticed where I'd been looking and turned to study the same spot.

"Seriously, run!" I shouted back to Janel and Teraeth.

"But this is where all the fun is." The laughter was forced and slightly hysterical, but I can't say I expected Janel to agree. That just wouldn't have been her style. Wouldn't have been either of their styles.

They don't fight because they care about you. They fight because they want to survive.

"You're really going to need to do better than that, asshole."

They don't have to die here with you. You're just luring them to their deaths.

I scowled as our swords slammed against each other. "All right. That was a little better."

Teraeth trotted over to the gray spot.

Vol Karoth suddenly turned away from me, all his attention focused on Teraeth. I stepped in front of him.

"Hey, I thought we were playing."

Get out of my way.

This was interesting. Naturally, I didn't get out of his way. But unfortunately, my main strategy for surviving fights with Vol Karoth involved not letting him hit me, so it wasn't terribly difficult for him to force his way past. But as Vol Karoth did, white outlined the side of his body. Vol Karoth flinched back. He turned.

Thurvishar had arrived.

I blinked. I was so used to seeing Thurvishar as only a mental construct that I'd sort of forgotten he could show up himself. And I wasn't sure what spell he'd just used, but Vol Karoth didn't like it. Not at all.

Thurvishar was also standing next to the gray area, looking at it curiously.

Stay away from that!

"Huh." Thurvishar tilted his head to the side. "This has an emotional pattern attached to it. Isn't that odd? I was wondering what I was feeling."

"You felt it too, huh?" Teraeth said. "I wonder what happens if I touched it–" He reached out a hand.

Vol Karoth started running straight for them.

Started. Janel appeared in front of him and slammed her shield down into the ground. A wall of magical force shot up from the ground, blocking Vol Karoth's way.

Huh. Why did that bother Vol Karoth so much? He seemed weaker than the last time we'd fought. Still monstrously powerful, but less monstrously powerful. I found myself wondering if destroying the city had cost him.

You cannot stop me that easily.

Vol Karoth snapped his thumb and forefinger together, and the wall shattered, each piece dissolving like sugar floss in water. He grabbed Janel's shield and disintegrated it.

"It's jealousy," Thurvishar said. "This spot is just soaked with jealousy." He turned back to Vol Karoth. "I can actually feel him, Kihrin. He's jealous of you. Jealous of Teraeth and Janel. Jealous of what you have."

Vol Karoth stopped fighting. I still couldn't see his expression, but he had tilted his head in a way that made me think he was staring at Thurvishar in a very unfriendly manner.

Why don't you step inside? You'll see how jealous I am. But clearly, I'm going to need to do something about meddling little ants.

He vanished.

"Why does that not feel like a victory?" Teraeth asked.

"We still drove him off," Janel said.

"We didn't drive him off," Thurvishar said. "He left. But we should take advantage of the opportunity." Without waiting on the rest of us, he stepped into the gray space.

Teraeth shook his head. "You wouldn't think the two of you were anything alike, but then he goes and does something like that."

"We all have our moments." I followed Thurvishar.

I let out the breath I'd been holding. Stepping into the area of grayness had felt exactly like stepping into any other section of street, just with less color. I had more than half expected blinding pain or a wall of flames to erupt in front of us or . . . something. This was anticlimactic in the extreme.

I glanced back, saw Janel and Teraeth holding hands as they waited for me. I felt a flash of irritation that they'd let me go first. "It's safe," I said.

They nodded, stepped in together. Thurvishar followed a heartbeat later, walking slower, inspecting the colorless walls on either side.

"It's a street," Teraeth said with a smirk. "Because the city wasn't full of those already."

Janel giggled at his "joke," leaning on his arm.

I turned away and looked ahead. The street continued on, tree-lined and all, for roughly two hundred yards before ending in a small courtyard. A fountain threw water into the air, but the mist failed to create a rainbow.

Of course, that might have had as much to do with a lack of direct sunlight as anything else. It was hard to tell.

Something about the place seemed vaguely familiar, but I couldn't concentrate on it; Janel and Teraeth hanging all over each other was simply too distracting. As I glanced at them, he brushed a strand of her hair over her ear, and she smiled and leaned her head against him.

It had been years since I'd wanted to punch him right in his stupid, pretty face as badly as I did right then. My hand balled into a fist.

"This isn't Karolaen," Thurvishar said.

The utter nonsense of that proclamation cut through my irritation. "Is this another 'it's called Karolaen before and Kharas Gulgoth after' thing?" I asked, doing my best Thurvishar voice.

His brow creased in a frown, but then he shook his head. "No," he said. "I mean, this isn't voras architecture. Look."

My lip curled into a sneer, but my eyes followed his pointing finger. I opened my mouth to say something scathing, but the words never left my throat.

He was right.

"He's right," Janel said, once more agreeing with anyone but me. "Look." She pointed at a window frame. "This is older. This is . . ."

"Nineawen," I said. "The first city we founded back on Nythrawl." I frowned at the window, then looked again down the street. Suddenly, I realized why it looked familiar. "Oh fuck," I said. "That's—" I pointed to the house at the end of the street.

"En'dassin's house," Janel finished for me.

"Who is En'dassin?" Teraeth asked.

"C'indrol's lover," I spat. Hate began building inside me, and I found my blade in my hand. I took a step toward the offending house, then another. Then I found myself in midair, my feet churning on nothing.

"We need to get out of here," C'indrol said as she turned and carried me, still held over her head, toward the edge of the colorless area.

"Why?" asked En'dassin, as clueless and horrible as ever.

I struggled to get free. I'd kill him, if only I could reach him. I just needed to—

We exited the gray area. Color washed back over us like a wave at the beach. The hate washed away in its wake.

Janel looked up at me. "Feeling better?"

"Yes," I said. I looked at Teraeth, who didn't seem angry that I'd been swinging my sword in his general direction moments ago so much as he just looked confused.

"What just happened?" he asked.

"Jealousy." Thurvishar spoke up. "As I said, there was an emotional overlay of jealousy there." He looked at Janel, then at me. "Care to explain?"

Janel set me down, and I put my sword away. I couldn't make eye contact with her, so she shrugged and spoke. "C'indrol and S'arric were lovers," she said, "but we'd had to hide it because . . . well, politics. It would have been a huge scandal, and that's not even considering how upset Rev'arric would have been. So C'indrol took another lover, En'dassin, as a cover." She looked at me, bending and stepping in front of me so I had to look at her. "I thought you understood that it wasn't serious between her and me," she said. "You told me you were okay with it."

"I was," I protested. Then I waved my hand at the area of grayness. "At least, I thought I was."

"Now we're gaining ground," Thurvishar said. "Jealousy is a victory."

I raised my eyebrows. "I'm going to need you to explain your definition of victory to me."

"You can't be jealous of something you don't want to possess yourself," Teraeth said softly.

I paused. "You . . . you mean—"

"Love," Teraeth said. "Thurvishar's right. If Vol Karoth's jealous of love? That's . . . yeah. That's a good sign."

"For values of 'good sign' that include having an angry god trying to kill us," Janel said.

"Feh." I waved a hand. "He was already trying to do that."

Before I could say anything else, the world changed.

Galen's story
The Lighthouse at Shadrag Gor

Before sleep could happen, they had to raid the linen closet and make all the beds. The linens were all House D'Lorus make—which meant fine linen dyed black—of the generally high quality one would expect of a Royal House.

Several rebellious sheets in other colors had been tucked into the back of the closet—a set of white sheets, dark blue, and a floral print that Senera immediately claimed with a glare at anyone who might object.

Galen avoided the dark blue set as though it were soaked in poison sumac and carried off one of the black sets.

Most of the rooms held two narrow beds, clearly not meant to be shared. With several of the walls removed, the space began to feel a bit like a dormitory. The beds themselves departed from the classic Quuros designs, which would have required hemp or bamboo or some other sort of organic, ultimately decomposing material. Instead, the beds were marble stone, beautifully carved.[1] Making them usable for sleep required pulling out stuffed mats that had been rolled up and left in storage along with padded bolsters.

It felt a bit like when Galen and Kihrin used to sneak off with stolen food to hide out in the storeroom, that feeling of turning something uncomfortable and hard into something soft and friendly. Galen had no idea if he'd actually manage to sleep on such a bed, but going through the motions felt soothing.

Then Sheloran marched over to Galen, all but dragging Qown by the scruff of his neck. "I'm going to stay with Kalindra. I think she needs the company. So Qown can sleep here." She let go of the man and turned around without waiting for either of them to respond.

"Wait, I didn't agree—!" Qown started to call out after her.

"You could always switch with someone else if you'd rather not," Galen suggested.

Qown turned around and regarded Galen as if he were something sharp and prickly that would absolutely draw blood if Qown wasn't careful. "It's, um . . . I mean, it's not—"

"I'm sure what my lovely wife meant to say was: Would you two idiots please talk?" Galen smiled tightly and gestured over to the other bed. "And we probably should." Galen tried to ignore the way his stomach was wrestling to switch places with his heart. Evidently, he was going to have to be the adult here, and just because he didn't want to be didn't change the reality of it.

"I don't—" Qown inhaled and managed to look anywhere but at Galen. "I'm sorry if I embarrassed you earlier. Please believe I had no intention of ever putting you in a situation where it seemed like I was just—"

"You know my wife and I are not sexually intimate with each other, yes?"

Qown's eyes widened. "I'm sorry? I don't need to know—" But he didn't move, and this time, he did look at Galen directly. "Really?"

"Really," Galen said. "I adore her. I can quite honestly say I owe her my life many times over. She not only taught me how to survive Darzin, I quite literally wouldn't have been Returned after Khaeriel murdered me if not for her. She is my best friend. She's like a sister to me. But we've never slept with each other, and we have no intention of ever doing so."

---

[1] Again, assuming this was your work, Thurvishar.

"Oh." Qown swallowed and looked away. "And you're telling me this be-cause . . . ?"

"Veils, Qown. I really haven't been subtle. As Senera would say, 'You're not this stupid.'" Galen stood up from his bed and walked over to Qown's. He sat down next to him. "If there is one good thing about these gods-damned dreams or memories or whatever you might want to call them, it's that it's made it rather difficult for either of us to pretend nothing is happening between us."

Qown studied him, uncertain and clearly uneasy. His expression turned anxious. "Galen, I-I can't! I. Took. A. Vow. Please respect that."

Galen blinked. "You took a vow to a fake religion founded by Relos Var. I would respect the vow if it meant something. I would respect the vow if it were necessary. But honestly, what is this 'vow' doing for you except to make you exceedingly frustrated and probably qualify you as top-ranking candidate for any number of demonic sacrifices?"

Qown turned bright red. "That was a reference to being a virgin, wasn't it?"

"Yes!" Galen lowered his voice, since he was in serious danger of starting to shout. Instead, he reached over and picked up Qown's hand, tightened his hold when the other man started to pull away. "Surely hand-holding is not forbidden to the Vishai faith?"

"No, I just–" Qown visibly swallowed. "No. It's not."

Galen interlaced his fingers with Qown's. The priest had beautiful hands, with long, delicate fingers. They were a bit callused and dry from all the salt-sea air and ship life of recent weeks, but still gorgeous and warm enough to make Galen wonder why he even needed to make a fire for cooking when he could just use the heat radiating out from that point of contact between them.

"Why Relos Var?" Galen asked quietly. "Help me understand."

Qown's mouth worked silently for a moment as the man stared at Galen in surprise. Galen was putting him in a spot, since he could either tackle this subject or go back to talking about their relationship, and Galen was reasonably sure he knew which one would win.

"I just . . . I realized that the gods weren't doing anything. That they didn't know what to do or how to fix the situation with Vol Karoth. They were just–" Qown laughed. "I should probably point out the hypocrisy of that. Because the Vishai faith has always claimed that the gods are nothing more than powerful wizards. And yet here I was, thinking the gods were going to 'fix' everything. As if they weren't just . . . really powerful wizards. So even as I was claiming I didn't believe in the sanctity of gods, I clearly . . . did . . . believe . . . that."

Galen smoothed his thumb over the back of Qown's hand. "It's hard to shake off what everyone else tells you is important. Even if you think you have, it's . . . it's not easy. You think you're fine, and then it ambushes you."

"Are we still talking about Relos Var?" Qown asked doubtfully.

"It was a statement with a broad range of applicability," Galen replied. "But let's touch back on Relos Var for a moment. Because okay, you realized the gods weren't going to solve this. And so you decided to side with the man who was. I suppose I can see the logic of that. But how do you know you can trust him?"

"Of course I can trust him." Qown started to pull his hand away from Galen, but only for a second. "I trust him to get us through this, and I don't–"

"I don't think you do."

Qown stared at Galen and didn't respond.

"I don't think you trust him," Galen continued. "I think he was the best option you thought you had. I think it's really easy, when everything is this horrible, to throw all your faith behind the person you think can solve all your problems. 'Just follow me,' he says, 'and I'll do all the heavy lifting. All you have to do is follow my every command.'"

"It's not like that," Qown said.

"I think if it wasn't exactly like that, Senera would still be on his side," Galen retorted. He set Qown's hand back in the other man's lap, untangled his fingers, and stroked a single line across the back of Qown's hand. "And if she was still on his side after all that, then yes, they probably deserve to win. Qown, I like you."

Qown had been staring at his hand, but at those words, he looked up, wide-eyed.

"I really like you," Galen repeated. "You're smart and you're beautiful and you like my poetry, and that last one is not easy to find. Sheloran thinks you're great, and she's already suggested we should adopt you–although in her case, I have to be honest: she's really thinking of how useful all your abilities would be in the larger Sheloran Mother-Hens the Whole Damn World project she's working on. I think you and I could be happy–if you'd let yourself."

Qown stood up and Galen could see–ah, but damn–that the man's arms were trembling. Not in a good way. Not in an excited way. Something quite different and quite unwelcome.

"It's not about . . . it's not about the religion," Qown said. "It's about me making a promise and keeping that promise. And I can't just . . . I can't just switch sides every time the wind blows a different direction. I like all of you–okay, not . . . not Talon, and Xivan is still quite scary, but–"

"Qown, please–"

"No! No, I can't just–" Qown bit his lip, and damn it, now those liquid eyes were genuinely wet and he was crying, the tears streaking down his cheeks. "I can't! Please don't try to make me! You're a . . . you're a high lord! A Royal House high lord! And I am never going to be someone's . . . I don't even know what I'd be. A concubine? A lover, I suppose, which . . . which sounds quite nice until I think about how we'd never be able to walk down a street together. Never even be able to–" He angrily gestured to the bed. "Never even be able to hold hands like this! Not in public. Maybe the idea of wearing masks your entire life is fine for you, but it's not for me!"

"I see," Galen said. A solid burning weight lodged itself in his chest, dragging downward with oppressive intensity. Because he'd never understood the religion angle. Not after it became clear that Qown's religion was nothing more than an elaborate con game. But embarrassment? Shame? Those were emotions that Galen understood far too well.

"Let me ask you something," Galen said. "Do you think what I'm proposing between us is a sin?" The moment condensed down to this. To this question.

To this answer. It felt like taking a candle flame to his flesh, knowing the pain would take a minute to kick in before flaring bright and raw.

"I . . ." Qown's mouth worked silently. He didn't answer.

"I'll take that as a yes," Galen said. He gave Qown a small, sad smile. "You didn't learn that from Relos Var. You learned that from Quur. You learned that how you feel about me is wrong. And you believe it."

"Galen, I–" Qown was still crying, but Galen forced himself to ignore it. For some reason, comforting the man who'd just admitted he was too ashamed of his feelings to admit them felt beyond Galen's capacity.

"I'll go find a different pair of beds," Galen said, and left.

31: Rainbow Lake

Qown's memory[1]
The Upper Circle of the Capital City, Quur
Just after the Lysian gas attack at the Culling Fields

They ended up stealing a horse and wagon from behind the Culling Fields and steering it into a back alley.

"That could have gone better," Galen said.

Anlyr just pressed his lips together and shook his head.

"Go ahead and say it," Galen said.

"Never underestimate stupid people," Anlyr said.

Sheloran sat up and straightened her agolé. "I'm reluctant to call Gerisea stupid when we're the ones hiding behind a chandler's."

"Can't we just go back to the Veil?" Qown asked.

"I wouldn't recommend it," Anlyr said. "If Gerisea is smart"—he gave Galen a look—"then she'll have people watching the exits to the Lower Circle. There aren't that many of them."

Galen sighed. "No, you're right. That would be the smart thing to do." He chewed on his lip before turning to Qown. "How did you know? Just before the gas erupted, you knew something was wrong."

"I've seen Lysian gas before," Qown explained. "I've seen it wipe out entire towns. That's why I—" He swallowed. "That's why I knew how to deal with it."

"You are my new official favorite person," Sheloran murmured.

"Anyone have any suggestions on where we can go? Since House D'Talus is out of the question and I just made the significantly viler of my two aunts a high lord?"

Qown swallowed. "Rainbow Lake."

Galen raised an eyebrow at him.

"The Temple of Light. My temple, on the shore of Rainbow Lake." Qown forced an entirely fake smile on his face. "We've been hiding out in a brothel. Let's try the opposite."

"It would be nice to go home again," Anlyr murmured.

Galen took a deep breath. "Sold. Now we just have to get there." He fished a small, flat piece of jade out of an inside pocket. "Fortunately, I know just how to do that." He saw the questioning look on Qown's face and smiled. "As it happens, any family members of House D'Aramarin can use the portal system at any time, to any location, no questions asked." He held

---

[1] Please note that this vison happened while we were all asleep.

up the jade token. "And my mother was a princess of House D'Aramarin. Bring the wagon."

Galen hadn't been exaggerating. Not a single House D'Aramarin servant asked questions. Qown thought it odd; after all, Galen was dressed in blue and had blue eyes. He clearly wasn't House D'Aramarin. But that token was apparently the only identification that mattered.[2] Within minutes, they were walking up to the afternoon gate attendant.

The Gatestone system was the transportation hub of the entire empire. Most locations might have a single circular area that was cordoned off to form an octagon of green tiles. Qown knew that magical transportation arrays were engraved on the underside of the tiles, but outsiders were never allowed to see them. This, however, was the hub of the Gatestone system, and so there were no fewer than eight such gates, all of which could be operated simultaneously.

Qown had only used the gates a few times in his life, and later, it seemed that almost everyone he knew could open a gate themselves. So this was a weird feeling. Still, everything went correctly, and they (and their horse and wagon) made it to the other side. By this time, it was late afternoon, so the easiest thing to do was find a hospitality house, reserve rooms for the night, and head out to the temple itself in the morning. Qown ordered the three poison victims to bed early—he'd cured the main issues, but that didn't mean their systems hadn't taken a dangerous shock. Given the healing he'd given them, they would sleep deeply through the night. Gerisea hadn't been taking chances. Qown let Anlyr fuss over defenses and perimeters and all the other security issues that his heart desired, and also retired early. Bluntly, he was tired.

However, he wasn't so tired that he didn't wake up in the middle of the night to a deafening roar, the ground shaking, and a sound roughly analogous to boulders shattering. He ran out to the balcony, watching as people all over the city unshielded mage-lights and opened windows. Dogs started barking. The upset murmurs of people echoed around them. In the distance, the sky lit up several times, lightning flashing in all the wrong colors: lavenders and blues and greens.

Then came the flash that silhouetted a giant draconian shape, head swooping down to bite at something. The roar rolled over the town a moment later, loud enough to shake walls, easy to mistake for violent thunder if one didn't know the truth was so much worse.

Qown stared in mute shock. Then a fact filtered through the horror: direction. That direction was Rainbow Lake. That direction was the Temple of Light.

"No! Oh no!" He turned to head inside and ran smack into Anlyr, who was also frowning, but not at the direction of the devastating dragon attack. The House D'Mon guard was frowning specifically at him. Then, like someone had pulled a veil across Anlyr's face, he smiled, any sign of anger or disapproval gone.

---

[2] In a sense, yes. They are magically keyed: Galen wouldn't have been able to use it if he hadn't been of close D'Aramarin descent.

"Anlyr, let me pass—"

"What would you do?" Anlyr's voice was surprisingly soft. "What difference could you make? All you would do by heading that way is put your own life in danger, and your job is here, alive."

"People will be injured over there—"

"Wait until the dragon leaves," he said.

Qown inhaled. "I am a healer. I'm not going to turn my back on people who need me."

Anlyr rolled his eyes. "Don't make me tie you down," he said. "I'll do it."

"I'm not the person you're assigned to protect!" Qown snapped.

Anlyr laughed.

Qown started to shove past him. No sooner had he than the man grabbed him by the arms and pulled them behind his back. Qown knew Anlyr didn't actually intend to hurt him, but that didn't mean the guard was being gentle. "I'll start screaming!" Qown threatened. Even as he made the threat, he remembered that Galen and Sheloran had enough damage to their lungs from the Lysian gas that he'd sent them to bed with a sleeping tincture. They weren't going to wake, even under threat of dragon attack.

Anlyr dragged him back inside. "Go right ahead," Anlyr said pleasantly. "And given what's going on outside, I'll be very impressed if anyone even bothers to check on you. They're all too busy hoping the giant dragon doesn't decide to go after this town next."

"Anlyr! Stop this right now!" But he didn't; Qown found himself being forced into a chair with his arms twisted behind him. He tried to escape as Anlyr began binding his hands with a cord. "You have rope? Who carries rope on them in the middle of the night?"

Anlyr stopped for a moment, and Qown felt something lean against him from behind. He realized Anlyr was resting his head against Qown's and laughing, hard, his whole body shaking from it.

"I'm so happy this amuses you," Qown said through clenched teeth.

"Oh, you have no idea the . . . restraint . . . I'm showing right now." Anlyr said happily as he moved Qown's hair out of the way so it wouldn't be caught on the ropes or the chair pressing against his back. He smoothed his hand down the side of Qown's head as if he were a dog on a leash while Qown could only sit there and seethe.

Seethe and . . . think about Anlyr's hands touching him. Truthfully, Qown was starting to feel a little uncomfortable. And then angry about that feeling because he was quite sure Anlyr knew perfectly well that he was making Qown feel uncomfortable.

Anlyr finished tying his knots and came around to Qown's front, crouched back on his heels between Qown's legs while he rested his elbows on Qown's thighs.

"Comfortable?" Anlyr asked.

"No!" Qown said. "You can't leave me here all night, you know."

"No?" Anlyr thought about it. "Hmm. Pretty sure I can. Also, I don't trust you not to run off and do something stupid and heroic. Seriously, you need to break this habit. It's only going to get you into trouble." He looked to the side past Qown, where the lights and roaring shook the skies in the distance. "I'm probably saving your life, and lucky me, you won't even be grateful."

"You have me tied up," Qown pointed out.

"You won't be grateful for that either."

Qown choked.

The corner of Anlyr's mouth quirked up as he stared into Qown's eyes. It left absolutely no doubt in Qown's mind that yes, Anlyr knew exactly what he was doing, and yes, he was doing it on purpose.

"Don't . . . I don't–" Qown started to stammer.

Anlyr sighed and wrinkled his nose. "Relax, Qown. Forcing someone is only fun when it's pretend. Besides, I make a personal point to never rape anyone who could kill me with a hard look."

"I can't–"

"Oh, you could. You just don't have the motivation. I'm not stupid enough to provide you with any either." He studied Qown thoughtfully. "Although we could still do that pretend bit, if you wanted."

"I'm sorry?" Qown hated how panicked he sounded.

"Come now. I know Vishai take a vow of chastity, but I also thought you were supposed to be honest about your emotions. And whether or not you're happy about the idea, you have to admit that you are interested. You're just burning up with how interested you are, aren't you?"

Qown felt a stab of guilt. Honesty was important. So was breathing, he reminded himself. Breathing was important. He needed to remember to do that. "Whether I am or not doesn't change anything."

"I rather think it does," Anlyr said, moving his hand farther up Qown's thigh without actually touching him. Qown could all but feel the heat radiating from the man's hand. "Say yes, and then we can pretend you said no to your heart's desire. Ah, it wouldn't be your fault at all. You were helpless. My prisoner."

"I am helpless and your prisoner," Qown pointed out.

Anlyr smiled and looked up at Qown through his eyelashes. "Are you, though?"

Qown's throat felt very dry.

"I . . . I thank you for the courtesy of your polite offer," Qown finally managed to say, "but I'm afraid I shall have to decline."

It had been so much easier to say that in Jorat.

Anlyr laughed. "Gods, you're adorable." He glanced back behind him toward the cots. "So which one of them are you saving yourself for? Galen or Sheloran? Hmm. A little of both, I think, but mostly Galen. Can't say I blame you. Those D'Mon boys are awfully pretty."

Qown's heart rate increased. "That's . . . He's not . . . Nothing is going to happen."

Those eyes turned serious, even stern. The change was so startling it felt like being doused in cold water. "Good. Keep it that way."

That stopped Qown. "Wait. Is this some kind of weird test? Was all this to try . . . Are you protecting him?"

"No, I'm protecting you," Anlyr said. "You know you don't get to have him, right? There is no scenario where someone like him ends up with someone like you. It's just not how this world works." This time, his hand did come down on Qown's thigh, did stroke upward, and Qown couldn't stop himself from shivering. "Now, if it's just a matter of you having a late coming of age, I am generously offering you the opportunity to get it all out of your system."

"Ha! Generous?"

"I'm a giver," Anlyr admitted.

"You're a terrible person!" Qown said.

Anlyr leaned forward and put a finger against Qown's lips, the action so intimate it silenced Qown better than a gag.

"Shh," he said. "Let that be our little secret." Anlyr winked at Qown before he stood up and walked back out toward the balcony. "Now try to get some sleep. I suspect tomorrow will be very trying for everyone."

Qown woke when he heard movement. That turned out to be Galen, who'd been the least injured and so presumably needed the least sleep. He walked over in front of Qown and squinted at the man, bemused. "Um, do I want to know why you're tied up?"

"Your stupid guard did this to me. He's a menace! Don't let the face fool you. He's evil! You have to untie me right now!"

Anlyr began to talk mid-yawn, and then started over. "There was ... Sorry—looks like some sort of dragon was fighting something over by Rainbow Lake, so our very own personal saint here decided he wanted to go up there while the dragon was still stomping around. I apologize if I overreached, my lord, but you seem to like him, so I assumed you'd want him to stay among the living."

Galen blinked at Anlyr. "Right. Yes, thank you. You did the right thing." He frowned, looking at Anlyr, then Qown, then back to Anlyr again. He didn't seem very pleased by whatever he saw, and scowled. Then to Qown, he said, "Don't be like my brother Kihrin. Nobody likes a hero."

Behind him, Anlyr chuckled.

"Must I point out that in fact everyone likes a hero?" Qown said as he pulled on his restraints.

Galen shook his head. "No. Everyone likes to tell stories about heroes. That's not the same thing at all. Didn't your Father Zajhera tell you a dead physicker heals no one? Even I know that rule."

Qown snorted and didn't answer. In part because yes, Father Zajhera had told him that rule. And reminded him about it regularly since. But ... he didn't know. Maybe he'd spent too much time around Janel.

Anlyr frowned. "Question?"

"Yes, Anlyr?"

"Apologies, but I thought Kihrin was your uncle."

Galen waved a hand. "Whatever. Calling him my uncle feels weird when he's only a year older. He's my brother until he tells me to stop. Would you kindly untie my man, Anlyr? If there's been trouble over at the temple, we should go see if we can help."

"Thank you!" Qown said. "Must I mention that all those healers who were supposed to help out House D'Mon are over there? Or at least were?"

Galen inhaled, suggesting that no, he hadn't thought about that at all. "All right. Let's wake up Sheloran. We'll leave immediately."

Qown couldn't stop himself from gasping when they came around the bend.

He'd known it would be bad. For the prior hour, they'd been encountering refugees along the road, petitioners who had gone to the Temple of Light for various reasons and had fled in horror when the attack had begun. Qown had healed people until Galen ordered him to save his strength.

Anlyr said nothing, but Qown saw him fingering the thin cord wrapped around his waist—which turned out to be what he'd bound Qown's arms with the night before. When Anlyr noticed Qown looking, he returned the priest's stare with a smirk. Hot-faced, Qown looked away.

But he forgot all that when he saw the ruins before him, the result of nothing so simple or clean as Sharanakal's fire or Morios's blades. The shore by the lake was strewn with rubble, but some of that rubble was melted and some shattered. Electrical arc burns tore apart rock, while ash spiraled in dust devils twisting though the wreckage. And then there were the bodies . . .

The bile rose in Qown's throat. He saw a person caught halfway through a stone block, as if they had turned insubstantial and then solid again while still melded through the rock. Another person lay dead, screaming, half their body twisted like long strings of sugar candy. Another body was—literally—turned inside out. No two people seemed to have died the same way, but it was all universally horrifying, people trapped halfway into transition to . . . something else. Animals and insects or masses of slick, gelatinous tumors.

Galen ran off to be sick, and Qown had to stop himself from following to do the same. Qown swallowed and shut his eyes.

He wasn't sure if he should take comfort in the fact that there didn't seem to be nearly enough bodies. Did that mean more of his people had survived the devastation? Or did that just mean those bodies weren't in a state to be recognized as such?

"There's someone over there," Sheloran said. "I saw movement." She left the horse and wagon and started picking her way through the rubble.

Everyone followed her. It took them nearly fifteen minutes just to make their way the several hundred feet to where, Qown realized with sinking dread, the main heart of the temple had once stood. It wasn't recognizable as anything but a horror-splattered canvas.

But Sheloran was right; a single person stood in the middle of the destruction, pacing out the length of the temple confines while blocks of stone magically moved around him. He was clearing room for bodies.

It was Relos Var.

Not Father Zajhera. He didn't look like the patriarch of the Vishai faith. He wore the form that Qown knew from Jorat, from Yor. The form of the wizard whom Qown was not supposed to publicly admit was his boss.

"Um, hello," Galen said. "Who are you?"

Relos Var looked up, seemingly surprised. His eyes were bloodshot. Light, had he been crying? The truth of that struck Qown in the gut, punched the air from his lungs. Var studied their group, frowning, eyes narrowed.

"What are you doing here?" Relos Var demanded. "What happened?" He gestured toward Anlyr. "Tell me."

The man cleared his throat, momentarily uncomfortable, then straightened. "There was a problem with the sisters. Unfortunately, the result is that Tishenya is dead, Galen D'Mon isn't high lord, and Gerisea is. Also, Galen may be wanted for the assassination of Tishenya and illegal use of Lysian gas. Gerisea was responsible for both, but I'm sure she'll waste no time blaming the person not in a position to defend themselves."

"Anlyr!" Galen looked furious. "What the hell are you doing?"

"What I asked," Relos Var said dryly.

"That's Relos Var," Qown said, because he'd told Galen enough to be able to say that without jeopardizing his cover. "Galen, that's Relos Var. I don't know if you—"

"I know who Relos Var is," Galen said coldly.

Relos Var rubbed an eye and sighed. "Gorokai attacked last night. And Rol'amar—" He drew in a sharp, shuddering breath as he stared out in to the middle distance before pulling himself back. "Anyway, apparently Gorokai's been hiding out in Rainbow Lake for centuries pretending to be a damn fish and I had no idea.[3] None. Just . . . incredible. Fucking incredible! For over a thousand years, Skyfire was guarded by four thousand wizards, but the night they're all sent to the Capital, that's the night a dragon attacks." He made a vague gesture behind him.

Qown followed the line of his hand while his brain tried to fill in all the gaps in the destruction and piece together the floor plan of the temple as it had originally been.

And that spot . . .

"The Sacred Lamp?" Qown gasped. "The dragon . . . Gorokai the dragon stole the Sacred Lamp?"

"No, that's currently twisted into a puzzle ring over to the side there. Gorokai stole what was inside the Sacred Lamp. He stole the Cornerstone Skyfire. Which means . . ." Relos Var growled. "Which means my plans have to change." He stopped and turned back to the group, his gaze speculative.

Qown . . . really didn't like the way Relos Var was looking at them.

"Skyfire," Qown said, gulping. "Right. Aeyan'arric's Cornerstone. I don't know much about . . . Really? The Sacred Lamp housed a Cornerstone? All this time?"

Sheloran started to say something. Galen put a hand on her arm and shook his head. He watched the two men talk without saying a word.

"I created each Cornerstone," Var said, "to supplant the power of one of the Eight Immortals. And Skyfire is linked to S'arric. Do you understand

---

[3] There are a shocking number of legends and god-king tales endemic to the Rainbow Lake area that speak of magic fish that will grant wishes, give advice, or murder entire villages on a whim, depending on the story. In hindsight, we all should have paid more attention.

what that means? Skyfire can destroy entire cities in a flash of bright light, and it has been stolen by fucking Gorokai!"

Qown had never seen Relos Var like this before. It was more than just annoyed or inconvenienced or even angry.

He was panicked.

"What was that about Rol'amar?" Qown asked. "You started to say something about Rol'amar."

Relos Var sneered. "It's not important."[4]

"But I thought–" Qown shook his head. "Okay. But how did Gorokai . . . ? Don't you control dragons?"

"Not when Vol Karoth's awake![5] Which he is. So Gorokai is probably on his way to Kharas Gulgoth as we speak to try to break his *master* free from his prison."

"We have to stop him," Sheloran said. "There . . . there is a way to stop him, isn't there?"

"Wait," Galen said. "Who's Vol Karoth?"

Everyone paused.

"The Hellwarrior," Sheloran offered as if Galen would of course know what that meant. "I mean, not really, but–"

"I thought Relos Var was trying to help the Hellwarrior, though." Galen made a skeptical face at the wizard.

"Young man, you mustn't believe everything Jarith told you. It's not like he had any idea what was really–" Relos Var stopped and blinked at the prince several times.

The wind howled and pushed the ash in circles around them.

"What?" Galen said.

"She's right," Relos Var said, pointing to Sheloran. "We do need to stop Gorokai. But it won't be any of you who does it. He's out of your league. I'm going to have to take care of him myself." His eyes glinted. "But that doesn't mean you can't help in a different way."

Galen let out a nervous, disbelieving laugh. "What?"

"Yes," Relos Var said. "I think that might just work. So a change of plans is in order."

Galen shook his head. "I don't know who the hell you're–"

"He's . . . Gods . . . Galen, you don't even know." Sheloran was holding the fan in her hand so tightly that if it hadn't been metal, she'd have broken it. Her hands were shaking.

Clearly, Sheloran knew exactly who Relos Var was. Which was . . .

Which was really interesting, now that Qown thought about it. Galen knew the name too, but it was likely because of Jarith, and in that context,

---

[4] Note the timing here. Comparing this with your account, Gorokai began his rampage at Rainbow Lake at roughly the same time as Rol'amar's attack on the Lakehouse in the Manol. Indeed, one cannot help but speculate that Rol'amar's death (at the hands of Kihrin, and by proxy, possibly Vol Karoth) may have *precipitated* Gorokai's rampage. Relos Var likely also sensed his son's death, so I think we can all agree he was having a particularly bad day.

[5] I can only imagine how frustrated Relos Var must have been the first time he discovered that Vol Karoth could wrest control away from him.

he knew of Relos Var as Azhen Kaen's court wizard. Sheloran, though? She seemed to know exactly how dangerous Relos Var really was.

"Anlyr, I'm changing your assignment," Relos Var said. "I need you with me."

"Yes, Lord Var," Anlyr said.

Qown's focus snapped back to the guard. What.

"What the—" Galen didn't actually say the next word, just mouthed it silently.

Anlyr calmly walked over to stand next to Var, shrugging to the others in a gesture that didn't even begin to count as an apology.

He winked at Qown.

Qown's lungs felt like they were on fire. In a heated rush, he realized that he'd had it all wrong. Anlyr *had* been there to protect Qown. He'd been there to both protect Qown and also watch him and make sure he did the job to which he'd been assigned. A hidden monitor, checking on the performance of the new recruit.

"Now the rest of you—"

"You had a spy?" Galen said, his tone venomous and his hands closed into fists. "You had a spy watching me?"

Relos Var pursed his lips. "In a manner of speaking. Don't take it personally."

"I suppose it does explain how you know who we are," Sheloran murmured.

"Don't sell yourself short, Your Highness," Relos Var told her. "You're quite special, after all."

Galen just stared. "There is nothing you can say that would ever convince me to help you."

"I know how to resurrect Jarith," Relos Var said.

Qown closed his eyes. Oh. Yes, that would do the job nicely.

"What?" Galen asked carefully. He took a step forward.

"I know how to resurrect Jarith," Relos Var repeated. "Shall I say it louder?"

"That's not necessary," Sheloran said, "but it is very uncalled for to make that kind of claim when we both know perfectly well—"

"Red," Galen said. "Shut up."

Sheloran flashed her husband a deeply worried look.

Galen turned back to Relos Var. "How would you get around Thaena?"

The wizard smiled. "As I said, every Cornerstone was meant to supplant one of the Eight Immortals. The Cornerstone that does so for Thaena is called Grimward, and I know where it is. I was in fact, on my way to retrieve it when"—he angrily flicked his fingers toward the horrors and debris—"this happened. So it's simple: if you recover Grimward for me, I'll show you how to use the Cornerstone to Return your cousin."

Anlyr glanced over at Var. "Can't Senera—?"

"No, she's busy."[6]

Anlyr sighed.

Relos Var continued, "You're seeking a pirate known as the Lash who operates near Zherias. He shouldn't be too difficult to track down. I understand he's

---

[6] Which is true. I was with Talea and Xivan, looking for Suless.

rather infamous. I'll give you a way to contact me once you have Grimward, and we'll arrange for the rest of the deal." He paused. "Every Cornerstone has a specific set of requirements that are necessary to fulfill in order to steal the stone. I won't lie; Grimward's are somewhat macabre. You'll need to kill its owner and then destroy the body before the Stone can regenerate it back to life again. Fire is traditional, but I leave that up to you."

Galen stared at the man. "And what else?"

Var blinked, surprised. "What else?"

"Naturally. I want to see Jarith Returned, yes, but that doesn't really help me on a personal level, does it? Not when, as Anlyr pointed out, we were forced to flee the Capital."

Qown blinked at Galen.

"I see." Relos Var looked faintly surprised. "Obviously, I can take care of the situation with your aunt Gerisea for you. You'll have your title and position restored to you and any threat to that position eliminated. Is that enough for you?"

"Hm." Galen studied Relos Var thoughtfully. "Yes, that would be more than enough."

"So we have a deal?"

"No."

Relos Var looked taken aback. "What did you just say?"

"I said no, we don't have a deal," Galen said. "And we will never have a deal. Because I *have* heard of you. And while you think Jarith couldn't possibly know who or what you really are—and you're probably right—he had figured out one thing: nobody who makes a deal with you ever comes out on top of it. I'm not so arrogant as to think I'd be any different. So no deals. Find someone else to be your lackey. I don't like the price tag attached to anything you're selling."

Galen turned around and started to walk away. He turned back to address the others. "We're leaving. Clearly, we're going to have to find someplace else to spend the night, anyway."

"Um, but, my lord . . . ," Qown started to say.

"Now, Qown."

Sheloran gave Relos Var one last, suspicious look before she did the same. Which left Qown standing there, looking at him.

Relos Var didn't seem upset. He had a faint smile playing on his lips. When he saw Qown still remained, he made a shooing motion. "Follow your little friends," he ordered.

"And remember what I said," Anlyr told Qown.

Qown stared at the two men for a beat longer, not responding. Then he turned and fled, running to catch up to the others.

They returned to the horse (which they had technically stolen when they'd taken the attached wagon), turned it around, and walked back to town.

Galen stopped just outside of city limits and looked at both Sheloran and Qown. He had a scowl affixed firmly on his face. "All right. How do you both know him?"

Sheloran raised her eyebrows. "Blue, he's *Relos Var.*"

"Explain that like it's not perfectly obvious to a three-year-old."

"He's not human. He's not even kind of human. He's responsible for–" Sheloran sighed. "He is older than the empire, responsible for the creation of the Immortals, and basically a god himself. To say he's dangerous is a bit like saying an erupting volcano is a tiny bit warm. At least, so my mother says."

Galen swung his attention to Qown. "And you?"

"I told you I was being kept hostage in Yor," Qown said. "Relos Var was the court wizard there."

"Yes, that part I'd heard," Galen scoffed. "I'm supposed to believe that the Duke of Yor has a millennia-old almost-god as his court wizard?"

"Had," Qown corrected. "The Duke of Yor's dead. The witch-queen Suless killed him."

The two royals both stared at him blankly.

"Blue, much as I do support your decision, don't you think–?"

"There's nothing to talk about, Red," Galen said. "My father was part of the group of cackling would-be villainous idiots that bastard leads. And that is all the endorsement I need to know that any enticement he offers is a trap. Men like that don't think they need to play true with anyone else. People don't matter to them."

"Oh, I don't . . . I don't know if that's fair–" Qown started to say.

"Don't start!" Galen scowled at Qown. "He had that man spying on me, Qown. People with good intentions don't do that. So drop it. We'll find some other way to get what we want. And as for Jarith–he was my friend. Words cannot even begin to describe how unhappy I am that he's gone, but he is. And no vague promises of a manipulative wizard with a world-conquering agenda is going to bring him back."

Qown swallowed. He didn't know if Relos Var was lying or not, but he knew of exactly two people who had managed to defy Thaena and come back from the dead–Gadrith and Xivan. Neither had done so as living beings. Would Jarith be grateful or even want to be returned in such a condition? He didn't know.

"Let's go back to town," Qown suggested. "I'm sure there's another inn where we can stay until we figure out what our next steps are."

Galen nodded. "Yes. A meal might be nice too." He seemed defeated, tired, even a bit broken.

But Qown couldn't help but admire him, a little, or maybe a lot, for doing what so many others hadn't and sticking to his convictions. He just wished . . .

Qown was well aware that it would be his job to convince Galen to change his mind.

He just had to figure out how.

Later that night, they settled in to a rented room. One room, because previously Anlyr had been staying with Qown, and now Galen didn't want to leave any of them alone just in case he came back. The chance meeting with the wizard had turned him deeply paranoid.

But Qown was grateful, because honestly, he wasn't sure Anlyr wouldn't come back either.

That night, after Qown had used Worldhearth to allow Sheloran to check in with her people in the Shadowdancers, Qown insisted on continuing their treatment.

"I've treated Lysian gas," Qown explained, "but never as a swallowed substance. I don't know what long-term effects it will have on either of you." He gave them each a cup of brewed medicine. "This will help."

Sheloran took hers with grace. The problem, naturally, was Galen.

"If that's going to make me sleep," Galen said, "then I don't want it."

"You need to heal," Qown chided.

"I don't like . . . I don't like being helpless," Galen said. He gave Qown a sharp look. "Last night, with Anlyr . . . he didn't do anything, did he?"

Qown exhaled. Light. "No. No. That would be pretty silly of him, wouldn't it? I mean, out of character. He would have given the whole charade away. No, he just tied me up. That was bad enough." He gestured toward the medicine. "I should drink one of those myself, with how little sleep I had last night."

"Not a problem. You can have mine." Galen held up the cup and offered it to Qown.

"Galen," Sheloran chided. "Don't be a child."

Qown wrapped his hand around Galen's and pushed it gently back toward the man. "Drink it, my lord. Please. I don't want you unconscious if anything serious should threaten us either. If anything happens, you'll wake."

Galen grimaced. "It's not you. I'm just not feeling very trusting right now."

Qown smiled. "If I were going to try something, I could have done so last night. Or for that matter, I could do something now. Do you think I need to use this to send you to sleep? Because I really don't."

Galen stared at him in consternation. "Fine. Against my better judgment."

"As long as you drink," Qown said.

Galen did, tipping the cup back, wincing at the taste. "Why . . . why do these always taste so terrible?"

"It's tradition," Qown said. "You should feel a little sleepy soon. If you make the effort, you can ignore the impulse, although I don't recommend it."

It would also make Galen more than a little suggestible. That would be harder to ignore.

"Fine," Galen said and started stripping off his clothes, which made Sheloran giggle. And then she started undressing too.

Qown spun around.

"You're a physicker," Sheloran teased, amusement floating through her voice. "How can you possibly be embarrassed by a naked person?"

"I just, it's that . . . Are you two in bed yet?"

"We are," Galen admitted.

When Qown turned back, he found that true enough. Galen had left on his misha, Sheloran her raisigi. None of them had had opportunity to grab clothing when they'd been forced to leave the city so precipitously.

"We should probably try to pick up some clothing tomorrow," Qown said. "Something less identifiable."

"Mmm," Sheloran agreed. "Are you getting undressed, or do you intend to sleep in your agolé?" Her lips curved. "Not that it matters to me, but Galen deserves nice things."

Galen batted Sheloran's arm. "Stop," he told his wife. "Stop teasing."

Qown knelt next to the mattress. "I thought we might talk about Jarith."

Both of them stopped laughing and turned back to him. Galen's stare was not at all friendly this time.

"It's just . . ." Qown cleared his throat. "It seems to me that Relos Var gave us all the information we need. Is there anything stopping us from . . . going ahead and finding Grimward on our own?"

Galen blinked at him. "You mean . . . leave Quur?" He said it like it was an impossible, ridiculous idea. Who could leave Quur? Who could even think of such a thing?

"My lord, given what we left behind, taking time to lie low and allow matters to calm seems prudent. Gerisea will have her people looking for you."

Sheloran tugged on Galen's sleeve. "You know, we can keep in contact with everyone at the Veil using Qown's Cornerstone. It's not a terrible idea."

Qown beamed at her. "Thank you."

"But–" Galen seemed to still be grappling with the whole "leaving Quur" idea. He shook his head as if to clear his thoughts. "I don't think the three of us versus an infamous pirate king are good odds, Qown."

Qown grimaced, because Galen was right about that.

"But we don't know, do we?" Qown said. "Besides, you're a fantastic swordsman, I can heal, and Sheloran is just terrifying–"

"Aw, thank you," she said happily.

"Y-you're welcome," Qown said. "As long as we have to keep a low profile, anyway, why not investigate if this is possible?"

Galen chewed on the inside of his lip. "Huh. You may have a point."

32: DEATH'S GRAIL

Qown's reaction
The Lighthouse at Shadrag Gor

Qown hadn't been prepared to have Vol Karoth continue the story. He'd assumed they'd skip . . . certain parts. But he should have known better. He could have slapped himself for being so naïve. Of course, Vol Karoth would want to show exactly those elements, right on the heels of their talk, because that was naturally the perfect time for it. The betrayals. The facts that Galen hadn't known. The proof that Qown had never been on Galen's side, not once.

The moment Qown woke, he threw off the covers and lurched down the hallway in a fluttery panic to find Galen. He'd run perhaps a hundred feet when he stopped. His heart pounded, his blood roared in his ears.

And the next bedroom shouldn't have been twenty feet down the hall from his own, let alone a hundred.

Qown turned around.

The hallway stretched forever, but in the distance, he saw a black silhouette of a man outlined by a blue-violet halo.

Qown didn't have to ask who that was; he ran.

As he stumbled forward, the hallway continued to stretch out before him, elongating and drawing away into the distance. The light started to dim. He knew, knew on a fundamental gut level, that it was too late. They were too late. Vol Karoth was free. He'd escaped, and now he was coming for everyone . . .

He stumbled, and as he caught himself, Qown realized there wasn't anyone behind him anymore. He wasn't being chased at all.

The hallway looked perfectly normal. He could see the other doors. He was standing in front of the one where Galen had been sleeping. Had probably been standing there for minutes while he thought he was running for his life.

Qown chuckled in relief and turned around.

Vol Karoth stood in front of him.

Qown screamed and woke up. He wasn't the only person screaming. Someone else was too.

Sheloran.

He stumbled out of bed, but this time, Qown saw what he'd missed in his dream: the rooms joined up now. He wouldn't have had to run out into the hallway to see everyone else because they'd removed large sections of the walls the night before. The others were waking, throwing off covers. They all converged on the room where the screaming was occurring.

Sheloran's scream choked off as everyone entered the room. The reason for those screams was embodied in the form of Galen D'Mon, still in bed, eyes staring sightlessly.

"No, no, no," Qown stammered. "That's not . . . He can't–"

Xivan didn't say a word. She folded Galen's arms over his chest, closed the man's eyes, and tucked the blankets tighter around him.

Everyone watched in silence.

Talon–Talon!–looked like she might cry.

Qown couldn't believe it. He hadn't thought it would be this bad–

"Qown, might I have a word?" Sheloran asked as she wiped her eyes.

"Sheloran?" Talea said. "Don't do anything rash . . ."

"Rash? I'm never rash." Sheloran's hand gripped her metal fan so hard her knuckles stood out stark white against her brown skin.

Qown wondered if he was still dreaming. This was a nightmare. It had to be a nightmare.

"Don't go off alone," Senera ordered.

"We'll be right there," Sheloran said. She pointed that same fan to the next room over, clearly still visible through the large open space where a wall had once stood.

Sheloran grabbed Qown roughly by the arm and dragged him with her.

Qown didn't argue. He didn't have the right to argue. This was all his fault. He walked over to the other room without looking back. In theory, the others might be able to eavesdrop if they really tried, but they were far enough away that they could pretend at some modicum of privacy.

Sheloran sat Qown on one bed, then sat across from him on another. For some unfathomable amount of time, neither spoke. Her whole body was rigid. He thought she might have been trying to calm herself, perhaps even meditate.

Qown wasn't ungrateful, but it gave him too much time to think. Too much time to realize the enormity of his mistakes.

"What did you say to him?" Sheloran's voice was soft. If one didn't know her, one might even make the mistake of thinking she wasn't angry.

"I don't–" He shook his head. "Say to who?" He was honestly confused. He hadn't said anything to Galen before he'd collapsed. He hadn't even been in the same room.

"Galen. When we retired for sleep last night. What did you say to Galen to make him look like he'd been stabbed when he told me good night? What happened? Don't try to pretend you didn't say anything to him."

Qown's throat felt scraped raw, the act of swallowing like sandpaper rubbed across an open wound. "I-I just–" He inhaled. "Yes, it's my fault."

"I know that. I also don't care. What did you say to him?"

Qown blinked and looked over at her, startled.

"I really can't be bothered to care whose fault it is right now. Yes, fine. We now all know you did in fact betray us and you were working for Relos Var the whole time. You performed your job with admirable dedication. But Galen would just be angry at you if that's all it was. It wouldn't be personal. He's a Quuros prince, Qown. He's grown up around more politics and subterfuge than you will *ever* know. He was born to backstabbing from the cradle." She shifted, moving from the bed to slump down to the floor in front of him, a stunningly artless slide that was in itself shocking. "Damn it all, Qown. What happened?"

He wiped his eyes. "I don't think . . . Sheloran, I don't think we should talk about this."

"No," Sheloran snapped. "You don't get to decide that."

Qown blinked again.

"Talking about this is the only thing that will make any difference. What did you two say to each other? Did he tell you how he feels about you?"

Qown's eyes widened. "I-I didn't . . . You–" He paused. "I'm sorry. I guess I shouldn't be surprised that you would know how he felt."

"Feels," Sheloran corrected. "Damn it all, Qown. He isn't dead. Not yet. And not only did I know, but fool that I am, I encouraged him." She laughed darkly. "I had this idiotic idea that you'd be good for him. Can you imagine?"

"Oh." He didn't know what to say.

"So Galen said that he likes you, yes?" Sheloran tilted her head. "And what excuse did you give him for why it couldn't possibly work?"

"I . . ." He shut his eyes.

"Hmm, so it's to be a guessing game? Fine. I'm happy to play. Perhaps it was your classic go-to of 'I can't possibly because I belong to a fake celibate order that apparently only ever existed to guard the Cornerstone Skyfire,' or was it the simpler 'I don't know how to deal with the idea I'm attracted to men, so I'm hoping if I just ignore the issue, it will go away'?"

"I'm not just attracted to men!" Qown said, then winced at the intrusion of that word "just." "It's a long leap from 'sex is sinful' to–" He made a vague, noncommittal gesture.

"Oh, I wish I lived in a universe where I could take a whip to Relos Var," Sheloran muttered. "I do hope you realize that even he doesn't expect you to stand by those vows anymore?"

"I–" He closed his eyes tightly and fought back the burning in his throat, the stinging of his eyes. Everything was horrible. "I did mention my faith. And he–Galen–just wouldn't stop pressing. Until finally I admitted . . . I admitted it wasn't just that."

"And what was your reason?"

"I don't–"

"What was it?"

He choked out a sob. "I told him I didn't want to hide. I told him I couldn't stand a life where I was constantly having to conceal what we were, and that would always be true–"

"You dirty little liar."

Qown drew back. "I beg your pardon?"

"As well you should," Sheloran said. "Because Galen wouldn't have hidden you, and you must know that. Do you think he gives a damn what the rest of the world thinks of him? The man who would stand up in front of all those high lords at Jarith Milligreest's funeral and tell them that he hopes they'll burn because they all deserve it? There's only a handful of people whose opinions Galen cares about, and none of those people are on that list. No, he wouldn't have hidden what you are to him. But I'm not going to let you lie to yourself, Qown: you're the one who would have wanted to hide your relationship, not Galen. You'd have told yourself it was for his own good when the whole time it was for yours. And because you didn't want to ever look at that fact about yourself, you accused him of what was always true of you instead. So you could use it as an excuse."

Qown felt the words slice into his skin, sink into his blood with each thump of his painfully loud heart. He knew that tears had started flowing down his cheeks. "I . . . That's not true—"

"You know the world is larger than Quur."

That time, he frowned at her.

"Idiot," Sheloran repeated. "You've seen Zherias. Da'utunse. You know not every place is like Quur. Not every place will care if two men want to be in love. Hell, there are parts of the Quuros Empire where no one cares, and that's assuming the Royal Houses even exist by the time we return. So this idea that you two can't end up together and happy? That excuse has evaporated. What lie would you like to tell yourself next?"

"I don't know what you mean—"

"You don't have some other poor justification for why you and Galen can't be together? Be honest with me here. If we go back to Quur tomorrow and you can snap your fingers and be legally with Galen—publicly so—would you?"

"I—" He swallowed.

Sheloran leaned forward. "That feeling is called shame. It's what happens when what society tells you is correct and what your heart tells you that you need don't align. But I know enough about Vishai to know that you have no problem pushing back on commonly held beliefs. Your faith has always savored heresy."

"Not that kind of heresy!"

"I see no reason why not. You can accept a woman isn't a witch without blinking, so why would you balk at love?" Sheloran tapped her fan against his knee. "Galen is in love with you."

Qown's eyes snapped open again. "What. No, he's not—"

"He is," Sheloran said. "You caught his eye right away, and I watched as he became more and more charmed by you. And my darling boy has never loved except with all his heart and souls. Now it also happens he has terrible taste in men, and I could argue has an unfortunate habit of picking impossible relationships, but he does at least commit to the idea."

Qown felt a sense of horror and guilt. Shame. He couldn't bear to look Sheloran in the eyes.

"Oh, but it's more than shame, though, isn't it? It's fear too. Because at some point this vow of yours became a symbol of your faith, and as long as you can hold on to it, your faith still exists. And as long as your faith still exists, then you have to be true to your vows. And if you do that, then you can pretend that you didn't throw it all away for all the wrong reasons. You can pretend that your life isn't a lie, that the man you trusted and loved like a father hasn't betrayed you, and, most importantly, that everything you've gone through was worth it. That the world makes sense and is fair and rewards the just and punishes the wicked."

"Stop! Stars, please, stop!" He curled up on himself, unable to stop himself from crying. Unable to stop the tears.

For a split second, the world started to turn black, a gray slide into oblivion.

He felt arms wrap around him, a warmth against his side. "Galen loves you," Sheloran whispered. "And I love you, and Janel loves you, and Thurvishar loves you, and Talea loves you. I bet deep down in her bitchy little heart, even Senera loves you, and we won't talk about Kalindra, but she'll come around. It is not too late for us to make this right. For you to make this right. We can create our own justice and goodness. There is still hope."

The darkness faded. He could almost hear the angry snarl of disappointment.

Qown reached up to where Sheloran's hand was on his shoulder and grabbed it. He pulled her to him and sobbed into her chest. She smoothed his hair back and rocked him gently. "It is okay," she whispered, "to admit that people we love have hurt us. It doesn't make it our fault, you understand. It doesn't mean you deserved it. You did not."

"He . . . he . . . gaeshed—" Qown couldn't stop himself from crying. It was as though those gentle words had in fact been so sharp they didn't hurt at all as they sliced open the sutures on a hundred wounds. What flowed out was putrid bile and every hidden cancer that had been festering inside him. It was the knowledge that what Relos Var had done to him was not forgivable, not justifiable, and had always been indefensible.

"I know, sweetheart, I know."

He didn't know how long he cried. Forever. Probably less than a minute. When he leaned away from her, Qown saw she was crying too. She wiped at his eyes with a length of her agolé. "You were hurt," she said, "and you tried to protect yourself. I don't blame you for that. But you're a healer. You know how this works. At some point, the medicine becomes the poison. So now's the part where we rip the bandages off so the wound can finally heal, hmm?"

"How are you—" He took a deep breath. "How are you so good at this?"

"I don't know." Sheloran brushed his hair back from his eyes. "I always thought I got it from my mother, and now—" Her face twisted with bitterness. "Now I don't know what to think."[1]

Qown cleared his throat. He felt scrubbed out. "What do we do?"

"Oh, I think first we're going to get some food in you. Possibly some tea." She smiled kindly at him. "And after that, well . . . do you really think that's the right question right now? You asking someone else to tell you the next step? I realize it's easier, but . . ."

"But it's what got me into this mess," Qown finished.

"Exactly. So what do you think we should do?"

Qown floated in a space of almost shocking clarity, still numb but in a way

---

[1] Much as Sheloran would hate me for saying this, she clearly does take after her mother in this regard. Her grandmother too, for that matter.

that felt freeing instead of suffocating. "We should . . ." He nodded to himself. "We should find him. We should find Galen and bring him back."

She squeezed his hand. "You're damn right, we will."

Talea didn't say anything when they stepped back out into the main gathering area. She been standing close by–close enough that she must have been listening to every word, but she just gave them a nod as she continued lacing that gold coin of hers over and under her fingers. Down the way, Xivan stood next to the main group, always keeping Talea in sight.

Qown didn't think that would mean much if Vol Karoth tried something, but it made him feel better to know they were watching.

Qown cleared his throat. "If everyone would like to follow me downstairs, I'll make breakfast."

Which he did. Qown made rice porridge in the Joratese style. Everyone ate, even Senera, who pretended it wasn't one of her favorites and snuck another bowlful when she thought Qown wasn't looking.[2]

And the tea only turned to blood once, so that was nice.

Everyone was tired and out of sorts. No one needed to ask why.

Qown almost tried to reassure people that it would be better the next night, when he remembered that there was a strong likelihood none of them would see a next night. At the rate Vol Karoth was emerging . . .

Well. He'd be free by then.

"He didn't torture Galen," Senera said out of nowhere.

"What was that?" Qown asked, surprised.

"Vol Karoth tortured Teraeth and made sure we knew about it. Why didn't he do the same to Galen?"

"If I would hazard a guess," Sheloran said, "it's because when he did that before, we promptly sent people to try to rescue Teraeth."

"But we have no idea if that even worked," Kalindra pointed out.

"No, we don't," Senera said. "But it is interesting. Something to keep an eye on."

"Noted! Who's next?" Talon said, trying to sound chipper and cheerful and failing miserably.

"Still me," Talea said. "No sense waiting."

The mimic studied her face for a moment and then nodded. "All right."

The world changed.

Talea's memory
The Capital City of Quur
One week after the Battle of the Well of Spirals

"I don't understand," Talea said. "Why are we going back to the Upper Circle? That's where Xivan is."

"Possibly," Eshi allowed, "but there's something we need to find there.

---

[2] He's just very good at cooking, all right?

Don't worry, though. The odds that we'll run into Xivan are low, and I don't feel like helping them along any."

Talea made a face and didn't reply to the little girl's comment. She had a different issue to worry about—namely, how she was going to return. The problem was that the Watchmen guards were careful to make sure no one entered the upper area without the proper clearances, the proper passes, or the proper bribes, none of which she possessed. She wasn't even dressed nicely—a thing she was going to need to do something about.

"Any ideas about getting past them?" she said, frowning at the Prayer Gate, which was the easiest way to get into the Upper Circle.

"Of course," the little girl said. "Go over to that merchant stall. There's a line in the back where they wash their sallí cloaks in preparation for selling them. If you time it correctly, there's a 79.69 percent chance the boy who normally watches the merchandise will have left to relieve himself. Grab one of the cloaks, wrap it around yourself, and come back. Keep your head down."

Talea walked around to the side, and sure enough, there were indeed several wash lines strung up with white sheets of fabric hanging from them to bleach dry in the sun. Even as she watched, the little boy standing on the porch ducked inside.

She grabbed a sallí cloak and wandered back to the gate. As she approached, a large group of Thaenan priests in white robes came up to the gate, part of a group that had apparently been performing last rites in the Lower Circle and were now going home. The smell of ash fires and fecal matter rolled out in a circle from the men and women, many of whom wore robes whose red trim was now stained a much less pleasant color.

"Hold . . . Hold . . . Now!" Eshi ordered.

Talea merged in with the group and kept her head down as she passed through. Nobody questioned her, even if she wasn't technically wearing the right sort of robe. Evidently, it was close enough.

"Walk with them up to the top of the stairs, then leave them behind and go right behind the Temple of Tavris."

Talea did this.

She didn't need to be told what to do next. A fire had left the tall fence that normally separated the Ivory District from the rest of the Upper Circle burned to a shell of itself and all too easy to circumvent. She left behind the mingling incenses of the Ivory District as she headed into the areas beyond.

Talea still had to keep a careful watch out for the guards; she still looked unusual enough that they might stop her for that alone. But Eshi evidently kept luck on her side, and no one noticed her.

When she was at Arena Park, Talea asked, "Now what? Are we going to the Culling Fields?"

"Not exactly. I want you to go over to Arena Park and put your hand up to the magical barrier."

Talea blinked at that, but she'd played along this far, so it seemed a shame to quit now just because the magical girl nobody else could see had said something weird. She looked around to make sure she was alone and set her hand against the barrier.

Starting at her hand, a rainbow line of energy drew a door in the air. The energy field inside that inscribed circumference vanished.

Talea blinked. "Wait—"

"Hurry. Step inside."

Talea did and found herself inside Arena Park. She knew enough about this place to understand that she shouldn't have been able to do what she just had. Only the emperor and the Voices had the power to open doorways in the field— and the Voices only had that power because the emperor granted it. She was reasonably certain that Empress Tyentso hadn't granted her any such ability.

Talea exhaled.

"The next part's easy," Eshi said. "And you're doing great."

Talea rolled her shoulders as if warming up for a fight as she walked farther into the Arena. It was quite pretty, she thought, then immediately took that back. The trees were mutated and strange, the grass grew in odd shapes and colors. It was weird and a bit creepy, especially since those were human bones on the ground.

"What's next?"

"You're looking for a grouping of abandoned buildings in the center of the park. There should be four of them."

"The Emperor's Vaults?" Talea asked. When Eshi blinked at her, Talea said, "I lived at the D'Lorus palace for a while. One hears things."

"Ah." Strangely, Eshi didn't seem pleased by the idea that she wouldn't have to explain.

"What don't I understand?" Talea asked.

"Let's find them first," Eshi said.

Talea nodded and kept walking.

The park wasn't large, so it didn't take much time. She probably would've been able to see the buildings from the path outside the park if it hadn't been for the trees and the odd detritus remains of ancient wizard battles that still littered the grounds. The sunlight was warm against her skin; it was a beautiful day.

This was a lovely spot for a picnic.

The vaults weren't much more than square boxes with doors, really. They managed to look impossibly ancient while not having much of an architectural style. Maybe it was the way the brickwork had worn smooth or the patina over the lintels. The doorways opened into blackness, giving no hint of what lay beyond.

"You have certain advantages," Eshi explained. "Because of who you are and because of your link to me. Consider me a sort of key. So. I want you to walk through the doorway of the last house, the one on the left."

Talea stopped in her tracks. "You want me to what?" She pushed her tongue against her teeth and contemplated that this was why Eshi hadn't been pleased that she knew what these were. If Talea hadn't known, Talea wouldn't have questioned. She'd just have done it.

Walked right into one of the buildings famous for killing anyone who did so.

"Please trust me," Eshi said. "This isn't going to harm you. You are, in fact, one of the few people in the whole world who can enter these buildings safely."

"I thought only the emperor could enter these buildings safely?"

"The emperor and nine others," Eshi corrected quietly.[3] "These places weren't built for the emperor. Not really. They were built for another group, with the emperor acting as custodian to keep a few important items safe. A task that—" She looked sad. "Well. I think that job is almost done, honestly."

"I see—"[4]

Eshi motioned for Talea to enter.

Talea knew the stories. Anyone other than the emperor who entered these buildings died. No exceptions.[5] Thurvishar had certainly believed that to be the case, and if that story he'd put together about Kihrin was true, then Gadrith had believed it too. Believed it well enough to assassinate and switch bodies with the emperor in order to make it happen.

She took a deep breath, then stepped through the doorway.

And felt nothing.

Since she was pretty sure someone would have told her if she were emperor, that either meant the stories were wrong in general, or Eshi was telling the truth when she claimed that more than just the emperor could safely enter.

Anyway, the room was filled with treasure.

Multiple chests were piled high with jewelry and gold rings and plates and goblets and all sorts of lovely, precious, wrought things. Inlaid wooden boxes and rare carved statues. Beautifully cut gems and, yes, tsali stones (ones she most sincerely hoped were empty of souls).

Talea pointed. "Are we—?"

"No, we don't care about any of that," Eshi said. "And whatever you do, don't take any of it. Don't even touch it. The curses on that rubbish would make your ears bleed for a thousand years, and the emperor will be able to track you down no matter where you went. Best to just leave it alone. Let Quur have what is Quur's. We're here for what belongs to us." The little girl walked over to the side and pointed to a carved stone cabinet. "Open that, please."

Talea did and then blinked at the objects inside. They were interesting, even nice, but they didn't seem that valuable compared with the other items in the treasure vault. There was a red glass sword that could only be purely decorative. A walnut seed, still in the shell, either molded from gold or more likely dipped in gold. A small, beautifully made leather book. An agolé made from rainbow-colored silk. A carved globe of the world, made from lapis lazuli and jade, seemed the most valuable thing there.

Eshi swore. Then she started demanding Talea pick up objects, look around, check at the back, search behind the wardrobe.

"Is something wrong?"

---

[3] It took me a minute, but then I realized she was likely counting Grizzst, and almost certainly S'arric (even if that last one wouldn't have been intentional).

[4] That seems unlikely.

[5] It's been tried five times, according to my research: thrice during the Great Contest to decide the next emperor and twice during duels. As only three instances are listed in official historical records, I have to assume that two of those attempts simply went unnoticed in the mass slaughter that decides who will be the next emperor.

"Yes!" Eshi seemed as furious as it was possible for a small child to be. "Something's very wrong. Where's the cup? There's supposed to be a cup!"

"What kind? Like a goblet?"

"It's just . . . a cup. A ceramic cup. Simple. White pottery with a red glaze trim."

Talea wasn't sure what she was really looking for, but certainly Eshi seemed extremely upset to find that it was gone. Talea felt around the side of the wardrobe. She started to pick up a sword that someone had set to lean against the side of the stone case. The moment her fingers touched the hilt, she thew her whole body backward as though accidentally setting her hand on a working forge.

"What is it?" Eshi asked.

Talea stumbled back and had to fight not to put her hands down in the stack of gold bits and bobs in case just touch alone was enough to activate the curses Eshi had mentioned. She pointed back toward the sword. It looked entirely at home here, meaning it was chased with gold, had a large diamond in the pommel, and every inch screamed ostentatious wealth. In theory, she'd never seen the sword before, but one touch told her that first impression was entirely incorrect. She'd know that fucker anywhere.

"That's Godslayer," Talea accused.

Eshi blinked and looked back at the weapon. "Are you sure?"

"I've held that sword before," Talea said. "I'm very sure." She frowned. "I thought Kihrin had it. What's it doing here?"[6]

"That . . . is an excellent question," Eshi said. She stared at the blade for a good long time, hardly seeming to breathe.

"What are you thinking?" Talea asked.

"I'm thinking there's a very high chance that Kihrin has . . . done something unanticipated," Eshi said carefully, "and I don't know what." The little girl drew in a deep breath and then started talking to herself. "Focus. The cup's not here. Why isn't the cup here? Because Khaemezra was a damn coward, that's why. She couldn't destroy it. Where would she hide it, though?"

"Would you please explain?" Talea pleaded.

Eshi sighed. She climbed on top of the pile of gold jewelry and made a spot for herself, until she looked like a very small queen on a very large throne. "As I said, when the remaining seven Immortals Returned to life, they realized that they needed to do something to make sure that if it happened again, it wouldn't take a thousand years to Return them next time. Bluntly, they didn't think they would have a thousand years next time. So Taja and Tya put their heads together and came up with those." She pointed to the cabinet. "It was supposed to help bring the Immortals back. That's why besides the emperor, the only people who can enter this building are consecrated to the other seven Guardians." She smiled at Talea. "That's you, by the way."[7]

---

[6] I'm guessing you gave it to Tyentso for safekeeping, yes? Which means the sword is now hilariously exactly where Gadrith thought it would be.

[7] Ah yes, except if that were the case the number of people who could enter would be fourteen plus the emperor, Grizzst, and S'arric. Which is not at all what Eshi said.

"So you mean–" Talea walked over to the cabinet and pointed to the seed. "Galava, I assume?"

Eshi nodded. "Yes."

"If I took that, I could use it to resurrect Galava?"

"For lack of a better word," Eshi said carefully, "but it's not so simple or fast. Faster than thirteen hundred years, but still slow by most standards. That's part of why some of the gods–Thaena, for example–didn't like it. Because she thought it would be too slow and because–" Eshi sighed. "Because she was always capable of rather extraordinary amounts of selfishness. But still, I thought hers would be useful." Eshi pointed out the sword, the veil, and the globe. "Those can't be used. Their linked Guardians are still alive. The others are available, but we have to find the right people to act as heralds. There has to be a . . . a synergy, if you will. Not just anyone can be the Herald of Death."[8]

"No, I would imagine not," Talea said. "But you have no idea where Thaena would have hidden this cup?" She paused. "It's not the cup the Black Brotherhood uses, is it?" She spoke with her hands, miming out the shape of a goblet. "There was this large grail thing that Teraeth apparently used to use for their rituals . . ."

Eshi stared at her for a moment. "Cute. No, nothing that gaudy. Just a regular cup."

"Hmm." Talea gave the vault one last look. "There's nothing here like that. Wherever she hid it, it's not here."

"That is a real shame," Eshi mourned. "Ah well, who knows? Maybe it will turn up."

"Right," Talea said brightly. "We might get lucky."

Eshi gave her such a look.

---

[8] I have no trouble whatsoever believing that Talea synergized perfectly with Luck.

33: THE HERALD OF DEATH

Talea's reaction
The Lighthouse at Shadrag Gor
Just after Talea's memory

When the vision ended, everyone was staring at Talea. Then, almost as one, everyone turned and stared at Xivan.

Xivan narrowed her eyes at Talea. "Herald of Death?"

Talea shrugged. "It cured your gaesh, didn't it?"

"So this is supposed to bring back Thaena and Taja?" Sheloran looked torn between skepticism and concern.

"It's supposed to resurrect them," Senera said, "*for lack of a better word*, to quote what the young not-a-goddess said. If we take her literally, then we should assume it will not be resurrection, just something functionally similar."

"One problem," Xivan said. "Shall I point out that no one at any point has given me a damn cup?"

"But we did," Sheloran said quietly. "Or rather Talea did. It's just we changed its form so it was something you'd accept." She pointed to the sword at Xivan's side.

Xivan glanced down at her blade. "You're claiming you changed a cup into a copy of sword?"

"Not the sword," Talea said. "The scabbard."

"We thought it best that it remain a container," Sheloran admitted. "And it's not the entire scabbard, just the ceramic lining on the inside. Rather thin stuff, but we were trying to stretch a small cup into a much larger shape."

Talea watched, feeling a bit nervous. She could already tell the sword was sitting a bit . . . loose . . . in the scabbard. More than it had been when she'd first given the sword back to Xivan. And this time, she knew what that meant.

Xivan unsheathed her sword and this time concentrated on the scabbard itself, looking critically at the opening. "There's no ceramic lining to this," she said.

There it was.

"There isn't?" Qown blinked. "What happened to it?"

Everyone turned and stared at Talea.

Talea smiled and held out her hands. "If I had to guess, I'd say it went the same place as the coin—wherever that is—when it healed Xivan's soul and removed the gaesh."

Xivan met Talea's eyes. "And is that all it did?"

Talea chose her words carefully. "I imagine it did the same thing to you the coin did to me. You know, made you a sort of angel of the memory of an Immortal? Just, not Taja. In your case, Thaena."

"Thaena." Xivan stared at her in shock. "You're saying I'm an angel of Thaena."

"No," Kalindra said. "You're not. Because that's not how that works."

The room focused on the assassin.

"What do you mean?" Sheloran asked.

Kalindra's face was a sneer. "Eshi's story. What she told Talea. That's a load of dragon shit."

Talea pursed her lips and glared. *Honestly. Why did Kalindra have to be like this?*

Kalindra returned the glare with her own. "I was an angel of Thaena, Talea! I know how this works. The position allows for communication, control, and resurrection. Do you think I can enter the Arena at will? No. No, I cannot. Eshi was lying to you."

"Probably," Senera agreed.

"Senera!" Talea pouted at the other woman.

"I'm sure it's a lie of omission, but a lie all the same," Senera said. "Please note, Kalindra, that this 'herald' position seems to be functionally different from 'angel.' We shouldn't assume your own experience is applicable."

"Okay," Kalindra said. "So what is a 'Herald of Death,' then?"

"I have no idea." Senera bit the side of a finger as she considered the matter. "I am truly fascinated by the fact that Talea and Xivan have found a way to simply ignore a gaesh. Grateful, even. I simply worry it may have some unforeseen and unpleasant side effects down the line."

Talea grinned. "Because you care."

"I do not. This is intellectual curiosity," Senera said.

"No, it isn't. You like us."

"Shut up." Senera glared. She stared down at the Name of All things, so clearly torn.

Talea bit her lip. She wasn't sure if Senera asking was a good thing or not. It was certainly too late to do anything about it, but . . . Talea didn't really want to have that conversation just then. Still, she held her breath.

Senera set the stone to the side.

"You're not going to ask?" Sheloran said.

"I'm considering how to word the question," Senera admitted, frowning. "I don't think it would be healthy to make a mistake about the phrasing." Senera pointed toward the food. "Don't think I haven't noticed you eating normal food, Xivan. Any other changes besides the return of a regular appetite?"

Xivan cleared her throat, looking embarrassed as she gave Talea a sideways glance. "I haven't been hungry. What I mean is, I haven't been hungry for souls."

"That's wonderful!" Talea said. "I didn't know it would do that."

Xivan smiled at her, and their eyes met. Talea felt a frisson of delight slide over her, because this was . . . different . . . from the way Xivan normally looked at her. Not kind or concerned or sternly serious. Not soft and loving. This was a look Talea knew exactly how to interpret.

Desire.

Before Talea could suggest that more than one sort of hunger might have returned to Xivan, the world changed.

Xivan's memories
The Capital City of Quur
Twelve days after the Battle of the Well of Spirals

Xivan left the Culling Fields after interviewing anyone who claimed to be there for the massive disaster that was the D'Mon meeting. Everyone except the tavern's owner and a few others who'd survived it had been convinced that Galen D'Mon had been responsible for the Lysian smoke. Xivan found herself agreeing with the tavern owner at first blush, but that's where things then became interesting. Because while Galen was unlikely to know an obscure spell used by only a select few of the Quuros army's war wizards, several witnesses described Galen and his associates escaping the fumes wearing round spheres of clean air around their heads.

Xivan was also familiar with that spell. If Galen knew that glyph, it meant he might also have been in a position to know how to create Lysian gas. He might have learned it from his father Darzin.[1] It was . . . interesting.

Maybe Galen had done what he was accused of. He was a D'Mon, after all.

But his guilt or innocence didn't make him easier to track down, especially when the trail was already weeks old by the time she'd even begun looking.

Gerisea had said her sources had tracked a group of the rough description of Galen and his companions leaving the Capital by the east gate, presumably traveling to Khorvesh. But Xivan thought that an odd choice when attempting to hide from a woman whose husband was the second son of the Duke of Khorvesh. And if Gerisea had been watching any of the gates leading from the Upper Circle to the Lower Circle, how had she managed to let them slip through her fingers?

House D'Talus? Possibly, but Gerisea seemed certain that they hadn't gone to ground there, and admittedly, it would have been one of the first places the High Council would have looked. So was there any other house that might have sheltered them? Lady Lessoral D'Talus hadn't been listed as being from any other royal families and—given her real identity—that was almost certainly true. But what about Galen? Who was his mother? Darzin's mother had been Khorveshan—Xivan remembered that because it was likely the reason that Darzin had started taking her son, Exidhar, under his wing, to the consternation of both Xivan and Azhen. But Darzin never talked about his wife.[2]

She ended up having to spend a bit more money asking around and finally came up with the knowledge that Galen's mother was deceased but also daughter to the High Lord of House D'Aramarin.

Which changed the landscape considerably. A royal would be able to use the Gatestone network but would be noted and tracked. The grandson of the D'Aramarin high lord was a different story.

But when she arrived at the Gatestone, she found there was a different problem: the place was in chaos. The entire site had been blocked off, with signs everywhere announcing the gate was shut down. Several groups of

---

[1] If Darzin had known it. Fortunately for everyone, he hadn't.
[2] I'm given to understand they'd always hated each other.

House D'Aramarin servants were busy using the gate to go . . . somewhere. Somewhere not in the Capital.

"Can someone help me?" she shouted.

They ignored her at first, but eventually, she got someone's attention.

"We're not open!" they shouted.

"I have a pass!" she shouted back. "You can't shut this down for me."

The servant sighed, clearly exasperated and annoyed. "I don't care if you're the Duchess of Yor, we're closed."

"As it happens, I am."

"What?"

"I *am* the Duchess of Yor," Xivan said, "so let's go over that one more time. Why's everyone in a titter? The Hellmarch isn't new at this point. Did something else happen?"

The House D'Aramarin servant blinked at her, then shook his head. "You haven't heard?"

"Assume not," Xivan replied.

"The emperor executed the high lords," the man said.

That sentence was so unbelievable that it took a moment to sink in. "I'm sorry, what? All of them?"

"Yes! I mean—" The man squinted. "I'm not sure. But High Lord D'Aramarin's dead, that's for certain."[3]

"What about D'Mon? D'Talus?"

"Well, how would I . . . ?" His eyes widened as he saw the gems Xivan was piling in her hand. He called behind him. "Hey, did High Lord D'Mon or D'Talus make it?"

A woman carrying a huge stack of clothes shouted back, "It was everybody! It's just the empress's people now."

The man looked back at Xivan and shrugged.

"I'm looking for High Lord D'Aramarin's grandson," Xivan said. "He's House D'Mon now. He would have used a gate several weeks ago." She held up the gems. "All for you if you tell me."

The man eyed her for a moment, then looked behind him to see if anyone was paying attention.

"I'll check," he said.

Later, after she'd gotten her answers and bought herself a gate to follow Galen and Sheloran, she traveled by gate to Eamithon. The city seemed typical of western Quuros except it was cleaner and friendlier than she was used to. But even so, there was an odd, stale taste of panic to the air.

She asked around. There'd been a dragon attack in the previous weeks.[4] Even for people who had seen more than their share of demons in the last few months, a dragon was a bit much to expect them to swallow down without vast quantities of sugar.

---

[3] I am not sure, and I will believe otherwise only when I see Havar D'Aramarin's tsali stone and not a moment before.
[4] Thirty days previous, to be precise.

It was another unwelcome complication. A lot of panicky refugees made it far more difficult to track the specific refugees she sought. They would all blend together.

It was just dumb luck that she heard someone complaining about how the dragon had attacked the Vishai temple complex over by Rainbow Lake.

"Excuse me, what was that?" She reached over and tugged on a woman's sleeve, who flinched back as though slapped.

"Hey!"

"I'm sorry, what did you say about the Vishai?"

"They're all gone now," the woman said. "If you were thinking about making a pilgrimage, think again." She hurried off.

Xivan pondered that. Gerisea had mentioned Galen's deal with the Vishai. It was possible that Galen had thought to turn that agreement into an offer of shelter as well. But if that was the case, then the dragon attack—and especially the timing of the dragon attack—was troubling. It would have been around the right time.

Still, it was the only thing even approaching a lead she had, so there was nothing to be done but to tromp out to the site and see if there was anything interesting to learn.

The road was empty. Anyone who could flee the area had already done so, and evidently, the idea of a dragon in the vicinity was more than sufficient to keep most people uninterested in returning.

Even Xivan was taken aback by the extent of devastation she encountered, the malignant chaos of it. She didn't know which dragon was responsible, but she had a much better idea of which dragon was not. This wasn't Aeyan'arric or Sharanakal. This wasn't Baelosh or Morios. This wasn't Rol'amar. She wasn't sure about the others.

Xivan wandered around the temple ruins. Someone had cleaned up the place and built an extremely large pyre to burn the bodies. Now the debris had been cleared away and used to create a large cairn, upon which were marked names. It looked like it had taken either thousands of man-hours or a very skilled wizard.

"Xivan? What are you doing here?" Relos Var asked.

So that answered that question. Xivan turned around to face the very skilled wizard.

Relos Var stood in front of a magical gate, which irised closed behind him. He wore traveling clothing that had seen some wear and appeared to have seen some wear himself. He looked ragged and not in a good mood.

"I'm looking for someone," she admitted, "and I didn't expect to find you here." She frowned. "But then I didn't, did I? How did you know I'd be here?"

"I didn't," he said. "I warded the area in case the dragon returned."

"Ah well. I didn't realize—" She frowned. There was a connection here, something she hadn't previously made. Relos Var's apprentice back in Yor, Qown—he had been Vishai. She supposed that must have been how Relos Var had come to be interested in this location.

"Clearly, I'm no dragon," Xivan said, "so I'll leave you to it."

He narrowed his eyes. "Actually, the dragon in question is a shape-shifter."

Then he waved a hand. "But even so, it's unlikely he would have a clue what you look like or that we would know each other, so I suspect it's safe enough."

"I see. Well. I wish you luck." She turned around and sighed in relief to herself, because she'd assumed that her next meeting with Relos Var wouldn't be nearly this friendly.

She'd only made it a few feet when Relos Var's voice rang out behind her. "Were you looking for anyone in particular? Perhaps I can help."

Xivan turned around. "Your help comes with a price tag, Relos."

"Anyone's help comes with a price tag. I'm simply honest enough to name the price before the sale." Relos Var cocked his head to the side. "Where's Talea, by the way? I never see her away from your side."

Xivan kept her expression fixed. "We've parted ways."

"Ah. Well, perhaps it's for the best. I always thought she was a little too soft for you."

"Hm."

"My condolences, by the way. Senera told me what Suless did to Azhen."

"Thank you," Xivan said.

"So." Relos Var motioned for her to keep talking. "You might as well tell me. Who are you looking for? No one's been through here in weeks."

She narrowed her eyes. "And did that 'no one' happen to include several teenage royals belonging to House D'Mon?"

Relos Var raised an eyebrow. "Now why would you be hunting children? That hardly seems like your normal predilection."

"My reasons are my own," Xivan said, because she literally couldn't explain even if she wanted to. "I'm only interested in one of them: Sheloran D'Talus."

"What a dangerous young woman to be interested in."

"I wasn't planning to fight her."

Var smiled. "And I suppose it's just coincidence that she happens to be Suless's granddaughter?"

Xivan didn't answer.

"Yes, I'm aware of her lineage. And apparently you are too."

"I didn't say anything."

Relos Var shrugged. "That was an answer of its own. Caless has always been delightfully adept at staying out of my business. We've never had a problem with each other."

Xivan returned to her silence.

Relos Var watched her.

Finally, Xivan sighed. "You know where Sheloran is, don't you?"

Relos Var sat down on a marble slab and set his ankle across the opposite knee. "I do."

"And what would it cost me for this information?" Xivan forced herself to ignore how smug he looked.

"Hmm. Now that is a question. I have been magnanimous and helpful before, Xivan. As I recall, the result of that generosity didn't work out in my favor. Indeed, it cost me my favorite sword."

"I'm under the impression Godslayer was never your sword to begin with."

Relos Var shrugged. "You're misinformed. I created that weapon, by any possible definition you might care to use." The smile vanished from his lips; his stare hardened. "I'm not inclined to give you any gifts today."

"Stop playing around. You've never given a gift in your life."

He let that statement pass without comment. "I think you're on the right track with Sheloran. Given Suless's personality, it's unlikely Suless won't soon hunt down the child. I know you think Suless was a disaster with your family, but trust me, she'll be as bad if not worse with her own."

Xivan felt something inside her freeze. "What?"

Relos Var pursed his lips. "Does that surprise you? Did you think the horrible, abusive witch-queen is vile and vindictive to her enemies but kind and sweet to those she loves? She loves no one. She is horrible to everyone. Why wouldn't she lash out against the offspring Cherthog forced upon her? And since a grown and powerful Caless isn't so easy to abuse anymore, why not switch that malice to Caless's daughter, Sheloran, instead?"

Xivan exhaled. "Gods. That girl has enough problems."

"Of which you're one, I'm sure. If only the flow of pain stops because one's cup is already full."

Xivan kicked a piece of marble, which skittered across the charred and melted ground. She'd thought of using Sheloran against Caless, yes, but it had never occurred to her that the young woman had a more immediate use as a lure against Suless herself. Although she still needed the Stone of Shackles, didn't she? But did it matter whether or not she was the one holding the Cornerstone? If Caless was the one taking revenge, revenge was still had. Xivan was fine with that.

"Name your price," Xivan said.

Var thought about it for a second. "You."

Xivan gave the wizard a sardonic smile. "I didn't think I was your type."

Relos Var actually looked charmed. "I have many types, and under different circumstances . . ."

Xivan blinked.

Relos Var waved a hand. "Neither here nor there. Despite the debacle with Godslayer, you still have your uses. So this is my price, Your Grace. I will tell you how to find Sheloran. I'll even send you to the closest location to her I'm able to reach. I'll give you every tool I can for your own success—and in return, you will serve me for the rest of your days."

"That seems a steep price for what you're providing, Var."

"I treat my people well, Xivan. You would not be gaining a onetime, temporary benefit."

Xivan stared at the man and pondered if that could possibly be true. Her husband suggested otherwise, but her husband hadn't been one of Var's people, had he? At least, not knowingly so. Would it be worth the price of revenge?

"I think you could give me what you're promising but still engineer matters so I fail," Xivan said.

Relos Var sighed. "I have encouraged Sheloran and her friends to chase after a pirate named the Lash. He's in possession of a Cornerstone called Grimward. You have a connection there."

"I do?"

"Grimward happens to be how I raised you from the dead."

Xivan straightened.

Relos Var looked at the sky, admiring the color. He waited a beat before adding, "Here's an interesting fact about Grimward, which I may have neglected to tell my unwilling and overly suspicious helpers. I don't even think Qown realizes—"

"Qown's with them?" Xivan scowled.

"Indeed. As I was saying, Grimward will kill any living being who picks up the stone. As it happens, only the dead can wield it."

Xivan stared. "Why wouldn't you tell them that?"

"Oh, I would have, if they'd agreed to find it for me. But Galen D'Mon is much less trusting than I'd anticipated. So it seems they'll be discovering that bit of trivia the hard way. When they do, they'll need someone to show them how to use the stone to fix that situation—since Thaena's no longer alive to help put matters to right. I suspect it will be Galen who falls victim, but who knows? It could just as easily be Sheloran. Probably not Qown. He already has a Cornerstone; he knows better than to try to claim another."

Xivan scowled as she thought over the matter. "Why tell me this? Why tell me any of this when I haven't agreed to your terms yet?"

"Because you can't stop it without my aid, of course," Var explained, laughter in his voice. "You'll never reach them in time. They have a several-week head start on you. And it's a shame, because honestly, you're the perfect person to take the stone. In your hands, Grimward is utterly safe. I can make sure you reach them in time to both warn and assist them."

Xivan scoffed. "I think you've made a serious miscalculation, because I really don't give a damn what happens to those people. It's not my problem if they die."

"Ah, so hard-hearted and full of hate, living only for revenge." Var's expression was fond. "Is that what I'm supposed to believe you are? Very well. But you don't get Sheloran unless you save them. And without Sheloran, I very much doubt that this notion of revenge you've been carrying around with you is going anywhere. Without something Suless wants, you're just an old, grim warrior chasing shadows." Relos Var chuckled. "I can imagine how your meeting with Caless went. Senera told me you were asking after the Stone of Shackles."

Xivan knew the smart play was to turn around and leave. To walk away from this man and his gifts and favors and promises.

"I'm sure she did," Xivan replied, "but you're going to have to do a little more for me than promise to teleport me to Sheloran's last known location if you want me to swear to serve you."

"Now, Xivan," Relos Var said softly, "you already know I want Suless dead. Nearly as much as you do, I imagine."

"I doubt that."

He didn't bother to argue the point with her. "I know a great deal more about killing demons than Caless does. Or you." He held out a hand. "All I want is your word, Xivan. That's quite enough guarantee for me."

Xivan scratched at the corner of her mouth as she eyed the wizard. "My word?"

"Yes." His expression was mild.

Neither of them said anything for a long while.

"You have it," she finally said. "Help me with this and I'm yours."

She felt nothing except the vague knowledge that Talea would be disappointed in her.

Relos Var nodded in satisfaction. "Excellent. Now let me open a portal for you."

34: THE CONSEQUENCES OF REBELLION

Xivan's reaction
The Lighthouse at Shadrag Gor
Just after Xivan's vision

Xivan barely had a chance to focus on Talea's eyes when the world changed again, chasing down the first vision without warning.

Talon's prison
Inside Vol Korath's prison

She swam.

The structures of the Capital crept past as Talon fled; coral-crusted and swathed in sargassum, rough arcs led into the caves and grottos of the Royal Houses, each teeming with small fish in their house colors. The Upper Circle was crowded, awaiting the upcoming tournament that would decide the next emperor, and people from all across the empire were in attendance. Everyone, from lowly mollusks to high-swimming whales, thronged around the barrier of the Arena, making it hard for Talon to push through the crowd.

The baby in her arms stirred, several tentacles lashing fitfully. He was hungry, but she had no time to stop and feed him. She rolled one of her eyes back to look behind her, and sure enough, there were her pursuers. She pushed harder against the bodies blocking her way, elbowing a hammerhead shark right between the eyes as she shoved past him.

The child wasn't hers. It belonged to a sister, a clutch-mate. The mother, however, was dead, slain in the horrible war with the surface dwellers.

Rounding a corner, she found a pocket of empty water and picked up speed with a thrash of her tail. But the freedom was an illusion, for the hollow had no other exits; a recent rockfall had collapsed the tunnel she could have used to escape. That fall hadn't been there the last time she swam this part of the Capitol.

It was new.

She turned, ready to press back into the teeming hordes, but the way was blocked.

Darzin D'Mon stood there in his red-and-gold armor, flanked by soldiers. Behind him, his father, Therin, strode up the street, unhurriedly.

"Great Lord," Talon begged, her skin flashing with heat and color as she spoke silently to him. "Please. It is just a hatchling! Help us. Please!"

Darzin cocked his head. No, wait, it wasn't Darzin; it was Kihrin. He looked at her, then at the child cradled in her tentacles, clasped to her thorax. Behind him, Therin came to a halt and put his hand upon his son's shoulder.

"Kill them," he ordered.

"But–" Kihrin said.

"They are the enemy, Captain," Therin said. "Are you disobeying an order?"

Kihrin shook his head. "No, sir," he said. He turned to Talon and the baby kraken in her arms. "Kill them," he ordered his soldiers.

They raised their weapons and unleashed bolts of pure energy that tore into her flesh, severing tentacles and burning out her eyes. The last thing she saw was the child she held, screaming in orange flashes across his skin.

The water around her boiled as they killed her and the child.

She swam.

Senera's reaction
The Lighthouse at Shadrag Gor
Just after Xivan's vision

Senera startled as the vision ended. She turned around. "Talon?"

Talon had already slid to the floor.

"Fuck," Senera cursed.

"Is she . . . ?" Qown's eyes were very wide.

"Dead? No, I imagine she's like the others." Senera stood, shaking her head. What had triggered that? She drew a blank. Xivan's deal with Var? No, it couldn't have been. But what else . . . ?

The Royal Houses. That was the only trigger Senera could identify. But how the hell had Talon been so fond of the Royal Houses that the idea of Tyentso wiping out their leaders proved enough to throw her into Vol Karoth's grip?[1]

"Senera!" Sheloran shouted, quite unnecessarily since she was still in the same room. "Is it true? About the Royal Houses?"

Ah yes. The other person who might react strongly to the idea the Royal House high lords had been executed.

Senera sighed.

Sheloran didn't wait for her to answer. "That man said Tyentso executed all the high lords. Did that happen? I need to know!"

Senera managed, barely, not to roll her eyes. She had that much self-control. Whatever Senera thought of Quur's Royal Houses, she understood that this was the young woman's family.

"I'll check once we're finished dealing with Talon," Senera said firmly.

"But–" Sheloran started to protest.

"I'm sure your parents are fine," Talea said. "Even Tyentso would have a hard time killing a god-queen without–" Talea paused. "Oh right. I guess she does have Godslayer, doesn't she?"

"Not helping, Talea," Xivan murmured.

"But Tyentso wouldn't know that, would she? There's no reason she'd use

[1] If I may add: Tyentso is truly living up to my every expectation.

Godslayer if she didn't think she was facing a god-queen." Sheloran's voice was defensive, brittle; Talea wasn't the person Sheloran was trying to convince.

Kalindra barked out a laugh, an ugly, mocking sound. When Sheloran turned to her, narrow-eyed, the former Black Brotherhood assassin was still chuckling. "Tyentso is also an angel of Thaena," Kalindra pointed out. "So I wouldn't bet on Tyentso's ignorance."

"Also not helping," Xivan muttered.

Senera sighed and rubbed her temples. She felt so old.

Kalindra shook her head. "She's your mother and you love her. And from what I can see, she seems to have done a decent job of raising you, which is kind of a miracle, considering. But you said it yourself: she's had centuries to do some good and what has she accomplished? Nothing. If Tyentso did take her down? Don't expect me to mourn."

"I don't." But Sheloran's lower lip trembled, even as her eyes were hot knives.

Kalindra leaned forward. "Half the women who entered this damn Lighthouse are former slaves. If she died—"

"They both lived," Senera interrupted. "I don't need to use the stone. I asked about your parents yesterday, for other reasons. Your parents were alive the day that the Lash attacked Devors. So they survived." Indeed, it seemed that both of Sheloran's parents had been involved in setting up the massacre, but Senera didn't feel like having that conversation just then.[2]

Nobody could say Caless wasn't very, very good at knowing which way the wind would blow and aligning all her sails in the proper direction in advance of the change in weather. A survival skill no doubt learned from her mother.

Sheloran slumped in relief.

"What a shame," Kalindra said.

Sheloran turned to the woman with blazing eyes. "How dare you."

"She's the God-Queen of Whores," Kalindra replied coldly. "Don't expect me to be happy for her survival."

"Oh, just shut up," Senera said.

"I don't take orders from you," Kalindra snapped.

"But Veils help you, you *will* take them from me," Xivan growled. Her voice was quiet, but razor-sharp. "You've done enough damage. Stop."

Senera fought down her own desire to lose her temper. "Also, you're wrong."

She probably should have kept silent, Senera realized. Xivan and Kalindra had been locked in some sort of stare-duel for dominance, and Xivan had been winning. Kalindra might have behaved.

But Senera had just distracted her. Kalindra's upper lip twitched but never quite managed to graduate to a full sneer. "How so, Mistress Know Everything?"

Senera ignored the jab. She only wished she knew everything. "She's not the God-Queen of Whores. She's the God-Queen of Love," Senera said, forcing herself to sound utterly bored about the whole subject. "But a god-king isn't the same as an Immortal. A god-king's portfolio can shift with popular opinion, as the reasons for offerings change. At some point, people stopped

---

[2] Although perhaps I should have. After all, it seems Caless has finally decided to *do* something.

worshipping Caless to find true love or stop a roving eye or—whatever—and started giving her offerings with more prurient motives. She couldn't say no."

"She could," Kalindra protested.

"No, she couldn't," Senera said. "That's not how it works. She had no choice at all if she wanted to survive. She became the God-Queen of Lust and Whores and Sex." Senera looked down her nose at Kalindra. "Given the things you've done for survival, you have no right to judge her."

"She has all that power," Kalindra pressed, "and she's done what with it?"

Senera shrugged. "If you think she's the only god-king in the Upper Circle, you're sorely mistaken. Even Relos Var only ventures into that cesspool of snapping crocodiles when absolutely necessary. I guarantee you that Tyentso didn't kill all the high lords, and the poor little lamb is about to find out Quuros politics is more . . . complicated . . . than she realized." Senera sniffed. "Someone really should have let her know, but I suppose they've all been distracted."

Talea frowned. "Didn't you grow up in the Upper Circle, Senera?"

"And it made her everything she is," Kalindra said, ignoring Senera's glare. Senera couldn't bring herself to deny it, however.

Xivan, meanwhile, crossed over to the young princess. "Sheloran, look at me."

Sheloran did, with eyes still full of tears.

"Okay," Xivan said. "Here are some things you need to understand about being a mother. First, it can change your priorities. What is best for your children becomes very important. Now I don't know if your mother has ever had any other children besides you, but you're right—" She ignored Sheloran's surprised blink. "Caless has had millennia, and Quur is still the way it is. But perhaps—just perhaps—you're the reason she's decided that she wants Quur to change. Because even if she never had a problem with the way women were treated before you were born, now she's being forced to watch you grow up in that same world. Clearly, she's willing to do a lot to protect you." She pointed at herself for emphasis.

Qown handed Sheloran a handkerchief, which she used to wipe her eyes. "Thank you," she told him, then turned back to Xivan. "I want to believe that," Sheloran said, "I really do. But she lied to me."

"Parents do that too," Xivan admitted. "We want our children to be a reflection of what we wish we were, not what we really are, so we lie about our weaknesses and our sins in the hopes that they'll emulate our example. We don't want our children making the mistakes that we made, and sometimes that means pretending we've never made any." Xivan swallowed and added, "I'm not saying it's a particularly good system. It's just an easy trap to fall into. Also, Kalindra's being a bitch. Don't let her get to you."

"Oh, I don't blame her," Sheloran said. "She's scared."

"I'm right here, and also: fuck you," Kalindra snapped. "If you're not scared, you're not paying attention."

"But we're not lashing out." Talea tilted her head and examined Kalindra. "And you are. Please stop. We're not your enemy."

"Then who is?" Kalindra was near to shouting. "I thought I knew! Demons? Apparently, the man I love and my sister-in-law are both *demons*. Relos Var?

We're being awfully chatty with two of his henchmen, aren't we?" She angrily gestured at Senera and Qown. "And Thaena—" She choked and turned away, standing so stiffly there was little doubt in Senera's mind that Kalindra was doing everything in her power not to break down crying.

Senera despised the fact that she knew exactly why. Senera knew it the way she knew the color of the sky. More than Kalindra losing her husband or the risks to her child, although those things were almost certainly important, Kalindra's real problem was so simple: she was a devotee who'd been stripped of her god.

It was almost a shame she was being so belligerent to Sheloran. They had so much in common.[3]

Then Xivan did something unexpected. Senera would have thought Talea would have been the one, but no. Xivan walked up to the former angel and put a hand on the woman's shoulder. Nothing more than that.

Kalindra collapsed into her arms, sobbing.

Senera sighed and turned to everyone else. "Let's give them a moment," she said. "But after, we need to discuss what we're going to do about Talon."

"Talon?" Talea asked, looking confused. "Why do we need to do anything about . . . Oh."

"Yes," Senera agreed. "Oh."

Qown's solution to every emotional problem that had ever existed was usually the same: food. Senera almost laughed when she realized how he was seemingly able to materialize so much food so quickly: he'd left dish after dish in food storage from his last visit there. Yes, that was probably centuries ago, as the Lighthouse tracked time, but the food pantry there had been enchanted to keep food perfectly unspoiled for millennia.

So even though they'd only eaten breakfast a short time previously, he still presented everyone with small finger foods. Rolls and pastries. Tea. Ironically, he never ate much of what he cooked himself, but then, he never had, had he? Senera found herself wondering if Caless had been right about it being a metabolism issue.

Xivan grabbed a handful of nut-stuffed rice dumplings. "Should I be flattered that a scene of me cutting a deal with Relos Var was enough to send Talon over the edge?" Xivan said.

Senera snorted. "I very much doubt it had anything to do with you and everything to do with the death of Gerisea D'Mon." She paused. "Although we're absolutely going to be having a discussion about you vowing to serve Relos Var for the rest of your life."

Xivan grimaced and looked away only to meet Talea's judging gaze. She sighed. "Of course we are."

Sheloran blinked. "Why would Talon care about Gerisea D'Mon?"

"Thank you," Qown said. "That was confusing me too."

Senera immediately regretted having said anything at all. Talking was

---

[3] In hindsight, I should have included Qown on that list. And myself.

such a bad habit. She much preferred sarcastic footnotes. "Do you have any idea what Talon's background is?"

Sheloran cocked her head. "Uh . . . why no."

"Before she became a mimic—" Senera waved a hand. "There's a whole story. I'm not getting into it right now. Before she ended up as a mimic, she was a slave in the D'Mon household. She would have been the same age as Gerisea. It would be foolish to assume they had no contact, especially given that Lyrilyn had been something of a"—her nose wrinkled in distaste—"procurer for the high lord at the time, Pedron."

"Oh." Sheloran looked ill. "I've heard about him. Not . . . good . . . things."

"So perhaps Lyrilyn and Gerisea were once close. Maybe it wasn't Gerisea at all but some other high lord. Who knows?"

"Often it can take a while for the full impact of a trauma to make itself known," Sheloran volunteered quietly.

"Unfortunately for us," Senera said. "But now we have a problem. Because we only have two telepaths," Senera said, "and now both of them are trapped out there in Vol Karoth's mental prison. Which means I need to find a way to wake Thurvishar up."

Kihrin's story
Inside Vol Korath's prison
Just after Talon's vision

"Okay," said Teraeth as we walked down a side street on the outskirts of the city, "I get that Talon loves herself some tentacles, but since when is she a Daughter of Laaka? I'm pretty sure I know where little baby mimics come from, and that's not it."

"That felt different from the other visions," Thurvishar said. "It felt more like . . ."

"Like his," I said, pointing at Teraeth.

"Yes," said Janel.

"So what? Talon's been taken like Teraeth was?" I asked.

Thurvishar scowled and stopped walking. "That is a problem."

I motioned for everyone to join me on a stairway that led down into some kind of basement space. It wasn't cover, but at least we wouldn't be immediately visible from the street. "Why?" I asked. "She's not exactly in the top ten of my most-well-loved entities."

"Because she's the one projecting the 'rebuttal' visions," Thurvishar said. "Since I've been here, she's been handling it. If Vol Karoth's kidnapped her, it means that the 'good' visions must be having some sort of effect, possibly tied to that." He waved an arm at the gray, colorless street. "Which means we can't stop."

"I see what you mean," Janel said. "A problem."

"Not really," I said. "I'll just start doing them again."

Thurvishar immediately shook his head. "You're the only one who shares Vol Karoth's memories. It would be better if you concentrated on using that knowledge, so we can track down Talon and anyone else he tries to grab in the future, and find out how to use the gray places against him. That technique is showing promise. He hasn't been as active. It's possible that we've weakened him."

I studied Thurvishar. "Is that the only reason?"

"Isn't that enough?" Thurvishar had his defensive hackles up right away.

Teraeth and Janel glanced at each other.

"Thurvishar—" I said.

"I'm worried about Senera," he admitted. "It's probably nothing. I just want to be there."

"You think Vol Karoth going to target her next?" Janel asked.

Thurvishar tilted his head. "I think it's odd he hasn't already. I understand why he hasn't gone after Xivan or Kalindra—he can't exploit their memories for more visions unless they're in the Lighthouse. Senera though? He should have targeted her by now."

"Why?" Janel asked. "Senera seems like she had a better handle on this than almost anyone."

Thurvishar gave her a skeptical look. "Things aren't always what they seem."

I leaned back against the railing of the stairs and chewed on my lip. I didn't want to argue with him. As far as I could tell, Senera seemed fine—or as fine as anyone could be who'd just given up her life's work and switched sides—but my ability to go reading through her "book" didn't automatically translate into a deep understanding of her mental state. So maybe Thurvishar had a point.[4]

"I guess then . . . see what you can do to help," I said.

Thurvishar nodded. In a blink, he vanished.

"Meanwhile, what should we do?" Janel asked. "I'd say we hit a nerve with the city beautification project, but that might not be a nerve we want to hit again, given how Vol Karoth reacted last time."

"What's that?" Teraeth asked.

"Oh, you remember." She nudged him gently in the ribs with her elbow. "Big ball of fire in the sky, obliterated everything, we only just found each other again . . ."

"No," Teraeth said, pointing up the street, "what's that?"

We turned to look. "That" appeared to be a handful of white lions walking down the street toward us in a staggered V formation. In the silence as we took in this spectacle, hard click-thumps echoed as if two pieces of stone were being clapped together repeatedly.

Then I realized that was exactly what was happening; the lions were made of stone.

"Yeah, uh . . . run?" I suggested.

For once, no one argued with me. We ran.

Several blocks later, Teraeth pulled Janel who pulled me into a large house-looking structure. We scampered inside, then up the stairs. Crouching by the

---

[4] If you ever say I told you so, I will hit you.

window, tilting our heads to peer out without exposing more than a sliver of our heads from below, we held hands and watched.

The troop of stone lions rounded the corner, but they continued down the street without spotting us. We all breathed sighs of relief.

"So that's new," Teraeth said. "You know, Vol Karoth's really starting to annoy me with his 'I can change the rules whenever I feel like it' bullshit."

"How did you know they wouldn't follow us in here?" I asked.

"They're made of stone," he replied. "I can't imagine they can smell very well."

"I'm sure they smell just fine," Janel said, "assuming you polish them regularly."

I groaned and rolled my eyes.

"Really," Teraeth said, "you should have seen that coming."

35: Denials and Distractions

Kihrin's story
Inside Vol Karoth's prison

Later, Janel said, "I recognized something from Talon's vision."

We were jogging down one of the city streets, avoiding lion prides and keeping an eye out for gray patches. The gray spots seemed to be points of emotional intensity related to S'arric's life. While they seemed to be an exploitable weakness, we hadn't yet figured out how to make that work for us. Certainly, traveling through them was problematic for me, since I tended to drown in whatever the emotion and its associated memories happened to be.

Anyway, when Janel said this, Teraeth and I stopped.

"Like what?"

"The uniforms those soldiers were wearing weren't House D'Mon. Those were voras guard uniforms, and I remember where their headquarters was."

"Great!" I said. "Let's see if Talon's there and free her."

Janel gave me a thin look. "Do we have to?"

"Janel, she only did what I asked her to do."

"That's not the excuse you seem to think it is."

Coward me, I chose not to deal with that right then. I cleared my throat. "Pretty sure I remember where the headquarters is also," I said. "Follow me."

We slipped down an alleyway and started zigzagging our way across town. I didn't take us on a straight path because I assumed Vol Karoth wasn't that stupid; he had to realize we were capable of looking at the visions he was sending out and drawing correct conclusions.

"I still don't get the kraken connection," Teraeth said. "I'm telling you, that's not where mimics come from."

"Oh, I don't think that had anything to do with Talon," I said. "Something Thurvishar said; Vol Karoth seems to have a problem with abstract thinking. That wasn't a scene from Talon's life; it was one from mine."

"Wait, what?" Teraeth asked, while Janel nodded. "Bullshit, you're not a kraken either."

"Are you sure about that?" I waggled my eyebrows at him teasingly. Then, "No, of course I'm not. That was a pastiche of two different events: Lyrilyn's failed escape from the D'Mon house with baby me, and . . ." I trailed off.

Something that had happened. Something terrible. I didn't remember the full details, but I knew they'd been horrible enough that I didn't want to remember.

Janel put her hand on my shoulder, both for support and to urge me to resume walking.

"The second half, the kraken part, was something that happened to S'arric a long, long time ago," Janel said as we slipped through an ease way between alleys. "In the early days, there was a war between the vor and the Daughters of Laaka."

Teraeth frowned. "How is that possible? The god-kings . . . and -queens . . . didn't arrive on the scene until after the voras became, well, humans. And S'arric was long gone by then."

"Laaka wasn't a god-queen. She wasn't human at all," Janel said and then stopped when I made a cutting gesture with my hand.

"Enough," I said. "We can't focus on that; it's just fodder for Vol Karoth. Concentrate on finding Talon and freeing her."

Janel gave me a concerned look but didn't push the issue.

We came to the military command center, which looked more like a museum than a military base. I noticed that it wasn't an empty or abandoned area. There had been large statues of lions out front, and those lions now roamed, visibly animated.

"I guess this means we've found the right place," Teraeth muttered.

Janel narrowed her eyes as she looked out over the scene. "I'll distract the statues while you and Teraeth fetch Talon. Keep in mind that when I did this with Teraeth, he was locked inside his own illusions, so it's possible she won't see you at first. You'll need to do something to grab her attention."

"So stab her. Easy enough," Teraeth said, testing the edge on a knife.

Janel looked like she was about to object, but then she just laughed. "Whatever works for you." She turned to me. "Don't worry; I don't plan on fighting those statues. Just baiting them into chasing me."

"I don't think it counts as stupid to fight them when you can melt rock, my love," I told her.

She kissed the side of my head. "In this place, anyone can do that. Let's aim for maximum distraction. Ready?"

I nodded. "Ready."

"Go!" Janel ran out into the center of the area and started waving her hands.

"Our turn," Teraeth said. "And remember. We're being quiet—eh?"

I'd already started sneaking over to the back of the building—although I did slow down enough to allow him to catch up with me.

Even with the animated lions, I wasn't sure we were in the right place until I peeked through a basement window and saw a gray space. In the center of it, a pale-skinned Kirpis vané man paced back and forth in a garden, waiting for someone.

Right. Because all mimics had originally been vané.[1]

I motioned for Teraeth to confirm what I was seeing, then unlocked the window and slipped inside. It felt oddly like being back with the Shadowdancers as a Key, and extremely satisfying. I took a perverse joy in not making any

---

[1] While I can't get direct answers from the Name of All Things because it happened so long before the stone's creation, I have pieced together that it was some kind of controlled experiment in radical neural imprinting that went extremely wrong or, arguably, extremely right. At least until the killing started.

noise, in the way Teraeth and I were silent shadows. I mean, we wouldn't have fooled Vol Karoth, but it was still nice to keep up old habits.

"Talon," I whispered when I was close enough.

The vané man ignored me.

"Do we have any idea what his real name was?" Teraeth asked.

"Nope," I whispered back.

"Not ideal." Teraeth waved a hand in front of the man's face. "Come on, friend. We're here to help you escape."

The vané man looked up, focused on Teraeth. "No, I need to wait for D'meera."[2]

I blinked and felt a chill. I was reasonably sure that was a voras name, not a vané one. But if he was as old as that, he'd have known voras too, wouldn't he?

"No, Talon, snap out of it."

Talon went back to ignoring us.

Something roared outside, followed by the sound of fighting. Janel had graduated from baiting the lions to actually fighting them, despite her insistence on not doing that.

This would be easier if we joined her and easier still if we could just leave.

"Talon!" I grabbed the man's shoulders.

He looked away. "D'meera," he muttered under his breath.

"How did Janel wake you?" I asked Teraeth.

Teraeth made a face. "She kissed me."

I shared his opinion. It's not that I thought Teraeth would have a problem with kissing someone he didn't know very well—just the opposite. But it was one thing to kiss a stranger and quite another to kiss someone you knew perfectly capable of eating you back. Especially when there was no emotional connection there to restrain their hunger.

Janel shouted.

"We have to trust that she can handle herself," Teraeth said, but he sounded as uncertain as I felt.

I shook Talon, who folded to the ground and began sobbing.

A scream echoed.

Teraeth ground his teeth. "This isn't working. If we can't figure out a way to get through to this asshole . . . Who did Talon care about?"

"Me," I said, "but I think we're past that now. Ola—I mean, she and Lyrilyn used to be lovers . . ." I blinked. "Wait."

Teraeth cocked his head. "Yes?"

"It's a trap," I said. "This isn't Talon."

The vané on the ground turned black—not in skin color but in outline, in composition, like the shape of him had fallen away from reality itself.

Vol Karoth attacked.

"Fuck!" I said as I tried to dash out of the way. I wasn't fast enough, though; I felt a searing pain as Vol Karoth grabbed my ankle. He tried to pull me in, to absorb me into himself. I screamed.

---

[2] I have no idea who that is, and no easy way to find out either.

"No!" Teraeth attacked Vol Karoth's hand with his daggers, which immediately disintegrated. Teraeth then used his hand. Which also disintegrated. But Vol Karoth flinched back as though burned.

Why would you try to save him? He's nothing to you. He cannot love you. He cannot ever be what you want.

Teraeth didn't bother answering. He dragged me back with his one remaining hand, long enough for me to climb to my own feet again. "Regrow your arm," I told him.

"Give me a second," Teraeth said. "I'm not a demon, you know."

"In this place, we're all demons," I said as I held out my sword in front of me.

"That doesn't mean I'm used to it. Hold on." He stepped behind me, delaying for the time he needed to recover before Vol Karoth attacked.

But Vol Karoth didn't go for the strike.

Instead, he made a low, growling noise and vanished.

A shout echoed from outside the building. "Janel," I said.

Teraeth was already running. Together, we made it outside in time to see a disturbingly large number of statues ganging up on Janel.

Janel gave us both a suspicious look as we ran up. I raised my arms. "It was a trap," I told her, probably unnecessarily. "Let's get out of here. Then we can fix up Teraeth."

Janel scowled as she noticed Teraeth's missing hand. "After you."

"This way," I said. "Let's pick a place at random."

So we did.

Senera's reaction
The Lighthouse at Shadrag Gor
After Talon's collapse

Senera studied Thurvishar as he lay unconscious on the stone bed she was certain he'd created in the first place.

Thurvishar was . . . frustrating. An itch she kept scratching without meaning to, even knowing that nothing good would come of worrying away at that same point again and again. He bothered her on a visceral level, and now that she knew his relationship to Relos Var, she couldn't stop comparing the two men.

They were so different and so much alike.

The similarities: They were both brilliant men with an aptitude for planning, logic, and formidable willpower. They were practical and deeply passionate about helping humanity. They both liked people—because Relos Var *did* like people, even if he had little patience for fools. They were realists with a keen understanding of human nature, neither one naïve or prone to succumbing to cliché bigotries or prejudices.

The differences: Relos Var was patiently willing to manipulate the whole world to gain what he wanted. Thurvishar was capable of such acts but had decided for moral reasons that he wanted no part in them. He was a rebel, but whereas Relos Var's arrogance came in the form of a superior (and not necessarily incorrect) belief in his own genius, Thurvishar's rebellion seemed to stem from a sense of humility. That he wasn't so much better than the rest of humanity that he alone should decide its fate.

She still didn't understand what he saw when he looked at her, but she was starting to feel . . .

What? What was she feeling? Gratitude? Relief?

She'd never been interested in sex. She never would be interested in sex. Too much ugliness was tied up in the experience, and she had spent too many years building up walls against any weakness in her defenses that sexual attraction might welcome. She was extremely good in bed—but it was a skill that gave her no personal satisfaction beyond its utility as a tool of persuasion. After her witchgift had first manifested, after Relos Var had found her, she'd gladly put that particular skill up on a shelf with the certain belief she'd never have to bring it back down again. And she'd assumed that with sex removed from the picture, any expectation of romance would be as well. She'd been fine with that. Why wouldn't she be?

And then this strange, odd man had walked into her life and bluntly told her that those two ideas didn't have to be connected. And that idea . . .

She mentally shook herself and set about the more immediate task of waking the man, but right away, she ran into problems.

Namely, she couldn't.

Senera tried shaking him, shouting, slapping him on the cheek, and splashing cold water on his face. He continued sleeping.

"If I find out you'll only wake up when kissed, brat, I'm turning you into a frog," Senera muttered.

"Perhaps you might try using your witchgift," Sheloran suggested from a few feet away. She'd been standing there so quietly Senera had forgotten she was there, even though it had been Senera's idea to bring Sheloran with her. As Senera herself had said, no one was to go off alone.

Senera met the princess's eye. "Whatever you think my witchgift is, assume you're wrong."

Sheloran stepped fully inside the room. "Oh yes, of course. I'm probably thinking of someone else. I'm so silly sometimes." Her voice was a parody of coquettish simpering, the proper behavior of proper Quuros princesses.

Senera sighed, grateful at least that Sheloran wasn't bothering to put too much effort into the acting routine. "And just who is it that you think I am?"

"When I was a little girl—"

"You still are."

Sheloran chuckled as if Senera had said something extremely funny and tapped the closed edge of her fan against her palm. "As I was saying, when I was a little girl, the High Lord of House D'Jorax died under the most embarrassing circumstances. My mother laughed about it for days. Said it was the most poetically appropriate assassination she'd ever seen.[3] She wouldn't tell me how he died, but as I grew older, I simply assumed that it must have occurred during some sort of sexual encounter. House D'Jorax, after all, licenses all the velvet houses."

---

[3] I still don't want to talk about it.

Senera glanced back at Thurvishar and let her expression be offended rather than the other more revealing emotions that might have otherwise taken up residency. "You'd better not be suggesting—"

"Oh no, no, no!" Sheloran held up both hands, looking wide-eyed at the idea she was being misunderstood. "Nothing like that. But I do very specifically remember Mother saying that the person responsible was a talented Doltari girl with a dangerous witchgift. She was a *spell thief.*"

Senera stood perfectly still. The two women stared at each other.

"A spell thief," Senera repeated, keeping her face blank. Not screaming. "And what is that?"

Sheloran squinted. "Is this really the time or place to be feigning innocence? I mean, I'm not inclined to let go of secrets either—I completely understand why you'd react this way. But we are very much all in this together at the moment."

"At the moment," Senera emphasized.

"I misspoke," the young royal said, her voice no longer pretending to be light and playful. "What I should have said was, 'Until the bitter end,' because there's no going back after this, and you and I both know it. House D'Jorax doesn't own you, and Relos Var doesn't own you, and you have *chosen* to be with us. So do that, and act like we're all on the same side. It happens to be true."

"Words cannot even begin to describe how much I'm regretting the decision to bring you all here." Senera was torn between chagrin and relief. Chagrin that a god-queen had taken notice of her back when she'd been a slave in the Capital. Relief that the topic of conversation had slid away from the events leading up to High Lord D'Jorax's death. It was a topic she would be perfectly happy to never discuss for the rest of her life.

"Regret is such a waste of energy," Sheloran said. "Now I personally don't care if you assassinated the High Lord of House D'Jorax or not. I might be confused about why you're not telling people that right after the polite introductions are out of the way—'Hello, I'm Senera. Did you know I once murdered a high lord?'—but I'm not going to question motives. That said, my understanding of how a spell thief works is that it's risky—I mean, any spell is risky; you're literally reshaping your own brain—"

"A point would be nice. Is that possible before Vol Karoth frees himself?"

Sheloran tsked. "Being a spell thief is just a skip and a whistle away from being a telepath. That's my point. You said earlier that we only have two telepaths, and I'm calling your bluff. The only reason we don't have three is because you're being stubborn. We need Thurvishar awake, so wake him."

Senera clenched her teeth and turned away. She bit down hard on the impulse to just scream. Damn it all, she had to stop underestimating that little girl. It was so easy to forget that she was also a wizard, that Sheloran had been trained by a god-queen, whether or not she'd known it at the time. Caless's power was inferior to that of any of the Eight Immortals, but her magical knowledge and skill was easily their equivalent—if not greater. Sheloran had probably had a better magical education than most Academy graduates. Although she hadn't been able to stop Khaeriel from killing her, had she? But perhaps she'd tried. Thurvishar's account of the D'Mon massacre hadn't exactly been the height of reliable testimony considering the lack of living witnesses.[4]

Sheloran wasn't wrong about the telepathy. Senera would never be as instinctively good at such magics as someone like Thurvishar or Talon, but she could learn the basic spell for it if she'd ever chosen to do so.

It's just that she'd never wanted to. Veils, why the hell would she ever want to do something that would almost certainly deepen her empathy for the people around her? She was barely sleeping at night as it was.

Senera cursed under her breath for at least ten minutes. Then she turned to Thurvishar and began casting.

Kihrin's story
Inside Vol Karoth's prison

We made it to shelter, or a shelter, far enough away that we hoped Vol Karoth wouldn't quickly find us. At least it bought us enough time for Teraeth to heal his missing hand. There was no couch this time, or any other significant furniture, but Janel had formed cushions and rugs from mind stuff. She'd piled them all together into something Teraeth and I could lean against while she paced the room, a tense, tightly wound bundle of angry hunting cat. I wasn't sure if she was upset because Teraeth had been injured or because she'd been overwhelmed by the statuary earlier. I was about ten seconds from demanding she join us on the pillows for a long-overdue hug when we were interrupted.

[I haven't found Talon. And each time I try to leave, he blocks me. I can't get out.]

"Thurvishar? You're back?"

[More or less. I'm projecting instead of manifesting directly. Hoping that'll make it easier to get out, but so far no luck. If I can't get out, we'll need Talon.]

"Who would have thought the phrase 'We'll need Talon' is something we'd ever say?" Teraeth muttered as he twisted and flexed his fingers.

"I didn't say it," Janel commented. "And I won't say it either. I've hardly forgiven her for—" She gestured toward me angrily.

"If it's any consolation, she protested a lot." I rested my head on Teraeth's shoulder, with the intention that I'd only have to face Janel's reaction to my defense. It didn't work: maybe I couldn't see his face, but I felt Teraeth's chest move as he scoffed under his breath.

Janel just stared. It still amazed me how good she was at conveying "Are you really this stupid?" without changing her expression at all.

[Would it be possible for you to distract Vol Karoth? Because if you could, then I might manage to escape. He's only partially focused on me.]

Janel's expression shifted into something inscrutable as she examined Ter-

---

[4] The more I think over this, the more I'm convinced that your account, Thurvishar, is highly suspect, and, I believe, intentionally so. Even if you had correctly deduced that Sheloran actively used magic to try to defend herself, I can't help but think you would've left it out rather than outing her as a witch during a time period when such knowledge would have absolutely been grounds for execution. It didn't matter who knew Khaeriel or Tyentso knew magic, after all—their positions protected them in various ways. Sheloran, though? I find it easy to imagine you purposefully edited the account in order to not put her life in jeopardy.

aeth and me. "Now that you mention it, yes. I believe we can. Give us a few minutes to figure out logistics."

[Please hurry. I can't imagine what Senera and the others are going through right now.]

There was a feeling of absence. I suppose that meant Thurvishar had telepathically withdrawn to give us a few minutes to sort things out.

"So what did you have in mind?" I asked her. "Am I supposed to run up on a rooftop and shout? He'll eventually find me, but if we want to lure him out—"

"I was thinking sex." Janel's eyes traced the outline of where Teraeth and I tangled up with each other.

I choked and started to sit up. "Janel! This isn't exactly the time—"

"No, no," Teraeth said, stopping me with a hand. "Let's hear her out."

I swallowed nervous laughter as Teraeth pulled me back. Hilarious. "Okay, I suppose I deserve the continued teasing."

"Teasing would imply I'm joking." Janel tilted her head and regarded me critically. "Vol Karoth's sensitive to your moods. While I don't think sex is going to make the flowers bloom and spring arrive early, it *would* distract him."

"You know, much as I love this plan," Teraeth said, "and please believe I really, really love this plan—I'm not keen to have Vol Karoth catch me with my pants down. Literally."

Janel chuckled. "I agree. But while it has to be Kihrin, it doesn't have to be both of us. In fact, I'll argue it shouldn't be me. That might qualify as 'attracting too much attention.' I thought perhaps I'd keep watch while you two played. You're both creative. I'm sure you can find a way to keep each other entertained without resorting to full nudity. Or you might remember that this is all in our minds and going from naked to clothed is an eyeblink. Your choice." Only then did Janel's smile turn bright and mischievous. She caught my gaze and trapped it in the blazing fire of her eyes. "Don't feel shy on my account."

All my thoughts stuttered to a halt as I realized that Janel was serious. "But wait, would that—" I cleared my throat. It's not as though Teraeth and I weren't already in each other's arms. We'd fallen into that embrace without any hesitation, without any thought or planning. But that had been comfort, and this was something else. "I mean, none of this is real. How would that even work? You can't . . . We can't . . . It doesn't—"

Teraeth's chest moved under my head as he started laughing. He wrapped his arm around me and ran his fingertips over my back. That moment left me vividly aware of how close we were, how I could feel the heat of his body and smell his skin. How for something that "wasn't real" this all felt so very real. "Oh, you're so adorable when you're flustered," Teraeth said as he stroked my hair. "This isn't so different from being in the Afterlife, and believe you me, you can have sex in the Afterlife."

Janel's expression turned smug. She leaned against the wall, crossed her feet under her. It wasn't a good spot for keeping a lookout, I noticed. Or rather, not a good spot for looking at anything that wasn't Teraeth and me. She gazed at us with heavy-lidded, burning intensity. Her stare could only be described as hungry.

Oh, I thought. *She* wants *to watch.*

My pulse quickened. I'd never considered myself much of an exhibitionist, but this was different.

"Sex isn't nearly as much of a physical act as people seem to think," Janel added, "and if we do succeed in rescuing that mimic, this is also the last time it's going to be just the three of us . . . for a while."

I swallowed. Or ever. Depending on how . . .

Well, I knew. I knew how this was going to work. If everything went perfectly, then I still wasn't going to be in a position to do anything with either of them. Which hurt. They were right here. Right here with me, fierce and beautiful. They'd braved Vol Karoth himself to be here with me.

I raised my head. Truthfully, I was glad for the excuse—Teraeth isn't that much taller than I am, so forcing my head to rest on his shoulder was starting to give me an imaginary crick in my apparently imaginary neck. But hey, I liked having his fingers in my hair.

"Hey, Thurvishar?" I had to hope that he could hear me. Meanwhile, Teraeth's mouth was hovering less than an inch away from mine. I felt his breath on my lips. It was all I could do to keep my concentration; I suspected Thurvishar wouldn't appreciate the direction that my thoughts—and blood—were trying to flow.

[Yes? Are you ready?]

"Yes. I think so. It might take a few minutes to catch his attention, but once we do, he should leave wherever he is now and head in our direction. Probably fast."

[I'll keep watch. Good luck and be careful.]

I started laughing. I couldn't help it. Teraeth immediately bit my lip as punishment, although honestly, he would have done that anyway. I'd practically done him a favor by providing the excuse.

He tipped my chin up as I pressed my lips to his, deepened the kiss, felt one hand tighten its hold on my waist while the other wandered past my jaw to tangle in my hair. Then he made the most amazing gasp when I yanked him closer and slipped my tongue into his mouth. There were all sorts of rules to this that I didn't really know, and I felt a moment of . . . not confusion exactly, because I was not at all confused about what we were doing—but disorientation. When we finally came up for air, he didn't stop kissing me but simply transferred his attention to the corner of my mouth, my cheeks, my jawline.

"Wait, wait," I said. "Are we supposed to do the reins or saddle thing?"

Janel laughed from the other side of the room.

Teraeth put on an extremely serious air. "But then we wouldn't have to fight each other to figure it out."

I felt a tension deep inside me release. "It's a contest, is it?"

"Well, it can be," Teraeth allowed. "But if we do it right, it's one of those contests where everyone wins." Even as he spoke, he flipped the two of us so I was under him. As he slid down the length of my body, his hands paused on my hips. His fingers slid along the front of my kef and began unfastening buttons. "Since I'm assuming you've never done this before, mind if I take the lead?"

I wasn't about to argue, but I felt an odd lurch, like the floor had tilted just slightly, when he said that. I inhaled and reached out touch his cheek. "Yeah, that would be—"

He didn't wait for me to finish the sentence.

"Oh damn." I moaned as he grabbed my hands and deliberately put them on his head. "Well, if that's an invitation . . ." I laced my fingers through his beautiful, sleek hair. If I pulled too hard, he'd let me know with his teeth.

Politely, that was the one time Teraeth didn't bite.

Janel's gaze burned as she watched us, slowly dragging her teeth over her lower lip. Her breathing was ragged. We locked stares.

The three of us had up until this point done a remarkably good job of not talking about certain things. Oh, we'd talked about individual components—Teraeth and me, Janel and me, Teraeth and Janel—but not the whole. Not the three of us together, how that would work, or what that would mean. It had made it easy to think that I could be removed from those equations without affecting the balance. That Teraeth and Janel would still have each other, and so would be fine without me.

I really had been such a fool.

She must have seen the darkness come back into my eyes, the shadowy-slick sheen of guilt as the regret of what I'd given up sank its claws in deep and held on. Janel crossed over to us in a heartbeat, sinking down onto her knees next to the two of us. She set one hand against Teraeth's head, gentle and adoring. She laced the fingers of her other hand into the hair at the back of my neck, and damn near yanked—pulling my head up to meet her own.

"You're *ours*," she whispered heatedly. "You understand? We're never going to leave you behind. *Never.*"

I knew the claim was ludicrous and illogical, blatantly indefensible, but the defiant passion in her eyes refused to bend before any attempt at what was practical or possible. I opened my mouth to say something anyway—I had no idea what—and her lips sealed themselves against mine in a fiery kiss. Teraeth's hands tightened on my hips, fingers digging in as emphasis to Janel's pronouncement as he took me deeper and hummed something against my skin.

It was more than enough to send me over the edge. Janel never stopped kissing me, muffling the noises I made with her mouth while my whole world went white around the edges.

I twisted my fingers in Teraeth's hair as he raised himself up to smile at me. I chuckled at the look on his face. Smug bastard. I suppose I couldn't blame him. He'd probably been waiting to do this for the last four years.[5]

"Since I was talking with my mouth full," he told me, "let me repeat: I agree with what Janel said."

I pulled him in for a kiss too. "Thank you for the translation," I said, "but I believe now it's your turn—"

---

[5] Four years or five hundred years. One of those.

An angry roar echoed from somewhere down the street.

I growled. Even though this had in fact been the whole point of our assignation, that didn't mean I was happy to find it successful quite so quickly. I wasn't anywhere close to being "finished."

Teraeth chuckled as he started buttoning my kef. "You can return the favor next time."

My heart twisted. Next time. The likelihood that there would be a next time . . . I didn't want to think about those odds.

Janel stood and held out her hands to both of us. "That's our cue to leave."

So then we ran.

36: COINCIDENCE AND CARD TRICKS

When Senera and Sheloran came back downstairs, Thurvishar was with them.

"I wasn't sure you'd be able to contact him," Xivan said. She hadn't been certain—Senera often astonished her with her capacity for magical problem solving—but it was still a pleasant surprise.

"I never doubted it," Sheloran replied.

Senera ignored the princess and sat down at the table.

"Given the progress we were making in the mindscape—" Thurvishar started to say.

"In the what?" Kalindra said.

Thurvishar rubbed a knuckle into the corner of his eyes and yawned. "Oh, thank you," he said as Qown handed him a cup of tea. "That's what I'm calling the other place. The mindscape. I'm not sure that it's progress, exactly, but Vol Karoth does seem to have some vulnerabilities. At least, the evidence of that is exhibited in the fact he grabbed Talon."

Talea frowned. "I don't follow."

"Grabbing Talon means we had to call Thurvishar back," Senera explained. "Now maybe that's just a fortuitous coincidence for Vol Karoth—"

Thurvishar snorted.

"Yes, I agree," Senera said. "I think we can assume you were annoying him. You're good at that."

Thurvishar raised an eyebrow at her. "Thank you." He smiled. "Did I miss anything else?"

"Vol Karoth took Galen too," Xivan said.

Thurvishar cursed under his breath. "We didn't see a torture vision."

"No, we didn't either," Senera said. "But Galen's in the same condition as the others."

"Did Janel rescue Teraeth?" Sheloran asked.

Thurvishar gave the princess a wary look. "Yes, she did, and no, you are not going to try the same with Galen."

Sheloran drew herself up. "Do you think I can't do it?" She set her hands on her hips and glared at the wizard.

Thurvishar rubbed his upper lip and looked away. He seemed supremely uncomfortable. "It has nothing to do with whether or not you can do it. Vol Karoth's making it difficult to leave. Once you enter, you aren't coming back out."

"I don't care," Sheloran protested. "He's my best friend."

Thurvishar mumbled something under his breath.

"What was that?" Qown asked.

Xivan looked up from polishing her sword and squinted. "He said, 'You're as stubborn as your mother.'" Thurvishar has almost certainly run into High Lady Lessoral, a.k.a. Caless, but that seemed like an unusually familiar comment—then she remembered: in Thurvishar's past life, he'd been Emperor Simillion. And Emperor Simillion had famously been lovers with two god-queens: Dina . . . and Caless.[1]

Given the choking sound Senera had just made, she'd made that connection too.

Sheloran looked peeved, but certainly not like she understood the reference. Xivan sure as hell wasn't going to explain it to her.

Senera cleared her throat. "Perhaps we pause for a bit and return to our conversation Xivan swearing an oath of loyalty to Relos Var? Because I feel that does need a conversation."

"I agree," Qown said, which earned him a surprised look from everyone.

"Oh, well, if the two traitors think we need to talk," Kalindra said.

Xivan exhaled and leaned back in her chair. "If you must."

Talea just rolled her eyes and went into the kitchen. She seemed . . . uninterested.

Which wasn't at all what Xivan expected. "Talea?" Xivan shouted after her. "Don't you want to yell at me too? I assumed you'd want to attend this party."

"I'd rather talk about how we're going to deal with Vol Karoth," Talea called back. "I checked on him, you know. We're up to the biceps."

Nobody had anything to say about that.

Xivan said, "She has a point. My oath to Relos Var sounds like tomorrow's problem."

"Besides," Talea said as she came back with two cups of tea, one of which she sat in front of Xivan, "it's not like you were telling him the truth when you promised you'd be loyal to him."

Xivan winced. No one else in the room said a word. Senera had leaned back in her chair, her expression appraising. She'd probably meant to drop that lure and let Talea carry the full weight of the actual conversation, a tactic that was working well for her so far.

"Wait," Talea said. "You weren't telling him the truth, were you?"

Xivan shifted uncomfortably. "I made a promise." It was a promise that would come due at some point and that she now deeply regretted, but it was a promise.

"You made a promise to a lying, evil bastard who sees you as nothing more than a tool and an asset."

Xivan flinched.

"You can break that kind of promise. No one will think less of you," Talea said. "Certainly, I won't."

Sheloran made a moue. "I'm with Talea on this. I don't think you need to be held to task for keeping your vow under such circumstances."

---

[1] Xivan also had access to our first two chronicles while she stayed in the Manol.

"He'll kill me," Xivan elaborated.

"Only if he finds it convenient," Senera said, "otherwise, he won't waste the energy."[2]

"Ouch," Talea told her.

Senera paused in the middle of pouring tea. "I'm not wrong. He's not stupid enough to think you'll keep that promise. I'm sure he'd love you to, but hinging anything important on your cooperation would be foolish after what happened before. This wasn't about turning you. It was about making sure that everyone else doubted your loyalties, including yourself."

Xivan sighed. Unfortunately, that made a great deal of sense. "I see," she said.

"Relos Var cannot be trusted," Thurvishar said. "He is a man who thinks of morality only in terms of scale, and he means to save humanity."

Qown frowned at him. "But that's . . . that's a good thing, isn't it?"

Thurvishar stared at the healer and sighed. "No. No, Qown, it is not a good thing. What happens if you tell yourself that the win condition is the survival of an entire race?"

Qown shrank against the back of the couch. "Well, I–"

"The larger your win condition," Senera said, "the more variables can fail within that definition and still be considered a 'success.'"

"Yes," Thurvishar said. "So what if a person dies? You've still saved the human race. Or if a hundred people die. Or a thousand people. A million people. A billion people. How many people can die, as long as you've still saved humanity? So many. Almost all of them, in fact."

Qown's throat bobbed as he inhaled.

"Don't try to tell me Relos Var wouldn't be willing to make such sacrifices," Thurvishar said. "Because he would. You and I both know it."

Sheloran reached over and patted Qown's shoulder.

Senera snorted. "He'd sacrifice that and more. And not too long ago, I agreed with him." She sighed. "Part of me still agrees with him. It's not that I think the philosophy is wrong. It's that he turned out to be a hypocrite in the implementation. He always made it seem like he was just as much of an acceptable loss as anyone else, but I now realize he never really believed that at all."

"A man who believes that the ends justify the means is capable of anything as long as he thinks his intentions are pure," Thurvishar said. "Even Gadrith thought he was going to create a better world."

Qown snorted.

"No, it's true," Thurvishar said. "He really did think that. Or at least he told himself that. And I'm sure it would have been a better world–at least for Gadrith."

"He saved my life," Senera said. "Relos Var, I mean. Not Gadrith."

Thurvishar stopped and looked at her. Xivan found herself staring as well.

"I assumed it had to be something like that," Sheloran said. "That he freed you from slavery or the like."

"He faked my death," Senera said. "I was to be executed, you see. As a witch."

---

[2] What can I say? He's not a petty man. Arrogant yes, but not petty.

Considering the number of women in the room who qualified as "witch" until just recently, it was almost funny to see how many blank stares Senera won with that statement.

"Ah," Sheloran said. "Can't have a slave learning magic. That would be terrible."

"Exactly. So he saved my life, and he did it in a way that made sure House D'Jorax never came looking for me. Why would they? I was already dead." A rueful expression stole over her features. "They almost didn't catch me. They couldn't believe a slave would have been able to do something that required that level of spell sophistication. But Relos Var saw the . . . the value . . . right away. So he recruited me."

"And while I'm grateful for that . . . ," Thurvishar began to say.

Senera looked pained. "You don't need to say it. And quite frankly, Thurvishar, if you had been in my place, you'd have followed him to the ends of the earth and beyond. Don't try to deny it."

Thurvishar's expression was unreadable. "I'm sure you're right."

Xivan sighed. "Well, now that this conversation has turned fucking awkward, shall we talk about what happens next?"

"Oh, might as well make it mine again," Talea said. "At least for the next bit."

"Yes, very well," Thurvishar agreed.

Kihrin's story
Inside Vol Karoth's prison

We ducked and dodged and ran for what seemed like forever. Previously, the lions had maintained a steady quick-walk, and we had been able to outrun them easily. This time, either because they were getting stronger or because Vol Karoth was pissed, they dogged our heels for much longer.

Me limping didn't help. If we could only have a second to rest, we could heal ourselves, but the damned statues never let up. After a dozen blocks, and numerous lacerations to our various backs and legs, Janel lost her temper.

"Enough!" she yelled, turning and slamming her doubled fists into the ground. The resulting shock wave knocked Teraeth and me off our feet, shattered the three lions in the lead, and sent the rest tumbling tail over mane half a city block. She followed this display by pointing at the wall of the three-floor building next to where the pack had come to rest. Her eyes blazed red. The stone at the base of the building followed suit; glowing, melting, slagging. The entire structure leaned, groaned, and then collapsed, burying the lion pack in rubble.

"Or we could do that," Teraeth agreed, picking himself up. He tried to dust himself off, realized he was still down a hand, and concentrated.

I got to my feet and did the same. Our wounds closed, my flesh regrew as did Teraeth's hand. "Thanks," I said to Janel, who nodded wearily.

"That . . . wasn't easy," she said. "Let's try not to make that a habit, yes?"

"Sounds good to me," I agreed.

We stood in silence for a few moments, surveying Janel's handiwork.

"So," Teraeth said finally, "what now?"

"We keep looking for Talon," I said.

"Right," he agreed, "but how? Our one lead was a bust. Also, who builds a jail with windows that open?"

I stared at him for several heartbeats, then began to laugh. "Good point," I said at last. "I was so caught up in the moment, it didn't even occur to me."

"Is that another element of Vol Karoth's lack of imagination?" Teraeth asked. "Did S'arric not spend a lot of time in jails?"

"As a prisoner? Hardly any at all," Janel said with a playful grin. "I mean, there was that one time after that beach party . . ."

I had to think about that one for a moment, then I chuckled. "Being ordered to attend my brother's lecture on spatial-temporal ley tracking[3] is hardly 'jail.'" I said. Then my grin faded, and I said, "But Teraeth has a point; where do we look next?"

Janel crossed her arms and lowered her head in thought. "You didn't spend any time in jails in Karolean," she said after a while. "You'd been promoted too high for such scut work by the time we came here. Which means Vol Karoth has only the most rudimentary idea of what the jails in Karolaen are even like. So . . ."

"So," I said, "we're not looking for a jail in Karolaen; we're looking for one in Nineawen.[4] Which is a problem, since this is all Karolaen."

"It's not *all* Karolaen," Janel mused. "We have seen some areas that were clearly from the other continent. Which means we need to look—"

"In a gray zone," we said at the same time. Grimly, we began searching.

Talea's memory
The Lower Circle of the Capital City, Quur
Nine days after the Battle of the Well of Spirals

Despite Talea's inability to just help herself to any of the empire's treasure hoard, raising money turned out to be a reasonably simple matter:

Talea went gambling.

She didn't have a coin to her name, but she found a gold throne someone had dropped on their way out, just sitting there in the middle of the road. That had paid for her first toss of the dice. Which she'd won. And then turned those winnings over to her next game.

Talea left that house before she'd upset too many people with her lucky streak, and wandered up the road to a card house. There, guided by Eshi's hilariously adult side commentary, she won several more hands, until she'd bought herself a place at one of the high-stakes tables.

Talea found herself fascinated by the entire process. She didn't always win. But her losses were minor and her wins were not. Bonus: the card house offered an extremely decent lunch menu. Still, she had started receiving some jealous, resentful looks that didn't bode well, so she decided it would be best to leave while they were still letting her walk out under her own power. Talea

---

[3] I need to know what this is. Desperately.

[4] Apparently the name of the voras capital on Nythrawl, prior to the demonic invasion and the subsequent relocation to these continents.

thought she might head over to the Copper Quarter and see what she might find in a nice agolé. They might even have some other clothing that fit her, although she wouldn't have time for tailoring.

As she walked out of the card house, she had just enough time to notice a shadow detach itself from a nearby wall and brush up against her. Then there was a dagger's point pricking her in the ribs and a familiar voice in her ear.

"You don't know how hard," Merit said, "it was to find you. Don't," he warned as Talea started to reach for her sword.

"Ah, and here I thought we were friends," she said pleasantly. Meanwhile, her heartbeat raced. She couldn't see Eshi anywhere.

"Friends don't run off and leave me holding my privates while I try to explain to my bosses just how I got out of that mess back at the Octagon." His hand was firm on her arm, his grip tight enough to bruise. "Oh, you know how it is: this mysterious, beautiful woman came out of nowhere, saved my life, saved the whole mission, in fact, and then ran off without reward or thanks before I could so much as ask her name."

"Talea."

"Talea? That's a pretty name—" Merit cleared his throat. "Not the point. Now hand over your sword, please."

"And what happens then? You take me back as proof that I'm real?"

"Yes, in fact. That's exactly the plan. The boss is away right now, but he checks in every evening to make sure I'm being a good boy." He pressed a little harder with the point of that dagger. "The sword. Don't make me ask again."

Talea unbuckled her scabbard and handed it over.

He gazed at the curved blade with grudging respect as he looped the belt over his shoulder and wore it cross-body. "Khorveshan sword, huh?"

"I'm Khorveshan."

"Right. Well, let's go. This way." He pulled her along with him. Merit kept a good pace, quick enough that she was having trouble stopping to get her bearings. "How were you doing that back there, anyway? Magic?"

"Doing what?" Talea was willing to play dumb.

Unfortunately, he was having none of it. "Oh no, you were my good luck charm escaping the Octagon and your own back there at that card table. I've never seen anything like it. Don't try to claim you weren't doing anything."

Talea almost smiled. Thurvishar could twist luck, and yes, the wizard absolutely would have used magic. On the other hand, she hadn't. At least, not that she knew.

Eshi probably counted as magic, but she wasn't about to explain how she ended up with a miniature Goddess of Luck helping her.

"I really wasn't, though. I'm just lucky. Blessed by—" She made a face, unable to stop herself.

Merit gave her an odd look. She felt a shudder sweep over her as she realized he didn't know. Most people didn't know. Taja's clergy were probably throwing fits, sure, but it was unlikely the priests were stopping to explain to anyone that their goddess had just stopped answering their prayers. Merit thought Taja was still alive.

"I get it. Blessed by Taja. Well, that's fine. We're going to come back to my place. You can make yourself comfortable. I'll check in with people. Then you can go. Easy."

Talea sighed. "And when they don't believe me and we're both in trouble? Then what? They leave our bodies in the harbor for the crocodiles to eat?"

Merit rolled his eyes. "The people I work for aren't monsters. We don't do that sort of thing anymore."

She gave him a studied look as she noted that last word.

They marched through the length of the Copper Quarter, until Talea began to wonder just where this rogue actually lived. She'd assumed somewhere close to where he'd gone with the slaves to that Blue House, but evidently she'd assumed wrong. Her curiosity was further piqued when he took the road away from the harbor and headed into Velvet Town.

"I'm being nice right now, but if you push things, I'll forget my manners. You'd better not be taking me to a velvet house."

Merit stopped and pulled her over to the side of the road, out of the way of most pedestrians. "I *am* taking us to a velvet house," he said, "but not like that. It's just where my check-in spot is located. And anyway, the velvets there are free people. Courtesans. It's all very expensive."

"Yes, how extravagant—the idea that sex might involve choice."

"I mean, as much as it still costs metal, I suppose."

Talea sighed. He was missing the point.

They walked along the roads of Velvet Town, and Talea pretended to not be interested. But truthfully, she'd never been there before. Not when she was a slave and not after she'd been freed. Talea felt keenly aware that she might have ended up there if things had gone just slightly differently for her. That her sister, Morea, had gone there, had in doing so gone to her death.

In a moment of bravery, she had once asked Darzin D'Mon why he bought her and not her sister. Darzin had said that he'd thought about buying them both, but thought the pain of separating them would be just that much more exquisite.

He'd tossed a coin to decide which one of them to keep.

Most of the velvet houses were demure, safely tucked away behind high whitewashed brick and clay walls that gave no hint to what pleasures and horrors might lurk beyond their doors. Harkers on the streets battled each other for the right to usher visitors inside their particular establishment, each singing the praises of their velvets over all others. A few houses didn't advertise at all, which Talea could only assume meant they didn't need to or want to; their customers would find them.

It was to one of these latter buildings that Merit took her, pulling her into a side entry that presumably was not the way in for customers. It didn't seem threatening. There was a courtyard of white stone, with a fountain in the center and benches. Orange trees and roses. Shaded colonnades that presumably led to other areas of the brothel.

And then Merit made his only serious mistake, which was to smile, let down his guard, and say, "Here we are. Welcome to the Shattered Veil Club."

Talea's heart skipped. The world darkened at the edges all around her.

Before she knew what she'd done, she'd grabbed Merit's wrist and twisted the knife from his fingers. She caught it before it fell, kicked the man's legs out from under him, and followed him down. She landed on his chest, shins pinning his arms, knife at his throat.

"Who the fuck are you?" she demanded. "Why did you bring me here?"

Merit blinked at her, wide-eyed and clearly confused. "Um ... I don't ... Okay, let's not ..." He took a deep breath and tried again. "While I'm going to admit here that I've never been so turned on in my entire life, this isn't how I want to die. So why don't you explain what you think I've done wrong, and we'll work something out."

"This is the Shattered Veil Club," Talea repeated.

Merit looked up at her and waited.

Talea inhaled, deep and shuddering. "My twin sister was murdered here."

Merit blinked at her, and then his eyes went wide. "What? Are you ... are you serious? Here? But how–?"

"Miss Morea?"[5]

Talea kept the dagger at Merit's throat as she looked up. Standing on the far side of the courtyard was a large man who looked like he probably worked at the brothel in some sort of enforcement capacity. He was a thick, broad man with a large, flat nose and unattractively bulbous eyes. He wore very odd bracers with narrow porcupine-like spikes.

Except no, Talea realized. Those were morgage arm spikes.

"Raorin, don't move," Merit said. "We're just having a conversation."

Talea removed the dagger and stood up. "Morea was my sister."

"Oh," Raorin said.

"Raorin?" Merit rubbed his neck as he scrambled backward away from her and then to his feet. "What are you talking about?"

"The murders in the mask roon, kid. Morea was one of the people killed, the whole reason the place was shut down a few years ago." Raorin shrugged helplessly. "A bunch of good folks died. Some of the girls, the velvet house's owner, the minstrel who used to play here. And the rest of us were told to get the hell out if we knew what was good for us–which we did, for a while. Then the kid here opened the place back up–"

"I kept telling him that squatting in an abandoned building was not the same as reopening for business, but he never listened."

"A lot of us didn't have any other place else to go," Raorin said.

"Because you were slaves," Talea said. She saw the way Raorin tensed and held up a hand. "I used to be one too. I understand."

Which she did. If the person who owned all their marks had suddenly gone missing, it didn't mean they were *free*. Anyone who found them as runaways would either be able to claim them for themselves or try to return them for a reward. If their owner was dead, then they could again be claimed, and if their owner wasn't dead, then they were potentially in serious trouble for running.

Either way, the most sensible solution was staying in place as if nothing had changed.

---

[5] I'm honestly surprised Raorin remembered Talea's sister. She hadn't been there long.

Merit rubbed his arm. "We pretended the old owner was still around and freed everyone," he said. "Let the ones who wanted to go do so, and the others reopened the shop. Except turns out one of the Royal Houses had legally confiscated the place, and they'd sold it. The new owners came around and—" He smiled wryly.

"They're not so bad," Raorin allowed, "for what they are."

Talea turned the dagger around and offered it back to Merit, who looked at the proffered weapon with undisguised shock.

"As if I'd be leaving, after that," Talea said. "Show me the room where it happened."

"Are you sure . . . ?"

"Now," Talea ordered.

Merit hooked a thumb over his shoulder. "Right this way."

Several hours and glasses of brandy later, Talea found herself in the mask room outside what had once been the bedroom of the brothel's madam. The room where her sister had probably been murdered. It was a storeroom now. Nobody had wanted to sleep there after the club reopened, and a different bed had been moved to the main room instead. A persistent rumor painted the spot as haunted—which, who knows? Might have even been true.[6] A great many people had died there. At least six, if Talea was remembering the story correctly.

Other than the bed, the rest of the room fit the description in Thurvishar's book almost exactly. It hadn't occurred to Talea that Merit was *that* Merit, but she guessed she could understand why he'd taken to living in the abandoned brothel when he needed a place to stay after Kihrin had freed him. Convenient, easy, and nobody was going to kick him out. At least not right away.

Talea found herself with a lot of questions and the knowledge that asking them would likely get her killed. Was Merit still involved with the Shadowdancers? Did the Shadowdancers still even exist? And if they did, who controlled them, since the last she'd read, it had been Darzin? The idea that this was a kinder, gentler group of criminals who didn't dump their victims into the Senlay River certainly suggested someone else had taken over. But maybe she was being overly optimistic.

"Why am I here?" Talea asked.

Merit blinked at her. "Um, I thought I explained this . . . ?"

"I wasn't talking to you," Talea said.

Eshi swung her legs back and forth from the edge of the bed. "I'm sorry this is painful for you. I promise it'll all make sense soon."

Talea tapped her empty glass at the edge of the glass table where they'd been playing cards. She had a high stack of metal in front of her, considerably larger than the stack in front of Merit. Honestly, the man had no one to blame but himself. He'd seen her at the card club. "I've had four years to come to terms with what happened to my sister. You'd think it wouldn't hurt. It still does."

---

[6] I suppose it's technically possible, but I rather doubt any ghosts that might have lingered would have survived demons hunting in the Hellmarch.

"I'm sorry," Merit said. "I heard about what happened. It was pretty shitty."

"I've met her killer," Talea said and then frowned. "Well, I suppose who killed her is somewhat open to debate. The woman who killed her was not the one who ordered her death. I've tried to remember that distinction." She tilted her head. "Darzin D'Mon is dead. I don't know if you know who that is or if that would even mean anything . . ."

"Oh no," Merit said. "I know who that is."

"Well, I–"

"Talea? What are you doing here?" Qown's voice was clear and distinct. He sounded as if he were sitting across from her on the other side of the burning candle. But there was no one there.

"Qown?" Talea frowned. "What–? I don't–"

"Wait," Merit said. "You two know each other?"

"Hmm. Funny story," Talea murmured. "Also a bit sad. But where are you?"

"Oh, I'm not here," Qown said.

"I can see that. Or rather, I *can't*."

"I mean, I'm using my Cornerstone to check in. As a favor from, uh–" His voice choked. "What are you doing here?"

"I was trying to get back home," Talea said, "but this man insisted I come here to talk to his bosses because I guess I'm his alibi?"

Merit leaned toward the candle. "Look, Qown, I just need to talk to the boss. The last slave sale went sideways–"

"I told you that you couldn't keep using the bills of sale because they'd catch on–"

"I know, I know," Merit agreed. "You were right. You were absolutely right. But Talea here helped get my ass out of the fire. All those slaves too. Except Scabbard's acting like the only way that could have happened is if I sold everyone out and House D'Erinwa let me go because I rang on people. Which I didn't do! So yeah, Talea's my alibi."

"I hope no one was hurt?" Qown sounded distressed.

"No, no. Everyone's fine. Really, your friend has Taja's own luck."

There was a protracted beat of silence. Talea suspected that Qown was talking to his "boss," whoever that was.

Wait. Wasn't Qown's boss Relos Var?

Talea started to get an ugly, sick-to-her-stomach feeling.

"Merit," Qown said as he returned–or at least his voice did, "would you mind giving Talea and me the room? There's something we need to discuss."

"Sure." Merit's expression suggested more than a little uncertainty, but he walked outside, anyway.

"Qown, really, what are you doing?"

"Talea, what are you doing?"

They both stopped talking. Talea waved. "You go first."

"I'm just surprised to see you here." Qown paused. "Where's Xivan?"

Talea exhaled. "I have no idea. I left her."

"Oh, I'm so sorry to hear that."

She sighed and shrugged. "Me too. So how is your 'boss' involved in all this?" She gestured around the room with a finger.

"My boss–" Qown seemed confused. "Oh no. Oh light. You haven't mentioned Relos Var to Merit, have you?"

Talea narrowed her eyes. "No."

"Good. I would appreciate it, as a friend, if you didn't. And anyway, that's not who Merit means. I'm working with Galen D'Mon, actually. I don't know if you ever met Darzin's son, but he's not anything like his father. In fact, you and Galen could probably talk for hours about how much you both hate Darzin. And Sheloran isn't even a D'Mon. I mean, she is, she's Galen's wife, but she's House D'Talus originally; I don't think it counts."

Talea sighed. Qown not wanting to mention Relos Var almost certainly meant that Qown was in fact still working for Relos Var. And Talea's feelings about that wizard/dragon were increasingly unkind. Still, Qown was a grown man, and it wasn't her place to lecture him about the company he was keeping–

Talea interrupted her own train of thought. "Wait. Did you just say House D'Talus?"

"Yes. Why?"

"Is she related to . . . I mean, um. Who's her mother?"

"Uh, I don't remember her first name. The high lady? I mean, Sheloran is the daughter of the high lord and lady."

Tale exhaled a shuddering breath. How to explain this without . . . explaining this. At the very least, what were the odds–she gave the little girl in the corner a dirty look–what were the odds that she just happened to run into the man who was working with Qown who was assigned by Relos Var to do something dealing with Galen D'Mon, whose wife, Sheloran, just happened to be Lessoral's daughter, Suless's granddaughter?

That was a string of coincidence it would take Taja herself to unravel.

"She's in danger," Talea murmured. She'd never met Sheloran D'Mon, but she felt the odds of Sheloran being in extreme danger were high. Very high. If not by Suless, then certainly from Xivan. Maybe 84 percent. No, 85.

Xivan wouldn't stop just because she'd been gaeshed, and she'd search for any advantage . . .

"Where are you right now, Qown? Can I travel to where you are? I think–" She grimaced. "I can't explain right now, but I think your friend Sheloran is in a lot of danger."

"You can't explain?"

"No." She paused. "Remember how there were certain things you couldn't explain to Janel? Things Relos Var wouldn't allow you to explain?"

The silence was deafening.

"Qown, are you still there?"

His voice was fractured and hollow when it returned. "Are you . . . are you all right? Are you safe?"

"Much better than I'd expect, honestly. I mean, under the circumstances. And I'm safe enough. You know how it is."

"So it re-formed." He sounded gutted.[7]

---

[7] "It" being the Stone of Shackles, naturally.

"Mmm," she agreed.

"I'm glad you're all right, at least." His breath caught. "I'm in Zherias right now. We just arrived in town, and honestly, I don't know how long we'll be staying for. But it's two weeks from the Capital to Pivilana Bay by ship. If we're still here—which I can't promise—then you know I'd love to see you. I just wish I still had some of those sweets you like."

"Oh, Qown. You know you're sweet enough all on your own." Talea glanced down at the coins sitting on her side of the table. She was pretty sure that she had enough to pay for ship's passage. "I'll see you in two weeks. With luck."

"With luck," he agreed. "I have to go. Be safe."

"Thanks," she said, but he was already gone.

37: The Abbess of Devors

Talea's reaction
The Lighthouse at Shadrag Gor
Just after Talea's memory

Talea blinked as the vision faded and found Xivan staring at her, open-mouthed. "You . . . guessed? You just guessed I'd go after Sheloran?"

"And you did!" Talea pointed out, grinning. She couldn't help but be deeply amused by Xivan's indignation. "So you see, that was the right strategy. You've always said I should play to my strengths, you know."

She did hope Xivan would grow to accept the wild coincidences. They weren't going away anytime soon.

"Yes, but I didn't think you just assumed . . ." Xivan waved a hand. "Never mind. As you said, I did. So you weren't wrong."

Talea started to say something when she caught a flash of shadow out of the corner of her eye. She glanced over in that direction, but there was nothing there.

Nor the second time, when she saw it again.

Screaming echoed from upstairs.

It was Janel.

Talea was almost through the door when Xivan caught her arm. "Whoa! What are you doing?"

"Janel! Didn't you hear her?" Talea stopped and examined every face in the room. No one had stood. No one looked the slightest bit concerned.

Clearly, no one else had heard the noise.

Talea bit her lip and slotted herself against Xivan's side. "Why don't I . . . not go running off by myself all alone, then? Since I'm apparently hearing things?"

Senera scowled. "Oh, I'm sure the problem isn't you." She turned to Thurvishar. "Please tell me that they've figured out something on the other side?"

Thurvishar grimaced.

"Unfortunately–"

The world changed.

Kihrin's story
Inside Vol Karoth's prison

Nothing was working.

The second time we found Talon, it was also a trap.

That time, we'd been walking down a street when I'd noticed that one of the gates to a building was exactly the same as the main gate to the Octagon in

Quur. Something that didn't belong, and something that one might reasonably expect to find featuring heavily in the nightmares of a slave turned mimic. Also, it was gray.

The way beyond it was a literal maze of traps and dead ends, one we wandered for hours trying to find the center.

"Surely, this is the right way, though," Janel said. "I mean, we're going through all this effort . . ."

Teraeth paused from examining the tiled floor pattern. "Damn it. I don't think this is the right way."

"You mean you think we should have gone left back at—" I started to turn.

"This is all bullshit," Teraeth said. "My prison was in a place that was significant to Vol Karoth, to S'arric. This place isn't. It's something pulled from Talon's memories, but it's not something pulled from *his*."

I chewed on my lip. "The problem with that is that it assumes Vol Karoth isn't capable of changing his strategies on the fly. That he'll keep going with something that betrays his motivations even after we've discovered him."

Janel rubbed the bridge of her nose. "So destroy the maze, Kihrin."

I cocked my head. "I would if I could."

"You can," she said. "This land is responding to you as much as to Vol Karoth. Tell the city you don't want a maze here. Tell the city there is no maze here. You have that power."

I frowned. Turned out it was easier said than done.

"You know what concerns me," Teraeth said, "is that this all feels like a delaying action. Like he's stalling for time. Have you noticed he's stopped attacking himself? *Where is he?*"

"Why would he care how long it takes?" Janel asked. "Doesn't he have all the time in the world? Or no time or—" She scowled. "Why would he need to delay us?"

"That's a very good question," Teraeth agreed.

I was still concentrating on what Janel had said about my connection to the wasteland. Was it possible that I could just . . . wish walls away?[1] Was that something within my power? I sat down on the floor and concentrated.

But try as I might, nothing happened.

Janel watched me.

I met her stare. "I can't," I told her.

She pressed her lips together and nodded. "So we shall do this the old-fashioned way. Let us find a way through these traps."

We kept going.

Kalindra's memory
After her arrival on Devors

Kalindra decided the moment Oliyuan walked away from the cell door that she was going to kill him. And whoever had given Oliyuan these orders.

---

[1] Why not? Kihrin was perfectly capable of adding or redesigning elements. I would have thought this easier.

And possibly every monk in the entire damn monastery. She would take what she needed from their damn library and leave. Let them just try to stop her.

Oliyuan had made a terrible mistake. Not just treating her this way but a more specific mistake. These cells were not designed with jailing in mind. As such, the hinges for them were on the inside, not the outside.

She used the butt of a dagger to hammer out those same hinges, after which point it was a reasonably simple matter to lift away the door and lean it against a wall. There didn't seem to be any guards stationed outside or, indeed, anywhere in the hall, so it seemed safe to assume that Oliyuan had thought the door enough to keep them trapped.

Nikali clapped his hands together and squealed—he found the door trick delightful. She bent down next to him. "Shall we go find some food?"

Nikali grinned. "Sugar apples!" which he pronounced "sugar abbles" because he hadn't quite figured out the *p* sound yet.

Kalindra rolled her eyes. She was reasonably sure her son loved sugar apples less for the flavor than because eating them made an absolute mess. "We'll see." She knelt before her son. "Niki, things may get a little loud soon. People may start shouting. If that happens, you know what to do, right?"

Nikali's smile faded, and he stared at her with large brown eyes. "Hide."

"That's right, little cub. I want you to hide." She smiled and caressed her son's cheek. "Let's hope there's no need." She picked up her son and carried him outside the cell.

Kalindra made her way back upstairs and didn't encounter another soul the entire time, although she did hear the sound of snoring and the soft sputtering breaths of sleeping monks coming from other cells. She somehow doubted their cells had been locked, however. At some point, she was going to run into someone who wasn't asleep, and that's when things would become . . . interesting.

Oliyuan had only complained about the dagger he'd seen and hadn't tried to search her, probably because that would have meant touching her. Kalindra suspected that Oliyuan liked his women quiet and hypothetical. She adjusted her daggers and checked the rings on each hand, which could be twisted in such a way to attach to the ends of a garrote. Not that she could effectively use a garrote while balancing a toddler on her hip. Ah well, life was full of compromises.

She was definitely going to have to have a word with her father-in-law about his definition of *safe*.

Kalindra found herself curious to know if all the monks lived in the same squalid little cells, or if there were more high-ranking brothers who rated better quarters. If there were, then that seemed like a fine place to start the conversation. So she began touring the grounds, acting for all the world as though she had every right to be there, was permitted to go where she liked. Which should have been true, even if the front door man had other ideas.

Tya's Veil filled the night sky, but there was little light otherwise. No one moved on the grounds. The air was warm and still and quiet, interrupted only by the soft whispers of distant waves crashing against the cliff faces. The salt air was rich with the scent of jasmine. Kalindra frowned as she entered a large cloister—a wide, green space where monks probably did morning exercises or contemplated universal mysteries. In the center stood a statue.

Probably a goddess. But even as the thought occurred to Kalindra, she dismissed it. Shouldn't it have been a statue of Argas? Tya was never associated with the prophecies, but she supposed possibly someone might link Taja with fate and thus make that connection. But the closer she approached to the statue, the odder it seemed. This wasn't a goddess or least showed none of the attributes Kalindra would associate with any of the Eight Immortals. The woman was dressed in a simple gown of archaic style, hair worn braided back, a crown on her head.

Kalindra frowned. A queen? Except Quur didn't have queens . . .

Something had been carved at the base of the statue. Curious, Kalindra moved forward to read the words.

> WITHIN LIES, UNCOVER TRUTH;
> FROM DESPAIR, FIND HOPE;
> AFTER HATRED, DISCOVER LOVE;
> IN DARKNESS, CREATE LIGHT.[2]

She frowned. Presumably that was meant to be an inspirational koan to aid in meditation, but it seemed an odd inscription for a monastery dedicated to prophecies. Just as she started to shake her head and move on, Nikali put his hands over his eyes and buried his face against her shoulder.

"Ew!" he shrieked.

"What? Why—" Her voice trailed off as she noticed what else was at the base of the statue, on the other side, which had been out of her line of vision.

Kalindra liked to think of herself as a woman immune to shock, who couldn't be startled. She had seen too much, done too much. Her hands were drenched in blood, which had been quite literal at various points in her life. And yet here she stood, frozen, blinking mutely at the bleeding pile of flesh spread out on the ground before her. Had that ever been a person? The light was poor, but she was fairly certain it had. Not just one person either. Those were weapons scattered on the ground and far too much blood for one person. People had died here. Recently.

"Good boy, Nikali," Kalindra whispered, stroking the back of his head. "Keep your eyes closed." She felt her stomach try to heave. Those were corpses to haunt nightmares. How had no one heard that? The attack must have been bestial . . . the whole courtyard seemed haunted by a palpable darkness, as though whoever was responsible still lingered.

"What are you doing—?" A man asked behind her. The voice cut off, shocked. No doubt he'd just seen the lumps of broken flesh and bone farther along the path too.

Kalindra's heart wanted to choke her, panic telling her to run. But there was no running, not while carrying Nikali. She instead turned to him. It wasn't

---

[2] I honestly do wish I'd had a chance to better research this. Alas.

Oliyuan, thank the gods. This was a younger man, with elegant features and soft eyes. If there was anything about him to mar the perfection of his appearance, it's that one of the sleeves of his robe was pinned to his side, empty. The remaining arm was raised, pointing toward the corpse. It was a moment crouched on the edge of a cliff, needing only the slightest nudge to turn into something fatal.

"What have you done?" the monk asked. He looked horrified as he put a hand to his waist.

Kalindra's eyes widened. He wore a sword. Most of the monks hadn't been armed, but this one . . .

Nikali, with perfect, perfect timing, took that moment to start bawling his eyes out. The monk's eyes visibly widened, and he took a step back, seeming to realize that the idea of a woman with her hands full of small child committing such awful violence was unlikely at best.

"I just . . . I was looking for . . . We just saw . . ." Kalindra did her very best impression of young and upset and bewildered. It wasn't a difficult impersonation. "Shhh, it's okay, little cub. Don't look. Don't look. Everything's fine." She rocked her boy in her arms to calm him.

The man's hand relaxed away from his weapon. "You—" He inhaled. "You're Lady Milligreest. We weren't expecting you until tomorrow morning."

Kalindra raised both eyebrows. "Apparently not. And when I arrived, one of your people threw me in a cell and locked the door on me. I didn't think I was coming here to be a prisoner."

It was at least a bit gratifying to see the look of horror that stole over the man's face. "What? Oh no, I'm so sorry. That wasn't what was supposed to happen at all. Who—who did this?"

"This? The murder?" She determinedly did not, would not, look back at the body. "I don't know. The person who locked me up was named Oliyuan."

The man's eyes widened, and he looked past her toward the corpse on the ground, then back to her. "I see. Why don't I take you someplace safe? This is no sight for widows and babies."

"No, it isn't." She paused. "But who are you? You can't blame me for being suspicious under the circumstances."

"Wixan. Again, I am sorry. Caerowan said you would be here in the morning. I would never have sent Oliyuan to attend you. Not ever." The man's expression was apologetic. "Oliyuan has little experience with the outside world."

"Oliyuan thinks women are evil," Kalindra corrected. "How does he deal with monks who are female?"

The man tilted his head. "Um . . . this is the men's section of the monastery. Oliyuan rarely comes into contact with anyone female. To be perfectly honest, he should never have been at the Gatestone, so I'm going to have words with the man assigned that duty."

Kalindra turned her head toward the corpse, just slightly, still not looking at it. "Let's hope that's not the corpse of the man in question."

The man, Wixan, visibly winced. "We'll find out. But please, follow me. I must put you somewhere safe and tell the abbess what's—" His gaze flickered back, toward the body. "What's happened here."

"Thank you," Kalindra said, swallowing unease and dread. "That would be appreciated."

The second room was much better—a large, elegant space where not a single decoration or piece of furniture was out of place, all of it planned down to the inch. (Probably in accordance with some prophecy, Kalindra thought uncharitably.) It seemed like the sort of place that would not even be a tiny bit appropriate for a handsy two-year-old whose favorite foods were all sticky, but that wasn't Kalindra's problem. It was infinitely better than a literal cell.

"The men's dormitories are to the north and the women's to the south," Wixan explained as he pulled out bedding from one of the cabinets, doing so quite adroitly in spite of only having one hand. Kalindra thought about offering her help, but he didn't seem to need it and might even take offense.

"This is sort of—" He stopped and gave her a blinding smile. If this were some other time, some other place, that smile alone would be enough. She would have pursued him relentlessly, just for the pleasure of seeing that smile turned on her while waking next to him in the mornings. She'd always been helpless before a beautiful smile.

Now it just reminded her of Jarith, and her stomach clenched.

The smile faded from his lips as he saw her expression. He clearly knew who she was, the circumstances that had led to her being there. She thought he intended to offer condolences. He didn't, and she liked him just a little more for it. So short a time and she was already sick to death of the false sympathy of strangers.

"This is neutral ground," Wixan said, his tone much more somber, "meant for guests or the highest-ranked visiting scholars. This is where you should have been taken."

It was an apology, but she was in no mood to savor it.

"When you go off and wake up the whole monastery, would you mind seeing if there is anyone who might be able to bring some food?" Kalindra asked. "I understand mealtimes are in the mornings, but he ended up skipping his dinner."

"Sugar apples!" Nikali suggested gleefully.

Wixan's mouth quirked. "I'll see what I can do." He bowed and left.

Afterward, it went pretty much the way Kalindra suspected it would. A lot of lights turned on as people were woken and unmasked mage-lights (there were a great many of those, which made Kalindra suspect one of those "rules" Oliyuan hadn't had a chance to warn her about was a stipulation against open flame). Voices echoed through the cloister as people ran about, doing . . . something.

A young woman, clearly distracted, brought them sugar apples and a towel with which to clean up the mess afterward.

Kalindra curled up around her son and tried to sleep. It had been a long day and would be an equally early morning.

The persistent knocking at the door woke her. Kalindra gave serious consideration to just how much trouble she would be in if she killed whoever that was. Probably a lot.

The "who" ended up being the same woman who had dropped off the fruit the night before. She at least seemed friendly and not inclined to lead Kalindra to a cell. She came with a change of clothes for Kalindra, in the form of the same tan robes that everyone on the island seemed to wear.

At least she'd blend in.

Once Kalindra changed, she followed the woman, Lenah, to another, grander building, which might have been a great hall or temple space in a different location. It seemed important. Kalindra had brought Nikali with her, because she didn't have anywhere else to leave him. He was yawning and sleepy, not used to being up so early. Neither of them were, she thought as she stifled her own yawn.

The main room was much like the quarters she'd been given: simple to the point of extreme elegance. The smell of sandalwood incense filled the air. The only decoration was another statue in the room, much like the one she'd seen in the cloister the night before. This one was a marble statue of a woman holding a book in one hand, using a naked sword rather like a walking stick with the other. In front of the statue sat a woman, cross-legged on the floor in front of a low table. She looked middle-aged except for her eyes, which were ancient. Cushions and low padded sofas were placed around the room, but the area directly in front of the woman, where any guest would sit, was bare. Which meant Kalindra either had to stand there the whole time or rest on the floor.

Kalindra bowed and then sat down on the floor.

She also wasn't going to come here and act like some sort of petitioner, begging for favors. That wasn't at all how she needed this relationship to evolve; it was already off to a terrible start. At this rate, the odds they'd let her search the library on her own were looking less and less likely.

Monks (or servants, she couldn't tell which) rushed forward to serve her tea, presenting her with a simple porcelain cup filled with tea so pale it was very nearly the color of water. She would far rather have had some sort of breakfast rice porridge or fruit.

"I am Niyabe, abbess of the Devors Monastery, and please, allow me to give my sincerest apologies for the"—the abbess paused a moment—"bureaucratic error that occurred last night. The idea that a Milligreest would come to us for shelter and be treated this way is an embarrassment beyond imagination. We want you to be comfortable and safe here." Her smile was gentle and kind, the face of every grandmother.

Nikali began fidgeting and clearly wanted to go to the old woman, probably because he found something about the abbess—ah, the jade pendant around her neck—just the thing he had always wanted to put in his mouth. He clearly hungered for it.

Kalindra sighed and shifted the boy. "No, little cub. That's not yours."

There was never a two-year-old alive who understood the difference, however, so he just fretted and then started crying until she handed him his favorite wooden doll to chew on. Then he calmed down, mostly, although he was clearly still playing with the idea of throwing a tantrum about not laying hands on that necklace.

"He's still teething," she explained to the abbess.

The old woman looked like she'd never seen a child before. She didn't stare at Nikali with distaste or disgust, but the look on her face was best described as bemused. "Of course. We don't . . . really have good facilities for children here. There's a village a few hours from here where we—" She left off whatever she'd been about to say. "I mean, if you need for anything, we will send for it."

"Thank you," Kalindra said. "I do need something."

"Yes?"

"Information. Who died last night, and does that sort of thing happen often here? I don't think my father-in-law would have sent me here if he'd known."

"Ah." The abbess's expression faltered, just for a second, just for the briefest pause, and then the warm smile was back on her face, the calm, gentle reassurance in her eyes. "We're still attempting to discern that, but please believe me, this is not at all normal. Rest assured we will find those responsible and make sure they are brought to justice. It's nothing you need to concern yourself over."

Kalindra blinked. She was standing in the one place in the world, short of god-king sanctum or Immortal haven, supposedly immune to demonic invasion. She had just witnessed the aftermath of deaths that very much appeared to be the work of a demon, of which, again, none were supposed to be capable of reaching the Devors Monastery. Deaths that had occurred just minutes before she and her child would have passed through that exact same area.

But she wasn't supposed to concern herself over this.

Kalindra leaned forward and drank her tea, which turned out to be surprisingly good. It didn't make up for the fury that boiled in her heart, but she smiled and pretended everything was fine. "Thank you, Abbess. You're very kind."

The abbess returned that smile with a proper one of her own. "Of course. Please let my people know if you need anything else." It was clearly a dismissal. "Wixan, please escort Lady Milligreest back to her rooms."

"Yes, Abbess," the man said as he helped Kalindra pick up Nikali and climb to her feet.

They walked in silence back to her room while Kalindra kicked herself for both not asking about the library or calling the abbess on her shit. Whatever was going on, the abbess didn't want to tell Kalindra about it.

"Lady Milligreest—" They arrived at the door to her rooms.

"Please, call me Kalindra."

The man swallowed, smiled tightly. "Yes, thank you. I just—"

Kalindra paused and reexamined the man. He seemed to be worrying something over in his mind, torn as to which decision he would make. "Yes, Wixan? Is there something you'd like to tell me?"

He wasn't smiling now. "I believe Oliyuan was one of the people killed. When we searched his room last night, we found several large promissory notes. Far more metal than he should ever have been able to acquire on his own." Wixan hesitated again. "And among the bodies last night, we found a gag. One sized for a small child."

A snake of pure adrenaline twisted its way up her spine, and yet she was paralyzed. A wave of concentrated, distilled horror swept over of her, chased down by an equally burning anger. There were no children here in the monastery. The abbess had made that clear enough. So such a restraint could only have been meant for . . .

"So it was to be a kidnapping," she said, then corrected herself. "No, an assassination first and then a kidnapping."

Wixan winced. "I don't want to assume, and yet I find it difficult not to leap to that conclusion. I thought . . . I thought you should know."

Kalindra met the man's eyes. He seemed both guilty and apologetic, which made sense, as he was absolutely betraying the abbess's wishes. She hadn't wanted to tell Kalindra the truth. Why? Was she afraid Kalindra would go screaming back to her father-in-law, or did the abbess simply want to make sure Kalindra was still around for a second attempt? Who had the motive to kidnap the high general's grandson?

Everyone. Every Royal House in Quur had such a motive.

The Devors Monastery wasn't safe. This place was, in fact, the opposite of safe. If one monk could be bribed, any of them might have been. She was in far greater danger here than she was back in the Capital. But a tiny worm of doubt threaded itself into the back of her mind. What if that wasn't true?

It didn't matter. She couldn't leave. She needed information only the library here could provide. So Kalindra smiled as Nikali made knots in her hair. "Thank you, Wixan. You're too kind."

38: The Toppling Cards

Kalindra's reaction
The Lighthouse at Shadrag Gor
Just after Kalindra's memory of meeting the abbess

"–we've made some progress, but not nearly enough," Thurvishar finished.

Kalindra made a face and pushed down her profound and very real desire to retch. She'd so hoped that maybe Vol Karoth had forgotten about her, would just skip going over those memories, but that had always been a fool's desire.

"Kalindra?" Xivan's stare was far too perceptive. She'd been watching Kalindra carefully.

Waiting for her to break.

But no sooner had Kalindra thought that than she mentally corrected herself. She knew better. She really did. Xivan seemed genuinely concerned. Kalindra could tell herself that it was for pragmatic reasons–any weakness in one of them could be exploited against all of them–but no one was making Xivan give a damn about her. She'd decided to do that all on her own.

"No," Kalindra said to her. "I'm not okay."

Xivan just nodded, her expression perfectly stern. Not judging or approving. Just . . . acknowledging.

It wasn't so unreasonable, after all, that Kalindra wouldn't be fine at all.

Then Kalindra noticed the silence. She looked up to see that no one was talking, and they were so pointedly not staring at her that it was painfully obvious they were attempting not to be rude.

"Your son's adorable," Talea said.

Kalindra's response was automatic, but Nikali was the one subject she never tired of discussing. Her little boy. "He really is."

"He has your smile," the woman added.

Kalindra felt the sticky, sick twist of her gut at what was supposed to be a compliment. She sniffed. "He's has Jarith's smile."

"If you say so," Talea agreed pleasantly.

Kalindra looked away. As she did, she saw a length of shadow in the kitchen detach itself from the wall and cross the room, like someone moving just beyond the light's edge.

But of course, she could see everyone present.

Kalindra inhaled and rubbed her eyes. She didn't ask if the others had seen anything. None of them had been looking in the right direction. And Kalindra knew she wasn't just seeing things.

"We'll take a small break," Thurvishar suggested. "Then start again. It is working, just . . . slowly."

Kalindra knew she wasn't the only person wondering if they would run out of time first.

Kihrin's story
Inside Vol Karoth's prison

Janel and Teraeth staggered as we emerged from the gray area yet again. It had been the most promising one yet: a re-creation of a barracks S'arric had lived in on Nythrawl, early in his career. He . . . I . . . had often referred to it as "my prison" when sending messages to Rev'arric.

"I really wish Thurvishar were here," Janel said, leaning against a wall and spitting to clear the taste of vomit from her mouth. "He could have warned us what sort of 'emotional connection' this had for Vol Karoth."

"What was that?" Teraeth asked, wiping his own mouth on the back of his sleeve.

"It's called hunko," I explained. "It's a sort of fermented worm paste mixed with sour apples, overripe bananas, and ipecacuanha roots, and I told you not to drink it."[1]

"Why was it even there?" Teraeth asked.

"It's a thing they use to haze new recruits," I said, shaking my head.

"I can still taste it," Janel whined. "Oh gods, that's never going away."

"It does," I said. Then I grinned an evil grin as I finished with, "In about an hour. Or two."

"Two hours? Kill me now," Teraeth said. "Fuck it. Vol Karoth's right; any species who would do that to a person doesn't deserve to live."

"Hey, not funny," I said, frowning.

He held a finger and thumb less than a quarter inch apart.

I shook my head. "No."

He shrugged, coughed, spat. "Fine," he said, some strength returning to his voice. I knew it was bravado, but I appreciated the effort. "And that emotion was . . . ?"

"Humiliation," I said. "In the real world, I'm pretty sure I was the one forced to drink that cup." I was equally sure that hadn't been the worst of it by a long shot, which made me grateful that we hadn't seen any of that. But it also made me nervous, because why *hadn't* we seen any of that?

"What I want to know is, how did they make it smell so good?" Janel asked.

"Illusions," I replied with a shrug. "Why does vané food taste good?"

"Hey now," Teraeth protested.

"Excuse me," I corrected myself. "Why does *Kirpis* vané food taste good?"

Teraeth closed his mouth and shrugged. "Fair," he said.

"Are we sure finding Talon is worth this much effort?" Janel asked.

---

[1] I believe that is a combination *guaranteed* to induce vomiting. Which has some uses medicinally, but hell, that sounds foul.

"Yes," I said. "One, we don't leave anyone behind." She looked unconvinced, so I continued, "And two, if we find her, then we get Thurvishar back."

"Fine, I'm sold. Shall we continue?" Janel said, straightening from the wall and marching with determination and purpose in an entirely random direction.

Talea's memory
Out at sea
Ten days after the Battle of the Well of Spirals

Talea's luck ran out when it came time to find a ship to Zherias. She wouldn't have thought it difficult–the Capital City was a major harbor, *the* major harbor, really, for the entire empire. But the first three ships she approached either wouldn't take her or seemed too eager to take her, with such a leer on the captain's face that she wouldn't have stepped on their ships for any price. The fourth ship said they had room, but it meant she'd be leaving on the evening tide, rather than the morning's–most of a day wasted.

Most merchant ships leaving Quur did so with reasonably light cargoes, since the main trade routes ran to Quur rather than away from it. The currents did no one any favors in this regard, so there was an advantage to running high when leaving the city, in order to shave as much time as possible off the voyage. This ship actually carried a cargo, which was the whole reason it hadn't been one of her top choices.

A cargo meant the ship would be slower. But it seemed it was either that or not go at all. And on the plus side, it had given her the time to do that shopping she had wanted, even if it was only a small stop to pick up a backpack and several new sets of clothes, all light enough and thin enough to help with the tropical weather, which would be even worse in Zherias than it was in the Capital. It all seemed frightfully thin and underdressed. She never thought she'd miss the cold.

The ship itself was best described as homely, but as Talea had never been on a ship before, she didn't really have much to measure it against. The captain had flirted, but not to an extent that made her think she'd be knocked upside the head and sold into slavery the first night she fell asleep. She even had a room with a lock.

She tried, as much as possible, not to think about Xivan. She also failed. Which meant she spent the first couple days on the forecastle of the ship, staring out at the water, brooding.

After a while, she noticed the little girl was there too, mimicking her head on her hand as she stared out at the sea. It was difficult not to think she was being mocked.

Although it was also adorable, so there was that.

"Do you think people will start to gossip about the crazy lady who hears voices?" Talea whispered conversationally.

"Oh, they're not paying attention."

"That's not true."

"Staring at your ass doesn't count."

Talea covered her face with a hand and growled through the fingers. "Am I doing the right thing?"

Silence.

"This is what you wanted me to do, isn't it? I have to assume you orchestrated that utterly ridiculous set of coincidences. Wasn't this the whole point?"

"I've told you my agenda," Eshi said. "And it's nothing malicious." The little girl hopped up on the railing, which would have made Talea nervous if it had been anyone but the imaginary ghost of a goddess. "I'll let you in on a secret," Eshi said. "Taja can't control fate."

Talea glared at her sideways. "Really? Then how did I end up in the same brothel where my sister was murdered? That was a low blow, by the way."

"I didn't do that," Eshi insisted. "Not directly."

Talea huffed.

"The D'Mons sold a property, and later, Galen D'Mon met a girl he felt understood him, so he married her. And Sheloran's mother bought him the velvet house, because she knew it would have sentimental value. After all, Lessoral D'Talus isn't just any old god-queen, is she?"

"No," Talea said. "She's not." As the God-Queen of Whores, Caless—Lessoral D'Talus—would have indeed been in a position to understand the Shattered Veil Club's "sentimental value." And the funny thing was, if anyone had asked Talea who she worshipped four years earlier, she'd have said Caless before Taja. How many offerings had she given to Caless over the years? How many times had she prayed for deliverance, for her and her sister? Caless hadn't answered those prayers.

But for that matter, neither had Taja.

"The only coincidence in all of that is what happened at the Octagon, and I will admit to shifting the odds a little there. But the rest? Merit staying at the Shattered Veil Club? How the club itself ended up in Galen's possession? None of that is coincidence. It's a string of tipped levers, with each trigger tripping the next in a very predictable fashion. It's not truly random at all. I mean, can you imagine if Taja truly controlled fate? Oh, Relos Var would never stand a chance."

Talea frowned at the blue waters of the sea, sparkling gem-bright and dazzling before her. "I thought that's what luck is."

"In part. And Taja was able to tip the odds, shift the probabilities, but she could never control how people reacted." The little girl shook a finger. "Which is something for you to remember. You can tip the odds of an event happening, but not how people react to the event itself. People have facets. We're complicated and shifting. Difficult to predict."

"Me?" Talea shook her head. "I'm not tipping anything."

"Just as well, really. It's not exactly reliable, although in some ways that's an advantage. I know that seems odd, but people always underestimate Taja. They think her powers are card tricks and rolls of the dice." She grinned. "Who pays attention to the pebble that makes the horse bolt? All they notice is the rider who gets thrown and cracks his skull."

Talea scoffed. "Perfect. I'm already used to everyone underestimating me."

"I would imagine so." Eshi traced her fingers over the ship's wooden railing. "I'll teach you a few tricks to help."

"Tricks?" Talea leaned out just to make sure she wasn't easily viewed by anyone who might be curious about the crazy lady talking to herself. "Spells?"

"Sort of? You'll want to know how to do certain things, but we have to go slowly. I don't dare rush this faster than your body can handle." The little girl sighed. "Taja thought we'd have more time, I think, but she was always such an optimist. Yet here we are." Eshi put her little fingers on top of Talea's.

Talea closed her eyes.

"You should know that anything involving the ritual that created Vol Karoth is almost impossible to predict. So Vol Karoth himself? Any of the dragons, including Relos Var? Blank spots. You have to understand, they are distortions—corruptions—creatures of pure chaos. Trying to see past an event that involves them is just . . . impossible. But!" The little girl grinned. "The very fact that you can't see past an event tells us something. It tells us that this is an event that involves dragons."

"Or Vol Karoth?"

"Right. Or Vol Karoth," Eshi said.

Talea nodded and watched the sea. After a pause, she said, "I assume one of these events is coming up."

Eshi laughed. "Yes, as a matter of fact! A kind of convergence, all pointing in the same direction, to a big, blank null. So you should be there."

"Wait. You don't think Relos Var will show up?"

"There's a chance," Eshi emphasized. "There's also a chance that Xaltorath may show up. Or Suless. Or both. Like I said, it's a nexus point. Anything could happen. And I think the odds of Xivan being involved are rather high."

"I don't want to see Xivan hurt," Talea said.

"Then I think you'll have to make a choice," Eshi said, "because saving Sheloran from Xivan and keeping Xivan from being hurt are not necessarily compatible goals. And then there's that other thing."

"What other thing?"

"What. Do. You. Want?" Eshi leaned against her shoulder. "Do you want Xivan to come to her senses and leave with you so you both can settle down somewhere in a lovely little cottage by a lake? Do you want to lead a fierce band of warrior women and carve a path through the empire? What do you want?"

Talea thought about it. "I don't want people to grow up the way I did," she finally said. A sailor passing by behind her gave her a strange look; she'd spoken too loud.

"I'm pretty sure Senera wants the same thing," Eshi said.[2]

"Yeah, but Senera believed Relos Var when he said he would fix everything." Talea slapped her hands against the wooden railing, pushed herself up until she was leaning on both wrists. "I'm not that naïve."[3]

---

[2] She's not wrong.
[3] Words cannot even begin to express how much exception I take to *Talea* calling me naïve. Even

Eshi giggled. "Oh, I'd love to see Senera's face when she learns you think she's naïve."

"Oh, it's not her fault." Talea shrugged. "Var told her that she was special. Who wouldn't be charmed by that? I would be." She squinted as she looked out toward the horizon. "Hmm. You know, I think there's another ship out there."

"It's the ocean," Eshi said. "That happens."

The sailor up in the crow's nest started raising the alarm.

Talea frowned at Eshi. "That happens, huh?"

Eshi grinned and raised both hands in a helpless gesture. "Oh yes."

A sailor came running up behind Talea. "You can fight, yes?"

Talea glared at the man. He took a step back, eyes wide.

"I mean–" He swallowed and pointed. "Pirate ship, headed this way. Anyone who can fight should. Especially a pretty lady like you."

"What if they like pretty boys better?"

The man laughed a little hysterically. "Thank Laaka I'm not one of those. They'll probably just kill me straight off."

Those were the last rational, sane words anyone said for some time. Sailors opened up closets and hauled out large, verdigrised statuary, setting up two of them on the deck facing the incoming ship. They moved with panicked haste, clearly not practiced at this, and regretting it more with every passing second.

Talea blinked at what she was looking at. They weren't shaped the same—someone had crafted them to look like fish instead of insects–but these were absolutely the same as Quuros scorpion war machines. She watched more sailors run in with casks they began loading while each man's driver picked up a control crystal.

"Fire when ready!" the captain ordered.

Talea could see right away that a scorpion engine (fish engine?) was not exactly an ideal siege weapon for use when at sea. The beam of light that marked the impact point for the engine's firing arc kept skipping about as the ship heaved on the waves, while the other ship moved counterpoint. They'd be lucky if they managed to hit the ocean with the way the deck was pitching under them.

Talea checked her sword and hoped the pirate ship wasn't armed with similar equipment.

The war machines were nearly silent as they fired, just the shouting of the men and the whistling noise they made as casks sailed through the air. Talea watched the small casks fly out–and vanish just before two large booms echoed.

For a second, it seemed like no one dared even breathe. Then the captain was shouting again. "It's a trick! Raise fog! Raise fog right now!"

Talea was sure he hadn't actually needed to shout. The ship's mage was standing right next to him.

---

more infuriating: that she was right.

Talea heard whistling.

There was nothing to dodge. No way to know when to dodge or where to go. And she didn't see exactly when the pirate ship's return fire hit, just saw the explosion and the rapidly expanding flame. Then the fogbank swept over the ship like a mother covering her child with a blanket. Talea could barely see the end of her arm. The captain gave more orders. Presumably something to the effect of "Go forward, as fast as you can, and take us out of here."

Or at least, that's what should have happened.

A loud splash carried, followed by a shudder that swept through the entire ship as it began to list to the side.

"What's going on?" the captain cried out. "Why are we turning?"

"Something's caught on the rudder chain, sir! I can't . . . I can't stop it!"

"Cap'n! The anchor's been dropped!"

The sound of movement, of creaking ropes and groaning wood, reached Talea's ears. She had no idea how far away that sort of noise could carry over the waves. It seemed close, however. It seemed to grow closer with every passing second.

More booms sounded, and an angry shout. Someone cried out, "I said wait!"

Talea unsheathed her sword.

"Get rid of the fog! Get rid of it!" The captain apparently had already decided that was a bad tactical decision. Talea was inclined to agree. If her ship had the services of a mage, well, apparently the pirates did too.

And something more.

As the fog began to clear, Talea looked down at the deck to see a wet footprint. She had that much warning before someone large and angry rushed her with a harpoon. She let momentum and the assumption that he'd caught his prey by surprise carry him too far forward, then she sliced down and around one of his wrists. He had fins and webbed fingers. His skin looked gray and thick, less like human skin than something appropriate to a shark's.

He screamed like a man, though.

Sadly, he wasn't alone. The sounds of shouting people, the clash of metal hitting kind or wood or flesh, was all too familiar even before the last of the fog lifted. The pirate ship was still closing, but these attackers had swum over and climbed the hull.

The human pirates began swinging over while Talea was still preoccupied with the advance party. She didn't like anything about her odds in this situation—that first wave had been smart enough to concentrate on the sailors manning the scorpion engines. That left only the ship's mage and the hope that the other side would be reluctant to use any weapons that might damage the cargo they'd come to steal.

The captain cried out, "Weapons down! We surrender!"

Talea looked over to see that a pirate had a sword to the man's throat. At least a dozen knives floated in midair around the ship's mage as well, with the clear understanding that he'd be skewered if he so much as flinched. The sound of groaning, injured men echoed on the water, punctuated with the sharp scissor sounds of the few men who hadn't felt like following orders or hadn't heard in time.

Silence, then the sound of weapons being dropped to the ground.

"Sword down, little girl," one of the pirates told her. "Your mother said playtime is over."

"Come try to take it," Talea said with a smile, "and we'll see how much you like my toys."

A large Zheriasian man with his hair in braids crossed over from the other ship, taking his time and clearly enjoying himself. He had a cutlass resting on his shoulder insouciantly. "Well. I have to say this is the easiest I've ever taken a ship. Nicely done." His gaze fell on Talea. "But there's always the one person who has to go and spoil things. And that would be you, wouldn't it?"

"Perhaps if you guaranteed her safety, she might be more willing to stop fighting?" The woman who'd asked the question was not Zheriasian, nor did she even especially look like a pirate. She looked like a courtesan of some sort, used to wearing fine things, not at all used to physical labor.

"I can't imagine why I would think I might not be safe with pirates," Talea said.

"Talea? Light! Talea, is that you?" Qown asked.

Half the ship, Talea included, must have stopped to turn and stare at the man who peeked his head out from behind the ship's captain. He was pretty, with extremely long black hair and soulful brown eyes. Since Galen showed up to the meeting with his aunts with blue eyes, I have to assume they switched back to their natural eye colors before that meeting.

She stared at him for several seconds before she realized she did in fact recognize him.

"Qown? What–? You have hair!"

The pirates all looked nonplussed. The man whom Qown had apparently been hiding behind twisted. "What? You know her?"

"Uh, yes!" Qown came out of hiding and motioned for Talea to put down her sword. "It's all right. Talea's a friend. Talea, you're safe."

She didn't lower her sword. Instead, she looked at the pirate captain. "Well?" she asked him. "Am I safe?"

He pondered her. "Don't hurt any more of my men and we'll talk."

Meanwhile, Qown had rushed over to one of the fallen sea folk. Talea didn't know if he was already dead or not. She hoped not, simply because it would make negotiations easier if she hadn't killed any of the pirates. But she hadn't been trying to keep them alive either. It could go any number of ways.

Talea cleaned off the edge of her sword and tipped the blade back into its scabbard. The pirate gave the weapon an appreciative look.

The merchant ship's captain was being tied up, along with the ship's mage, while most of the sailors were being herded into some of the smaller rooms in the back of the ship. They seemed rather surprised to find they weren't being tossed overboard.

The man who had been holding a sword to the captain's throat sheathed his weapon and came over. Even before he'd walked close, something about him had raised Talea's hackles. She wasn't quite sure what it was. He was handsome enough, tall and trim and with a carriage that spoke of quick reflexes and a better-than-average familiarity with a blade. Then she saw the sunlight glitter off eyes bluer than the sea and knew why she'd felt the urge to go for her sword again.

Because this *had* to be Darzin D'Mon's son Galen.

He'd grown since she'd last seen him, but it had never been close up. Thurvishar's book had made him seem like a timid rabbit, and this man was every bit the hawk she'd have expected from a D'Mon, all laughing grin, flushed with success. That grin only slipped when he glanced down at the deck and saw the blood.

"So this is my friend—"

"Perhaps introductions can wait for later," Galen D'Mon told Qown.

Talea snorted. He wasn't as stupid as he looked. "That sounds like a wise idea."

"Well!" The pirate captain clapped Galen and Qown on the shoulders. "That went very well. I'll keep my end of the bargain. Are you sure I can't persuade you to stay on? Or maybe just your wife?" He grinned.

Galen laughed.

"I'm right here," said the woman Talea had taken for a courtesan.

Wait a minute.

Talea gave her another look. She had to squint to see the resemblance to Caless, but it was there. Maybe, if nothing else, it shone through in an undeniably sensual beauty. Sheloran was hiding behind an open fan, which had the net effect of drawing attention down to her small waist, her voluptuous figure. Talea was amused to note she'd been warped enough from her time spent training with the Spurned that the first thing she thought was a dismissive "But it doesn't look like she can even use a sword."

Which reminded her of Xivan. She scowled and looked away.

"So what do you say?" The captain propositioned Sheloran. "Stay on with me? I promise it'll never be boring . . ."

"Oh, trust me. My life's never boring now." She gave Talea a thoughtful look, an unvoiced question in her eyes.

The pirate captain said, "Fine, the girl can stay, but it's on your heads to make sure she behaves herself. I'm not a passenger ship, despite what it's seemed like lately." He stalked off, probably to search rooms for the captain's strongbox.

"How can you be sure they're not going to kill everyone here the moment your back's turned?" Talea asked Galen D'Mon.

The prince sighed. "I'm not. But what would be the point of it? They'll get their cargo, and they mostly got it without a fuss. Plus, he kept his word so far and kept it when he didn't have to. Frankly, after seeing what we can do, I'd like to think the captain's not stupid enough to make us angry."

Talea chewed on her lip. "I suppose I don't have a choice. So, um . . ."

"Yes?" Galen gazed at her with evident amusement.

"Where are we going?" Talea asked. "Zherias?"

"Not exactly," Galen said.

Sheloran laughed. "What my darling husband means to say is we have no idea."

39: The Prince in Hiding

Kihrin's story
Inside Vol Karoth's prison
An indeterminate time after Galen's collapse

[Everyone, Vol Karoth's taken Galen.] Thurvishar's voice came through as if heard from a long way away. I didn't have the sense that he'd be able to hear any of us if we said something back. This had been a one-shot, a message tied to a brick and thrown over the wall. He'd have no way to know if we'd received it.

"Yeah." I sighed. "Figured that might be the case when we found this."

We were staring at the Court of Princes in the Blue Palace. Needless to say, it hadn't been difficult to figure out this wasn't a spot that had any place existing in Vol Karoth's mental architecture. I'd been hoping that the Blue Palace had appeared because it was emotionally important to me, but Thurvishar's warning suggested a different reason.

I was a little concerned, though. We hadn't seen any vision of Galen. No sign that he had been taken, the way we'd seen for everyone else. And if I was really feeling paranoid . . .

If I was really feeling paranoid, then I had to admit that I had no way to know if that was really Thurvishar's voice I'd heard. It seemed awfully convenient that we'd hear that just as we happened to all but trip over the spot where we were most likely to find Galen.

"Vol Karoth didn't brag about this," Janel mused. "Why wouldn't he have bragged?"

"I don't like it," Teraeth said.

"Nothing for it," I finally said. "Let's go take a look around."

Which we did. We quickly found Galen. He was in the middle of the main hall, sitting among a pile of bodies—everyone who had died that day in the Capital, either at the hands of Gadrith or Khaeriel. Sheloran's body, his sisters' bodies, all his uncles—including me.

Belatedly, I realized that one of the bodies off to the side was Darzin's. Someone had gone after him with a large cleaver or ax of some kind, so it was difficult to recognize what was left of him. I wouldn't have been able to do it except for his hair and the richness of his clothing.

Galen was holding my body in his arms and wailing.

"Shit," I muttered. "Galen? Galen, come on. None of this is real. Wake up."

Galen didn't seem to hear me.

"We haven't had a great record of success at this so far," Teraeth pointed out. "Any ideas?"

Janel just shook her head, looking concerned.

I touched Galen's shoulder. When he didn't react, I tried to pry the dead body away from him. "This isn't me, Galen. Look, I'm right here."

He didn't pay any attention.

I tried again.

That time, I managed to pull the body away. "Galen, please look at me." I took a deep breath. "Galen, I'm sorry. I really didn't mean to leave you behind. That wasn't my intention at all. Please believe—"

Galen pulled a dagger from his belt and slashed it across his throat.

"No!" I screamed and grabbed him. He'd cut deep. Blood fountained out of the wound. I tried healing him, but even as I did, I could tell right away that I was going to fail; he was fighting me.

Galen wanted to die.

I was left gasping, with Galen's corpse in my arms, the light faded from his eyes. What—? No. This couldn't—

"Get away from that bullshit, Kihrin," Teraeth snapped. "That's not real."

"He—" I blinked at her. "He killed himself."

"Did he, though?" Janel was staring at the body.

Teraeth stalked over to my position and grabbed my face. "Listen to me. I know what this is like. I know what it feels like to think everything is so hopeless and dark that oblivion seems like a mercy. And I also know Vol Karoth is a dirty fucking liar. So if you want to bet metal on which option is more likely, bet on this isn't real." He pointed around us. "You've been seeing the same visions I have, and your nephew might have his issues, but quite frankly, he was dealing with them a whole lot better than I was. Than any of us, for that matter. That kid is a survivor, and anyone who can claw his way out from under Darzin D'Mon's grip isn't going to turn around and take his own life like this."

I gave him a hard look. "They might. Don't presume to know someone else's pain, Teraeth."

He exhaled. "No. No, I don't. But I still know this isn't real."

"How? How do you know that?" I started shouting. "You have no idea—"

"That isn't Galen. I know that isn't Galen because Vol Karoth isn't here gloating," Teraeth said calmly. "He would be."

I stopped. More than anything else Teraeth had said, that made me pause. Because yes, Vol Karoth absolutely would be there to gloat if Galen had taken his own life. He'd be there to remind me that he didn't need to hurt the people I loved if they were going to do all the work themselves.

Janel put her hand on my arm. "Teraeth's right. We should listen to him."

Teraeth raised an eyebrow at her and smiled. "You have to warn someone if you're going to keep sweet-talking them like this. I could get ideas."

"Remember that," Janel said. "We still might find that bed."

Galen's prison
After going to sleep in the Lighthouse at Shadrag Gor
Just after Qown's vision

Galen woke in the dark to the feeling of having a pillow shoved into his face, of being smothered.

"Fucking pretty boy thinks he's so special," someone hissed. There was more than one pair of hands holding him down, keeping him from struggling.

"Tie him up! Don't let him get away!"

Something slammed into his stomach, forcing the air out of his lungs. He thought it might have been a knee. The pillow came away, just for a second; he gulped air.

"Let's see your mommy save you now, huh?"[1] That was followed by a sharp, stinging pain in his jaw as someone hit him.

"No time for that! Get the bag over his head. Come on, come on!"

He was being carried somewhere. He struggled, but there were at least five of them, all decently strong. He didn't have a chance. He tried screaming, but that just earned him a piece of cloth crammed into his mouth, which, from the smell, was apparently a dirty sock.

"Hurry! Hurry!" More shouting, and then he was thrown down on the ground. They started kicking him. There wasn't much he could do other than try to brace for it. His hands and feet were still bound.

"Fucking asshole," someone said to him. "Teach you to snitch on us again. Just remember it can get a lot worse."

More cursing. More names. Not one of them was a voice Galen recognized.

Galen heard a strange noise he couldn't identify then, just before something warm and wet began splashing over him.

Someone was pissing on him.

Galen turned his face away from it, but at least the kicking had stopped—no one wanted urine on their legs. After a moment, the flow stopped. Someone spit on him. Then the footsteps faded.

The door slammed shut.

He was left alone.

Galen pulled at the cloth around his wrists. They hadn't tied him very well. He was free in a few seconds, then pulled the bag off his head. It was a pillowcase. Fortunately, it had absorbed the worst of the urine. He tossed it in a corner, far away from him.

The lights were out. Galen rolled over on his back and stared up at the ceiling. It was covered in a strange white tile with an embossed design he didn't recognize. He wouldn't have considered it attractive, although maybe that was just a cultural preference. The room was small—probably meant to be some sort of supply closet. It was astonishingly clean. Almost certainly not meant to hold prisoners. But with the darkened room and the small spaces pressing in, it would have been terrifying . . .

---

[1] Based on other comments, and this one, I am increasingly under the impression that S'arric and Rev'arric's mother was herself someone "important"—but have no more information than that.

For someone else.

Galen propped himself up on his elbows and began laughing.

"Is that all you've got?" he said out loud. "I have to say, I don't feel like you're really giving this your full effort here. No forced sex acts? What about my father showing up to beat me? My mother? Honestly, I'm giving you so much to work with, and this is all you can come up with? Disappointing!" He untied his feet and stood. Then he grabbed a giant white bottle of something from one of the lower shelves and threw it hard against the door. He didn't expect it to do much.

The entire wall shattered.

It was like watching a mirror crack slowly, the sharp shards of glass careening through the air a half inch at a time. And beyond was . . . someplace else. Not any of the rooms he had seen before but someplace he didn't recognize. He was in the middle of an impossibly long hallway that ran in front and behind, a cold and undecorated place whose purpose seemed unfathomable. Ahead of him in the hallway, a black silhouette phased through the wall and stood there. Galen had the sense that it had turned to look at him, but he couldn't make out any features, any details. It was just that black cutout shape.

He recognized the descriptions, though. Vol Karoth.

So Galen ran.

He stopped running when he was panting and out of breath, his sides a burning ache. He leaned against a withered old tree that was valiantly trying to sprout a few green buds. Where was he? Galen didn't recognize any of the architecture, the streets, any surroundings. It seemed like an abandoned city, but he had no idea where he was.

He'd seen Vol Karoth, so he could make certain guesses. Galen even had a fairly good idea what he was doing there, although that was also an unpleasant reminder. He didn't really want to think about Qown just then, especially if that was the sort of thing Vol Karoth might be able to home in on.

Maybe Galen could find Kihrin, though.

He started walking this time, noticing the empty streets, the faint but present stirrings of life in the weeds and old, not-quite-dead trees lining the streets, the straggling flowers and ivy creeping up walls and sprouting from abandoned window boxes. The city must have been beautiful in its heyday.

Galen was crossing the street when he stopped, blinked, and walked backward until he could look down the road he'd just passed. He took a minute and studied the scene in front of him.

What Galen saw was a small section of fence that opened up on to a park, across the street from a walled building with a single door. Galen recognized the door: it didn't belong there.

It was the door to the Culling Fields.

Galen sucked on his teeth for a moment. Yes, that was definitely the door to the Culling Fields, and it definitely didn't belong. That seemed like a fantastic place to look for Kihrin.

He approached the door but immediately ran into a problem. There was no handle on the door. No way to open it at all. He tried pushing. Nothing. Galen had no way to pull against it.

He heard noises behind him.

Galen turned. Something moved in the park across the way. He waited and saw a flash of color. It was a person, someone he didn't recognize. Another person joined them. This rapidly turned into a large crowd of people dressed in Quuros-style clothing of all colors and types, pushing and shoving against each other while they jostled to see what was going on. It felt a bit like a large crowd gathering to watch a street brawl.

Which . . . okay. That was a good place to start. Galen walked across the street and began his own shoving match to see what all the fuss was about. Then he nearly tripped. A body lay on the ground, which people largely ignored. The crowd shifted around the dead man's body as if he were a log fallen off the back of a cart in the middle of the road. They also ignored the living woman on her knees next to him. She looked just a little older than his own age. She held her hands to her neck, sobbing. It wasn't Kihrin or Janel or anyone else he'd expected to run across after being swept up into Vol Karoth's mindscape.

Still, Galen recognized her.

Because it was Lyrilyn, better known as Talon.[2]

Talea's reaction
The Lighthouse at Shadrag Gor
After Talea's memory of being attacked by pirates

Senera narrowed her eyes at Talea when the vision ended. "You don't think Eshi was messing with probability? After that?"

"Oh no," Talea said, "I think she was. Is. I mean, that coincidence seems a bit much for anyone, don't you think? But since it's all working in my favor, I don't feel like complaining."

"Thurvishar," Sheloran said. "If we're going to keep telling the story of what happened next, I should point out that Talea was here for all of it."

Thurvishar squinted. "Meaning?"

"Meaning," Qown said, "that you don't need us. Sheloran and I could go find Galen. Let us at least tell everyone else that he's missing. They don't know!"

"I tried to pass along a message to them," Thurvishar said. "It may have worked."

"So allow us to make sure," Sheloran said.

Most of the others seemed to have no strong opinion on this, although everyone was frowning because lately—well, everyone had been frowning.

"Let them," Talea told Thurvishar. "It might help."

Thurvishar scowled and studied the ceiling for a moment. "Fine," he finally said.

Qown also stood. "Should we, uh . . . What should we—?"

Senera rolled her eyes. "The two of you go upstairs and lie down on a bed. It'll be easier that way. We'll escort you and come back down after."

---

[2] Talon did take her form as Lyrilyn earlier in the Lighthouse, so that's likely why Galen was able to recognize her.

"Yes, naturally," Sheloran said before adding, "Are you going to do it or shall Thurvishar?"

Senera narrowed her eyes. "I can't."

Sheloran fanned herself slowly. "Oh. That's right."

Thurvishar frowned at the two women. "Am I missing something?"[3]

"No," Senera said. "You aren't." The look on her face suggested that was absolutely a lie.

Talea frowned as well. What was going on?

Sheloran smiled, waving her fan idly. "I just feel I should remind you–"

"You really don't need to say anything," Senera said.

Sheloran smiled. "This is a place where secrets play to Vol Karoth's strengths. They will be used against you." Her gaze slipped to Xivan, to Kalindra, before landing once more on Senera. "Perhaps you might feel more comfortable discussing such matters in a smaller crowd."

"There's nothing to discuss," Senera said.

"Sheloran, we should go–" Qown said.

Sheloran nodded. "As you say, Qown." She still stared at Senera for a moment longer, though, until she finally nodded to herself, tucked the fan away, and elegantly walked upstairs as though she were about to attend a party.

"I'll go with them," Talea volunteered, touching Xivan's shoulder as she passed. Xivan touched her fingers as she went with a hand that was shockingly warm. At least for Xivan.

They arrived upstairs without incident, although at the door to the sleeping area, Sheloran turned to Thurvishar.

"I'm frankly surprised that you're putting up with her denial about this."

Thurvishar shook his head. "I know you mean well, but please let it be. There's such a thing as pushing someone too quickly and before they're ready."

Sheloran looked chastised. "I'm sorry. Of course, you're right. I wasn't thinking. She comes off as rather unbreakable."

Qown blinked. "What are you two talking about?"

"Nothing," Thurvishar said quickly. He gestured for the two to lie down in one of the bedrooms. "Just lie down and close your eyes. It will feel a bit like falling asleep."

Talea wasn't sure if Thurvishar succeeded in linking them with the mindscape or not. Before she had any chance at all the confirm matters, the world changed.

[3] Evidently not.

40: A Ruthless Focus

Kalindra's memories
One month after arriving on Devors

If the monks at the Devors Monastery ever contacted the high general to let him know that someone had tried to assassinate the man's daughter-in-law and kidnap his grandson, Kalindra never heard about it. She pretended at brightness and innocence, or at least the humble dedication of the grieving widow. She found herself ignored except for the occasional lapse best described as "small toddler in a library." But mostly, Nikali behaved himself and left her to read.

There were a truly astonishing number of books dedicated to the Devoran Prophecies, and under the best of circumstances, they existed in a constant state of scholarship, rearrangement, and analysis. In times like these? With demons on the loose and the very events the prophecies seemed most concerned with finally coming to pass? The library was full to capacity with scholars, including at least two Voices.

The library itself claimed to be the largest in the whole world, and while just on principle Kalindra doubted that was true, it was impressive enough to make such a claim plausible. The building was three stories high, each floor equal to two stories in any other building. All of it the most beautiful glowing white marble, veined with gold. It was all pillars and tall shelves and soft, quiet areas filled with tables and couches where one might read undisturbed. No fire was allowed inside the building–not that fire was prohibited, but that some magic simply made lighting a fire impossible–and the air smelled of old books and ink.

She hadn't a clue in all the seas where to start looking.

Since everyone was reading, it was no particular obstacle to include herself in that number. In theory, she should have had advantages the others didn't. For example, being able to definitively recognize certain passages that had already come to pass, as well as pinpointing exactly how. That should have made it relatively easy.

If there just weren't so damn many books. She'd been looking for weeks, and still found nothing.

Then one day, while sitting on one of the cushioned couches, Nikali playing in her lap, Kalindra overheard something interesting. She'd been listening to the steady drone of scribes arguing the merits and origins of the prophecies. Did they mean anything? Were they predictions? The age-old prescriptive versus descriptive debate was alive and well here, with several of them arguing the prophecies were recipes and completely alterable, while others thought they described inviolate events.

"Bah!" a querulous voice protested. "Idiots, the lot of you. They're none of that. They're not prophecies at all. They're histories." Something hard, possibly a cane, tapped angrily against the tile floors.

A chorus of groans met this pronouncement. "Master Linyuwan, not this again!" someone much younger complained.

"Histories," the first man, Linyuwan, repeated. "Histories of what have come before! Time is not what you lot think it is. I've memorized every prophecy. Every single one! I know what they really are." A Devoran sect known as the Preservers once existed who used to attempt this very thing, although they typically divided the prophecies into sections rather than for any single person to attempt to memorize the entire collection.

More complaints. Nervous laughter.

Kalindra didn't care much about the old monk's statement on the true nature of the prophecies, but she was exceedingly interested in his claim to have memorized all of them. That might be the break she needed.[1]

So after the group broke up and the younger scholars retreated to their respective cells, she set Nikali on her hip and followed Linyuwan. He evidently had a room in the library itself–proof of his seniority.

Just as she was about to knock on the doorway, he said, "Come in, Kalindra."

As "wise old seer" tactics went, that one was effective, even if it was logical that he would know who she was.

She walked inside.

The office was a scrambled mess of messages and writing pinned to walls, or in several cases, written directly on to the plaster. And much of it did indeed seem to discuss the prophecies.

"You're not safe here, you know," Linyuwan said. Then he looked up from his papers. "Do you want something to drink? I have brandy and ginger wine." He pursed his lips at a pile of bottles in a corner. "At least, I had ginger wine. Might be out now."

"Uh, I just wanted to, uh–" She collected herself and repositioned a squirmy Nikali, who'd spotted the beautifully carved dragon inkstone on the monk's desk with a determined hunger. "I was going to ask you about some prophecies, but what was that about not being safe?"

"Close the door behind you and have a seat."

She did. The monk piled a mass of scrolls to the side, then wiped ink-stained fingers on his robes. "Ah, sorry, sorry," he said. "Place is a bit of a mess." He gave her a keen look. "Of course you're not safe. There's a whole gaggle of monks here who want to kill you. Idiots."

She blinked. Kalindra had been operating under the assumption that it was the Royal Houses that were trying something and bribing the right monks for access. This implied . . .

"Why . . . why would monks want to kill me?"

---

[1] I, too, think Linyuwan may be helpful in the future. Assuming he survived, we should find him again.

It really wouldn't do to forget that this man might just be lost in fantasies, considering his previous statements about the prophecies really being "histories."

Nor would it do for her to lower her guard.

"Hmm," he said, making a face. "You spend centuries collecting every scrap you can find that talks about the End Times. Not you you. Us you. We've spent centuries doing that. How long do you think it takes before some of us decide that maybe it's possible to change things? To stop the impending catastrophe?" He sighed. "If only it worked that way. Those idiots just don't understand."

She was starting to feel distinctly uneasy. "What don't they understand?"

"There's a pattern," Linyuwan explained, pointing to rows and rows of quatrains tacked up on the walls in messy columns. "Spent my whole life studying it, trying to piece together the connections, until finally I did: each loop, he leaves notes to himself for the next time."

"He? Who's he?" Kalindra asked.[2] Nikali started to grow antsy, so Kalindra pulled one of his favorite toys out of her agolé and gave it to him.

"Not sure," the old man muttered, "but that's not important. Someone's doing it. It's not what will happen. It's what *has* happened." He taped a stack of papers to the side. "And you, Daughter of Death, have been a very naughty girl in some of these previous cycles. Pretty easy, I think, to look at all this and think, Might be best for everyone to just kill her now and get her out of the way before she marries her demon husband and starts killing gods."[3] Linyuwan shook his head, tsking.

Kalindra's throat felt dry. She had known the prophecies hinted at things that might reference her. Mother had never denied it. But Mother had always made it sound like those were slight, unimportant references, easily overlooked and not at all certain. Nothing like . . .

Demon husband? Really?

She clenched the fist she wasn't holding Nikali with and let herself be grounded by the sharp bite of nails digging into her skin.

"I–" She cleared her throat. "I'm only staying as long as it takes to find out a piece of information. I'm trying to locate a Cornerstone called Grimward. I thought the prophecies–or histories–might hold a clue." She kissed the top of Nikali's forehead. "No, you can't have that, dear."

He sighed and chewed the ear of his toy elephant.

"Hmm. Grimward, Grimward, Grimward . . ." The old monk stood from his desk and walked over to one of the columns of paper, searching for a few seconds before he plucked a half dozen little stanzas off the wall. "Here we go. Any of these help?"

She scanned the list. She started to say no, then she noticed the last one.

> The stone of death
> Will chain the lash

---

[2] That would be Xaltorath.

[3] What are the odds, I wonder, that in a universe where Janel and Kihrin hadn't existed–or at least hadn't existed as the reincarnations of Elana/C'indrol and S'arric–that Relos Var would have tried to turn Kalindra? Fairly high, I'd wager.

Of favored daughters
And the wide, haunted sea[4]

Kalindra pressed a hand over the passage. Linyuwan had put a notation in the marginalia suggesting the passage might be referring to the Cornerstone Grimward, as well as a note that the normal (and apparently "ridiculous") interpretation of the passage assumed it spoke in metaphor.

Like Linyuwan, Kalindra did not assume it was metaphor.[5]

Kalindra chewed on her lip. She had led a life that might charitably be called "interesting" and done things that she had hoped never to reveal to her husband, Jarith. Not all those sins could be laid before the doors of the Black Brotherhood. In her youth, for example, fresh from her own escape as a slave, she had taken a fellow escaped slave named Kohi Luzaka as a lover, and together they had plotted vengeance on all the spoiled, rich bastards who had ever profited off putting one human in chains for the pleasure of another. Later, Luzaka and Kalindra had parted ways, as lovers sometimes do. He'd become too violent, too unstable. A cult of assassins had seemed like a less violent choice.

A few years later, she'd heard he'd taken to calling himself the Lash.

Kalindra leaned back and stretched. If the Lash had Grimward . . .

She set Nikali down for just long enough to stand and then picked up her son. "Thank you," she told the old man. "But I'm afraid none of that seemed familiar."

He snorted, and she knew that he didn't believe her even a little. Still, he didn't press, for which she was grateful.

She made her farewells and hurried to pack.

The next day, Kalindra went down to the village, escorted by Wixan and several other monks he was quick to assert were most certainly not guards, even if they held swords no monks wore normally.

Kalindra looked out over the rolling green hills of the islands and found herself frowning.

"Yes, Lady Milligreest? Do you have a question?" Wixan smiled gently at her.

"I just—" She sighed. "It's a shame Quur never let anyone build a city here."

Wixan shrugged. "The currents here make that awkward."

She adjusted Nikali on her hip. "On the western side of the islands, of course, but not everywhere. And this would be so much closer to Zherias, to Doltar. Why not use the islands as more than just—" She scowled. "What do they use the islands for? According to your maps, there are a few villages here and that's it, but these islands could support so many more people than that."

Wixan made a moue. "Oh. I honestly hadn't considered that. I mean, I suppose it's probably just . . . I mean . . ." He seemed at a loss.

Kalindra looked back at him. "You know what it is, right? Someone didn't

[4] As every quatrain in the prophecies is a transcription of spoken word, homophones are rampant.
[5] Even worse in a case like this, where only in hindsight is it obvious that "the Lash" was meant to be a proper noun. Indeed, we're fortunate some well-meaning scholar didn't decide it was a typographic or pronunciation error, and correct it to "last."

want to give the islands to Khorvesh, and letting them be their own dominion would break that sacred 'eight' number we're so fond of. It would throw all the prophecies off."

He laughed. "Maybe so! I never really gave the matter any thought, to be honest."

Kalindra shook her head. "Never mind. Let's go find Aego."

Nikali clapped his hands together. "Aego!'"

"That's right, little cub. We're going to go play." She smiled at her son and used blowing kisses into his hair as an excuse to look at the fishing boats tied up in the small harbor. While most of the boats were too small to be any more than local fishers, meant to be taken out for an hour or two and then returned, the larger ones seemed capable of proper ocean voyages.

Manning one by herself would be difficult. Not impossible. Just difficult.

"You really didn't need to escort me yourself, you know," she told Wixan. "I'm sure your men are more than up to the task."

He nodded, the smile bright and warm on his lips. "I know that. But I know how it must seem here, with no familiar faces and with so much going on. After–" He paused and grimaced before forcing himself to continue, "After everything that's happened, I would feel terrible if anything bad were to occur. So this is really the least I can do."

Kalindra sighed. She liked Wixan.

"Of course," she said. "It's very kind of you." She let that be the last of their conversation while they finished the walk to the village, where all the locals looked at her and her soldiers with a kind of thoughtful wariness. It wasn't fear so much as the natural caution of a small village that had existed for years in a large shadow. Kalindra wondered if they even realized they were part of the empire, or what they thought about the idea.

Together, the group found Aego's small cottage and knocked on the door. There was an almost immediate squeal of delight as soon as the child opened the door, as Nikali wiggled out of Kalindra's arms to go run after his new best friend for all time. Really, Kalindra had been so pleased with how the boys had immediately gotten along. Nikali had a few friends at the duke's palace in Khorvesh too, but they had been nobility, and their keepers quick to point out that Nikali was not.[6] Aego probably didn't even know what nobility was. The boy's mother only cared that her son was happy, and that Kalindra was paying good metal to have her watch over Nikali.

"I'll be back in a few hours," Kalindra told her as she placed several coins on the table next to the door. "Thank you so much."

Wixan frowned slightly when Kalindra left. "I've never seen you leave him behind before. Do you want me to leave some of the guards?"

She paused. "Would you? I don't really want to leave him, it's just . . ." She paused and gave him a weak, watery smile. "One does occasionally need a bit of time to oneself. All the stress–honestly, I just wanted to go back to our room and have a long, hot bath."

---

[6] Seriously? The boy's a Milligreest. That's a more storied name than most Khorveshan nobles could even dream of having.

Wixan smiled. "Of course." He gestured for two of his guards to stay, and they peeled off and took up positions, one at the front of the cottage, one at the back.

She resisted the urge to lecture them on their work. As if any assassin worth their metal would be so foolish as to attack so obviously. They were really worse than useless.

But it meant two fewer guards, so she let them be.

As she started to walk back to the monastery, she paused. "Hmm. Would you mind if we took a slight detour? I would very much like to look out at the waves."

Wixan gestured for her to lead the way.

So she did, bringing the men along with her to a narrow, private little stretch of cliff overlooking ocean rocks, not quite up to the monastery's high vantage point but out of the view the valley and its village below.

Kalindra checked the basket she'd brought with her, wondering why Wixan hadn't asked about it. Maybe he assumed that she'd prepared to go on a picnic and had changed her mind. He'd have thought something very different if he'd seen the contents or felt how heavy they were, but when he'd offered, she'd pointed out that there was no sense in having guards if they were going to keep their hands too occupied to do any good.

As she reached into the basket, Kalindra heard the sound of a sword being drawn.

She looked up. All the men had unsheathed their weapons and were slowly starting to circle her, to draw close.

She met Wixan's gaze. "Why?"

His smile was kind. "I am sorry. You seem lovely. But you cannot be allowed to live."

Kalindra snorted. "You were in league with Oliyuan."

"I was detained," he mourned, "but don't worry; we'll make this fast."

She allowed the concern she felt to show. "What happens to my son?"

Wixan smiled. "I promise you that we have no issue with him."

She exhaled. He didn't seem to be lying. He had no reason to. "That is a comfort." Kalindra pulled her dagger from the basket as the men closed on her.

When she was finished, she collected her basket and Wixan's sword and made her way back down the hill, toward the village harbor. She resisted the urge to check in on the cottage, to see her son one last time before she left. She'd have to take Wixan's word that the guards meant her son no harm.

She had a boat to steal and an old lover to find.

Qown's story
Inside Vol Karoth's prison
After volunteering to find Galen

Sheloran and Qown appeared in the middle of a city street. The architecture was strange, and the road was paved with some unknown substance that resembled stone but seemed too elastic for that to be true. The city was even pleasant looking but had a neglected air about it, as though all its residents had simply set down their belongings and walked away one day.

Qown realized Sheloran was giving him a startled look.

"What's wrong?" he asked her.

She pointed to him.

Qown looked down at himself.

He looked the way he used the look, the way he'd look when he first arrived in Jorat. Which was to say, overweight.

It made sense, he supposed. He'd grown up plump, and the only reason that had stopped being the case was because he'd nearly starved himself to death while he lived in Yor. Whatever Caless had done to him had kept him slender, and he'd certainly been extremely active since then. But in his mind, in his heart, he always pictured himself as he'd been for most of his youth—an overweight boy who'd become an overweight man.

Qown felt himself blush. "Oh."

He supposed at least this would simplify the situation with Galen. There seemed little possibility the royal prince would have any interest in carrying on a relationship once he knew what Qown really looked like.[7]

Sheloran had a small, sad smile on her face. "This is how you see yourself? This isn't even what you looked like when we first met."

"This is what—" Qown shrugged. "I'm used to this. I'm sorry—"

"Why are you apologizing? This isn't anything to be ashamed of," Sheloran said. "If you're more comfortable this way, then that's how you should look."

"I don't know that I would say—" He trailed off. "It's not important."

Sheloran narrowed her eyes at him but didn't press the point. She waved down the street. "Let's head that way."

"Do we know where we're going?" Qown asked.

"Oh, not in the slightest," Sheloran admitted, a wide grin on her face. "But why should we let that stop us?"

Which is precisely when their friends attacked.

Kihrin came first, sword out, screaming at the top of his lungs as he lunged straight at Qown, who barely got out of the way. Janel was right behind him, her hands heated to molten levels, attempting to grab Sheloran. She caught the edge of the woman's agolé, which immediately fried to a crisp, flakes of ash floating away in the air.

"What are you doing?" Qown cried out.

But neither of them answered. They kept attacking.

Qown grabbed the back of Sheloran's raisigi and pulled her toward him, then made a cutting gesture with his hand.

In front of him, a wall tumbled into place, cutting them off from Kihrin and Janel's path.

"Run!" He grabbed Sheloran's hand to make sure she kept up.

"What? But you—!"

Taking her hand was the right call, clearly. "Later," he promised her. "Now we run!" He pulled her after him, pausing only after several street blocks. Qown turned around, took a deep breath, and concentrated.

---

[7] The boy really has no idea, does he?

A giant section of building and block just flipped upside down, shifted, and reslotted into place in an entirely new position.

Sheloran gaped.

Qown didn't have time to explain. Honestly, he didn't understand why this was even something to be surprised about. Surely, she'd been paying attention to the explanation of what this place was?

They stopped an interminable distance from the point of the attack. Qown led them inside a building, summoning up a table and chairs for them to use. Sheloran continued to stare at him like she'd never seen him before.

"It's a mental construct," he explained.

She continued staring.

"None of this is *real*," Qown explained. "It's a mental construct created by someone. That means that it can be modified. It can be controlled. There's nothing particularly mysterious about it."

"It's a god's mental construct," Sheloran told him with wide eyes.

Qown paused. Oh.

"Oh," he said out loud. "I suppose I just didn't really, uh . . . look at it that way."

"Clearly not." Sheloran leaned back in her chair. She was still watching him with a look that wasn't quite wariness as much as confusion. "So if this is all so easy to manipulate, why do you still look like that when it clearly bothers you?" She gestured toward him.

He felt himself flush again, this time as much with anger as embarrassment. "Because this is what I look like. Or at least, I looked like this for a lot longer than I've looked like anything else. Why wouldn't I be most comfortable this way?"

"Comfortable?" she repeated.

Qown grimaced. "I'm used to it."

"Very well," Sheloran said. She leaned forward and took his hand. "I need you to stop and think about this before you answer. Is this the appearance you want or the appearance you deserve?"

Qown snatched his hand back. "Oh, fuck you." He put his hand to his mouth. "I'm sorry. I'm sorry. I shouldn't have said that."

"It was honest," she said, smiling. "And I was being rude. There's nothing wrong with being overweight. A better option than when we first met. You looked like you'd been starving yourself."

Qown shuddered. "I, um, sort of had been."

"Well, I want you to understand something—however you look is fine as long as it's what *you want*. And it's not going to injure you. Poor health would be unacceptable, in my opinion."

Qown swallowed thickly. "Thank you. That's sweet of you to say."

Sheloran stared. "You think Galen will care, don't you?"

"Of course he would. Why wouldn't he? He's—" Qown waved a hand. "He's gorgeous and a royal prince, and he can have anyone he wants. So of course it would matter."

"And if—say, hypothetically—it didn't?"

"But it does," Qown insisted.

"No." Sheloran batted him on top of his head with her fan. "We're playing my game, and in my game, the rules are that it Does. Not. Matter. If it didn't matter and you could look however you wanted. Like whatever you wanted at all. What would you look like?"

"You can't remove the context of society, Sheloran," Qown told her. "You can't remove how people act and react. I just . . . oh hell, you're really going to make me sit down and figure this out *now*?"

She nodded. "I really am, yes."

"Fuck." Qown lifted a finger. "You're both a terrible influence on me. I hope you realize that. *Dorna* wasn't this poor of an influence on me!"

"It's what you love about me," Sheloran said.

Qown's eyes widened for just a moment, and then he quickly looked away.

Sheloran tucked her closed fan under his chin and turned his face back to meet hers. "My oh my, what a complicated relationship you and I are going to have," she told him. "I like to think we'll be such good friends. And I am already so fond of you. Can you handle that? Just friendship? It can't be anything else. Not unless you decide you'd really rather be a woman, and that would rather wreck things with Galen, I suspect."

"No," Qown agreed. "I wouldn't want to be female. I had that conversation with Dorna once. Not for myself—"

"Who's Dorna again?"

"Oh, Janel's nurse. Elderly woman I met in Jorat. Only it turned out that she hadn't been born a woman. She'd petitioned the goddess Galava to turn her into one. It's a thing they do over there. I asked her why she'd done it. I mean—" He blushed. "I was rude. I didn't know any better. I actually asked why she would turn into a woman if she sexually preferred other women when she could just have stayed a man and no one would have questioned it."

"I do hope she hit you," Sheloran said.

"Oh, she did. She said it had nothing to do with who she liked to, uh, sleep with—she'd grown tired of lying to everyone, including herself, about who she really was. So that's why she did it."

"That sounds perfectly sensible to me. And who are you?"

"I don't know," Qown answered honestly. "I think I've been letting other people tell me that for all my life. It was just so much easier when no one was paying attention to me. When I was just . . . invisible."

"Hmm. I understand."

"Do you?" Qown blinked at her. "Everyone looks at you. All the time."

"Yes," Sheloran said. "That's why I understand. What you're saying sounds so very appealing. I have no trouble imagining the lure of it." She tapped his knee. "But that doesn't seem healthy. Everyone needs to be seen, at least a little. Everyone should be comfortable in their own shell. You looking like this"—she waved at him—"that's fine. If that's comfortable. But if you're using it as a sort of security blanket, a way of running from something you're scared of, as a way of maintaining that invisibility, then you may want to ask yourself if it's what you really want."

"And if it is?" Qown asked. "If it's what I really want?"

Sheloran smiled. "Then you'll still be perfectly beautiful."

Kalindra's reaction
The Lighthouse at Shadrag Gor
After Kalindra's memory of escaping Devors

Kalindra sighed. If only that had been the worst of it. She didn't really think anyone there would blame her for defending herself. "I really want to go back and talk to that old monk."

"Oh indeed," Thurvishar agreed.

"You don't think he set you up, do you?" Senera mused.

"You have a very paranoid mind," Talea told her.

Kalindra snorted at the same time Senera said, "You do know me, yes?"

Xivan and Thurvishar chuckled.

Then Kalindra stood up. "Someone want to escort me to the restroom?" Because they had all agreed not to be alone, and even she understood the wisdom of that.

As she did, her eye caught a flash of red, and she realized her hands felt wet.

Kalindra looked down to see her hands were covered in blood. Just sopping in it, crimson, thick, and shiny. She gasped. Kalindra hadn't felt . . . what . . .

"Fuck," Senera cursed and rushed over to her. She grabbed a blanket on her way and began wiping Kalindra's hands, looking for the injury.

There was none.

"Maybe this is just Vol Karoth's way of saying, 'Don't forget me.'" Kalindra's laughter fooled absolutely no one.

"Why don't we take that break," Thurvishar said, "and then we'll continue?"

41: Uncomfortable Truths

Talea's memory
Still out at sea
Just after the pirate attack

"—so we looked around on Zherias and found a man that was going to introduce us to this pirate king, but it turned out to be a trap," Qown explained as they walked below decks on the *Angel's Spite*. "Not from the pirate, you understand. They just wanted to rob us and leave us for the sharks. But then Captain Rima showed up and saved us. Only it turned out—"

"That your rescuer was still a pirate," Talea said.

"Yes, exactly," Qown said. "Which honestly hadn't even occurred to us at first, until, you know, he was attacking ships and we were on board and being expected to pull our own weight or find ourselves tossed overboard."

"Awkward," Talea agreed sympathetically.

"Yes! Exactly so. I *never* meant to become a pirate, Talea."

"Don't worry," she said, "I won't tell the Quuros navy. But why are you looking for this 'Lash'?"

Qown brought them into a small room that seemed to be used for either meetings or private meals, given it housed nothing more than a table and chairs. All the furniture was luxurious, and little of it matched, leaving Talea with the distinct feeling that most of it had probably started out its life on merchant ships that had come to a bad end.

"Oh, it's complicated," Qown said to her question, "but basically, we're looking for a Cornerstone."

Talea gave him a canny look. "You are? Or your new master is?"

Qown's eyes widened in panic as Galen walked into the room.

"We can talk here," Galen said to Talea, "since we don't have a proper room of our own. We're all sleeping in hammocks down in the hold."

Sheloran giggled as she sat in one of the chairs. "If Captain Rima really wanted to sway us, he should have offered a cabin."

"The rest of the crew would murder us out of jealousy. Do you want to 'accidentally' fall overboard?" Galen seemed amused.

Qown didn't sit at first. Instead, he fretted, and the gesture was so like the Qown that Talea remembered she had no trouble recognizing him. He was, Talea realized, worrying over the idea she was going to mention Relos Var.

She watched as the healer decided on a misdirection. "Are we . . . are we not going to talk about how we just engaged in piracy?" Qown asked.

Talea leaned back in her chair. She was willing to play along. She admitted to feeling some curiosity about what had led to that whole "Sure, let's help the pirates" idea.

Sheloran sighed. "It's not as though we had a choice. Also, that's not important right now."

Qown looked confused. "It isn't? Then what is?"

Sheloran pointed at Talea. "We have a guest. Talea, wasn't it?"

Galen frowned and softly murmured, "Why is that name familiar?"

"My apologies for being a bit rude," Sheloran said, "but isn't it just a tiny bit suspicious that the first random ship we attack has an old friend of Qown's on board? What are the odds?"

Eshi started laughing, and Talea had to fight not to throw the little girl a dirty look. At least Eshi did not, in fact, answer the question. Talea didn't want to know.

Talea spread her hands. "And yet coincidence happens. I promise I don't have any malicious motives for being here. Quite the opposite."

"Would you like some tea?" Qown asked. "I could fetch some tea . . ."

"Thank you, but no," Talea said. "Maybe later?" She paused. "They have tea here? I wouldn't have expected that."

"Oh, I brought my own," Qown said.

"Now that makes more sense."

Galen sat back at the table and kicked his feet up on a chair. "So why don't you tell us about yourself, Talea." He smiled at her roguishly. If it had been anyone else, she might have found it charming. He was undeniably a handsome man, after all, just like all the men in his family.

But Talea felt the blood drain from her face. She took a step back, her reaction taking her utterly by surprise.

She couldn't help it. He looked like . . .

Galen looked like his father. And for just that moment, Galen had acted like him too.

It was too much.

Talea couldn't breathe. Her heart was beating so quickly she thought it might pound its way right out of her chest, the rush of blood a roar in her ears.

"Talea?"

"Talea!" Eshi screamed. "Talea, he's not here, that's not Darzin!"

Talea looked down at herself. She'd drawn her sword, the blade trembling in her white-knuckled grip. She'd backed up all the way until she'd hit the door, and if anyone had approached her, she'd have swung at them. Taja only knew how long Qown had been shouting at her. Everyone was standing. Sheloran looked alarmed and wide-eyed, and Galen . . .

Galen looked understandably concerned.

Talea exhaled in a long, slow stream, tried to wrestle her pulse back under control. She sheathed her sword.

"Explain yourself," Sheloran said. "Quickly."

Talea let out a shaky laugh. "Yes, I suppose you do deserve one." She spat out the truth like the curse it was. "I was a slave owned by Darzin D'Mon."

Utter silence fell over the room.

Galen cursed under his breath.

"Oh gods." Sheloran closed her fan and set it down on the table.

"I can . . . I can vouch for her," Qown said softly. "That's how we met. Not . . . not that she was still a slave then. I've never known Talea when she wasn't free. Just . . ."

Talea gave him a bitter smile. "It's disconcerting how much His Highness resembles his father at times, isn't it?"

"Yes," Qown agreed, "but you grow used to it quickly. Most of the time they have completely different attitudes."

"Wait." Galen frowned at Qown. "You've met my father?"

Qown looked like he wanted to climb under the table. Talea would have felt a little sorry for him, except she knew perfectly well he had to be there under false pretenses.

"Yes," Qown finally said, grimacing. "When I was in Yor. I didn't want to say anything because, um . . . well . . ." He visibly fidgeted. "I didn't have a very good relationship with your father."

Galen pulled out a chair, almost violently, and sat down. "That's not a mark against you, Qown."

Talea sat down again and began laughing.

She knew this wasn't exactly helping her portray herself as someone steady, reliable, or particularly sane, but it was all just a bit much.

"I'll . . . fetch that tea," Qown said.

Talea pushed her hair away from her eyes, her laughter still threatening to overflow and drown her. "I honestly can't believe I ever thought I'd kill him. I couldn't even be in the same room with his *son* without losing control." She paused and muttered. "At least Kihrin didn't really look like him that much."

Talea looked up to see Galen staring at her flatly, while Sheloran seemed ready to commit murder with her glare. Talea held up a hand. "I'm sorry. I–"

"Why on earth are you apologizing?" Galen said angrily. "My family kept you as a slave."

Talea sighed. "Yes, but you didn't, and I knew–" She hung her head. It's not like she hadn't known Galen would be there. She had. She absolutely had. She had no excuse. And yet . . .

She looked around the room, but Eshi had vanished after snapping her out of her panic attack. Talea would have to work through this by herself.

The silence was awkward and stifling. Galen must have felt the need to fill the air with something other than guilt. "How do you know Kihrin? He was only at the Blue Palace for a short–" His eyes widened. "Oh, that's where I know your name. You're that Talea. You're *Kihrin's* Talea!"

Talea's mouth twisted. "I would rather appreciate it if you never worded it like that ever again."

That revelation absolutely transformed Galen. He beamed, a sunshine-bright smile, and he arrested a motion forward that might very well have been him fighting back the temptation to lean forward and give Talea a hug. "You made it!" he exclaimed. "You survived! I just . . ." He shook his head. "I assumed they'd killed you. D'Lorus freed you? Really?"

Sheloran raised her chin. "Well, now I'm lost."

Galen grabbed his wife's hand and squeezed. "Red, this is the slave girl that Kihrin was trying to free when he was taken, or ran away, or whatever it was that happened to him." He was still laughing, short little bursts of surprise escaping in between smiles. "I know I only met you the one time, but I apologize for not recognizing you. You've . . . you've cut your hair."

Talea bit her lip as she shook her head. "We've never met."

"No," Galen said, "we have. There was this tavern—"

"I understand, but we've truly never met," Talea repeated. "That person you thought was me was actually a mimic—an assassin who worked for your father. The whole thing was just one of your father's sadistic games to try to trick Kihrin into giving up the Stone of Shackles. And if it had worked? Well, you saw what happened when your father and Gadrith finally managed it. That, but probably no one would have stopped them."

Galen stopped smiling. "Oh."

Qown returned from another room with a pot of tea and cups, which he served with surprising elegance considering the nature of the swaying ship. Talea took her cup gratefully, inhaling the steam before drinking.

Sheloran hid behind her fan, her posture so perfect and stiff it was a brilliant counterpoint to her discomfort. "So what brings you here?" Her tone was a great deal less interrogatory than it had been earlier, but still held the suggestion that it could return there quickly.

Talea gave her a rather uncomfortable smile. "You do." She inhaled. "I suppose I'd better explain."

Sheloran stared at her contemplatively while she drank her tea.

Talea paused. She hadn't really given much thought as to how to explain this, what she would say. Especially since there were certain names and facts—Caless, Suless—that the gaesh would prevent her from saying out loud. "Up until just recently, I was traveling with the Duchess of Yor, Xivan Kaen, first wife of Duke Azhen Kaen. The very same Duke Kaen who was working with Darzin D'Mon, Gadrith D'Lorus, and a wizard named Relos Var."

Sheloran's expression, what could be seen of it above her fan, went perfectly blank, while Galen sat up straighter. Both, Talea was certain, had been reacting to that last name.

"Xivan is dedicated to avenging the death of her late husband and her son—"

"Oh, Talea," Qown said. "I'm so sorry. They died?"

Talea frowned at him. "Last you saw him, Duke Kaen was ordering your execution, Qown. Are you really so sad?"

"Well"—Qown cleared his throat—"that's not . . . that's beside the point. I know how much Xivan cared for him. And I know how much you care for Xivan."

"Yes." Talea swallowed that little truth down and tried not to think about it. "So you must understand that Duke Kaen was murdered by one of his slaves, who was freed from her gaesh when the Stone of Shackles was broken."

Talea was not surprised to see the D'Mons share a look at that piece of news.

"Seems to be a lot of that going around," Galen murmured.[1]

---

[1] Quite a lot. Khaeriel and Suless are just two of the more extreme examples.

"In this case," Talea said, "it was particularly bad because the slave in question was a god-queen. The, um—" She made a motion with her hand as if she were searching for the words.

"Suless," Qown helpfully supplied. "God-Queen of Witchcraft, Malice, and Betrayal."

Talea exhaled in relief. "That's the one. Thank you, Qown. So Xivan has been hunting her."

Galen scoffed. "Is the duchess especially suicidal or just that arrogant?"

"She had Godslayer," Talea answered.

"I take it back," Galen said, "but since you're giving this to us as background for why you're here, I assume that didn't work." He frowned. "What does any of this have to do with us?"

"Xivan thinks she needs an artifact, a Cornerstone, to complete her revenge," Talea said, "and it's currently in the hands of Sheloran's mother."

"The Stone of Shackles," Galen said. "You're talking about the Stone of Shackles?"

Qown coughed, and a number of thoughts seemed to go through the healer's mind in quick succession. "The blue rock that the high lady was wearing? That was—" He inhaled sharply and stopped talking.

"I'd have recognized it anywhere," Galen said matter-of-factly. "I'm not sure how she ended up with it, but it didn't seem an opportune moment to ask."

"Yes," Talea said, pleased that they were all using proper nouns so she wouldn't have to. "Exactly so."

Sheloran squinted at Talea. "So Xivan wants the Stone of Shackles from my mother, and you're here . . . for what? To ask me to put in a good word?"

"Oh no," Talea said. "I'm here to keep Xivan from kidnapping you."

Her dramatic statement was rewarded appropriately with looks of shock from Qown, surprise from Galen, and that extremely guarded lack of expression from Sheloran that Talea had already tagged as the woman's "surprised and upset" face.

"Xivan wouldn't really do that . . ." Qown blinked, looking lost.

"She really would," Talea corrected gently. "She's not thinking clearly right now. She is so focused on her revenge that she's not considering who she might hurt getting there. I'm hoping that if I'm here with you, then maybe I can talk her away from that cliff she's trying to leap off before she has to be destroyed."

"You mean killed, don't you?" Galen asked.

Talea cleared her throat again. Across the table, Qown visibly winced.

"I suppose . . ." Talea sighed. "I suppose I should mention Xivan's a soul vampire, of the same sort as Gadrith."

"What." Galen's voice was very faint.

"Yes, um, she was, uh . . . resurrected, of a sort. Because Thaena refused." Talea chewed on her lip and left off the part about being raised by Relos Var. His name had come up enough during the conversation. "So no, I mean destroyed. It would break my heart."

"You care for her," Sheloran said. Talea noticed the lack of question mark.

Talea thought about it for a second before she decided that no, she really wasn't interested in half-truths or evasions on this subject. "She's the love of my life."

Sheloran looked surprised, then sympathetic.

"When did that happen?" Qown asked.

Talea gave him a good, hard stare.

Qown blushed and looked down at his hands. Then he made a face as a thought seemed to occur to him. "You said she 'had' Godslayer. She doesn't anymore? Who does?"

"Kihrin," Talea said.

He turned absolutely white. "Oh. I see."

Talea stood up and circled around the table until she could pat Qown on the shoulder. "Honestly, that's the one thing that's gone right. I hated Xivan having that stupid sword. And I hate that stupid sword. Give me a weapon I can wield without the uncontrollable urge to kill every sorcerer, mage, and wizard within five miles any day, thank you."

"You've . . ." Sheloran's voice held the faintest tremble. "You've wielded Godslayer?"

Talea shrugged. "It's really not all it's made out to be." She picked up her bag. "The hammocks are down in the hold, you said?"

Galen nodded. His eyes were distant. "Yes. You know, Talea—"

She turned around, not sure what he wanted to say, not sure if it was anything she wanted to hear. She really hoped he wouldn't mention his father again.

But he didn't. "I'm not exactly sure of our destination. I know it's not the mainland, or even Zherias. I don't mind that you're here, but you should know that it's basically impossible that we're going to run into Xivan Kaen."

Sheloran put away her fan. "Yes, but wasn't it basically impossible that we'd run into Talea?" She didn't look mad about the situation, so that was good.

Talea sighed. "Please believe me when I say I know the odds. If she's coming for you, then it's not a question of if we'll run into Xivan. It's only a question of when."

Talea's reaction
The Lighthouse at Shadrag Gor
Just after Talea's memory

Xivan stared at her. "You . . . you seriously caught up to them just by catching the first random ship to Zherias and letting them find you?"

"That is not a thing an angel should be able to do," Kalindra said. "I don't care if you're angel of Taja or not, that shouldn't be possible."

"Well, apparently, I'm a *herald* of Taja," Talea corrected.

"And just what is that again?" Senera had her ink brush in her hand, staring at Talea as if she were deciding whether to take notes or ask the Name of All Things questions.

"I haven't the faintest idea," Talea said.

"I think I know," Thurvishar said. "Or at least, I'm beginning to suspect."

Kalindra stood up and began to pace. "Please, is there any way you can block him? Keep him from accessing my memories? I don't want—"

The world changed.

Inside Vol Karoth's prison

Galen didn't attempt to reason with Lyrilyn or even talk to her. He simply picked her up bodily and carried her out of the park. She fought him a bit, but she didn't change shape, and she didn't have the strength to force him to drop her. After several blocks, he set her down on a flight of stairs.

"You . . . you—" She was furiously wiping tears from her eyes.

"I'm sorry if I offended," Galen lied, "but I didn't think leaving you there was a good idea."

Lyrilyn stared at him with wide eyes. "Oh fuck. It's you."

"Yes," Galen agreed. "It's me."

"Why would you save me?" Lyrilyn asked. "That doesn't make any sense. Don't you realize who I am? What I've done?"

"What you did?" Galen asked. "Or what Talon did?"

Lyrilyn dropped her hands into her lap and studied her fingers. "I'm not . . . I can't . . ."

"Any idea where we are?" Galen asked her.

Lyrilyn shook her head. "No."

"Me neither," he admitted. "So we should probably keep walking. I have to think Vol Karoth will come looking for us now that we've both escaped."

"Vol Karoth," Lyrilyn repeated numbly.

"Hmm." Galen narrowed his eyes. "You didn't look like you were doing so well back there."

She just looked at him and stared for a few seconds. Then she burst into tears and covered her face with her hands.

Galen was taken aback. He was having trouble thinking of this as the same creature who'd made jokes about cannibalism and murdering people close to him. He reached out to touch her shoulder.

Lyrilyn flinched away from him. "Don't touch me! Gods, don't touch me! Why are you—" She backed away from him. "Don't you realize what a monster I am?"

Galen took her place, sitting down on the stairs. The sky that he could see through the tall buildings was a drab fluffy gray, like a baby's blanket that had been used once and never washed again. "Hmm. Are we talking on a scale here? Because I've known so many monsters. Some of them weren't even human. But most—" He shrugged. "Most were."

Lyrilyn was still staring at him, wide-eyed and horrified. "I've done things."

"Yes, I've gotten that impression."

"I ate your mother."

Galen froze. That was indeed a piece of information he hadn't known. "I thought my father had her poisoned."

"No," Lyrilyn said, shaking her head frantically from side to side. "He sacrificed her souls to the demon Xaltorath and then had me eat her body afterward so I would have all her memories when I took her place. Which I did for . . . six months? Until Darzin decided he needed me for something else. And so he had me fake being poisoned so I could move about more freely. I'm so sorry—"

Galen was having trouble breathing. He reminded himself of Sheloran's exercises. He looked around and described to himself what he was seeing, shaped the objects in the window of his mind until his pulse was under his control again. Did he even have a pulse here? Apparently, he could imagine he did. Close enough.

He started chuckling.

"It's not funny," Lyrilyn said.

"You know, I always wondered why my mother suddenly started being nice to me. Isn't that just priceless? It's because you weren't being completely faithful to my mother's sterling personality." Galen tilted his head. "My parents were terrible people. Both my parents. No child should ever go through what I did."

Lyrilyn swallowed thickly and nodded. "I know. I . . . I didn't . . ." She shuddered. "You didn't deserve any of that."

"I know," Galen said. "I really do know. Took me a while, and I do on occasion backslide, but I'm aware that terrible things can and do happen to the undeserving." He paused. "You might want to tell yourself that. Maybe repeat it more than once."

She blinked, her eyes widening. "What? No, we're talking about you."

"Not anymore." Galen leaned forward. "You know, I heard about you. Not Talon the mimic. Lyrilyn the slave. The one who betrayed Pedron."

Lyrilyn started breathing rather fast.

"It's all right," Galen told her. "I happen to admire you for it. I think my grandfather Therin must have as well, or he wouldn't have given you to Khaeriel." He paused. "He should have freed you. That would have been a much better thanks, in my opinion. But my point is that those few stories about you I'd heard all agreed that you were one hell of a survivor."

"That's not an admirable quality," she said. "You don't know the things I've had to do to survive."

"You think I can't imagine?" Galen said. "Because you'd be wrong. I'm guessing you had to hurt a lot of people. I'm guessing you had to make Pedron think you were just like him. Just as sick. Maybe . . . maybe you even learned to like it."

She exhaled a shuddering breath.

"I'm not saying that what you did is excused," Galen said, "but you had no choice about being there. You were a slave. You didn't have any choice at all, except for one thing: to live or die. You chose to live. I can't call that a sin. You didn't deserve what happened with Talon."

"With all respect, my lord," Lyrilyn said, "you don't know what the fuck you're talking about."

He grinned. "You think not? You think we weren't both prisoners in that damn palace performing for our survival? Because I beg to differ."

She sat down next to him. "I'm not a good person, Galen. Not like you."

"By whose criteria?" Galen said. "I'm not a good person. Too much of my parents in me. Sheloran's the good one. I'm just trying to keep her alive. Did you know I wrote a poem about you?"

"I'm sorry. You what?"

"I wrote a poem about you," Galen said. "Here."

"I saw a woman at market
a beauty of the age
with skin like summer honey
and a mind filled with rage.
I saw a woman at market
with eyes sunken as a well,
her hope long abandoned
to a life lived deep in Hell.
I saw a woman at market,
bereft of anyone to trust,
with iron around her collar
and a heart filled with dust.
In darkness she will weep now,
her tears they'll never see,
her weaknesses are hidden,
her anguish never free
I wonder does she dream now,
of iron and of knives,
of the copper taste of vengeance,
of the day she'll end their lives.

Hey, that wasn't supposed to make you cry."

"Well maybe you shouldn't have said it, then!" She rubbed her eyes. "Seriously? Why would . . . you–"

"You're welcome," Galen said.

She hit him.

He laughed and pretended it didn't hurt.

Then she was crying again, for real, her whole body shaking from the sobs. Galen pulled her into his arms. He could feel his own tears welling at the corners of his eyes, pooling there before spilling down his cheeks. "Shhh," he told her. "You're braver than you give yourself credit for being, Lyrilyn. You should use that."

"Use that?" She looked up at him. "*Use that?* How? What does Lyrilyn have to offer anyone? She's not useful or powerful. She's not a shape-changing mimic who can read minds! Lyrilyn was a slave who was very good at sex and very bad at knowing who to trust. That's not a useful quality, Galen. It won't win us any battles. You need Talon, not Lyrilyn."

"Lyrilyn had a willpower made from stone and an ability to survive horrors that would have broken most people," Galen corrected. "I'm not saying you should be proud of what happened to you. But I will tell you the same thing that I've had to learn: you're not a victim. You can have bad things happen to you and refuse to let those bad things win."

She put a hand to her mouth, rubbed the flesh there before blinking and looking away. "I wouldn't know where to start," she murmured.

"Who am I to say?" Galen agreed. "But this is who you are." He poked her arm. "Not those people whose memories you've consumed. You can be better than those voices. Maybe, I don't know, think twice before you kill someone and eat them?"

"That is, uh ... that is easier said than done," Lyrilyn admitted. "Those voices are strong."

"Bet not one of them is stronger than the slave girl who took down a high lord."[2]

Lyrilyn huffed, but she didn't tell him that he was wrong.

Galen stood and offered her a hand. "Come, then. Shall we go see if we can find my brother?"

"Your brother? But–" Lyrilyn drew short. "Is that how you see him?"

"Well, I'm not going to call him uncle. That would just be weird."

---

[2] That is a rather generous interpretation, but I suppose had she not betrayed Pedron's deeds to Therin the Affair of the Voices would have gone very differently.

42: Deadly Dark Desires

Kalindra's memory
Zherias
Three days after leaving Devors[1]

When Kalindra arrived on the coast of Zherias, she was exhausted, dehydrated, and very badly wanted everything—food, a bath, a nap, buckets of water. She was trying hard not to think about how frantic with worry her son must be. She was trying harder not to think about the severing she'd felt on that first day out at sea, when her silent connection to Thaena had simply vanished. As though Thaena was no longer ignoring her, but had cast her out, cut the ties between them.

What a fool she'd been to think Thaena wouldn't notice Kalindra's defiance.

She dragged herself ashore, not much caring what happened to the boat after she disembarked. She climbed a coconut tree, cut down several nuts, and used those to quench her thirst. Then she hunted for enough wild game and vegetables to salve her hunger.

She rested a full day before she took her bearings and began hiking toward the nearest fishing village. Finding a real fishing village in Zherias was always tricky. Because most towns and cities on Zherias weren't.

Weren't real, that was. They were distractions, illusions, meant to fool idiots, slavers, pirates, and the Quuros navy with a nicely accessible target. The real villages and towns lay tucked away in isolated lagoons and grottoes, hidden in cave networks, or shaped along lost valleys. Most outsiders had never and would never see a true Zheriasian town. Most never wondered that they visited towns where not a single Zheriasian person actually seemed to live. It was charade and illusion on a national scale, and under normal circumstances it filled Kalindra with warm delight.

In at least three cases Kalindra knew of personally, the villages were deep underwater, and no one could go there who wasn't more than a little Ithlané.

She dreaded returning, but she needed the resources she could command there. She just had to hope that she could do so without anyone questioning it enough to seek out Mother. Kalindra was reasonably certain that no amount of justifications or rationales would fool Khaemezra, and that would be the end of Kalindra's little adventure.

The chapter house was, not unpredictably, a fish shop. She gave the man at the counter the pass code, which she hoped was still current—it had been

---

[1] Also three days after the Battle of the Well of Spirals.

when the Capital Hellmarch had occurred, the last time she'd been in contact with her goddess.

They immediately brought her into a back room and made her comfortable. They even cooked her a meal, and if said meal was predictably fish, that was hardly a matter for complaint.

The man who worked the shop out front had been Zheriasian, but the woman in the back must have been part Ithlané, wearing the veil even in private. She was hunched over, her hands to her face. Her breathing was ragged and uneven.

Kalindra frowned. Was the woman crying?

"Are you . . . all right?"

The woman jerked her head upward. A moment later she was on her knees in front of Kalindra, reaching out a hand only to jerk it back at the last moment as afraid of burning herself.

"Is it true?" she asked Kalindra. "Is really true?"

Kalindra had no idea what to say. She felt like she'd been slammed into the middle of a conversation with no preparation. "I'm sorry, but—"

"Is Thaena really dead?" The woman's voice was scraped raw with grief.

Kalindra's whole body stuttered.

"Where . . . what . . ." Kalindra bent down next to the woman, pulled her back up to her feet. Her mind refused to make any progress toward a rational thought. "What have you heard?"

The woman rubbed at her face through her veils. "There's a rumor that she's dead. That she was killed. One of the priestesses said she felt Thaena die . . ."

A dark void stretched out in front of her. Kalindra felt like she might fall any second. "When?" she finally asked. "When did this happen?"

The woman turned away. "So you don't know either."

"When did this happen?" Kalindra repeated. "Was it three days ago?" Three days ago, when Kalindra had assumed that Thaena's withdrawal was condemnation.

The woman looked back over her shoulder. "You felt it?"

Kalindra shuddered, but she managed to nod. "I did. I can't tell you . . . I can't." She tried to collect herself. She didn't know what was worse: the impending horror at the idea that Thaena might be dead or the sense of relief that Thaena's silence might have had nothing to do with Kalindra's behavior after all. "I don't know."

The woman's shoulders began shaking. She was likely crying again.

Kalindra grit her teeth. "We'll find out." She made her voice snap, wrapped herself up in authority. She wasn't some timid petitioner. She was one of Thaena's *angels*. "But in the meantime, I need to go to Da'utunse."

The woman didn't seem to hear her at first, but after a long, awkward gap of silence, raised her head. "Tonight?"

"It doesn't have to be. Tomorrow will be fine." Kalindra waved a hand. "I'll need the usual equipment." She added, "I'm sure there's an explanation. She's Thaena. She is Death. Have faith, sister."

Kalindra felt none of that faith herself, but she knew the right words to say. She knew the words that the other woman would want to hear.

The woman trembled and bowed. "Yes, hunter. We have a small cot up-stairs you can use for tonight. Unless you'd prefer different accommodations?"

Kalindra nodded. "A cot will be fine."

The next morning brought with it another wagon ride, this one to the deep jungles of Zherias. There lurked one of the ancient network gates that the god-king Ynis had once built across his kingdom. The gates had been expanded; there were several more now than when he'd originally created the system. Several led to locations beyond the knowledge of even most Zheriasians. One led to the pirate haven of Da'utunse, which was a useful spot to know if you were looking to sell or buy something illegal everywhere else.

The Black Brotherhood often found themselves on both sides of that equa-tion. And the Black Brotherhood controlled this gate.

She exited in an underground grotto on the ocean bottom, with an entry pool taking up the largest area on the floor and mage-light mimicking can-dles lining the coral stone walls. A Black Brotherhood agent waited on the other side, alert in case of an unauthorized access. Kalindra frowned at the sight that greeted her. There should have been guards, trained Brotherhood members keeping the gate safe. Instead, there was but a single man who seemed unsure of himself and was possibly performing his duties for the first time. Bluffing her way past him would be easy. The agent had no idea who Kalindra was. She looked the part and seemed confident, and that was close enough.

"Welcome," the man said, stepping forward. "How may this one be of service?"

Kalindra motioned the man over. "Do we have a list of everyone who's in port?"

"Of course." He motioned over to the pool with the clear implication: yes, such a list existed. Such a list did not, however, exist at their present location.

Kalindra's mouth twisted to the side. "Very well." She held out her hand.

The agent went to the far side of the room and fished through a bowl before coming back with a token of a red fish on a gold chain. He handed it to her. "Wait at the exit. There's an Ithlané guide who will take you the rest of the way."

She nearly snapped that this wasn't her first time visiting Da'utunse, but she realized there was little point in taking out her anger on the man. Bad enough that he'd already been subjected to this particular posting, which couldn't have been much fun. She didn't ask where everyone else was either. She suspected she wouldn't like the answer.

She took her weapons but left her agolé. It would only get in the way.

Kalindra bowed to the man and then dove into the seawater.

The water below filled a tunnel, lit at regular intervals. At slightly larger spans, the tunnel curved up above the waterline, allowing pockets of air to linger where someone might surface if they needed to take a quick breath. None of the Ithlané would need it, but humans were a different matter.

When she finally emerged from the tunnel, she was still underwater. Spread out around her were dark waters, with the flickering hint of sunlight coming from a faraway place above. Lights filled the darkness, suggesting houses and buildings of all sorts built up from the ocean floor. But that wasn't her destination.

A young Ithlané boy swam over to her, his hand waving to touch her. This boy was too old and the wrong race, but it was so hard not to think of Nikali. It felt like when she wasn't being reminded of Jarith, she was being reminded of her son.

But she pushed those feelings aside and held out her hand to him and let him lace his fingers with hers. She didn't feel him cast the spell, but she knew it had happened from the moment she felt a rush of air hit her lungs like the sweetest of daggers, a sharp, beautiful pain. Kalindra motioned up toward the light.

The boy motioned toward his neck, then pointed at her.

Kalindra showed him the necklace, and he broke into a wide grin, silver eyes sparkling. She found his concern both endearing and silly—if she hadn't been wearing the necklace, the pressure would have already been in the process of killing her, no surfacing required. But probably the boy had been told not to take any humans down to the Everdark who wasn't wearing a protective talisman, and he'd assumed the reverse must be true as well.

He started swimming upward, pulling her along with him.

As Kalindra rose toward the surface, fish swam lazily in the distance through kelp forests that reached toward that feeble sunlight. Enormous objects floated above, some tethered down to the ocean bottom with thick chains, while others floated on rising curtains of air bubbles, magically held in position. Not all the creatures that swam in the distance were piscine. The traffic between the Everdark and Flotsam flowed nonstop.

They surfaced outside the floating ring the boy had steered them toward, which seemed to be a guesthouse from the smell of food and the sound of people merrily drinking. She thanked the boy and pulled herself from the water. Dripping wet, she set out in search of an innkeeper.

It was indeed a Black Brotherhood chapter house. Once the owner realized who she was, everything was provided. Yes, of course she'd been expected. Yes, naturally there was a room put aside for her. Yes, her clothing would be sent up as soon as it arrived (and was pulled out of a Brotherhood storeroom). Food would be sent up, or she could eat downstairs, as she preferred.

She preferred the room.

No one mentioned Thaena, but it was impossible to miss the subdued tone. Everyone held themselves with the breathless expectation of people waiting for the army to arrive, the siege to begin. For the rumor of tragedy to become the reality of grief.

She ordered a bottle of sassibim from the bar and took it to her room, where she sat at the window and watched the floating buildings wander up and down in a lazy dance across the water. Da'utunse wasn't a location she'd had cause to visit often, but it was soothing in its way. True, she could hear the rowdy shouts and cheers of sailors enjoying themselves in taverns and brothels echoing from every part of the floating city, but it all had a lazy feel to it. Da'utunse was a safe place. The Quuros navy had never discovered its location in over a thousand years of looking. They said no one came to Da'utunse to start a fight, only to finish one.

Most of the permanent residents were Ithlané. Indeed, Da'utunse was an Ithlané word. They took the money of pirates and traders and in turn gave them a place where they could go outside the normal searching gaze of all the naval enforcers who would otherwise hunt them down. The pirates who havened here called the floating sections of raft lashed together and anchored to the ocean floor Drift Town. The area at the bottom where the tethers hooked into the bedrock was called Lagan. Not exactly original, but it served its purpose. Da'utunse was one of the few places in the whole world where the Black Brotherhood had a known, permanent address.

She wouldn't be using it. Maybe the woman on Zherias had been wrong. Maybe Thaena wasn't dead. Depending on how her task here went, it would be best for everyone if her actions didn't reflect back on the Black Brotherhood at all.

She took a few sips from the bottle, but not enough to slow her down. A human girl brought her roasted salmon and an accompanying fish stew starter, and by the time she was finished, another errand runner had dropped off appropriately piratical attire. They'd even found her a war chain. She dressed herself, an oddly satisfying task after so many years spent away from this life. But she'd left it for a reason, and with luck, once she'd gotten what she came for, she'd never have to return. Her only worry was that the Lash might not be in port—in which case she'd have little choice but to wait.

But even if that was the case, sooner or later, the Lash's ship, *the Cruel Mistress*, would return to Da'utunse.

When it did, she would be waiting.

Kalindra's reaction
The Lighthouse at Shadrag Gor
Just after Kalindra's memory

Everyone seemed surprised when the vision ended. Startled, blinking, perhaps a bit confused. After all, that wasn't so bad, was it? And yet it seemed likely to have been one of the visions Vol Karoth had triggered.

Kalindra shut her eyes and tried to push it all away. She failed. The pain and guilt welled up around her, horrible and sharp, not what she'd just seen but what she knew she would see the next time. It was like being bled out, a single cut at a time, slowly. Oh gods, she was the only person in the room who knew what the next vision would show. But even as she thought that, she saw Thurvishar staring at her . . .

So no. Probably not the only person. At least one other, who saw her. Who knew.

It didn't make her feel better.

"Kalindra?" Talea said.

"I don't like this game anymore," she whispered. "I want to stop playing." She wasn't sure when she'd ended up sitting on one of the benches in the

THE HOUSE OF ALWAYS

kitchen, but she'd pulled her legs up to her chest, resting her head against her knees.

"That's nice," Senera said. "If only what you wanted mattered."

"Senera!" Talea scolded.

Senera shrugged.

"What's the problem here?" Xivan asked. "That last vision seemed fine. And finding out that Thaena's dead isn't new, so what is it?"

"It's not that," Kalindra said.

"Then what? Was it the vision before that? Because again, sure, you killed those monks, but they weren't exactly innocent. They seemed pretty comfortable with the idea of murdering you just because of some idiotic prophecies. Are you worried about your son?"

"I hope he's safe," Kalindra murmured. In theory, yes, her son was safe. In practice? It would depend who had told the truth and who had lied. Did that little Devoran cabal truly not care about Nikali? And would they return in time to be able to do anything about the attack on Devors? Because everyone on the island was in terrible danger. Including her little boy.

The plan had been to get him out, and that plan now tasted like ash.

"So what's the problem?" Senera asked. "Perhaps you should talk about it now."

"Fuck off," Kalindra snapped.

Senera rolled her eyes. "Do you seriously think I am going to judge you? Do you have any idea some of the things I've done?"

"Now that the kids are gone," Xivan said, "there's nobody in this room who hasn't killed somebody. Hell, we ask Talea to step into the hall, and there's nobody in this room who isn't a murderer. Although I suppose Thurvishar's a bit borderline, since he was never willing."

Thurvishar made no comment.[2]

Talea did, though. "You know, I would have murdered Darzin if I'd had the opportunity. Suless too."

Kalindra started laughing. *Fuck, Xivan was right.*

In the end, though, Kalindra knew this had nothing to do with body counts and everything to do with trust. The real betrayal was yet to come, and Vol Karoth had set the scene for that revelation with all the tender care of a chef bringing out courses at a banquet. The people who would *really* understand—Qown and Talon—weren't in the room anymore.[3]

It had been such an easy trap to fall into. She would have done anything to bring Jarith back. She very nearly had.

Kalindra had lived her whole life thinking the ends justified the means, and maybe that was still true, but if so . . .

If so, then it meant failure brought no excuses. Failure made every sin and every sacrifice an act of hubris. Failure meant it had all been for *nothing.*

"It's our turn," Thurvishar said. "So whenever you're ready, Talea."

---

[2] I hope you realize Ola Nathera doesn't count. Killing her was an accident.
[3] Sweet of her to leave me out of it, but we both know I'm now on this list too.

Qown's story
Inside Vol Karoth's prison
An unknown time after their arrival

Qown and Sheloran had been attacked five times and still hadn't come any closer to tracking down anyone—not Galen, not Kihrin, not Janel. They'd been attacked by fake versions of all those people, however.

The sixth time, however, when Sheloran shifted a whole mass of metal that Qown had created for her into shackles that she hurled at the group, Janel screamed, "Qown, what the are you doing? Let us go!"

"We don't know if it's really them," Teraeth said.

Sheloran narrowed her eyes. Qown understood why easily enough. This group was more convincing than most. The previous groups had been a lot more inclined to just froth excessively at the mouth.

Janel immediately melted through her shackles. Which she had on previous occasions as well. It's just that this time, she wasn't following it up with a counterattack.

"Hey, Sheloran," Not-Kihrin said amiably. "Remember how we met?"

Sheloran paused. "Yes?"

"You were dressed up as a dragon in that scaled red gown with metal wings, and I was dressed like a chicken?"

Sheloran stared. "Oh Veils. You're really Kihrin."

"We don't know—" Qown started to say.

Sheloran pursed her lips. "No, this is really Kihrin. Can you imagine Vol Karoth willingly referring to himself as a chicken? And gods, you did look like a big chicken." She laughed. "Prettiest chicken I ever saw."

"Excuse me, but would you mind?" Teraeth shook his new shiny metal bracelets.

Sheloran waved a hand; the metal shackles that hadn't already been destroyed by that point fell to the ground.

"So . . . ," Kihrin said, rubbing his wrists. "How have you been, Qown?"

Qown felt himself blush furiously. He . . . oh god. "I'm . . . good?"

"Glad to hear it. And back on our side, I hope?"

"Kihrin," Janel said. "This isn't—"

Qown rushed over to Janel. He started to take her hand, stopped, felt his face scrunch up on the verge of tears. "I'm sorry."

Janel stopped whatever it was she'd been about to say and instead just looked at him. She didn't say a word.

"I'm sorry," he continued. "I was wrong. I just . . . I thought . . . I thought he—" He felt his throat threaten to close up again.

Janel pulled Qown into her arms and held him close. "Stop it. You don't need to apologize. This is Var's fault, not yours. I don't blame you."

"Uh, you know, actually it is sort of Qown's fault—" Teraeth started to say.

"Not. Now." Janel growled.

Teraeth nodded as if he completely expected that response and didn't say another word.

"He's right, though," Qown said as he backed away at least enough to look at Janel at arm's length. "It is my fault. Maybe Relos Var used me, but I let him. I thought . . . I just thought if he was right, it would all be okay. Everything would be—" Qown looked over at Kihrin. "I'm sorry."

Kihrin shrugged. "We all make mistakes. I mean—" He gestured around the city as if it proved his point. "Who am I to judge?"

Qown nodded. "I'm just—" He shook his head. "I can't make this right."

"Sure you can," Teraeth said. "Help us fix this. That'll make it right. We're not turning Senera away. Hell, we're not turning *me* away. You think you're too irredeemable to join the save-the-world club? Please."

Janel shrugged. "If you still feel bad about it when this is all done, you can help me with the rebellion in Quur. I'll call that even."

"Rebellion in Quur?" Sheloran questioned.

Janel looked at the Quuros royal with a smile on her face. "Don't worry. You're invited too."

Sheloran paused. "Oh. That's fine, then. I didn't want to be left out."

Qown felt a genuine smile force its way on to his face, but then he realized who was missing. "You haven't found Galen yet."

"No," Kihrin said. "Nor Talon. Vol Karoth's doing a much better job of hiding them from us. But we are looking."

"We'll find him," Sheloran said. "Both of them."

43: Dinner with the Lash

Talea's memory
The pirate haven of Da'utunse.
Eighteen days after the Battle of the Well of Spirals

Their destination proved to be a city called Da'utunse.

Talea hadn't been prepared.

That wasn't entirely her fault. None of her companions had the faintest idea where they were headed except that it was a sort of refuge used by pirates, part of a nation Talea had never even heard of before: Ithlakor.

She immediately found herself taken aback both by the size of the city and by its basic construction. She'd assumed that any port of call would be attached to, well, to land.

And she was absolutely wrong.

If one wasn't paying attention, it was possible to fool oneself into thinking that the city was stable and permanent. Some of the buildings even looked like they may have been made of materials far too heavy to float on water. As to what kept the city afloat, she could only assume the answer was magic. Lots of magic.

The dockside of the city was just lousy with ships. Every single one of them had the predatory air of people who made their livelihood attacking others. She didn't doubt that this was a town that saw more than its share of fights, although maybe that was an incorrect assumption on her part. Maybe they saved their hostility for outsiders and treated each other as family.

Probably not, though.

She was surprised, however, when Captain Rima came back and handed each of her companions a bag.

"What's this?" Sheloran asked him.

The captain shrugged. "You helped. You get a share. That's how it works." He grinned. "That's the reason the crew tends to be a bit picky about just letting any old person on board, but you lot made this run just about risk-free and healed the people who were injured besides. No one's begrudging you a cut." He gestured at Talea. "Except you. No offense."

"Ah," Talea said. "None taken." When the captain left, she clapped Qown on the shoulder. "I see that look. Don't feel bad about this."

He startled from examining the bag of coins in his hands to look at her, wide-eyed and skittish. "But I do feel bad about it! People were hurt . . ."

Talea sighed. "Trust me when I say odds are good a lot more people would have died if you hadn't been there. You chose the option that saved the most lives." She chucked him under the chin. "It's okay. No reason why you should feel bad about any of this. Besides, maybe that pirate whose tooth you cured–Shortie?–maybe Shortie's going to go settle down in Zherias, marry his childhood sweetheart, and have a daughter who'll invent a new kind of sail that will revolutionize transportation for the next century." She paused as she realized Qown's expression had frozen into a perfect mask of bemusement.

"I mean," Talea added, "theoretically. Who can say?"[1]

"Yes. Maybe so. Thank you, Talea," Qown said. "That's kind of you." He still looked at the point of tears by the idea that he'd made a profit off hurting other people.

Talea needed to do something about him. Poor boy was going to stress himself straight into some sort of terrible illness at this rate.

"I don't want you to think I don't appreciate everything you've done," Galen told the captain just before they all left the ship for good, "but, uh . . . we have no idea where to go next."

"Yeah, that occurred to me," the captain said. He paused a minute, and when it started to seem like Galen might lose his temper, he grinned. "Don't worry. I'll ask around. I didn't see the Lash's ship when we came in, but that doesn't mean much; the Lash has a habit of anchoring a distance away and rowing in on a smaller boat. Makes him harder to track." He pointed toward the city. "I recommend you lot make yourselves comfortable at an inn. The Scarlet Gull's a good choice. Once I have that information, I'll drop in and let you know."

Talea pursed her lips. She looked to the side, where Eshi was playing with a starfish someone had pulled up onto the dock. She didn't seem to be paying any attention. She also didn't seem to be particularly distressed. Talea thought she would be if following along with Captain Rima's plan would prove to be a really, really bad idea. A look of distrust came over Galen's face. This did seem like the sort of scenario that would make it spectacularly easy for Captain Rima to sell them out.

Rima held up a hand. "I can sympathize with your wariness. Tell you what. Pick whatever lodgings you want. Come back by the ship tomorrow morning at first light. The docks will be busy. There'll be a lot of people. I'll be out here, and if I've found any information, I'll tell you then. Fair?"

Galen squinted. "You could still have a group of people waiting for us."

"My darling," Sheloran said gently, "if his intentions were unpure, he could have simply made sure we didn't wake up one morning when he had us at his mercy. Waiting until we're ready for the attack would be very civilized of the man. Also very stupid."

"Thank you for appreciating that I'm neither," Captain Rima said, grinning. Sheloran inclined her head in his direction.

"All right. The Scarlet Gull, you said?" Galen pointed in the right direction.

"Sure," the captain said. "Big sign. You can't miss it."

Which proved to be the case. Talea immediately decided that she liked being in the city much more than she liked being on board a ship. Some of this was

---

[1] I'm beginning to understand why Argas found Taja so infuriating.

for purely hygienic reasons—the hospitality house gave her access to a bath, and since these were a people who evidently placed a great deal of pride and skill in all sorts of magic dealing with the channeling and controlling of water, they had the sort of plumbing that would have made House D'Laakar foam with jealousy. So a hot bath of the sort one could comfortably luxuriate in for hours is exactly what Talea took.

She spent much of the time thinking about Xivan and how she could possibly persuade the woman to give up her quest for revenge. It wasn't that Talea didn't also want to see Suless dead. She passionately hated the bitch. But it wasn't worth what Xivan had already proven she was willing to give up in exchange. There had to be a way to walk Xivan back from the cliff.

And Sheloran seemed nice, frankly. They all did. Maybe a bit young— even Qown was striking her as young these days—but so well-intentioned. She couldn't even hate Galen, and oh, she'd *wanted* to hate Galen.

When she had finished wrinkling up her skin as much as humanly possible, she toweled herself off, mourned the fact that even her spare clothing needed to be cleaned, and made her way downstairs. The tavern was rowdy, as one might expect of a place frequented by pirates, but honestly also endearingly homely. Someone was playing the flute along with a zither in the front of the room, which was much more melodic than Talea would have suspected.

Her companions had staked out a table for themselves and ordered several rounds of food. This included a strange fish dish that they told her was Zheriasian, eaten with various dipping powders and sauces. The fish was eaten raw, but that was also true of several Quuros dishes, so she didn't mind. And honestly, anything became edible with enough peppers on it.

And . . . they had a lovely evening. Neither Qown nor Galen drank, but Sheloran enjoyed a glass of wine. They laughed and sang and even danced a little.

Captain Rima was good for his word; he met them on the crowded docks at dawn the next morning. He looked bright and fresh; Talea suspected he probably woke up around this time every day.

She didn't necessarily mind the hour, it was just the whole "didn't really get any sleep from the night before" thing that was an issue. But in spite of that, she felt surprisingly spry, and Sheloran had bought all of them cups of coffee, tar thick and shockingly sweet, from a street vendor. They had to drink the coffee while they were at the stall, handing over the cups where they were finished so they could be cleaned and used for the next customer. The coffee was strong enough to wake the dead.

Rima looked like he'd probably had three cups. At least.

"Good news," he said, spreading his arms to include the group before landing his fists to his hips. "You lot are in luck, if you want to call it that. The Lash sailed into port early this morning. He's here."

"That is good news," Galen said. "Where can we find him?"

"No, no," the captain said. "I don't recommend you just go barging in there. He's here. That doesn't make him friendly, and the Captain's Council is largely hands-off when it comes to the Lash. Don't expect anyone to come running to your rescue if you get into trouble. Next step is to hire a messenger to go in and see if he'll consent to a meeting. If he does? Great. You go in and be polite. Be very polite. And if he tells you to get out, you do that." Rima sighed. "Mind you–I don't recommend you do any of this. Never heard of a meeting with the Lash that went well. Ever. But you can try."

Talea was only half paying attention. Mostly because she was watching the crowd and making sure no one came too close to Sheloran. Xivan was smart enough not to attack them outright given the size of the group; she was also smart enough to hire help.

It occurred to Talea that she had not the slightest idea in the world what Galen, Qown, and Sheloran were actually trying to accomplish. Why were they in the middle of the ocean on an artificial floating pirate city trying to arrange to meet with a pirate king?[2] Something about a Cornerstone, sure, but to what end?

Probably questions she should have asked the night before.[3]

Galen said, "Thank you. We'll start with that. Where would we send the message, though?"

Captain Rima sighed. "The Shark's Mouth. Don't make me regret telling you. And I shouldn't have to say this, but make sure you're not wasting the man's time. He has a notoriously short temper."

"We promise we'll behave," Sheloran said, smiling softly.

The pirate captain gave her a bow before heading back to his ship. The whole group stood there, drank their coffee, and watched him leave.

"So. We're killing the Lash, right?" Galen asked amiably.

"Oh, most definitely," Sheloran answered.

"*Why* are we killing the Lash?" Talea asked later as they waited for the messenger to return. It was afternoon, and the tavern hadn't yet started filling up with all the people who would come later for drinks and food. Which meant they'd had most of the day to just sit around and talk.

"He owns a Cornerstone that we need," Galen explained.

Qown frowned and looked uncomfortable about the idea.

Talea squinted. "Which one again?"

"Grimward," Galen said.

"I'm not familiar with that one."

"It can raise people from the dead," Galen supplied.

"There's a Cornerstone that can do that?" Talea said. "I didn't know that." She set aside her drink.

Qown cleared his throat. "I'm not as familiar with Grimward as some of the other Cornerstones, but I know its powers deal with death so . . . it's possible?"

"I thought you couldn't steal a Cornerstone," Talea said.

"If we kill the Lash," Galen explained, "the Cornerstone no longer has an owner."

Then Qown looked really uncomfortable. "I worry that just possibly a pirate king who's been able to evade the Quuros and Zherias navies for all this time might be more than we can handle? Also, although I realize I might be

---

[2] An excellent question she really should have asked much earlier.
[3] Or back on the ship.

speaking to the wrong crowd here, *killing is bad*." He started chewing on a nail.

Galen turned to him. "You do remember that this was your idea, yes?"

Talea leaned back in her chair. "We want to try talking to the man first? See if we can convince him to cooperate?"

Sheloran fanned herself. "I'd like that, but I can't imagine how we could entice the man to give up such an item. Or come back with us willingly to Quur."

"It would have been a lot easier if Thaena just agreed to bring Jarith back to life," Galen groused.

Talea froze.

She looked around the table and realized that, once again, she was the only person present who knew what had happened at the Well of Spirals. She was the only one of them who knew Thaena, Galava, Argas, and Taja were all dead.

Should she say anything? Should she say nothing? And what would it change? She felt paralyzed by indecision.

A teenage boy ran into the shop, looked around, and came over to their table. "I was told to give this to you."

"Thank you." Sheloran tipped the young man and took the note from him. He stood for a minute, staring wide-eyed at the royal princess. Talea had to stop herself from laughing. It was as if the poor boy had discovered puberty at precisely that minute. To be fair, it would be difficult not to, with a figure like Sheloran's.

Eventually, Sheloran noticed the messenger was still standing there. "You may go," she said.

"What?" He shook himself. "Right. Sorry." He wandered out, looking back over his shoulder.

Sheloran read the note. "The Lash has agreed to a meeting." She passed the note to Galen. "I say we go, try to see if he'll accept payment for use of Grimward, and scout out his protection and guards. Going in blind would be foolish. Once Qown has seen what the pirate looks like, we can use World-hearth to follow the Lash back to his lair, whether that be ship or some-place else. And only then, once we're confident of our ability to deal with his defenses—then we will make our move. Agreed?"

Galen grinned. "Sheloran, you're a genius."

She leaned over and touched Galen's hand. "You are so lucky you married me."

"I tell myself that almost every day. Did he say where he wants this meeting to happen?" Then Galen blinked, clearly realizing she'd already handed him the note. "The Black Dolphin. Tonight. I suppose someone here will know where that is."

It turned out to be an entertainment hall, and the meeting was to take place only a few minutes after it opened for the evening, meaning they'd have no time to arrive early and scout the lay of the land.

"Is 'entertainment hall' a euphemism for brothel?" Qown asked.

It seemed like a fair question.

Galen shrugged. "I honestly have no idea."

"Probably not," Sheloran said. "I have no doubt plenty of those exist here, but it's likely a combination of dining house and theater. People who've been at sea for weeks if not months do like their diversions."

"How is that not a velvet house?" Qown asked.

"They may not sell sex there?" Sheloran shrugged.

Galen bit his lip. "Sounds like a place that would have security."

"And we'll see if that's a good thing or not," Sheloran agreed.

The Black Dolphin turned out to be a fancy octagonal building with its own guards and a lot of customers eager to use the excuse to dress in their nicest clothing, eat delicacies, and be entertained. Talea felt incredibly under-dressed, but also amused, because what constituted "nicest clothing" covered a shockingly wide spectrum. Some of it could only be described as hilarious. Talea was distinctly amused to note that in many cases, the men had taken to wearing their agolé as wide sashes around their waists, with scabbards belted on top. Talea felt reasonably certain that sex was indeed not a service for sale here. She'd have worried about Qown if that had been the case.

They gave their name at the front, and the man in charge of seating actually blanched a little before bringing them into the back, to one of the private rooms. The room itself wasn't level but had risers on all sides, each level with seating for diners. The seats themselves were backless and low to the ground, so one had to kneel to use them. Instead of one large table, each person had their own personal table, also low to the ground. Lush tapestries and drapes covered every wall but the entrance.

The pirates had arrived first. They were dressed in the local style, but each of them also wore a mask. Indeed, each of them had their skin completely covered, with no sign of flesh visible anywhere. Their leader—or at least the woman in front—dressed in lace and silk, the mask drowned in the shadows lurking under her wide-brimmed hat. She nodded at them, then seemed to lurch forward as if she'd seen something unexpected.

"We have chilled wine for you," the waiter said. "And food. Your host"—he gestured back toward the woman—"has paid for entertainment. Please be comfortable."

"Hmm. The Lash has good taste, it seems," Sheloran said, looking at the bottle of wine. "It's Kirpis."

Galen shrugged. "Bring us a pot of tea."

"Tea?" The man seemed taken aback.

"You know. Leaves. You add hot water and steep until the color changes?"

The waiter cleared his throat. "Of course. Right away."

The man left, and . . . nothing happened. The pirates watched them. No one said a word. It began to verge on creepy.

Talea had been under the impression that the Lash was male, but the woman seemed in charge. She motioned to one of her people, who stepped forward and bowed. He was a small, thin man, and the way he moved was more like a scurry than a normal walk.

"The Lash welcomes you," he said.

Galen's head popped up. "Wait. I know that voice. Boji, is that you?"

The man in question chuckled nervously before taking off his mask.

The dark-skinned Zheriasian revealed looked sickly, like he hadn't slept for many days.

"What an unexpected reunion," Boji said. "Truly, it's a small world."

Talea leaned over to Qown. "Who's that?"

"Remember when I mentioned that pirate who wanted to rob and kill us?" Qown whispered back.

"Boji, you little turd!" Galen stood.

"It's so nice to be remembered," Boji said.

Every one of the seated pirates—except for the Lash herself—stood and drew their swords. There seemed to be a great many more of them than there'd been just a few moments earlier. They weren't just outnumbered; they were stunningly outnumbered. Even more so when several of the pirates made their way to the entrance.

There was something wrong with them too. They moved oddly. It was as if they were synchronized.

"Wait," Galen said, backing away. "Let's not be hasty."

The door opened. Several musicians and a troop of veiled dancers came in. They all paused in the doorway with the age-old experience of people who knew when not to interrupt an argument.

Galen refocused his attention back to the speaker. "We're just surprised to see you after our last parting. You have to admit we didn't part on the best terms."

The man—Boji, apparently—wagged a finger. "You should be grateful I refused to bring you to see the Lash." A look of fear flashed over his face as he looked back at the woman sitting behind him. "But since you're all so determined, the Lash has agreed to hear your petition. Although you might not want her to think you're being rude." He glared at Sheloran.

"I would never," Sheloran protested.

"Maybe just for special occasions," Galen amended. He turned back to Boji. "Would you mind telling your people to stand down? We're here to bargain, not to start a fight. If you weren't interested in hearing us out, why even invite us?"

The Lash laughed. Talea felt her gut twist.

She recognized the laugh.

"Oh no," Talea said.

No, no, no. She *hated* being right.

The thing that had been bothering Talea since they entered the room finally clicked into place. One of those niggling little details that had crept up on her unaware. The Lash was wearing a Khorveshan curved sword, an imchii, and although she'd largely tucked the scabbard behind her body, the hilt was still visible. Talea recognized the hilt as much as the laugh, and she'd know both anywhere.

It was *Xivan's* sword.

As Talea stood, Xivan made a motion with her hand. All around the edges of the room, the curtains dropped, demonstrating that they were even more outnumbered than they'd initially thought.

And most of the people doing that outnumbering were dead.

"I'm not interested in anything you want," the Lash—*Xivan*—said. "But you have something I want. Turn Sheloran over and there's no need for anyone to die." She didn't so much as turn her head in Talea's direction.

Talea stepped in front of Sheloran, aware even as she did that there were now enemies on both sides of her. "Galen, that's Xivan."

"What?" Galen and Qown said at the same time.

Something popped loudly. Billowy clouds of smoke began to fill up the room. Someone—probably one of the dancers—screamed.

"Don't run off!" Talea shouted. "Don't let them separate us." Footsteps moved around them in the smoke. Xivan cursed—the smoke evidently hadn't been her idea—and anyone who hadn't already drawn a blade remembered to do so. The smoke was the sort that choked the throat and stung eyes, far more annoying to the living people in the room than to the undead. Someone—maybe Boji—started coughing.

A pirate with half a face ran out of the fog, sword swinging. Then another one from the opposite side. That was the only warning they had before the dead husks all rushed at once. In the middle of this, however, the fog began to dissipate. Too fast to be anything but magic.

Talea was caught by surprise as the smoke cleared. A woman—one of the dancers, face still obscured by her veil—was fighting Xivan. From the tears in Xivan's clothing, she'd been stabbed several times, but Talea knew it took more than a few stab wounds to put Xivan out of commission. Or even slow her down.

Still, Talea could have kissed the dancer. She was doing a brilliant job of keeping Xivan busy so they could escape.

"Come on!" Talea yelled to the others. "We're leaving!"

Xivan stabbed the dancer through the abdomen.

"Run!" Galen called out as he decapitated one of the pirates. His sword wasn't nearly as good for that sort of thing as a Khorveshan sword, but he was trying his best. "Qown!"

Qown, Talea realized, was running to the injured woman.

Because of course he was.

"Qown!" Talea shouted, but he wasn't listening. She ran after him.

Which was how she found herself blocking Xivan's killing blow, the one meant to end the dancer's life. "What are you doing?" she asked Xivan, desperate and hurt, not understanding how this had come to be. What was Xivan even doing here? How had any of this happened?

"Get out of my way," Xivan spat.

"No," Talea said.

Talea didn't know if Xivan would have attacked her or not. Before she had a chance to test that particular bit of resolve, Xivan's sword twisted in her hand, the metal warping like a ribbon of sugar candy cooled too quickly. Xivan's eyes widened in horror, and she tossed the weapon aside before it could curl back and trap her hand or attack her.

Sheloran stepped up next to Talea. She didn't speak, but there could be no doubt in Talea's mind as to who had just ruined Xivan's family sword.

No doubt in Xivan's mind either, it seemed. "We're leaving. Now," she said.

"Oh yes, my lordship," Boji said, still coughing. "You're so very wise."

"Shut up, Boji," Xivan said. She walked away as the pirates who remained stepped in behind her to cover her escape.

Kihrin's story
Inside Vol Karoth's prison
After meeting up with Qown and Sheloran

We finally located Galen while in the middle of being ambushed by a whole contingent of animated flying statues that had dived off one of the taller buildings nearby.

Well, more like he found us.

"Look out!" shouted Janel, her sword materializing in her hands. She swung it at a swooping monster, shattering a curved horn and notching her blade in the process.

She blinked in surprise at the minimal damage done to the unnecessarily ambulatory statue. Vol Karoth was changing the rules again.

"I can do this!" Qown said. He stepped forward and lifted his hands. The paving stones of the street began to shift and quiver ahead of him. One lifted free and then flung itself violently at a gargoyle. Both shattered in an explosion of dust and rubble. He started to raise another one when suddenly, the paving stones collapsed back into place.

"Uh," Qown said, eyes wide.

"Not your fault," I told him, pointing. Up the street, the blacker-than-black silhouette that was Vol Karoth stood, his own arms outstretched.

Adorable. What a happy reunion.

Vol Karoth was countering Qown's control of the environment, which was at least better than fixing the situation by lobbing pieces of the sun at us.

Teraeth's shoulder-rolled to the side to avoid the claws of a goat-headed statue, while Sheloran D'Talus—excuse me, *D'Mon*—flung metal pellets at high velocity, knocking holes in the left wing of a gargoyle shaped like a leering demon. The sudden damage to one wing caused it to veer slightly to the left, missing Teraeth by a foot.

This is my world. My rules. My will. None of you have any chance against me.

With Qown and Vol Karoth locked in a struggle for control over "reality" itself, Janel's strength returned, and she smashed her opponent to dust with three brutal two-handed strikes.

Still, there were a lot of them, and they had razor-sharp claws and horns, a fact that Sheloran had cause to discover when one with snakes for arms managed to score a cut on her shoulder when she didn't block it in time. "Ow," she muttered, gritting her teeth.

"Hey, ugly," a voice called from across the street, "fangs off my wife!"

Galen D'Mon charged forward, swinging his sword. Sadly, it glanced harmlessly off the gargoyle. His rapier, excellent for duels in the Arena or aboard pirate ships, lacked the pure physical mass and strength to smash stone.[4]

---

[4] But really, don't most swords?

"Galen!" I called, ducking the tail whip of a scorpion-man gargoyle. "Nice timing. But you need to make your blade bigger."

"Oh sure," he called back. "I'll just . . ." But his blade did grow in size and the handle extended so he could use it two-handed if he wanted. He glanced at Sheloran, who smiled sweetly at him. "Oh," he said. "Thank you, Red!"

I lost track of him for a moment, wrapped up in my own problems. I ducked another sweep of the tail, jumped over a claw swipe at my leg, and grabbed my opponent by the curved horns on its head. Lifting it, I began smashing it as hard as I could against the ground, chipping and shattering it until all that remained was gravel.

I looked around to see how everyone else was doing. Things looked good; we were all dealing with our demons in our own ways. So to speak.

I noticed a figure across the street, where Galen had come from. A slender girl with honey-wheat skin.

I went cold as I recognized her.

Before I could say anything or otherwise make an ass of myself, more stone monsters began emerging from the open doorways of the buildings around us.

"Oh, for fuck's sake," Janel snarled.

"Yeah," I said, "screw this. Everyone! Run!"

Everyone did, including, I noticed, Lyrilyn.

After a few dozen blocks, we stopped running.

And we stood there for a few seconds just kind of looking at each other.

Galen had, I realized, been laughing, although less from an exuberant joy of life sort of sense and more "Can you seriously believe this shit?"

I respected the difference.

"Hey, nice to see you," I said.

"Yeah, you look pretty good for a dead man," he acknowledged.

"Ouch."

"Am I wrong?" Galen grinned at me.

"Let's just say I hope so." I held on to his shoulders and looked him over. He was almost as tall as I was, I realized, and his hair had taken on a decidedly red tone that spoke to his mother's influence. He was starting to look more and more like his father, but I hoped to god Galen never earned the same smirk of casual cruelty.

I gave him a hug.

He shook his head at me in mock exasperation when he finally pulled himself away. "You are such a troublemaker."

"It runs in the family."

"I have no idea what you're talking about—" He stuttered then, and when I looked over, I realized why. Ah. He'd spotted Qown.

"He got you too?" Galen asked him. He sounded like he was ready to go beat up Vol Karoth for the very idea.

Qown blinked at him. "What? Who?"

"Vol Karoth!"

"No, Qown and I volunteered," Sheloran said. She shrugged. "We had this ridiculous idea that we'd come rescue you. That you would need rescuing. Clearly not the case." She waved her fan at him.

Galen just smiled at that. I noticed he was still looking rather wistfully at Qown, however. Qown blushed and started to look away, then squared his shoulders and drew himself up. He walked over to Galen and picked up his hands.

Suddenly, I felt like I was about to be eavesdropping on a private conversation. So I walked away . . . and it didn't help. I still heard every word.

"Qown, what are you—"

"Please let me talk," Qown said. He took a deep breath. "I owe you an apology. I'm sorry. I just . . . I was scared."

Galen's voice was subdued. "It's fine. I know what that's like. I don't want to make you uncomfortable—" His voice cut off with a surprised muffled noise.

I looked back to see Qown was kissing him.

Sheloran spread her fan in front of her face. "Isn't that sweet?"

Qown and Galen paid no attention whatsoever.

They were still kissing when the next vision hit.[5]

Talea's reaction
The Lighthouse at Shadrag Gor
After Talea's memory of the Lash's ambush

Talea was pacing. She almost didn't notice when the vision ended.

"So . . ." Senera cleared her throat. "I realize I'm probably going to regret asking this, but how exactly did you end up pretending to be the Lash, Xivan?"

"It's a long story," Xivan said.

Everyone stared at her.

Talea smiled at the woman. "Sweetheart . . ."

Xivan crossed her arms over her chest, looking disgruntled. "What's there to explain? Var sent me to Zherias, I tracked down the same lying little thief who tried to rob Galen, Sheloran, and Qown, and he offered to take me to the Lash so I could get ahead of them."

Kalindra pursed her lips. "Sounds like he did."

"Yes, exactly," Xivan said, "but I didn't realize I was being volunteered as the next replacement. And since the Lash has Grimward, and I'm dead, she could control me and I had no power to tell her no. Thus, my new career as a pirate."

"So it's not a long story at all," Thurvishar said mildly.

Xivan bared her teeth.

Senera tapped on the edge of the table with the Cornerstone in a way that would have made Talea flinch if she hadn't known how indestructible the damn thing was. "What are we going to do?"

"That's my line," Kalindra growled. "What are we going to do if we run out of story before Kihrin . . . does whatever Kihrin needs to do?"

"We still have a fair bit of story to go," Talea pointed out.

"Not that much," Xivan said.

"It's helping," Thurvishar said. "It really is."

---

[5] Someone needs to have a chat with those boys about priorities. Vol Karoth wasn't that far behind them.

"I just worry that we're playing into his hands. I mean, obviously, we know why he's trying to delay"–Senera gestured vaguely in the direction of the tower–"but this feels like he's also trying to keep us from finding out something."

Thurvishar pointed to the stone in her hand.

"You don't think I've asked?" Senera said. "Vol Karoth's like Urthaenriel: immune to the Cornerstone's ability to predict or describe. I have no idea what his motivations or plans might be."

"Well, fuck," Kalindra muttered.

"Why don't we take a break," Talea suggested. "We can make something to eat, walk away from this for a few minutes. Maybe something will come to us?"

"That's just what he'd like us to do," Xivan pointed out. "Draw things out."

Talea shrugged. "Sometimes you have to take a step back to see the whole picture. Even if he's trying to delay things, he may also be trying to keep us so panicked and rushed that we're not thinking clearly."

Xivan met her eyes, held them, and smiled. Talea felt herself flush.

Ah, she wished she had more time for all sorts of reasons.

Kalindra shook her head. "I think you all are forgetting that this isn't our turn–"

The world changed.

44: SULESS'S GAME

Xivan's memory
The ocean near Da'utunse
Just after the failed attempt to kidnap Sheloran

Xivan stalked out of the Black Dolphin, fury coursing through every part of her. She ignored the startled or terrified looks of restaurant patrons, most of whom were reacting more to the undead crew she'd brought with her than herself.

She'd been so close! The idiots had marched right into the meeting, completely unprepared, with no idea what they were stepping in. Sheloran had been right there. *Right there!*

But so had Talea. Xivan had no idea how the woman had managed that particular miracle. Talea should have been back in Quur. How the hell had she ended up in the middle of the ocean?

"So, um, you don't need me anymore, yes, Captain?" Boji said, his voice tremulous. "It's been such a pleasure, but I'll just take my leave—"

Xivan grabbed the back of his shirt before he could run off. "I'm not finished with you just yet."

"Ah, of course, my captain. It's my honor to serve." He bowed as best he could under the circumstances.

"You really are a fawning little toad, aren't you, Boji?" She kept heading toward the ship. Once they were outside, most of the others shrugged into sallí cloaks and pulled up their hoods. In the dim light of Tya's Veil, they were basically indistinguishable from any other sailor out for a night of fun. Only Xivan and Boji were recognizable as anything other than mannequins—which happened to be closest to the truth.

His laughter was surprisingly genuine. "My mother always said if you're good at something and it makes you happy, you don't just have a job, you have a calling."

Xivan almost laughed. Fuck. She hated it when the little bastard reminded her that he'd once been a child. That someone, somewhere, might have cared what happened to him.

Xivan stopped in the middle of the street. People swirled around her in the night, full of pent-up energy and eager for entertainment. Night vendors in stalls lining the sides of the road offered delicacies to anyone with the metal to pay—some of it was even Quuros. If she'd still been capable of enjoying food, she'd have been salivating. As it was, this was a street filled with life. Shipowners shouted and customers haggled. A child screamed, which quickly transformed into the sound of a child laughing, the initial shriek indistinguishable from a more anguished noise. Xivan was surrounded by people; she had never in her life felt so alone.

It had been a mistake to track down the Lash. She knew that now. She just hadn't suspected–

She'd been stupid. Of course Grimward could be used to control undead. Of course Grimward could be used to control *her*. The Lash didn't need to gaesh Xivan, because Xivan came already bound, the control automatic and unbreakable.

So here she was, playing decoy because the last person playing the role had ended up so damaged he'd been all but useless, begging for the solace of a real death. Xivan's own wishes in the matter had been inconsequential.

"Would you like me to find someone for you?" Boji's voice was as soft and hesitant as a man trying to pet a shark.

"No," Xivan answered. She turned to him. "When did you eat last?"

"Oh, I–" He grimaced and made a dismissive motion. "I'm fine."

Xivan studied the man. Too thin. "We should buy you dinner–and some extra provisions for the trip. I'm sure no one on board is used to having passengers who still need to eat."

Boji seemed shocked. "Uh . . . thank you? Your generosity humbles me beyond–"

"Shut up, Boji. You're no good to me if you die from starvation."

"Yes, Captain."

Xivan stuck around just long enough to make sure Boji didn't try to run. Not that she blamed him. He had to be wondering if his reward for this misadventure would be a one-way invitation to join the Lash's crew as a mindless husk–which was a possibility. Unfortunately, Xivan needed someone who knew their way around the various factions of the ocean communities. Boji, for better or worse, filled that role. She couldn't trust him, but that would have been true of anyone. Almost anyone.

She had to stop thinking of Talea.

How had the woman found her? She hadn't been following Xivan. She'd somehow embedded herself with Sheloran, and the only way that made any sense was if . . .

Xivan did start laughing that time.

"Captain?" Boji eyed her as if he was contemplating whether or not running was the safe bet.

"She knew what I would do," Xivan murmured. "She knew I'd go after Sheloran. She must have contacted Qown and used . . . no, not Var. Perhaps Senera? Maybe even Thurvishar. But used one of those damn wizards to get ahead of me. And then she just had to wait." A warm, strange feeling filled her, and Xivan laughed again. Oh, but she was proud of Talea and more than a little rueful of how she'd underestimated the woman. She of all people should have known better. Talea was much more dangerous than she appeared.

Boji paused from eating a kelp-wrapped piece of fish. "You . . . know those people? The Quuros people we just left?"

"Yes, I know them." Xivan clasped his shoulder. "But we're not going to let that stop us. Let's head back to the ship."

"I was going to buy sweet-glass grapes," Boji whined.

"Hurry." Xivan moved her hand to the hilt of her sword only to remember that someone had wrecked it. Her father had made that sword—it had been his finest work.

She'd have to find a replacement, but that was a problem for later. For now, she concentrated on buying food for her single living crew member.

Xivan found no small amount of irony to the fact that they had to keep Boji alive. The Lash could and did use Grimward to astonishing effect when it came to puppeting undead, but she was terrible at creating them. It was the very quality that had made Xivan so valuable—she still possessed all her mental faculties. If the Lash raised Boji, he would lose the skills they needed.

Part of her was tempted to free him. What did it matter? But it mattered to the Lash. The only reason the pirate queen hadn't already killed the little shit was because Xivan had reminded her that Boji would be more useful if he still had a pulse. If the Lash had been hoping Xivan could also create undead of the same caliber as Xivan herself, well, Xivan had quickly disabused her of that notion. Although politely, because if the Lash had ordered Xivan to slowly dismember herself, Xivan would have done it without hesitation.[1]

The Lash's control—Grimward's control—was total. Already she could feel the Lash's impatience, the creature's will looping around her limbs like skeins of invisible thread pulled taut. The Lash wanted Xivan back. She began moving again toward the harbor and the ship. It didn't matter if Xivan didn't want to go or not. Go she would.

Xivan had tried to convince herself that this wasn't so bad. Xivan had explained that Sheloran was from a rich family and could be ransomed— she already knew that the royal princess was looking for the Lash, so it was simply a matter of arriving at the harbor to which Captain Rima Latemé was most likely to take them. The Lash had been intrigued enough by the idea to agree.

"Leave Boji in his room," Xivan told one of the men when they'd both returned to the ship. At least she hoped that's what she said. Her Mazhei was still a bit rusty, although she'd had quite an immersive introduction in recent weeks.

"That's not really necessary," Boji said. His mouth was sticky with fruit juice.

Xivan quirked her mouth and didn't dignify that with a response.

"Come talk to me."

"Now?" Xivan looked around. They were still in the harbor. They'd left the Lash quite a distance away, because no matter how cosmopolitan and sophisticated a pirate haven might be, the Lash—the real Lash—would never be welcome.

"Now."

The dead sailors around the ship didn't even wait for orders, although to be fair, they weren't truly under Xivan's control. They were nothing more than puppets controlled by the Lash. So they began casting off, immediately ready-

[1] Or even the ability to hesitate. Grimward is very different from the effect of a gaeshe in that regard.

ing to sail right back out of town. Xivan couldn't contradict the Lash's orders. She was a mouthpiece and nothing more.

She sat on the prow of *the Cruel Mistress* and watched the lights of Da'utunse fade, the low creak of wood as the wind caught the sails. The ship pulled out of the harbor on its way to make the Lash's rendezvous.

Find me.

Xivan didn't send for Boji. He wouldn't be coming along. Instead, she stripped off her most fragile finery and dove over the side. They'd left the Lash in a cave she used whenever she visited the pirate haven. It was large enough to accommodate her and even held a small pocket of air the Lash could use if she felt like having a conversation with guests less well adapted to life underwater.

Xivan, for instance.

When she reached the air pocket, Xivan pulled herself out of the water and looked around. As lairs of pirate queens were concerned, it fulfilled every cliché Xivan had ever heard—treasure littered every inch of the place. It very much struck Xivan as the sort of thing she might have expected to see created by an immortal being who had been told it was important to collect gold and jewels without anyone ever stopping to explain to her why. The Lash liked to pretend, but she wasn't human and never would be.

The Daughter of Laaka pulled herself out of the water.

The kraken looked a little like an octopus, if an octopus were pulled straight from a nightmare. She was the darkest abysses of the ocean brought to life, a rolling, squirming mass of tentacles flashing with glints of blue and green. On the underside of those writhing limbs, bony spikes made it easy for the monster to climb up on to ships or cliffs or anything with a surface to rend and crack. And there was one more detail that became noticeable only upon close observation.

The Lash was very dead.

As dead as Xivan, anyway. She had acquired the same gray cast to her skin, the same festering injuries, the same cataract eyes. It's just that the Lash was an undead creature the size of Arena Park. Breathtaking, in more than one sense.

Xivan sent a gold cup tumbling to the floor in her passage, the sound of water dripping off her clothing melding with the wet sound of the water from the cave. The kraken opened her glowing eyes and stared at her.

"You failed to bring back the princess," the Lash said. Not a question, of course. She already knew.

"She was more heavily protected than I anticipated," Xivan said. "We can find other marks . . ."

"It has nothing to do with treasure," the Lash said, slamming a tentacle against the stone hard enough to make the ground jump. **"What intrigued me about the princess wasn't treasure, it was knowledge. You said her family included powerful wizards!"**

Xivan paused. "I did, but . . ." She frowned. The Lash didn't want treasure? Xivan had promised wealth because she'd been trying to convince the Lash that ransoming Sheloran would be profitable. "What would you want with a Quuros Royal House?" She'd misunderstood something. Xivan knew very little of the nature of kraken, but she'd always assumed that they'd been created by the god-queen Laaka, who, as far as she knew, was very much still around. With that kind of close relationship with a god-queen, why would a kraken, basically immune to magic, anyway, need wizards?

Well, since she didn't have Senera in her pocket, there was only one way to find out. "May I ask what you needed her for? Perhaps someone else can help . . ."

The kraken's thrashing tentacles stilled, and she settled back into the water. Her eyes glowed like moonstones in the reflected illumination of the mage-lights set up in the chamber. **"I have a lover,"** the kraken explained. **"She's been acting oddly. I . . . worry."**

Xivan blinked. It was a toss of the dice as to which idea was more shocking: that the Lash had a sexual partner or that she'd worry about their welfare. "Another Daughter of Laaka?" It would have to be, wouldn't it? Few things in the ocean were large enough to compete with a kraken for size.

"No. I need to know what's wrong with her. I need to *fix* her."

Xivan looked away. "What if she doesn't want to be fixed?" she whispered.

"What was that?"

"I'm sorry. It was nothing. You think a wizard might know how to help?"

"Unless you know how to contact a god-king?" the Lash snapped. **"Or an Immortal? Are you good friends with Argas?"**

Xivan cleared her throat. She found herself extremely grateful that Grimward—which she could see twinkling like a small star just above the Lash's right eye—seemed to only give its owner the power to control undead, not the power to read their minds.

"Argas is dead," Xivan said.

"Dead?" The Lash once again demonstrated why she was named such. The cave was lined with the scratched evidence of years of this behavior. **"Are you certain?"**

"Yes." Xivan was certain. Xivan had, after all, been the one who'd slain him. Which had seemed like a good idea at the time. Xivan was starting to wonder.

"Doesn't matter," the Lash finally muttered. **"I just want my Drehemia back."** The monster stared balefully at Xivan. **"Make that happen and I will give you anything you want."**

ANYTHING? BECAUSE I THINK WE COULD WORK SOMETHING OUT.

Xivan turned around.

They weren't alone, impossible as that idea should have been. A woman sat on one of the mounds of treasure, leaning back against gold plates and trinkets as if they were pillows in a royal princess's boudoir.

The woman was unfamiliar. She had very pale skin, nearly white, and hair red as arterial blood. What she wore on her body could only laughably be called clothing.

XIVAN, MY DEAREST. HOW ARE YOU?

Xivan froze.

A demon? What was a demon—but there was only one demon who would know Xivan by name, who would greet her as someone familiar.

There was only one demon this could be.

"Suless," Xivan whispered. She reached for her sword, only to remember she didn't have one anymore, thanks to whichever one of those children had dabbled in sorcery enough to know how to warp metal. Probably Sheloran.

The demon grinned—a far wider grin than a human face should have allowed, done deliberately to be unsettling. A long, too-red tongue wagged at her before retreating into that black orifice. **AH, XIVAN. HOW WONDERFUL TO SEE YOU. I WAS JUST STOPPING BY TO CATCH UP WITH THE LASH HERE.**

"Catching up implies that we're friends," the Lash said. **"We've never met."**

NO, I SUPPOSE NOT. TRUTHFULLY, I WANTED TO SEE XIVAN. SHE'S ALWAYS GOOD FOR A LAUGH.

Xivan felt herself start to shake with anger.

AND ANYWAY, I THINK WE COULD BECOME FRIENDS. ESPECIALLY SINCE I HAVE SOMETHING YOU WANT.

"Do you?" The Lash pulled herself up.

"She's lying," Xivan said. "She's always lying. Her greatest pleasure in life is to sow chaos and pain."

YOU SAY THE NICEST THINGS.

Xivan ignored the demon and focused her attention on the pirate kraken. "Anyone she has ever claimed to befriend has come to a foul end. She is a vindictive monster who exists to manipulate others and cause malice."

WELL, I WON'T DENY IT. Suless cocked her head and smiled at the Lash. **SPEAKING OF VINDICTIVE MONSTERS, HOW IS YOUR GIRLFRIEND?"**

"If you're trying to convince me to let you live, you need to do better."

I'M A DEMON, Suless explained as if to a child. **YOU CAN'T HURT ME.**

"Is that so?" The Lash reached out with a tentacle and very delicately moved it toward the demon.

At the last minute, Suless stepped away, her expression disturbed.[2]

Xivan paused. This visit had just become interesting. She'd assumed a kraken could only affect a demon as much as any physical creature could—destroy the temporary physical shell and the demon would be forced to retreat back to the Afterlife. The level of Suless's hesitation, though . . .

YOU SAID YOU WOULD GIVE ANYTHING TO HAVE YOUR DREHEMIA BACK, Suless said. **I CAN MAKE THAT HAPPEN FOR YOU.**

At this, the Lash drew herself fully out of the water. Half her tentacles latched on to the stone wall of the cave, while the other half waved in the air. **"What do you know of it?"**

I KNOW IT'S ONLY GOING TO GET WORSE. DREHEMIA ISN'T ACTING THIS WAY BECAUSE SHE HAS ANY CONTROL OVER HERSELF. SHE DOESN'T. THIS IS ALL HAPPENING BECAUSE VOL KAROTH IS AWAKE. HER CONDITION WON'T IMPROVE.

---

[2] I believe we shall have to reexamine a great many of our assumptions about Daughters of Laaka.

The waters stilled and grew silent. The Lash had not moved at all.

"Go on," she finally said.

THE MONASTERY AT DEVORS HAS THE LARGEST COLLECTION OF BOOKS ABOUT PROPHECIES, DRAGONS, AND THEIR CREATION IN THE ENTIRE WORLD, Suless said. **THEY WOULD KNOW EXACTLY HOW TO RESTORE DREHEMIA. AND IN EXCHANGE, I ONLY ASK FOR ONE TINY THING.**

"No!" Xivan said. "You can't listen to—" Her whole body froze. Her throat ceased to function.

The Lash had paralyzed her.

Suless smiled at Xivan. It wasn't her normal broad grin. This was a tiny smile, just at the corners of her mouth, her eyes shining with delight. A real, genuine smile.

"It seems to me that all you're doing is giving me a suggestion and then asking me to do all the work."

OH, BUT IT'S SUCH A GOOD SUGGESTION. AND I DON'T WANT A FAVOR YOU WOULDN'T BE WILLING TO GIVE ME.

"You don't?"

NO. I WAS GOING TO ASK FOR XIVAN HERE, Suless admitted. **BUT WHAT YOU'RE DOING HERE IS WORSE THAN ANYTHING I COULD DEVISE.** She paused. **WELL, NO. BUT I'M TOO BUSY AT THE MOMENT. IT'LL KEEP ME WARM AT NIGHT TO IMAGINE XIVAN HERE, TOTALLY UNDER SOMEONE ELSE'S CONTROL . . .**

She walked in a circle around Xivan, trailing a finger around her shoulders, her back, the front of her body.

Then Suless looked back at the Lash. **ALL I ASK AS REWARD IS THE SAME YOU WERE GOING TO DO FOR XIVAN HERE. I WANT SHELORAN. YOU WON'T NEED HER ANYMORE. YOU'LL HAVE THE ENTIRE LIBRARY AT DEVORS.**

Xivan ground her teeth. No. Because even if she could never claim that her own intentions toward the royal princess had been pure, she knew that it would be better than what Suless would do to her. Turn her into a witch-mother at the very least. Possibly something quite a bit worse than that, given how little Suless probably cared about spare bodies now that she'd made her ascension.

"Fine. But you will help with the attack." That wasn't a question either.

Suless shrugged. **SURE. WHY NOT?** Suless leaned over and kissed Xivan's cheek. **SEE YOU AROUND.**

Xivan's reaction
The Lighthouse at Shadrag Gor

"What?" Thurvishar straightened. "Suless? What's Suless's involvement with all this?"

"Trying to have the Monastery of Devors destroyed, apparently," Senera said. "But why is the question I'd like to know." She paused and stared down at her paper as if contemplating the idea that it might have the answers that she was seeking.

"You're forgetting petty revenge and whimsy," Xivan pointed out.

"Janel has always claimed the Devoran Prophecies are Xaltorath's work," Thurvishar said. "Do you suppose that might be the connection?"

Senera narrowed her eyes as she regarded the other man. "You think Suless knows the truth? That she's figured out her connection to Xaltorath?"

Kalindra shook her head and walked over to the two wizards. "What are you two talking about? Fill it in for the rest of us, because we were never given the target briefing."

Senera scratched her forehead, sighing. She looked like she was searching for the words. "That monk you met back on the island. Linyuwan."

"What about him?" Kalindra narrowed her eyes.

"He's right." Senera pulled a blanket off one of the couches and wrapped it tightly around herself. The fire had burned low, and it was growing colder in the room. "Xaltorath has claimed that they are looping time, replaying events until they've manipulated the result they want. Which means your Linyuwan's theory about the prophecies truly being records of previous histories has validity."

Thurvishar didn't seem surprised. Instead, the look on his face suggested he agreed with Senera's statement.

"What does that have to do with Suless?" Xivan asked.

Senera looked helplessly over at Thurvishar. "Would you like to try this?"

"Fair," Thurvishar said. He pondered the matter for a moment. "So assume Xaltorath was telling the truth. That they have some way of traveling back in time. Clearly not to whenever they like. Were that the case, they'd have defeated all their enemies long before any of us were born. But there is some period of time—millennia, probably—that they can loop and start over when some as-yet-unknown condition is met. We have a rough idea of when the entry point is, because we have no prophecies earlier than that date.[3] But—according to Janel—the non-time-traveling not-yet-Xaltorath who is native to our version of history is Suless."

Everyone in the room was silent.

"Never mind. I should have explained it," Senera said.

"You're saying Suless is Xaltorath?" Xivan growled.

"More like Xaltorath's little sister who's never really going to be able to compete," Senera said. "Suless is the person who might have become Xaltorath under different circumstances. Not now though. Xaltorath won't tolerate the competition."

Kalindra ran the edge of a nail along the bottom of her lip, eyes lost as she gazed at something far away. "So I have a theory."

"All right," Senera said.

Xivan waited. Everyone waited.

Senera slammed her hand against the table. "Kalindra!"

The Black Brotherhood assassin visibly jumped. "Sorry."

"It's fine. We're all tired," Talea said.

---

[3] Just after Grizzst resurrected the Eight Immortals, which I am increasingly beginning to suspect may not be a coincidence.

"What is your theory?" Senera asked, sounding like she was trying not to grind her teeth.

Xivan saw Kalindra start to answer. She also saw the moment when Kalindra stopped herself, a flash of mischief dancing across her dark eyes.

"Oh," Kalindra said, smiling. "So you'd like to hear it, then?"

Senera growled.

"Because I wasn't sure," Kalindra continued.

"Kalindra, don't tease the short-tempered wizard," Talea scolded gently. "She knows dangerous spells."

Kalindra cleared her throat. "Whenever Jarith wanted to memorize something, he'd make a little game of it. Turn a list of things to be memorized into a sentence or a poem. 'Rebellious Kids Eager for More Justice Killed the Yellow King' becomes the Eight Dominions of Quur: Raenena, Kirpis, Eamithon, Marakor, Jorat, Kazivar, Yor, and Khorvesh. Make it a mnemonic device. If Suless has always been in a habit of doing something similar to that, what if she recognized the same behavior in the prophecies? Looked at them and thought: oh, I know what those are. Enough to know that if she destroys those notes, Xaltorath loses their playbook."

Xivan leaned back and stared at the ceiling. It was . . . possible. She liked to think she was reasonably familiar with how Suless's mind worked by now, although it was like sticking her hand in a bucket of slime. And Suless would never, ever let herself just be "Xaltorath's little sister"–if she knew that Xaltorath was competition, she would do whatever it took to eliminate that competition.

She straightened as she remembered how seriously Relos Var had taken Suless when almost no one else had. Like he had known . . .

Xivan turned to Senera. "You knew. You already knew the connection between Suless and Xaltorath."

Senera pressed her lips together in a thin, tight line. "No," she said. "If the Name of All Things doesn't work on anything prior to its creation, it certainly doesn't work on events that happened in the shadowy realms of might-have-been or has-been. We didn't know for certain–"

"But you suspected," Xivan said. "That's the real reason Relos Var wanted me to kill Suless so badly. He wanted to make sure he wasn't fighting *two* Xaltoraths."

Senera slowly nodded. "Yes."

"Oh, wow," Talea said. "We're really going to need to do something about her."

Senera laughed. "I've been saying that for years."

Kihrin's story
Inside Vol Karoth's prison

Galen and Qown didn't break their embrace so much as stumble backward from it. Galen shook his head and laughed. "Talk about your mood killers," he said.

"Why yes," Janel said, nodding, "Suless often has that effect on people."

"Does this 'whatever we're doing gets interrupted by a vision' thing ever grow less annoying?" Galen asked the group at large.

Teraeth and I exchanged a glance. We both started laughing.

"What?" Galen asked.

We didn't elaborate, but I thought the meaning was obvious enough:

No. No, it never did.

"Vol Karoth has a marked tendency to act quickly after he ends a vision," Janel said. "We should relocate before he . . . Oh. Never mind."

A group of statues, mostly lions and a few thriss drakes, loped up the boulevard toward us.

"What do you think the others are doing right now?" Qown asked, brushing marble dust off himself.

The battle had been short but fierce. We picked our way out of the field of rubble we'd created with care. No one wanted to survive an attack by stone monsters only to fall because we twisted an ankle on their remains. Not permanently crippling—not here, anyway—but downright embarrassing, under the circumstances.

"Senera's probably asking her magic rock something that really doesn't matter right now, but she just can't resist the urge to learn every bit of minutiae involving something—," Sheloran said, flicking away dust from her shoulder.

"Kalindra's growling about something," Galen added, shaking gravel from his hair. "And she's probably found a way to blame Xivan for it."

"And Talea's saying something cryptic but profound," Qown said with a grin.

The rest of us stared at them. Then Janel asked slowly, "Is . . . is everything . . . all right . . . back there?"

Teraeth frowned. "What the fuck happened while we've been gone?"

Sheloran made a dismissive wave with her fan. "Place that many people with massive 'I'm always right' complexes in the same room, and one's bound to have personality conflicts."

"So anyway," Galen said, "what are you all up to? I mean, before you went looking for me. Anything exciting?" The blue eyes were full of sharp mischief and irony.

"We're looking for gray spots," Teraeth said.

Galen stared at him for a moment, trying to decide if the vané man was joking or not. Finally, he said, "So . . . that's a no, then?"

I chuckled. "We've discovered that some locations in the city are even grayer than others, with all color missing. Those spots seem to be memories or . . . something . . . important to Vol Karoth. They're usually dangerous, but we think that exploring them is weakening him."

"How dangerous?" asked Qown.

"It varies, but they tend to fall somewhere between 'a half-dozen Dedreughs' and 'Relos Var' on the catastrophe scale," Janel opined.

Qown blanched.

"My, then. So what are we waiting for?" Sheloran asked brightly. "We're here, you're here . . . shall we make a party of it?" She pointed her folded-up fan at Kihrin and said, "No chicken costumes this time."

"Party found us," Teraeth said, pointing.

Vol Karoth had raised an entire army of marble soldiers, complete with shields and pikes, and they were marching up the street toward us in perfect formation.

"Oh, for fuck's sake," I said, sighing. "Run!"

We were still running when the inevitable vision hit us.

45: Under the Sea

Talea's memory
The pirate haven of Da'utunse
Just after fighting Xivan

The dancer sat up as Qown healed her injury and pulled the veil from her head. The woman underneath was a handsome woman of mixed Khorveshan and Zheriasian ancestry. Her expression was murderous.

"Galen, what are you doing here?" the woman demanded.

Galen's eyes widened. "Kalindra?"

"Let's have a reunion later," Talea suggested. "Right now, we need to find someplace secure. Any suggestions?"

Sheloran bent down and picked up Xivan's discarded sword, now shaped like a spring. "Pick a hospitality house at random. But any brothel will have rooms rentable by the hour or night with better security than a hospitality house."

"Why do we keep ending up in brothels?" Qown asked plaintively.

Sheloran was clearly still waiting on Galen's answer. "Agreed?"

"Agreed," Galen said. He stopped and narrowed his eyes at both Talea and Kalindra. "And then we're going to have a talk."

They found a brothel that looked fancy enough for discretion and good security and paid for their own room. It was probably cleaner than a room at a hospice would have been. The room was large, the bed enormous. The velvet house owner never even blinked at their party size or when they suggested that they would need dining arrangements for everyone.

Talea had to admit, the low chairs and individual tables did make it much easier to accommodate their numbers. A velvet house probably wouldn't have had a table large enough for them to all sit together.

"Let me look at your wound again," Qown said to Kalindra.

"I'm fine."

"You're fine when I say so," Qown snapped.

Talea smiled. Qown had lost his patience.

"So if that was your Xivan, one assumes it wasn't the real Lash," Galen said. "And you weren't kidding when you said Xivan would find us. I apologize for not taking you more seriously."

"I don't . . . I don't know what happened back there," Talea admitted. "But I agree Xivan is not the Lash. And she definitely can't control the dead. So someone else must have had Grimward." She chewed on her lip. "You don't think it was the ratty little man, do you?"

"I think if it were Boji, we wouldn't have survived our first ambush," Sheloran said. "So no."

Meanwhile, Qown had finished looking at Kalindra and pulled World-hearth from under his shirt. "We have a problem."

Galen waited for a moment, then motioned for him to continue.

"I follow heat sources," Qown explained. "And the dead don't really . . . have any. That's going to make it difficult–if not impossible–to figure out where Xivan went. Our plan hinged on that." He grimaced. "It never occurred to me that the entire crew would be dead."

"Xivan isn't the one you need to follow," Sheloran said. "Boji is. Boji looked alive."

Qown opened his mouth and then closed it again. "Right! Right." He hurried over to a chair, sat down, and started staring into the rock's heart.

Galen watched him for a moment before motioning for everyone else to pay attention to him. "Okay," he said. "Now, Kalindra . . . mind explaining what the hell you're doing here?"

Kalindra stared at him with narrowed eyes. "You first."

Galen didn't answer.

Kalindra leaned back and crossed her arms over her chest.

Finally, Sheloran rolled her eyes. "We're here to find Grimward so we can raise your husband from the dead."

Kalindra blinked at her. "That's . . . How do you even know about Grimward?"

"Weirdly enough, the wizard Relos Var told us," Galen said. "And we're not helping him, but I haven't stopped looking over my shoulder. Figure he could show up at any time. Now you, Kalindra."

"So this is Jarith's wife?" Talea said, desperately hoping for an explanation before she accidentally said the wrong thing. She only knew of one Kalindra, and that was a Black Brotherhood assassin and . . .

Okay. Probably the same Kalindra. Small world.[1]

"Yes," Galen said, "and what have you done with Nikali?"

"I left him in good hands," Kalindra said. She rubbed her forehead and chuckled. "And as it happens, I'm here for the same reason you are. The exact same reason. Even before Thaena–" She closed her eyes. "Grimward's my only chance."

"I'm sorry, Kalindra," Galen said. "I really am. But hey, at least we're much closer than we were, and it's looking like someone in the Lash's organization really does have it, so . . . just a matter of convincing them to give it up." He gave Kalindra a hard look. "Although to be perfectly clear, we're not handing over Sheloran."

"Thank you, darling," Sheloran said distractedly as she concentrated on the ruined sword.

Kalindra frowned. "Why does the Lash want Sheloran?"

"Not the Lash. Or yes, I suppose the Lash, but Xivan was hunting for Sheloran before she started pretending to be the Lash," Talea said. "It's not about

---

[1] Oh not at all, but it's easy to mistake causation for coincidence.

Sheloran at all. Xivan just needs help, and she's being incredibly stupid about how she's asking for it." She felt a flash of heat, of anger and frustration.

"Okay, well, then I say our situation hasn't especially changed," Kalindra said. "We're still trying to locate and kill the Lash."

"No!" Talea protested.

Sheloran ran her hand over Xivan's imchii, straightening it, or rather returning it to its original gentle arc. "This is Vanaj Mezian's work. I'd know it anywhere."

Talea blinked. "Xivan's father made it."

"So her father is Mezian? Well, then. Huh." Sheloran laughed, although its edge was a little too dark to be considered delight. "He was one of our best weaponsmiths. Quite famous for the fine quality of his blades." She smiled at the sword. "It is unfortunate for Xivan that her father chose to make this sword out of a rare alloy that my father invented. I imagine she'd grown rather used to most wizards having no idea what her sword was made from and thus no idea how to warp the blade."

Talea seemed intrigued in spite of herself. "What's the alloy?"

"My father's idea of humor," Sheloran explained. "It's called sheloran."[2]

Galen coughed.

"Really?" Qown leaned away from the table, eyes wide and unblinking.

"Oh, it could have been worse," Sheloran said. "Can you imagine if he'd named me shanathá? Or drussian." She mock shivered.

"No, not that," Qown exhaled and covered his face for a moment before lowering his hands. "I meant I found her. I found Xivan."

Talea's heart skipped. She immediately crossed over to the table and sat down across from Qown, taking his hands. "Is she all right? Where is she?"

Kalindra scowled at the man. "What are you—" Her mouth dropped open as she saw what the healer was holding. "You have Worldhearth? How do you have Worldhearth?"

Qown blinked at the two women, clearly unsure who he should be answering. Finally, he said to Talea, "She seems well? I mean, sort of well. Well maybe isn't a word I would ever use to describe Xivan, though."

"It's fine," Talea said. "She's been dead for years."

"Anyway, it was tough finding Boji, but fortunately the nice thing about us being out here in the middle of the ocean is that fire really stands out, heat-wise, and Boji lit a fire to keep warm. Finding Xivan still would have been impossible, but—" Qown chewed on his lip. "I'm getting ahead of myself."

"Go on," Talea urged.

"It looks like she's being controlled," Qown said, "by the real owner of Grimward. She has no choice but to do whatever it says."

"I can't help but notice their interests seemed to have aligned when it comes to kidnapping me," Sheloran commented.

"Yes, well . . ." Qown squeezed Talea's hands back. "Remember how everyone says the Lash has a kraken? It's kind of . . . true."

[2] I have to wonder which came first. Probably the metal.

"Oh, how lovely," Galen said.

"I know it's true," Kalindra said. "That's why the best time to move against the Lash was after he came to port." The woman frowned. "But the Lash I knew was a man. And not undead.[3] That's who I'd expected to find. That's who I expected to kill."

"Right," Qown said, "but everyone has it wrong. You see, it's the kraken. The kraken *is* the Lash."

No one said anything.

"What?" Galen said.

"The kraken. The Daughter of Laaka—she's the Lash. She's also undead and has Grimward."

Kalindra sat down slowly. "Are you telling me that someone took a creature that's almost entirely immune to magic and made her almost entirely immune to physical damage as well? And gave her the ability to animate the dead?" Her voice went up several octaves on the last part of that sentence.

". . . yes?" Qown said, wincing.

"Right. Just checking." Kalindra slammed a fist against one of her legs. "Perfect. Really, really love this development. Taja just fucking loves me."

"It's nothing personal," Talea muttered.

"It gets worse," Qown said.

"Of course it does," Galen said.

"Suless came to visit."

Talea felt her pulse skip so hard she felt faint. Then she noticed that no one else seemed to be reacting the same way. Except for Qown, of course.

"The witch-queen Suless," Talea whispered, then shook her head. "But that makes no sense. Xivan hates Suless."

"Are we . . . are we talking about the god-queen Suless?" Kalindra looked bemused.

"Yes," both Qown and Talea said together.

"I thought she was dead," Kalindra said.

"She's not," Qown assured her. "And Xivan does still hate Suless, but the Lash wasn't allowing Xivan to attack. Suless wants to work with the Lash, and the Lash seems to be agreeing because she thinks Suless can help her cure her girlfriend's insanity." He made a face. "Uh, I didn't realize that Daughters of Laaka could—"

"What? Do you think it can't work without a Son of Laaka?" Talea laughed. "You know better than that, Qown."

"Yes, you're right, of course," Qown agreed. "Apparently, said girlfriend is . . . uh . . . Drehemia. I assume she means the dragon."

"I'm not really, uh, up on my dragons," Galen said. "Which one's Drehemia?"

"Oh, she's the dragon of shadows," Qown said. "Of secrets and lost knowledge. If Drehemia traveled near, you'd likely never realize it until she attacked. She's darkness and mystery."

[3] Oh, I sincerely doubt that. Xivan does a wonderful impersonation of a living person just after she's fed. I imagine it was much the same with Kalindra's former lover.

"Sounds lovely," Sheloran said.

"Vol Karoth's awakening—" Qown shut his eyes for a minute and seemed to collect himself. "Vol Karoth's awakening has affected Drehemia, and she's gone on a rampage. The Lash is concerned—desperately worried—and wants to know how to fix her. And for some reason, she thought your mother would have that ability? Although honestly, I don't see how."[4]

"My mother's made it something of her life's work to study and cure mental troubles," Sheloran murmured. "If it were any normal case, I would say there was no one better, but I fear this isn't any normal case."

"No," Galen agreed. "I would say not."

"So Suless convinced the Lash that the library at Devors has the cure and that the Lash should . . . attack it." Qown flailed a bit.

Kalindra closed her eyes. "Nikali. My son is there."

"Okay, so that's a problem," Galen said. "Not that I think we should just let a Daughter of Laaka attack the Monastery at Devors, but surely their defenses can handle that, right?"

"Why would they?" Kalindra replied. "Quur is concerned with practical defenses. Who would suggest putting up wards meant to deal with a kraken? Those are creatures of myth. If you live in the empire, you probably don't believe they exist. The idea that one would attack an entire island—that's ludicrous."

"And yet," Sheloran said. "The monastery is warded against dragons and demons. If it can keep them out, it can almost certainly stop the Lash. The real problem is that any Quuros ships in those waters won't have those protections."

"We have to warn them," Qown said.

Talea scowled and threw her arms over her head and she walked around. "Why . . . why did Thaena have to move her stupid cup? I could fix this if only I had it!"

"Cup?" Qown asked.

"I suppose technically it's a grail," Talea allowed.

Kalindra turned in her seat. "Thaena's Grail? You're talking about Thaena's Grail, aren't you?"

Talea tilted her head. "Yes? I mean . . ." She paused to consider Kalindra again.

Kalindra was an angel of Thaena. Kalindra knew Thaena was dead.

"Yes," Talea said, "I'm talking about Thaena's Grail."

"Huh." Kalindra's mouth twisted. "As it happens, I do know where that is, but there's no way to recover it. I didn't think . . . I was never really sure what the cup did. If anything. She always made it sound like—"

"I believe the cup would supersede Grimward's control," Talea said truthfully. "If we can get Xivan to take it." And if it liked her. If Xivan and the cup resonated.

"So where is it?" Galen asked.

"Oh, well, you know how it is," Kalindra said with entirely false humor.

---

[4] The knowledge that Sheloran's mother was Caless would have explained a great deal, I imagine.

"It's a small world. Last I knew—and I see no reason why this would have changed—it was in the lair of the *shadow dragon Drehemia.*"

Talea rubbed a thumb into her temple. "I'm really starting to hate dragons."

"What if I could find out where Drehemia's lair is?" Qown asked quietly.

As soon as he asked the question, Talea knew exactly what he was suggesting. Contacting Senera. Asking the Name of All Things. She wasn't entirely certain it would work on the cup, but then again, why wouldn't it? It worked on the Eight Immortals themselves. The only reason it had never been used on the cup was because Relos Var hadn't known to ask.

Thaena must have thought giving the cup to the dragon of secrets to be delightfully appropriate.

"It's a dragon," Galen said. "We don't have a way of dealing with a dragon."

"We might not have to," Sheloran said. "If the Lash is right and Drehemia is out rampaging, then she's not in her lair. Why couldn't we sneak in, steal a single cup, and walk right back out? We wouldn't confront Drehemia at all."

"Qown could check," Talea said. "Once we know the location, he could make sure she's not at home."

"Huh." Galen crossed his arms over his chest, looking thoughtful. "That could work. Just possibly. And you think this cup will really make a difference?"

"It doesn't matter," Sheloran said. "We have no way to make Xivan take the cup, and even if we did, no way to reach Devors first. The Lash is almost certainly already on her way. And we're sitting here in an inn in pirate land, where, I must remind you, we don't own a ship."

Talea felt herself deflate. It was still possible, but it would mean asking Senera for not only a favor involving the Name of All Things but also transportation. That latter one was far more likely to have her asking inconvenient questions about what they were doing. Questions Talea didn't want to answer.

"I know a quick way back to Zherias," Kalindra said. "From there, it's a short stretch to cross the Galla Sea to Devors. We shouldn't take our time, but depending on where Drehemia's lair is, we'd be able to make it there days before the Lash." She paused. "Drehemia's lair is almost certainly near here."

"What makes you say that?" Sheloran inquired.

"Because . . ." She paused and seemed to be considering her words. "The Lash lairs near here. That's where the cup was last seen, and the ship it was on was attacked at sea. Drehemia wouldn't be attacking ships at random. She'd be attacking ships that were convenient. And if her girlfriend is the Lash, well, I think we can assume she's normally close by."

"I bet someone in Ithlakor knows exactly where Drehemia lairs," Sheloran said.

Galen stared at her. "The dragon of secrets and shadows? You're sure about that?"

Sheloran's face twisted. "Oh. Never mind."

"But your logic was good up until that point," Qown said. "She probably does live close to the Lash, and I'm sure her hunting grounds are convenient. It's just that she could probably be living directly under this city and nobody would realize it. It's a trait she shares with Gorokai."

"Which one's Gorokai?" Galen asked.

"The dragon who destroyed the Temple of Light." Qown's expression was stricken.

"Oh. That Gorokai."

"So Senera, then?" Talea said.

Qown nodded. "Yes, this may take longer. She can be difficult to track down, but I'll see what I can do."

It did take longer. Nearly four hours. During which time, everyone was antsy and increasingly discomforted by the loud sex noises that migrated through the walls from their neighbors.

"Are we going to sleep here?" Qown looked at the room like he was in danger of melting if he touched the wrong surface.

Galen picked up an enormous pillow and shrugged. "Don't fool yourself. A regular hospitality room wouldn't be any cleaner."

"Hmm." Qown wrinkled his nose.

"Why don't we order dinner while we wait," Sheloran suggested. "None of us had the opportunity to eat at that lovely establishment we were forced to leave so dramatically."

"I think I'm beginning to understand why Qown lost so much weight," Talea murmured, looking at the man. He looked better than the last time Talea had seen him—the hair was a good look for him—but she remembered when he'd first arrived in Yor. He'd been all shyness and baby fat, and then she'd watched the hope drain from his eyes even as the pounds had melted from his body. It hadn't been healthy, and she'd been tempted to lay all the blame on the food, but now she began to suspect a different reason: self-inflicted starvation. He'd probably just grown accustomed to the idea of going without.

Everyone else was enjoying a positively opulent spread of food, but Qown was too busy using Worldhearth. Qown still crouched down on the embroidered pillow by one of the long sofas, curled up around the stone in his lap the way one might around a good book. If it took much longer—and there was no reason to think it wouldn't—then the meal would be over long before he was finished.

Galen frowned. "Lost weight?"

Talea shrugged. "When he was trapped in Yor." Her expression turned morose. "He wasn't eating. Yor isn't a great place to be stuck if you don't eat meat."

Galen sent down to the kitchen for a dish of pastry-wrapped vegetable pies, which seemed like they would probably survive the wait.

After some time, Qown woke and blinked wearily. He looked around the room as if he'd forgotten where they were, forgotten what they were doing. He looked exhausted.

Galen picked up the pies and brought them over to Qown. "Eat one, then tell us what you found out."

Qown's expression lit up. "Oh? Oh, thank you. I'm famished." His fingers paused as he was about to touch one of the pies. "But what is—?"

"Some kind of spinach, I think," Galen said. "Not spicy enough, though."

Qown glared. "You think it's not spicy enough unless it will melt your teeth."

Galen shrugged. "Guilty."

Sheloran bapped both men on the head with her closed fan. "Enough of that. What did you find out?"

Qown cleared his throat. "Ah, well, it's like Kalindra suspected. Drehemia does have her lair near here, and Thaena's Grail is there."[5] He took a delicate, exploratory nibble on the pastry before deciding it was acceptable and biting off a larger piece. "But it's at the bottom of the ocean. Now I happen to know a glyph—uh, I mean a spell—that's fantastic for breathing underwater, but it's terrible for actually, you know, seeing underwater. It would be extremely difficult to navigate. Imagine trying to see to the bottom of a lake from the outside. That's—that's what it's like."

"That won't be an issue." Kalindra sat to the side, managing to convey a sense of isolation.

"It won't?" Galen cocked his head.

Kalindra's wry smile suggested she just might possibly have been enjoying herself. "There's an Ithlané temple here in town. That means we can work something out."

Kalindra took them to the docks, a rambling, multilevel structure that looked like exactly what it had probably been: an improvised collection of independent buildings lashed together with compromise, magic, and good intentions. Eyes lingered on them as they walked, focused on the hundreds of telltale clues that betrayed their outsider status. They didn't belong, and these people knew it.

The night air smelled of salt and fresh ozone. To Talea's pleased surprise, it smelled not at all of dead fish and offal. Kalindra was the only one of them who clearly knew where she was going and what she was doing. Talea found herself wondering what the woman planned to do now. Did the Black Brotherhood even still exist? Or would it become a secular organization, exactly what they had pretended to be on the surface—assassins for hire?[6]

"Here's how it will go," Kalindra explained to the rest of them. "The priestess will ask for a donation. It will be expensive. Pay it, anyway. We're going to ask her to give us the blessing of the sea daughters—"

"Please don't tell me you're going to ask her to turn us into kraken," Galen said.

Kalindra glared. "Would you rather we didn't do this?"

Galen stopped talking.

"As I was saying," Kalindra continued, "be reverent and respectful. I should warn you that she will ask us to disrobe. That's perfectly normal. Anyone who has a problem with nudity should wait at the temple door."

It was almost comical how many of them turned and looked at Qown. He didn't seem to find it nearly as amusing. "I'll be fine."

"They will put the possessions we leave behind in a chest. Don't take any-

---

[5] I am curious what he used as a focus, but I suppose that curiosity will have to go unsatisfied for the moment.
[6] I assume at least some of them will go that route. They do have marketable skills, after all.

thing you don't mind dunking under water for several hours. Conversely, take everything with you that you reasonably can. I've never personally heard of anyone robbing one of the priestesses, but that doesn't mean it never has nor never will happen." Kalindra continued on then, not waiting to see if anyone declared that they were staying behind. Likely she assumed the truth: that everyone was committed.

Eventually, Kalindra stopped at the end of a pier, then motioned for the rest of them to continue following her as she ducked down a ladder. Talea would've never noticed it.

At the base of the ladder, a small wooden platform floated just above the waves, so cramped that Talea had to stoop. She could only imagine how un-comfortable Galen found the experience. Ropes secured an altar to the end of the platform, although it might be more accurate to say that it hung down from the timbers of the pier above. The altar consisted of offering bowls, a statue of a woman who was half fish, and various artistically draped fishing nets and corals. The woman tending the altar was ancient, her skin a pale, chalky gray, her eyes silver with no whites at all.

The old priestess picked up an offering bowl and thrust it in their direction.

Galen took the coin pouch that Captain Rima had given him, weighed it in his hand for a moment, and then placed it into the bowl. One by one, ev-eryone else did the same.

"We would like a blessing of the sea daughters, please," Galen said carefully.

She squinted at him, then seemed about to turn around.

Kalindra said something.

The woman paused and turned back.

"What did you just say?" Sheloran asked.

"I said we would like a blessing of the sea daughters," Kalindra said. "Evi-dently, the priestess on duty tonight doesn't speak Guarem."

The woman sniffed. Her nose wasn't just small, it was nearly absent—more like a protrusion with nostrils than an actual nose. The priestess said some-thing unintelligible.

Kalindra answered, clasped her hands in front of her stomach, and bowed. Talea didn't need to understand the language to guess that Kalindra was probably placating the woman about performing services for outsiders.

"Bah! Not one of them knows the sea," the old woman growled.

Talea bit her lip and looked around. Nobody else gave any sign that they'd suddenly begun comprehending the old woman's words. And it wasn't like the priestess had suddenly begun speaking Guarem. Rather, Talea had suddenly started understanding Ithlané. Across the platform, she saw Eshi standing there very still, watching.

Eshi put a finger to her lips to indicate silence.

"Our intentions are good," Kalindra assured, "and our need great."

The old woman huffed, then began opening the bags. Her eyes widened at the quantity of metal contained inside. "I admit this is . . . respectful." She closed off each bag and set them carefully in front of the altar. "Fine. Tell them to disrobe."

Talea ignored the instruction until Kalindra translated. For Talea's part, undressing happened without much fuss or interest. She hadn't found nudity embarrassing for years. She doubted it was anything the others hadn't seen. Including Qown.

The old woman motioned. Kalindra indicated they should each stand next to the edge of the platform, the sea at their backs.

"Don't surface again until the spell ends," the old woman warned. "You'll choke to death on air. And it won't last more than four hours, so don't be caught on the bottom when it ends or you'll die for sure. Understand?"

Kalindra translated this, basically as spoken.

The old woman began to pray and mumble something under her breath, making passes with her hands in the air that lingered, ghost images trailing behind her movements.

Then she knocked Galen on the head with the flat of her hand and pushed him back into the water.

"This is normal!" Kalindra shouted a quick assurance.

The priestess knocked back Sheloran next, then Qown, finally Talea, and then, presumably, Kalindra.

Admittedly, Talea was a little too distracted to pay much attention by that point. Her first sensation was, predictably, wetness.

Her second sensation was pain.

Her legs itched, and then that itching turned into a screaming, piercing horror of agony. She screamed, unable to stop herself, and choked as she found herself breathing in water instead of air. Everything about the experience told her to get out, to escape, to struggle to stay afloat.

"Stop fighting it," Eshi commanded in a tone quite at odds with the little-girl voice delivering it.

Talea held on to her sword with all her might. She probably had tears streaming down her face, but since she was underwater, she couldn't really tell. Everything hurt.

Until, quite suddenly, everything didn't.

She jerked and ended up doing a movement more like a shimmy than a scissor kick as she tried to move her legs. Talea looked down and realized that moving her legs was impossible.

She no longer had legs.

A long, iridescent fish's tail now flowed from her hips to past where her feet should have been. And she was breathing perfectly well, although she had no idea how. She also saw clearer in the dark water than she'd ever been able to on land.

She laughed. Notably, this didn't have the normal effect of drowning her. Everyone else had a fish tail too, the same as she.

"Well, this is weird," Galen said. "Pretty sure I've never been a fish before."

"You're only half-fish," Sheloran assured him.

The language was odd. While Talea thought that she normally wouldn't have been able to understand it (at least not any more than she could understand anyone speaking underwater), everyone's speech was perfectly intelligible.

"You know which way to go?" Kalindra questioned Qown.

"West," Qown said, "but I'm not sure which way is west."

"Follow the cold current," Kalindra said. "It comes from the west." She pointed. "That way."

"Right." Qown nodded. "Then we need to go that way. We're looking for an underwater mountain. It shouldn't be more than a few miles from here."

"Then let's get moving," Galen said.

Talea was more familiar with dragons than most people, for whom the very idea of a dragon was a god-king tale to be dismissed as the province of children. She knew better. She hoped Qown was right about Drehemia being away from her cave. It wasn't a mistake they were likely to survive.

Talea had seen five dragons in her life: Aeyan'arric, Baelosh, Sharanakal, Relos Var (in dragon form), and Thaena (in Talea's opinion, she counted, even if she wasn't a dragon in the same way as the others).[7] The closest Talea had ever come to dying was at the hands of the dragon Baelosh. She had great respect for the power of dragons.

She had no desire to meet a sixth.

Talea pulled short, arms moving in circles as she kept her place in the ocean water. In the distance, fish and larger animals—dolphins, turtles—went about their lives. And although she would have assumed she wouldn't have a sense of smell, in fact, her olfactory senses seemed to be her most acute. For example, she could tell in which direction she needed to swim if she wanted to find where people had gathered or had dumped their waste into the sea. She knew where to find blood.

"I checked," Qown said, "and Drehemia is miles away right now, attacking a city in Zherias. She's rampaging, just as the Lash claimed. So in theory, there's no one to stop us."

"In theory," Galen repeated.

"The theory being she lives alone?" Talea asked.

Galen nodded. "Pretty much, yes. Let's hope that's true. And that Taja likes us."

"As much as she likes anyone," Talea said mournfully, but she rather doubted that Galen caught the subtext. She thought the odds were in their favor, though: easily an 87 percent chance that Drehemia wouldn't catch them in her lair. If they hurried.

"We need to move," Talea announced and started forward without waiting to see if anyone was following.

Being a mermaid was remarkably fun once one got used to it. It took a while. The swimming was tricky—she kept trying to move her legs separately. But after she got used to the right motions, she found it remarkably easy to swim for hours—which was convenient, because she was reasonably sure that would be required by the time they'd finished.

Eventually, after what seemed like a much larger distance than "just a few miles," they found the lone mountain in the middle of the sea, an island that just hadn't quite managed to grow tall enough to break the surface of the ocean.

---

[7] It's an interesting semantical debate. I'm of the opinion that Thaena didn't count, but I recognize how someone else might not agree.

"There's a cave opening, like a gash," Qown said, "but I'm having trouble seeing inside."

Which was true. They were so far down it was nearly dark. The creatures that swam there were either very small and brought their own lights with them, or very large and didn't seem to need them.

Talea had a feeling there was probably more than one Daughter of Laaka hiding in these depths.

"I see it," Galen said. "Everyone link hands. I'll lead us there."

He pulled everyone to a cave mouth, pitch-black, almost invisible in the already dark area, and swam inside. It was still far too dark for Talea to see.

The cave itself was as underwater as anything else, but it managed to be even murkier than the water outside.

"Wow," Galen said.

"Wow?" Talea said. "What does 'wow' mean?"

"I'd create a light," Qown said, "but I'm not sure it's a good idea."

"It should be safe enough," Sheloran reassured him. "If she comes back early, she'll spot us regardless of the light levels."

"Good point."

Qown created a light, and as soon as he did, Talea gasped. She was standing front of the wealth of an empire.

Every kind of metal and gemstone was before her, just heaped about like piles of rubbish that someone had forgotten to tidy before company arrived. It was the kind of dragon's hoard the stories always described but that Talea had yet to see.

Except . . .

A section of the floor had been smoothed out, polished, and inlaid to form a checkerboard of squares. Next to this area, a number of boxes shaped like coffins lined the walls of the cave. Unlike the rest of the cave, this area had been kept immaculately, scrupulously clean.

"I spotted those earlier," Qown whispered. "The tenyé signatures . . . there are people trapped inside those coffins." He started swimming in that direction.

Kalindra grabbed his arm. "Hold on there. You don't know what will happen if you free them. You don't know if they can breathe down here. You don't know what's keeping them alive. And most importantly: *this isn't why we're here.*"

"They're people." It was clearly all the reasoning that Qown needed, and Talea couldn't even say that he was wrong. Unfortunately, Kalindra wasn't wrong either. "We can't just leave them. What is she even doing with—"

Galen swam over and took Qown's hand, who immediately stopped talking and stared at Galen, wide-eyed.

"We'll come back," Galen promised. "You have my word. We will come back."

Qown swallowed, his throat moving visibly. He nodded.

Talea studied the magically enchanted game board, life-size, and then at the boxes lining the walls. A lifetime of catering to the desires of horrifying, sadistic royals had left her with an innate understanding of such whims. So she felt confident in her assessment of the boxes' purpose. They protected and preserved Drehemia's game pieces. It's just that her game pieces happened to also be people.

Talea fought down the taste of bile. She clenched and opened her hands several times, fighting the desire to open every box. Even if it killed the people inside, that would be a kindness by comparison to this . . . and if Drehemia was truly gone off attacking cities . . .

Talea said, "When you do, please let me know. I'll help you deal with her." She didn't look over to the side, not that anyone else could see Eshi. "What's her matching Cornerstone?"

Galen frowned. "I don't know what you mean . . . ?"

"The Name of All Things," Eshi and Qown both answered together.

Talea flinched. She'd never convince Senera to give that up in a million years, but it was the only way to kill Drehemia. They'd have to destroy the Name of All Things and Drehemia simultaneously.

So they wouldn't be killing Drehemia. Fine. That didn't mean they couldn't still come back there and take away her toys.

Galen didn't let go of Qown's hand. "So how do we find this cup?"

"Easily," Qown said. "Just have to look past the First Veil. It's been touched by tenyé from one of the Eight Immortals, so it shines out like a light." He briefly closed his eyes, concentrating, and then gazed at the far side of the room.

Nothing unusual about that except for when his vision crossed Talea's path, and he visibly flinched. He spent a few moments staring at her with a dropped jaw, his expression unnerved.

Talea pressed her lips together and didn't look at him. She was quite sure her tenyé didn't look the same anymore. But what of it? Everything changed.[8]

"There." Qown pointed into a corner. "It's behind that pile of coins."

Talea nodded. She saw it too, crammed under a heap of metal carelessly tossed to the side, unimportant and unvalued. Talea could tell right away that the cup was nothing like a normal cup. It was a solid knot of tenyé potential.

It occurred to her as she picked the thing up that she'd never looked at the coin from the other side of the First Veil. Would it have looked the same?

Did she look the same?

Sheloran gazed at the piles and piles of precious metals speculatively.

"I wouldn't," Qown advised.

"Maybe just a small pile of priceless treasures?" Sheloran queried.

"Do you want to take the chance the dragon has memorized every single item in her hoard?" Talea asked with a bright smile. She carefully pushed the coins away and felt around until her fingers touched where the ghostly tenyé glow told her the cup would be. She tugged it free.

---

[8] There are limits. I'm sure her aura was starting to look notably different by this point.

The cup itself was an ugly little thing carved from something that looked like bone, glazed with a dark red polish around the rim. It looked like the misshapen clay had been thrown by someone still learning the craft. She clasped it to herself and wouldn't let anyone else touch it.

Fortunately, no one else tried.

"Right," Galen said. "Let's go."

46: Game Pieces

Xivan's reaction
The Lighthouse at Shadrag Gor
After Talea's memory of retrieving the Grail of Thaena

They'd settled in on the couches in the keeping room, with Talea tucked in against Xivan, and Thurvishar and Senera aggressively not sitting next to each other. Kalindra balanced on the other side of the couch from the cuddling women. No one said anything. The room fell into quiet.

"I think Qown left some food," Talea said. "Xivan, help me out here?"

Xivan normally would have waved that off as something that didn't interest her, but she was rather unnerved to find that food had begun to interest her a great deal—and more and more seemed to be something she wanted. So she followed Talea into the kitchen, then frowned as Talea walked to the other side of the kitchen, into a storeroom.

"What are you—"

Talea pushed Xivan up against a wall and began kissing her furiously.

Xivan felt a second of surprise, and then her body insisted that there was only one correct response to this situation and that was to kiss Talea back. Enthusiastically. Gods. She'd all but forgotten how good this felt. Her whole body felt flushed, tingling, each touch of Talea's fingers a fire racing under Xivan's skin.

Talea paused, just once, to look at Xivan. "If this isn't doing anything for you, you'd tell me, right?"

Xivan growled, "Why are you stopping?"

But Talea wasn't ready to be pulled back. "You'd tell me, wouldn't you?"

Xivan dug her fingers into the other woman's hips. "I would tell you. But there's no need, because as it happens, this is doing a lot for me. Or it would be, except we've stopped."

"We shouldn't be doing this at all," Talea said.

"Agreed. But, uh . . . yeah, don't stop, anyway."

Talea grinned and began unbuckling Xivan's pants. "Only for the moment."

Xivan felt her knees turn watery. "We don't have time—"

"We have time for this," Talea said. "If we're very dedicated and focused." She grinned impishly. "You've always taught me to be focused."

"Ha!" But she gasped as she felt Talea's hand slip under the hem of her pants, rub down in between Xivan's legs. "Fuck."

Talea grabbed the edges of both kef and uisigi and yanked them down over

Xivan's hips, baring her thighs to the naked air. Then she sank to her knees and began peppering Xivan's skin with kisses.

"I should be doing this to you," Xivan murmured, one hand tangling in Talea's short hair.

"Next time," Talea promised a second before she lowered her mouth to Xivan's slick skin and made speech impossible for either of them.

Xivan could barely stand upright, but she was being given plenty of motivation to make the effort; if she fell, Talea would have to stop. And Xivan had forgotten how amazing sex felt, how amazing this kind of sex felt. Her whole body was singing, waves of pleasure radiating outward.

Talea started using her fingers in addition to her tongue, and it was more than enough to send Xivan over the crest. She bit down on one of her hands to keep her keening from turning into a loud scream as euphoria crashed through and her whole world turned sparkling white. Xivan's body arched and tightened as she orgasmed. She gave out a choked moan.

"Gods . . ."

Talea grinned and rested her head on Xivan's thigh. She didn't say a word, but her smug expression made that unnecessary. She looked very pleased with herself.

Xivan didn't move. She didn't even bother pulling up her pants. She was still catching her breath when she looked over at the far side of the room and saw a black silhouette.

What?

She blinked. It was gone, but Xivan didn't think for a moment she'd imagined it. She pulled up her kef and readjusted her clothes. "We need to check the tower."

Talea didn't question her, although the look on her face said she wanted to.

"Xivan?" Kalindra's voice called out. "Are you okay?" Xivan was surprised to note that Kalindra actually sounded worried.

"No," Xivan said as they returned to the main room. Xivan ignored the droll look on Senera's face that suggested just possibly Xivan hadn't been as quiet as she should have been. "Senera, I need you to check the Lighthouse," Xivan said. "I saw him. I fucking *saw* him."

Xivan didn't bother explaining who "he" was.

Senera's amusement vanished. The wizard cast spells in quick succession as she followed Xivan and Talea out into the hallway. The entrance to the Lighthouse was shrouded in darkness, an impenetrable void.

"Can you see?" Xivan asked.

Kalindra and Thurvishar followed them out into the hall as well.

Senera cast one last spell and then lowered her hand, her expression twisted in disgust.

"He's only trapped by a leg," she said. "And not by much. You say you saw him?"

"Probably a projection," Thurvishar said. "He can do that."

"Oh, well, isn't that lovely," Senera said. "So we'd better figure something out fast. We're officially out of time."

Kihrin's story
Inside Vol Karoth's prison
Also after Talea's memory of retrieving the Grail of Thaena

"Ow," Galen said as he prodded the scrape on his chin he'd gained falling flat on his face when that last vision ended.

"Stop being such a baby," Qown teased. "You'll be fine. You just need to–" But the wound healed before Qown could even begin to prepare his magic.

Galen grinned at him. "I'm not an idiot, you know. I've figured out how this place works. How do you think I got away from the prison-vision-thing Vol Karoth put me in?"

"For my part, I still can't believe that's what my voice sounds like," Sheloran said.

We were in a room we'd found in a building, after outrunning the army. Memory-conjured couches and cushions in an otherwise barren chamber gave us a place to sit and rest for a few minutes before the next, inevitable assault.

"Right?" Teraeth nodded at Sheloran. "Every time I see myself in someone else's memory, my first thought is, 'Why are they making me sound like that?'"

"Your voice is lovely," Janel said. She looked at me then. "You're uncharacteristically quiet," she said.

"Those coffins," I said, shaking my head and fighting the urge to vomit. "Living game pieces? And here I thought the Old Man was bad."

"Eternally screaming semi-petrified people arranged to produce a chorus of agony is pretty bad too," Teraeth said, putting his arm around my shoulders. "In case I never said it before, by the way, I'm proud of you for destroying those."

I flashed him a small, tight grin, leaned my head against his shoulder.

"We shouldn't stay here for long," Janel said. "He'll find us."

"He always does." Forcing myself to my feet, I said, "Come on. There's got to be another gray spot around here somewhere we can exploit. And if not, at least we can paint the town blue." I paused, looked at Qown. "I mean that literally."

"Are you sure?" Janel frowned at me. "After the last time?"

"We're still around," I said, "but he's weaker. I think we came out ahead in the long run. The more we do that, the better our chances."

"Assuming his next reaction doesn't just kill us," Teraeth said. But then he nodded and stood up also. "Well, we always knew this might be a one-way trip. Let's go bait the not-at-all-bearlike god of destruction in his own lair."

"It's not a lair, strictly speaking . . . I'll shut up now," Qown said, seeing the glare Teraeth shot him.

"Wise man," the vané said.

We made our way back out into the world.

Kalindra's memory
Devors, Quur
Three days after leaving Da'utunse

Kalindra returned to Devors expecting her immediate arrest, but it seemed fate had a sense of humor.

Arriving at that point had been easy. They'd used the Black Brotherhood gate system—no questions asked—and then had "hired" a boat for the rest of the journey.

The Quuros sailors they encountered first at least had the common sense not to clap irons on any of them. Not only because of the whole "hurting the dignity of a royal" thing but because Kalindra had no doubt Sheloran could melt her way through such trivial restraints in seconds. But no, the sailors were clearly concerned enough that they'd engaged in a behavior quite beyond their normal attitude: politeness.

And as far as anyone knew, Kalindra had been kidnapped.

It didn't put her in any better mood as she watched them sail into Atamer Harbor, the main port of call for the entire island. Kalindra had avoided using it for that very reason, because no one could come or go through the harbor's gates without being noticed. The place was so sticky with Quuros it was like shoving one's hands into a barrel full of tar.

The moment they docked, a runner sprinted away, no doubt to deliver the miraculous news to all the people who needed to know it. Kalindra readied her story. She'd decided to continue with the kidnapping angle; that seemed the easiest to justify. And as long as she didn't have to explain herself in front of the wrong people, everything would be fine.

Kalindra had utterly failed, but everything would be fine.

So they stood there on the docks and waited. A storm was blowing in from the west, and it looked to be ugly, turning the sky a dark gray-green. The wind had begun to pick up, tossing hair and sallí cloaks with equal abandon. When the rain started—which might well be any second—it would come down like having the whole ocean dumped on their heads.

The first group to arrive was the abbess and her people, most of whom wore stern, severe expressions, except for the abbess herself, who wore a look of vast relief. Kalindra could only assume she'd been fielding no small amount of heat from having managed to lose the high general's daughter-in-law on an isolated island.

One of the monks held Nikali, who began wriggling furiously as soon as he caught sight of his mother.

The monk holding him clearly had only minimal experience with a squirming toddler. In a matter of seconds, the small boy was waddling over to Kalindra. She ran out to pick him up, bouncing him against her hip. "Did you miss your mommy?" she asked him.

He immediately scrunched his hands up into his eyes and began crying.

"Shhh, shhh," she whispered, stroking his head. "It's all right, sweetheart. I'm here now."

He bawled into the crook of her neck while the others stepped forward. The abbess stared at the small boy with a perplexed expression. "I'd been told he was well behaved." The statement carried a faint whiff of accusation, implying someone might have lied.

"He's a good boy," Kalindra said, because it happened to be the truth. He'd just been through a lot. She'd really gotten incredibly lucky to have such a well-mannered son. She laid the blame entirely on Jarith. Heaven knew the boy didn't get it from her.

She tried to ignore the way her throat tightened at the thought of her husband.

"I hate to interrupt," Galen D'Mon said, "but might we move this indoors before it starts raining in earnest? I can't imagine any conversation will be improved with the addition of sopping wet clothing."

"Uh, yes, of course," the abbess agreed. "The soldiers will wish to speak with you as well, but—" She quickly scanned the group of them, evidently trying to make up her mind about what to do with them. "Follow me," she said and motioned for her people to do likewise.

Kalindra released a breath she hadn't known she was holding. That could have gone badly.

She concentrated on quieting her son. He'd want to meet everyone—he always wanted to meet everyone—but those would be introductions best handled once he'd finished with his extremely emotional moment. And had been bribed with a treat.

The abbess took them to her main receiving room, the same one she'd used while lying to Kalindra about the dangers of staying at the monastery. For the others, who had never been here before, there was undoubtedly a lot to stare at. The monastery was a magnificent place in its way. The care that had gone into its construction still impressed Kalindra.

"Please, be seated." The abbess motioned to the low benches. She turned to one of the monks. "Bring tea for everyone."

"And fruit, please," Kalindra added.

"Yes," the abbess agreed. "And some fruit."

The abbess schooled her expression into a mask of sympathetic concern as she sat across from Kalindra. "What . . . what happened, my dear?"

"Someone from my past," Kalindra explained, which was almost true. "I'd have come to a bad end if it hadn't been for these people. Oh, I'm sorry. Abbess, this is Galen D'Mon and his wife, Sheloran, Galen's personal healer, Qown, and Talea Ferandis—did I get that right?"

"Yes," Talea beamed at her. "You did."

"Excellent," Kalindra said. "They rescued me and brought me back."

"And as glad as we are to do that," Galen said, "we didn't return just because of Kalindra. We're here because we learned that the monastery is about to come under attack."

The abbess stared at him. "What."

"The monastery is about to come under attack," he repeated. "We know it's going to be soon. Under a week, in all likelihood."

"There's nothing in the prophecies about an attack on the Devors Monastery." The abbess punctuated that statement with a small, indignant huff.

"That's because the prophecies are a ridiculous pile of offal designed to distract and confuse, and you weren't supposed to be studying them because you believed them; you were supposed to be studying them to find out what Xaltorath wanted people to do." The woman who made that irate statement crossed into the room despite the presence of a half dozen or so monks who seemed to be seconds from bodily throwing themselves in front of her. In fact, two monks had grabbed her by the arms and were pulling. She simply ignored them.

Kalindra's eyes widened. She knew who this was. How could she not? Kihrin had described the damn woman enough times, moon-eyed the whole while. She was shorter than Kalindra had expected but took up a lot of space by personal magnetism. Everything else was exactly as Kihrin had described: Joratese horse mane hair, sienna-brown skin, black-stockinged hands, red eyes. Behind her stood the reason the monks were likely wringing their hands: Thurvishar D'Lorus, looking as tired and out of sorts as Kalindra had ever seen him. And standing just to the other side of Janel–

Teraeth noticed Kalindra, eyes widening fractionally, and then ignored her.

"Who are you?" the abbess demanded. "Who let you–" She paused as she noticed Thurvishar. "Lord Heir D'Lorus."

Of course, the monks would know the Royal House that supplied paper and books on sight.

"It's high lord now," Thurvishar said as he walked into the room. He looked over the rest of them and frowned, perplexed. He straightened and returned his focus to the abbess.

"Well," the woman said, "with all respect, perhaps you might exercise some control over your–" She seemed to be searching for the right word to call Janel.

Janel paused and blinked. "Talea?"

Talea grinned and waved. "Janel!"

"Um–?" Janel gestured in a way that clearly meant "What the fuck?"

"Oh, it's a long story."

"Where's Xivan?"

"That's a shorter story." Talea stopped smiling. "She'll be here soon, though. But why are you here?"

"That's a question you're going to have to ask Thurvishar," Janel said, giving the wizard a thoroughly vicious look.

Thurvishar looked uncomfortable, but didn't answer.

"This is not a social club!" The abbess had clearly lost what little patience she had ever had. "I don't know who you people are–"

"You have two high lords standing in your receiving room," Galen snapped, "so I wouldn't be so quick to claim that we're being rude. We are, in fact, attempting to warn you that your lives are in peril!"

The abbess started to retort and visibly wrestled herself back under control. "I am touched by your concern for our welfare, but in five hundred years, no attack against this island has ever come even close to being successful. And we would know if the prophecies–"

Janel shook her head. "Amazing. I came here to look through the stacks, and I find you dismissing the idea of an attack because it's not written down on some moldy old quatrain? You're really woefully underprepared for dealing with what's about to arrive, aren't you?"

"Outrageous!" The abbess slammed her hand down on a table. Any chance of diplomacy evaporated.

Thurvishar leaned toward Janel. "Perhaps you're not helping?"

Janel made a face. "Do you know who founded this monastery?" The question was aimed at the abbess and seemed rhetorical.

The abbess's eyes flickered over to Kalindra and then back to Janel. "Of course I do. Now I'm going to ask you to leave, companion to a high lord or not. This is a sacred place, and I will not have you barging in here and disrupting everything!"

"Oh, but she's so good at it," Teraeth muttered under his breath.

Kalindra wished they'd brought the tea. That fruit, perhaps. This was turning into a show.

Nikali had also decided that since his mother was here, everything was fine, and therefore, it was time to work the crowd. He climbed down off his mother's chest and waddled over to Galen, whom he had at least met before. Kalindra rather doubted her son recognized the D'Mon royal, though. He'd been a baby when Galen had last stopped by.

"Oh, hello there." Galen regarded the boy solemnly. "I'm afraid I don't have anything—"

Sheloran silently passed Galen a filigree metal ball filled with metal beads, too big for the boy to fit in his mouth (although Kalindra knew he would try). "Never mind," Galen said. He held the toy up to Nikali, whose eyes went wide with delight at the prospect of shaking the damn thing every second of every minute of the next year.

Kalindra's mouth twisted. Sheloran and she were going to have a *talk*.

Meanwhile, Janel seemed equal parts furious and amused. She turned to Teraeth. "Elana Milligreest," she said. "That's who founded the Monastery at Devors."

Teraeth blinked. "Are you serious?"

"Dead serious. After Atrin died, of course. Years later. These people had one job, and they've stampeded it off the side of a cliff."

The abbess stood. "Who told you—"

"Are you kidding me?" Kalindra narrowed her eyes. "That's the reason Qoran Milligreest sent me here? Because we're *Milligreests?* What's the damn purpose of this place, anyway? I thought you were recording the prophecies."

"We are," the abbess said. "We have for almost five hundred years! And who founded us isn't—" She sputtered. "We are losing focus on the point!"

"Now, that I agree with," Janel said. She walked over to Galen. "You were saying something about an attack? Would you mind elaborating, my lord?"

"Yes. Thank you. There's a Daughter of Laaka who's acquired a Cornerstone—Grimward—and she's planning to attack the monastery. She thinks she can find a way to cure her lover's insanity. Her lover being the shadow dragon, Drehemia."

Thurvishar whistled.

Galen gave the wizard a wary look, but nodded. "The Lash—that's the Daughter of Laaka—is undead herself, and she can control any undead she encounters and create more out of the bodies of the slain. She's been pretending to be a pirate for years, using Grimward to control and manipulate animated corpses from a distance."

Talea added, "Currently, her ship is being captained by Xivan."

"Why are you carrying Xivan's sword?" Janel asked Talea.

Talea glanced down at the second Khorveshan sword she wore, the blade kept snug in a gorgeous scabbard. "She dropped it."

"Even if a dragon attacks," the abbess said, grimly determined to keep to the topic at hand, "the wards will stop them. And a kraken–" She paused.

"The wards may not stop a kraken," Thurvishar said. "They've never been tested for that."

"No, but the cliffs will," the abbess replied. "And the navy. Her ship and her undead will never break through the barrier. We are perfectly safe." She gestured elegantly toward her people. "Now, please let these good people see you to visitors' quarters, where you can rest and be refreshed. Kalindra, your father-in-law has asked me to see you and Nikali escorted back to the Capital."

Kalindra raised her eyebrows. "Oh, that's not happening."

The abbess gave her an even look. "You're refusing to cooperate?"

Kalindra found herself fighting off a smile. "I would love to see Nikali removed from this place, except I don't trust one of your people not to take the opportunity to kidnap him."

"How dare–"

"You claim that won't happen? Yes, indeed. How dare you."

The abbess closed her mouth with a sharp, unhappy snap of teeth. She'd walked right into that one.

The abbess was clearly just too tired to argue this anymore. She waved them off, probably so she could write any number of extremely stern letters to the high general of Quur.

Kalindra managed to convince Nikali to go to bed early after dinner, although he made her tell him three stories until he was finally so heavy-lidded he fell asleep before she finished the tale of how the smallest mermaid defeated a dragon. Kalindra ventured out onto the balcony afterward to watch the waves crash against the rocks offshore, spraying white foam so far up in the air that she occasionally imagined it licking against her face.

A squawk broke through the normal sound of seagulls calling, and a bird landed on the railing. At first, she thought it might have been a parrot, but the beak was all wrong; it had a crimson head and bright blue body, with red wing tips. Other than the coloring, it resembled a magpie. Some of the bright red feathers on the side of its head were missing. Its single eye winked at her, an unhealthy gray.

It was dead.

Then it opened its beak and spoke: "Ka . . . Kalindra."

Kalindra stepped back.

The bird repeated her name and cocked its head at her.

Kalindra looked back inside. Nikali was still asleep. She said, "This is new. I've seen talking parrots before, but even then, they were still alive. So I assume I'm speaking to the Lash? How did you get past the wards?" She contemplated next steps. Shouting for the guards? What would that do for her, really?

The magpie hopped up and down. "They're not designed . . . to stop birds. Birds are too small."

"Ah, a serious oversight on their part, I suspect," Kalindra said. "How did you find out my name?"

The magpie laughed, which would have been eerie no matter what the bird's status. "I overheard someone call you that. Should I not call you that?"

"No. Kalindra is fine." She closed the door to the patio and sat down on a chair.

"Good! Hate to be rude."

Kalindra could only stare. This was ridiculous. The damn magpie—but of course it wasn't a damn magpie. It was an impossibly old, immortal kraken talking through a dead magpie. "You would hate to be . . . Okay, so what's your name? It can't really be the Lash."

"You can't pronounce it." The magpie actually managed to sound indignant, although Kalindra wasn't sure if it was over Kalindra's lack of vocal ability or that she would even have to ask such a ridiculous question.

"I guess Lash it is, then. So, Lash: What do you want?"

The magpie trilled and looked at Kalindra with its one good eye. "Same question I'm here to ask you. When you tried to kill me—futile though it was—what motivated you? I thought money, but then why are you still here?"

The Lash must have been asking Xivan questions. Finding out as much information as possible about everyone in the group. Who they were, what they wanted. Xivan would've been able to answer questions about most of them: Sheloran and Galen, Qown and Talea. But she'd have had no information on Kalindra.

Kalindra had to respect the Lash's audacity. She'd gone right to the source. So she answered with a question. "Do you know Thaena's dead?"

The magpie hopped back, just once. "No. I hadn't heard."

Kalindra exhaled. "She is. Which makes Grimward the only way to Return people we've lost. That's why I came after you. That's why the others came after you too."

"You don't have to kill me for that," the Lash answered.

Kalindra scoffed. "Who would have thought you could be so reasonable?"

"I understand wanting back a loved one," the Lash retorted.

Kalindra's laugh was bitter. "Oh hell. I suppose you do."

The magpie hopped closer. "I propose a trade."

"What sort of trade?" Here it was. Whatever the Lash was really here for. Kalindra could assume it wasn't just to satisfy a question about ambiguous motives.

"Help me restore my love, and I will restore yours." The magpie rattled off this promise like it was the most obvious and easily fulfilled bargain that had ever been made.

Kalindra shut her eyes. It was a lie. It had to be a lie but—

"Exactly how would I help you?"

"Take down the wards surrounding the island."

Kalindra's fingers clutched at the fabric of her agolé, so hard she felt her nails scratch against her thighs. That was a preposterous idea, a price that should have had her immediately grabbing the damn bird and wringing its neck before vigorously smacking it against the wall.

The Lash must have been able to see through the bird's eyes. She saw Kalindra's hesitation—and her indecision. "Do these people matter to you? I only want information, but we both know they won't cooperate. Do you think they'll wait while I peruse their house of knowledge?"

A surreal image entered Kalindra's mind. She couldn't stop herself from laughing. "How exactly do you intend to . . . I'm sorry. I'm just having a difficult time imagining a kraken reading tiny little books. Do you even know how to read Guarem?"

"I don't need to," the Lash pointed out. "The monks know how."

"But they won't–"

"They'll do what they're told once they're dead," the kraken answered.[1]

Kalindra felt her heart stutter. "Oh. Oh, I see. Of course. Because of Grimward."

"Help me," the Lash/magpie said, "and when I am finished, I will bring your loved one back. We'll both have what we want."

Kalindra stood and walked over to the railing, unable to help herself, needing to do something. She watched the waves crash, the rain slamming down on a darkened sea. She'd once been told by Mother—by Khaemezra— that these islands were entirely artificial, created by Ompher to staunch the currents that otherwise would have driven life-giving rains to the shores of Khorvesh. Because Quur had waged war against Ynis, and his people, the thriss, had liked their jungles.

Thaena had always been a massive bitch.

And Kalindra had never cared about Quur at all.

"You have to promise safety for my family. Myself and my son." Which meant Kalindra had already made her decision. It was quite probably the stupidest of her life. She couldn't guarantee the Lash would carry out her end of the bargain, and if she reneged on the deal, what was Kalindra supposed to do? Go whine about it to the high general? But it was a chance of bringing Jarith back. Her chances otherwise rested firmly at zero.

"Do we have a deal?" the bird chirped.

Kalindra closed her eyes in despair. "Yes, we do."

---

[1] One must assume "read book out loud" is not outside the realm of capability for undead the Lash has animated.

47: THE LIST

Senera's reaction
The Lighthouse at Shadrag Gor
Just after Kalindra's memory

Kalindra didn't wake when the vision ended.

Senera's only surprise was that it had taken so long. It had been obvious for a while that Kalindra hadn't been coping with the stress. But this had no doubt been the last grain of sand: the reminder that she'd been the one who'd sold out everyone, that in doing so she'd put her son in mortal danger, and that it had all been for nothing.

"Oh, no wonder she didn't want to talk about it," Xivan mourned.

Kalindra sat up again and opened her eyes.

The remaining four people backed away from the body with all the haste of those who had been dealing with demons and dark fallen gods for weeks. When Xivan started to draw her sword, Senera held out her hand. "Wait," she advised.

Kalindra stood. She was in no way elegant about it, but moved jerkily like someone who'd forgotten how to walk. Senera had seen this sort of behavior before. She knew what it meant.

"Jarith?" Senera said.

"*Now* you show up?" Xivan said. Talea elbowed her and made a shushing sound.

For several long, protracted beats, nothing happened. Then they all heard:

I am still very new to ... this. And there is much I don't ... I don't re-member.

"But you know who you are?" Thurvishar asked. His voice was thick with pity.

I do. Despite using Kalindra's body, small swirls of black smoke kept escaping, swirling around her legs, flowing outward like a cloak. **But only as facts. I know she was important to me.** The demon looked down at himself, wearing Kalindra's body. **She *is* important to me.**

"So that's why he waited," Thurvishar murmured.

Senera looked at the man. He had an infuriating habit of not explaining what the hell he was talking about, as if he expected that everyone would just follow his logic without any explanation. "And he is ... ?"

Thurvishar looked up. "Oh? What?"

Senera pressed her lips together. "Who is he? The 'he' who waited?"

"Oh!" Thurvishar said. "Vol Karoth. As long as Kalindra was awake and aware here, Jarith wouldn't leave, wouldn't come out. I don't think Vol Karoth wants Jarith here."

"Why?" Xivan asked. "He's a demon. Vol Karoth *eats* demons. Literally eats demons. Wouldn't Jarith be the most vulnerable among us?"

"Maybe," Thurvishar said, "but maybe not. I don't know if the rules are different for Xaltorath's 'children.'"

Send me to Kalindra. I must bring her back.

Thurvishar's eyes widened. "I don't know if that's a good idea."

Please. She is the only— The shadows around Kalindra's legs thrashed angrily. **She is my anchor.**

Talea sighed. "Thurvishar—"

"I can try," Thurvishar acknowledged. "I've never—" He gave Senera a rueful look. "As someone I know once pointed out, I've never read a demon's mind before. I don't know if I can do this."

"You read Janel's mind. She's a demon," Senera reminded him. "And Talon read Jarith's mind earlier. If Talon can do it, you can."

"Oh," Thurvishar said. "Good point." He didn't look any happier by the reassurance, however. He wore a pensive, upset look on his face.

"But as for him—" Senera gestured toward the possessed body of Kalindra. "I feel obligated to point out we also don't know if it's a trap. We don't know anything about what Xaltorath's done to this . . . man. What he's become. You can't touch him that way without making yourself vulnerable. And maybe that is what Vol Karoth really wants."

"If it is," Thurvishar said, "I think Vol Karoth would have done it earlier. He's made no secret of the fact that he'd like to have me out of the way."

"We could toss a coin for it." Talea pulled a gold coin seemingly from thin air to give emphasis to the suggestion.

"No, Talea," Senera and Xivan both said at the same time.

Talea rolled her eyes. "Fine. But let's help him out if we can. Kalindra would want that. Kihrin too, for that matter."

Thurvishar inhaled. "All right." He turned to the demon. "We shall see if we can do this. Be ready for anything."

Kalindra's prison
After Kalindra's memory of agreeing to help the Lash

Kalindra opened the door to her suite and paused in confusion.

The room looked as it always did—bright and airy with windows both high and low. The sunken central entertaining area, carpeted in red and gold with matching pillows for sitting or reclining against, was as it always looked when not filled with laughing guests drinking wine and chatting, the old wooden bar to the left sported unopened bottles and a single carafe filled with a deep red from the Shendola region. Pegs protruded from the wall to her left, ready to receive hats or coats or cloaks. Doors opened from the main room into the bedrooms and the bath on the left and right walls, respectively.

The only thing out of place was the pile of luggage by the door to the bedroom. That was unusual and unexpected.

"Hello?" she called out, shrugging out of her cloak and hanging it on the wall. "Are you home?"

Jarith Milligreest emerged from the bedroom, setting a small valise down atop the pile of luggage already there. "Hi," he said, not making eye contact.

"What's all this?" she asked, stepping forward and sweeping an arm broadly. "Are we going on a trip I didn't know about?"

"No," Jarith said, still not looking at her. "Just me."

A stone tied itself around her heart and threw itself into a deep, dark well. She felt a sinking feeling as well as a sudden splash of cold that made the hairs on her arms stand up. "Excuse me?" she asked, stepping forward again.

"I had hoped to be done before you got home," Jarith admitted sheepishly. "I left a . . . There's a note." He gestured over his shoulder toward the bedroom. "I wanted to avoid a scene."

"A scene?" Kalindra scoffed. "Is that what this is? What's going on? Talk to me, my love."

"I'm . . . I'm leaving," he said as if the luggage didn't make that obvious.

Kalindra shook her head. "I don't understand. I thought . . . I thought we were doing well. Was it something I did?"

"No," Jarith said quickly, glancing up at her for the first time. She saw a wetness in his eyes as if he were holding back tears. "No, it's just . . . you're busy with your work all the time, and I . . . I have realized that I'm not happy here."

"In this house?" Kalindra asked.

"In this city," Jarith said. "I . . . I'm going to join F'elana's project."

Kalindra had to think for a moment. "The world tree thing?" she asked. "You're going to the other continent?"

"Sky trees," Jarith said, "and yes."

"But, love," she said, taking another step forward with her hand outstretched, "you know it's not safe. There's so much about that land, the nature of those trees, that we still don't understand. Never mind the creatures that live there."

"And we'll never learn as long as we keep treating them like enemies." Jarith's voice rose, becoming strident. "We've all but exterminated the Daughters of Laaka. What's to stop us from committing genocide on the sky trees and the gryphons and whatever else we find over there?"

"Hey, the Daughters attacked us first," Kalindra protested. That stone around her heart was continuing to sink deeper into the apparently bottomless well. "We are only defending ourselves."

"The voramer invaded their lands," Jarith said, shaking his head. "How did we think they'd react?"

"They could have tried to communicate first," Kalindra said. "But no, they went straight to mass murder. They collapsed the entire voramer cavern. You know this!"

"And none of them actually died, because we can't die!" Jarith screamed. "We're wrong. We're unnatural. We're the abomination!"

Silence filled the room uncomfortably. Jarith hung his head, staring at the carpet beneath his feet. "We need to find a way to become part of this world," he said. "And we think . . . I think . . . that the sky trees are the answer."

"So you're going to just leave this?" Kalindra asked, indicating the house. "Leave us? Leave me? Without even talking to me about it?"

"Please," Jarith said. "You're a soldier; it's what you do. You'd never be happy with us."

"I was happy with you," Kalindra said as the stone finally found the bottom.

Jarith looked up, forced a sad smile. "You'll find someone else," he said.

"I don't want someone else," Kalindra said, anger igniting in her breast. "I want you! I love you!"

Jarith shook his head. "If that were true, you'd be happy for me. I've finally figured out my place here." When Kalindra didn't reply, he said, "Goodbye, Solan."

He left, leaving Kalindra there. The tears took a long while to come, and when they did, they were the harsh, angry kind. They didn't go away for a long, long time.

Kalindra opened the door to her suite and paused in confusion as it all began again.

Jarith's story
Inside Vol Karoth's prison
After Kalindra's collapse

The demon found itself in the middle of a street that was barren and devoid of life. The lines were clean, neat, precise, but there was a sterility to the place that made it uneasy. There was no warmth, no life; nothing to eat.

It felt the essence of the place picking away at it, seeking loose threads to tug and unravel into so much tenyé to be devoured.

It was a demon; it knew hunger better than any. And this was a hunger so far beyond its comprehension–

His. His comprehension, the demon reminded himself. **I am Jarith Milligreest. I am a man. My wife's name is Kalindra. I love her.** He repeated this mantra to himself as he drifted down the street, looking for her.

He looked, but not with eyes. He didn't really have those anymore. Rather, he used his other senses. The ones that showed him every scrap of tenyé, every frisson of terror or misery.

It was with this last one that he found her. He recognized the taste of her fear and despair across miles of this endless city. He knew that taste well. It had sustained him through the weeks since his escape from . . .

. . . since his escape. Every time Kalindra thought of her dead husband, every time her heart broke just a little more, it fed him.

Me, he said to himself. **I am that dead husband. My name is Jarith Milligreest. I am a man. My wife's name is Kalindra. I love her.**

Love? Love wasn't something a demon was supposed to care about, or even understand. He'd learned that at his creator's knee, one of his first lessons.

But . . .

I am a man. I love my wife. He chanted the words as he floated in the direction of his wife's distress.

He hated this place, he decided. A place where nothing was real and, therefore, nothing was as it should have been. He should have been able to flash across the magnetic lines, crossing miles in moments of thought, but there were no magnetic lines here. No glorious sun sending tenyé in the form of warmth down upon the world. There was just . . . nothing. Hunger and emptiness and a faint, shallow regret too thin and soupy to provide nourishment.

He had to float slowly. No faster than a mortal might run.

It was agonizing. There was an irony there; but self-cannibalism was a last-resort-only option, and he wasn't there yet.

Besides, he'd fed well at the Lighthouse. The air had reeked of emotions, both pale and thin and more nourishing emotions too: fear, sorrow, hate.

Maybe when he was done here, he would go back there and—

No! I am not like that. I am a man. I am . . . My name is . . . ** Shit. What was his name? **Jarith! That was it. **Jarith Milligreest. My wife's name is Kalindra. I love her. I love her.**

He floated along the streets of the city, the city that was the mind of a demon-god so much hungrier and more powerful than he.

More powerful, but strangely less clever in some ways, he decided after a time. He'd passed several places where fake Kalindras writhed in pain or sobbed in anguish. But not one of those had so much as a flicker of life to them, not so much as a hint of actual emotion. Who were these flat, painted simulacrums meant to fool?

Finally, he arrived at the "place" where she was. Animated statues patrolled the street outside, stone eyes keen to spot any intruder. But Vol Karoth thought it was dealing with mortals. Beings who were convinced of their own flesh, even in this place where such things were meaningless. They would think themselves visible, and so they would be.

The demon knew better. The demon—

Jarith, he thought to himself and almost ruined everything. Great stone heads turned toward him briefly. He paused, letting his mind go perfectly blank.

The statues resumed their restless patrol, and the demon floated into the building they guarded, the one from which the magnificent flavors of agony and despair wafted.

If the demon had had a mouth, it would have begun to water.

Inside was a room like the rest of the city—empty and sterile and fake. There stood a human, dark brown skin and hair matted into long tendrils tied back with a leather cord. She moved her lips, and the vibrations in the air that mortals called speech happened from her. The demon—

Jarith! My name is Jarith Milligreest. I am a man. My wife's name is Kalindra. I love her.

Jarith focused that part of his essence in the proper way so that he could receive those air vibrations, far too weak and diffuse to provide even a hint of flavor. He heard her talking to someone.

There was no one else there.

Annoyed, Jarith focused on that part of his essence in the proper way so that he could "see" as mortals did. He "saw" that she faced a bipedal figure, a human covered in cloth the way that their kind did. He wasn't an expert, but from the shape of the body, he believed it was of the "female" type like the one he was there to eat.

Save.

That he was there to save.

His wife spoke to a figure without a face. And Jarith knew it was extremely disconcerting to look upon someone who didn't have a face. He would know.

He focused that part of his essence in the proper way to manifest. As he did, he chanted part of his mantra to himself. **I am Jarith Milligreest. I am a man. I am Jarith Milligreest. I am a man.**

Parts of him began to appear. Torso, arms, shadows instead of legs. He ran into the problem he always ran into when he reached his face: Jarith didn't remember what he looked like. He left it blank, only to remember again that humans found such blankness disconcerting.

But before he could correct the problem, the human saw him and began screaming. Her horror was delicious, and for a moment, he lost himself in the flavors. Then he remembered what he was there to do.

Kalindra. He projected the thought into her mind. He wasn't yet skilled enough at manipulating his essence to vibrate the air in the way that humans communicated. He hadn't quite managed to figure out how to keep both lungs and a larynx in his mental image in clear enough focus at the same time, so this was his only option.

She continued screaming. He glanced down and realized he'd lost the arms; they'd gone back to being shadows again.

This wasn't going well.

He dropped the image entirely, vanishing from sight. **Kalindra,** he spoke again. **It is Jarith. I am here to . . . to save you.** He'd almost lost that train of thought. Her fear and despair were so distracting. **Please, Kalindra, my wife. You are a prisoner of . . . of . . . this place. I can save you, but we must go.**

He concentrated so hard on the words, on remembering who he was and why he was here, that he only distantly noticed when she stopped screaming. He did notice, however, when she plunged a dagger right into the center of his essence.

It was laughable. A dagger could no more hurt him than a light breeze could.

So why did it hurt so much?

Oh right, he remembered; nothing here was real.

That included him.

Kihrin's story
Inside Vol Karoth's prison

We were in the middle of searching for another one of Vol Karoth's memory points when shadows began to swirl in an entirely unnatural way in the road in front of us.

"Wait, what's that?" Janel said.

We all readied ourselves, because hey, there was one thing we could count on: whatever it was, it wouldn't be friendly.

Then it started to take on a man-shaped mass. Around the time the mask started to form, his identity became obvious.

"Jarith?" Galen stepped forward, his voice trembling.

I am Jarith. I am— He seemed to pause as if trying to remember the rest of his lines.

"Oh gods," Janel whispered. She looked sick.

I am Jarith Milligreest. My wife is Kalindra. I love her. She's in danger—

"Jarith!" Galen screamed.

The demon stopped.

"It's me," Galen said. "I'm your friend. Don't you remember me?"

Janel came up behind Galen and put a hand on his shoulder. "Don't. You don't know how dangerous this is."

"I need to do this." Galen shrugged away from her. I'm not sure he noticed how Jarith flinched forward toward him. Galen turned back to Jarith. "Please, Jarith. It's me. You remember me, right?"

I don't remember— The demon seemed to shake his head. **I don't remember . . .**

"Come on!" Galen said. "You know I followed you around like a damn puppy! You were one of my only friends!"

"Galen," I said carefully. "I need you to listen to me."

He was most definitely not listening to me.

Jarith floated closer to Galen. I wasn't so naïve as to think it was familial or friendly concern. Galen was anguished; Jarith wouldn't be able to help himself.

"Jarith has been through a terrible ordeal," Janel said, "and he's been damaged by it. It's not your fault if he doesn't remember you. The fact that he can remember anything at all is . . . amazing. It took me years to deal with the damage done to me, and Jarith's been through so much worse. My brother has a really strong will."

Galen paused and blinked. "Right. He's your brother, isn't he?"

"Yes, he is."

I am Jarith Milligreest. I am a man. I love my wife, Kalindra. Jarith wasn't saying that with any strong emotion. He was reciting it. To make sure he remembered. Then, in a voice that did have emotion: **I couldn't wake her. I couldn't help her. I couldn't save her.**

Galen made a strangled sound. "We need to help him."

"We're going to try." I sympathized with Galen. I did. Hell, I wanted to grab Jarith by his insubstantial, shadowy sleeves and shake him until he returned to normal, but I also knew that wasn't happening.

At least not easily.

"But it sounds like he knows where Kalindra is," Teraeth interrupted. "That is what you're trying to say, isn't it, Jarith? You know where Kalindra is?"

Yes. Help me. No. Help her.

I honestly paused for a minute and wondered if it was a trick, a trap.

But what choice did we have?

48: The Doomsday Solution

Senera's story
The Lighthouse at Shadrag Gor
After talking to Jarith

"Can we undo the glyphs?" Thurvishar asked.

Senera turned to him. "What?"

"Can we undo the glyphs?" he repeated. "The sigils you created that are binding Kharas Gulgoth and Shadrag Gor together. Presumably, you needed to paint the glyphs at both locations to create the link. If we removed the glyphs at this end, we could break the link—"

Senera considered the idea. "Possible."

"No," Talea said. "It would work, but you'll kill everyone in the mind-scape."

Senera stopped to give Talea a gimlet stare. She hated that Talea was right. Senera chewed on her lip and considered their options. Nothing good.

Lost in her own thoughts, she hadn't noticed that Thurvishar was also lost in his. Until at last the man raised his head and said, "What if we linked Vol Karoth's prison to the Nythrawl Wound?"

"I'm sorry," Xivan said. "The what?"

Senera felt the idea like an electric shock. "The Nythrawl Wound is where the demons first entered this universe. It's the gaping wound in reality that Relos Var is attempting to close. Why he created Vol Karoth. It's on the other continent—Nythrawl." She shook her head. "It wouldn't work, Thurvishar. Even if we had sigils at the site of the wound—which we don't have a way to carry out—transporting Vol Karoth to the wound isn't the goal. We need to transport Vol Karoth to the other side. To the other universe. And we don't have a way to do that."

"We'd need something that originated in that universe," Thurvishar mused.

The four people stared at each other. Then Talea stuck her head out the door and looked down the hall toward the Lighthouse. When she ducked back, she said, "Um, isn't S'arric originally from that same universe?"

"Xaltorath certainly implied that," Thurvishar said.

Xivan leaned forward. "Are you saying we can rid the world of Vol Karoth ourselves? Right now? Just draw a few of those glyphs and banish him to that other universe forever?"

Thurvishar thought about it for a minute. "Yes?"

"No," Senera said. "No, wait." She inhaled. "We can remove the sigil link here that ties the Lighthouse to Kharas Gulgoth, but not the one at Kharas

Gulgoth itself. If we send Vol Karoth to that universe, it will cascade. The Lighthouse will go too." She paused. "We'll all go. We'll *all* die."

Everyone paused.

"But the world will be saved," Xivan said.

"Maybe." Senera hesitated. "Probably. At least from Vol Karoth."

"I suppose that is a solution," Thurvishar said carefully. "Just not a very good one."

Kihrin's story
Inside Vol Karoth's prison

Vol Karoth had moved Kalindra.

Jarith threw an absolute fit about it when we reached the spot where he'd claimed Kalindra waited, howling, screaming, and tearing apart the nearby stonework. The pain of his open yearning for his wife was hard to be near.

I sat down on a nearby bench and let the demon get it out of his system. This was a good place for it. The city streets here were especially dilapidated and ruined, with cracked roads and diseased trees.

Janel came over and put an arm around my shoulders. "You okay?"

I gave her a smile I knew was probably far too thin and weak to ever be taken as sincere. "I'll be fine. He was a friend. This . . . Oh, this hurts."

"Yes, that was the whole point," she said bitterly. "And it's my fault."

"Janel, it's not–"

"Xaltorath didn't do this to Jarith to hurt *you*," Janel whispered. "Don't pretend otherwise."[1]

We both took a moment to stare at the raging demon. Teraeth walked up then and sat down next to me, legs touching. He didn't say a word. He just wanted me to know he was there. I set my hand on his leg.

I checked to make sure Galen wasn't in hearing range. "Can he be cured?"

"I was," Janel said, "but I was much younger when it happened, and I had Relos Var as my own personal mind physicker." She took a deep breath. "Jarith hasn't forgotten, you realize. I'll tell you that right now. Nobody forgets. But Xaltorath has almost certainly locked those memories behind associations so painful Jarith's mind is refusing to go anywhere near them. You can't blame a person for not wanting to put their hand in a fire after they've been badly–" She paused and blinked. A funny look came over her face as her eyes slowly took in the scene in front of her. She looked around as if she hadn't realized where we were. "Burned," Janel finished, so softly I only heard her because I was right there.

"Are you all right?" Teraeth asked her.

She pulled herself up, but her eyes were shiny bright. "Fine. Just–" Janel glanced at me. "I think . . . I think Vol Karoth's doing something similar. Separating out the memories too painful for him to face. That's what the gray spaces are." A flash of heartbreak seared across her eyes, a low and torturous

---

[1] But as pointed out in earlier conversations, I don't think Xaltorath did it for Janel either. It's quite possible Jarith earned this entirely on his own–at least, in a previous time line.

piece of agony and grief. Whatever she'd just remembered, it had been bad; Jarith halted his tantrum as if Janel had started screaming and stared in her direction.

She had to be thinking about C'indrol, about S'arric. It had never really occurred to me how much this must be like . . . I didn't know. Being a widow, I supposed, walking through the corpse of your memories of the man you once loved. Still loved.

Janel stood, suddenly. "Jarith, enough!" she shouted. "You've had your fun. Now it's time to find your wife."

"You've got to be joking," Teraeth said.

I exhaled as I took in the scene in front of us. "Yeah," I said. "Agreed."

When Jarith finally located Kalindra, she wasn't trapped in a dungeon or locked away in a vault or hidden in any of the illusion, trap-filled lairs that we'd become so familiar with.

She was on a roof.

Now the thing to understand was that a lot of these buildings were really tall. I'd always thought the buildings in the Capital were the tallest anywhere, since it wasn't uncommon for buildings in the city to be five, six stories tall in places. But Karolaen's buildings? Some of them were easily a dozen stories tall or higher. It was like someone had decided to build on a sky tree but instead of using a tree had just built the structure that tall. I assumed magic and lots of it kept the damn things up.

So this may explain why we didn't go rushing in, even though it seemed like Kalindra was all by herself, not tied up, and without a single guardian in attendance anywhere.

"What happens if we fall from this height?" Galen asked. "Nothing's real, right?"

"Nothing's real, and everything's real," Teraeth said. "That's the problem."

"That doesn't even make sense," Galen growled.

"Belief is important," Janel said, "so yes, we can die here."

Everyone looked at the woman standing on the roof.

Kalindra.

Before anyone could do anything else, the world changed.

Xivan's reaction
The Lighthouse in Shadrag Gor
After discussing how to destroy Vol Korath

The room was quiet—grave quiet, sepulchre quiet—when Xivan felt it.

She didn't know quite how to describe the feeling except that it was the opposite of feeling like someone was walking over your grave.

It felt like she was walking over theirs.

"Kalindra," Xivan murmured. "Kalindra's in trouble." She hadn't meant to say it out loud, or at least not loudly, but evidently, in the morgue-quiet space, it had been more than loud enough.

"Yes," Senera snapped, "I think we all know that."

"No, there's something—" Xivan stood and found herself pacing, her skin awash with the prickling feeling of ghostly premonition. She felt like she could hear Kalindra screaming, crying, begging. And yet, Xivan knew she wasn't hearing any of that. Not with her ears. Not with her body.

"No," Xivan whispered. *"He's lying to you. Don't you dare believe him."*

That silence stretched out, pulled tight.

Snapped.

"Fuck it," Senera said. She grabbed her brush and the inkstone and ran out of the room.

Xivan felt a rush of dread. She knew exactly where the wizard was heading.

"Senera!" Thurvishar yelled out and went chasing after her. So they all went. There were only the four of them left, after all. Might as well make it a party.

Entering the Lighthouse was painfully difficult. Xivan watched as the wizards started casting spells—a lot of spells—to protect themselves. It was so cold Xivan suspected the temperature itself would instantly freeze almost anything left out. The whole area was pitch-black, and any mage-light created died in seconds.

Oddly, as they approached the doorway, Vol Karoth was still visible. The inky blackness surrounding him only made the delicate blue halo around his body more obvious.

Xivan felt certain that anyone stepping into that room without wards would have died on the spot.

Senera didn't try to erase any of the sigils on the walls, but she knelt at Vol Karoth's feet and started sketching out sections on the floor.

"Senera," Thurvishar said, "you can't."

She leaned back on her heels. "How does this change anything? If we get rid of the sigils to escape this place, everyone dies, and we don't even know for sure it will work. If we stay, we're no closer to doing something about Vol Karoth, he escapes, everyone dies. This is the only choice where he dies too."

"Along with everyone else," Talea said.

"That's going to happen, anyway!" Senera shouted.

Xivan cleared her throat. "I agree with Senera—" she said.

"Thank you!" Senera crossed her arms over her chest.

"Which means it's the wrong thing to do," Xivan finished. She shrugged at the pale woman's glare. "Look, I know myself well enough to know I don't make the right call about these sorts of things. And neither do you, Senera." Xivan gestured to Talea and Thurvishar. "So what do you two think?"

"I think this isn't a decision that we get to make by ourselves," Talea said. "It doesn't just affect us."

"Finish everything but the last part," Thurvishar finally said. "Then come back inside. We're done with stories. I'll contact one of the others, and we'll find out what everyone thinks. And if everyone agrees—*everyone*—then we'll finish this." He wore a sick, ugly expression as he glanced at Vol Karoth, still locked in place. "We'll finish this once and for all."

Kalindra's story
Inside Vol Karoth's prison

Kalindra ran. The broken stones of the ruined city lacerated her feet until each step left red footprints behind her. All around her, her sins crowded closer, while behind . . . something worse pursued.

To her left, a man whose throat had been slit reached out for her, words blowing wetly from the gash across his neck. "I had a child who depended on me." To her right, a younger man, barely more than a boy, held his head under one arm as he said, "My mother killed herself after my death." Next to him, a man and woman rasped through throats crushed by her garrote, "We were going to get married."

Ahead and behind were more, hundreds more. She knew each face. She'd killed each one. And behind that front line, hundreds more, thousands more; the faceless hordes of friends, families, loved ones. Those who had to live on in the aftermath of her murders, most of them never knowing why—why did their friends and families and loved ones have to die? And she couldn't tell them, for she no longer knew herself.

The whim of a fickle, treacherous goddess, who didn't even care enough to Return the loved ones of her own servants? Maybe there was no reason at all; maybe Thaena just liked it when people died.

She stumbled, caught herself before she went down. A hand brushed her shoulder, cold and clammy from the grave. She wrenched free and ran. The dead—her dead—pressed in on both sides.

But that wasn't the worst part. The worst part was what followed behind her, keeping pace. Whispering to her. "Kalindra," it said to her in a horrible parody of her dead husband's voice. "Why didn't you have me Returned? Why do you run from me, Kalindra? Kalindra the assassin. Kalindra the murderer. Kalindra the betrayer!"

The one time she had glanced back, she'd seen him. Not as he'd been in life but pale and worm-eaten, clothed in the wrong uniform, half of his jaw hanging off, infinite darkness where his eyes should have been.

How long had he chased her? It felt like days. Days of hearing the dead call out to her for justice, beg her for the life she stole back.

"Just let me see my sweetheart one last time."

"My momma needs me; she's old and won't survive the winter without me."

"It was just a candlestick. Did I need to die for so little?"

"Please, my baby is crying for me. Can't you hear him?"

She stumbled again at that last one: she did hear a baby crying. Worse, she knew that voice.

Nikali.

She looked and saw him ahead of her. A basket sat on a stone plinth ahead, and her son fussed inside of it. She redoubled her speed, bleeding feet slapping wetly on the jagged stones as she raced for him. If she could reach him ahead of the tide of dead, she could keep him safe.

She would . . .

A darkness swept over everything and then retreated.

She leaned back as she stopped suddenly. In front of her was a cliff–the cliff outside the monastery at Devors. Below, far below, the sea crashed against the tumbled stones. She looked around. Where was Nikali?

But all she saw were the hordes of dead. Then she heard the voice again. Jarith's voice. Only it wasn't his voice; it was deeper, harsher, and dissonant, like a thousand souls in pain crying out simultaneously.

"Where is our son, Kalindra? He's gone."

"He . . . he was safe!" she cried out. "I . . . I made arrangements!" She whirled to face him, tears blurring her sight.

He laughed, dark and bitter as he pushed through the throng of corpses. "A deal? With the Lash? With the new goddess of death? You never learn, do you, Kalindra? Thaena was willing to sacrifice her own son; you think she cares one whit for ours? No, Kalindra, you left him there, alone and scared, while you brought down the wards. While you let the Lash and Drehemia and all these dead people into the monastery. They didn't care who he was; he was just another annoying mortal to them. They didn't even notice when they destroyed him."

With every step he took, he changed. Step, and now he was a peasant who's crime was owning land a Brotherhood client coveted. Step, and now he was a woman who had thought to cheat Death by having the Blue House make her young again, over and over. Step, and now he was a fellow killer, sent to eradicate the same target as she, but the Brotherhood brooks no competition, so she'd eliminated him as well.

"No!" Kalindra screamed. "It's. . . . it's not true!"

"Do you think Drehemia's breath cared about your 'deal' with the Lash? Do you think that a Daughter of Laaka, animated by an artifact created by Rev'arric, cares about our child? He's gone, Kalindra. He's gone, and you killed him!" Now the creature who pursued her sounded empty and hollow, echoing as if speaking from inside a dark, fathomless cave.

Someone cried out behind her. She spun to look and saw, far below, the nacreous, rotting form of the Lash holding her baby high in the air for a moment . . . and then plunging him underwater and holding him there.

"No!" Kalindra screamed again until her throat gave out. Arms outstretched toward Nikali, her heart, already cracked almost to the point of no return from her husband's death, shattered. She fell to her knees.

No. Thaena's voice sounded harsh but more tender than she'd heard in years. *He's lying to you. Don't you dare believe him.*[2]

"Thaena?" But no, that was wrong. That had to be wrong. Thaena was dead.

Wait. She blinked and looked around.

How much of this was real? Was any of this real?

Kalindra, Jarith's voice said. She almost turned to look at him. But no; he was dead, Nikali was dead. Tears streamed down her face to be washed

---

[2] Under the circumstances I suppose I can understand why Kalindra reinterpreted Xivan's voice as Thaena's. The really interesting part is that she heard the other woman.

away in the driving rain atop the cliff on Devors. Around her, the dead shuffled, moving toward her. They began to push her over the edge.

A hand grabbed her arm.

Everything changed. Kalindra blinked and looked around, perplexed. She was on top of a building somehow, in a gray and broken city. She felt cored, sliced open, hollowed out.

A hand touched her face. Kalindra flinched, before she saw the hand was attached to a man clothed in shadows and wisps of darkness, his face hidden behind a ceramic mask with no eyes.

Kalindra.

"Jarith," she said, knowing it was he. Somehow, it was really he. How? She didn't know, and right then, she didn't care. "Nikali?" she croaked.

Still alive, still on Devors. Our son is alive, the voice said directly into her mind, but it was his voice. She would know Jarith anywhere. She collapsed in his arms, crying.

The demon held her.

49: The Easiest to Break

Kihrin's story
Inside Vol Karoth's prison

We all watched, horrified, as Kalindra dropped from the edge. None of us would have been able to stop her. None of us could have gotten to her in time. Maybe Thurvishar, if he'd been there.

But I had forgotten about Jarith.

The demon moved faster than any of the rest of us and grabbed Kalindra even as she dropped off the edge. Better still, it was clear that she saw him and knew who he was.

Which meant we just needed to get out—

Vol Karoth appeared in front of me.

I win.

I crossed my arms over my chest. "How do you figure? We saved Kalindra."

Did you, though? Vol Karoth said. *She realized the truth; her life was too painful to allow to continue. Life is too painful to allow to continue. She was willing to take her own life, and even if you've stopped her this time, you can't watch her forever.*

"You crazy mother—" I muttered under my breath, then said louder, "That's a cheap cop-out, and you know it. Life is hard, so just cancel life? People are mean to each other, so the solution is no more people? No."

We had a deal.

"And you haven't proved anything!"

She abandoned you, she abandoned her husband, she abandoned her child. She didn't love them enough to survive for any of you. Love is a mortar too weak to hold when the foundations of our lives crumble.

"Oh, don't you dare blame her for this. She made some mistakes. Bad ones. Maybe she'd have fixed them on her own if you hadn't literally pushed her over the edge. But you don't get to shove her over a cliff and then say she had it coming because she didn't dodge fast enough."

Fine. Then we are through playing games.

Vol Karoth vanished.

Everything started moving again. The wind whipped past us.

And I knew, deep in my gut, that everything had just gone terribly wrong.

Senera's story
The Lighthouse at Shadrag Gor
After starting the final glyph

Senera retreated to one of the empty bedrooms while she waited for Thurvishar to finish getting a message to the others in the mindscape. She sat on the edge of a bed, elbows on her knees, fingers steepled together under her chin. Her mind was blank and too full, and nothing had worked out the way she'd wanted. She wrote a letter to Thurvishar, immediately regretted it, and crumpled the paper into a tight ball.[1]

"Senera?" Thurvishar's voice, from the doorway.

"Done so soon?" Senera's voice cracked, because the sad expression on his face told her what the answer had been. Gods-damn bunch of self-sacrificing fools, all of them.

Herself included.

"I thought we might talk about . . . that thing we haven't been talking about."

Senera rolled her eyes. "Any relationship between us—"

Thurvishar winced. "No, I meant the other thing. You being a spell thief."

Senera froze. "There's nothing to talk about."

"You can hardly expect me not to have noticed," Thurvishar said. "I don't think there's a single one of us who hasn't noticed you copying one of our spells. I don't think Talea or Xivan really understand how rare it is. Or what that means—"

"If you're going to tell me that I'm a telepath, you can just turn around and walk away," Senera said. "I'm not."

"How did you wake me?"

"I used a glyph," Senera said, staring hatefully at him. "Next question?"

"I'm sorry," Thurvishar said, "but we both know that's a lie."

He reached out and touched the side of her head.

The world changed.

Senera's memory
The Opaline Palace of House D'Jorax, Quur
Sixteen years earlier

Senera sat perfectly still. She had to sit still; there were wards all around her. If she so much as moved an inch, the result was pain. She wasn't technically tied up, but in all the ways that mattered, her chains were the size of the entire room.

Senera was going to die. She knew she was going to die. There was only one outcome for a witch, and since that was what she was, it wasn't difficult math. She considered herself fortunate that they'd never really figured out—or believed—the full extent of her crimes because of her age, her sex. But it didn't matter, they'd still kill her for casting spells, and dead was dead. They were taking her power seriously too. The wards proved that.

---

[1] No, I'm not going to tell you what it said.

The only reason they hadn't killed her yet was because they were still try-ing to find the lord heir to let him know that he was now high lord.

Two men entered the room.

One of them was Emeran D'Jorax, who was a distant cousin of the current—err, former—high lord. He had a real talent for bootlicking. He'd probably go far. Senera didn't recognize the other man. He was average looking, and to judge by the eyes, not a member of any Royal House.

The wards didn't stop her from feeling the extraordinary power emanat-ing from him, hard and crisp and sharp enough to cut. He was annoyed, and thought Emeran D'Jorax wouldn't go far at all if the royal had wasted his time. Emeran was thinking of metal, a lot of it, and just exactly how he planned to spend it.

"You told me, Lord Var, that if I ever found anyone of a certain sort of magical talent, I should contact you immediately." The sycophantic little toady gestured toward her. "She murdered the high lord."

"Really." The wizard (with that aura, Senera just assumed he must be a wizard) seemed skeptical of the idea. He sat back on his haunches to look at her closer, like she was a well-bred horse.

"She knew exactly how to get through the wards, Lord Var, and no one knew that information but the high lord himself. No one could cast the spell but the high lord himself. It was unique."

Senera cursed. She hadn't known that. It explained a lot. It explained their panic.

"I see," Relos Var says. "And are you a telepath, little girl?"

She didn't dare move her head.

"No need to answer," Var said. "I can tell. A telepath and yet you were still able to commit a murder. Rather extraordinary. It's almost a pity I have no need of telepaths."

"Lord?" Panic from Emeran, who was now worried about losing his grand reward.

"The problem with telepaths," Relos Var said casually as he stood, "is that they either go insane and become something like mimics, or they go . . . soft. Too much empathy. Too much ability to understand *every* point of view. And why would I want a servant who might actually be able to tell if I was lying to them? Stars no."

"So you're not interested in her, then?" Emeran looked upset by the idea, probably because what he was doing would also get him killed if the rest of House D'Jorax ever found out about it.

"Oh no, I'll take her. Please remove these wards." Relos Var gave Senera what she thought was meant to be a comforting smile. She couldn't bring herself to return it, although at least he thought that Emeran was a fool, which endeared the wizard to Senera at least a little.

The D'Jorax sorcerer took down the wards and then said, "Now don't move. He's powerful enough to stop your heart just by looking at you, you little whore." It was the first time he's said a word to Senera.

"Oh, not her," Relos Var corrected. "She might be a child, but her aura is much too strong. You, though?"

Emeran D'Jorax collapsed into an untidy little heap of flesh.

Senera made a small sound and shied back. The light of Emeran's mind had simply vanished, snuffed out. He was dead. Senera didn't scream. There was no point. The wizard could kill her as easily as he killed the D'Jorax fool, strong aura or not.

The wizard who murdered him did something then. Senera wasn't quite sure what, but she watched as he gathered strands of light from the man's body, which coalesced into a small, hard indigo jewel with a sparkling star in the center. "Now that's a surprise," Var said amiably. He held the star tear up to the light. "Don't see many of these anymore. Certainly not in idiots too weak to protect their sense of self."

The wizard had taken that man's souls, Senera thought, and she cringed at the injustice of it. No reincarnation, no rebirth. No Return, if he had family who cared enough about him to try. And no one inside House D'Jorax would have any idea what happened there. They'd just find the body.

But she underestimated the wizard. He kept casting, and this time, he did something that changed the shape of Emeran's corpse. She watched intently as he transformed Emeran's body into something that looked–

"I thought you said you didn't need a telepath." Senera said the words before she could stop herself. Because the body on the ground was hers now, dead because she'd struggled too hard against the wards chaining her in place. There was only one reason Senera could think of why Relos Var would do this–because he'd planned on taking her with him.

"I don't," Var told her, smiling warmly. "But don't worry, by the time we're done, you won't be one anymore."[2]

Senera's reaction
The Lighthouse at Shadrag Gor

Senera gasped and came back to her own mind. She was still sitting there on the edge of the bed, but it wasn't Thurvishar who crouched down next to her, so close he's almost touching.

It was Vol Karoth.

You should have listened to Sheloran.

"That didn't happen," Senera said. "That's not–" She should have cast spells, tried to fight, done something. She couldn't make herself move.

Not what you remember? He sounded amused. *Shall we give you back your memories? Every single one that my dear, sweet brother stole? I saved you for last, you know.*

"Saved me for last?" Her heart was beating so fast she could hear the pounding in her ears. She could feel Thurvishar down the hall, the dawning horror in his mind as he must have realized he left her alone for just a damn minute too long.

---

[2] The interesting thing about this vision, ignoring my own personal involvement, is that it marks one of the only times that Vol Korath invoked a memory from one of us which predated his awakening. Interesting, but not, I think, significant: Vol Korath had always been capable of changing the rules of the game to suit his needs.

Oh yes, Val Karoth said. *I left you for the end because I always knew you'd be the easiest to break.*

The bastard let her remember the truth. He reached inside her mind and brushed away all the cobwebs, every dusty, boarded-up, abandoned part of her mind. Because Relos Var never stopped her from being a telepath. He didn't stop her from hearing the voices, the screams. All those screams. Every time she killed someone. Every single time anyone died near her. She had always, all these years, felt every single one.

Relos Var just stopped her from remembering them after. Until now.

She started screaming.

By the time Thurvishar reached the room, it was too late.

Senera's prison

She slammed open the door to the ritual room. "What in all the void do you think you're doing?" Senera spat.

The room had been recently cleaned; she could smell the astringency of the antiseptics. The floor and walls were marked off, sigils placed in all the right locations, each slightly incomplete as they waited for the final stroke to finish them and bring them to full potency.

In the center of the glyphs lay the unconscious body of a boy of around ten or eleven years old. He wore a plain, unadorned robe too small for him, and his hair was matted. Clearly, he had been kept unconscious for some time.

A handsome man in dark, severe clothing looked up from the scroll he was reading when she entered. He was tall, bald, with eyes that were pure black. He held the scroll with hands that seemed strong despite the long, delicate fingers.

Any fond greeting he might have offered died a quick death at her opening words. "What do you think?" Thurvishar snapped back. "I'm doing what has to be done. And don't look at me like that; you know I take no pleasure in this. With how rare children are? This breaks my heart."

"But you're still going to do it," Senera said. She refused to look at the child, although a part of her wondered if he had the same eyes as D'eras, the man he'd been before the accident a decade ago. There's still so much they don't understand about reincarnation.

"Of course I'm still going to do it," Thurvishar said. "Someone has to, and you know it."

"There has to be another way," Senera said, shaking her head. "He's the first child since . . . He's a miracle."

"A miracle with a tragic flaw." Thurvishar mirrored her head-shake. "Telepathy in one so young is problem enough," he continued, "but the boy is so much more than that. He need but see a spell performed once and he can cast it also. But he's a child, with a child's understanding of consequences. That's a tragedy waiting to happen."

"So remove it. Take away his ability to cast," Senera begged. "You don't have to—"

"It's not enough, and you know it," Thurvishar interrupted her. "Even if I could—which I cannot—it wouldn't be enough. He hears voices, constantly. But they're not voices, are they? They're thoughts." He rolled up the scroll and placed it on a cluttered desk against the far wall. "This won't hurt him. He simply won't remember," he continued. "This will let him lead a normal life."

"Who are you to define what qualifies as normal?" Senera said with a sour taste in her mouth. "You're not removing the telepathy . . ."

"As I said, I cannot," Thurvishar said mildly. "But what I'm doing is a valid compromise. I will create a buffer around that part of his mind. The thoughts of others will simply be . . . locked away."

"That's too close to his emotional center," Senera was almost yelling in her passion. "You're going to create a monster, you know that, right? If it spills over into his emotional core—and it will—you'll be killing his empathy. It's . . . it's criminal!"

His eyes flashed with rage, briefly, before he took a deep breath. "It's not criminal," he said as he exhaled. "I have his parents' permission. And that of the Assembly. So I'd kindly ask you to get the fuck out of this room and let me work!"

She did, her vision blurring with anger.

She slammed open the door to the ritual room. "What in all the void do you think you're doing?"

Thurvishar's story
The Lighthouse at Shadrag Gor
Just after Senera's collapse

Thurvishar recognized his mistake the moment it occurred. He'd felt it, the way one might feel an itch in the middle of one's back when being watched. He'd been concentrating on trying to reach one of the people whose bodies were there in the Lighthouse, attempts that had, one and all, proved fruitless. Vol Karoth fooled them all. Thurvishar had thought the dark god was weakening, but it was the opposite: he'd become too strong, and it was ultimately his mind that Thurvishar was attempting to breach. He could no longer send messages.

He opened his eyes. "Where's Senera?"

The other two women stared at him in surprise and then looked around. It was clear that neither had realized Senera wasn't with them.

"Fuck," Xivan said.

Then the screaming started. It cut off abruptly.

"Damn it all," Thurvishar cursed and ran out the door. He was forced to search from room to room because he could no longer feel Senera. Finally, he found her body in one of the empty bedrooms, laid out on one of the stone beds.

It was all he could do not to collapse. He'd been fine as long as Senera was fine. Even when they were potentially planning a final act that would qualify as suicide, she was there with him, and that made it fine. Now . . .

"What happened?" Xivan said.

"Oh, she's been crying," Talea said, motioning toward Senera's cheeks.

Talea was right. She had indeed been crying. And Thurvishar had a good idea why. He'd known from very nearly the first moment he'd met Senera, years ago at the court of Duke Kaen, but he'd never said a word. He'd always assumed she'd had her own reasons for blocking that side of her abilities or figured that she'd run afoul of an early magical ritual gone wrong or some kind of psychic trauma. And then, later still, he began to realize the sort of advantages one might gain from having a telepath as a servant, if only one removed all those icky, inconvenient "feelings."

"Vol Karoth took her," Thurvishar said, just to spell out the obvious. "Which I'm going to interpret as an indication that the final sigil idea will work."

Xivan scowled and looked away.

"Did you talk to any of the others?" Talea folded Senera's arms on top of her chest and brushed away the tears.

"I couldn't reach them," Thurvishar said. "He's blocking me."

"I felt Kalindra," Xivan said.

Thurvishar stared at her. What.

"I felt Kalindra earlier. Felt her mind. Felt her calling for help," Xivan said. "He can't be blocking that hard. He wants us in the mindscape, because then we're not here."

Thurvishar chewed on his lip. "There's a chance . . ." He inhaled. "There's a chance that he's only blocking communication. I might still be able to transfer minds."

"You mean going after Senera."

"While she completed all but the final glyph, we still need her for that final symbol," Thurvishar said.

Xivan rolled her eyes and pulled a sheet of parchment out of Senera's skirt. "You honestly think she didn't allow for that?" She flashed the sheet in front of him. It had the final sigil drawn on it, each component divided so it wouldn't accidentally activate. "I mean, I'd say you should just use the Name of All Things, but I don't know if that would count as borrowing."

"I still want to go after Senera." Talea pulled on Xivan's sleeve. "We can't leave her in there."

"No," Thurvishar said. "Xivan's right. Vol Karoth wants us there."

"The point is she saved us," Xivan said, stabbing a finger in Senera's direction. "She saved us all. Let Vol Karoth chew on that. We can't do anything here, but you can. So we'll go rescue Senera and find the others. You can pull one of us back and we'll tell you the happy news." The happy news being whether or not the others had agreed to destroy themselves to save all of mankind. Nothing significant.

Talea reached over and laced her fingers in Xivan's.

"Fine," Thurvishar agreed. "Bring her back to me."

PART II

ENDINGS IN THE
HOUSE OF ALWAYS

50: Necessary Sacrifices

Talea's story
Inside Vol Korath's prison
After Senera's collapse

Talea and Xivan appeared on a disused but not unpleasant city street, with overgrown weedy verges and wild trees lining the thoroughfare. The architecture was like nothing Talea had ever seen before. It all had a sameness to it, though, as if it had been built at the same time by the same team of stonemasons. Pretty, but repetitive.

"Okay, so now we just need to find Senera or any of the others!" Talea said. She pulled a coin from her sash and flipped it at random. "That way," she said, pointing.

Xivan stared. "Talea, that wasn't a binary choice. We could go any direction."

"Yes, but I was thinking of going this way or that way," Talea admitted. "So the coin said that way." She shrugged. "Basically, any way is as good as any other."

"Fine." Xivan pulled out her sword and began stalking that way. After a few minutes of walking, she paused. "Someone's over there."

"Well, only one way to find out who it is," Talea said, grinning broadly. "Let's go take a look."

They rounded the corner and found themselves in the midst of an entire platoon of armed soldiers.

"I didn't see that coming," Talea said.

Each of the footmen was armed and armored the same, in red-and-gold uniforms of a make and style unknown to her. Open-faced helmets protected the heads of the men . . . and women, Talea noticed. Some of those faces, however, lacked *faces*.

"What the—?" she asked.

Xivan shrugged. "Fight now, discuss existential horror later," she ordered. Putting actions to words, she stepped forward and swung her imchii toward the nearest soldier. The man put up his arm to defend himself, and Xivan's sword rebounded from striking his armor, which was a lot sturdier than it looked.

"Right," Talea said. "Aim for seams. Got it. Thanks for that sage advice."

"So glad I could provide one more lesson for you." Xivan grinned wildly as she spun, ducked her opponent's riposte, and slashed upward into the exposed underside of his arm. Cloth and flesh tore.

But he didn't bleed. The grin on Xivan's face faded. This was suddenly not nearly as much fun.

Talea parried a thrust, struck back one-handed only for her blade to skitter off her enemy's armor. He chopped at her legs, forcing her to jump back. He had reach on her, as well as a good sixty pounds. If she couldn't find a way to close inside his guard, this was going to be a highly unpleasant bout on her end.

She feinted high to force him to lift his blade to protect that blank face. Then she rolled under him, coming up beside and ramming her blade two-handed into the joint between his helmet and his pauldron. With a hard, sideways tug, she severed his spine.

This seemed to bother her enemy only slightly.

"Um, Xivan?" Talea said, allowing a note of worry to creep into her voice.

"Yeah, I'm having the same problems," Xivan replied. "I suggest we switch to plan J."

Talea parried another swing, backpedaled as she caught a second soldier moving to flank her on her left. "But I didn't bring a bladder of goat's milk with me. Did you?" she replied, ducking under a lateral cut from the newcomer.

"Ha," Xivan replied. Then, "Run!"

"Running!" Talea agreed, smashing her sword against that of her first enemy to put him out of line so she could turn and flee.

They ran side by side, clattering footsteps behind letting them know they were pursued. Talea felt something was wrong as they sprinted away from the battle. It came to her; Xivan wasn't holding back to "let" Talea keep up.

Talea glanced over and saw Xivan panting for breath.

Oh. Right.

Well, that's not ideal, she thought. The one time it would be helpful for her to be dead . . .

Wait. That's it. Dead.

"Hey," Talea forced out between gasps. "Can you just. . . . you know . . . kill them? Herald of . . . Death . . . and all . . . that?"

"Can't," Xivan panted, her breathing even harsher than Talea's. But that made sense; she hadn't needed to breathe in years. Her dear teacher was out of practice. "Not . . . alive . . . can't . . . die . . . ," Xivan finished.

Talea craned her head to look behind. Somewhere in the last several turns, they'd managed to lose their pursuers. She put a hand on Xivan's arm and slowed, stopped, bent over holding her sides and gasping loudly.

Xivan did the same.

After what felt like several minutes, they'd both recovered enough to talk.

"What?" Talea asked.

"I said they're not really 'alive,'" Xivan said. "Probably why I didn't sense them until we ran into them."

"Problematic." Talea chewed on her lower lip. "Okay, so our swords are basically useless, and your powers won't help us here. That leaves me. Give us a moment to–" She looked around, frowning.

She still hadn't seen Eshi since Thurvishar had sent them to this place.

"Er, I mean, give me a moment," she corrected herself. She tried to figure the odds of a wall collapsing in the right direction if pushed or of there being a runaway cart at just the right time if they . . .

Nothing.

Nothing happened by "luck" in this world, because it wasn't a world.

"It's no good," she said, shaking her head. "I'm powerless too. Damn." She kicked at an imaginary rock and liked to believe it would have flown a good distance had there actually been anything there to kick.

"Okay," Xivan said. "So we go at this a different way."

"What way?" Talea asked. "No weapons, no powers . . . Are we going to just ask politely and rely on the good manners of people with no faces?"

"Nope," Xivan said. "We're going to do this really old style. For me, I mean."

"I have no idea what you're saying."

"Before I met Azhen, I was your typical Khorveshan swordmaster's daughter," Xivan said.

"Meaning?" Talea prompted.

"Meaning," Xivan said, "I had to sneak in and out of the house to meet up with my lovers, just like any other girl my age." Xivan grinned again, that same wild, feral grin as earlier. Talea almost swooned when she realized what it meant; Xivan was having fun. "Here's what we're going to do," Xivan said, and she explained the plan.

"Hello," Talea said, waving at the soldiers from the corner of the building. "Say, you folks don't happen to know where a girl could get a spiced sag roll in this city, do you?"

Several heads turned her way. A faceless man in slightly more ornate armor, which Talea took to mean he was an officer of some sort, pointed. Swords were drawn, and half the platoon ran toward her.

"Oh, this way? Okaythanksbye!" Talea turned and ran. Only this time, she ran slower than her flat-out sprint, letting the charging horde of heavily armed creatures stay just far enough away that they wouldn't realize they stood no chance of catching her.

She ran to the edge of the block, made a right, and kept going. Halfway down the street, she glanced back. Sure enough, the group was still only a dozen or so yards behind her. She picked up just a little speed, so by the time she made the next right, the gap had widened to twenty yards.

It was almost thirty by the time she made the next right, running along the road toward the rest of the soldiers.

This had better work, she thought to herself, *or I'm going to have to have a "I'm hole-y-er than you" talk with Xivan.*

The soldiers still milling around the front turned to face her, seeing her running toward them. "Oops," she said loudly. "Did I make a wrong turn?"

Most of that group drew weapons and ran toward her.

"Now or never!" she yelled.

Now, as it turned out.

From the building the soldiers were guarding, Xivan emerged with Senera, who looked like shit. What didn't look like shit, however, what looked simply magnificent and beautiful and perfect, was the way the sorceress lifted her arms and made a sweeping motion with her downward-trailing fingers. Fire erupted from them and fanned out, catching most of the contingent of faceless goons.

Talea smiled. They might be hard to cut, but it turned out that they burned quite prettily.

Then she stopped smiling. Because behind those soldiers?

Were more soldiers.

Kihrin's story
Inside Vol Korath's prison

We'd all felt it when Vol Karoth took Senera. He'd wanted us to feel it. He was practically rubbing our noses in it.

Teraeth came over and put his arm around me. "We'll find her," he whispered. "We're getting pretty good at this."

"You're lying," I said. We were not getting pretty good at this.

As if to emphasize the point, Vol Karoth appeared in the middle of the room. "Fuck." Galen went for his sword.

I think Qown tried to do something, rearrange reality until we were someplace else, but Vol Karoth just . . . stopped it.

I felt my heart sink. At some point, Vol Karoth had become a lot more powerful, and I'd missed it. When had that happened?

I've just saved your lives.

"Excuse me?" Teraeth said. "Call me skeptical, because that doesn't seem like your style." He looked uncomfortable for any number of reasons, not least of which was because Vol Karoth hadn't been stopping by for friendly chats. This was a break in pattern.

I, for one, assumed a break in pattern was bad.

Senera intended to link the Lighthouse and everyone in it to the other side of the Nythrawl Wound. Which wouldn't kill either of us, but it most certainly would kill all your friends.

"So that's why you took Senera," I said.

Do you want to spend eternity locked away in a dying universe while Rev'arric takes over this one? I don't. Aren't you grateful? I saved you. His mockery was almost as black as his body.

The others were silent. I supposed I couldn't blame them for that. "Fine, so now she's here. Let her go. There's no reason to keep her in that . . . loop."

Vol Karoth circled around me. I had to turn to keep him in view. *It accomplished what I wanted. I have all Three Sisters now.*

I blinked. "What did you say? Tya, Taja, and Thaena aren't—" But Taja and Thaena.

Damn it. *Taja* and *Thaena.*

It had been so cute of Eshimavari to refer to what Talea was becoming as a "herald," but I could see the truth of matters easily enough now.

Tya and Taja had indeed learned from all Grizzst's attempts to resurrect the Eight. The wizard had been wrong about one thing—maybe the Eight hadn't found a cure in three thousand years, but they hadn't spent that time being idle either. They hadn't tried to force an Immortal's souls, with all that copious and overabundant tenyé, into a mortal body that couldn't contain it. Grizzst had proved that couldn't be done. They hadn't tried to save their immortal souls at all, which had undoubtedly been the reason Thaena had sabotaged their plan at every opportunity.

They'd taken an entirely different tactic—turning mortal bodies into something else. The talismans were never meant to resurrect the Eight; they were meant to transfer their positions to new souls and new hosts.

Taja and Thaena were dead. Long live Taja and Thaena.

I checked the Lighthouse and realized he was right. Both Xivan and Talea were gone, which could only mean that they'd gone after Senera. And while Senera wasn't Tya, since the Goddess of Magic was still very much alive, it was still easy enough to make the comparison when Senera's two closest friends were well on their way to replacing Luck and Death.[1]

"Kihrin," Janel said. "What's he talking about?"

"Talea and Xivan . . . are becoming Taja and Thaena. Not the people. The roles. Luck. Death. Being tied to those concepts are what gave the Eight Guardians their powers. Eshimavari and Irisia must have figured out a way to transfer that bond to new hosts."

Impossible to do while they were still alive. Khaemezra would never have given up that position, no matter what she told herself in the quiet, still hours when she gave life to her regrets. But dead? Ah, dead, they can't fight it. And so now Eshimavari and Khaemezra are truly dead. Never to return.

I realized right away the problem. There was no chance at all that either Talea or Xivan were anywhere near close to full strength. Hell, I was pretty sure Xivan hadn't reached the stage where a friendly Khaemezra version two started showing up to give her advice—assuming that would ever happen. They were at best proto-Immortals, who had control over only a small fraction of their full powers. And that meant that here, in Vol Karoth's literal mind, they were vulnerable. So vulnerable.

If Vol Karoth had those concepts under his control . . . breaking free of his prison would be the easiest thing in the world.

I'm here to make a deal. Offer you a final chance. You give yourself up and I'll release them. You'll be proving friendship has value, that you'd be willing to save them. But ask yourself: Why would you give yourself up for people who were perfectly willing to kill you?

My stomach knotted. I could almost admire the elegance of the logic trap. If I gave myself up, I lost, no matter if Senera, Talea, and Xivan survived for the moment. If I refused, then I proved Vol Karoth's point—and still lost. A perfect Nemesan gambit. Any choice I made led right down the road to my own failure.

Honestly, Relos Var would have been so proud.

Could Vol Karoth have been lying about having the three women? I didn't think so. No, scratch that. I knew he wasn't lying. He absolutely had them. Which meant—

"Take me," Janel said. "Take me instead."

What.

---

[1] I feel obligated to make a token protest about the assumption that Xivan and Talea are my closest friends, but no one seems to believe me. Least of all Xivan and Talea.

What.

"Janel!" I said through clenched teeth. That was not going to help the situation at all.

But she ignored me, instead staring at the dark god. "You know this is all my fault. We've talked about this. I'm the one you're angry with, so why don't you just leave them alone and take me? We have so much to catch up on."

"Janel, no–" Teraeth said, wide-eyed.

"Kihrin's not the only one who can make boneheaded sacrifices," Janel said, her voice thick and self-deprecating. She shuddered and looked over at Kihrin. "You'd better not waste the time I'm buying you."

"No!" I shouted. "It's a stupid idea, and he's not stupid enough–"

I accept.

Vol Karoth and Janel both vanished.

51: UNANIMOUS CONSENT

S'arric's memories

He walked down a long, broad hallway tiled with weathered, cracked marble, the dim light bouncing off dust and ash in the air. Everything was gray and washed out, all the color pulled from it. Students hurried on their way to classes, pausing only to give S'arric dirty looks, glares.

It was the uniform. It was out of place there. Truthfully, it was out of place everywhere. People all over were debating if the military was even necessary anymore. After all, they'd found their happy ending, their promised land. Everyone was settling in just fine; it'd been years since they'd needed anything resembling a military. If there were a few problems—what was happening with the children, for example, or rumors of sea monsters bothering the voramer— everyone knew they'd figure it out eventually. The kids who roamed the halls were . . . not kids. There were no children. Not anywhere.

That was kind of the problem, wasn't it?

But hey, they'd survived the death of an entire universe. What *couldn't* they do?

Have children, apparently. Or die.

He ignored the resentful looks and continued until he reached the last doorway down the hall, shoving the double doors open.

"Hey, Revas, you about done?" he called down.

The large, wide room was unsettling, disconnected, as if someone had taken two different classrooms and taped them together with ragged seams. It was empty. Almost empty. His brother was down there. S'arric was always amazed at how little Rev'arric looked like him for someone who looked so much like him.[1] Attitude was everything.

He looked up from his papers. "Solan? What are you doing here?"

S'arric sighed as he walked down the steps, taking them two at a time. "Right. Smartest man in two universes and you'd still forget to eat if someone didn't remind you. I'm taking you to that new restaurant." He pointed. "You asked me to rescue you, remember?"

Rev'arric blinked at him as though he didn't quite understand the language S'arric was speaking. "I'm in the middle of something."

"If it's grading papers, I'm not just rescuing you, I'm saving your life."

---

[1] It never occurred to me that the two brothers might resemble each other, but based on Grizzst's account in your last chronicle, it does seem like Relos Var has consciously chosen to take on a less "remarkable" appearance for the sake of anonymity.

He was about to say something when they both heard a voice from the top of the stairs. "Professor? Do you have a moment?"

And then . . . nothing. A gap in the universe. Someone walked into the room. They didn't have a face. They didn't have . . . anything.

S'arric walked through the door and sank down in a chair, letting his arms fall at his sides as the temptation to succumb to exhaustion nearly took control. He resisted, but it was by the finest of margins.

He felt a hand on his shoulder and smiled, clasping it. "I didn't think you'd make it," he said, returning to smile at . . .

The person standing there didn't have a face.

There was a gap, a blank spot. Nothing.

S'arric ran into the headquarters. The city was on fire, and nobody'd come close to stopping it. It was like an entire city had become haunted, all at the same time, spirits materializing out of nowhere and wreaking havoc again before vanishing as if they'd never been. And the dead bodies . . . the dead bodies should have been impossible, but the proof couldn't be denied.

After how many thousands of years, finally they'd met an enemy that could kill them. And was. By the *thousands* . . . Up ahead, he saw . . . nothing. There's a spot clipped out of the universe. He didn't remember what happened next.

Janel's story
Inside Vol Korath's prison

Do you understand?

The voice lodged in Janel's mind, an angry, furious roar.

Every blank spot is you.

"No, I–"

You didn't just steal my memories of you. You stole flowers and sunshine. You took my memories of my parents, my lovers, and any good days I ever had with my brother. You took all the things that were bright and beautiful.

You stole hope.

Janel gasped, unable to keep it inside anymore. "I didn't know," she whispered.

Is it better because you thought you were saving me? Because you thought that you could just excise pain and trauma like a gangrenous wound? I don't remember the day we met, but I remember the day you died. I don't remember the birth of our child, but I remember her screams as she turned into a monster.

I don't remember love, but you left me all the hate.

"S'arric, please . . . please . . ." Janel didn't know what to say. The guilt was nearly overwhelming, because what had he said that was a lie? "I never meant to hurt you. I didn't realize what it would do. Please forgive me."

Never meant to hurt me? Forgiveness? His voice sounded incredulous. *Why would you need forgiveness? Why wouldn't you want to hurt me? I deserve your hate!*

Janel lifted her head. "What?"

Are you forgetting I murdered you? How can you forget that I killed you! It's one of the only memories of you I have left!

She didn't understand what he meant for a second. When had he . . . But then she remembered the explosion. The explosion that had wiped Karolaen from the map, sent the whole globe into an early and prolonged winter, and, of course, sent C'indrol on from their first life to a succession of much shorter mortal ones.

Janel closed her eyes. "That was an accident," she whispered. "I don't blame you."

She felt a whisper of a touch against her cheek, and a voice she very much recognized said, *I do.*

She opened her eyes and really looked at the creature who so terrified her.

Vol Karoth didn't have a face. He didn't have a face or a body, here, in this place, where he could look like anything he wanted. He could have looked like Kihrin if he wanted. He could have looked like S'arric, if he wanted. The only limit was his imagination.

But he was like Jarith, so tortured by pain and despair that he'd forgotten himself. *Vol Karoth didn't remember what S'arric looked like.* He had nothing left of himself.

Except . . .

Except he had remorse. He had grief. He had jealousy and sorrow. And not all those qualities were bad. They were emotions that hadn't been there when Elana Milligreest had finished with him all those years ago. This, like the intelligence, was new.

And Janel finally understood why.

"I'm so sorry," she whispered. "We didn't understand."

Thurvishar's story
Inside Vol Korath's prison

Thurvishar kept pressing and pressing, the whole time, knowing it was futile but trying with all his might to break through Vol Karoth's defenses. If he could just get a message through.

And then he did.

There was no warning and no explanation for why Vol Karoth's blocks were suddenly gone. They just were. Thurvishar didn't hesitate. He grabbed at every mind he found.

[We have a chance to destroy Vol Karoth permanently,] he said to them. *[But it's not without cost.]*

"Vol Karoth told us," Kihrin said. "Was he telling the truth? Senera figured out a glyph that would hurl the entire Lighthouse into the Nythrawl Wound?"

[Yes. He was telling the truth.]

"Okay, then here's what we're going to do," Kihrin said. "Thurvishar, you start getting people back into their bodies and get out of the Lighthouse. Me and one other person—"

"Kihrin, no," Teraeth said.

"There's no reason we all have to die, Teraeth!"

Teraeth took a larger-than-normal breath. He forced a smile on his face. "Idiot," he told me, "if we start vanishing from this place, Vol Karoth will feel it, and I guarantee you that will snap him out of whatever lovely moment he is currently having with our girlfriend. If defeating him means staying here and dying, that's what I'm going to do. We are in this together. I didn't agree to be reincarnated just so I could watch you leap off a cliff without me."

Kihrin made a small, choked noise.

"I'm staying too," Qown said.

Kihrin stared at him. "You . . . you're not the person who I expected to say that."

Qown shrugged and looked embarrassed. "I don't see why not. Clearly, I'm willing to do things I find uncomfortable if it means saving the world." He turned to Galen and Sheloran. "You two should get out while you can, though."

"Oh, hell no," Galen said. "Have you met me? I'm a D'Mon."

"We're staying," Sheloran said.

"I am too," Lyrilyn said quietly. She gave Kihrin a sad smile. "It's the least I can do. Do we know how Senera, Talea, and Xivan feel, though?"

[They were there when we came up with the plan. Fine. I'm going to need time to finish this, so please keep him distracted. He's free in the tower at this point, so the only reason he won't be able to stop me is because he isn't trying.]

Kihrin sighed. "Yeah, I can do that."

Thurvishar immediately knew what Kihrin was about to do. He could have tried to stop him, but they needed the time.

And if it all worked out, it wouldn't matter, anyway.

Kihrin said, "Hey, Vol Karoth. You win. Let's talk."

52: Claiming Victory

Kihrin's story
Inside Vol Korath's prison
After Vol Korath took Janel

Vol Karoth wasted no time, reappearing in the middle of the room. He was holding on to Janel's arm. The impossibility of that lodged in my stomach for a moment like a molten slug of iron. She still had an arm. He was touching her. That didn't seem possible.

I didn't like it.

Teraeth stood and started to cross to her, only stopping because, well, Vol Karoth was standing right there. We let the silence wrap around us with no real idea what to say.

I made a deal. Unlike you, I keep my bargains. Vol Karoth waved his other arm in the air.

Senera, Xivan, and Talea appeared in the room.

"What the hell!" Xivan drew her sword, but she paused when she saw Janel.

It did look a bit like a hostage situation. I supposed it was.

I swallowed. "We did make a deal. I'll stay with you. You let them go. You let everyone go. You win. I'm here to stay, yours to do with whatever you want."

"Kihrin . . ." Janel's face was twisted with a mix of sadness and despair. "Kihrin, listen to me. This isn't what you think it is."

Vol Karoth shoved Janel away, then looked around the room, assessing each person. He paused for longer on Teraeth than the others. Teraeth confused him. I wasn't sure why.

"Kihrin, you can't go with him," Teraeth said.

"I have to," I said. "I'm so sorry. Please believe I love you. I wouldn't be doing this if I thought there was any other way."

"You asshole."

"Guilty."

Janel exhaled, ragged and shaken. "Kihrin, do you trust me?"

Come here. Vol Karoth gestured toward me.

"Always . . . ," I told her, but I knew I sounded uncertain. Maybe that was just the fear. There was certainly a lot of fear. I didn't want to do this. My only consolation was that, well, this would at least end it.

For everyone here after Thurvishar finished the glyph array, but still. I mourned that I wasn't going to be clever enough to give Janel and Teraeth that happy ending they deserved.

It would have been nice.

"It's a bit like ripping off a bandage, all at once," Janel told me. "We've been trying to do it slowly, but maybe that's not the right way."

My thoughts stuttered and tripped, confused. "What are you talking about?"

"Agreed. What *are* you talking about?" Teraeth asked.

On the other side of the room, what little color had ever existed in Senera's face drained right out of it. "Oh gods," she said.

Janel gave her a fond smile. "You see it, don't you? But everything will be fine."

For some reason, I had my doubts.

Come here now, Vol Karoth bellowed.

"I'm not doing another loop," Janel said. "It ends here."

I honestly had no idea what she was talking about. "Okay, just . . . give me a minute." I started walking toward Vol Karoth. How long did it take to finish a sigil, anyway? And would we even know if it worked and we ended up in another universe? I wanted to think that Vol Karoth would have said something. As a professional courtesy, if nothing else.

I had almost reached him when I felt a sharp pain. Someone shouted.

No!

I looked down at myself. There was a sword sticking through my chest.

Janel had shoved her sword through my back.

Everything went black.

Janel's story

Everyone was yelling, which Janel thought was perfectly understandable. Teraeth was staring at Janel like . . . well . . . like she'd just done what she'd done. Probably everyone was, but she didn't check. She didn't bother pulling the sword out. The sword didn't truly exist, anyway. It was just a metaphor. She let it and the body it pierced drop to the ground.

"I'm sorry," she mouthed to Teraeth. Janel wished she'd had time to explain. But would Teraeth have believed her? Probably not. Some things were hard to accept, and "I have to kill the man we love, but really it's for his own good" definitely qualified.

Then a roar filled the whole world. Vol Karoth, enraged. Vol Karoth, ready to kill them all, starting with Janel, who had given him one last unforgivable betrayal.

At least, that's the way he saw it.

Vol Karoth's voice was the rasp of despair honed against rage. *Don't you understand? If you would have just given him back to me, I could have been whole again! I could have incorporated him and been healed!*

"No, my love," Janel said as tears spilled down her cheeks. "You're the one who refuses to understand. You did that a week ago."

Everything stilled. Everything became so quiet. So empty.

"What," Teraeth whispered.

"He did it days ago," Janel repeated. "Kihrin returned to Kharas Gulgoth. Talon killed him, his souls walked into Vol Karoth's prison, and Vol Karoth and Kihrin *merged*. It's done. It's been done this whole time."

No. That's not—

"But you couldn't accept that you were healed," Janel told him. "It was too much. The memories were too painful. It was all too new. How long has it been for you? Millennia have passed in seconds while you've been frozen in time. You've had no time to heal. So you shoved it all away. You remade Kihrin. And you've been fighting yourself ever since."

Vol Karoth didn't say anything that time. He stood perfectly motionless, absolutely silent, just a perfect black silhouette.

But at Janel's feet, Kihrin's body vanished as if it had never been.

Teraeth made a sound that squeezed tight around Janel's heart.

Janel began crying in earnest then, tears spilling down her cheeks in a steady stream. Her eyes stung, so she closed them. She couldn't stand to look anymore, anyway. "You've been Kihrin this whole time. That's why Vol Karoth suddenly became smart again. That's why Kihrin's moods affected this place. Why you could never quite kill him. Why we could weaken you by supporting Kihrin. Because it was always *you*."

I don't–

"I won't leave you. I promised you that. Just let the others go. Gods, let Teraeth go. But I love you. I'll stay."

But– There was a note of hesitation, a confused stumble. And something–a register in the dark god's voice–changed.

"I'm not going anywhere." Teraeth walked over and put his arm around Janel. "I'm staying too."

No. You should . . . you should go.

"Gods damn it, Monkey," Teraeth said, "I fell in love with S'arric first. Why the fuck would I leave you now?"

"Wait," Galen said. "You're saying this is Kihrin? He's Kihrin right now?"

"Yes," Janel said. "That's exactly what I'm saying."

"Well, I guess I'm not leaving either, then," Galen said. "Red, you good here? I'm good here. I'm not leaving my brother."

Vol Karoth turned to Galen. Janel could feel him staring. She held her breath. Brothers were always going to be a bit of a sore spot for S'arric. For Kihrin too. So this . . .

"Guess you can't get rid of us that easily," Senera said. She had a complicated, stubborn look on her face. "We're in this together."

Slowly, one by one, everyone in the room made a similar comment.

Vol Karoth folded in on himself, collapsing down to the ground, all but fetal except for the fact that his feet were still on the floor.

Teraeth shook his head, seemed to steel himself, and then put his arm around the god. Which should have disintegrated him.

It didn't.

A wave spread out around them, widening out in a massive push of energy and color. Janel didn't doubt that all around the city, trees were sprouting and flowers were blooming and probably a whole lot more of this place looked like the Capital City than had been true just a few minutes earlier. This time, there would be no giant fireball to scour the earth clean.

Vol Karoth stopped being a silhouette–

–and stopped being Vol Karoth.

53: The Last Possible Moment

Thurvishar's story
The Lighthouse at Shadrag Gor
After everyone else had gone

Thurvishar moved to dip the brush into the paint for the last time. He hesitated. Who wouldn't hesitate? He'd never planned for this to be his end. He had wanted . . . different things. But if this was how it was meant to be, so be it.

Vol Karoth was all but free. Thurvishar could almost see the dark god move, and he knew his hourglass was down to its last grains of sand. He studied the drawing and moved to make one more mark . . .

Vol Karoth vanished.

For a split second, all Thurvishar could do was stare, and then he hurried to complete the sigil. It could be a trick. It might even be a clever trick, one Vol Karoth might exploit to escape.

Then a slender, delicate hand grabbed his wrist holding the paintbrush.

Senera said, "Let's not get carried away. It's not the end of the world."

She was smiling. Senera was *smiling at him.*

Thurvishar knew this wasn't a trick. Because Vol Karoth could fake a lot of things, but he couldn't fake joy. And the light shining from those beautiful eyes couldn't be anything else.

"Did we win?" Thurvishar asked.

She chuckled. From farther inside the Lighthouse, people laughed and moved about as they woke from enchanted sleeps.

"Yeah, funny thing, that," Senera said. "Turns out, it wasn't a contest."

Kihrin's story

In the memory of Karolaen, flowers bloomed.

The streets echoed with the sounds of a lifetime of past experiences—good, bad, and somewhere in between. Sometimes the sights were fuzzy at the edges, worn smooth by the polish cloth of time, but the colors still shone bright.

Everyone was gone. Except for three people.

Teraeth and Janel stood at the entrance to the park, and I waited until they saw me. Teraeth had an expression of disbelief on his face. At least until I grinned at him. The relief on his face reminded me of someone waking from a nightmare. Which, fine. Probably an obvious metaphor. Galen's the poet, not me.

"Kihrin," he said as he approached. Just that one word, but so much emotion had been packed into it.

I'd chosen to look like Kihrin, you see.

Why shouldn't I? Kihrin had a lot more friends and loved ones than S'arric did by this point, that was for sure. And just like Janel was and yet most definitely was *not* C'indrol, I was making my choice too. I would always be S'arric, which wasn't the worst thing in the universe. I would also always own S'arric's rage, his pain, and his grief, which kind of was.

And while that wasn't good, it didn't have to be evil. But old me, old just-turned-into-a-dark-god me, had lost everything, or anyway, it had felt like I had. I'd been tossed by the winds, blown away, and I hadn't known how to right myself.

Which was a problem when you had the power to destroy the universe.

Teraeth reached me and put his hand on the side of my face. "Monkey, why are we still here?"

I kissed him first. I had a lot I wanted to say, but one had to have priorities. "I wanted to say goodbye," I said when we parted.

"Kihrin—" Janel's voice was stricken, broken. Anguished.

"Oh no, no." I ran my hand down the side of her head. "Not that kind of goodbye. But I kind of have to pretend to be an insane god of darkness for a while. And that means we can't touch. Honestly, it, uh . . . still may not even be *safe* for us to touch. I'll have to experiment. We can't give Rev'ar—" I wrinkled my nose. "Relos Var. We can't give Relos Var any reason to think that I'm not the dumb Vol Karoth he's come to know and love. The one he thinks he can control."

"Can't he, though?" Janel asked. "If you're . . . you again. Are you sure he won't be able to control you?"

"I'm more Kihrin than S'arric, if I'm being honest," I said. "Both, absolutely, but . . . no, I don't think Urthaenriel's going to be able to control me. And as long as Kihrin's right there in front of him, he won't try to fix that."

"As long as Kihrin—" Janel narrowed her eyes. "You mean Talon."

"I need her to return to impersonating me for a while. And then afterward, she'll go back to the vané and ask them to do a tsali transfer on her. I think Lyrilyn's ready to stop hiding behind all those other lifetimes."

Janel stood there looking like she'd just eaten a lemon. "I'm not sleeping with that thing."

"Good," I agreed. "I'm perfectly comfortable with that."

"Oh, I don't know," Teraeth said, the quirk of his lips suggesting he was teasing. Probably. "I could probably talk myself into it. Have you seen your ass?"

I laughed. "Don't ever change, Teraeth."

But it was time to return to the serious talks about serious matters. I picked up their hands. "I'm going to try my damnedest to find a solution to all of this. One that includes being around to enjoy it with the two of you afterward."

"Really?" Teraeth said. "Because you just said you weren't sure we could physically touch. That doesn't make a relationship impossible, but it certainly complicates things."

"Yes, well, Tya and Taja's trick with handing off guardian duties to a new generation has some interesting implications. Thurvishar had some ideas before all this started too. And honestly, Talon had a great suggestion involving the Well of Spirals. We'll figure something out." I squeezed Janel's hand. "Seven months, right?"

"Let's not wait that long," she said. "I don't want to have to be out there defeating the forces of evil while eight months pregnant." She paused. "But don't think I won't do it."

"Don't worry. I doubt Relos Var or Xaltorath will want to wait that long either." I leaned over and kissed her too. Then I pulled Teraeth close. I whispered, "Thank you. Both of you."

I sent them back.

After they were gone, I pulled the third person to me. No, I hadn't been counting myself. It was my mind, after all. I didn't think that fair.

I pulled him together into a shape and knelt next to the man who was still understandably shocked and upset. But I could work with that.

"Okay, Jarith," I told him. "Let see what we can do about patching you up."

54: BACK TO THE BEGINNING

Talea's story
The Lighthouse at Shadrag Gor

"Hey, welcome back." Talea smirked at Janel and Teraeth as they joined the others. She didn't think they'd had time to get up to anything sexy in the mindscape, but they were the last to wake by a significant degree.

Janel squeezed Teraeth's hand as she smiled at Talea. "We're ready."

"I hope everyone realizes," Senera said, "that the moment we're back, we're going to be staring down Drehemia and her lovely tentacled girlfriend."

"You're not going to gate us right back to where we left, are you?" Qown asked with indignation. "That would be a terrible idea. She was about to unleash her madness breath. Why would we—" He narrowed his eyes as he noticed everyone else shaking their heads and/or snickering. He scowled at the smile on Senera's face. "Oh. You're teasing."

"I'm teasing," Senera said. The smile melted then. "But we should talk about what, if anything, we are going to do about them." She paused and looked at each of them meaningfully. "We could just leave it to the imperial military."

Janel scoffed. "Last I checked, the imperial military was getting trampled like a gopher hole in a stampede."

"My son's there." Kalindra's voice was soft but scratchy. Her eyes looked haunted, shaken still by her experiences in Vol Karoth's dreamland.

Talea cleared her throat. "I wonder if it might be worth it to spend another day here in the Lighthouse before heading out? We could use the time to recover." She gestured at Xivan and added, "And also grow accustomed to uh . . . new skills?"

"Speaking of . . ." Teraeth stared directly at Xivan. "We're going to need to have a conversation when all this is over."

"Might be a good idea." Janel ignored Teraeth's comment in favor of replying to Talea. "If we take the day, we can sit down, figure out a strategy for dealing with not one but two city-smashing monsters."

"Can't Kihrin just send Drehemia home?" Qown protested. "I mean, doesn't he uh . . . he . . ."

"No," Teraeth said.

"No, he doesn't control the dragons?" Senera's tone was skeptical.

"No, he's not going to send her home," Teraeth corrected. "Because Vol Karoth *wouldn't do that*. He can't jeopardize that by having Vol Karoth suddenly break pattern and start helping people."

Qown made a face and nodded. Talea wanted to pat the man on the shoulder. This wouldn't be easy for any of them.

"Can't we just give the Lash what she wants?" Sheloran said.

In the brief silence that followed that remarkable query, everyone turned to look at her.

"Unfortunately," Thurvishar said slowly, sounding out the rebuttal even as he spoke it, "what the Lash wants is her girlfriend's insanity cured–"

"Wait," Sheloran said, "isn't that because of Vol Karoth? But with what's happened here, won't that stop?"

"First of all," said Talon, who had changed back into looking like Kihrin, "Teraeth already explained this: nothing will change. Nothing *can* change. Relos Var can't know what Kihrin has done, or this was all for nothing. So no, Drehemia will not be miraculously cured or sent elsewhere or talked down by Vol Karoth. And on that note, we need to not talk about what happened here outside of these walls, ever. To anyone. Period. Got it?"

Qown shifted his feet nervously, cleared his throat. "Um . . ."

Janel nodded to Talon, then looked at the Vishai priest. "Yes?"

Qown twisted his hands, blushed, and looked at his feet. "I feel like people should be asking me questions about my loyalties, and it's making me uncomfortable that no one is."

Galen pried Qown's hands apart, took one in his own. "That's because we don't have to."

"Well, *I* know that," Qown said, "but everyone else–"

"You're not going back to him." Teraeth softened his voice to make that sound like less of a threat than might normally be expected of him. "You were loyal to Relos Var because you thought he was the best option to save the greatest number of people. Now you know that's not the case." He shrugged as if that made the conclusion a foregone one.

Sheloran flanked the priest, putting her arm around his shoulder and fanning them both. "That's the difference between Relos Var and us. *He* demanded that you be on his side."

Qown looked confused. "And you don't?"

"Why no," Sheloran said. "We're on yours."

The former priest stared at her in shock for a moment, tears threatening to well in his eyes. He nodded, swallowed thickly, and tucked his head against Galen's shoulder. It was adorably cute, Talea thought.

"By the Veils," Senera said, rubbing her temples as if nursing a headache.

"So what's the plan?" Kalindra asked. "What can we do? Under normal circumstances, the Lash is entirely bribable, but what could we offer her? And how would we get her to stop smashing us into us-shaped smears on the ground long enough to offer her a bribe even if we came up with one she'd accept?"

If she were being honest with herself, and Talea liked to think she was normally quite honest with herself, she was only half listening to the conversation. Instead, she was staring at Senera as possible scenarios and likely outcomes flitted through her mind. Most of them were awful, terrible ideas filled with horrific body counts or acts of moral cowardice that would haunt them all and sabotage everything they were trying to accomplish.

Talea kept coming back to one idea that might work. One series of events that might possibly see them through this with skins and self-respects equally intact. The problem was that the odds were terrible. Not of the plan succeeding; the odds of that were decent. But of the group even trying the plan, even volunteering to enact it—those odds were abysmal.

It would require a sacrifice, one Talea didn't think would be offered.

Senera looked up, met her stare. Talea glanced down at the woman's waist and then back into her eyes. She nodded solemnly.

Senera frowned for a moment, and then her eyes widened.

Teraeth, who hadn't noticed that little interplay, replied to Kalindra's question. "I'm not sure we could. Maybe a stealth mission? We might not be able to stop them from destroying the monastery, but maybe if they're too busy—"

"You're all forgetting that it's not just Drehemia and the Lash." Xivan interrupted whatever terrible idea Teraeth had been about to propose. "Suless is there also."

"Shit," Teraeth spat. "Yeah, that complicates—"

The man was not having a good day when it came to finishing sentences.

"We can cure Drehemia," Senera said. She glanced at Thurvishar, her face contorted in anguish.

Qown must have been thinking along the same lines. He figured it out before anyone else, and gasped.

Thurvishar frowned at Senera, and then his eyes also widened. "Of course," he said. "But . . . are you sure?"

"I don't see another choice." Senera's voice cracked. "Not one I can live with. Sheloran's right: let's just give the Lash what she wants."

Talea grinned. Sometimes the long shots came through.

Janel's story
The Monastery at Devors

Senera's gate deposited them in the middle of the main library.

The library itself wasn't entirely deserted. Normally, the building was warded against most physical catastrophes such as fires, but with the scorpion casks being tossed about with abandon, and dragons and lunatics and undead rampaging through the buildings, it was merely a matter of time before those protections failed. A handful of monks and librarians stood by to begin the task of rescuing as many precious books as they could when the inevitable happened.

Janel looked around the room. She could feel a scowl growing. She found the place . . . unfamiliar. Belatedly, she realized that for all that Elana Milligreest had founded this library, it had changed and expanded too many times between then and now. Of course she wouldn't know where anything was anymore.

"It's over there." Thurvishar pointed toward a row of glass-fronted cases.

Janel nodded her thanks and marched over. A special alcove of the room had been set aside for books and documents valued less for their contents than their historical significance. The particular case she approached bore a small brass plaque that read, *"The first book donated to the library,"* and a date. It was well over four hundred years old. If there was any single object could be said to symbolically represent the entire library, it was this one.

Janel shattered the glass with her elbow, then reached inside and lifted out the book.

"Hey!" one of the monks shouted. "You can't—"

Xivan drew her sword and pointed it at him. "It's one book," she said. "Consider how many more you'll save if you're still alive to do so."

The monk swallowed and retreated to the company of his peers.

Janel examined the book in her hands. Thanks to magic and meticulous care, it was in as good a condition as it was when she'd donated it centuries before. Elana Milligreest's travel journal, filled with a highly edited and nearly fictional account of her journey into the Korthaen Blight.

Despite it being entirely nonsense, Janel hesitated for a moment. Then she opened the book to a page about one-third of the way from the end.

"I can't watch," Thurvishar said, looking away.

Janel tore the book lengthwise down the spine.

Qown made a wounded, choking sound as Janel handed the smaller piece to Teraeth before opening the book again in at the half-way point and ripping it apart a second time. She tapped Thurvishar on the shoulder with one-third of the mangled book twice before he would look at her.

He took his third. She kept the last one for herself.

"Everyone knows what they need to do," Janel said. "The tunnels are downstairs. Off you go."

Xivan saluted with her sword, jerked her chin, and led the others away.

Thurvishar opened another gate. "This will take us outside the monastery," he said, gesturing for Janel and Teraeth to precede him through the glowing portal.

"Thank you," Janel said. "Once we're through, split up. When we get the signal—" Her eyes met Teraeth's as she let out a brief, dry chuckle. "I cannot believe that I am again going to be waiting for an all-clear signal from Senera. I am not a fool, am I? I do have the capacity to learn from my mistakes, do I not?"

Teraeth winked and leaned over to kiss her on the cheek. "Let's just see how this turns out before we start deciding who is or is not a fool." He stepped through the portal.

"Exactly what I feared you'd say," Janel told the empty air.

She squared her shoulders and followed him.

55: THE SECOND PARLEY

Xivan's story
The Monastery at Devors

The hallways split outside the library. Xivan took Sheloran and ~~Talon~~ Kihrin with her, while Senera left with Talea, Galen, and Qown. Kalindra headed off on her own, deeper into the fortress in search of her son and, potentially, her father-in-law.

"Be safe, Red," Galen said as the group split.

"Will do, Blue." Sheloran smirked at her own silly rhyme.

"House D'Jorax you ain't," Fake-Kihrin said, shaking his head.

"Shut up and pay attention," Xivan ordered. "We have company."

The first group they encountered consisted of three Quuros soldiers maddened by Drehemia's influence. The frenzied soldiers fought viciously, with little thought to their own safety. Xivan sliced one through the gap between his helmet and cuirass. Kihrin performed an elaborate double feint, neither of which his foe fell for, before saying, "Fuck it," and simply stabbed the man through the eye. Sheloran flicked her fan, and her opponent fell to the ground, choking and bleeding for the moment before the D'Talus woman recalled her metal slivers.

No sooner had the men died than they started to rise again, powered by proximity to the Lash and Grimward.

Xivan cocked her head. "Are you seeing this?" she asked the others, gesturing.

"Yes," Sheloran said. "They're rising. Which I should point out they've been doing since your former employer arrived. Now shall we hurry along before we're forced to reduce them into chunks too insignificant to animate?"

"No, I mean . . ." Xivan frowned. No one else seemed to be aware of the wispy black filaments that stretched from each of the newly animated dead. She couldn't see where the filaments led, because they passed through walls, but she'd have bet significant metal they connected the undead to Grimward.

"Hang on," she said. She approached one, sidestepped a clumsy blow, and swept her hand through the space the black tendril occupied.

It snapped. The corpse fell to the floor, dead once more.

"Huh," Xivan said.

And so it went, Xivan disrupting Grimward's hold on the dead, while the others handled the living ferals with deft swordplay or pinpoint metal control.

They emerged from the monastery and ran down to the docks. Much of the area that hadn't been destroyed by the Lash was now on fire. Bodies were piled everywhere, most of them unable to even stand before Xivan had laid them back to rest again. She found that the more she used the ability, the greater her range and capacity for multiple exterminations at a time.

"Hey, Lash!" Xivan yelled. For a moment, she worried if the entire plan was doomed to fail because of the simple, prosaic, and overlooked reality of just how loud it was while standing on a burning dock in the middle of a raging storm surrounded by screaming people while a massive kraken thrashed about. The war engines had ceased firing, but the din was equal to any battlefield Xivan had ever witnessed. So where was Boji during all this? I have no idea. Certainly he'd been with Xivan when she first arrived, but she lost track of him. It's possible that he's dead, but also possible he took advantage of the chaos to escape.

She needn't have worried; the Lash heard her. **"Xivan,"** the kraken's voice thundered, **"why have you returned?"**

Xivan wasn't sure if she should be flattered or worried that the Lash was able to recognize her personally. Given the size difference, it was akin to recognizing an individual bee in a swarm.

"I've come to propose a bargain!" Xivan shouted. "I know how to cure Drehemia."

The Lash stilled. One giant, milky eye turned toward Xivan. All the undead that they could see stopped also, but sadly, this had no effect on the men and women rendered lunatic by Drehemia.

"Go on..."

"Here's the deal: You stand down. Recall or destroy your dead. And we will cure the dragon."

"Of all the creatures for whom the phrase 'I wasn't born yesterday' might apply...," the Lash drew herself partially out of the water. **"You expect me to believe you'd honor such an arrangement? Tell me why I shouldn't simply destroy you where you stand?"**

"You can kill us." Xivan nodded, although in truth, she wasn't sure that was true of herself anymore. "But you should know my friends have cast a ritual sympathetically linked to the entire library complex. If you don't agree, if you don't withdraw, they'll finish the ritual they've already begun, which will destroy the entire library and every book in it.[1] You won't get what you want. Your entire reason for this attack will go up in smoke."

The Lash let out a sound that vibrated Xivan to her very bones. The noise was so loud and deep it took her a moment to identify it as a growl.

"I don't mean to cause distress," ~~Talon~~ Kihrin said, "but, um..."

"I see them," Xivan said.

"Them" were four enormous, spiked tentacles roughly the size of pine trees, lifting from the water and falling toward them fast.

"Should we–" Sheloran started to ask.

---

[1] So. Would this have worked? Having given the matter considerable thought, I can confidently say: maybe. (While the principle is sound, improvised rituals can go wrong for a vast number of unforeseeable reasons. As Relos Var can attest.)

"Wait," Xivan said. Her gaze never left the Lash's clouded eye, but she could feel Sheloran and Kihrin exchanging worried looks behind her.

The tentacles stopped mere feet above their heads. The Lash had reconsidered.

Xivan looked at the monster, calm in spite of the spiked death dripping cold seawater onto their heads. "You're running out of time," she told the kraken. "If you agree to our terms, we will cure your dragon, but we'll need your help. Drehemia's treatment won't be instant. Someone—that is to say you—will need to keep Drehemia still long enough for us to do what needs to be done."

"And what, exactly, needs to be done?" asked the Lash, although her voice seemed a fraction less enraged than it had been moments before. Xivan knew they had her. **"How will you cure her?"**

Xivan smiled grimly. She glanced away, toward the top of the cliff where a flash of Drehemia's wing, or perhaps tail, moved. Screams, shouts, colored lights all came from atop the plateau. She turned her attention back to the Lash.

"We'll cure her the only way you can cure a dragon's madness," she said. "We'll reunite her with her Cornerstone."

Qown's story
Under the ocean near Da'utunse

"Beautiful," Senera said as she swished her hand back and forth through the water. Her voice sounded slightly muffled, but then Qown imagined that they all sounded like that.

Senera and Thurvishar had spelled them up with every bit of magic they could think of to protect them at the bottom of the ocean; from the old standby of Senera's air-bubble glyphs to the glyph that prevented the incredible pressure of being so far underwater from crushing them the moment they stepped from the gate into Drehemia's underwater lair. They even had their own light sources; each of them clutched a softly glowing coin in their hands. It was the play of this light on the water that had briefly entranced Senera.

"Are we sure this will work?" Qown asked.

"If it doesn't, at least we'll be incredibly rich for however long we have left before the world ends," Galen said. "I'm looting this entire place. It'll be a good learning experience for the old girl."

"This will work," Talea said absently as she looked around the cave. "Ninety-eight percent chance."

"Yeah, that's getting old really fast." Senera shook her head with a scoff. "What our dear friend Taj-alea is trying to say is that dragons love their hoards. There's effectively no chance at all that Drehemia won't realize that you're messing around with hers the moment you touch something, and she will come flying back here. Well, swimming. You get the idea."

"We'll start with those," Talea said, pointing to a line of caskets near the back wall.

"Oh, yes," Senera said. "I imagine Drehemia will be very upset if you mess with her favorite toys. Good luck with that. In the meantime, I have an appointment to keep." She cast the intricate knot of tenyé necessary to open a gate, but paused before stepping through. "I'll pick you up when I'm done. And, Galen?"

"Yes?"

"Legends say that a dragon can sense their hoard, even the smallest piece of it, anywhere in the world. And while it may just be a story, it also may not be. I can think of at least two different ways such a feat might be accomplished. So resist that temptation, would you?" She stepped through without waiting for a reply.

56: The Demon Witch

Sheloran's story
Atamer Harbor, Devors, Quur

While Xivan negotiated with the Lash, Sheloran and Talon Kihrin didn't stand idle. Yes, the undead ceased assaulting them once Xivan piqued the kraken's interest, but the crazed continued to attack them, soldier and civilian alike. Still, Sheloran kept half an eye on the parley session.

So far, as they said, so good.

She noticed a soldier, injured but not dead, struggling weakly. His legs were pinned beneath a heavy plank from the dock, and the very thing that trapped him seemed to have saved him from the dragon's madness breath.

"Kihrin, you can handle this, yes?" Sheloran remembered to use the correct name. "I'll be right back."

"Wait, what?" Talon scowled. "Hey, come back . . . damn it!"

Sheloran didn't answer. She dodged a feral who attacked her with a piece of burning lumber, holding it by the side that was engulfed in flames. She threw a metal spike into the former monk; it was a mercy killing. Half of the poor woman's body was on fire.

"Here, don't move. Let me help you," she told the soldier. She looked about for something to use as a lever.

Drehemia screamed and launched herself from the cliff, taking to the sky. Sheloran looked up.

The moment she did, the soldier grabbed her ankle and yanked, hard. She fell over backward onto the remains of the dock, her head slamming against the hard wood. She looked up, vision temporarily swimming. Something was very wrong. Maybe the soldier hadn't avoided Drehemia's breath, after all.

Except . . . except when the soldier she'd been trying to help stood over her now, he leered at her in a way that sent shivers down her spine. Or perhaps she was just in shock from the blow to her head. She tried to respond with spell and steel, but before she could, the soldier's eyes flashed blue.

Not as in they turned blue in a flashing sort of way like Galen's when he was being mischievous. No, this was a flash of blue from the man's eyes changing color entirely, if just for a moment.

Sheloran couldn't move.

"Hello, sweetie," the man said in a strangely feminine voice. "What, no kisses for your long-lost grandmother?"

Suless had revealed herself at last.

Janel's story

"The dead are pulling back," Thurvishar said as he emerged from a portal next to Janel. "Looks like the Lash accepted our deal."

"Oh, thank goodness," Janel said, fingering the tattered edge of her third of the journal. "I really wasn't looking forward to destroying this . . . or that." She gestured with her chin toward the distant monastery.

Footsteps fast approaching heralded the imminent arrival of Teraeth. "Are we good?" he called out, still some yards away.

Drehemia launched herself off the cliff and soared out over the harbor.

"We're good," Janel said.

"We're not good yet," Thurvishar corrected with a frown, although he didn't bother to explain his cryptic remark. Rather, he stepped forward, one hand on the green gemstone he wore around his neck: Wildheart. He concentrated.

Lines of kelp, like giant yellow-green ropes, flung themselves out of the sea and wrapped around Drehemia's right wing. She veered and spiraled down in that direction.

The Lash erupted from the ocean, leaping so high they saw her even from this distance. Tentacles wrapped around the dragon in a tight embrace, and both fell back into the ocean with a mighty, thunderous crash.

"Now we're good," Thurvishar said. "Let's hurry down there. We have a ritual to perform." He opened a gate.

Senera's story
Atamer Harbor, Devors, Quur

Drehemia struggled, naturally. Had the Lash been alive, the contest between them would have inflicted horrible injuries on the kraken, for while she wrestled to contain her lover without hurting her, the dragon felt no such restrictions.

Muscles and sinews tore, were reknit instantly by the magics that kept the Lash in her state of perpetual nonlife. Drehemia ripped free of the kelp muzzle Thurvishar had formed and bit the Lash, nearly ripping one of the Kraken's larger tentacles clean off.

Thurvishar stood on the remains of the dock, using sorcery on the cliff nearby to extrude sheets and columns of stone in an attempt to imprison the furious dragon.

Senera took all this in as she emerged from the portal, dripping wet except for her head.[1] "Where the hell is Sheloran?" Senera screamed to be heard over the roaring of surf and dragon alike. "Keeping the dragon from breathing on us was her job!"

Thurvishar was too busy to reply. Kihrin said something to Xivan and pointed, and the two of them ran off in that direction.

Senera could only hope they were going to hunt down the missing princess. She didn't have time to do it herself. She drew the Name of All Things from

---

[1] Because the air glyph kept that dry.

her misha and began preparing the ritual that would destroy the Cornerstone forever.

She blamed the salt water stinging her eyes on the crashing waves and not her own feelings on the impending loss.

Sheloran's story
Atamer Harbor, Devors, Quur

Sheloran fought uselessly as Suless dragged her under the boardwalk, through calf-deep water, and onto a small jetty some distance from the docks. The spell paralyzing her refused to relax its grip even when a particularly large wave buffeted them both.

"I'm so pleased we're able to spend some quality time together like this," Suless said as she dragged Sheloran over mollusk-encrusted rocks. The body still looked like the soldier, so Sheloran couldn't be completely certain it was Suless, but the "grandmother" comment was a giveaway. Suless decided they were far enough inland and dropped Sheloran, who hit her head again.

That was going to leave a mark. Assuming she survived.

"You seem like such a sweet girl." Suless didn't make it sound like a compliment, forcing the words out through a sneer. "So. Where shall we begin, hmm? Because I was thinking, the toes." The soldier's face twisted in a sickening grin. "Little familial advice for you, my dear: always start with the toes. If you start with the fingers, your prey will realize that they can't work, or play a musical instrument, or cast spells, or whatever it is that they feel gives their pathetic little life meaning. They may decide they have nothing left to live for and just die on you. But the toes"—she licked her lips and made a slurping noise—"a person can live a perfectly respectable life without their toes." She tapped the side of her nose with a finger. "The trick is to give them hope, you see, no matter how false. If they have hope, they'll—"

A soft click came from behind Suless—the sound of one rock gently touching another. The din of waves crashing against the jetty nearly drowned out the soft sound, but Suless heard. She spun, too late.

A much louder noise, that of metal cutting flesh and bone, heralded both the arrival of a razor-sharp sword and the departure of the soldier's head. It bounced and came to rest beside Sheloran with a sickening, wet thump.

"I have a few ideas where to start," Xivan said, shaking the blood off her blade.

Sheloran found herself able to move just in time to roll away from the soldier's falling body. She scrambled to her feet, swayed for a moment, and put her hand to the back of her head. She was bleeding. She made a mental note to have Qown fix that.

When Qown returned.

"Did you . . . Is she . . . ?" Sheloran couldn't quite manage full sentences.

"Is Suless dead?" Xivan asked. "Sadly, no. Not even slightly. She escaped into the Afterlife. That was the whole reason she became a demon in the first place." Xivan clapped Sheloran on the shoulder, then pointed back toward the fray raging a few hundred yards away. It was then that Sheloran noticed Kihrin standing several paces behind Xivan.

"Go help our friends, would you? That dragon's a handful," the Duchess of Yor said. "I need to finish something. Shouldn't take but a few minutes."

"But what—?" Sheloran didn't have a chance to finish. Xivan vanished.

"Come on," Kihrin said, approaching and putting an arm around her shoulders to support Sheloran. She was still a little wobbly on her feet. "He'll never admit it, but Thurvy needs your help."

They'd gone ten steps before Sheloran said, "Thurvy?"[2]

---

[2] I don't care what anyone says. Talon will always be the real demon here.

57: Promises and Freedom

Galen's story
The Lair of the Shadow Dragon Drehemia

Galen kept an eye on Qown as the man created lights at various spots around the cave. He'd told Qown they'd return, and he'd been able to keep his promise.

Talea watched as well, but her expression was unreadable. Galen wondered if she realized that she was slowly becoming . . . inscrutable.

"I thought we'd start from that side and work our way over." Qown gestured toward one end of the row of caskets. "They're magical, but I don't think they're trapped."

"Don't think?" Galen asked.

Qown shrugged. "Not really something I know a lot about, traps. They . . . might be?"

"Only one way to find out," Talea said. She put her foot on the lid of a casket and shoved.

Galen stepped back. Inside the coffin lay a thin woman covered in snake scales with multiple serpents instead of hair. She was dressed in a tattered, ancient green dress.

She opened her eyes and began screaming.

Galen didn't think she saw them. From the angle, she was staring at the ceiling. And unlike them, whatever kept her alive didn't involve a bubble of air surrounding her head, so her screams released a steady stream of the more mundane variety, which ascended quickly.

He drew breath to say something, but all the other caskets chose that moment to open and disgorge their contents. No two races were the same, and many Galen had believed existed only in legends. Here was a creature with a goat's legs and the upper body of a crab. There, a woman who would have been attractive if not for the three extra pairs of eyes and the arms replaced with long, stiff-haired legs like those of a wolf spider. A particularly large, oddly shaped coffin let loose what he suspected was an actual centaur.

All of the creatures were alike in three specific ways, however. First, all of them emerged from their caskets screaming.

Second, they all turned to face his little group.

Third, they all attacked.

Sheloran's story

Killing a dragon—even temporarily—was a monumental labor. The stuff of legends (the few that didn't claim it was flat-out impossible). It was so difficult, in fact, that the phrase "kill a dragon" meant to attempt the impossible.

And yet, there were people present who witnessed the deaths of as many as three dragons.

Capturing a dragon was much trickier.

Anyone who possessed so much as a witchgift had their hands full, and the rest were just as busy holding off the maddened and crazed and the just plain idiotic who sought to stop the sorcerers. If Kihrin was seen to throw a little more magic than it was popularly believed that Kihrin knew? Well, that was easily explained as him having learned more at Tyentso's knee than people had suspected.

The Lash did her best to keep Drehemia trapped, both with her own body and with the dead whom, individually insignificant, could simply weigh down the dragon by overwhelming numbers.

Sheloran did what she could, but the blows to her head made it hard to concentrate.

Time and again, Drehemia freed an arm or a wing, and time and again, she was re-imprisoned. Time, however, wasn't on their side, for while the dragon seemed to possess an infinite supply of rage-fueled strength, the mortals were beginning to tire.

Senera's story
Atamer Harbor, Devors, Quur

"Ready?" Thurvishar asked Senera when they completed the last of the preparations.

"No," Senera said and then sighed. "But I volunteered."

Her gut churned.

Relos Var would kill her for this. Actually kill her. She had no doubt whatsoever. It was possible he could forgive the betrayals she had committed so far, but if they did this, now, any hope of reconciliation with him was obliterated for all eternity.

"I'm proud of you," Thurvishar said.

"Oh, fuck off," she snapped. "Let's do this."

She began opening the ritual array when a light flashed overhead, centering on Drehemia. A second later, a scorpion cask slammed into the dragon and exploded in a burst of brilliant white light. Two more followed it, scorching dragon, undead, metal chains, and kraken with equal abandon.

Senera picked herself up off the ground, cursing.

The Quuros army had arrived to "help."

Galen's story

Galen swore as he yanked Qown away from the sword thrust of a cat-headed man. The only advantage Galen and his friends had was that the water slowed movements of friend and foe alike.

Two advantages, he corrected himself after a second. None of the game pieces seemed to be spellcasters. That was nice.

They were still outnumbered a dozen to one, and if their attackers managed to surround them, the relatively low velocity of the thrusts wouldn't matter in the slightest.

If they were surrounded . . .

Galen stared at the cat-man, who even now stepped forward for another strike while the lady with the snakes for hair shuffled to his left.

Stepped. Shuffled.

The "pieces" behaved as if they were on land. That made a degree of sense; one wouldn't want their Zaibur pieces swimming off the board, would they?

"Swim above them!" Galen yelled. He pushed Qown upward and then launched himself up as well. The cat-man's blade passed beneath his feet.

"They can't swim! We have a—" Galen never finished that thought. It was Qown's turn to save him, planting his feet in Galen's abdomen and pushing them in opposite directions. As he did, a tentacle-like blast of gold coins tore through the bit of water they'd been occupying a moment ago.

So Galen had been wrong about the lack of enemy spellcasters.

"Okay, this officially sucks," he declared. He sighed and drew his sword, swimming toward the centaur. "Sorry about this," he said, angling himself for a blow.

The centaur tried to dance away, and had he been surrounded by the more malleable air instead of water, he'd have pulled off the trick. As it was, Galen managed to score a long, shallow cut down the creature's right flank. Blood flowed, creating red ribbons in the water.

The centaur reared onto its front legs and lashed out at Galen. The water again slowed the blow, and Galen was able to get his sword between him and one of the hooves. The second one hit him in the shoulder, and he knew he'd have the mother of all bruises there tomorrow.

"Don't let them surround you!" Talea cried out.

"Sure," Galen said, leveling his blade and pushing himself into a swimming lunge at the centaur. He cut it again on the same flank, and the creature cried bubbles of pain. Several other clouds of blood floated in the water by this point, and it was getting increasingly hard to see.

An issue that became irrelevant to Galen a moment later when the coin pseudopod struck him from behind and engulfed his legs and waist. He kicked and hacked at it, but gold coins don't bleed or feel pain.

"Look out!" Talea yelled.

Galen looked up. A hulking white-skinned man with shark's teeth in a too-wide mouth leveled a trident at Galen's chest.

"Well, fuck," Galen said.

58: THE COST OF JUSTICE

Xivan's story
The Second World

Suless's mistake was thinking she was safe.

It was an easy mistake to make. This was the Afterlife, a place where only souls, demons, and Immortals wandered free. The very reason Suless had sought out the secrets of demonic soul transformation in the first place was to escape the annoyingly relentless Xivan by popping off into the Afterlife if she ever drew too close.

The Afterlife was the one place Xivan couldn't go, right? The nature of what Grimward did, by allowing the binding of upper souls to otherwise dead bodies, tied that soul to the Living World. The Cornerstone granted eternal half-life, but that existence was also a prison.

Logically, traveling to the Afterlife was quite beyond Xivan's ability.

But not, as it turned out, beyond the power of what Xivan was turning into, ever since Talea tricked her into accepting Thaena's Grail. Now such travel wasn't merely within Xivan's power, it was trivially easy.

Her first blow hit Suless in the right arm, severing it at the elbow with a satisfying, meaty chuck. Suless screamed in pain, but also surprise. She must not have expected the Afterlife to feel so . . . real.

Suless spun to face her attacker, and her eyes widened in shock.

"That's . . . that's not possible!" Suless cried.

"And yet, here we are," Xivan said with an amiable grin. "Now, my girlfriend is probably going to be mad at me if I don't offer you a chance to surrender," she said, the smile turning sardonic. "But let's be honest with each other, you and I: that was never an option."

"No, wait, I can–"

After everything Xivan had been through in the past few months (or decades, if she were to be entirely honest with herself), it would have been so satisfying to take a moment to spell out Suless's sins. To make a long, dramatic description of the pain and horror Suless had inflicted on Xivan and everyone she cared about. It would have been lovely to do so slowly, all the while carving off piece after piece of Suless until even a fellow demon wouldn't recognize what was left.

To make it hurt. To make it slow.

Torturing Suless wouldn't bring Azhen back. It wouldn't bring Exidhar back. And it wouldn't make them feel better, because they'd never know it happened.

But Xivan had friends who needed her back in the Living World. Friends who could still feel pain, loss, and love. So Xivan made a choice.

She chose them.

Her powers had crept up on her, growing swiftly but invisibly over the past few days. Most of the time, Xivan only vaguely comprehended how to control her new gifts; some skills seemed instinctive, others less so. In the Living World, she'd had no guide, no real idea what she could do or how to do it.

But this place felt more like home than anything she could remember in a long, long time. Here, she knew exactly what to do and how. It was if the very Afterlife itself spoke to her, guided her, nurtured her, taught her.

This land so desperately wanted to be loved.

Xivan grabbed Suless by the throat and reached inside her, hand passing right through metaphysical "flesh" as if were but smoke and mist. She began pulling out the souls that Suless had consumed; an impressive number for one so newly come into demonhood. An impressive number, but not enough to give Suless the power she'd have needed to survive this.

Not nearly enough.

When the last outside soul was released and Suless was merely herself, a sobbing, mewling, pathetic soul that squirmed and spewed promises, Xivan did one more thing that the Afterlife taught her.

And then, in the silence that followed, she turned her attention to more important matters.

Janel's story
The Monastery at Devors, Quur

"High General, what the hell do you think you're doing?" Janel yelled as she approached her father's position atop the cliffs. The scorpion war machines arrayed on either side of him like the wings of some massive raptor of doom weren't those that normally guarded the monastery. Those were overrun by the feral beasts who used to be soldiers. These were all new war machines, brought in through magic gates and now taking advantage of the opportunity to rain destruction on both the Lash and Drehemia.

And Janel's friends.

"That's what I've been saying!" Kalindra shouted. She held a squirming, crying, screaming Nikali in her arms. "Oh, for fuck's sake!" she yelled as soldiers moved to block Janel's way. "She's on our side! Move!"

The soldiers ignored her orders. One pushed Janel, hard, and she stumbled back.[1] Her eyes flashed red, and she pushed him back. He flew a good ten, twelve feet and landed on his back, the air knocked out of him.

Several other soldiers began to draw weapons, but Qoran Milligreest, High General of Quur, roared, "Enough!" and made an irritated gesture. The soldiers backed away and let her through.

She rather doubted any of them even noticed Teraeth circling around to take up position behind them. Even Kalindra probably hadn't noticed.

---

[1] Yes, she's incredibly strong, but she still only weighs as much as a person her size. That does make a difference.

"You need to stop with this nonsense before you make the Lash angry and she breaks the deal!" Janel shouted. "Those are my people down there."

"Then remove them," her father said, his face expressionless. "Do you have any idea how many people have died in the last couple of hours because of those two monsters? I may not be able to permanently kill Drehemia, but I am not passing up the opportunity to rid the world of the Lash."

Janel wondered who'd told him the Lash's real identity. Then she realized he might have just figured it out himself; the kraken hadn't exactly been quiet in her bellowing.

"You won't be able to destroy either of them," Janel said. "But we can make them leave. We're halfway there, but if you keep this up, there's an excellent chance we'll lose everything."

"Someone remove this woman," Qoran Milligreest said.

"I wouldn't recommend trying," Janel said. "The first one of you to touch me—"

"Father," Jarith said, his voice stern and commanding, "stop it."

Qoran Milligreest visibly paled as he turned and beheld his son standing between two scorpion war machines.

Jarith was dressed in funeral white, almost certainly the last thing his father had ever seen him wear.

Janel exhaled softly. *Teraeth, you sneaky son of a bitch. That's one Kirpis-worthy illusion.*

"Dada!" Nikali screamed. Janel couldn't tell if the tone in his voice denoted joy or desperation.

"What . . . How . . ." Qoran frowned. "This is a trick." He turned to Janel, leveling a finger at her. "It has to be a trick!"

"It's not a trick," Jarith corrected, his voice firm. He walked forward as Nikali wiggled free of his mother's stunned grasp and ran to him. He bent to scoop up "his" son. "Thurvishar D'Lorus is down there right now. Galen and Sheloran D'Mon are down there also. Kihrin D'Mon is down there. So please do what my sister said. Call off the damn attack. We're handling this."

Qoran stared at him for a moment, then started barking orders to his men.

59: Lessons in Metallurgy

Galen's story
Drehemia's Lair near Da'utunse

Galen kicked and squirmed, but the gold metal wrapped around his leg had him trapped. He raised his sword to parry the trident heading for his chest, and that worked . . . somewhat. He slowed the weapon's forward movement, but the larger, stronger shark-toothed man inexorably forced the deadly points of the fork closer and closer.

"A little help?" Galen cried out.

As if in answer, the shark-man paused, shook his head, and glanced wildly around himself as if seeing this place for the first time. He pulled the trident away from Galen, said something in a foreign tongue, and swam for the exit.

The gold released its hold on Galen, the coins reverting to normal coin behavior and tumbling slowly to the floor of the cavern.

Galen scanned the place for more threats.

There were none.

The majority of the "game pieces" were contorting in horrible-looking ways or clawing at their throats. "Oh damn," he said and then, "Qown!"

"I know," Qown said. He held a pile of wooden splinters in his hand, evidently torn from the various caskets, and he'd done something to break their connection to their former occupants. But doing so also removed the protections allowing them to survive underwater.

Qown extended his finger and drew a now-familiar glyph on the floor of the cavern, several orders of magnitude larger than Galen had ever seen it drawn before. A huge bubble of air pushed the water out and away, leaving them all dripping but able to breathe, in Drehemia's no-longer-entirely-underwater lair.

Galen let out a shriek–a very manly shriek–as he fell six feet and landed on a pile of coins.

He threw Qown a reproving look from where he lay, sprawled inelegantly on his royal throne. "That's it," Galen announced. "I've decided this is a very comfy bed, and I'm never leaving it."

"Sorry," Qown was explaining to one of the newly freed creatures, a dog-like creature the size of a Joratese pony with flat teeth and antlers coming out of its head. "I thought that if I could break Drehemia's control, you'd all be free. But you were about to kill me, so I had to do that first before I could do the spell that would let you breathe and not get crushed and–"

"Qown?" Talea said, putting her hand on his shoulder. "Qown, she doesn't speak Guarem. I doubt any of them do. But I think they get the idea."

The former pieces milled about, testing the confines of their new habitat. The cat-man poked at the wall of water being held at bay by the air from the glyph. A few, however, perhaps a half dozen of the creatures, lay or crouched in variations of the fetal position as their physiology dictated, lost to the trauma of what they'd experienced.

Despite his protestations otherwise, Galen heaved himself to his feet and approached, pulling Qown close. "You were perfect," he said. "Thanks."

Qown blushed. "What about them, though?" he asked, glancing about.

"We'll have to figure something out," Talea said. "But we've ruined Drehemia's game set . . . so I hope Senera is able to cure her. Also that Senera rescues us soon." She linked arms with Qown and said, "In the meantime, let's make some new friends."

Senera's story
Atamer Harbor, Devors, Quur

"Look out!" Thurvishar pulled Senera behind him roughly, throwing up his hands to form a magical barrier. A scorpion cask exploded in front of them, the blast partially deflected by his shield. The force still shoved them both back several feet.

Normally, scorpion fire was horrifyingly accurate. However, the spotter lights had never had to cope with a shadow dragon or a kraken before. Drehemia's form absorbed the light, preventing the war machines from focusing on her. Likewise, the lights slid off the Lash's magic-resistant skin as though she was made of mirrors. Even so, plenty of splash damage hit both monsters, and the casks were landing close enough to their own position to make completing the ritual impossible.

Senera and Thurvishar retreated, joining Sheloran and Kihrin farther up the quay.

"Xivan!" bellowed the Lash as another cask exploded and melted off part of her left-side flipper. **"Explain this betrayal!"** But Xivan was nowhere to be found.

Drehemia wrenched a leg free and slammed it into the harbor. She began dragging herself toward shore, bodily pulling the Lash with her.

"If she reaches the shore, the Lash will have to release her," Senera said.

"We can't let that happen," Thurvishar said. "You need to complete the ritual."

"I need to be much closer!"

"Can we just let High General Stupidhead and his stupidhead soldiers drive them off?" not-Kihrin asked.

"Even if they do, what makes you think that the Lash won't return for revenge after our 'betrayal'?" Senera shook her head. "This is our only chance, but as long as *that* continues"—she pointed toward the top of the cliff behind them—"we don't stand a chance."

"I can help." Sheloran stood from the barrel she'd been sitting on. She swayed and sat back down abruptly. "From here," she added. "I can help from right here."

"What do you need me to do?" Thurvishar said.

Senera faced him. "Can you keep them away from me for long enough?"

Thurvishar nodded, his face grim. "Absolutely," he said.

Senera knew he was lying. The strain would be too much. He was good, he was *so good*, but even Thurvishar had his limits. It was entirely possible to burn up every reserve of tenyé until the energy began to cannibalize one's own body. A powerful enough wizard with a strong enough will could cast their way right past the Second Veil and into their own grave.

What other choice did they have?

"We have another problem," Kihrin said. He pointed. The Lash's undead were heading their way. "I think she's really pissed at Xivan but is willing to take it out on, you know, us."

Sheloran forced herself to stand again. "Then that's our job," she said, nodding to Talon-disguised-as-Kihrin. "Luckily, there's plenty of metal around."

And indeed, there was. The weapons and armor of the fallen, hoops from shattered barrels, nails from crates and boxes, spikes from the very dock itself; Senera was willing to bet Sheloran hadn't had this rich an environment to work with since leaving the Rose Palace.

"Very well," Senera said softly, still looking at Thurvishar. "Shall we finish this dance?"

60: The Definition of Victory

Janel's story
The Monastery at Devors, Quur

The rain of scorpion casks ceased on the high general's order, but the damage was done. Drehemia's frenzy increased again, and she tried new tricks. Day turned to night and back as she strobed darkness. She turned invisible. She ripped and tore at the Lash's tentacles, severing many, although they grew back swiftly enough.

Someone down there–Janel assumed Sheloran–began melting all the metal and forming giant dragon-size shackles. The very cliff face itself had distended, providing cover from the scorpion attacks. She imagined Thurvis-har was responsible for that one.

Between the distance, the storm, the sea spray, the various shields, and the on-again, off-again light, it was impossible to say for sure what was happening down there. This didn't stop her, or dozens of other soldiers, from squinting down in an attempt to do just that. She was hard at it when Teraeth appeared by her shoulder.

"Think it'll work?" he asked.

"Maybe," Janel said. "Now that we're giving them a breather–" A baby's giggle from behind gave her pause. She looked over her shoulder to where her brother Jarith was bouncing his son in his arms. Jarith, Kalindra, and their son were being escorted to one of the temporary gates.

Janel looked at Jarith, then at Teraeth, then back at Jarith.

"Is that . . . Talon?" she whispered.

Teraeth followed her gaze. "I don't think so, no."

"But then, if that's not . . . and you're here, then . . ."

Jarith glanced up in her direction, and their eyes met. His expression was indecipherable, but he gave her a solemn nod. Then he left through the gate.[1] Janel didn't know if either Kalindra or Jarith intended on coming back, but she could understand the need to remove Nikali from the war zone.

Janel found herself smiling.

Shouts drew her attention back to the harbor. The wall extruded from the cliff side had begun to crumble, allowing better visibility. Also, the flickering darkness had ceased, and the storm appeared to be letting up. But the most

---

[1] I find myself curious to know if Jarith had formed a "shell" of a body, in the manner of most demons capable of creating temporary bodies for themselves when they manifest physically, or if (possibly with Kihrin's assistance) he re-created his old body in its entirety. The latter would make him more akin to Janel–a demon, but a demon possessing their own, dedicated life-form.

important element, that which drew startled exclamations, was the complete and utter absence of monsters—dragon or kraken.

Janel grabbed the spyglass from a nearby soldier and ignored his protests as she peered through it. Gathered on the shattered remains of the quay she saw Kihrin, Thurvishar, Senera, Talea, and Qown standing in a semicircle looking down. Galen knelt before them, and lying on the ground, her head in Galen's lap, lay the body of Sheloran D'Talus.

Teraeth's story
Atamer Harbor, Devors, Quur

In the minutes it took Teraeth to run down to the harbor, he decided he hated stairs. They weren't any more fun to run down than up and considerably scarier in some cases.

Out of breath for the first time in he couldn't remember how long, Teraeth approached the group, who hadn't moved the entire time it took him to get down there. He knew it was bad when he saw Galen, Talea, and Qown crying.

"What happened?" he asked Thurvishar, who leaned wearily on Senera's shoulder.

Thurvishar shook his head. He looked exhausted.

Senera answered for him. "She was already injured, and she overextended herself to hold Drehemia. She saved us at the cost of her life." She closed her eyes for a moment, then opened them again to glare at Teraeth. "Aren't you going to tell me this isn't my fault?"

"It isn't—" he started to say.

"I know it's not!" Senera snapped. "It's the fucking Quuros army's fault!" She looked past Teraeth and said, "Give me one good reason why I shouldn't go up there and just blow them all to—"

"I thought you were done helping Relos Var," Janel said from behind Teraeth.

Senera closed her eyes and shuddered.

Teraeth turned to look at Janel in confusion. He looked at the top of the cliff, at the never-ending stairs connecting "there" and "here," and then at her again.

She returned his gaze without expression.[2]

Teraeth shook his head and returned his attention to the tableau. "When this is all over . . . ," he said, but left the sentence unfinished. Janel's abilities would be the least of his problems when this was all over.

In the meantime, he regarded Galen's tear-streaked face and Sheloran's empty one. She hadn't been terrible for a Quuros royal. Neither of them were.

Sheloran inhaled.

Galen opened his eyes in shock. He put his finger to his wife's throat. He didn't need to announce if she had a pulse; Sheloran was visibly breathing.

"What just happened?" Qown asked.

---

[2] No, I don't know how she managed that either, although we shouldn't discount the idea she too simply ran.

Sheloran opened her eyes and stared at her husband. She tsked. "You shouldn't cry, Blue. It does unfortunate things to your complexion."

Galen drew in a shuddering breath. "You—" He lowered his head to hers. Teraeth didn't think he kissed her, but instead whispered something. He couldn't see the man's lips to read them and found himself glad of that; the scene was painfully private, and he didn't feel he had the right to watch.

Xivan stepped into the circle. "I take it everything worked out?"

Teraeth opened his mouth to reply, glanced at her, and froze.

He'd spent enough time in his mother's presence to recognize Death when he saw her. Xivan wasn't that—yet. Not fully, anyway. But the echoes were there, like seeing someone dressed up in the favorite gown of a person you loved. They don't look the same, but you couldn't help but be reminded of the original owner.

He wondered what the criteria had been; to be singled out to become the new Goddess of Death. Chance? Was she to become the new Thaena because she'd been "lucky" enough to be the lover of the new Taja? That would imply things about the relationship between Khaemezra and Eshimavari I'm reasonably certain never existed. Or was there more to it than that?

He suspected the latter. Xivan's link with death seemed too strong, her background too appropriate. And perhaps, if one was to be the Goddess of Death, it might be wise to understand the concept from every side; to lose and to have lost, to cut the threads of life and experience their severing in turn.

"You figured out how to Return," he said.

Xivan smiled, just a little bit. "Oh no," she said. "I haven't even begun to figure that out. But stiff-arming a soul that was still in the process of crossing the Veils back into a perfectly good body? That's not so tough."

"Thank you," Sheloran said, looking up at her.

"*Thank you*," Xivan said with an awkward shrug. "I kind of owed you for the whole 'trying to kidnap you to use you to blackmail your mother' debacle." She reached down, offering her hand. "Are we good?"

Sheloran took the hand and let Xivan pull her to her feet. She looked at Galen, then at Qown, Talea, and the rest. Her gaze returned to Xivan, and she smiled, for once without covering it with her fan. "We're good," she said. "The real question is: What are we going to do with them?" She pointed up the quay.

Teraeth turned to look, only just then noticing the cluster of some two or three dozen creatures standing around awkwardly. He didn't even recognize some of them, but others were all too horribly familiar. *Fuck. Is that a centaur?*

Janel laughed, put her arm around Teraeth's waist. "Come on, everyone," she said. "We're a long way from done."

61: Epilogue

Deep in the heart of the Korthaen Blight, seven streams of light converged over a building in the center of the city. Once called Karolaen, now Kharas Gulgoth, the city was tomb and prison, maintained for one purpose and one purpose only: to chain a corrupted god.

Seven streams of light converged over a building. In the center of that building, a dark god tilted his head as if stretching from a long nap. For the god that had once been, seven rays of light had been enough to keep him imprisoned.

But for the god that now was, those seven rays of light were nothing more than component pieces to a complicated lock.

And Kihrin had grown up a thief.

Vol Karoth performed an act he hadn't tolerated in all the many millennia or minutes of his existence—instead of absorbing tenyé, he released it. He sent that energy cascading up those seven streams.

In various locations scattered around the world, seven crystals cracked and shattered.

Escape had always been as easy as that.

It had just been impossible while Vol Karoth remained nothing more than a warped version of S'arric.

If anyone had been there, if anyone had dared, they might have seen something unexpected then. That just for a second, the dark god's shape had flickered. For that second, he had looked like a normal man. Then he remembered himself and became a silhouette again.

He hovered up into the air and laced his hands behind his back.

Vol Karoth, King of Demons, also known as S'arric, more recently known as Kihrin, floated out into the world at a leisurely pace. He wasn't in a rush, although he did wonder if Relos Var would be happy or upset to see him free and loose upon the world. He wished for the latter but suspected it was probably the former. At the very least, Relos Var would have planned for it. He was, after all, the smartest man in two universes.

Kihrin had work to do and a last game to run. The stakes were everything, the odds were grim, and there would be no second chances. His opponents were both geniuses who wanted to either rule or ruin the universe, and both had the power to make their dreams reality.

Though no one could see it, Kihrin smiled.

It was time to start the most important con of his existence.

GLOSSARY

A

Academy, the–famous school of magic in Alavel, Kirpis.

Aego (AI-goh)–a small boy living in a village on the largest of the Devors islands.

Aeyan'arric (EYE-ann-AR-ik)–ice dragon, also the daughter of S'arric and C'indrol.

Afterlife, the–a dark mirror of the Living World, souls go to the Afterlife after death, hopefully to move on to the Land of Peace.

agolé (a-GOAL-lay)–a piece of cloth worn draped around the shoulders and hips by both men and women in western Quur.

Alavel (a-la-VEL)–home city of the wizard's school known as the Academy.

Anlyr (AHN-leer)–a guard in the employ of House D'Mon.

ara (AHR-ay)–a potent distilled alcohol made from grain, popular in Jorat.

Arena, the–a park in the center of the Capital City that serves as battleground for the choosing of the emperor.

Argas (AR-gas)–one of the Eight Immortals. Considered the god of invention and innovation.

Aryahal (AHR-ah-hal)–a priest of Caless.

Atrine (at-rin-EE)–capital of the dominion of Jorat, originally built by Emperor Atrin Kandor.

B

Baelosh (BAY-losh)–a dragon, best known for the size of his hoard of treasure.

Battle of the Well of Spirals, the–a large-scale battle involving gods, demons, dragons, and mortals that occurred when Thaena attempted to wipe out the Manol nation using ritual magic. Argas, Galava, Grizzst, Taja, and Thaena all died during the fighting.

Bikeinoh (beh-KEEN-oh)–Duke Kaen's second wife, third in command of the Spurned mercenary company.

Black Brotherhood, the–a cult of assassins dedicated to Thaena, Goddess of Death.

Black Dolphin, the–an entertainment house in Da'utunse.

Black Gate of Thaena, the–the temple of Thaena in the Upper Circle of the Capital.

Blue Houses–generic name for any house of healing licensed by House D'Mon.

Blue Palace, the—the Upper Circle palace of House D'Mon.

Boji (BO-jhee)—a Zheriasian cad.

C

C'indrol (SIN-drohl)—a voras politician who conducted a prolonged love affair with S'arric, kept secret to avoid scandal. They were also one of Aeyan'arric's parents and died in the destruction of Karolaen when S'arric was transformed into Vol Karoth. Later reincarnated as Elana Kandor and again as Janel Theranon.

Caerowan (KAER-o-wan)—a rare Devoran priest involved in politics, elected to be a Voice of the Council. Had a close relationship with Emperor Sandus and was evidently a Gryphon Man.

Caless (kal-LESS)—depending on who's answering the question, either the Goddess of Sex, or the Goddess of Love.

caraba (ka-ra-BAE)—a small pastry made from layers of thinly rolled dough stuffed with nuts and honey.

Casar (KAZ-ar)—the alias used by Merit when he was pretending to be a member of House D'Erinwa.

Cherthog (cher-THOG)—a god of winter and ice, primarily worshipped in Yor.

Cimillion (seh-MIL-e-on) Emperor Sandus's son, originally believed killed as an infant by Gadrith D'Lorus, but in fact adopted by him as Thurvishar D'Lorus.

Citadel, The—headquarters of the Quuran Imperial Military.

City, the, a.k.a. the Capital City—originally a city-state under the control of the god-king Qhuaras, its original name (Quur) now applies to the whole empire.

Clarea (KLAR-ee-ah)—a velvet girl working at the Shattered Veil Club.

Colarin's (kol-AR-in's)—a bakery in Eamithon.

Copper Quarter—the mercantile district of the Lower Circle of the Capital City.

Cornerstones—eight magical artifacts; the Stone of Shackles and Chainbreaker are two of these.

Court of Gems—slang for the royal families of the Upper Circle represented by twelve different kinds of gemstones.

Crown and the Scepter, the—famous artifacts that may only be wielded by the Emperor of Quur.

Cruel Mistress, the—the pirate ship infamously used by the Lash.

Culling Fields, the—a tavern and inn situation just outside the Imperial Arena.

Capital City Hellmarch, the—the last Hellmarch that occurred before the breaking of the Stone of Shackles freed all demons. It was in fact still in progress when this happened. Afterwards, demons were free to attack anywhere, at any time, indiscriminately.

D

Da'utunse (dah-uh-TOON-say)—an Ithlakor floating city that has become (or possibly was always intended to be) a pirate haven. One of the few cities they have that is not underwater.

dakerra (dah-keer-AYE)–a generic name for roasted meats, usually marinated or covered with a dried spice such as Nakari powder.

D'Aramarin, Havar (hav-AR), High Lord of House D'Aramarin.

Daughters of Laaka (lah-KAH), a.k.a. kraken–enormous immortal sea creatures that resemble cephalopods, quite possibly native to Ompher in spite of stories that claim that they're the creations of a god-queen. Very difficult to hurt with magic.

demons–an alien race from another dimension that can, through effort, gain access to the material world. Famous for their cruelty and power. See: Hellmarch.

Dervala (der-VAHL-aye)–a teacher at the Ten Metals fighting school in Khorvesh.

Devoran Library, the (de-VORAN)–the largest library in the known world, dedicated primarily to the Devoran Prophecies, but containing a great many other books besides.

Devoran Prophecies, the–a many-book series of prophecies that are believed to foretell the end of the world.

Devors (de-VORS)–island chain south of the Capital City, most famous as the home of the Devoran priests and their prophecies.

Devors Monastery–the monastery where the Devoran priests live and study the prophecies.

dibis (dib-IZ)–sesame seed candies, often formed into cute shapes.

D'Jorax, Emeran (EM-er-an)–a member of House D'Jorax.

D'Kaje, Palnyr (PAL-neer)–High Lord of House D'Kaje.

D'Lorus (du-LOR-us)

    Cedric (KED-rik)–executed by Empress Tyentso for treason (it should be noted that he was her grandfather).

    Gadrith (GAD-rith)–Lord Heir of House D'Lorus, who was believed dead before contriving to switch bodies with Emperor Sandus, killing him in the process. He was finally slain (for good, this time) by Kihrin D'Mon, an event that also freed the demons.

    Raverí (rav-ear-EE)–wife of Gadrith D'Lorus. Officially listed as mother of Thurvishar D'Lorus. She was not, in fact, executed (nor was she Thurvishar's mother) but went into hiding, later re-emerging as Tyentso. While she was legally Gadrith's wife, they never consummated the relationship, and it seems both parties were fully aware that she was his biological daughter.

    Thurvishar (thur-vish-AR)–High Lord of House D'Lorus.

D'Mon (day-MON)

    Alshena (al-shen-AY)–wife of Darzin D'Mon, originally from House D'Aramarin. Alshena was murdered and replaced by Talon.

    Darzin (DAR-zin)–lord heir and conspirator with Gadrith D'Lorus. Darzin was slain by his younger brother, Kihrin D'Mon.

    Galen (GAL-len)–firstborn son of Lord Heir Darzin D'Mon. As Kihrin D'Mon was not, in fact, Darzin's son, the lord heir position would technically fall to Galen, not Kihrin, and under the assumption that Therin D'Mon was dead, Galen would legally be high lord. Galen was murdered by Khaeriel, but Returned at the behest of his wife, Sheloran.

Gerisea (ger-IS-ea)—Therin D'Mon's second-oldest daughter. She married the second son of the Duke of Khorvesh.

Kihrin (KEAR-rin)—youngest child of High Lord Therin D'Mon and only child of Queen Khaeriel of the vané. Also, the reincarnation of S'arric, one of the Eight Immortals.

Saerá (SAY-ra)—eldest daughter of Darzin D'Mon.

Saric (SAHR-ik)—a D'Mon ancestor, long since dead.

Sheloran (SHEL-or-an)—Galen D'Mon's wife, formerly of House D'Talus.

Therin (THER-rin)—technically still High Lord of House D'Mon, it seems likely that Therin is abdicating that position for good.

Tishenya (ti-SHEN-ya)—oldest daughter of Therin D'Mon. She married into House D'Kard, but had no children who survived the games of empire.

Doc—see: Terindel.

Doltar (dol-TAR)—a conglomeration of city-states to the south of Quur whom most Quuros believe are part of a single country (they are not). Ethnically tend to be much paler than their northern counterparts.

Dorna (DOR-na)—an elderly Joratese woman who served as Janel Theranon's nanny in childhood and is now assisting her adopted daughter, Ninavis.

Dragonspires, the—a mountain range running north-south through Quur, dividing the dominions of Kirpis, Kazivar, Eamithon, and Khorvesh from Raenena, Jorat, Marakor, and Yor.

Drehemia (DRAY-hem-EE-ah)—the shadow dragon.

dreth (dreth)—see: vordreth.

Drift Town—the portion of Da'utunse that floats above the waves.

D'Talus (day-TAL-us)

Lessoral (les-SOR-al)—High Lady of House D'Talus. A somewhat mysterious figure who married into the house from more common (possibly even velvet) origins.

Varik (VAHR-ik)—High Lord of House D'Talus. Unusual from his counterparts in that he actively works at his house's primary trade, which is possibly why House D'Talus has a significantly higher degree of loyalty than most royal houses enjoy.

E

Eamithon (AY-mith-ON)—a dominion just north of the Capital City, the oldest of the Quuros dominions and considered the most tranquil.

Eight Immortals, the—Eight beings of godlike power created by a ritual performed by Relos Var, who are now actively worshipped as gods throughout the world.

Empire of Quur (koor)—see: Quur.

En'dassin (END-ahs-in)—a lover taken by C'indrol in an attempt to deflect suspicion from their on-going love affair with S'arric.

Eshi (ESH-ee)—a nickname for Eshimavari.

Eshimavari (esh-EE-mah-var-EE)—the real name of the Goddess of Luck, Taja.

Everdark, the—the area below Da'utunse where surface light can't reach.

F

Ferandis (fur-AND-is)
  Morea (MOR-e-ah)–a slave girl murdered by Talon; Talea's twin sister.
  Talea (tal-E-ah)–a slave girl formerly owned by Baron Mataris, Talea was purchased by Darzin D'Mon and later bought (and freed) by Thurvishar D'Lorus, who helped apprentice her to swordmaster Xivan Kaen.
Festival of the Turning Leaves–a yearly celebration to the goddess Galava. Here petitioners may, after one year of service to the goddess, petition the goddess to change their biological sex.
Flotsam–a neighborhood in Da'utunse.
Four Races, the–four immortal, powerful races that once existed. Unfortunately this turned out to be a bit of propaganda, as there were in fact only three immortal races: the voras, the voramer, and the vordredd. None of them are still immortal.

G

gaesh (gaysh), pl. gaeshe (gaysh-ay)–an enchantment that forces the victim to follow all commands given by the person who physically possesses their totem focus, up to and including commands of suicide. Being unable or unwilling to perform a command results in death.
Galava (gal-a-VAY)–one of the Eight Immortals; goddess of life and nature.
gate, a.k.a. portal–the magical connection of two different geographic locations, allowing for quick travel across great distances. Only powerful wizards can typically create Gatestone-independent portals.
Gatekeepers, the–guild who controls and maintains gate travel. Ruled by House D'Aramarin.
Gatestone–a specially inscribed section of stone that somehow makes gate travel much less magically onerous. Exactly how this is accomplished is a proprietary, heavily protected House D'Aramarin secret.
Guarem (GOW-rem)–the primary language of Quur.
god-kings–wizards who have, through special rituals, given themselves the ability to collect tenyé offered through prayer and sacrifice. This typically allows them incredible power, up to and including immortality. Because the amount of tenyé sacrificed is not unlimited, competition for worshippers is fierce.
Godslayer–see: Urthaenriel.
god-touched–a gift or curse (depending on whom one asks) handed down by the Eight Immortals to the eight original, founding Royal Houses of Quur. Besides giving each house a distinctive eye color, the Royal Houses are forbidden from making laws.
Gorokai (GORE-o-kai)–a mercurial, shape-shifting dragon.
Grail of Thaena, the–one of the Great Talismans.
Great Talismans–seven talismans created by the Eight Immortals to help correct matters in the event that there would ever be a repeat of their deaths at the hands of Vol Karoth. Each of the Immortals has one, typically symbolic: a glass sword for Khored, a rainbow veil for Tya, a coin for Taja, etc.
Grimward–a Cornerstone. Grimward allows its wearer to control the dead and create undead, and makes the wearer extremely difficult to hurt. It cannot

be held by anyone who is living (or rather, it will immediately correct that problem).

Grizzst (grizt)—falsely considered to being one of the Eight Immortals; famous wizard, sometimes considered a god of magic, particularly demonology. Believed to be responsible for binding demons as well as making the Crown and Scepter of Quur. Died at the Battle of the Well of Spirals.

Gryphon Men—a cabal created by Grizzst whose members have included at least two emperors (Gendal and Sandus) that seems to be dedicated to helping the Hellwarrior. Considering Grizzst was theoretically in league with Relos Var and the Hellwarrior in question is Kihrin, it seems likely that Grizzst was either playing both sides against each other or had intended some other kind of scheme.

H

Harbor District—the harbor of the Capital City of Quur.

Hell—distinct from the Land of Peace. Where demons come from.

Hellmarch—the result of a powerful demon gaining access to the physical world, freely summoning demons and possessing corpses. This usually results in a runaway path of death and devastation. It typically stems from a demon escaping a summoner's control. Before the breaking of the Stone of Shackles, demons could only be summoned to the Living World by corporeal entities (such as humans or vané). But demons quickly discovered they could exploit a loophole by possessing a living body, and forcing that body to summon more of their kind. Demons can also possess corpses in the Joratese/Marakori area but cannot summon more demons in this manner.

Hellwarrior—a prophesied villain who will rise up to destroy the Empire of Quur and possibly the world. Also a prophesied hero who will rise up to save the world.

Hivar (HIV-ar)—a soldier who served as Jarith Milligreest's secretary while he was stationed at Stonegate Pass.

I

imchii (im-CHEY)—a distinctive Khorveshan sword with a thin, gently curving blade. Famous for being exceedingly sharp and good at slicing.

Irisia—see: Tya.

Ithlakor (ith-la-KOR)—an underwater nation composed primarily of Ithlané (a voramer offshoot).

Ithlané (ith-lan-AY)—a voramer offshoot race, probably the most like the original voramer of any of their cousin groups. Like most voramer-derived races, they are sequential hermaphrodites (meaning born male, and eventually becoming female as they age).

Ivory District, the—the temple district of the Upper Circle, in the Capital.

J

Jheshikah (jesh-eh-KAH)—one of the Spurned.

Jorat (jor-AT)—a dominion in the middle of Quur of varying climates and wide reaches of grassy plains; known for its horses.

K

Kaen (KANE)–the Yoran ducal line.

Azhen (AHJ-en)–Duke, or Hon, of Yor, grandson of the Joratese Quuros general who conquered the region. Murdered by Suless.

Exidhar (ex-ID-ar)–Azhen and Xivan Kaen's son, murdered by Suless.

Xivan (JI-van)–Azhen Kaen's first wife; her Khorveshan ancestry made her unpopular with the Yoran people, and she was eventually killed in an assassination attempt meant for her husband. Relos Var animated her using Grimward. Slayer of Argas, using Godslayer.

Kandor (KAN-dor),

Atrin (AT-rin)–an emperor of Quur who significantly expanded the borders of the Empire. Most famous for deciding to invade the Manol, which resulted in the destruction of virtually the entire Quuros army and himself, leaving Quur defenseless against the subsequent morgage invasion. Reincarnated as Teraeth.

Elana (eh-lan-AY)–Atrin Kandor's wife, responsible for ending the morgage invasion of Khorvesh. After her husband's death, she gave birth to his son and returned to using her maiden name, Milligreest. She later re-married a man named Terin (see: Terindel) but never had any other children.

Karolaen (KAR-o-lane)–former name of Kharas Gulgoth.

Kazivar (KAZ-eh-var)–one of the dominions of Quur, north of Eamithon.

kef (kef)–a style of trouser common in western Quur.

Kelanis (KEL-a-nis)–son of Khaevatz and Kelindel, younger brother of Khaeriel who attempted to have his sister assassinated and usurped her position. Murdered by Suless.

kevra (KEV-ray)–a tropical flower with a scent that is both fruity and rose-like. Often used to create kevra-water, which is popular for desserts and perfumes. Kevra hedges are popular in the Upper Circle.

Key–a specialist burglar working for the Shadowdancers trained at unlocking magical wards and enchantments.

Khaemezra (kay-MEZ-rah)–a.k.a. Mother–the High Priestess of Thaena, and leader of the Black Brotherhood; Teraeth's mother; the true name of Thaena. See: Thaena.

Khaeriel (kay-RE-el)–queen of the vané, assassinated by her brother, Kelanis. Because Khaeriel was wearing the Stone of Shackles, she ended up in the body of her assassin, and was later gaeshed and sold into slavery to Therin D'Mon by her grandmother, Khaemezra. Kihrin D'Mon's mother.

Khaevatz (KAY-vatz)–Manol vané queen, famous for resisting Atrin Kandor's invasion. She later married Kirpis vané King Kelindel, uniting (in theory) the two nations.

Kharas Gulgoth (KAR-as GUL-goth)–a ruin in the middle of the Korthaen Blight; believed sacred (and cursed) by the morgage; prison of the corrupted god Vol Karoth.

Khored (KOR-ed)–one of the Eight Immortals. God of Destruction, a.k.a. Mithros, who is Teraeth's grandfather.

Khorvesh (kor-VESH)–a dominion to the south of the Capital City, just north of the Manol Jungle.

Kirpis, the (KIR-pis)–a dominion to the north of Kazivar, primarily forest. Most famous for being the original home of one of the vané races, as well as the Academy. Also, home to a number of famous vineyards.

Kirpis vané (van-EH)–a fair-skinned, immortal race who once lived in the Kirpis forest. They were driven south to eventually relocate in the Manol Jungle.

Kishna-Farriga (kish-na-fair-eh-GA)–one of the Free States, independent city-states south of Quur, past the Manol Jungle; Kishna-Farriga is used as a trading entrepôt by many neighboring countries.

Korthaen Blight, the (kor-THANE)–also called the Wastelands, a cursed and unlivable land that is (somehow) home to the morgage.

kraken–see: Daughters of Laaka.

Kulma swamp (KUL-mah)–a lowland swamp area in southern Marakor.

L

Laaka (LAKE-ay)–goddess of storms, shipwrecks, and sea serpents.

laevos (LAY-vos)–a Joratese hairstyle consisting of a strip of hair down the center of the head and shaved sides, echoing a horse's mane. Some Joratese grow their hair this way naturally; it's considered a sign of nobility.

Lagan–a district in Da'utunse.

Land of Peace, the–Heaven, the place of reward souls go after they die and are judged worthy by Thaena.

Lash, the–an infamous pirate operating in the seas surrounding Zherias.

Lighthouse at Shadrag Gor, the–a highly magical lighthouse in Yor where time runs extremely fast.

Linyuwan (LIN-u-wan)–a Devoran priest.

Living World, the–the part of the Twin Worlds that living beings can see and interact with.

Lotus Court, the–a section of the Rose Palace famous for its man-made lake.

Lower Circle, the–area of the Capital City that exists outside of the safety of the table-top mesa of the Upper Circle, thus making it vulnerable to flooding.

Lyrilyn (LIR-il-in)–a slave girl owned by Pedron D'Mon, later transformed by the Stone of Shackles into the mimic Talon.

Lysian gas (LIS-e-an)–an extremely dangerous magical weapon of mass destruction capable of destroying the populations of entire towns. Looks like blue smoke.

M

Malkoessian (MAL-KOZ-ee-an),

   Aroth (AIR-oth)–Markreev of Stavira, one of the four quadrants that politically divide Jorat. Count Janel Theranon's canton, Tolamer, lies within Stavira's borders.

Manol, the (MAN-ol)–an area of dense jungle in the equatorial region of the known world; home to the Manol vané.

Manol vané (MAN-ol van-AY)–one of the vané races, who broke away from the Kirpis as a political protest and changed their appearance to underscore their new allegiance. Manol vané are typically dark-colored, but like all vané, not predictably so.

Marakor (MARE-a-kor)–the Quuros dominion to the southeast of the empire. Politically important because Marakor is the only (relatively) easy entry point to the Manol Jungle. Consolidating the various rival city-state clans, which originally made up the region, has proved difficult.

Merit (MER-it)–a thief with the Shadowdancers who now helps run the the Shattered Veil Club velvet house.

Mezian, Vanaj (MEZ-e-an, vahn-AJ)–a Khorveshan swordsmith famous for the quality of his blades. Xivan Kaen's father.

Milligreest (mill-eh-GREEST),

    Elana (e-LAN-ay)–a musician from Khorvesh who married Atrin Kandor. After his death, she returned to using her maiden name and journeyed into the Korthaen Blight to negotiate a peace settlement with the invading morgage people; responsible for freeing S'arric. Past life of Janel Theranon. See: Elana Kandor.

    Eledore (el-eh-DOR-ee)–Qoran Milligreest's youngest daughter.

    Jarith (JAR-ith)–only son of Qoran; like most Milligreests, served in the military; killed by Xaltorath during the Capital Hellmarch.

    Kalindra (KAL-ind-rah)–a half-Khorveshan, half-Zheriasian member of the Black Brotherhood and angel of Thaena, who married Jarith Milligreest.

    Nikali (ni-KAL-i)–1. Cousin of Qoran Milligreest, famous for his skill with a sword. See: Terindel. 2. Jarith and Kalindra Milligreest's toddler son.

    Qoran (KOR-an)–High General of the Quuros army. Biological father of Janel Theranon.

    Taunna (TAWN-nay)–a member of the Milligreest family who was adopted by Nikali Milligreest after the death of her parents. She now runs the Culling Fields tavern.

mimics–a mysterious shape-changing race that hides amongst humanity, typically selling their services as spies and assassins. Infamous for their fondness for devouring brains.

misha (MEESH-ah)–a long-sleeved shirt worn by men in Quur.

Mithros (MEETH-ros)–leader of the Red Spears, a mercenary company selling their services to the highest bidder for tournaments in Jorat; a Manol vané. Also, the real name of Khored, God of Destruction.

Miya (MY-ah)–nickname for Miyathreall

Miyathreall (MY-ah-threel)–A handmaiden to Queen Khaerial, sister of Queen Khaeriel's consort, Miyane. After she assassinated Khaeriel, they swapped places because of the Stone of Shackles, with the result that Khaeriel was now trapped in Miyathreall's body.

morgage (mor-gah-GEE)–a belligerent, aggressive race that lives in the Korthaen Blight and makes constant war on its neighbors. These are mainly Quuros living in the dominion of Khorvesh, but the morgage hold a special hatred for the vané.

Morios (MORE-ee-os)–the dragon of swords, brother of Mithros.

Mouse–a Key in the Shadowdancers, deceased.

Name of All Things, the—one of the Cornerstones. The Name of All Things can answer any question asked while holding it, with the caveat that it cannot answer questions about events that predate its existence, nor can it answer questions about Urthaenriel or Vol Karoth. Since there is no way to stop answering a question once it's asked, care must be taken not to ask a question so open-ended that one starves to death.

N

Nemesan (NEM-es-an)—a deceased god-king.

Nemesan gambit—any strategy so excellent that there is no way to lose, i.e. a mastermind play where every possible counterplay still results in a victory for the plotter.

Nightrunners—a Khorveshan mercenary company.

Nineawen (nin-e-AH-wen)—the name of the original voras settlement on Nythrawl, which had to be abandoned after the first demon invasion occurred.

Niyabe (NIGH-ah-bee)—Abbess of the Devors Monastery.

Nythrawl (NITH-rahl)—the original continent settled by the voras, now uninhabitable.

O

Octagon, the—the main slave auction house of the Capital City.

Ogenra (OH-jon-RAY)—an unrecognized bastard of one of the royal families. Far from being unwanted, Ogenra are considered an important part of the political process because of their ability to circumvent the god-touched curse.

Old Man, the—see: Sharanakal.

Oliyuan (OL-eh-wan)—a Devoran priest.

Ompher (OM-fur)—one of the Eight Immortals, god of the world.

ord—the main monetary unit of Kishna-Farriga.

P

Pajanya Cliffs (PAH-jan-ya)—the cliffs upon which the Devors Monastery and Library are built.

pepperleaf beer—a sweet alcoholic beverage made from the herb of the same name.

Pirate Queen of the Desolation—a famous and popular ribald play occasionally performed by House D'Jorax.

Pivilana Bay (piv-il-an-AY)—a harbor in Zherias.

Q

Qown, Brother (kown)—an acolyte of the Vishai Mysteries, originally assigned to guide Count Janel Theranon, now assigned to Galen D'Mon.

Quur, the Great and Holy Empire of (koor)—a large empire originally expanded from a single city-state (also named Quur), which now serves as the empire's capital.

Quuros High Council—the ruling body of Quur, elected from a pool of candidates who are themselves elected by the Royal Houses.

R

Raenena (RAY-nen-ah)–a dominion of Quur, nestled in the Dragonspires to the north.

Rainbow Lake–a large lake in Eamithon named because of its unusually clear waters and the rainbow sheen of the feldspar underneath. Home to Grizzst's tower, which he has hidden using illusions.

raisigi (RAY-sig-eye)–a tight-fitting bodice worn by women.

Raorin (RAY-or-in)–a morgage-blooded bouncer at the Shattered Veil Club.

Return–to be resurrected from the Afterlife, always with the permission of the Goddess of Death, Thaena.

Rev'arric–see: Relos Var.

Rima, Latemé (REEM-ah, la-TEM-ay)–a Zheriasian pirate, captain of the *Angel's Spite.*

Ritual of Night, the–a magical ritual designed to align an immortal race more fully with the universe, making them mortal and channeling the tenyé yield of that sacrifice into strengthening Vol Karoth's prison. All involved in the ritual itself die.

Rol'amar (ROL-a-mar)–the bone dragon, also the son of Relos Var and Tya.

Rose Palace, the–the palace of House D'Talus.

S

S'arric, (sar-RIC)–one of the Eight Immortals, mostly unknown (and deceased); god of sun, stars, and sky; murdered by his older brother, Rev'arric. Past life of Kihrin D'Mon.

sag bread (SAHG)–a flat unleavened bread, used to eat meals with.

sallí (sal-LEE)–a hooded, cloak-like garment designed to protect the wearer from the intense heat of the sun.

Sandus (SAND-us)–a farmer from Marakor, later Emperor of Quur. Thurvishar's biological father and Relos Var's son.

sassibim brandy (sass-ah-BIM)–a style of brandy made from sassibim berries.

Scabbard–the day-to-day commander of the Shadowdancers, a criminal organization.

Scarlet Gull, the–a hospitality house in Da'utunse.

scorpion war machines–a Quuros military invention that uses magic to hurl casks of magical munitions at great velocity at a target (usually) with a high degree of accuracy.

Selanol (SELL-an-al)–the solar deity worshipped as part of the Vishai Mysteries.

Shadowdancers, the–an illegal criminal organization operating in the Lower Circle of the Capital City.

shanathá (shan-NA-tha)–a light, hard metal used to make some kinds of armor and weapons.

Sharanakal (SHA-ran-a-KAL)–a dragon, associated with fire. Also known as the Old Man.

Shark's Mouth, the–a dive bar in Da'utunse.

Shattered Veil Club, the–a velvet house and entertainment hall.

Simillion (SIM-i-le-on)–First Emperor of Quur. Famous for many things, not
   least of which is conforming to the classic "farm boy hero slays gods" trope,
   Simillion was promptly murdered by the very people he'd meant to save.
   Reincarnated as Thurvishar D'Lorus.

Simillion's Crossing–a street named after the Emperor.

Skyfire–a Cornerstone with the ability to create intense bursts of heat and flame.

Soaring Halls–name of the Imperial Palace.

Solan'arric (SOL-an-AR-ic)–see: S'arric.

sorshi balls (SOR-shy)–dessert made of beaten rice flour with fruit stuffing.

Spurned, the–an all-female mercenary company consisting almost entirely of
   Yoran witches.

Stone of Shackles, the–one of the eight Cornerstones. The Stone of Shackles
   has power over souls, including the ability to exchange its wearer's soul
   with that of their murderer.

Stonegate Pass–the fortress and town built up at the easiest entry point into
   the Korthaen Blight.

sugar apple–a large fruit that can be split open to reveal fluffy, sticky white
   flesh wrapped around black seeds (which are discarded). The fruit is very
   sweet but can be messy to eat.

Suless (SUE-less)–god-queen of Yor, associated with witchcraft, deception,
   treachery, and betrayal; also associated with hyenas.

sweet-glass grapes–a popular street fruit in which a variety of round fruit on a
   stick (usually some sort of sour berry) is dipped in hot molten sugar, which
   is allowed to harden.

T

Taja (TAJ-ah)–one of the Eight Immortals. Goddess of Luck.

Talisman–an otherwise normal object whose tenyé has been modified to vibrate in sympathy with the owner, thus reinforcing the tenyé against enemies who might use magic to change it. This also means it's extremely
   dangerous to allow one's talisman to fall into enemy hands. One's ability
   to use magic, it's possible to wear so many talismans that one is rendered
   incapable of using any magic at all.

Talon–a mimic assassin and spy working for Darzin D'Mon.

tamarane (tam-a-RAN-ee)–a system of Joratese cooking with eight specific
   styles of heating.

Tavris (TAV-ris)–god-king of merchants and profit.

Tel, Kavis (KAV-is TEL)–pseudonym used by Galen D'Mon for publishing
   his poetry.

Ten Metals fighting school–a Khorveshan fighting school in Stonegate Pass.

tenyé, (ten-AY)–the true essence of an object. Vital to all magic.

Teraeth (ter-WRATHE)–hunter of Thaena. A Manol vané assassin and member of the Black Brotherhood. Son of Terindel and Khaemezra. The reincarnation of Atrin Kandor. Currently, King of the Manol.

Terindel (TER-in-del)–an infamous Kirpis vané king who sparked a civil war
   when he refused to conduct the Ritual of Night. Teraeth's father. Slain by
   Thaena after he revealed the truth about the Four Races.

Thaena (thane-AY)–one of the Eight Immortals. Goddess of Death.

Theranon (ther-a-NON)

Janel (jan-EL), a.k.a. Janel Danorak, a.k.a. the Black Knight–daughter of Qoran Milligreest and Tya. The reincarnation of Elana Kandor and C'indrol.

Ninavis (NIN-a-vis)–former outlaw turned duke.

Three Sisters, the–either Taja, Tya, and Thaena, or Galava, Tya, and Thaena; also, the three moons in the night sky.

thriss (thris)–a serpent-headed race created from humans by the god-king Ynis.

Tolamer (TOL-a-mear)–a canton in northeastern Jorat, ruled by the Theranon family for almost five hundred years.

tsali stone, (zal-e)–a crystal created from the condensed soul of a person.

Tumai (TU-mai)–Yoran word for knight.

Twin Worlds, the–name for the combination of the Living World and Afterlife, when referring to both realms as part of a larger whole.

Tya (tie-ah), a.k.a. Irisia (IR-is-EE-ah)–one of the Eight Immortals, the Goddess of Magic.

Tya's Veil–an aurora borealis effect visible in the night sky.

Tyentso (tie-EN-so)–formerly Raverí D'Lorus, now the emperor of Quur; the first woman to ever be emperor.

U

uisigi (YOU-sig-eye)–undergarments, specifically underpants or loincloths.

Upper Circle–the mesa plateau in the center of the Capital City that is home to the Royal Houses, temples, government, and Arena.

Urthaenriel (UR-thane-re-EL)–Godslayer, the Ruin of Kings, the Emperor's Sword. A powerful artifact that is believed to make its wielder completely immune to magic and thus is capable of killing gods. The sword used to turn S'arric into Vol Karoth.

V

Valathea (val-a-THE-a)–Terindel's wife, who cursed herself to become a harp following her fatal poisoning after having been sentenced to the Traitor's Walk by her brother-in-law. Kihrin's great-great-grandmother.

Valrashar (val-ra-SHAR)–vané princess, daughter of Kirpis vané King Terindel and Queen Valathea.

vané (van-EH), a.k.a. vorfelane–an offshoot of the voras who split over ideological differences in how to interact with the world's native species. Essentially, the voras changed the world to suit their needs, and the vané changed themselves to suit the world.

vanoizi (vah-NWA-zi)–a style of Eamithonian cooking, also a region of Eamithon.

Var, Relos (VAR, REL-os)–a powerful wizard, believed responsible for the ritual that created the Eight Immortals, and also the ritual that created both the dragons and Vol Karoth.

Var, Senera (SEN-er-AY)–a former House D'Jorax slave who was freed and trained by Relos Var.

Veil–1. see: Tya's Veil. 2. The state of perception separating seeing the "normal" world from seeing the true essence or tenyé of the world, necessary for magic.

velvet houses–Quuros slang term for brothels or bordellos.

Velvet Town–the red light district of the Lower Circle. Those who engage in the sex trade are commonly described as "velvet," i.e. velvet boys or velvet girls.

Vishai Mysteries, the (vish-AY)–a religion popular in parts of Eamithon, Jorat, and Marakor; little is known about their inner workings, but their religion seems to principally center around a solar deity; usually pacifistic; members of the faith will often obtain licenses from House D'Mon to legally practice healing.

Vol Karoth (VOL ka-ROTH), a.k.a. War Child–a demon offspring crafted by demons to counter the Eight Immortals; alternately a corrupted remnant of the sacrificed god of the sun, S'arric; both.

voramer (vor-a-MEER), a.k.a. vormer–an extinct water-dwelling race believed to be the progenitors of the morgage and the Ithlané. Of the two, only the Ithlané still live in water.

voras (vor-AS), a.k.a. vorarras–extinct race believed to have been the progenitors of humanity, who lost their immortality when Karolaen was destroyed.

vordreth (vor-DRETH), a.k.a. vordredd, dreth, dredd, dwarves–an underground-dwelling race known for their strength and intelligence; despite their nickname, not short. Believed to have been wiped out when Atrin Kandor conquered Raenena, but the fact that Thurvishar D'Lorus's mother was one suggests otherwise.

W

Warmonger–a Cornerstone that allows emotional control over large population groups.

Watchmen, the–guards tasked with policing the Capital City, under the auspices of House D'Kard.

Well of Spirals, the–a vané holy site where much of their biological magics are performed.

Wildheart–a Cornerstone that allows its owner to control plants.

witchgift–slang term for the first spell a sorcerer or wizard learns, which is usually wild and considered a sign of one's potential.

Wixan (WIKS-an)–a Devoran priest.

Worldhearth–a Cornerstone that allows its owner to see clairvoyantly using heat sources.

X

Xaloma (ZAL-o-may)–a dragon, associated with souls.

Xaltorath (zal-tor-OTH)–a demon king/queen who is manipulating events. Responsible for the death of Galava. Self-associated with lust and war.

Y

Ynis (y-NIS)–a god-king who once ruled the area now known as Khorvesh. Associated with death and snakes. Slain by Thaena.

Ynisthana (y-NIS-than-AY)—an island in the Desolation chain, used as a training grounds by the Black Brotherhood.

Yor (yor)—one of Quur's dominions, the most recently added and the least acclimated to imperial rule.

Z

Zaibur (ZAI-bur)—1. The major river running from Demon Falls and Lake Jorat all the way to the ocean, dividing Jorat from Marakor. 2. A strategy game.

Zajhera, Father (zah-JER-ah)—leader of the Vishai faith / Vishai Mysteries. Personally exorcised the demon Xaltorath, who possessed Janel Theranon when she was a child. An alternate identity used by Relos Var.

Zherias (ZER-e-as)—a large island to the southwest of Quur. Independent from Quur, and anxious to stay that way. Famous for their skill at piracy and trade.

Demon Classifications

NASCENT

A just-infected human soul, virtually powerless and often deeply traumatized, but still essentially a "person." Ironically, one rarely encounters a demon in the nascent development stage because their demon parent typically takes them to Imp stage immediately.

IMP

A breaking-in period of demonic development in which the soul's identity and personality are systematically destroyed through a combination of torture, forced inhumanity (a dog form is popular), and the devouring of other souls.

SPITE

An intermediate stage transitioning between the mindless beast nature of the Imp stage and the more polished next stage. Spite-level demons are still malleable in appearance, often taking forms that their victims find terrifying and changing those forms on the fly. They are a shifting mass of conflicting emotions, desires, and sadistic urges. Teenagers, if you will.

MALICE

The level at which demons begin to have real agency, opinions, and minds of their own. By this point a dominant personality has emerged from the gestalt of consumed souls. Later souls are subsumed into this personality rather than having a chance of taking control of it. Demons at this stage pick a name and a form and stick with it (mostly) unless being forced into a particular shape by magic or agreement (a thing much more common back when summoning was possible).

MALIGNANT

A sufficiently powerful demon develops the ability to infect human souls, and these are considered the "royalty" of the demon world (and often call themselves such). Malignant demons are typically able to cast magic with ease and open gates between the First and Second Worlds.

CALAMITY

There is something worse than Malignant. A demon of Calamity level is so powerful they can battle god-kings and, at least for a short time, Immortals. Very few Calamity-level demons exist, as most of those that did exist are believed to have been destroyed by Vol Karoth after they helped create him. Xaltorath definitely falls into this category, however.

DRAGONS

Aeyan'arric (linked Cornerstone: Skyfire)
Powers: Ice, storms, cold

While Aeyan'arric is hardly "good" in any sense of the word, of all the dragons she is the least actively malicious, which is to say she's exactly as dangerous as one would expect if a particularly sadistic house cat ended up in the body of a giant ice dragon. So dangerous, but animalistic in her rages and tantrums. If nothing else, the storms that accompany her passage are always devastating.

Baelosh (linked Cornerstone: Wildheart)
Powers: Plant life

Baelosh is one of the better known of the dragons thanks to his well-documented rivalry with Emperor Simillion. He is clever and cruel and takes a particular delight in collecting tsali stones of all types. While in theory his presence might be good for a region—his passage often results in lush, overgrown vegetation—the actively harmful nature of that foliage typically qualifies as "too much of a good thing."

Drehemia (linked Cornerstone: The Name of All Things)
Powers: Shadows, darkness, ignorance, secrets

The Queen of Secrets is seldom seen precisely because she is seldom perceived. Drehemia is perfectly capable of flying over a city without anyone realizing it, or attacking ships without anyone (even survivors) being able to describe their attacker afterward. She is exceedingly dangerous.

Gorokai (linked Cornerstone: Chainbreaker)
Powers: Shape-change, chaos, reality alteration

Like Drehemia, Gorokai is one of the most active dragons, but also one of the most subtle. He has spent several centuries living in Rainbow Lake, for example, shape-changed into the form of a particularly large carp (apparently because it amused him to mess with the periodic fisherman who might catch him). However, his shape-changing ability doesn't fully express the terrifying depth of his powers, since he seems to be able to force objects and people around him to change shape as well—destructively.

Morios (linked Cornerstone: Warmonger)
Powers: Metal, swords

Morios is a very straightforward dragon compared to the others—he's made of metal, exceedingly sharp, and devastatingly strong. It's his size (easily the largest of any of the dragons) and near invulnerability that makes him so difficult to deal with.

Rol'amar (linked Cornerstone: The Stone of Shackles)
Powers: Soulbinding

While it would be easy to assume that Rol'amar's powers deal with death or undeath, they seem to more specifically deal with manipulating souls and forcing souls to stay tied to their physical forms, even after death. So in much the same way that someone wearing the Stone of Shackles cannot die under certain circumstances (namely when there's no clear assailant), Rol'amar doesn't seem to be able to die no matter how much damage his body has taken.

Sharanakal (linked Cornerstone: Worldhearth)
Powers: Fire, volcano

He's the living embodiment of a volcano.

Xaloma (linked Cornerstone: Grimward)
Powers: Death

Very little is known about Xaloma simply because she so rarely leaves the Second World (better known as the Afterlife), which means that most of the people she encounters are in no position to tell anyone about the experience. The scope of her powers are unclear.

and

Relos Var (linked Cornerstone: Cynosure)
Powers: ??

Relos Var is a dragon, although, like Gorokai, he seldom runs around looking like one. That said, he is currently the only dragon who has been "cured" by being reunited with his Cornerstone, Cynosure (which thus, technically speaking, no longer exists). According to Grizzst, Cynosure allowed its owner to be all but immune to the powers of the other Cornerstones, and Relos Var has indicated that he himself possesses some ability to control the other dragons. However, we don't know if Relos Var has Cynosure's powers himself.

ACKNOWLEDGMENTS

There is no little irony to the idea that I started writing a book about a dozen souls trapped in a small space with each other just as Covid-19 decided to help me experience that claustrophobia firsthand. Thankfully, my own personal lighthouse comes equipped with internet, so I've been able to keep in touch with the people so vital to my peace of mind.

So many thanks once more to my editors, Devi Pillai and Bella Pagan, and to my agent, Sam Morgan, who have all been incredibly supportive and understanding of the psychological toll of trying to write while the whole world seems to be on fire. Y'all continue to be the absolute best, and I consider myself so incredibly fortunate to have the opportunity to work with you. I'd also like to thank all the marketing, sales, and production staff at Tor who so often go unsung—this is a job one does for love, and I am endlessly grateful that you have chosen to do so.

I'd like to thank everyone in the Author's Sack, who have done so much to help and support me. Your friendship means the world. (A special call-out to Freya Marske, for her continued willingness to help me make my books just a little bit sexier.)

Lastly, to everyone out there who've been generous enough to share how these books have touched their lives, often in ways I couldn't have predicted: Thank you.

219823198483341